W9-BKZ-823

CAPTAIN
Horatio Hornblower

BOOKS BY

C. S. FORESTER

THE GUN

THE PEACEMAKER

THE AFRICAN QUEEN

THE GENERAL

* BEAT TO QUARTERS

* SHIP OF THE LINE

* FLYING COLOURS

CAPTAIN HORATIO HORNBLOWER

(*Originally published in the three volumes starred above*)

CAPTAIN
Horatio Hornblower

BY C. S. FORESTER

WITH DRAWINGS BY

N. C. WYETH

Published in BOSTON *by*

LITTLE, BROWN AND COMPANY

1939

Published April 1939
Reprinted June 1939 (twice)
Reprinted July 1939
Reprinted September 1939 (twice)
Reprinted November 1939
Reprinted December 1939 (three times)

PRINTED IN THE UNITED STATES OF AMERICA

CONTENTS

Beat to Quarters

The Landfall–Captain Hornblower Aloft

Chapter I

IT WAS not long after dawn that Captain Hornblower came up on the quarterdeck of the *Lydia.* Bush, the first lieutenant, was officer of the watch, and touched his hat but did not speak to him; in a voyage which had by now lasted seven months without touching land he had learned something of his captain's likes and dislikes. During this first hour of the day the captain was not to be spoken to, nor his train of thought interrupted.

In accordance with standing orders — hallowed by now with the tradition which is likely to accumulate during a voyage of such incredible length — Brown, the captain's coxswain, had seen to it that the weather side of the quarterdeck had been holystoned and sanded at the first peep of daylight. Bush and the midshipman with him withdrew to the lee side at Hornblower's first appearance, and Hornblower immediately began his daily hour's walk up and down, up and down the twenty one feet of deck which had been sanded for him. On one hand his walk was limited by the slides of the quarterdeck carronades; on the other by the row of ringbolts in the deck for the attachment of the carronade train tackles; the space of deck on which Captain Hornblower was accustomed to exercise himself for an hour each morning was thus five feet wide and twenty one feet long.

Up and down, up and down, paced Captain Hornblower. Although he was entirely lost in thought, his subordinates knew by experience that his sailor's instinct was quite alert; subconsciously his mind took note of the shadow of the main rigging across the deck, and of the feel of the breeze on his cheek, so that the slightest inattention on the part of the quartermaster at the wheel called forth a bitter rebuke from the captain — the more bitter in that he had been disturbed in this, the most important hour of his day. In the same way he was aware, without having taken special note, of all the salient facts of the prevailing conditions. On his awakening in his cot he had seen (without willing it) from the telltale compass in the deck over his head that the course was northeast, as it had been for the last three days. At the moment of his arrival on deck he had subconsciously noted that the wind was from the west, and just strong enough to give the ship steerage way, with all sail set to the royals, that the sky was of its perennial blue, and that the sea was almost flat calm, with a long peaceful swell over which the *Lydia* soared and swooped with profound regularity.

The first thing Captain Hornblower was aware of thinking was that the Pacific in the morning, deep blue overside and changing to silver towards the horizon, was like some heraldic blazon of argent and azure — and then he almost smiled to himself because that simile had come up in his mind every morning for the last fortnight. With the thought and the smile his mind was instantly working smoothly and rapidly. He looked down the gangways at the men at work holystoning; down on the main deck, as he came forward, he could see another party engaged on the same task. They were talking in ordinary tones. Twice he heard a laugh. That was well. Men who could talk and laugh in that fashion were not likely to be plotting mutiny — and Captain Hornblower had that possibility much in mind lately. Seven months at sea had almost consumed the ship's stores. A week ago he had cut the daily ration of water to three pints a day, and three pints a day was hardly sufficient for men living on salt meat and biscuit in ten degrees north latitude, especially as water seven months in cask was half solid with green living things.

A week ago, too, the very last of the lemon juice had been served out, and there would be scurvy to reckon with within a month and no surgeon on board. Hankey the surgeon had died of all the complications of drink and syphilis off the Horn. For a month now tobacco had been doled out in half ounces weekly — Hornblower congratulated himself now on having taken the tobacco under his sole charge. If he had not done so the thoughtless fools would have used up their whole store, and men deprived of tobacco were men who could not be relied upon. He knew that the men were more concerned about the shortage of tobacco than about the shortage of fuel for the galley which caused them each day to be given their salt pork only just brought to the boil in seawater.

The shortage of tobacco, of water and of wood was nothing nearly as important, however, as the imminent shortage of grog. He had not dared to cut that daily issue, and there was only rum for ten more days in the ship. Not the finest crew in the world could be relied on if deprived of their ration of rum. Here they were in the South Sea, with no other King's ship within two thousand miles of them. Somewhere to the westward were islands of romance, with beautiful women, and food to be got without labour. A life of happy idleness was within their reach. Some knave among the crew, better informed than the rest, would give the hint. It would not be attended to at present, but in the future, with no blessed interval of grog at noon, the men would be ready to listen. Ever since the crew of the *Bounty* had mutinied, seduced by the charms of the Pacific, the captain of every ship of His Britannic Majesty whose duty took him there was haunted by this fear.

Hornblower, pacing the deck, looked sharply once more at the crew. Seven months at sea without once touching land had given an admirable opportunity for training the gang of jailbirds and pressed men into seamen, but it was too long without distraction. The sooner now that he could reach the coast of Nicaragua, the better. A run ashore would distract the men, and there would be water and fresh food and tobacco and spirits to be got. Hornblower's mind began to run back through his recent calculations of the ship's position. He was certain about his latitude, and last night's lunar observations had seemed to confirm the chronometers' indication of the longitude — even though it seemed incredible that chronometers could be relied upon at all after a seven months' voyage. Probably less than one hundred miles ahead, at most three hundred, lay the Pacific coast of Central America. Crystal, the master, had shaken his head in doubt at Hornblower's positiveness, but Crystal was an old fool, and of no use as a navigator. Anyway, two or three more days would see who was right.

At once Hornblower's mind shifted to the problem of how to

spend the next two or three days. The men must be kept busy. There was nothing like long idle days to breed mutiny — Hornblower never feared mutiny during the wild ten weeks of beating round the Horn. In the forenoon watch he would clear for action and practise the men at the guns, five rounds from each. The concussion might kill the wind for a space, but that could not be helped. It would be the last opportunity, perhaps, before the guns would be in action in earnest.

Another calculation came up in Hornblower's mind. Five rounds from the guns would consume over a ton weight of powder and shot. The *Lydia* was riding light already with her stores nearly all consumed. Hornblower called up before his mental eye a picture of the frigate's hold and the positions of the storerooms. It was time that he paid attention to the trim of the ship again. After the men had had their dinner he would put off in the quarter boat and pull round the ship. She would be by the stern a little by now, he expected. That could be put right tomorrow by shifting the two No. 1 carronades on the forecastle forward to their original positions. And as the ship would have to shorten sail while he was in the quarter boat he might as well do the job properly and give Bush a free hand in exercising the crew aloft. Bush had a passion for that kind of seamanship, as a first lieutenant quite rightly should. Today the crew might beat their previous record of eleven minutes fifty one seconds for sending up topmasts, and of twenty four minutes seven seconds for setting all sail starting with topmasts housed. Neither of those times, Hornblower agreed with Bush, was nearly as good as it might be; plenty of ships had set up better figures — at least so their captains had said.

Hornblower became aware that the wind had increased a tiny amount, sufficiently to call forth a faint whispering from the rigging. From the feel of it upon his neck and cheek he deduced it must have shifted aft a point or perhaps two, as well, and even as his mind registered these observations, and began to wonder how soon Bush would take notice of it, he heard the call for the watch. Clay, the midshipman on the quarterdeck, was bellowing like a bull for the afterguard. That boy's voice had broken since they left England; he was learning to use it properly now, instead of alternately squeaking and croaking. Still without taking visual notice of what was going on, Hornblower as he continued pacing the quarterdeck listened to the familiar sequence of sounds as the watch came tumbling aft to the braces. A crack and a yelp told him that Harrison the boatswain had landed with his cane on the stern of some laggardly or unlucky sailor. Harrison was a fine seaman, but with a weakness for using his cane on well-rounded sterns. Any man who filled his trousers out tight was likely to get a welt across the seat of them solely for that reason, especially if he was unluckily engaged as Harrison came by in some occupation which necessitated bending forward.

Hornblower's meditations regarding Harrison's weakness had occupied nearly all the time necessary for the trimming of the sails; as they came to an end Harrison roared "Belay!" and the watch trooped back to their previous duties. Ting-ting, ting-ting, ting-ting, *ting* went the bell. Seven bells in the morning watch. Hornblower had been walking for well over his covenanted hour, and he was aware of a gratifying prickle of sweat under his shirt. He walked over to where Bush was standing by the wheel.

"Good morning, Mr. Bush," said Captain Hornblower.

"Good morning, sir," said Bush, exactly as if Captain Hornblower had not been walking up and down within four yards of him for the last hour and a quarter.

Hornblower looked at the slate which bore the rough log of the last twenty four hours; there was nothing of special note — the hourly casting of the log had given speeds of three knots, four and a half knots, four knots, and so on, while the traverse board showed that the ship had contrived to hold to her northeasterly course throughout the day. The captain was aware of a keen scrutiny from his first lieutenant, and he knew that internally the lieutenant seethed with questions. There was only one man on board who knew whither the *Lydia* was bound, and that was the captain. He had sailed with sealed orders, and when he had opened and read them, in accordance with his instructions, in 30° N. 20° W., he had not seen fit to tell even his second in command what they contained. For seven months Lieutenant Bush had contrived to refrain from asking questions, but the strain was visibly telling on him.

"Ha — h'm," said Hornblower, clearing his throat noncommittally. Without a word he hung up the slate and went down the companion and entered his sleeping cabin.

It was unlucky for Bush that he should be kept in the dark in this fashion, but Hornblower had refrained from discussing his orders with him not through any fear of Bush's garrulity, but through fear of his own. When he had first sailed as captain five years ago he had allowed his natural talkativeness full play, and his first lieutenant of that time had come to presume upon the license allowed him until Hornblower had been unable to give an order without having it discussed. Last commission he had tried to limit discussion with his first lieutenant within the ordinary bounds of politeness, and had found that he had been unable to keep himself within those limits — he was always opening his mouth and letting fall one word too many to his subsequent regret. This voyage he had started with the firm resolve (like a drinker who cannot trust himself to drink only in moderation) to say nothing whatever to his officers except what was necessitated by routine, and his resolution had been hardened by the stress which his orders laid upon the need for extreme secrecy. For seven months he had held to it, growing more and more silent every day as the unnatural state of affairs took a firmer grip upon him. In the Atlantic he had sometimes discussed the weather with Mr. Bush. Round in the Pacific he only condescended to clear his throat.

His sleeping cabin was a tiny morsel of space bulkheaded off from the main cabin. Half the room was occupied by an eighteen pounder; the remainder was almost filled by his cot, his desk, and his chest. His steward Polwheal was putting out his razor and lather bowl on a bracket under a strip of mirror on the bulkhead — there was just room for the two of them to stand. Polwheal squeezed himself against the desk to allow his captain to enter; he said nothing, for Polwheal was a man of gratifyingly few words — Hornblower had picked him for that reason, because he had to guard against his besetting sin of garrulity even with servants.

Hornblower stripped off his wet shirt and trousers and shaved standing naked before the mirror. The face he regarded in the glass was neither handsome nor ugly, neither old nor young. There was a pair of melancholy brown eyes, a forehead sufficiently high, a nose sufficiently straight; a good mouth set with all the firmness acquired during twenty years at sea. The tousled curly brown hair was just beginning to recede and leave the forehead a little higher still, which was a source of irritation to Captain Hornblower, because he hated the thought of going bald. Noticing it, he was reminded of his other trouble, and glanced down his naked body. He was slender and well muscled; quite a prepossessing figure, in fact, when he drew himself to his full six feet. But down there where his ribs ended there was no denying the presence of a rounded belly, just beginning to protrude beyond the line of his ribs and of his iliac bones. Hornblower hated the thought of growing fat with an intensity rare in his generation; he hated to think of his slender smooth-skinned body being disfigured by an unsightly bulge in the middle, which was the reason why he, a naturally indolent individual who hated routine, forced himself to take that regular morning walk on the quarterdeck.

When he had finished shaving he put down razor and brush for Polwheal to wash and put away, and stood while Polwheal hung a ragged serge dressing gown over his shoulders. Polwheal followed him along the deck to the head-pump, removed the dressing gown, and then pumped up seawater from overside while his captain solemnly rotated under the stream. When the bath was finished Polwheal hung the dressing gown again over his dripping shoulders and followed him back to the cabin. A clean linen shirt — worn, but neatly mended — and white trousers were laid out on the cot. Hornblower dressed himself, and Polwheal helped him into the worn blue coat with its faded lace, and handed him his hat. All this was without a word being spoken, so well by now had Hornblower trained himself into his self-imposed system of silence. And he who hated routine had by now so fully called in routine to save himself from speech that exactly as he stepped out again on the quarterdeck eight bells rang, just as happened every single morning.

"Hands to punishment, sir?" asked Bush, touching his hat.

Hornblower nodded. The pipes of the boatswain's mates began to twitter.

"All hands to witness punishment," roared Harrison on the main deck, and from all parts of the ship men began to pour up and toe their lines in their allotted positions.

Hornblower stood rigid by the quarterdeck rail, setting his face like stone. He was ashamed of the fact that he looked upon punishment as a beastly business, that he hated ordering it and dreaded witnessing it. The two or three thousand floggings he had witnessed in the last twenty years had not succeeded in hardening him — in fact he was much softer now (as he was painfully aware) than as a seventeen year old midshipman. But there had been no avoiding the punishment of this morning's victim. He was a Welshman called Owen who could somehow never refrain from spitting on the decks. Bush, without referring to his captain, had sworn that he would have him flogged for every offence, and Hornblower had necessarily to endorse the decision and back up his officer in the name of discipline, although Hornblower had the gravest doubts as to whether a man who was fool enough not to be deterred from spitting on the decks by the fear of a flogging would benefit by receiving it.

Happily the business was got over quickly. The boatswain's mates triced Owen, naked to the waist, up to the main rigging, and laid into him as the drum rolled. Owen, unlike the usual run of seamen, howled with pain as the cat of ninetails bit into his shoulders, and danced grotesquely, his bare feet flapping on the deck until at the end of his two dozen he hung from his bound wrists motionless and silent. Someone soused him with water and he was hustled below.

"Hands to breakfast, Mr. Bush," snapped Hornblower; he hoped that the tan of the tropics saved him from looking as white as he felt. Flogging a half-witted man was not to his taste as a before breakfast diversion and he was sick with disgust at himself at neither being strong enough to stop it nor ingenious enough to devise a way out of the dilemma Bush's decision had forced him into.

The row of officers on the quarterdeck broke up as each turned away. Gerard, the second lieutenant, took over the deck from Bush. The ship was like a magic tessellated pavement. It presented a geometrical pattern; someone shook it up into confusion, and at once it settled itself into a new and orderly fashion.

Hornblower went below to where Polwheal had his breakfast awaiting him.

"Coffee, sir," said Polwheal. "Burgoo."

Hornblower sat down at table; in the seven months' voyage every luxury had long since been consumed. The coffee was a black extract of burnt bread, and all that could be said in its favour was that it was sweet and hot. The burgoo was a savoury mess of unspeakable appearance compounded of mashed biscuit crumbs and minced salt beef. Hornblower ate absentmindedly. With his left hand he tapped a biscuit on the table so that the weevils would all be induced to have left it by the time he had finished his burgoo.

There were ship-noises all round him as he ate. Every time the *Lydia* rolled and pitched a trifle as she reached the crest of the swell which was lifting her, the woodwork all creaked gently in unison. Overhead came the sound of Gerard's shod feet as he paced the quarterdeck, and sometimes the pattering of horny bare feet as some member of the crew trotted by. From forward came a monotonous steady clanking as the pumps were put to the daily task of pumping out the ship's bilge. But these noises were all transient and interrupted; there was one sound which went on all the time so steadily that the ear grew accustomed to it and only noticed it when the attention was specially directed to it — the sound of the breeze in the innumerable ropes of the rigging. It was just the faintest singing, a harmony of a thousand high-pitched tones and overtones, but it could be heard in every part of the ship, transmitted from the chains through the timbers along with the slow, periodic creaking.

Hornblower finished his burgoo, and was turning his attention to the biscuit he had been rapping on the table. He contemplated it with calm disfavour; it was poor food for a man, and in the absence of butter — the last cask had gone rancid a month back — he would have to wash down the dry mouthfuls with sips of burnt-bread coffee. But before he could take his first bite a wild cry from above caused him to sit still with the biscuit half way to his mouth.

"Land ho!" he heard. "Deck there! Land two points on the larboard bow, sir."

That was the lookout in the foretop hailing the deck. Hornblower, as he sat with his biscuit in midair, heard the rush and bustle on deck; everyone would be wildly excited at the sight of land, the first for three months, on this voyage to an unknown destination. He was excited himself. There was not merely the imminent thrill of discovering whether he had made a good landfall; there was also the thought that perhaps within twenty four hours he would be in the thick of the dangerous and difficult mission upon which my lords of the Admiralty had despatched him. He was conscious of a more rapid beating of his heart in his breast. He wanted passionately to rush out on deck as his first instinct dictated, but he restrained himself. He wanted still more to appear in the eyes of his officers and crew to be a man of complete self-confidence and imperturbability — and this was only partially to gratify himself. The more respect in which a captain was held, the better for his ship. He forced himself into an attitude of complete composure, crossing his knees and sipping his coffee in entire unconcern as Mr. Midshipman Savage knocked at the cabin door and came bouncing in.

"Mr. Gerard sent me to tell you land's in sight on the larboard bow, sir," said Savage, hardly able to stand still in the prevailing infection of excitement. Hornblower made himself take another sip of coffee before he spoke, and he made his words come slowly and calmly.

"Tell Mr. Gerard I shall come on deck in a few minutes when I have finished my breakfast," he said.

"Aye aye, sir."

Savage bolted out of the cabin; his large clumsy feet clattered on the companion.

"Mr. Savage! Mr. Savage!" yelled Hornblower. Savage's large moonlike face reappeared in the doorway.

"You forgot to close the door," said Hornblower, coldly. "And please don't make so much noise on the companionway."

"Aye aye, sir," said the crestfallen Savage.

Hornblower was pleased with himself for that. He pulled at his chin in self congratulation. He sipped again at his coffee, but found himself quite unable to eat his biscuit. He drummed with his fingers on the table in an effort to make the time pass more rapidly.

He heard young Clay bellowing from the masthead, where presumably Gerard had sent him with the glass.

"Looks like a burning mountain, sir. Two burning mountains. Volcanoes, sir."

Instantly Hornblower began to call up before his mind's eye his memory of the chart which he had so often studied in the privacy of this cabin. There were volcanoes all along the coast; the presence of two on the larboard bow was no sure indication of the ship's position. And yet — and yet — the entrance to the Gulf of Fonseca would undoubtedly be marked by two volcanoes to larboard. It was quite possible that he had made a perfect landfall, after eleven weeks out of sight of land. Hornblower could sit still no longer. He got up from the table, and, remembering just in time to go slowly and with an air of complete unconcern, he walked up on deck.

Chapter II

THE quarterdeck was thronged with officers, all the four lieutenants, Crystal the master, Simmonds of the marines, Wood the purser, the midshipmen of the watch. The rigging swarmed with petty officers and ratings, and every glass in the ship appeared to be in use. Hornblower realised that a stern coldblooded disciplinarian would take exception to this perfectly natural behaviour, and so he did the same.

"What's all this?" he snapped. "Has no one in this ship anything to do? Mr. Wood, I'll trouble you to send for the cooper and arrange with him for the filling of the water casks. Get the royals and the stun'sails off her, Mr. Gerard."

The ship burst into activity again with the twittering of the pipes, and Harrison's bellowing of "All hands shorten sail" and the orders which Gerard called from the quarterdeck. Under plain sail the *Lydia* rolled smoothly over the quartering swell.

"I think I can see the smoke from the deck, sir, now," said Gerard, apologetically raising the subject of land again to his captain. He proffered his glass and pointed forward. Low on the horizon, greyish under a wisp of white cloud, Hornblower could see something through the telescope which might be smoke.

"Ha — h'm," said Hornblower, as he had trained himself to say instead of something more conversational. He went forward and began to climb the weather foremast shrouds. He was nothing of an athlete, and he felt a faint dislike for this task, but it had to be done — and he was uncomfortably aware that every idle eye on board was turned on him. Because of this he was morally compelled, although he was hampered by the telescope, to refrain from going through the lubber's hole and instead to make the difficult outward climb up the futtock shrouds. Nor could he pause for breath — not when there were midshipmen under his command who in their follow-my-leader games thought nothing of running without a stop from the hold to the main royal truck.

The climb hand over hand up the fore-top gallant shrouds tried him severely; breathing heavily, he reached the fore-top gallant masthead, and settled himself to point the telescope as steadily as his heaving chest and sudden nervousness would allow. Clay was sitting nonchalantly astride the yard-arm fifteen feet away, but Hornblower ignored him. The slight corkscrew roll of the ship was sweeping him in a vast circle, up, forward, sideways, and down; at first he could only fix the distant mountains in snatches, but after a time he was able to keep them under fairly continuous observation. It was a strange landscape which the telescope revealed to him. There were the sharp peaks of several volcanoes; two very tall ones to larboard, a host of smaller ones both to starboard and to port. As he looked he saw a puff of grey steam emerge from one peak — not from the summit, but from a vent in the side — and ascend lazily to join the strip of white cloud which hung over it. Besides these cones there was a long mountain range of which the peaks appeared to be spurs, but the range itself seemed to be made up of a chain of old volcanoes, truncated and weathered down by the passage of centuries; that strip of coast must have been a hell's kitchen when they were all in eruption together. The upper parts of the peaks and of the mountains were a warm grey — grey with a hint of pink — lower he could see what looked like green cataracts which must be vegetation stretching up along gullies in the mountain sides. Hornblower noted the relative heights and positions of the volcanoes, and from these data he drew a map in his mind and compared it with the section of the chart which he also carried in his mind's eye. There was no doubting their similarity.

"I thought I saw breakers just then, sir," said Clay. Hornblower changed the direction of his gaze from the tops of the peaks to their feet.

Here there was a solid belt of green, unbroken save where lesser volcanoes jutted out from it. Hornblower swept his glass along it, along the very edge of the horizon, and then back again. He thought he saw a tiny flash of white, sought for the place again, experienced a moment of doubt, and then saw it again — a speck of white which appeared and disappeared as he watched.

"Quite right. Those are breakers sure enough," he said, and instantly regretted it. There had been no need to make any reply to Clay at all. By that much was his reputation for immobility diminished.

The *Lydia* held her course steadily towards the coast. Looking down, Hornblower could see the curiously foreshortened figures of the men on the forecastle a hundred and forty feet below, and round the bows a hint of a bow wave which told him the ship must be making four knots or very nearly. They would be up with the shore long before nightfall, especially as the breeze would freshen as the day went on. He eased himself out of his cramped position and stared again at the shore. As time went on he could see more breakers stretching on each side of where he had originally seen them. That must be a place where the incoming swell broke straight against a vertical wall of rock and flung its white foam upwards into sight. His belief that he had made a perfect landfall was growing stronger. On each side of the breakers was a stretch of clear water on the horizon, and beyond that again, on each side, was a medium-sized volcano. A wide bay, an island in the middle of the entrance, and two flanking volcanoes. That was exactly how the Gulf of Fonseca appeared in the chart, but Hornblower was painfully aware that no very great error in his navigation would have brought them anything up to two hundred miles from where he thought he was, and he realised that on a coast like this, littered with volcanoes, one section would appear very like another. Even the appearance of a bay and an island might be simulated by some other formation of the coast. Besides, he could not rely on his charts. They had been drawn from those Anson had captured in these very waters sixty years ago, and everyone knew about Dago charts — and Dago charts submitted to the revision of useless Admiralty draftsmen might be completely unreliable.

But as he watched his doubts were gradually set at rest. The bay opening before him was enormous — there could be no other of that size on that coast which could have escaped even Dago cartographers. Hornblower's eye estimated the width of the entrance at something over ten miles including the islands. Farther up the bay was a big island of a shape typical of the landscape — a steep circular cone rising sheer from the water. He could not see the far end of the bay, not even now when the ship was ten miles nearer than when he first saw the entrance.

"Mr. Clay," he said, not condescending to take his eye from the telescope. "You can go down now. Give Mr. Gerard my compliments and ask him please to send all hands to dinner."

"Aye aye, sir," said Clay.

The ship would know now that something unusual was imminent, with dinner advanced by half an hour. In British ships the officers were always careful to see that the men had full bellies before being called upon to exert themselves more than usual.

Hornblower resumed his watch from the masthead. There could be no possible doubt now that the *Lydia* was heading into the Gulf of Fonseca. He had performed a most notable feat of navigation, of which anyone might be justifiably proud, in bringing the ship straight here after eleven weeks without sighting land. But he felt no elation about it. It was Hornblower's nature to find no pleasure in achieving things he could do; his ambition was always yearning after the impossible, to appear a strong silent capable man, unmoved by emotion.

At present there was no sign of life in the gulf, no boats, no smoke. It might be an uninhabited shore that he was approaching, a second Columbus. He could count on at least one hour more without further action being called for. He shut his telescope, descended to the deck, and walked with self-conscious slowness aft to the quarterdeck.

Crystal and Gerard were talking animatedly beside the rail. Obviously they had moved out of earshot of the man at the wheel and had sent the midshipman as far away as possible; obviously also, as indicated by the way they looked towards Hornblower as he approached, they were talking about him. And it was only natural that they should be excited, because the *Lydia* was the first British ship of war to penetrate to the Pacific coast of Spanish America since Anson's time. They were in waters furrowed by the famous Acapulco galleon which carried a million sterling in treasure on each of her annual trips; along this coast crept the coasting ships bearing the silver of Potosi to Panama. It seemed as if the fortune of every man on board might be assured if only those unknown orders of the captain permitted it. What the captain intended to do next was of intense importance to them all.

"Send a reliable man with a good glass to the fore t'gallant masthead, Mr. Gerard," was all Hornblower said as he went below.

Chapter III

POLWHEAL was waiting with his dinner in the cabin. Hornblower meditated for a moment upon the desirability of a dinner of fat salt pork at noontide in the tropics. He was not in the least hungry, but the desire to appear a hero in the eyes of his steward overrode his excited lack of appetite. He sat down and ate rapidly for ten minutes, forcing himself to gulp down the distasteful mouthfuls. Polwheal, too, was watching every movement he made with desperate interest. Under his avid gaze he rose and walked through, stooping his head under the low deck, to his sleeping cabin and unlocked his desk.

"Polwheal!" he called.

"Sir!" said Polwheal, instantly appearing at the door.

"Get out my best coat and put the new epaulettes on it. Clean white trousers — no, the breeches and the best white silk stockings. The buckled shoes, and see that the buckles shine. And the sword with the gold hilt."

"Aye aye, sir," said Polwheal.

Back in the main cabin Hornblower stretched himself on the locker below the stern window and once more unfolded his secret Admiralty orders. He had read them so often that he almost knew them by heart, but it was prudent to make certain that he understood every word of them. They were comprehensive enough, in all conscience. Some Admiralty clerk had given his imagination loose rein in the wording of them. The first ten paragraphs covered the voyage up to the present; firstly the need for acting with the utmost possible secrecy so that no hint could reach Spain of the approach of a British frigate to the Pacific shores of her possessions. "You are therefore requested and required — " to sight land as little as possible on the voyage, and "you are hereby entirely prohibited — " from coming within sight of land at all in the Pacific until the moment of his arrival at the mouth of the Gulf of Fonseca. He had obeyed these orders to the letter, although there were few enough captains in the service who could have done and who would have done. He had brought his ship here all the way from England without seeing any land save for a glimpse of Cape Horn, and if he had allowed Crystal to have his way regarding the course to be set a week ago, the ship would have gone sailing into the gulf of Panama, completely forfeiting all possibility of secrecy.

Hornblower wrenched his mind away from the argument regarding the amount of compass-variation to be allowed for in these waters and forced himself to concentrate on a further study of his orders. "You are hereby requested and required — " to form an alliance as soon as he reached the Gulf of Fonseca with Don Julian Alvarado, who was a large landowner with estates along the western shore of the bay. Don Julian intended, with the help of the British, to rise in rebellion against the Spanish monarchy. Hornblower was to hand over to him the five hundred muskets and bayonets, the five hundred pouch-belts, and the million rounds of small arm ammunition which were to be provided at Portsmouth, and he was to dc everything which his discretion dictated to ensure the success of the rebellion. If he were to think it necessary, he could present to the rebels one or more of the guns of his ship, but the fifty thousand guineas in gold which were entrusted to him as well were only to be disbursed if the rebellion would fail without them, on pain of his being brought to a courtmartial. He was to succour the rebels to the utmost of his power, even to the extent of recognising Don Julian Alvarado's sovereignty over any territory that he might conquer, provided that in return Don Julian would enter into commercial treaties with His Britannic Majesty.

This mention of commercial treaties apparently had acted as an inspiration to the Admiralty clerk, for the next ten paragraphs dealt in highflown detail with the pressing necessity for opening Spanish possessions to British commerce. Peruvian balsam and logwood, cochineal and gold, were awaiting exchange for British manufactures. The clerk's quill had fairly dripped with excitement as it penned these details in a fair round hand. Furthermore, there was an arm of the bay of Fonseca, called, it was believed, the Estero Real, which approached closely to the inland lake of Managua, which was thought to communicate with the lake of Nicaragua, which drained to the Caribbean by the river San Juan. Captain Hornblower was requested and required to do his utmost to open up this route across the isthmus to British commerce, and he was to guide Don Julian's efforts in this direction.

It was only after Don Julian's rebellion should be successful and all this accomplished that the orders went on to give Captain Hornblower permission to attack the treasure ships to be found in the Pacific, and moreover no shipping was to be interfered with if doing so should give offence to those inhabitants who might otherwise be favourable to the rebellion. For Captain Hornblower's information it was noted that the Spaniards were believed to maintain in these waters a two decked ship of fifty guns, by name the *Natividad*, for the enforcement of the royal authority. Captain Hornblower was therefore requested and required to "take, sink, burn or destroy" this ship at the first opportunity.

Lastly, Captain Hornblower was ordered to open communication as soon as might be convenient, with the Rear Admiral commanding the Leeward Islands station for the purpose of receiving further orders.

Captain Hornblower folded up the crackling paper again and fell into contemplation. Those orders were the usual combination of the barely possible and quite Quixotic, which a captain on detached service might expect to receive. Only a landsman would have given those opening orders to sail to the Gulf of Fonseca without sighting other land in the Pacific — only a succession of miracles (Hornblower gave himself no credit for sound judgment and good seamanship) had permitted of their being carried out.

Starting a rebellion in the Spanish American colonies had long been a dream of the British government — a dream which had been a nightmare to the British officers ordered to make it a reality. Admiral Popham and Admiral Stirling, General Beresford and General Whitelocke, had, during the last three years, all lost in honour and reputation in repeated efforts to raise rebellion on the river Plate.

Opening up a channel to British trade across the Isthmus of Darien had long been a similar dream cherished by Admiralty clerks with small scale maps before them and no practical experience. Thirty years ago Nelson himself, as a young captain, had nearly lost his life in command of an expedition up that very river San Juan which Hornblower was ordered to clear from its source.

And to crown it all was the casual mention of the presence of a fifty-gun ship of the enemy. It was typical of Whitehall to send a thirty-six-gun frigate so lightly to attack an enemy of nearly double the force. The British navy had been so successful in single ship duels during these wars that by now victory was expected of its ships against any odds. If by any chance the *Natividad* should overwhelm the *Lydia* no excuse would be accepted. Hornblower's career would be wrecked. Even if the inevitable courtmartial did not break him, he would be left to languish on half pay for the rest of his life. Failure to capture the *Natividad*, failure to start a successful rebellion, failure to open the isthmus to trade — any one of these quite probable failures would mean a loss of reputation, of employment, of having to face his wife on his return condemned as a man inferior to his fellows.

Having contemplated all these gloomy possibilities Hornblower thrust them aside with determined optimism. First and foremost he must make contact with this Don Julian Alvarado, which seemed to be a duty involving some little interest and only small difficulty. Later there would be treasure ships to capture and prize money to be won. He would not allow himself to worry about the rest of the future. He heaved himself off the locker and strode back to his sleeping cabin.

Ten minutes later he stepped up on the quarterdeck; he noted with sardonic amusement how his officers tried without success to appear not to notice his splendid best coat with the epaulettes, his silk stockings, his shoes with the cut steel buckles, his cocked hat and his gold-hilted sword. Hornblower cast a glance at the fast-nearing shore.

"Beat to quarters, Mr. Bush," he said. "Clear for action."

The roll of the drum set the ship into a wild flurry as the watch below came tumbling up. Urged on by the cries and blows of the petty officers the crew flung themselves into the business of getting the ship ready for action. The decks were soused with water and strewn with sand; the bulkheads were knocked away; the fire parties took their places at the pumps; the boys ran breathless with cartridges for the guns; down below the purser's steward who had been appointed acting surgeon was dragging together the midshipmen's chests in the cockpit to make an operating table.

"We'll have the guns loaded and run out, if you please, Mr. Bush," said Hornblower.

That was only a sensible precaution to take, seeing that the ship was about to sail before the wind straight into Spanish territory. The guns' crews cast off the frappings of the breeches, tugged desperately at the train tackles to drag the guns inboard, rammed home the powder and the shot, depressed the gun muzzles, strained madly at the gun tackles, and ran the guns out through the opened ports.

"Ship cleared for action. Ten minutes twenty one seconds, sir," said Bush as the last rumble died away. For the life of him he still could not tell whether this was an exercise or in earnest, and it gratified Hornblower's vanity to leave him in doubt.

"Very good, Mr. Bush. Send a good man with the lead into the main chains, and make ready to anchor."

The breeze off the sea was strengthening every minute now, and the *Lydia's* speed was steadily increasing. With his glass from the quarterdeck Hornblower could see every detail of the entrance to the bay, and the broad westerly channel between Conchaquita Island and the westerly mainland which the chart assured him afforded twenty fathoms for five miles inland. But there was no trusting these Spanish charts.

"What have you in the chains, there?" called Hornblower.

"No ground with this line, sir."

"How many fathom have you out? Pass along the deep sea line."

"Aye aye, sir."

A dead hush descended on the ship, save for the eternal harping of the rigging and the chatter of the water under the stern.

"No ground, sir, within a hundred fathom."

The shore must be very steep-to, then, because they were within two miles of land now. But there was no purpose in risking running aground under full sail.

"Get the courses in," said Hornblower. "Keep that lead going in the chains, there."

Under topsails alone the *Lydia* crept in towards land. Soon a cry from the chains announced that bottom had been reached in a hundred fathoms, and the depth diminished steadily at every cast. Hornblower would have been glad to know what was the state of the tide — if he was going aground at all it would be far better to do so on the flow than on the ebb — but there was no possible means of calculating that. He went half way up the mizzen rigging to get a better view; everyone else in the ship save for the man in the chains was standing rigid in the blinding heat. They were almost in the entrance channel now. Hornblower sighted some driftwood afloat on the near side, and training his glass on it, he saw that it was floating in up the bay. The tide was making, then; better and better.

"By the deep nine," chanted the leadsman.

So much for the Dago chart which indicated ten fathoms.

"And a half eight."

The channel was shoaling fast. They would have to anchor soon in this case.

"And a half eight."

Plenty of water still for the present. Hornblower called down to the helmsman, and the *Lydia* swung to starboard round the slight bend.

"And a half eight."

Well enough still. The *Lydia* steadied on her new course.

"By the mark seven."

Hornblower's eyes searched the channel in an attempt to determine the line of deepest water.

"By the mark seven."

An order from Hornblower edged the *Lydia* towards the further side. Bush quietly sent the men to the braces to trim the yards on the new course.

"And a half eight."

That was better.

"By the deep nine."

Better still. The *Lydia* was well up the bay now, and Hornblower could see that the tide was still making. They crept on over the glassy water, with the leadsman chanting monotonously, and the steep conical mountain in the middle of the bay drawing nearer.

"Quarter less eight," called the leadsman.

"Are the anchors clear?" asked Hornblower.

"All clear, sir."

"By the mark seven."

No useful object could be served in going in farther.

"Let go the anchor."

The cable roared through the hawsehole while the watch sprang to furl the topsails, and the *Lydia* swung round to wind and tide while Hornblower descended to the quarterdeck.

Bush blinked at him as at a miracle worker. Seven weeks after sighting the Horn, Hornblower had brought the *Lydia* straight in to her destination; he had arrived in the afternoon with the sea breeze and a flowing tide to bring him in, and if there were danger for them here nightfall would soon bring them the ebb tide and the land breeze to take them out again. How much was fluke and how much was calculation Bush could not guess, but as his opinion of Hornblower's professional merit was far higher than Hornblower himself cherished he was inclined to give him more credit than was really his due.

"Keep the watch at quarters, Mr. Bush," said Hornblower. "Dismiss the watch below."

With the ship a mile from any possible danger and cleared for action there was no need to keep every man at his station. The ship broke into a cheerful buzz as the watch below lined the rails to stare out at this land of green jungle and grey rock, but Hornblower was puzzled for a moment, wondering what to do next. The excitement of bringing the ship into an unknown harbour had prohibited his usual careful planning of his next step. His mind was made up for him by a hail from the lookout.

"Deck there! Boat putting out from shore. Two points abaft the starboard beam."

A double speck of white was creeping out towards them; Hornblower's glass resolved it into an open boat under two tiny lateen sails, and as she drew nearer he could see that she was manned by half a dozen swarthy men wearing wide straw hats. She hove-to fifty yards away, and someone stood up in the stern sheets and shouted across the water with hands cupped round his mouth. It was Spanish that he spoke.

"Is that an English ship?" he asked.

"Yes. Come on board," replied Hornblower. Two years as a prisoner of Spain had given him the opportunity of learning the language — he had long before decided that it was merely on account of this accomplishment that he had been selected for this special service.

The boat ran alongside and the man who had hailed scrambled lightly up the ladder to the deck. He stopped at the side and looked round him with a certain curiosity at the spotless decks and the rigid order which prevailed on every hand. He wore a sleeveless black waistcoat aflame with gold embroidery; beneath it a dirty white shirt, and on his legs dirty white trousers terminating raggedly just below the knees. His feet were bare, and in a red sash round his waist he carried two pistols and a short heavy sword. He spoke Spanish as his native tongue, but he did not look like a Spaniard; the black hair which hung over his ears was long, lustreless, and lank; there was a tinge of red in his brown complexion and a tinge of yellow in the whites of his eyes. A long thin moustache drooped from his upper lip. His eyes at once picked out the captain, gorgeous in his best coat and cocked hat, and he advanced towards him. It was in anticipation of just such a meeting that Hornblower had donned his best, and he was pleased with his foresight now.

"You are the captain, sir?" asked the visitor.

"Yes. Captain Horatio Hornblower of His Britannic Majesty's

frigate *Lydia*, at your service. And whom have I the pleasure of welcoming?"

"Manuel Hernandez, lieutenant general of El Supremo."

"El Supremo?" asked Hornblower, puzzled. The name was a little difficult to render into English. Perhaps "The Almighty" might be the nearest translation.

"Yes, of El Supremo. You were expected here four months, six months back."

Hornblower thought quickly. He dared not disclose the reason of his coming to any unauthorised person, but the fact that this man knew he was expected seemed to indicate that he was a member of Alvarado's conspiracy.

"It is not to El Supremo that I am ordered to address myself," he temporised. Hernandez made a gesture of impatience.

"Our lord El Supremo was known to men until lately as His Excellency Don Julian María de Jesús de Alvarado y Moctezuma," he said.

"Ah!" said Hornblower. "It is Don Julian that I want to see."

Hernandez was clearly annoyed by this casual mention of Don Julian.

"El Supremo," he said, laying grave accent on the name, "has sent me to bring you into his presence."

"And where is he?"

"He is in his house."

"And where is his house?"

"Surely it is enough, Captain, that you should know that El Supremo requires your attendance."

"Do you think so? I would have you know, señor, that a captain of one of His Britannic Majesty's ships is not accustomed to being at anyone's beck and call. You can go, if you like, and tell Don Julian so."

Hornblower's attitude indicated that the interview was at an end. Hernandez went through an internal struggle, but the prospect of returning to face El Supremo without bringing the captain with him was not alluring.

"The house is there," he said sullenly, at last, pointing across the bay. "On the side of the mountain. We must go through the town which is hidden behind the point to get there."

"Then I shall come. Pardon me for a moment, General."

Hornblower turned to Bush, who was standing by with the half puzzled, half admiring expression on his face so frequently to be seen when a man is listening to a fellow countryman talking fluently in an unknown language.

"Mr. Bush," he said, "I am going ashore, and I hope I shall return soon. If I do *not*, if I am not back nor have written to you by midnight, you must take steps to ensure the safety of the ship. Here is the key of my desk. You have my orders that at midnight you are to read the government's secret orders to me, and to act on them as you think proper."

"Aye aye, sir," said Bush. There was anxiety in his face, and Hornblower realised with a thrill of pleasure that Bush was actually worried about his captain's well being. "Do you think — is it safe for you on shore alone, sir?"

"I don't know," said Hornblower, with honest indifference. "I must go, that is all."

"We'll bring you off, sir, safe and sound, if there is any hanky-panky."

"You'll see after the safety of the ship first," snapped Hornblower, visualising a mental picture of Bush with a valuable landing party blundering about in the fever-haunted jungles of Central America. Then he turned to Hernandez. "I am at your service, señor."

Chapter IV

THE boat ran softly aground on a beach of golden sand round the point, and her swarthy crew sprang out and hauled the boat up so that Hornblower and Hernandez could step ashore dry shod. Hornblower looked keenly about him. The town came down to the edge of the sand; it was a collection of a few hundred houses of palmetto leaves, only a few of them roofed with tiles. Hernandez led the way up towards it.

"Agua, agua," croaked a voice as they approached. "Water, for the love of God, water."

A man was bound upright to a six foot stake beside the path; his hands were free and his arms thrashed about frantically. His eyes were protruding from his head and it seemed as if his tongue were too big for his mouth, like an idiot's. A circle of vultures crouched and fluttered round him.

"Who is that?" asked Hornblower, shocked.

"A man whom El Supremo has ordered to die for want of water," said Hernandez. "He is one of the unenlightened."

"He is being tortured to death?"

"This is his second day. He will die when the noontide sun shines on him tomorrow," said Hernandez casually. "They always do."

"But what is his crime?"

"He is one of the unenlightened, as I said, Captain."

Hornblower resisted the temptation to ask what constituted enlightenment; from the fact that Alvarado had adopted the name of El Supremo he could fairly well guess. And he was weak enough to allow Hernandez to guide him past the unhappy wretch without a protest — he surmised that no expostulation on his part would override the orders given by El Supremo, and an unavailing protest would only be bad for his prestige. He would postpone action until he was face to face with the leader.

Little miry lanes, filthy and stinking, wound between the

palmetto huts. Vultures perched on the roof ridges and squabbled with the mongrel dogs in the lanes. The Indian population were going about their usual avocations without regard for the man dying of thirst within fifty yards of them. They were all brown with a tinge of red, like Hernandez himself; the children ran naked, the women were dressed either in black or in dirty white; the few men to be seen wore only short white trousers to the knee and were naked from the waist up. Half the houses appeared to be shops — open on one side, where were displayed for sale a few handfuls of fruits, or three or four eggs. At one place a black robed woman was bargaining to make a purchase.

Tethered in the little square in the centre of the town some diminutive horses warred with the flies. Hernandez' escort made haste to untether two of them and stood at their heads for them to mount. It was a difficult moment for Hornblower; he was not a good horseman, as he knew, and he was wearing his best silk stockings, and he felt he would not cut a dignified figure on horseback with his cocked hat and his sword. There was no help for it, however. He was so clearly expected to mount and ride that he could not draw back. He got his foot into his stirrup and swung up into the saddle, and was relieved to find that the tiny horse was submissive and quiet. He trotted alongside Hernandez, bumping awkwardly. The sweat ran down his face, and every few seconds he had to reach up hurriedly and adjust his cocked hat. A path wound steeply up the hillside out of the town, only wide enough for one horseman at a time, so that Hernandez, with a courteous gesture, preceded him. The escort clattered along fifty yards behind them.

The narrow path was stifling hot, hemmed by trees and bush on either hand. Insects buzzed round them, biting viciously. Half a mile up the path some lounging sentries came awkwardly to attention, and beyond this point there were other men to be seen — men like the first one Hornblower had encountered, bound to stakes and dying of thirst. There were dead men, too — mere stinking masses of corruption with a cloud of flies which buzzed more wildly as the horses brushed by them. The stench was horrible; gorged vultures, hideous with their naked necks, flopped along the path ahead of the horses, unable to fly, seeking escape into the forest.

Hornblower was about to say, "More of the unenlightened, General?" when he realised the uselessness of comment. It was better to say nothing than to say anything ineffectual. He rode silently through the stink and the flies, and tried to estimate the mentality of a man who would allow rotting corpses to remain, so to speak, on his doorstep.

The path rose over a shoulder of the mountain, and for a moment Hornblower had a glimpse of the bay below, blue and silver and gold under the evening sun, with the *Lydia* riding to her anchor in the midst of it. Then suddenly the forest at each side changed as if by magic into cultivated land. Orange groves, the trees laden with fruit, bordered the path, and through the trees Hornblower could gain a glimpse of fields bearing crops. The sun, sinking fast to the horizon, illuminated the golden fruit, and then, as they turned a corner, shone full on a vast white building, stretching low and wide on either hand, before them.

"The house of El Supremo," said Hernandez.

In the patio servants came and took their horses, while Hornblower stiffly dismounted and contemplated the ruin which riding had caused to his best silk stockings. The superior servants who conducted them into the house were dressed in clothes similar in their blend of rags and finery to those Hernandez wore — scarlet and gold above, bare feet and rags below. The most gorgeous of all, whose features seemed to indicate a strong dash of negro blood in his ancestry along with the Indian and the slight trace of European, came up with a worried look on his face.

"El Supremo has been kept waiting," he said. "Please come this way as quickly as you can."

He almost ran before them down a corridor to a door studded with brass. On this he knocked loudly, waited a moment, knocked again, and then threw open the door, bending himself double as he did so. Hornblower, at Hernandez' gesture, strode into the room, Hernandez behind him, and the major-domo closed the door. It was a long room, limewashed to a glittering white, whose ceiling was supported by thick wooden beams, painted and carved. Towards the farther end, solitary in the bleak bareness of the room, stood a treble dais, and in a canopied chair on the dais sat the man Hornblower had been sent half round the world to see.

He did not seem very impressive or dignified; a small swarthy man, restless and fidgety, with piercing black eyes and lank black hair beginning to turn grey. From his appearance one might have guessed at only a small admixture of Indian blood in his European ancestry, and he was dressed in European fashion, in a red coat laced with gold, a white stock, and white breeches and stockings; there were gold buckles on his shoes. Hernandez cringed before him.

"You have been a long time," snapped Alvarado. "Eleven men have been flogged during your absence."

"Supremo," sighed Hernandez — his teeth were chattering with fright — "the captain came instantly on hearing your summons."

Alvarado turned his piercing eyes upon Hornblower, who bowed stiffly. His mind was playing with the suspicion that the eleven men who had been flogged had suffered, unaccountably, because of the length of time it took to ride a horse from the beach to the house.

"Captain Horatio Hornblower, of His Britannic Majesty's frigate *Lydia,* at your service, sir," he said.

"You have brought me arms and powder?"

"They are in the ship."

"That is well. You will make arrangements with General Hernandez here for landing them."

Hornblower thought of his frigate's almost empty storerooms; and he had three hundred and eighty men to feed. Moreover, as with every ship's captain, he was already feeling irritation at dependence on the shore. He would be restless and uncomfortable until the *Lydia* was fully charged again with food and water and wood and every other necessary, sufficient to take her back round the Horn at least as far as the West Indies or St. Helena, if not home.

"I can hand nothing over, sir, until my ship's needs are satisfied," he said. He heard Hernandez draw in his breath sharply at this sacrilegious temporising in the face of orders from El Supremo. The latter's eyebrows came together; for a moment it seemed likely that he would attempt to impose his imperious will upon the captain, but immediately afterwards his expression cleared as he realised the folly of quarrelling with his new ally.

"Certainly," he said. "Please make known to General Hernandez what you require, and he will supply you."

Hornblower had had dealings with officers of the Spanish services, and he knew what they could accomplish in the way of fair promises not carried out, of procrastination and shiftiness and doubledealing. He guessed that Spanish American rebel officers would be proportionately less trustworthy. He decided to make known his wants now, so that there might be a fair chance of seeing a part at least of his demands satisfied in the near future.

"My water casks must be refilled tomorrow," he said.

Hernandez nodded.

"There is a spring close to where we landed. If you wish, I will have men to help you."

"Thank you, but that will not be necessary. My ship's crew will attend to it all. Besides water I need — "

Hornblower's mind began to total up all the multifarious wants of a frigate seven months at sea.

"Yes, señor?"

"I shall need two hundred bullocks. Two hundred and fifty if they are thin and small. Five hundred pigs. One hundred quintals of salt. Forty tons of ship's bread, and if biscuit is unobtainable I shall need the equivalent amount of flour, with ovens and fuel provided to bake it. The juice of forty thousand lemons, oranges or limes — I can supply the casks to contain it. Ten tons of sugar. Five tons of tobacco. A ton of coffee. You grow potatoes on this coast, do you not? Then twenty tons of potatoes will suffice."

Hernandez' face had grown longer and longer during this formidable recital.

"But, Captain — " he ventured to protest, but Hornblower cut him short.

"Then for our current needs, while we are in harbour," he went on, "I shall need five bullocks a day, two dozen chickens, as many eggs as you can provide, and sufficient fresh vegetables for the daily consumption of my ship's company."

By nature Hornblower was the mildest of men, but in any matter regarding his ship fear of being deemed a failure drove him into unexpected hardness and temerity.

"Two hundred bullocks!" said the wretched Hernandez. "Five hundred pigs?"

"That is what I said," replied Hornblower, inexorably. "Two hundred *fat* bullocks."

At this point El Supremo intervened.

"See that the captain's wants are satisfied," he said, with an impatient wave of his hand. "Start now."

Hernandez only hesitated for a further tenth of a second, and then retired. The big brass bound door closed silently behind him.

"That is the only way to deal with these people," said El Supremo, lightly. "They are no better than beasts. Any kind of refinement is wasted upon them. Doubtless you saw on your way here various criminals suffering punishment?"

"I did."

"My ancestors on earth," said El Supremo, "went to much trouble in arranging elaborate punishments. They burned people to death with elaborate ceremonial. They cut out their hearts to the accompaniment of music and dances, or pressed them to death in wrappings of raw hide exposed to the sun. I find all that quite unnecessary. A simple order to have the man tied up to die of thirst is sufficient. The man dies, and there is an end of him."

"Yes," said Hornblower.

"They are incapable of absorbing even the simplest of conceptions. There are some who to this very day cannot understand the very obvious principle that the blood of Alvarado and

Moctezuma must be divine. They still cling to their absurd Christs and Virgins."

"Indeed?" said Hornblower.

"One of my earliest lieutenants could not shake himself free from the influence of early education. When I announced my divinity he actually made suggestions that missionaries should be sent out to preach to the tribes so as to convert them, as though I were putting forward a new religion. He could never realise that it was not a matter of opinion but a matter of fact. He was of course one of the first to die of thirst."

"Of course."

Hornblower was utterly bewildered by all this. But he clung to the fact that he had to ally himself to this madman. The revictualling of the *Lydia* depended upon his acting in concert with him, if nothing else did — and that was a matter of the most vital primary importance.

"Your King George must have been delighted to hear that I had decided to act in concert with him," continued El Supremo.

"He charged me with messages to you assuring you of his friendship," said Hornblower, cautiously.

"Of course," said El Supremo, "he would not venture to push himself forward beyond that point. The blood of the family of Guelph naturally cannot compare with that of Alvarado."

"Ha — h'm," said Hornblower. He found that noncommittal noise as useful in conversation with El Supremo as with Lieutenant Bush.

El Supremo's brows approached each other a trifle.

"I suppose you are aware," he said, a little sternly, "of the history of the family of Alvarado? You know who was the first of that name to reach this country?"

"He was Cortez' lieutenant — " began Hornblower.

"Lieutenant? Nothing of the sort. I am surprised that you should believe such lies. He was the leader of the Conquistadores; it is only by the falsification of history that Cortez is represented as in command. Alvarado conquered Mexico, and from Mexico he descended upon this coast and conquered it all, as far as the Isthmus. He married the daughter of Moctezuma, the last of the Emperors; and as a direct descendant from that union I have chosen to select from my family names those of Alvarado and Moctezuma. But in Europe, long before the head of the house came to the Americas, the name of Alvarado can be traced back, beyond the Hapsburgs and the Visigoths, beyond the Romans and the empire of Alexander, to the ultimate sources of time. It is only natural, therefore, that in this present generation the family should have attained to the divine state in my person. I find it satisfactory that you agree with me, Captain — Captain —— "

"Hornblower."

"I thank you. And now I think we had better, Captain Hornblower, discuss the plans for the extension of my Empire."

"As you please," said Hornblower. He felt he must at least agree with this madman until the *Lydia* was revictualled, although his already faint hope of heading a successful insurrection in this country was fast becoming fainter.

"The Bourbon who calls himself King of Spain," said El Supremo, "maintains in this country an official who calls himself Captain General of Nicaragua. I sent to this gentleman some time ago a message ordering him to announce his fealty to me. This he had not done, and he was even misguided enough to hang my messenger publicly in Managua. Of the insolent men whom he subsequently sent to secure my divine person some were killed on the road and some died while attached to stakes, while a few were fortunate enough to see the light and are now included in my army. The Captain General is now, I hear, at the head of an army of three hundred men in the city of El Salvador. When you have landed the weapons consigned to me I propose to move on this town, which I shall burn, along with the Captain General and the unenlightened among his men. Perhaps, Captain, you will accompany me? A burning town is worth seeing."

"My ship must be revictualled first," said Hornblower, sturdily.

"I have given the orders for that," replied El Supremo with a trace of impatience.

"And further," continued Hornblower, "it will be my duty first to ascertain the whereabouts of a Spanish ship of war, the *Natividad,* which I believe to be on this station. Before I can engage in any operations on land I must see that she can do no harm to my ship. I must either capture her or know for certain that she is too distant to interfere."

"Then you had better capture her, Captain. I expect, from the information I have received, that she will be sailing into the bay here at any moment."

"Then I must go back to my ship immediately," said Hornblower, all agitation. The possibility that his frigate might be attacked in his absence by a fifty-gun ship threw him into a seething panic. What would the Lords of the Admiralty say if the *Lydia* were lost while her captain was on shore?

"There is food being brought in. Behold!" said El Supremo.

The door at the end of the hall was flung open as he spoke. A crowd of attendants began to walk slowly in, carrying a large table covered with silver dishes, and bearing four large silver candelabra each supporting five lighted candles.

"Your pardon, but I cannot wait for food. I must not," said Hornblower.

"As you will," said El Supremo indifferently. "Alfonso!"

The negroid major-domo came forward, bowing.

"See that Captain Hornblower goes back to his ship."

El Supremo had no sooner spoken the words than he relapsed into an attitude of contemplation. The bustle attendant upon the bringing in of the banquet he allowed to pass unheeded. He did not bestow another glance on Hornblower, who stood before him, regretting already his precipitation in deciding to rejoin his ship, anxious to cause no offence by a breach of good manners, worried by the need to revictual the *Lydia,* and acutely conscious that his present attitude of uncertainty before a man who was paying him no attention whatever was quite undignified.

"This way, señor," said Alfonso, at his elbow, while El Supremo still gazed blankly over his head. Hornblower yielded, and followed the major-domo out to the patio.

Two men and three horses awaited him there, in the half light.

Without a word, bewildered by this sudden turn of events, Hornblower set his foot in the linked hands of a half naked slave who knelt at his horse's side and swung himself up into the saddle. The escort clattered before him out through the gates, and he followed them; night was falling fast.

At the corner of the path the wide bay opened before them. A young moon was fast fading down the sky. A shadowy shape in the centre of the silver water showed where the *Lydia* swung to her anchor — she, at least, was something solid and matter-of-fact in this mad world. Eastward a mountain top suddenly glowed red, illumining the clouds above it, and then died away into darkness. They rode at a sharp trot down the steep path, past the moaning men tied to the stakes, past the stinking corpses, and into the little town. Here there was neither light nor movement; Hornblower had to leave his horse to the task of following the escort round the corners. The sound of the horses' hoofs ceased as they reached the soft sand of the beach; and simultaneously he heard the pitiful moaning of the first man he had seen tied to a stake and saw the faint phosphorescence of the edge of the sea.

He felt his way in the darkness into the waiting boat, and sat on a thwart while to the accompaniment of an explosion of orders the unseen crew pushed off. There was not a breath of wind — the sea breeze had died with the sunset and the land breeze had not yet sprung up. The unseen crew tugged at six oars, and the water sprang into view, the foam faintly visible as each stroke waked the phosphorescence. Slowly they made their way out into the bay to the rhythmical sound of the oars. Far out across the water he could see the faint loom of the *Lydia,* and a minute later he heard the welcome sound of Bush's voice as he hailed.

"Boat ahoy!"

Hornblower made a speaking trumpet of his hands and hailed back, "*Lydia!*"

The Captain of a King's ship calls himself by the name of that ship when he is on board a small boat.

Hornblower could hear all the expected noises now, could see all the expected sights; the bustle and clatter as boatswain's mates and sideboys ran to the gangway, the measured tramp of the marines, the flickering of lanterns. The boat ran alongside and he sprang to the ladder. It was good to feel solid oak under his feet again. The pipes of the boatswain's mates twittered in chorus; the marines brought their muskets to the present, and Bush was at the gangway to receive him, with all the pomp and ceremony due to a Captain arriving on board.

Hornblower saw, by the lantern light, the relief in Bush's honest face. He glanced round the decks; one watch, wrapped in blankets, was lying on the bare boards of the deck, while the other squatted by the guns ready for action. Bush had very properly maintained all precautions while thus at anchor in a presumably hostile port.

"Very good, Mr. Bush," said Hornblower. Then he became conscious that his white breeches were stained by the dirty saddle, and that his best silk stockings were in threads about his calves. He felt discontented with his appearance; he was ashamed of the fact that he had come back to his ship in this undignified fashion, and without, as far as he knew, having settled anything for the future. He was angry with himself; he feared lest Bush should have a worse opinion of him should he come to know the facts. He felt his cheeks go hot with self-consciousness, and he took refuge, as ever, in uncommunicativeness.

"Ha — h'm," he rasped. "Call me if there is anything unusual to justify it."

With that, and with no other word, he turned and went below to his cabin, where canvas screens replaced the torn down bulkheads.

Bush stared at his disappearing form. The volcanoes flickered and glowed round the bay. The crew, excited at their arrival in this strange land, and anxious to hear about the future, saw themselves doomed to disappointment, just like the officers, who watched with dropped jaws their captain descending the companion ladder.

For one brief instant Hornblower felt that his dramatic appearance and exit compensated him for his consciousness of failure, but it was only for an instant. Seated on his cot, having sent away Polwheal, he felt his spirits fall again. His weary mind set itself vaguely again to debate the question of whether he would be able to obtain stores on the morrow. He fretted about whether he would be able to raise a rebellion successful enough to satisfy the Admiralty. He fretted about the approaching duel with the *Natividad*.

And throughout these considerations he continually found himself blushing again at the recollection of his abrupt dismissal by El Supremo. He felt that there were few captains in His Britannic Majesty's service who would have submitted so meekly to such cavalier treatment.

"But what the devil could I have *done?*" he asked himself pathetically.

Without turning out his lantern he lay on his cot sweating in the still tropical night while his mind raced back and forth through past and future.

And then the canvas screen flapped. A little breath of wind came stealing along the decks. His sailor's instincts kept him informed of how the *Lydia* was swinging to her anchor. He felt the tiny tremor which ran through the ship as she brought up short to her anchor cable in a new direction. The land breeze had begun at last. The ship was cooler at once. Hornblower wriggled over on to his side, and slept.

Chapter V

THOSE doubts and fears which encompassed Hornblower while he was trying to go to sleep the night before vanished with the day. Hornblower felt a new strength running through his veins when he woke. His mind was teeming with plans as he drank the coffee which Polwheal brought him at dawn, and for the first time for weeks he dispensed with his morning walk on the quarterdeck. He had decided as he stepped on the deck that at least he could fill the water casks and restock with fuel, and his first orders sent parties of men hurriedly to the tackles to hoist out the launch and lower the quarter boats. Soon they were off for the shore, charged with the empty casks and manned by crews of excited chattering men; in the bow of each boat sat two marines in their red coats with their muskets loaded and bayonets fixed, and in their ears echoing their final orders from their sergeant, to the effect that if a single sailor succeeded in deserting while on shore every man among them would have his back well scratched with the cat.

An hour later the launch came back under sail, deep laden with her water casks full, and while the casks were being swayed out of her and lowered into the hold Mr. Midshipman Hooker came running up to Hornblower and touched his hat.

"The beef cattle are coming down to the shore, sir," he said.

Hornblower had to struggle hard to keep his face immobile and to receive the news as if he expected it.

"How many?" he snapped; it seemed a useful question to ask in order to waste time, but the answer was more surprising still.

"Hundreds, sir. There's a Dago in charge with a lot to say, but there's no one ashore who can speak his lingo."

"Send him out to me when you go ashore again," said Hornblower.

Hornblower spent the interval granted him in making up his

mind. He hailed the outlook at the main royal masthead to ensure that a careful watch was kept to seaward. On the one hand there was the chance that the *Natividad* might come sailing in from the Pacific, in which case the *Lydia,* caught with half her crew ashore, would have no time to clear from the bay and would have to fight in confined waters and with the odds necessarily against her. On the other hand there was the opportunity of filling up completely with stores and regaining entire independence of the shore. From what Hornblower had seen of conditions prevailing there he judged that to postpone regaining that independence would be dangerous in the extreme; at any moment Don Julian Alvarado's rebellion might come to a hurried and bloody ending.

It was Hernandez who came out to him, in the same boat with the two tiny lateen sails in which Hornblower had been ferried across last night. They exchanged salutes on the quarterdeck.

"There are four hundred cattle awaiting your orders, Captain," said Hernandez. "My men are driving them down to the beach."

"Good," said Hornblower, his mind still not made up.

"I am afraid it will take longer to assemble the pigs," went on Hernandez. "My men are sweeping the country for them, but pigs are slow animals to drive."

"Yes," said Hornblower.

"With regard to the salt, it will not be easy to collect the hundred quintals you asked for. Until our lord declared his divinity salt was a royal monopoly and scarce in consequence, but I have sent a party to the salt pans at Jiquilisio and hope to find sufficient there."

"Yes," said Hornblower. He remembered demanding salt, but he had no distinct recollection of the quantity he had asked for.

"The women are out collecting the lemons, oranges, and limes which you ordered," continued Hernandez, "but I am afraid it will be two days before we shall have them all ready."

"Ha — h'm," said Hornblower.

"The sugar is ready at El Supremo's mill, however. And with regard to the tobacco, señor, there is a good deal in store. What special kind do you prefer? For some time we have only been rolling cigars for our own consumption, but I can set the women to work again after the fruit has been collected."

"Ha — h'm," said Hornblower again, suppressing just in time the cry of delight which nearly escaped him involuntarily at the mention of cigars — it was three months since he had last smoked one. Virginia pigtail twist was what his men used, but that, of course, would be unobtainable on this coast. However, he had often seen British sailors chewing and enjoying the half cured native leaf.

"Send as many cigars as will be convenient to you," he said, lightly. "For the rest, it is of no importance what you send."

Hernandez bowed.

"Thank you, señor. The coffee, the vegetables, and the eggs will of course be easy to supply. But with regard to the bread —— "

"Well?"

Hernandez was obviously nervous about what he was going to say next.

"Your Excellency will forgive me, but in this country we have only maize. There is a little wheat grown in the tierra templeda, but it rests still in the hands of the unenlightened. Would maize flour suffice?"

Hernandez' face was working with anxiety as he gazed at Hornblower. It was only then that Hornblower realised that Hernandez was in terror of his life, and that El Supremo's light-hearted endorsement of the requisitions he had made was far more potent than any stamped and sealed order addressed to a Spanish official.

"This is very serious," said Hornblower sternly. "My English sailors are unaccustomed to maize flour."

"I know that," said Hernandez, his interlocked fingers working galvanically. "But I assure Your Excellency that I can only obtain wheat flour for them by fighting for it, and I know that El Supremo would not like me to fight at present. El Supremo will be angry."

Hornblower remembered the abject fright with which Hernandez had regarded El Supremo the night before. The man was in terror lest he should be denounced as having failed to execute his orders. And then, suddenly, Hornblower remembered something he had unaccountably forgotten to ask for — something more important, if possible, than tobacco or fruit, and certainly far more important than the difference between maize flour and wheat.

"Very well," he said. "I will agree to use maize flour. But in consequence of this deficiency there is something else I must ask for."

"Certainly, Captain. I will supply whatever you ask. You have only to name it."

"I want drink for my men," said Hornblower. "Is there wine to be had here? Ardent spirits?"

"There is a little wine, Your Excellency. Only a little. The people on this coast drink an ardent spirit with which you are perhaps not acquainted. It is good when of good quality. It is distilled from the waste of the sugar mills, from the treacle, Your Excellency."

"Rum, by God!" exclaimed Hornblower.

"Yes, señor, rum. Would that be of any use to Your Excellency?"

"I shall accept it in lieu of anything better," said Hornblower sternly.

His heart was leaping with joy. It would appear like a miracle to his officers that he should conjure rum and tobacco from this volcano-riddled coast.

"Thank you, Captain. And shall we begin to slaughter the cattle now?"

That was the question on which Hornblower had been postponing a decision ever since he had heard about the arrival of the cattle on the beach. Hornblower looked up at the lookout at the masthead. He tested the strength of the wind. He gazed out to sea before he took the plunge.

"Very well," he said at length. "We will start now."

The sea breeze was not nearly as strong as yesterday, and the weaker the breeze the less chance there was of the *Natividad* coming in to interrupt the *Lydia's* revictualling. And as events turned out the *Lydia* completed the work undisturbed. For two days the boats plied back and forth between the beach and the ship. They came back piled high with bloody joints of meat; the sand of the shore ran red with the blood of the slaughtered animals, while the half-tame vultures gorged themselves into coma on the piled offal. On board the ship the purser and his crew toiled like slaves in the roasting heat, cramming the brine barrels with the meat and tugging them into position in the storerooms. The cooper and his mates worked for two days with hardly a break, making and repairing casks. Sacks of flour, ankers of rum, bales of tobacco — the hands at the tackles sweated as they swayed these up from the boats. The *Lydia* was gorging herself full.

So obvious were the good intentions of those on shore that Hornblower was able to give orders that the cargo consigned to this coast should be released, and so the boats which bore the meat and flour to the ship returned laden with cases of muskets and kegs of powder and shot. Hornblower had his gig hoisted out, and was rowed periodically round his ship inspecting her trim, in the anticipation lest at any moment he would have to hoist up his anchor and beat out to sea to fight the *Natividad*.

The work proceeded by night as well as by day; in fifteen years at sea — every one a year of warfare — Hornblower had seen many opportunities lost as a result of some trivial lack of energy, some omission to drive a crew into exerting the last ounce of its strength. He had lost opportunities himself like that, for that matter. He still felt a revulsion of shame at the recollection of how he had missed that privateer off the Azores, for example. For fear of standing condemned again in his own eyes he drove his men to work until they dropped.

There was no time for enjoyment of the pleasures of land at the moment. The shore party did indeed cook their rations before a huge bonfire, and revel in roast fresh meat after seven months of boiled salt meat, but with the characteristic contrariness of British sailors they turned with revulsion from the delicious fruit which was offered them — bananas and paw-paws, pineapples and guavas, and considered themselves the victims of sharp practice because these were substituted for their regulation ration of boiled dried peas.

And then, on the second evening, as Hornblower walked the quarterdeck enjoying the sea breeze at its freshest, and revelling in the thought that he was free of the land if necessary for another six months, and looking forward with the sheerest joy to his imminent dinner of roast fowl, there came the sound of firing from the beach. A scattering volley at first; a few dropping shots, and then another ragged volley. Hornblower forgot his dinner, his feeling of well-being, everything. Trouble on the mainland, of whatever sort, meant that the success of his mission was being imperilled. In hot haste he called for his gig, and he was pulled to the shore by a crew who made the stout oars bend as they flung their weight on the handles in response to the profane urgings of Coxswain Brown.

The scene that greeted his eyes as he rounded the point excited his worst apprehensions. The whole landing party was clubbed together on the beach; the dozen marines were in line on one flank, reloading their muskets; the sailors were bunched beside them armed with whatever weapons had come to their hands. In a wide semicircle round them were the inhabitants, brandishing swords and muskets, and in the no man's land between the two parties lay one or two corpses. At the water's edge, behind the sailors, lay one of the hands with two of his mates bending over him. He was propped up on his elbow and he was vomiting floods of blood.

Hornblower sprang into the shallows; he paid no attention to the wounded sailor, but pushed his way through the mob before him. As he emerged into the open there came a puff of smoke from the half circle up the beach and a bullet sang over his head. He paid no attention to that either.

"Put those muskets down!" he roared at the marines, and he turned towards the gesticulating inhabitants and held up his hand, palm forward, in the universal and instinctive gesture of peace. There was no room in his mind for thought of personal danger, so hot was he with anger at the thought that someone was botching his chance of success.

"What's the meaning of this?" he demanded.

Galbraith was in command. He was about to speak, but he was given no opportunity. One of the sailors who had been attending to the dying man came pushing forward, discipline forgotten in the blind whirl of sentimental indignation which Hornblower instantly recognised as characteristic of the lower deck — and which he despised and distrusted.

"They been torturing a pore devil up there, sir," he said. "Lashed him to a spar and left him to die of thirst."

"Silence!" bellowed Hornblower, beside himself with rage not merely at this breach of discipline but at realising the difficulties ahead of him. "Mr. Galbraith!"

Galbraith was slow of speech and of mind.

"I don't know how it started, sir," he began; although he had been at sea since childhood there was still a trace of Scotch in his accent. "A party came running back from up there. They had Smith with them, wounded."

"He's dead now," put in a voice.

"Silence!" roared Hornblower again.

"I saw they were going to attack us, and so I had the marines fire, sir," went on Galbraith.

"I'll speak to you later, Mr. Galbraith," snapped Hornblower. "You, Jenkins. And you, Poole. What were you doing up there?"

"Well, sir, it was like this, sir —— " began Jenkins. He was sheepish and crestfallen now. Hornblower had pricked the bubble of his indignation and he was being publicly convicted of a breach of orders.

"You knew the order that no one was to go beyond the creek?"

"Yessir."

"Tomorrow morning I'll show you what orders mean. And you, too, Poole. Where's the sergeant of marines?"

"Here, sir."

"A fine guard you keep, sergeant, to let these men get by. What were your pickets about?"

The sergeant could say nothing; he could only stand rigidly at attention in face of this incontrovertible proof of his being found wanting.

"Mr. Simmonds will speak to you in the morning," went on Hornblower. "I don't expect you'll keep those stripes on your arm much longer."

Hornblower glowered round at the landing party. His fierce rebukes had them all cowed and subservient now, and he felt his anger ebbing away as he realised that he had managed this without having to say a word in extenuation of Spanish-American justice. He turned to greet Hernandez, who had come riding up as fast as his little horse would gallop, reining up on his haunches in a shower of sand.

"Did El Supremo give orders for this attack on my men?" asked Hornblower, getting in the first broadside.

"No, Captain," said Hernandez, and Hornblower rejoiced to see how he winced at the mention of El Supremo's name.

"I think he will not be too pleased with you when I tell him about this," went on Hornblower.

"Your men tried to release a man condemned to death," said Hernandez, half sullenly, half apologetically. He was clearly not too sure of his ground, and was nervous about what would be Alvarado's attitude towards this incident. Hornblower kept a rasp in his voice as he went on speaking. None of the Englishmen round him, as far as he knew, could speak Spanish, but he was anxious for his crew to believe (now that discipline was restored) that he was wholeheartedly on their side.

"That does not permit your men to kill mine," he said.

"They are angry and discontented," said Hernandez. "The whole country has been swept to find food for you. The man your men tried to save was condemned for driving his pigs into the bush to keep them from being taken and given to you."

Hernandez made this last speech reproachfully and with a hint of anger; Hornblower was anxious to be conciliatory if that were possible without exasperating his own men. Hornblower had in mind the plan of leading Hernandez out of earshot of the Englishmen and then softening his tone, but before he could act upon it his attention was caught by the sight of a horseman galloping down the beach at full speed, waving his wide straw hat. Every eye turned towards this new arrival — a peon of the ordinary Indian type. Breathlessly he announced his news.

"A ship — a ship coming!"

He was so excited that he lapsed into the Indian speech, and Hornblower could not understand his further explanations. Hernandez had to interpret for him.

"This man has been keeping watch on the top of the mountain up there," he said. "He says that from there he could see the sails of a ship coming towards the bay."

He addressed several more questions rapidly, one after the other, to the lookout, and was answered with nods and gesticulations and a torrent of Indian speech.

"He says," went on Hernandez, "that he has often seen the *Natividad* before, and he is sure this is the same ship, and she is undoubtedly coming in here."

"How far off is she?" asked Hornblower, and Hernandez translated the answer.

"A long way, seven leagues or more," he said. "She is coming from the southeastward — from Panama."

Hornblower pulled at his chin, deep in thought.

"She'll carry the sea breeze down with her until sunset," he muttered to himself, and glanced up at the sun. "That will be another hour. An hour after that she'll get the land breeze. She'll be able to hold her course, close hauled. She could be here in the bay by midnight."

A stream of plans and ideas was flooding into his mind. Against the possibility of the ship's arrival in the dark must be balanced what he knew of the Spanish habit at sea of snugging down for the night, and of attempting no piece of seamanship at all complicated save under the best possible conditions. He wished he knew more about the Spanish captain.

"Has this ship, the *Natividad*, often come into this bay?" he asked.

"Yes, Captain, often."

"Is her captain a good seaman?"

"Oh, yes, Captain, very good."

"Ha — h'm," said Hornblower. A landsman's opinion of the

seamanship of a frigate captain might not be worth much, but still it was an indication.

Hornblower tugged at his chin again. He had fought in ten single ship actions. If he took the *Lydia* to sea and engaged the *Natividad* on open water the two ships might well batter each other into wrecks. Rigging and spars and hulls and sails would be shot to pieces. The *Lydia* would have a good many casualties which would be quite irreplaceable here in the Pacific. She would expend her priceless ammunition. On the other hand, if he stayed in the bay and yet the plan he had in mind did not succeed — if the *Natividad* waited off shore until the morning — he would have to beat his way out of the bay against the sea breeze, presenting the Spaniards with every possible advantage as he came out to fight them. The *Natividad's* superiority of force was already such that it was rash to oppose the *Lydia* to her. Could he dare to risk increasing the odds? But the possible gains were so enormous that he made up his mind to run the risk.

Chapter VI

GHOSTLIKE in the moonlight, with the first puffs of the land breeze, the *Lydia* glided across the bay. Hornblower had not ventured to hoist sail, lest a gleam of canvas might be visible to the distant ship at sea. The launch and the cutter towed the ship, sounding as they went, into the deep water at the foot of the island at the entrance of the bay — Manguera Island, Hernandez called it when Hornblower had cautiously sketched out his plan to him. For an hour the men laboured at the oars, although Hornblower did his best to aid them, standing by the wheel and making as much use as possible of the leeway acquired by the ship through the force of the puffs of wind on the *Lydia's* rigging. They reached the new anchorage at last, and the anchor splashed into the water.

"Have that cable buoyed and ready to slip, Mr. Bush," said Hornblower.

"Aye aye, sir."

"Call the boats alongside. I want the men to rest."

"Aye aye, sir."

"Mr. Gerard, you have charge of the deck. See that the lookouts keep awake. I want Mr. Bush and Mr. Galbraith to come below with me."

"Aye aye, sir."

The ship was seething quietly with excitement. Everyone on board had guessed the captain's plan, even though the details of its execution, which he was now explaining to his lieutenants, were still unknown. In the two hours which had elapsed since the arrival of the news of the *Natividad's* approach Hornblower's mind had worked busily at the perfection of his plan. Nothing must go wrong. Everything that could possibly contribute to success must be done.

"That is all understood?" he asked, finally; he stood, stooping under the deck beams in his screened off cabin while his lieutenants fiddled awkwardly with their hats.

"Aye aye, sir."

"Very good," said Hornblower, dismissing them.

But within five minutes impatience and anxiety drove him up on deck again.

"Masthead, there? What can you see of the enemy?"

"She's just come up over the island, sir. She's more than hull down. I can only see her torps'ls, sir, below her t'garns."

"What's her course?"

"She's holding her wind, sir. She ought to make the bay on this tack."

"Ha — h'm," said Hornblower, and went below again.

It would be four hours at least before the *Natividad* reached the entrance, and before he could take any further action. He found himself pacing, stoopshouldered, up and down the tiny limits of his cabin, and checked himself furiously. The iron-nerved captain of his dreams would not allow himself to work himself into this sort of fever, even though his professional reputation was to be at stake in four hours' time. He must show the ship that he, too, could face uncertainty with indifference.

"Pass the word for Polwheal," he snapped, coming out through the screen and addressing a group by a maindeck gun; and when Polwheal appeared he went on, "My compliments to Mr. Bush, and tell him that if he can spare Mr. Galbraith and Mr. Clay and Mr. Savage from their duties I would be glad if they would sup with me and have a hand of whist."

Galbraith was nervous, too. Not merely was he anticipating a battle, but hanging over his head there was still the promised reprimand for his part in the skirmish of the afternoon. His rawboned Scotch figure moved restlessly, and his face was flushed over his high cheek bones. Even the two midshipmen were subdued as well as fidgety.

Hornblower compelled himself to play the part of the courtly host, while every word he uttered was designed to increase his reputation for imperturbability. He apologised for his shortcomings of the supper — the ship being cleared for action involved the extinction of all fires and the consequent necessity for serving cold food. But the sight of the cold roast chickens, the cold roast pork, the golden cakes of maize, the dishes of fruit, roused Mr. Midshipman Savage's sixteen year old appetite and caused him to forget his embarrassment.

"This is better than rats, sir," he said, rubbing his hands.

"Rats?" asked Hornblower, vaguely. For all his appearance of attention his thoughts were up on deck, and not in the cabin.

"Yes, sir. Until we made this harbour rats had become a favourite dish in the midshipmen's berth."

"That they had," echoed Clay. He carved himself substantial slices of cold pork, with plenty of crackling, and added them to the half chicken on his plate. "I was paying that thief Bailey threepence apiece for prime rats."

Desperately Hornblower jerked his mind away from the approaching *Natividad* and delved back into the past when he had been a half starved midshipman, homesick and seasick. His seniors then had eaten rats with gusto, and maintained that a biscuit-fed rat was far more delicate a dish than beef two years in cask. He had never been able to stomach them himself, but he would not admit it to these boys.

"Threepence apiece for rats seems a trifle dear," he said. "I can't remember paying as much as that when I was a midshipman."

"Why, sir, did you ever eat them yourself?" asked Savage, amazed.

In reply to this direct question Hornblower could only lie.

"Of course," he said. "Midshipmen's berths were much the same twenty years ago as now. I always maintained that a rat who had had the run of the bread-locker all his life made a dish fit for a king, let alone a midshipman."

"God bless my soul!" gasped Clay, laying down his knife and fork. He had never thought for a moment that this stern and inflexible captain of his had once been a rat-eating midshipman.

The two boys blinked at their captain with admiration. This little human touch had won their hearts completely, as Hornblower had known it would. At the end of the table Galbraith sighed audibly. He had been eating rats himself only three days ago, but he knew full well that to admit it would not increase the boys' respect for him, but would rather diminish it, for he was that sort of officer. Hornblower had to make Galbraith feel at home, too.

"A glass of wine with you, Mr. Galbraith," he said, raising his glass. "I must apologise because this is not my best Madeira, but I am keeping the last two bottles for when I entertain the Spanish captain as our prisoner tomorrow. To our victories of the future!"

The glasses were drained, and constraint dwindled. Hornblower had spoken of "*our* prisoner" when most captains would have said "*my* prisoner." And he had said "*our* victories." The strict cold captain, the stern disciplinarian, had for a moment revealed human characteristics and had admitted his inferiors to his fellowship. Any one of the three junior officers would at that moment have laid down his life for his captain — and Hornblower, looking round at their flushed faces, was aware of it. It gratified him at the same moment as it irritated him; but with a battle in the immediate future which might well be an affair of the utmost desperation he knew that he must have behind him a crew not merely loyal but enthusiastic.

Another midshipman, young Knyvett, came into the cabin.

"Mr. Bush's compliments, sir, and the enemy is hull up from the masthead now, sir."

"Is she holding her course for the bay?"

"Yes, sir. Mr. Bush says two hours ought to see her within range."

"Thank you, Mr. Knyvett," said Hornblower, dismissing him. The reminder that in two hours he would be at grips with a fifty-gun ship set his heart beating faster again. It took a convulsive effort to maintain an unmoved countenance.

"We still have ample time for our rubber, gentlemen," said Hornblower.

The weekly evening of whist which Captain Hornblower played with his officers was for these latter — especially the midshipmen — a sore trial. Hornblower himself was a keen good player; his close observation and his acute study of the psychology of his juniors were of great help to him. But to some of his officers, without card sense, and floundering helplessly with no memory for the cards that had been played, Hornblower's card evenings were periods of torment.

Polwheal cleared the table, spread the green tablecloth and brought the cards. When play began Hornblower found it easier to forget about the approaching battle. Whist was enough of a passion with him to claim most of his attention whatever the distraction. It was only during the intervals of play, during the deals and while marking the score, that he found his heart beating faster again and felt the blood surging up in his throat. He marked the fall of the cards with close attention, making allowance for Savage's schoolboy tendency to dash out his aces, and for the fact that Galbraith invariably forgot, until it was too late, to signal a short suit. One rubber ended quickly; there was almost dismay on the faces of the other three as Hornblower proffered the cards for cutting for a second one. He kept his face expressionless.

"You really must remember, Clay," he said, "to lead the king from a sequence of king, queen, knave. The whole art of leading is based upon that principle."

"Aye aye, sir," said Clay, rolling his eyes drolly at Savage, but Hornblower looked up sharply and Clay hurriedly composed his expression. Play continued — and to all of them seemed interminable. It came to an end at last, however.

"Rubber," announced Hornblower, marking up the score. "I think, gentlemen, that it is almost time that we went on deck."

There was a general sigh of relief and a scraping of feet on the deck. But at all costs Hornblower felt that he must consolidate his reputation for imperturbability.

"The rubber would not be over," he said, dryly, "if Mr. Savage had paid attention to the score. It being nine, Mr. Savage and Mr. Galbraith had only to win the odd trick to secure the rubber. Hence Mr. Savage, at the eighth trick, should have played his ace of hearts instead of risking the finesse. I grant that if the finesse had been successful he would have won two more tricks, but —— "

Hornblower droned on, while the other three writhed in their chairs. Yet they glanced at each other with admiration for him in their eyes as he preceded them up the companion ladder.

Up on deck everything was deathly still as the crew lay at their posts. The moon was setting fast, but there was ample light still as soon as the eye grew accustomed to it. Bush touched his hat to the captain.

"The enemy is still heading for the bay, sir," he said hoarsely.

"Send the crews into the launch and cutter again," replied Hornblower. He climbed the mizzen rigging to the mizzen top gallant yard. From here he could just see over the island; a mile away, with the setting moon behind her, he could see the white canvas of the *Natividad* as she stood in, close hauled, across the entrance. He struggled with his agitation as he endeavoured to predict her movements. There was small chance of her noticing, against the dark sky, the top gallant masts of the *Lydia*; and it was on the assumption that she would not that all his plans were based. She must go about soon, and her new course would bring her directly to the island. Perhaps she would weather it, but not likely. She would have to go about again to enter the bay, and that would be his opportunity. As he watched, he saw her canvas gleam brighter for a space and then darken again as she came round. She was heading for the middle of the entrance, but her leeway and the beginning of the ebb tide would carry back to the island. He went down again to the deck.

"Mr. Bush," he said, "send the hands aloft ready to set sail."

The ship was filled with gentle noises as bare feet padded over the deck and up the rigging. Hornblower brought the silver whistle out of his pocket. He did not trouble to ask whether everyone was ready for the signal and properly instructed in the part he had to play; Bush and Gerard were efficient officers.

"I am going forr'ard, now, Mr. Bush," he said. "I shall try and get back to the quarterdeck in time, but you know my orders if I do not."

"Aye aye, sir."

Hornblower hurried forward along the gangway, past the forecastle carronades with their crews crouching round them, and swung himself over onto the bowsprit. From the sprit sail yard he could see round the corner of the island; the *Natividad* was heading straight for him. He could see the glimmer of phosphorescence foam about her cut water. He could almost hear the sound of her passage through the water. He swallowed hard, and then all his excitement vanished and he was left deadly cool. He had forgotten about himself, and his mind was making calculations of time and space like a machine. Now he could hear the voice of a man at the lead on board the *Natividad*, although he could distinguish no word. The Spaniard was coming very close. By now he could hear the babble of the Spanish crew, everyone busy talking, like every Spaniard, and no one looking out sufficiently well to catch sight of the *Lydia's* bare spars. Then he heard orders being shouted from the *Natividad's* deck; she was going about. At the very first sound he put the whistle to his lips and blew, and the whole of the *Lydia* sprang into activity. Sail was loosed from every yard simultaneously. The cable was slipped, the boats were cast off. Hornblower, racing aft again, collided with the hands at the braces as the ship paid off. He picked himself off the deck and ran on, while the *Lydia* gathered way and surged forward. He reached the wheel in time.

"Steady!" he called to the quartermaster. "Port a little! A little more! Now, hard-a-starboard!"

So quickly had it all happened that the Spaniard had only just gone about and had gathered no way on her new course when the *Lydia* came leaping upon her out of the blackness behind the island and rasped alongside. Months of drill bore their fruit in the English ship. The guns crashed out in a single shattering broadside as the ships touched, sweeping the deck of the *Natividad* with grape. Overhead the topmen ran out along the yards and lashed the ships together. On deck the cheering boarders came rushing to the portside gangway.

On board the Spaniard there was utter surprise. One moment all hands had been engrossed with the work of the ship, and the next, seemingly, an unknown enemy had come crashing alongside; the night had been torn to shreds with the flare of hostile guns; on every hand men had been struck down by the hurtling shot, and now an armed host, yelling like fiends from the pit, came pouring onto the deck. Not the most disciplined and experienced crew could have withstood the shock of that surprise. During the twenty years the *Natividad* had sailed the Pacific coast no enemy had been nearer to her than four thousand miles of sea.

Yet even then there were some stout hearts who attempted resistance. These were officers who drew their swords; on the high quarterdeck there was an armed detachment who had been served out with weapons in consequence of the rumours of rebellion on shore; there were a few men who grasped capstan bars and belaying pins; but the upper deck was swept clear immediately by the wave of boarders with their pikes and cutlasses. A single pistol flashed and exploded. The Spaniards who offered resistance were struck down or chased below; the others were herded together under guard.

And on the lower deck the men sought blindly round for leaders, for means of resistance. They were gathering together in the darkness ready to oppose the enemy above them, and to defend the hatchways, when suddenly a new yelling burst out behind them. Gerard's two boats' crews had reached the *Natividad's* port side, and prising open the lower deck ports, came swarming in, yelling like fiends as their orders bid them do — Hornblower had foreseen that the moral effect of a surprise attack would be intensified, especially against undisciplined Spaniards, if the attackers made as much noise as possible. At this new surprise the resistance of the lower deck broke down completely, and Hornblower's prescience in detaching the two boats' crews to make this diversion was justified.

Chapter VII

THE Captain of the *Lydia* was taking his usual morning walk on the quarterdeck of his ship. Half a dozen Spanish officers had attempted, on his first appearance, to greet him with formal courtesy, but they had been hustled away by the *Lydia's* crew, indignant that their Captain's walk, sacrosanct after so many months, should be disturbed by mere prisoners.

The Captain had a good deal to think about, too — so much, in fact, that he could spare no time to rejoice in the knowledge that his frigate last night, in capturing a two decker without losing a man, had accomplished a feat without precedent in the long annals of British naval history. He wanted instead to think about his next move. With the capture of the *Natividad* he was lord of the South Sea. He knew well enough that the communications by land were so difficult that the whole trade — the whole life, it might be said — of the country depended upon the coastwise traffic; and now not a boat could move without his license. In fifteen years of warfare he had learned the lessons of sea power. There was at least a chance now that with Alvarado's aid he might set the whole of Central America into such a flame that the Spanish Government would rue the day when they had decided to throw in their lot with Bonaparte.

Hornblower paced up and down the sanded deck. There were other possibilities, too. Northwestward along the coast lay Acapulco, whither came and whence departed yearly galleons bearing a million sterling in treasure. The capture of a galleon would at a stroke make him a wealthy man — he could buy an estate in England then; could buy a whole village and be a squire, with the country folk touching their hats to him as he drove by in his coach. Maria would like that, although he could not imagine Maria playing the part of a great lady with any grace.

Hornblower tore his mind away from the contemplation of Maria snatched from her Southsea lodgings and settled in a country home. To the east was Panama, with its stored silver from Peru, its pearling fleet, its whitewashed golden altar which had escaped Morgan but would not escape him. A blow there, at the central knot of the transcontinental communications, would be the best strategy perhaps, as well as being potentially profitable. He tried to think about Panama.

Forward, Sullivan, the red haired Irish vagabond, was perched on a carronade slide with his fiddle, and round him a dozen sailors, their horny feet flapping on the deck, were setting to partners. Twenty five guineas apiece, at least, the men would get as prize money for the capture of the *Natividad*, and they were already spending it in imagination. He looked across to where the *Natividad* swung at anchor. Her waist was black with her crew, crammed on her upper deck. On her old fashioned poop and quarterdeck he could see the red coats and shakoes of his marines, and he could see, too, the carronades pointing down into the waist and the men posted beside them with lighted matches. Gerard, whom he had left on board as prizemaster, had served in a Liverpool slaver in his day and knew well how to keep a ship full of hostile humanity in subjection — although, parted from their officers, Hornblower for one did not anticipate trouble from that crew.

Hornblower knew that he must make up his mind about what to do with the *Natividad*, and more especially with his prisoners. He could not hand them over to the tender mercies of El Supremo; his own crew would hardly permit that. He tried to think about the problem. A long line of pelicans came flying by, more rigid in their formation than the Channel fleet at drill. A frigate bird, superb with its forked tail, came wheeling above them with motionless wings, and having obviously decided that they were not worth plundering, swooped away again towards the island where the cormorants were fishing industriously. The sun was already hot and the water of the bay was as blue as the sky above.

Hornblower cursed sun and pelicans and frigate birds as he tried to concentrate on the problems before him. He paced moodily up and down the deck another half dozen times. Then Midshipman Knyvett barred his way, touching his hat.

"What the devil is it now?" snapped Hornblower.

"Boat coming alongside, sir. Mr. — Mr. Hernandez on board."

That was only to be expected.

"Very good," said Hornblower, and went down the gangway to greet Hernandez as he came up the side. Hernandez wasted no time on felicitations for the late victory. In the service of El Supremo apparently even Spanish-Americans grew abrupt and businesslike.

"El Supremo wishes to see you at once, Captain," said Hernandez. "My boat is waiting."

"Indeed," said Hornblower. He knew well that dozens of his brother captains in the British service would be infuriated at such a cavalier message. He toyed with the idea of sending back to tell El Supremo to come out to the ship himself if he wanted to interview her captain. But he knew that it would be foolish to imperil his cordial relations with the shore, upon which so much of his success depended, upon a mere question of dignity. The captor of the *Natividad* could afford to overlook the presumption of others.

A compromise suggested itself to him; he could keep Hernandez waiting for an hour or two so as to bolster up his own dignity. But his commonsense rejected the notion. Hornblower hated compromises, and this one would only (like most compromises) irritate one side and do no good to the other. Far better to put his pride in his pocket and to come at once.

"Certainly," he said. "My duties leave me free at the moment."

But this time, at least, there was no need to dress up for the occasion. There was no call to put on his best silk stockings and his buckled shoes. The capture of the *Natividad* was a clearer proof of his bonafides than any gold-hilted sword.

It was only while giving final orders to Bush that Hornblower remembered that last night's success gave him adequate grounds for not flogging the erring Jenkins and Poole, and for not reprimanding Galbraith. That was an enormous relief, anyway. It helped to clear away the clouds of depression which always tended to settle on him after every success. It cheered him up as he mounted the minute horse which awaited him on shore, and rode past the mountain of stinking animal intestines, and along the avenue of dead men, up to El Supremo's house.

The appearance of El Supremo, sitting in his canopied chair on his dais, seemed for all the world to indicate that he had been sitting there, immobile, since the occasion four days ago (it seemed more like a month) when Hornblower had left him.

"So you have already done what I wished you to do, Captain?" were his opening words.

"I captured the *Natividad* last night," said Hornblower.

"And the provisioning of your ship, is, I understand, complete?"

"Yes."

"Then," said El Supremo, "you have done what I wanted. That is what I said before."

In the face of such sublime self assurance there was no point in arguing.

"This afternoon," said El Supremo, "I shall proceed with my plan for the capture of the city of El Salvador and the man who calls himself Captain General of Nicaragua."

"Yes?" said Hornblower.

"There are fewer difficulties before me now, Captain. You may not be aware that the roads between here and El Salvador are not as good as roads might be. At one place the path goes up one hundred and twenty seven steps cut in the lava between two precipices. It is difficult for a mule, to say nothing of a horse, to make the journey, and an evilly disposed person armed with a musket could cause much trouble."

"I expect he could," said Hornblower.

"However," said El Supremo, "El Salvador lies less than ten miles from the sea, and there is a good road from the city to its port of La Libertad. This afternoon I shall sail with five hundred men in the two ships to La Libertad. As this town is no more than a hundred miles away I shall reach there at dawn tomorrow. Tomorrow evening I shall dine in El Salvador."

"Ha — h'm," said Hornblower. He was wondering how best to present in argument the difficulties he could see ahead.

"You killed very few of the crew of the *Natividad*, Captain?" asked El Supremo, and thereby approached directly some of the very difficulties Hornblower had in mind.

"Eleven killed," said Hornblower. "And eighteen wounded, of whom four seem unlikely to recover."

"So you left enough to work the ship?"

"Ample, señor, if —— "

"That is what I wanted. And, Captain, human beings in addressing me do not use the expression 'señor.' That is insufficiently honorific. I am El Supremo."

Hornblower could only bow in reply. El Supremo's marvellous manner was like a stone wall.

"The navigating officers are still alive?" went on El Supremo.

"Yes," said Hornblower; and, because he could see trouble close ahead and was anxious to keep it to a minimum, he added, with a gulp, "Supremo."

"Then," said El Supremo, "I will take the *Natividad* into my service. I will kill the executive officers and replace them with men of my own. The others and the common sailors will serve me."

There was nothing intrinsically impossible in what El Supremo suggested; Hornblower knew from experience that the Spanish navy, old fashioned as always, maintained a rigid distinction (such as was fast dying out in his own service) between the officers who worked the ship and the gentlemen who commanded it. And Hornblower had no doubt whatever as to what choice the seamen and sailing master would make if asked to choose between death by torture and serving El Supremo.

Nor could it be denied that El Supremo's suggestion was in many ways a good one; to transport five hundred men in the *Lydia* alone would be difficult, to say the least, while the *Lydia* by herself would find it impossible to blockade completely all the thousand miles of coast — two ships would cause far more than twice as much trouble to the enemy in that way. Yet to hand over the *Natividad* meant starting an endless and probably unsuccessful argument with the lords of the Admiralty on the question of prize money. And he could not in honour hand over the Spanish officers to the death El Supremo had in mind for them. He had to think quickly.

"The *Natividad* is the prize of my King," he said. "Perhaps he would not be pleased if I let her go."

"He certainly would be displeased if he knew you had offended *me*," said El Supremo. His eyebrows came closer together, and Hornblower heard Hernandez beside him take a quick breath. "I have noticed before, Captain Hornblower, that you have verged upon disrespect towards me, and I have been mild enough to attribute it to your foreign breeding."

Hornblower was still thinking hurriedly. A little more opposition would cause this madman to order him out for execution, and if her captain were killed the *Lydia* would certainly not fight for El Supremo. There would indeed be a complicated situation in the Pacific, and the *Lydia*, with friends neither among the rebels nor among the government, would probably never reach home again — especially with the unimaginative Bush in command. England would lose a fine frigate and a fine opportunity. He must sacrifice his prize money, the thousand pounds or so with which he had wanted to dazzle Maria's eyes. But at all costs he must keep his prisoners alive.

"I am sure it is my foreign breeding which is to blame, Supremo," he said. "It is difficult for me to express in a foreign tongue all the delicate shades of meaning which it is necessary to convey. How could it possibly be imagined that I could be lacking in respect to El Supremo?"

El Supremo nodded. It was satisfactory to see that a madman who attributed almightiness to himself was naturally inclined to accept the grossest flattery at its face value.

"The ship is yours, Supremo," went on Hornblower, "she has been yours since my men first set foot on her deck last night. And when in the future a vast Armada sails the Pacific under El Supremo's direction I only wish it to be remembered that the first ship of that fleet was taken from the Spaniards by Captain Hornblower at El Supremo's orders."

El Supremo nodded again, and then turned to Hernandez.

"General," he said, "make arrangements for five hundred men to go on board the ships at noon. I will sail with them and so will you."

Hernandez bowed and departed; it was easy to see that there was no chance of El Supremo doubting his own divinity as a result of disrespect or hesitation on the part of his subordinates. His lightest order, whether it dealt with a thousand pigs or five hundred men, was obeyed instantly. Hornblower made his next move at once.

"Is the *Lydia*," he asked, "to have the honour of carrying El Supremo to La Libertad? My crew would greatly appreciate the distinction."

"I am sure they would," said El Supremo.

"I hardly venture to ask it," said Hornblower, "but could my officers and I aspire to the honour of your dining with us before our departure?"

El Supremo considered for a moment.

"Yes," he said, and Hornblower had to suppress the sigh of relief he was on the point of drawing. Once El Supremo was on board the *Lydia* it might be possible to deal with him with less difficulty.

El Supremo clapped his hands, and instantly, as though by clockwork, a knocking at the brass studded door heralded the arrival of the swarthy major-domo. He received in a single sentence orders for the transfer of El Supremo's household to the *Lydia*.

"Perhaps," said Hornblower, "you will permit me to return to my ship now to make arrangements for your reception, Supremo."

He received another nod in reply.

"At what time shall I be at the beach to receive you?"

"At eleven."

Hornblower, as he came out into the patio, thought with sympathy of the oriental vizier who never came out of the royal presence without feeling to see if his head were still on his shoulders. And on the *Lydia's* deck, the moment the twittering of the pipes had died away, Hornblower was giving his orders.

"Have those men taken below at once," he said to Bush, pointing to the Spanish prisoners. "Put them in the cable tier under guard. Call the armourer and have them put in irons."

Bush made no attempt to conceal his surprise, but Hornblower wasted no time on explanations to him.

"Señores," he said, as the officers came by him, "you are going to be harshly treated. But believe me, if you are as much as seen during the next few days you will be killed. I am saving your lives for you."

Next Hornblower turned back to his first lieutenant.

"Call all hands, Mr. Bush."

The ship was filled with the sound of horny feet pattering over pine boards.

"Men!" said Hornblower, "there is coming aboard today a prince of this country who is in alliance with our own gracious King. Whatever happens — mark my words, *whatever happens* — he is to be treated with respect. I will flog the man who laughs, or the man who does not behave towards Señor El Supremo as he would to me. And we shall be sailing tonight with this gentleman's troops on board. You will look after them as if they were Englishmen. And better than that. You would play tricks on English soldiers. The first man to play a trick on any of these men I shall flog within the hour. Forget their colour. Forget their clothes. Forget that they cannot speak English, and remember only what I say to you. You can pipe down now, Mr. Bush."

Down in the cabin Polwheal was waiting faithfully with the dressing gown and towel for his captain's bath, which ought according to time-table to have been taken two hours back.

"Put out my best uniform again," snapped Hornblower. "And I want the after cabin ready for a state dinner for eight at six bells. Go for'rard and bring my cook to me."

There was plenty to do. Bush and Rayner, the first and fourth lieutenants, and Simmonds the marine officer, and Crystal the master, had to be invited to the dinner and warned to be ready in full dress. Plans had to be made for the accommodation of five hundred men on board the two frigates.

Hornblower was just looking across to the *Natividad,* where she swung with her white ensign over the red and gold of Spain, wondering what steps he should take with regard to her, when a boat came running gaily out to him from the shore. The leader of the party which came on board was a youngish man of less than middle height, slight of figure and lithe as a monkey, with a mobile smile and an expression of indefeatable good humour. He looked more Spanish than American. Bush brought him up to where Hornblower impatiently trod his quarterdeck. Making a cordial bow, the newcomer introduced himself.

"I am Vice Admiral Don Cristobal de Crespo," he said.

Hornblower could not help but look him up and down. The Vice Admiral wore gold earrings, and his gold embroidered coat did not conceal the raggedness of the grey shirt beneath. At least he wore boots, of soft brown leather, into which were tucked his patched white trousers.

"Of El Supremo's service?" asked Hornblower.

"Of course. May I introduce my officers. Ship captain Andrade. Frigate-captain Castro. Corvette-captain Carrera. Lieutenants Barrios and Barillas and Cerna. Aspirants Diaz —— "

The dozen officers introduced under these resounding titles were barefooted Indians, the red sashes round their waists stuck full of pistols and knives. They bowed awkwardly to Hornblower; one or two of them wore expressions of brutish cruelty.

"I have come," said Crespo, amiably, "to hoist my flag in my new ship *Natividad*. It is El Supremo's wish that you should salute it with the eleven guns due to a vice admiral."

Hornblower's jaw dropped a little at that. His years of service had grained into him despite himself a deep respect for the details of naval pageantry, and he was irked by the prospect of giving this ragged-shirted rascal as many guns as Nelson ever had. With an effort he swallowed his resentment. He knew he had to go through with the farce to the bitter end if he was to glean any success. With an empire at stake it would be foolish to strain at points of ceremony.

"Certainly, Admiral," he said. "It gives me great happiness to be one of the first to congratulate you upon your appointment."

"Thank you, Captain. There will be one or two details to attend to first," said the Vice Admiral. "May I ask if the executive officers of the *Natividad* are on board here or are still in the *Natividad*?"

"I greatly regret," said Hornblower, "that I dropped them overboard this morning after courtmartial."

"That is indeed a pity," said Crespo. "I have El Supremo's orders to hang them at the *Natividad's* yardarms. You did not leave even one?"

"Not one, Admiral. I am sorry that I received no orders from El Supremo on the subject."

"There is no help for it, then. Doubtless there will be others. I will go on board my ship, then. Perhaps you will be good enough to acompany me so as to give orders to your prize crew?"

"Certainly, Admiral."

Hornblower was curious to see how El Supremo's subordinates would deal with the problem of changing the allegiance of a whole ship's crew. He gave hurried orders to the gunner for the saluting of the flag when it should be hoisted in the *Natividad*, and went down into the boat with the new officers.

On board the *Natividad* Crespo swaggered on to the quarterdeck. The Spanish sailing master and his mates were grouped there, and under their startled eyes he walked up to the image of the Virgin and Child beside the taffrail and tossed it overboard. At a sign from him one of the aspirants hauled down the Spanish and British ensigns from the peak. Then he turned upon the navigating officers. It was a dramatic scene on that crowded quarterdeck in the brilliant sunshine. The British marines stood in rigid line in their red coats, with ordered arms. The British seamen stood by their carronades, matches smouldering, for no orders had yet relieved them of their duty. Gerard came over and stood beside Hornblower.

"Which is the sailing master?" demanded Crespo.

"I am," quavered one of the Spaniards.

"Are you his mates?" rasped Crespo, and received frightened nods in reply.

All trace of humour had disappeared from Crespo's expression. He seemed to expand and dilate with cold anger.

"You," he said, pointing at the youngest. "You will now hold up your hand and declare your faith in our lord El Supremo. Hold up your hand."

The boy obeyed as if in a trance.

"Now repeat after me. 'I swear ——' "

The boy's face was white. He tried to look round at his superior officer, but his gaze was held by Crespo's glaring eyes.

" 'I swear,' " said Crespo, more menacingly. The boy's mouth opened and shut without a sound. Then convulsively he freed himself from the hypnotic stare. His hand wavered and came down, and he looked away from Crespo's pointing right forefinger. Instantly Crespo's left hand shot out; so quick was the motion that no one could see until afterwards that it held a pistol from his sash. The shot rang out, and the boy, with a pistol ball in his stomach, fell to the deck writhing in agony. Crespo disregarded his convulsions and turned to the next man.

"*You* will now swear," he said.

He swore at once, repeating Crespo's words in quavering tones. The half-dozen sentences were very much to the point; they declared the omnipotence of El Supremo, testified to the speaker's faith, and in a single sweeping blasphemy denied the existence of God and the virginity of the Mother of God. The others followed his example, repeating the words of the oath one after the other, while no one paid any attention to the dying boy at their feet. Crespo only condescended to notice him after the conclusion of the ceremony.

"Throw that overboard," he said curtly. The officers only hesitated a moment under his gaze, and then one stooped and lifted the boy by his shoulders, another by his feet, and they flung the still living body over the rail.

Crespo waited for the splash, and then walked forward to the quarterdeck rail with its peeling gilt. The herded crew in the waist listened dumbly to his uplifted voice. Hornblower, gazing down at them, saw that there would be small resistance to Crespo's missionary efforts. To a man the crew were of non-European blood; presumably during the many years of the *Natividad's* commission in the Pacific the original European crew had quite died out. Only officers had been replaced from Spain; fresh hands had been recruited from the native races. There were Chinese among them, as Hornblower recognised, and negroes, and some whose physiognomy was unfamiliar to him — Filipinos.

In five minutes of brilliant speaking Crespo had won them all over. He made no more attempt to enunciate the divinity of El Supremo than was involved in the mention of his name. El Supremo, he said, was at the head of a movement which was sweeping the Spaniards from the dominion of America. Within the year the whole of the New World from Mexico to Peru would be at his feet. There would be an end of Spanish misrule, of brutal domination, of slavery in mine and field. There would be land for the asking for everybody, freedom and happiness under the benign supervision of El Supremo. Who would follow him?

They all would seemingly. Crespo had them all cheering wildly at the end of his speech. Crespo came back to Hornblower.

"Thank you, Captain," he said. "I think there is no more need for the presence of your prize crew. My officers and I will be able to attend to any insubordination which may arise later."

"I think you will be quite able to," said Hornblower, a little bitterly.

"Some of them *may* not easily be enlightened when the time comes for that," said Crespo, grinning.

Pulling back to the *Lydia* Hornblower thought bitterly about the murder of the Spanish master's mate. It was a crime which he ought to have prevented — he had gone on board the *Natividad* expressly to prevent cruelty and he had failed. Yet he realised that that kind of cruelty would not have the bad effect on his own men that a coldblooded hanging of the officers would have done. The crew of the *Natividad* was being forced to serve a new master against their will — but the pressgang had done the same for three-quarters of the crew of the *Lydia*. Flogging and death were the punishments meted out to Englishmen who refused to obey the orders of officers who had arbitrarily assumed command over them — English sailors were not likely to fret unduly over Dagoes in the same position, even though with English lower-class lack of logic they would have been moved to protest against a formal hanging of officers.

His train of thought was suddenly interrupted by the sound of a gun from the *Natividad*, instantly answered by another from the *Lydia*. He almost sprang to his feet in the sternsheets of the launch, but a glance over his shoulder reassured him. A new flag was flying now from the *Natividad's* peak. Blue with a yellow star in the middle, he saw. The sound of the saluting guns rolled slowly round the bay; the salute was still being fired as he went up the *Lydia's* side. Mr. Marsh, the gunner, was pacing up and down the foredeck mumbling to himself — Hornblower guessed at the jargon.

"If I hadn't been a born bloody fool I shouldn't be here. Fire *seven.* I've left my wife, I've left my home and everything that's dear. Fire *eight.*"

Half an hour later Hornblower was at the beach to meet El Supremo, who came riding down, punctual to the minute, a ragged retinue of a dozen riding with him. El Supremo did not condescend to present his suite to the captain, but bowed and stepped straight into the launch; his suite introduced themselves, in a string of meaningless names, in turn as they came up to Hornblower. They were all nearly pure Indians; they were all Generals save for one or two Colonels, and they were all clearly most devotedly attached to their master. Their whole bearing, every little action of theirs, indicated not merely their fear of him but their admiration — their love, it might be said.

At the gangway sideboys and boatswain's mates and marines were ready to receive El Supremo with distinguished military formality, but El Supremo astonished Hornblower as he was about to go up the ladder, with the casual words —

"The correct salute for me, Captain, is twenty three guns."

That was two more guns than His Majesty King George himself would receive. Hornblower stared for a moment, thought wildly of how he could refuse, and finally salved his conscience with the notion that a salute of that number of guns would be entirely meaningless. He sent a message hurriedly to Mr. Marsh ordering twenty three guns — it was odd, the way in which the ship's boy almost reduplicated Hornblower's reactions, by staring, composing his features, and hurrying off comforted by the thought that it was the captain's responsibility and not his own. And Hornblower could hardly repress a grin as he thought of Marsh's certain astonishment, and the boiling exasperation in his voice when he reached — "If I hadn't been a born bloody fool I shouldn't be here. Fire *twenty three.*"

El Supremo stepped on to the quarterdeck with a keen glance round him, and then, while Hornblower looked at him, the interest faded from his face and he lapsed into the condition of abstracted indifference in which Hornblower had seen him before. He seemed to listen, but he looked over the heads of Bush and Gerard and the others as Hornblower presented them. He shook his head without a word when Hornblower suggested that he might care to inspect the ship. There was a little awkward pause, which was broken by Bush addressing his captain.

"*Natividad* hoisting another flag to the main yard-arm, sir. No it's not, it's —— "

It was the body of a man, black against the blue sky, rising slowly, jerking and twisting as it rose. A moment later another body rose at the other end of the yard. All eyes instinctively turned towards El Supremo. He was still gazing away into the distance, his eyes focussed on nothing, yet everyone knew he had seen. The English officers cast a hasty glance at their captain for guidance, and followed his lead in lapsing into an uncomfortable pose of having noticed nothing. Disciplinary measures in a ship of another nation could be no affair of theirs.

"Dinner will be served shortly, Supremo," said Hornblower with a gulp. "Would you care to come below?"

Still without a word El Supremo walked over to the companion and led the way. Down below his lack of stature was made apparent by the fact that he could walk upright. As a matter of fact, his head just brushed the deck beams above him, but the nearness of the beams did nothing to make him stoop as he walked. Hornblower became conscious of a ridiculous feeling that El Supremo would never need to stoop, that the deck beams would raise themselves as he passed rather than commit the sacrilege of bumping his head — that was how El Supremo's quiet dignity of carriage affected him.

Polwheal and the stewards assisting him, in their best clothes, held aside the screens which still took the place of the discarded bulkheads, but at the entrance to the cabin El Supremo stopped for a moment and said the first words which had passed his lips since he came on board.

"I will dine alone here," he said. "Let the food be brought to me."

None of his suite saw anything in the least odd about his request — Hornblower, watching their expressions, was quite sure that their unconcern was in no way assumed. El Supremo might have been merely blowing his nose for all the surprise they evinced.

It was all a horrible nuisance, of course. Hornblower and his other guests had to dine in makeshift fashion in the gunroom mess, and his one linen tablecloth and his one set of linen napkins, and the two last bottles of his old Madeira remained in the after cabin for El Supremo's use. Nor was the meal improved by the silence that prevailed most of the time; El Supremo's suite were not in the least talkative, and Hornblower was the only Englishman with conversational Spanish. Bush tried twice, valiantly, to make polite speeches to his neighbours, putting a terminal "o" on the ends of his English words in the hope that so they might be transmuted into Spanish, but the blank stares of the men he addressed reduced him quickly to stammering inarticulation.

Dinner was hardly finished; everyone had hardly lighted the loose brown cigars which had been part of the stores handed over to the *Lydia* when a new messenger arrived from the shore and was brought in by the bewildered officer of the watch who could not understand his jabbering talk. The troops were ready to come on board. With relief Hornblower put away his napkin and went on deck, followed by the others.

The men whom the launch and the cutter, plying steadily between ship and shore, brought out, were typical Central

American soldiers, barefooted and ragged, swarthy and lank-haired. Each man carried a bright new musket and a bulging cartridge pouch, but these were merely what Hornblower had brought for them; most of the men carried in their hands cotton bags presumably filled with provisions — some bore melons and bunches of bananas in addition. The crew herded them onto the main deck; they looked about them curiously and chattered volubly, but they were amenable enough, squatting in gossiping groups between the guns where the grinning crew pushed them. They sat on the planking and most of them incontinently began to eat; Hornblower suspected them to be half starved and to be devouring the rations which were expected to last them for several days.

When the last man was on board Hornblower looked across to the *Natividad;* it appeared as if her share of the expeditionary force was already embarked. Suddenly the babble on the main deck died away completely, to be succeeded by a silence surprising in its intensity. Next moment El Supremo came on the quarterdeck — it must have been his appearance from the after cabin which had quelled the noise.

"We shall sail for La Libertad, Captain," he said.

"Yes, Supremo," replied Hornblower. He was glad that El Supremo had made his appearance when he did; a few seconds later and the ship's officers would have seen that their captain was awaiting his orders, and that would never have done.

"We will weigh anchor, Mr. Bush," said Hornblower.

Chapter VIII

THE voyage up the coast was completed, La Libertad had fallen, and El Supremo and his men had vanished into the tangle of volcanoes surrounding the city of the Holy Saviour. Once again in the early morning Captain Hornblower was pacing the quarterdeck of His Britannic Majesty's 36-gun frigate *Lydia,* and Lieutenant Bush as officer of the watch was standing by the wheel rigidly taking no notice of him.

Hornblower was gazing round him, and filling his lungs deep with air at every respiration as he walked. He noticed that he was doing this, and grinned to himself at the realisation that what he was doing was to savour the sweet air of liberty. For a space he was free from the nightmare influence of El Supremo and his cut-throat methods, and the feeling of relief was inexpressible. He was his own master again, free to walk his quarterdeck undisturbed. The sky was blue, the sea was blue and silver — Hornblower caught himself making the old comparison with heraldic argent and azure, and knew that he was himself again; he smiled once more out of sheer high spirits, looking out to sea, nevertheless, so that his subordinates should not see that their captain was walking the deck grinning like a Cheshire cat.

There was just the gentlest wind abeam pushing the *Lydia* along at three or four knots; peeping over the horizon on the port side were the tops of the interminable volcanoes which formed the backbone of this benighted country. Perhaps after all El Supremo might accomplish his wild dream of conquering Central America; perhaps after all there might be some solid foundation in the hope that good communications might be opened across the Isthmus — by Panama if the Nicaraguan scheme proved impracticable. That would make a profound difference to the world. It would bring Van Diemen's Land and the Moluccas into a closer relation to the civilised world. It would open the Pacific to England by evading the difficulties of the journey round the Horn or by the Cape of Good Hope and India, and in that case the Pacific might see squadrons of ships of the line cruising where hardly a frigate had penetrated up to that moment. The Spanish Empire of Mexico and California might acquire a new importance.

Hornblower told himself hastily that all this was only a wild dream at present. As a kind of punishment for dreaming he began to take himself to task regarding his present movements, and to subject himself to a severe examination regarding the motives which had brought him southwards towards Panama. He knew full well that the main one was to shake himself free from El Supremo, but he tried to justify his action in face of his self-accusation.

If El Supremo's attempt upon San Salvador should fail, the *Natividad* would suffice to bring off what few might survive of his army. The presence of the *Lydia* could in no way influence the land operations. If El Supremo should succeed, it might be as well that while he was conquering Nicaragua there should be a diversion in Panama to distract the Spaniards and to prevent them from concentrating their whole strength upon him. It was only right that the *Lydia's* crew should be given a chance of winning some prize money among the pearl fishers of the Gulf of Panama; that would compensate them for their probable loss of the prize money already gained — there would be no screwing money out of the Admiralty for the *Natividad*. The presence of the *Lydia* in the Gulf would hamper the transport of Spanish forces from Peru. Besides, the Admiralty would be glad of a survey of the Gulf and the Pearl Islands; Anson's charts were wanting in this respect. Yet for all these plausible arguments Hornblower knew quite well that why he had come this way was to get away from El Supremo.

A large flat ray, the size of a table top, suddenly leaped clear of the water close overside and fell flat upon the surface again with a loud smack, leaped clear again, and then vanished below, its pinky brown gleaming wet for a moment as the blue water closed over it. There were flying fish skimming the water in all directions, each leaving behind it a momentary dark furrow.

Hornblower watched it all, carefree, delighted that he could allow his thoughts to wander and not feel constrained to keep them concentrated on a single subject. With a ship full of stores and a crew contented by their recent adventures he had no real care in the world. The Spanish prisoners whose lives he had saved from El Supremo were sunning themselves lazily on the forecastle.

"Sail ho!" came echoing down from the masthead.

The idlers thronged the bulwark, gazing over the hammock nettings; the seamen holystoning the deck surreptitiously worked more slowly in order to hear what was going on.

"Where away?" called Hornblower.

"On the port bow, sir. Lugger, sir, I think, an' standing straight for us, but she's right in the eye of the sun —— "

"Yes, a lugger, sir," squeaked midshipman Hooker from the fore top gallant masthead. "Two masted. She's right to windward, running down to us, under all sail, sir."

"Running down to us?" said Hornblower, mystified. He jumped up on the slide of the quarterdeck carronade nearest him, and stared into the sun and the wind under his hand, but at present there was still nothing to be seen from that low altitude.

"She's still holding her course, sir," squeaked Hooker.

"Mr. Bush," said Hornblower. "Back the mizzen tops'l."

A pearling lugger from the Gulf of Panama, perhaps, and still ignorant of the presence of a British frigate in those waters; on the other hand she might be bearing a message from El Supremo — her course made that unlikely, but that might be explained. Then as the ship lifted, Hornblower saw a gleaming square of white rise for a second over the distant horizon and vanish again. As the minutes passed by the sails were more and more frequently to be seen, until at last from the deck the lugger was in plain view, nearly hull up, running goose-winged before the wind with her bow pointed straight at the *Lydia*.

"She's flying Spanish colours at the main, sir," said Bush from behind his levelled telescope. Hornblower had suspected so for some time back, but had not been able to trust his eyesight.

"She's hauling 'em down, all the same," he retorted, glad to be the first to notice it.

"So she is, sir," said Bush, a little puzzled, and then — "There they go again, sir. No! What do you make of that, sir?"

"White flag over Spanish colours now," said Hornblower. "That'll mean a parley. No, I don't trust 'em. Hoist the colours, Mr. Bush, and send the hands to quarters. Run out the guns and send the prisoners below under guard again."

He was not going to be caught unawares by any Spanish tricks. That lugger might be as full of men as an egg is of meat, and might spew up a host of boarders over the side of an unprepared ship. As the *Lydia's* gun ports opened and she showed her teeth the lugger rounded-to just out of gunshot, and lay wallowing, hove to.

"She's sending a boat, sir," said Bush.

"So I see," snapped Hornblower.

Two oars rowed a dinghy jerkily across the dancing water, and a man came scrambling up the ladder to the gangway — so many strange figures had mounted that ladder lately. This new arrival, Hornblower saw, wore the full dress of the Spanish royal navy, his epaulettes gleaming in the sun. He bowed and came forward.

"Captain Hornblower?" he asked.

"I am Captain Hornblower."

"I have to welcome you as the new ally of Spain."

Hornblower swallowed hard. This might be a ruse, but the moment he heard the words he felt instinctively that the man was speaking the truth. The whole happy world by which he had been encompassed up to that moment suddenly became dark with trouble. He could foresee endless worries piled upon him by some heedless action of the politicians.

"We have had the news of the last four days," went on the Spanish officer. "Last month Bonaparte stole our King Ferdinand from us and has named his brother Joseph King of Spain. The Junta of Government has signed a treaty of perpetual alliance and friendship with His Majesty of England. It is with great pleasure, Captain, that I have to inform you that all ports in the dominions of His Most Catholic Majesty are open to you after your most arduous voyage."

Hornblower still stood dumb. It might all be lies, a ruse to lure the *Lydia* under the guns of Spanish shore batteries. Hornblower almost hoped it might be — better that than all the complications which would hem him in if it were the truth. The Spaniard interpreted his expression as implying disbelief.

"I have letters here," he said, producing them from his breast. "One from your admiral in the Leeward Islands, sent overland from Porto Bello, one from His Excellency the Viceroy of Peru, and one from the English lady in Panama."

He tendered them with a further bow, and Hornblower, muttering an apology — his fluent Spanish had deserted him along with his wits — began to open them. Then he pulled himself up; on this deck under the eye of the Spanish officer was no place to study these documents. With another muttered apology he fled below to the privacy of his cabin.

The stout canvas wrapper of the naval orders was genuine enough. He scrutinised the two seals carefully, and they showed no signs of having been tampered with; and the wrapper was correctly addressed in English script. He cut the wrapper open carefully and read the orders enclosed. They could leave him in no doubt. There was the signature — Thomas Troubridge, Rear Admiral, Bart. Hornblower had seen Troubridge's signature before, and recognised it. The orders were brief, as one would expect from Troubridge — an alliance having been concluded between His Majesty's Government and that of Spain, Captain Hornblower was directed and required to refrain from hostilities towards the Spanish possessions, and, having drawn upon the Spanish authorities for necessary stores to proceed with all dispatch to England for further orders. It was a genuine document without any doubt at all. It was marked "Copy No. 2"; presumably other copies had been distributed to other parts of the Spanish possessions to ensure that he received one.

The next letter was flamboyantly sealed and addressed — it was a letter of welcome from the Viceroy of Peru assuring him that all Spanish America was at his disposal, and hoping that he would make full use of all facilities so that he would speedily be ready to help the Spanish nation in its sacred mission of sweeping the French usurper back to his kennel.

"Ha — h'm," said Hornblower — the Spanish viceroy did not know yet about the fate of the *Natividad,* nor about the new enterprise of El Supremo. He might not be so cordial when he heard about the *Lydia's* part in these occurrences.

The third letter was sealed merely with a wafer and was addressed in a feminine hand. The Spanish officer had spoken about a letter from the English lady in Panama — what in the world was an English lady doing there? Hornblower slit open the letter and read it.

The Citadel,
Panama.

Lady Barbara Wellesley presents her compliments to the captain of the English frigate. She requests that he will be so good as to convey her and her maid to Europe, because Lady Barbara finds that owing to an outbreak of yellow fever on the Spanish Main she cannot return home the way she would desire.

Hornblower folded the letter and tapped it on his thumb nail in meditation. The woman was asking an impossibility, of course. A crowded frigate sailing round the Horn was no place for females. She seemed to have no doubt about it, all the same; on the contrary, she seemed to assume that her request would be instantly granted. That name Wellesley, of course, gave the clue to that. It had been much before the public of late. Presumably the lady was a sister or an aunt of the two well-known Wellesleys — the Most Hon. the Marquis Wellesley, K.P., late Governor General of India and now a member of the Cabinet, and General the Hon. Sir Arthur Wellesley, K.B., the victor of Assaye and now pointed at as England's greatest soldier after Sir John Moore. Hornblower had seen him once, and had noticed the high arched arrogant nose and the imperious eye. If the woman had that blood in her she would be of the sort to take things for granted. So she might, too. An impecunious frigate captain with no influence at all would be glad to render a service to a member of that family.

Maria would be pleased as well as suspicious when she heard that he had been in correspondence with the daughter of an Earl, the sister of a Marquis.

But this was no time to stop and think about women. Hornblower locked the letters in his desk and ran up on deck; forcing a smile he approached the Spanish captain.

"Greeting to the new allies," he said. "Señor, I am proud to be serving with Spain against the Corsican tyrant."

The Spaniard bowed.

"We were very much afraid, Captain," he said, "lest you should fall in with the *Natividad* before you heard the news, because she has not heard it either. In that case your fine frigate would have come to serious harm."

"Ha — h'm," said Hornblower. This was more embarrassing than ever; he turned and snapped out an order to the midshipman of the watch. "Bring the prisoners up from the cable tier. Quickly!"

The boy ran, and Hornblower turned back again to the Spanish officer.

"I regret to have to tell you, señor, that by evil chance the *Lydia* met the *Natividad* a week ago."

The Spanish captain looked his surprise. He stared round the ship, at the meticulous good order, the well set up rigging. Even a Spanish frigate captain could see that the frigate had not been engaged in a desperate action lately.

"But you did not fight her, Captain?" he said. "Perhaps —— "

The words died away on his lips as he caught sight of a melancholy procession approaching them along the gangway. He recognised the captain and the lieutenants of the *Natividad*. Hornblower plunged feverishly into an explanation of their presence; but it was not easy to tell a Spanish captain that the *Lydia* had captured a Spanish ship of twice her force without receiving a shot or a casualty — it was harder still to go on and explain that the ship was now sailing under the flag of rebels who had determined to destroy the Spanish power in the new world. The Spaniard turned white with rage and injured pride. He turned upon the captain of the *Natividad* and received confirmation of Hornblower's story from that wretched man's lips; his shoulders were bowed with sorrow as he told the story which would lead inevitably to his courtmartial and his ruin.

Bit by bit the newcomer from the lugger heard the truth about recent events, about the capture of the *Natividad*, and the success of El Supremo's rebellion. He realised that the whole of the Spanish overlordship of the Americas was in jeopardy, and as he realised that, a fresh and harassing aspect of the situation broke in upon him.

"The Manila galleon is at sea!" he exclaimed. "She is due to arrive at Acapulco next month. The *Natividad* will intercept her."

One ship a year crossed the wide Pacific from the Philippines, never bearing less than a million sterling in treasure. Her loss would cripple the bankrupt Spanish government hopelessly. The three captains exchanged glances — Hornblower was telling himself that this was why El Supremo had agreed so readily to the *Lydia's* sailing southwestward; he had doubtless been pleased at the thought of the *Natividad* to the northeastward acquiring this wealth for him. It would take the Spaniards months to bring round the Horn a ship capable of dealing with the *Natividad*, and in the interval El Supremo would enjoy all those advantages of sea power which Hornblower had foreseen for the *Lydia*. The rebellion would be so firmly rooted that nothing would put it down, especially as, apparently, the Spaniards of Spain were engaged in a life-and-death struggle with Bonaparte and would have neither ships nor men to spare for America. Hornblower could see where lay his duty.

"Very well," he announced abruptly. "I will take my ship back to fight the *Natividad*."

All the Spanish officers looked their relief at that.

"Thank you, Captain," said the officer of the lugger. "You will call in at Panama to consult the Viceroy first?"

"Yes," snapped Hornblower.

In a world where news took months to travel, and where complete upheavals of international relationships were not merely possible but likely, he had learned now by bitter experience to keep in the closest contact with the shore; his misery was in no way allayed by the knowledge that the present difficulties were occasioned merely by his strict obedience to orders — and he knew, too, that the Lords of the Admiralty would not allow that point to influence them in their opinion of a captain who could cause such terrible trouble.

"Then," said the captain of the lugger, "I will bid you goodbye for the time. If I reach Panama first, I will be able to arrange a welcome for you. Perhaps you will allow my compatriots to accompany me?"

"No, I won't," rasped Hornblower. "And you, sir, will keep under my lee until we drop anchor."

The Spaniard shrugged and yielded. At sea one can hardly argue with a captain whose guns are run out and whose broadside could blow one's ship out of the water, especially as all Englishmen were as mad and as domineering as El Supremo. The Spaniard had not enough intuition to enable him to guess that Hornblower still had a lurking fear that the whole business might be a ruse to inveigle the *Lydia* helpless under the guns of Panama.

Chapter IX

It was not a ruse at all. In the morning when the *Lydia* came stealing before a three knot breeze into the roadstead of Panama the only guns fired were the salutes. Boatloads of rejoicing Spaniards came out to greet her, but the rejoicing was soon turned to wailing at the news that the *Natividad* now flew El Supremo's flag, that San Salvador had fallen, and that all Nicaragua was in a flame of rebellion. With cocked hat and gold-hilted sword ("a sword of the value of fifty guineas," the gift of the Patriotic Fund for Lieutenant Hornblower's part in the capture of the *Castilla* six years ago) Hornblower had made himself ready to go ashore and call upon the Governor and the Viceroy, when the arrival of yet one more boat was announced to him.

"There is a lady on board, sir," said Gray, one of the master's mates, who brought the news.

"A lady?"

"Looks like an English lady, sir," explained Gray. "She seems to want to come aboard."

Hornblower went on deck; close alongside a large rowing boat tossed and rolled; at the six oars sat swarthy Spanish Americans, bare armed and straw hatted, while another in the bows, boat hook in hand, stood waiting, face upturned, for permission to hook onto the chains. In the stern sat a negress with a flaming red handkerchief over her shoulders, and beside her sat the English lady Gray had spoken about. Even as Hornblower looked, the bowman hooked on, and the boat closed in alongside, two men fending off. Somebody caught the rope ladder, and the next moment the lady, timing the movement perfectly, swung onto it and two seconds later came on deck.

Clearly she was an Englishwoman. She wore a wide shady hat trimmed with roses, in place of the eternal mantilla, and her grey-blue silk dress was far finer than any Spanish black. Her skin was fair despite its golden tan, and her eyes were grey-blue, of just the same evasive shade as her silk dress. Her face was too long for beauty, and her nose too high arched, to say nothing of her sunburn. Hornblower saw her at that moment as one of the horsefaced mannish women whom he particularly disliked; he told himself that all his inclinations were towards clinging incompetence. Any woman who could transfer herself in that fashion from boat to ship in an open roadstead, and could ascend a rope ladder unassisted, must be too masculine for his taste. Besides, an Englishwoman must be unsexed to be in Panama without a male escort — the phrase "globe trotting," with all its disparaging implications, had not yet been invented, but it expressed exactly Hornblower's feeling about her.

Hornblower held himself aloof as the visitor looked about her. He was going to do nothing to help her. A wild squawk from overside told that the negress had not been as handy with the ladder, and directly afterwards this was confirmed by her appearance on deck wet from the waist down, water streaming from her black gown onto the deck. The lady paid no attention to the mishap to her maid; Gray was nearest to her and she turned to him.

"Please be so good, sir," she said, "as to have my baggage brought up out of the boat."

Gray hesitated, and looked round over his shoulder at Hornblower, stiff and unbending on the quarterdeck.

"The captain's here, ma'am," he said.

"Yes," said the lady. "Please have my baggage brought up while I speak to him."

Hornblower was conscious of an internal struggle. He disliked the aristocracy — it hurt him nowadays to remember that as the doctor's son he had had to touch his cap to the squire. He felt unhappy and awkward in the presence of the self-confident arrogance of blue blood and wealth. It irritated him to think that if he offended this woman he might forfeit his career. Not even his gold lace nor his presentation sword gave him confidence as she approached him. He took refuge in an icy formality.

"Are you the captain of this ship, sir?" she asked, as she came up. Her eyes looked boldly and frankly into his with no trace of downcast modesty.

"Captain Hornblower, at your service, ma'am," he replied, with a stiff jerk of his neck which might charitably be thought a bow.

"Lady Barbara Wellesley," was the reply, accompanied by a curtsey only just deep enough to keep the interview formal. "I wrote you a note, Captain Hornblower, requesting a passage to England. I trust that you received it."

"I did, ma'am. But I do not think it is wise for your ladyship to join this ship."

The unhappy double mention of the word "ship" in this sentence did nothing to make Hornblower feel less awkward.

"Please tell me why, sir."

"Because, ma'am, we shall be clearing shortly to seek out an enemy and fight him. And after that, ma'am, we shall have to return to England round Cape Horn. Your ladyship would be well advised to make your way across the Isthmus. From Porto Bello you can easily reach Jamaica and engage a berth in the West India packet which is accustomed to female passengers."

Lady Barbara's eyebrows arched themselves higher.

"In my letter," she said, "I informed you that there was yellow fever in Porto Bello. A thousand persons died there of it last week. It was on the outbreak of the disease that I removed from Porto Bello to Panama. At any day it may appear here as well."

"May I ask why your ladyship was in Porto Bello, then?"

"Because, sir, the West India packet in which I was a female passenger was captured by a Spanish privateer and brought there. I regret, sir, that I cannot tell you the name of my grandmother's cook, but I shall be glad to answer any further questions which a gentleman of breeding would ask."

Hornblower winced and then to his annoyance found himself blushing furiously. His dislike for arrogant blue blood was if anything intensified. But there was no denying that the woman's explanations were satisfactory enough — a visit to the West Indies could be made by any woman without unsexing herself, and she had clearly come to Porto Bello and Panama against her will. He was far more inclined now to grant her request — in fact he was about to do so, having strangely quite forgotten the approaching duel with the *Natividad* and the voyage round the Horn. He recalled them just as he was about to speak, so that he changed at a moment's notice what he was going to say and stammered and stuttered in consequence.

"B-but we are going out in this ship to fight," he said. "*Natividad's* got twice our force. It will be d-dangerous."

Lady Barbara laughed at that — Hornblower noted the pleasing colour contrast between her white teeth and her golden sunburn; his own teeth were stained and ugly.

"I would far rather," she said, "be on board your ship, whomever you have to fight, than be in Panama with the *vomito negro*."

"But Cape Horn, ma'am?"

"I have no knowledge of this Cape Horn of yours. But I have twice rounded the Cape of Good Hope during my brother's Governor-Generalship, and I assure you, Captain, I have never yet been seasick."

Still Hornblower stammered and hesitated. He resented the presence of a woman on board his ship. Lady Barbara exactly voiced his thoughts — and as she did so her arched eyebrows came close together in a fashion oddly reminiscent of El Supremo although her eyes still laughed straight into his.

"Soon, Captain," she said, "I will come to think that I shall be unwelcome on board. I can hardly imagine that a gentleman holding the King's commission would be discourteous to a woman, especially to a woman with my name."

That was just the difficulty. No captain of small influence could afford to offend a Wellesley. Hornblower knew that if he did he might never command a ship again, and that he and Maria would rot on the beach on half-pay for the rest of their lives. At thirty seven he still was not more than one eighth the way up the captains' list — and the goodwill of the Wellesleys could easily keep him in employment until he attained flag rank. There was nothing for it but to swallow his resentment and to do all he could to earn that goodwill, diplomatically wringing advantage from his difficulties. He groped for a suitable speech.

"I was only doing my duty, ma'am," he said, "in pointing out the dangers to which you might be exposed. For myself there would be nothing that would give me greater pleasure than your presence on board my ship."

Lady Barbara went down in a curtsey far deeper than her first, and at this moment Gray came up and touched his cap.

"Your baggage is all on board, ma'am," he said.

They had hove the stuff up with a whip from the main yard-arm, and now it littered the gangway — leather cases, ironbound wooden boxes, dome-topped trunks.

"Thank you, sir." Lady Barbara brought out a flat leather purse from her pocket, and took from it a gold coin. "Would you be so kind as to give this to the boat's crew?"

"Lord love you, ma'am, you don't need to give those Dago niggers gold. Silver's all they deserve."

"Give them this, then, and thank you for your kindness."

Gray hurried off, and Hornblower heard him bargaining in English with a boat's crew who knew no tongue but Spanish. The threat of heaving a cold shot hove down into the boat compelled it at length to shove off still spattering expostulations. A new little wave of irritation rose in Hornblower's mind. He disliked seeing his warrant officers running to do a woman's bidding, and his responsibilities were heavy, and he had been standing in a hot sun for half an hour.

"There will be no room in your cabin for a tenth of that baggage, ma'am," he snapped.

Lady Barbara nodded gravely.

"I have dwelt in a cabin before this, sir. That sea chest there holds everything I shall need on board. The rest can be put where you will — until we reach England."

Hornblower almost stamped on the deck with rage. He was unused to a woman who could display practical commonsense like this. It was infuriating that he could find no way of discomposing her — and then he saw her smiling, guessed that she was smiling at the evident struggle on his face, and blushed hotly again. He turned on his heel and led the way below without a word.

Lady Barbara looked round the captain's cabin with a whimsical smile, but she made no comment, not even when she surveyed the grim discomfort of the after-cabin.

"A frigate has few of the luxuries of an Indiaman you see, ma'am," said Hornblower, bitterly. He was bitter because his poverty at the time when he commissioned the *Lydia* had allowed him to purchase none of the minor comforts which many frigate-captains could afford.

"I was thinking just when you spoke," said Lady Barbara, gently, "that it was scandalous that a King's officer should be treated worse than a fat John Company man. But I have only one thing to ask for which I do not see."

"And that is, ma'am —— ?"

"A key for the lock on the cabin door."

"I will have the armourer make you a key, ma'am. But there will be a sentry at this door night and day."

The implications which Hornblower read into this request of Lady Barbara's angered him again. She was slandering both him and his ship.

"*Quis custodiet ipsos custodes?*" said Lady Barbara. "It is not on my account, Captain, that I need a key. It is Hebe here whom I have to lock in unless she is directly under my eye. She can no more keep from the men than a moth from a candle."

The little negress grinned widely at this last speech, showing no resentment and a good deal of pride. She rolled her eyes at Polwheal, who was standing silently by.

"Where will she sleep, then?" asked Hornblower, disconcerted once more.

"On the floor of my cabin. And mark my words, Hebe, the first time I find you not there during the night I'll lace you so that you have to sleep on your face."

Hebe still grinned, although it was evident that she knew her mistress would carry out her threat. What mollified Hornblower was Lady Barbara's little slip in speaking of the "floor" of her cabin instead of the deck. It showed that she was only a feeble woman after all.

"Very good," he said. "Polwheal, take my things into Mr. Bush's cabin. Give Mr. Bush my apologies and tell him he will have to berth in the wardroom. See that Lady Barbara has all that she wants, and ask Mr. Gray with my compliments to attend to putting the baggage in my storeroom. You will forgive me, Lady Barbara, but I am already late in paying my call upon the Viceroy."

Chapter X

THE Captain of the *Lydia* came on board again to the accompaniment of the usual twitterings of the pipes and the presenting of arms by the marine guard. He walked very carefully, for good news just arrived from Europe had made the Viceroy pressingly hospitable while the notification of the first case of yellow fever in Panama had made him apprehensive so that Hornblower had been compelled to drink one glass of wine too much. A naturally abstemious man, he hated the feeling of not being quite master of himself.

As always, he looked sharply round the deck as soon as his feet were on it. Lady Barbara was sitting in a hammock chair on the quarterdeck — someone must have had that chair made for her during the day; and someone had rigged for her a scrap of awning in the mizzen rigging so that she sat in the shade with Hebe crouching at her feet. She looked cool and comfortable, and smiled readily at him as he approached, but he looked away from her. He would not speak to her until his head was clearer.

"Call all hands to weigh anchor and make sail," he said to Bush. "We leave at once."

He went below, checked himself with a gesture of annoyance at finding that habit had led him to the wrong cabin, and as he turned on his heel he hit his head a shattering crash on a deck beam. His new cabin from which Bush had been evicted was even smaller than the old one. Polwheal was waiting to help him change his clothes, and the sight of him reminded Hornblower of fresh troubles. He had been wearing his best gold laced coat and white breeches when Lady Barbara came on board, but he could not afford to continue to wear them lest they should grow too shabby for use on ceremonial occasions. He would have to appear before this woman in future in his old patched coats and cheap duck trousers. She would sneer at his shabbiness and poverty.

He cursed the woman as he stripped off his clothes, all wet with sweat. Then a new trouble came into his mind. He had to leave Polwheal to keep watch while he had his shower bath under the pump lest she should surprise him there naked. He would have to issue orders to the crew so as to make sure that her fastidious eyes would not be offended by the state of undress which they habitually affected in the tropics. He combed his hair and cursed its curliness as drawing additional attention to the way his hair was receding from his forehead.

Then he hurried on deck; he was glad that the need for looking after the ship saved him from meeting Lady Barbara's eyes and seeing her reaction to his shabby clothes. He felt her gaze upon him, all the same, as he stood with his back to her attending to the business of getting under weigh. Half of one watch were at the capstan with all their weight upon the bars, their bare feet seeking holds on the smooth deck while Harrison bellowed encouragement and threats, and stimulated the laggards with cuts from his cane. Sullivan the mad fiddler, the two Marine fifers and the two drummers were playing some lively tune — to Hornblower one tune was much the same as another — on the forecastle.

The cable came steadily in, the ship's boys with their nippers following it to the hatch-coamings and scuttling back immediately to take a fresh hold on cable and messenger. But the measured clank-clank of the capstan grew slower and slower and then came to a dead stop.

"Heave, you bastards! Heave!" bellowed Harrison. "Here, you fo'c'sle men, bear a hand! Now, heave!"

There were twenty more men thrusting at the bars now. Their added strength brought one more solemn clank from the capstan.

"Heave! Christ damn you, heave!"

Harrison's cane was falling briskly first here and then there.

"Heave!"

A shudder ran through the ship, the capstan swung round so sharply that the hands at the bars fell in a tumbling heap to the deck.

"Messenger's parted, sir," hailed Gerard from the forecastle. "The anchor's foul, I think, sir."

"Hell fire!" said Hornblower to himself. He was certain that the woman in the hammock chair behind him was laughing at his predicament, with a foul anchor and the eyes of all Spanish America on him. But he was not going to abandon an anchor and cable to the Spaniards.

"Pass the small bower cable for a messenger," he shouted.

That meant unbearably hot and unpleasant work for a score of men down in the cable tier rousing out the small bower cable and manhandling it up to the capstan. The calls and curses of the boatswain's mates came echoing back to the quarterdeck — the warrant officers were as acutely conscious of the indignity of the ship's position as was their captain. Hornblower could not pace the deck as he wished to do, for fear of meeting Lady Barbara's eyes. He could only stand and fume, wiping the sweat with his handkerchief from his face and neck.

"Messenger's ready, sir!" hailed Gerard.

"Put every man to the bars that there's place for. Mr. Harrison, see that they heave!"

"Aye aye, sir!"

Br-r-r-rm. Boom! Br-r-r-rm. Boom! The drum rolled.

"Heave, you sons of bitches," said Harrison, his cane going crack-crack-crack on the straining backs.

Clank! went the capstan. Clank-clank-clank.

Hornblower felt the deck inclining a trifle under his feet. The strain was dragging down the ship's bows, not bringing home the anchor.

"God —— " began Hornblower to himself, and then left the sentence uncompleted. Of the fifty five oaths he had ready to employ not one was adequate to the occasion.

"Avast heaving!" he roared, and the sweating seamen eased their aching backs.

Hornblower tugged at his chin as though he wanted to pull it off. He would have to sail the anchor out of the ground — a delicate manœuvre involving peril to masts and rigging, and which might end in a ridiculous fiasco. Up to the moment only a few knowing people in Panama could have guessed at the ship's predicament, but the moment sail was set telescopes would be trained upon her from the city walls and if the operation failed everyone would know and would be amused — and the *Lydia* might be delayed for hours repairing damage. But he was not going to abandon that anchor and cable.

He looked up at the vane at the masthead, and overside at the water; the wind was across the tide, which gave them a chance, at least. He issued his orders quietly, taking the utmost precaution to conceal his trepidation, and steadily keeping his back to Lady Barbara. The topmen raced aloft to set the fore topsail; with that and the driver he could get sternway upon the ship. Harrison stood by the capstan ready first to let the cable go with a run and then second to have it hove in like lightning when the ship came forward again. Bush had his men ready at the braces, and every idle hand was gathered round the capstan.

The cable roared out as the ship gathered sternway; Hornblower stood rooted to the quarterdeck feeling that he would give a week of his life for the chance to pace up and down without meeting Lady Barbara's eyes. With narrowed eyes he watched the progress of the ship, his mind juggling with a dozen factors at once — the drag of the cable on the bows, the pressure of the wind on the driver and the backed fore topsail, the set of the tide, the increasing sternway, the amount of cable still to run out. He picked his moment.

"Hard-a-starboard," he rasped at the quartermaster at the wheel, and then to the hands forward, "Smartly with the braces now!"

With the rudder hard across the ship came round a trifle. The fore topsail came round. The jibs and fore staysails were set like lightning. There was a shuddering moment before the ship paid off. Her sternway checked, the ship hesitated, and then, joyfully, began slowly to move forward close hauled. Up aloft every sail that could draw was being set as Hornblower barked his orders. The capstan clanked ecstatically as Harrison's men raced round with the bars gathering the cable again.

Hornblower had a moment to think now, with the ship

gathering forward way. The drag of the cable would throw her all aback if he gave her the least chance. He was conscious of the rapid beating of his heart as he watched the main topsail for the first signs of flapping. It took all his force of will to keep his voice from shaking as he gave his orders to the helmsman. The cable was coming in fast; the next crisis was at hand, which would see the anchor out of the ground or the *Lydia* dismasted. He nerved himself for it, judged his moment, and then shouted for all sail to be got in.

All the long and painful drill to which Bush had subjected the crew bore its fruit now. Courses, topsails and top gallants were got in during the few seconds which were left, and as the last shred of canvas disappeared a fresh order from Hornblower brought the ship round, pointing straight into the wind and towards the hidden anchor, the way she had gathered carrying her slowly forward. Hornblower strained his ears to listen to the capstan.

Clank-clank-clank-clank.

Harrison was driving his men round and round the capstan like madmen.

Clank-clank-clank.

The ship was moving perceptibly slower. He could not tell yet if all this effort was to end ignominiously in failure.

Clank-clank.

There came a wild yell from Harrison.

"Anchor's free, sir!"

"Set all sail, Mr. Bush," said Hornblower; Bush was making no attempt to conceal his admiration for a brilliant piece of seamanship, and Hornblower had to struggle hard to keep his voice at the hard mechanical pitch which would hide his elation and convince everyone that he had had no doubt from the very start of the success of his manœuvre.

He set a compass course, and as the ship came round and steadied upon it he gave one final glance of inspection round the deck.

"Ha — h'm," he rasped, and dived below, to where he could relax and recover, out of Bush's sight — and out of Lady Barbara's, too.

Chapter XI

STRETCHED flat on his back in his cabin, blowing thick greasy wreaths of smoke from one of General Hernandez' cigars towards the deck above him where sat Lady Barbara, Hornblower began slowly to recover from the strain of a very trying day. It had begun with the approach to Panama, with every nerve keyed up lest an ambush had been laid, and it had ended so far with this trying business of the fouled anchor. Between the two had come Lady Barbara's arrival and the interview with the Viceroy of New Granada.

The Viceroy had been a typical Spanish gentleman of the old school — Hornblower decided that he would rather have dealings with El Supremo any day of the week. El Supremo might have an unpleasant habit of barbarously putting men to death, but he found no difficulty in making up his mind and one could be confident that orders issued by him would be obeyed with equal promptitude. The Viceroy, on the other hand, while full of approval of Hornblower's suggestion that instant action against the rebels was necessary, had not been ready to act on it. He was obviously surprised at Hornblower's decision to sail from Panama on the same day as his arrival — he had expected the *Lydia* to stay for at least a week of fêtings and junketings and idleness. He had agreed that at least a thousand soldiers must be transported to the Nicaraguan coast — although a thousand soldiers constituted practically the whole of his command — but he had clearly intended to postpone until the morrow the issuing of the orders for that concentration.

Hornblower had had to use all his tact to persuade him to do it at once, to give his instructions from his very banqueting table, and to put his favourite aides de camp to the pain of riding with messages under a hot sun during the sacred hours of the siesta. The banquet had in itself been trying; Hornblower felt as if there were no skin left on his palate, so highly peppered had been every dish. Both because of the spiciness of the food and the pressing hospitality of the Viceroy it had been hard to avoid drinking too much; in an age of hard drinking Hornblower stood almost alone in his abstemiousness, from no conscientious motive but solely because he actively disliked the feeling of not having complete control of his judgment.

But he could not refuse that last glass of wine, seeing what news had just come in. He sat up on his cot with a jerk. That business with the anchor had driven the recollection out of his mind. Good manners compelled him to go and communicate the news to Lady Barbara, seeing how closely it concerned her. He ran up on deck, pitched his cigar overboard, and went towards her. Gerard, the officer of the watch, was in close conversation with her; Hornblower smiled grimly to himself when he saw Gerard hurriedly break off the conversation and move away.

She was still seated aft by the taffrail in her hammock chair, the negress at her feet. She seemed to be drinking in the cool wind against which the *Lydia* was standing out of the gulf close hauled. On the starboard beam the sun was nearly at the horizon, a disc of orange fire in the clear blue of the sky, and she was exposing her face to its level beams with a total disregard for her complexion which accounted for her sunburn and, presumably, for the fact that she was now twenty seven and still unmarried despite a trip to India. Yet there was a serenity in her expression which seemed to show that at the moment at least she was not worrying about being an old maid.

She acknowledged his bow with a smile.

"It is heavenly to be at sea again, Captain," she said. "You have given me no opportunity so far to tell you how grateful I am to you for taking me away from Panama. To be a prisoner was bad enough, but to be free and yet to be confined there by force of circumstances would have driven me out of my mind. Believe me, Captain, you have won my eternal gratitude."

Hornblower bowed again.

"I trust the Dons treated your ladyship with all respect?"

She shrugged her shoulders.

"Well enough. But Spanish manners can grow trying. I was

in the charge of Her Excellency — an admirable woman, but insupportably dull. In Spanish America women are treated like Mohammedans. And Spanish-American food —— "

The words recalled to Hornblower the banquet he had just endured, and the expression on his face made Lady Barbara break off her sentence to laugh, so infectiously that Hornblower could not help but join in.

"Will you not sit down, Captain?"

Hornblower resented the suggestion. He had never once during this commission sat in a chair on his own deck, and he disliked innovations in his habits.

"Thank you, your ladyship, but I prefer to stand if I may. I came to give you good news."

"Indeed? Then your company is doubly pleasant. I am all eagerness to hear."

"Your brother, Sir Arthur, has won a great victory in Portugal over the French. Under the terms of a convention the French are evacuating the whole country and are handing over Lisbon to the English army."

"That is very good news. I have always been proud of Arthur — this makes me prouder still."

"It gives me great pleasure to be the first to congratulate his sister."

Lady Barbara contrived miraculously to bow although seated in her hammock chair — Hornblower was conscious of the difficulty of the feat and grudgingly admitted to himself that it was well done.

"How did the news come?"

"It was announced to the Viceroy while I was at dinner with him. A ship has reached Porto Bello from Cadiz, and a messenger rode express by the waggon road. There were other news as well — how true is more than I can say."

"To what effect, Captain?"

"The Spaniards claim a victory, too. They say a whole army of Bonaparte's has surrendered to them in Andalusia. They are already looking forward to an invasion of France in company with the English army."

"And how true do you think it is?"

"I distrust it. They may have cut off a detachment by good luck. But it will need more than a Spanish army to beat Bonaparte. I can foresee no speedy end to the war."

Lady Barbara nodded a grave approval. She looked out to where the sun was sinking into the sea, and Hornblower looked with her. To him the disappearance of the sun each evening into those placid waters was a daily miracle of beauty. The line of the horizon cut the disc now. They watched silently, as the sun sank farther and farther. Soon only a tiny edge was left; it vanished, reappeared for a second like a glint of gold as the *Lydia* heaved up over the swell, and then faded once more. The sky glowed red in the west, but overhead it grew perceptibly darker with the approach of night.

"Beautiful! Exquisite!" said Lady Barbara; her hands were tightly clasped together. She was silent for a moment before she spoke again, returning to the last subject of conversation. "Yes. One gleam of success and the Spaniards will look on the war as good as over. And in England the herd will be expecting my brother to lead the army into Paris by Christmas. And if he does not they will forget his victories and clamour for his head."

Hornblower resented the word "herd" — by birth and by blood he was one of the herd himself — but he was aware of the profound truth of Lady Barbara's remarks. She had summed up for him his opinion both of the Spanish national temperament and of the British mob. Along with that went her appreciation of the sunset and her opinion of Spanish-American food. He actually felt well disposed towards her.

"I hope," he said, ponderously, "that your ladyship was provided today during my absence with everything necessary? A ship is poorly provided with comforts for women, but I hope that my officers did their best for your ladyship."

"Thank you, Captain, they did indeed. There is only one more thing that I wish for, which I should like to ask as a favour."

"Yes, your ladyship?"

"And that is that you do not call me 'your ladyship.' Call me Lady Barbara, if you will."

"Certainly, your — Lady Barbara. Ha — h'm."

Ghosts of dimples appeared in the thin cheeks, and the bright eyes sparkled.

"And if 'Lady Barbara' does not come easily to you, Captain, and you wish to attract my attention, you can always say 'ha — h'm.' "

Hornblower stiffened with anger at this impertinence. He was about to turn on his heel, drawing a deep breath as he did so, and he was about to exhale that breath and clear his throat when he realised that he would never again, or at least until he had reached some port where he could get rid of this woman, be able to make use of that useful and noncommittal sound. But Lady Barbara checked him with outstretched hand; even at that moment he noticed her long slender fingers.

"I am sorry, Captain," she said, all contrition, "please accept my apologies, although I know now that it was quite unforgivable."

She looked positively pretty as she pleaded. Hornblower stood hesitating, looking down at her. He realised that why he was angry was not because of the impertinence, but because this sharp-witted woman had already guessed at the use he made of this sound to hide his feelings, and with that realisation his anger changed into his usual contempt for himself.

"There is nothing to forgive, ma'am," he said, heavily. "And now, if you will forgive me in your turn, I will attend to my duties in the ship."

He left her there in the fast falling night. A ship's boy had just come aft and lighted the binnacle lamps, and he stopped and read on the slate and traverse board the record of the afternoon's run. He wrote in his painstaking hand the instructions with regard to calling him — because some time that night they would round Cape Mala and have to change course to the northward — and then he went below again to his cabin.

He felt oddly disturbed and ill at ease and not merely because of the upsetting of all his habits. It was annoying that his own private water closet was barred to him now so that he had to use the wardroom one, but it was not just because of this. Not even was it merely because he was on his way to fight the *Natividad* again in the certain knowledge that with Vice Admiral Cristobal de Crespo in command it would be a hard battle. That was part of what was troubling him — and then he realised with a shock that his disquiet was due to the added responsibility of Lady Barbara's presence on board.

He knew quite well what would be the fate of himself and his crew if the *Lydia* were beaten by the *Natividad*. They would be hanged or drowned or tortured to death — El Supremo would show no mercy to the Englishman who had turned against him. That possibility left him unmoved at present, because it was so entirely inevitable that he should fight the *Natividad*. But it was far different in Lady Barbara's case. He would have to see that she did not fall alive into Crespo's hands.

This brief wording of his difficulty brought him a sudden spasm of irritation. He cursed the yellow fever which had driven her on board; he cursed his own slavish obedience to orders which had resulted in the *Natividad's* fighting on the rebel's side. He found himself clenching his hands and gritting his teeth with rage. If he won his fight public opinion would censure him (with all public opinion's usual ignorance of circumstances) for risking the life of a lady — of a Wellesley. If he lost it — but he could not bear to think about that. He cursed his own weakness for allowing her to come on board; for a moment he even dallied with the notion of putting back to Panama and setting her on shore. But he put that notion aside. The *Natividad* might take the Manila galleon. His crew, already discomposed by all the recent changes of plan, would fret still more if he went back and then went to sea again. And Lady Barbara might refuse — and with yellow fever raging in Panama she would be justified in refusing. He could not exercise his authority so brutally as to force a woman to land in a fever-stricken town. He swore to himself again, senselessly, making use of all the filthy oaths and frantic blasphemies acquired during his sea experience.

From the deck came a shrilling of pipes and a shouting of orders and a clatter of feet; apparently the wind had backed round now with the fall of night. As the sound died away the feeling of oppression in the tiny cabin overcame him. It was hot and stuffy; the oil lamp swinging over his head stank horribly. He plunged up on deck again. Aft from the taffrail he heard a merry laugh from Lady Barbara, instantly followed by a chorus of guffaws. The dark mass there must be at least half a dozen officers, all grouped round Lady Barbara's chair. It was only to be expected that after seven months — eight, nearly, now — without seeing an Englishwoman they would cluster round her like bees round a hive.

His first instinct was to drive them away, but he checked himself. He could not dictate to his officers how they spent their watch below, and they would attribute his action to his desire to monopolise her society to himself — and that was not in the least the case. He went down again, unobserved by the group, to the stuffy cabin and the stinking lamp. It was the beginning of a sleepless and restless night for him.

Chapter XII

MORNING found the *Lydia* heaving and swooping lightly over a quartering sea. On the starboard beam, just jutting over the horizon, were the greyish-pink summits of the volcanoes of that tormented country; by ranging along just in sight of the coast the *Lydia* stood her best chance of discovering the *Natividad*. The captain was already afoot — indeed, his coxswain Brown had had apologetically to sand the captain's portion of the quarterdeck while he paced up and down it.

Far away on the port side the black shape of a whale broke surface in a flurry of foam — dazzling white against the blue sea — and a thin plume of white smoke was visible as the whale emptied its lungs. Hornblower liked whales for some reason or other; the sight of this one, in fact, led him on his first step back towards good temper. With the imminent prospect of his cold shower bath before him the prickle of sweat under his shirt was gratifying now instead of irritating. Two hours ago he had been telling himself that he loathed this Pacific coast, its blue sea and its hideous volcanoes — even its freedom from navigational difficulties. He had felt himself homesick for the rocks and shoals and fogs and tides of the Channel, but now, bathed in sunshine, his opinion changed once more. There was something to be said in favour of the Pacific after all. Perhaps this new alliance between Spain and England would induce the Dons to relax some of their selfish laws prohibiting trade with America; they might even go so far as to try to exploit the possibility of that canal across Nicaragua which the British Admiralty had in mind, and in that case this blue Pacific would come into its own. El Supremo would have to be suppressed first, of course, but on this pleasant morning Hornblower foresaw less difficulty in that.

Gray, the master's mate, had come aft to heave the log. Hornblower checked in his walk to watch the operation. Gray tossed the little triangle of wood over the stern, and, log line in hand, he gazed fixedly with his boyish blue eyes at the dancing bit of wood.

"Turn!" he cried sharply to the hand with the sand glass, while the line ran out freely over the rail.

"Stop!" called the man with the glass.

Gray nipped the line with his fingers and checked its progress, and then read off the length run out. A sharp jerk at the thin cord which had run out with the line freed the peg so that the log now floated with its edge towards the ship, enabling Gray to pull the log in hand over hand.

"How much?" called Hornblower to Gray.

"Seven an' nigh on a half, sir."

The *Lydia* was a good ship to reel off seven and a half knots in that breeze, even though her best point of sailing was with the wind on her quarter. It would not take long if the wind held to reach waters where the *Natividad* might be expected to be found. The *Natividad* was a slow sailer, as nearly all those two-decker fifty gun ships were, and as Hornblower had noticed when he had sailed in her company ten days back—it might as well be ten years, so long did it seem — from the Gulf of Fonseca to La Libertad.

If he met her in the open sea he could trust to the handiness of his ship and the experience of his crew to out-manœuvre her and discount her superior weight of metal. If the ships once closed and the rebels boarded their superior numbers would overwhelm his crew. He must keep clear, slip across her stern and rake her half a dozen times. Hornblower's busy mind, as he paced up and down the deck, began to visualise the battle, and to make plans for the possible eventualities — whether or not he might hold the weather gage, whether or not there might be a high sea running, whether or not the battle began close inshore.

The little negress Hebe came picking her way across the deck, her red handkerchief brilliant in the sunshine, and before the scandalised crew could prevent her she had interrupted the captain in his sacred morning walk.

"Milady says would the captain breakfast with her," she lisped.

"Eh — what's that?" asked Hornblower, taken by surprise

and coming out of his day dream with a jerk, and then, as he realised the triviality for which he had been interrupted, "No no no! Tell her ladyship I will *not* breakfast with her. Tell her that I will *never* breakfast with her. Tell her that on *no* account am I to be sent messages during the morning. Tell her you are *not* allowed and neither is she on this deck before eight bells. *Get below!*"

Even then the little negress did not seem to realise how enormous had been her offence. She nodded and smiled as she backed away without a sign of contrition. Apparently she was used to white gentlemen who were irascible before breakfast and attributed little importance to the symptoms. The open skylight of the after cabin was close beside him as he walked, and through it he could hear, now that his reverie had been broken into, the clatter of crockery, and then first Hebe's and then Lady Barbara's voice.

The sound of the men scrubbing the decks, the harping of the rigging and the creaking of the timbers were noises to which he was used. From forward came the thunderous beat of a sledgehammer as the armourer and his mate worked upon the fluke of the anchor which had been bent in yesterday's misadventure. He could tolerate all the ship's noises, but this clack-clack-clack of women's tongues through the open skylight would drive him mad. He stamped off the deck in a rage again. He did not enjoy his bath after all, and he cursed Polwheal for clumsiness in handing him his dressing gown, and he tore the threadbare shirt which Polwheal had put out for him and cursed again. It was intolerable that he should be driven in this fashion off his own deck. Even the excellent coffee, sweetened (as he liked it) to a syrup with sugar, did not relieve his fresh ill temper. Nor, most assuredly, did the necessity of having to explain to Bush that the *Lydia* was now sailing to seek out and to capture the *Natividad*, having already been to enormous pains to capture her and hand her over to the rebels who were now their foes.

"Aye aye, sir," said Bush gravely, having heard the new development. He was being so obviously tactful, and he so pointedly refrained from comment, that Hornblower swore at him.

"Aye aye, sir," said Bush again, knowing perfectly well why he was being sworn at, and also knowing that he would be sworn at far worse if he said anything beyond "aye aye, sir." Really what he wanted to utter was some expression of sympathy for Hornblower in his present situation, but he knew he dared not sympathise with his queer-tempered captain.

As the day wore on Hornblower came to repent of his ill humour. The saw-edged volcanic coast was slipping past them steadily, and ahead of them somewhere lay the *Natividad*. There was a desperate battle awaiting them, and before they should fight it would be tactful for him to entertain his officers to dinner. And he knew that any captain with an eye to his professional advancement would be careful not to treat a Wellesley in the cavalier fashion he had employed up to the present. And ordinary politeness dictated that he should at this, the earliest opportunity, arrange that his guest should meet his officers formally at dinner, even though he knew full well that she had already, in her emancipated manner, conversed with half of them in the darkness of the quarterdeck.

He sent Polwheal across to Lady Barbara with a politely worded request that Lady Barbara would be so kind as to allow Captain Hornblower and his officers to dine with her in the after cabin and Polwheal returned with a politely worded message to the effect that Lady Barbara would be delighted. Six was the maximum number that could sit round the after cabin table; and superstitiously Hornblower remembered that on the eve of his last encounter with the *Natividad* Galbraith, Clay, and Savage had been his guests. He would never have admitted to himself that it was for this reason that he invited them again in the hope of encountering similar good fortune, but it was the case nevertheless. He invited Bush as the sixth — the other possible choice was Gerard, and Gerard was so handsome and had acquired somehow such a knowledge of the world that Hornblower did not want to bring him into too frequent contact with Lady Barbara — solely, he hastened to assure himself, for the sake of peace and quiet in his ship. And when that was all settled he could go on deck again to take his noon sights and pace his quarterdeck in his consuming restlessness, feeling that he could (after this exchange of polite messages) meet Lady Barbara's eye without the embarrassment that would previously have prevented him, unreasoningly.

The dinner at three o'clock was a success. Clay and Savage passed through the stages of behaviour that might have been expected of boys their age. At first they were brusque and shy in Lady Barbara's presence, and then, when the novelty had worn off and they had a glass of wine inside them, they moved towards the other extreme of over-familiarity. Even the hard-bitten Bush, surprisingly, showed the same symptoms in the same order, while poor Galbraith was of course shy all the time.

But Hornblower was astonished at the ease with which Lady Barbara handled them. His own Maria would have been too gauche ever to have pulled that party together, and in a world where he knew few women Hornblower was prone to measure the ones he met by Maria's standard. Lady Barbara laughed away Clay's bumptiousness, listened appreciatively to Bush's account of Trafalgar (when he had been a junior lieutenant in the *Téméraire*) and then won Galbraith's heart completely by displaying a close knowledge of a remarkable poem called "The Lay of the Last Minstrel" by an Edinburgh lawyer — every line of which Galbraith knew by heart, and which Galbraith thought was the greatest poem in the English language. His cheeks glowed with pleasure as they discussed it.

Hornblower kept his opinion of the work to himself. His model author was Gibbon, whose *Decline and Fall of the Roman Empire* was to be found in the very locker on which he sat, and he was surprised that a woman who could quote Juvenal with ease should be so interested in a barbaric romantic poem with no polish about it whatever. He contented himself with sitting back and watching the faces round the table — Galbraith tense and pleased, Clay and Savage and Bush a little out of their depth but interested in spite of themselves, and Lady Barbara completely at ease, conversing with a fearless self-confidence which nevertheless (as Hornblower grudgingly admitted to himself) seemed to owe nothing to her great position.

She made no use of her sex, either, Hornblower realised, and yet she was, marvellously, neither cold nor masculine. She might have been Savage's aunt or Galbraith's sister. She could talk to men as an equal, and yet could keep from her manner both invitation and hostility. She was very different from Maria. And when dinner was over and the officers rose to drink the health of the King, stooping under the deck beams (not until twenty five more years had passed would a King who had been a sailor himself give permission to the Navy to drink his health sitting) she echoed "God bless him!" and finished her single glass of wine with exactly the right touch of light-hearted solemnity which befitted the occasion. Hornblower suddenly realised that he was passionately anxious for the evening not to end.

"Do you play whist, Lady Barbara?" he asked.

"Why, yes," she said, "are there whist players on board this ship?"

"There are some who are not too enthusiastic," replied Hornblower, grinning at his juniors.

But nobody had nearly as much objection to playing in a four with Lady Barbara, the more so as her presence might moderate the captain's dry strictness. The cut allotted Lady Barbara as the captain's partner against Clay and Galbraith. Clay dealt and turned up a heart as trump; it was Lady Barbara's lead. She led the king of hearts, and Hornblower writhed uneasily in his seat. This might well be the play of a mere tyro, and somehow it hurt him to think that Lady Barbara was a bad whist player. But the king of hearts was followed by the king of diamonds, which also took the trick, and that by the ace of hearts, followed by the seven. Hornblower took the trick with the queen — his last heart, making a total of eleven played, and returned a diamond. Down came Lady Barbara's queen. Next came the ace of diamonds, and then two small ones to follow. At his first discard Hornblower dropped the seven from his suit of four clubs headed by king and knave. His opponents each discarded small spades on that remorseless string of diamonds. From doubt Hornblower changed instantly to complete confidence in his partner, which was entirely justified. She led the ace of clubs followed by the three, Hornblower finessed his knave, played his king, on which his partner discarded her singleton spade and then claimed the last two tricks with her remaining trumps. They had made a slam even though their opponents held every trick in spades.

Lady Barbara had shown that she could play a good hand well; later she proved that she could fight out a losing hand with equal brilliance. She watched every discard, noted every signal, finessed boldly when there was a chance of profit, returned her partner's leads and yet resolutely ignored them if her hand justified the risk; she played low from a sequence and led high. Not since the *Lydia* had left England had Hornblower had such a good partner. In his pleasure at this discovery Hornblower quite forgot to have any qualms at the fact that here was a woman who could do something well.

And the next evening she displayed another accomplishment, when she brought out a guitar onto the quarterdeck and accompanied herself in the songs which she sang in a sweet soprano — so sweet that the crew came creeping aft and crouched to listen under the gangways and coughed and fidgeted sentimentally at the close of each song. Galbraith was her slave, and she could play on his musical heartstrings as on her guitar. The midshipmen loved her. Even the barnacle-encrusted officers like Bush and Crystal softened towards her, and Gerard flashed his brilliant smile at her and made play with his good looks and told her stories of his privateering days and of his slaving adventures up the African rivers. Hornblower watched Gerard anxiously during that voyage up the Nicaraguan coast, and cursed his own tone deafness which made Lady Barbara's singing not merely indifferent to him but almost painful.

Chapter XIII

THE long volcanic coast line slid past them day after day. Every day brought its eternal panorama of blue sea and blue sky, of slaty-pink volcanic peaks and a fringing coast line of vivid green. With decks cleared for action and every man at his post they ran once more into the Gulf of Fonseca and sailed round the island of Manguera in search of the *Natividad*, but they did not find her. They saw no sign of life on the shores of the bay, either. Someone fired a musket at the ship from the cliffs of Manguera — the spent bullet thudded into the main-chains — but they did not see the man who fired it. Bush steered the *Lydia* out of the gulf again and northeastward in his search for the *Natividad*.

The *Natividad* was not to be found in the roadstead of La Libertad, nor in any of the little ports farther along. There was much smoke to be seen at Champerico, and Hornblower, training his glass upon it, could see that for once it was not volcanic. Champerico was in flames, so that presumably El Supremo's men had come there spreading enlightenment, but there was no sign of the *Natividad*.

Storms awaited them in the Gulf of Tehuantepec, for that corner of the Pacific is always stormy, lashed by the wind which blows hither from the Gulf of Mexico through a gap in the sierras. Hornblower was made aware of the change by an increase in the motion of the ship. She was rising and swooping more violently than usual and a gusty wind was heeling her sharply over. It was just eight bells, and the watch was being called; he could hear the bellowings of the master's mates — "Show a leg! Show a leg! Lash up and stow! Lash up and stow!" — as he ran up to the quarterdeck. The sky was still blue overhead and the sun was hot, but the sea was grey, now, and running high, and the *Lydia* was beginning to labour under her press of sail.

"I was just sending down to you, sir, for permission to shorten sail," said Bush.

Hornblower glanced up at the canvas, and over towards the clouds towards the coast.

"Yes. Get the courses and t'gallants off her," he said.

The *Lydia* plunged heavily as he spoke, and then rose again, labouring, the water creaming under her bows. The whole ship was alive with the creaking of timber and the harping of the rigging. Under shortened sail she rode more easily, but the wind on her beam was growing stronger, and she was bowing down to it as she crashed over the waves. Looking round, Hornblower saw Lady Barbara standing with one hand on the taffrail. The wind was whipping her skirts about her, and with her other hand she was trying to restrain the curls that streamed round her head. Her cheeks were pink under their tan, and her eyes sparkled.

"You ought to be below, Lady Barbara," he said.

"Oh, no, Captain. This is too delicious after the heat we have been enduring."

A shower of spray came rattling over the bulwarks and wetted them both.

"It is your health, ma'am, about which I am anxious."

"If salt water was harmful sailors would die young."

Her cheeks were as bright as if she had been using cosmetics. Hornblower could refuse her nothing, even though he bitterly remembered how last evening she had sat in the shadow of the mizzen rigging talking so animatedly to Gerard that no one else had been able to profit by her society.

"Then you may stay on deck, ma'am, since you wish it, unless this gale increases — and I fancy it will."

"Thank you, Captain," she replied. There was a look in her eye which seemed to indicate that the question as to what would happen if the gale increased was not nearly as decided as the captain appeared to think — but like her great brother she crossed no bridges until she came to them.

Hornblower turned away; he would clearly have liked to have stayed there talking, with the spray pattering about them, but his duty was with his ship. As he reached the wheel there came a hail from the masthead.

"Sail ho! Deck, there, a sail right ahead. Looks like *Natividad*, sir."

Hornblower gazed up. The lookout was clinging to his perch, being swung round and round in dizzy circles as the ship pitched and swooped over the waves.

"Up you go, Knyvett," he snapped to the midshipman beside him. "Take a glass with you and tell me what you can see." He knew that he himself would be of no use as a lookout in that wild weather — he was ashamed of it, but he had to admit it to himself. Soon Knyvett's boyish voice came calling down to him through the gale.

"She's the *Natividad,* sir. I can see the cut of her tops'ls."

"How's she heading?"

"On the starboard tack, sir, same course as us. Her masts are in one line. Now she's altering course, sir. She's wearing round. She must have seen us, sir. Now she's on the port tack, sir, heading up to wind'ard of us, close-hauled, sir."

"Oh, is she," said Hornblower to himself, grimly. It was an unusual experience to have a Spanish ship face about and challenge action — but he remembered that she was a Spanish ship no longer. He would not allow her to get the weather gage of him, come what might.

"Man the braces, there!" he shouted, and then to the man at the wheel, "Port your helm. And mark ye, fellow, keep her as near the wind as she'll lie. Mr. Bush, beat to quarters, if you please, and clear for action."

As the drum rolled and the hands came pouring up he remembered the woman aft by the taffrail, and his stolid fatalism changed to anxiety.

"Your place is below, Lady Barbara," he said. "Take your maid with you. You must stay in the cockpit until the action is over — no, not the cockpit. Go to the cable tier."

"Captain —— " she began, but Hornblower was not in the mood for argument — if indeed she had argument in mind.

"Mr. Clay!" he rasped. "Conduct her ladyship and her maid to the cable tier. See that she is safe before you leave her. Those are my *orders,* Mr. Clay. Ha — h'm."

A cowardly way out, perhaps, to throw on Clay the responsibility of seeing his orders carried out. He knew it, but he was angry with the woman because of the sick feeling of worry which she was occasioning him. She left him, nevertheless, with a smile and a wave of the hand, Clay trotting before her.

For several minutes the ship was a turmoil of industry as the men went through the well learned drill. The guns were run out, the decks sanded, the hoses rigged to the pumps, the fires extinguished, the bulkheads torn down. The *Natividad* could be seen from the deck now, sailing on the opposite tack towards her, obviously clawing her hardest up to windward to get the weather gage. Hornblower looked up at the sails to mark the least shiver.

"Steer small, blast you," he growled at the quartermaster.

The *Lydia* lay over before the gale, the waves crashing and hissing overside, the rigging playing a wild symphony. Last night she had been stealing peacefully over a calm and moonlit sea, and now here she was twelve hours later thrashing through a storm with a battle awaiting her. The wind was undoubtedly increasing, a wilder puff almost took her aback, and she staggered and rolled until the helmsman allowed her to pay off.

"*Natividad* won't be able to open her lower deck ports!" gloated Bush beside him. Hornblower stared across the grey sea at the enemy. He saw a cloud of spray break over her bows.

"No," he said, heavily. He would not discuss the possibilities of the approaching action for fear lest he might be too talkative. "I'll trouble you, Mr. Bush, to have two reefs taken in those tops'ls."

On opposite tacks the ships were nearing each other along the sides of an obtuse angle. Look as closely as he would, he could not decide which ship would be to windward when they met at the apex.

"Mr. Gerard," he called down to the lieutenant in charge of the port side main deck battery. "See that the matches in your tubs are alight."

"Aye aye, sir."

With all this spray breaking aboard the flint lock trigger mechanism could not be relied upon until the guns grew hot and the old fashioned method of ignition might have to be used — in the tubs on deck were coils of slow-match to meet this emergency. He stared across again at the *Natividad*. She, too, had reefed her topsails now, and was staggering along, close-hauled, under storm canvas. She was flying the blue flag with the yellow star; Hornblower glanced up overhead to where the dingy white ensign fluttered from the peak.

"She's opened fire, sir," said Bush beside him.

Hornblower looked back at the *Natividad* just in time to see the last of a puff of smoke blown to shreds by the wind. The sound of the shot did not reach them, and where the ball went no one could say — the jet of water which it struck up somewhere was hidden in the tossing waves.

"Ha — h'm," said Hornblower.

It was bad policy, even with a well-drilled crew, to open fire at long range. That first broadside, discharged from guns loaded carefully and at leisure, and aimed by crews with time to think, was too precious a thing to be dissipated lightly. It should be saved up for use at the moment when it would do maximum harm, however great might be the strain of waiting inactive.

"We'll be passing mighty close, sir," said Bush.

"Ha — h'm," said Hornblower.

Still there was no means of telling which ship would hold the weather gage when they met. It appeared as if they would meet bow to bow in collision if both captains held rigidly to their present courses. Hornblower had to exert all his will power to keep himself standing still and apparently unemotional as the tension increased.

Another puff of smoke from the *Natividad's* starboard bow, and this time they heard the sound of the shot as it passed overhead between the masts.

"Closer!" said Bush.

Another puff, and simultaneously a crash from the waist told where the shot had struck.

"Two men down at number four gun," said Bush, stooping to look forward under the gangway, and then, eyeing the distance between the two ships, "Christ! It's going to be a near thing."

It was a situation which Hornblower had visualised several times in his solitary walks on the quarterdeck. He took a last glance up at the weathervane, and at the topsails on the point of shivering as the ship tossed on the heaving sea.

"Stand by, Mr. Rayner. Fire as your guns bear," he called. Rayner was in command of the starboard side main deck battery. Then, from the corner of his mouth to the men at the wheel — "Put your helm a-weather. Catch her! Hold her so!"

The *Lydia* spun round and shot down the lee side of the *Natividad* and her starboard side guns went off almost simultaneously in a rolling crash that shook the ship to her keel. The billow of smoke that enveloped her momentarily was blown away instantly by the gale. Every shot crashed into the *Natividad's* side; the wind brought to their ears the screams of the wounded. So unexpected had the manœuvre been that only one single shot was fired from the *Natividad*, and that did no damage — her lower deck ports on this, her lee side, were closed because of the high sea.

"Grand! Oh, grand!" said Bush. He sniffed at the bitter powder smoke eddying round him as if it had been sweet incense.

"Stand by to go about," rasped Hornblower.

A well-drilled crew, trained in months of storms under Bush's eagle eye, was ready at sheets and braces. The *Lydia* tacked about, turning like a machine, before the *Natividad* could offer any counter to this unexpected attack, and Gerard fired his battery into her helpless stern. The ship's boys were cheering aimlessly in high piping trebles as they came running up from below with new charges for the guns. On the starboard side the guns were already loaded; on the port side the guns' crews were thrusting wet swabs down the bore to extinguish any residual fragments of smouldering cartridge, ramming in the charges and shot, and heaving the guns up into firing position again. Hornblower stared across the tossing water at the *Natividad*. He could see Crespo up on her poop; the fellow actually had the insolence to wave his hand to him, airily, while in the midst of bellowing orders at his unhandy crew.

The *Lydia* had wrung the utmost advantage out of her manœuvre; she had fired her two broadsides at close range and had only received a single shot in reply, but now she had to pay for it. By her possession of the weather gage the *Natividad* could force close action for a space if resolutely handled. Hornblower could just see her rudder from where he stood. He saw it kick over, and next moment the two-decker had swung round and was hurtling down upon them. Gerard stood in the midst of his battery gazing with narrowed eyes into the wind at the impressive bulk close overside. His swarthy beauty was accentuated by the tenseness of the moment and the fierce concentration of his expression, but for once he was quite unconscious of his good looks.

"Cock your locks!" he ordered. "Take your aim! Fire!"

The roar of the broadside coincided exactly with that of the *Natividad's*. The ship was enveloped in smoke, through which could be heard the rattling of splinters, the sound of cut rigging tumbling to the deck, and through it all Gerard's voice continuing with his drill — "Stop your vents!" The quicker the touch holes of the muzzle loaders were plugged after firing the less would be the wear caused by the rush of the acid gases through them.

The guns' crews strained at the tackles as the heave of the ship bade fair to send them surging back against the ship's sides. They sponged and they rammed.

"Fire as you will, boys!" shouted Gerard. He was up on the hammock-netting now, gazing through the smoke wreaths at the *Natividad* rising and swooping alongside. The next broadside crashed out raggedly, and the next more raggedly still, as the more expert gun crews got off their shots more quickly than the others; soon the sound of firing was continuous, and the *Lydia* was constantly a-tremble. At intervals through the roar of her cannon came the thunderous crash of the *Natividad's* broadside — Crespo evidently could not trust his crew to fire independently with efficiency, and was working them to the word of command. He was doing it well, too; at intervals, as the sea permitted, her lower deck ports were opening like clockwork and the big twenty four pounders were vomiting flame and smoke.

"Hot work, this, sir," said Bush.

The iron hail was sweeping the *Lydia's* decks. There were dead men piled round the masts, whither they had been hastily dragged so as not to encumber the guns' crews. Wounded men were being dragged along the deck and down the hatchways to where the horrors of the cockpit awaited them. As Hornblower looked he saw a powder boy flung across the deck, dissolved into a red inhuman mass as a twenty four pounder ball hit him.

"Ha — h'm," said Hornblower, but the sound was drowned in the roar of the quarterdeck carronade beside him. It was hot work indeed, too hot. This five minutes of close firing was sufficient to convince him that the *Natividad's* guns were too well worked for the *Lydia* to have any chance against her overpowering strength broadside to broadside, despite the damage done in the first few minutes of the action. He would have to win by craft if he was to win at all.

"Hands to the braces!" he yelled, his voice, high-pitched, cutting through the din of the guns. He stared narrow-eyed at the *Natividad* with the smoke pouring from her sides, he estimated the force of the wind and the speeds of the ships. His mind was making calculations with delirious rapidity, keyed up by the excitement, as he began the new manœuvre. Throwing the main topsail aback a trifle allowed the *Natividad* to shoot ahead without taking so much way off the *Lydia* as to make her unhandy, and then the next moment Hornblower tacked his ship about so that his waiting starboard battery was able to fire into the *Natividad's* stern. The *Natividad* came up into the wind in the endeavour to follow her opponent round and keep broadside to broadside with her, but the frigate was far quicker in stays than the clumsy, stumpy two-decker. Hornblower, watching his enemy with his keen gaze, tacked once more, instantly, and shot past the *Natividad's* stern on the opposite tack while Gerard, running from gun to gun, sent every shot crashing into the shattered timbers.

"Glorious! Damme! Damn my eyes! Damn my soul! Glorious!" spluttered Bush, thumping his right fist into his left hand and leaping up and down on the quarterdeck.

Hornblower had no attention to spare for Bush nor for Bush's good opinion, although later he was to remember hearing the words and find warm comfort in them. As the ships diverged he shouted for the *Lydia* to go about again, but even as the sheets were handed and the helm put over the *Natividad* wore round to pass her to leeward. So much the better. At the cost of a single exchange of broadsides he would be able to assail that vulnerable stern again, and if the *Natividad* attempted to circle, his was the handier ship and he could rely on getting in at least two effective shots to his opponent's one. He watched the *Natividad* come foaming up; her bulwarks were riddled with shot and there was a trickle of blood from her scuppers. He caught a glimpse of Crespo on the poop — he had hoped that he might have been killed in the last two broadsides, for that would mean, almost for certain, a slackening in the attack. But her guns were run out ready, and on this, her weather side, her lower deck ports were open.

"For what we are about to receive —— " said Bush repeating the hackneyed old blasphemy quoted in every ship awaiting a broadside.

Seconds seemed as long as minutes as the two ships neared. They were passing within a dozen yards of each other. Bow overlapped bow, foremast passed foremast and then foremast passed mainmast. Rayner was looking aft, and as soon as he saw that the aftermost gun bore on the target he shouted the order to fire. The *Lydia* lifted to the recoil of the guns, the ears were split with the sound of the discharge, and then, even before the gale had time to blow away the smoke, came the *Natividad's* crashing reply.

It seemed to Hornblower as if the heavens were falling round him. The wind of a shot made him reel; he found at his feet a palpitating red mass which represented half the starboard side carronade's crew, and then with a thunderous crackling the mizzenmast gave way beside him. The weather mizzen rigging entangled him and flung him down into the blood on the deck, and while he struggled to free himself he felt the *Lydia* swing round as she paid off despite the efforts of the men at the wheel.

He got to his feet, dizzy and shaken, to find ruin all round him. The mizzenmast was gone, snapped off nine feet from the deck, taking the main top gallant mast with it, and masts and yards and sails and rigging trailed alongside and astern by the unparted shrouds. With the loss of the balancing pressure of the mizzen topsail the *Lydia* had been unable to keep her course on the wind and was now drifting helplessly dead before the gale. And at that very moment he saw the *Natividad* going about to cross his stern and repay, with a crushing broadside the several unanswered salvoes to which earlier she had been forced to submit. His whole world seemed to be shattered. He gulped convulsively, with a sudden sick fear of defeat at the pit of his stomach.

Chapter XIV

BUT he knew, and he told himself, at the moment of his getting to his feet, that he must not delay an instant in making the *Lydia* ready for action again.

"Afterguard!" he roared — his voice sounding unnatural to himself as he spoke — "Mr. Clay! Benskin! Axes here! Cut that wreckage away!"

Clay came pounding aft at the head of a rush of men with axes and cutlasses. As they were chopping at the mizzen shrouds he noticed Bush sitting up on the deck with his face in his hands — apparently a falling block had struck him down, but there was no time to spare for Bush. The *Natividad* was coming down remorselessly on them; he could see exultant figures on her deck waving their hats in triumph. To his strained senses it seemed to him that even through the din on board the *Lydia* he could hear the creaking of the *Natividad's* rigging and the rumble of her reloaded guns being run out. She was steering to pass as close as possible. Hornblower saw her bowsprit go by, felt her reefed fore topsail loom over him, and then her broadside crashed out as gun after gun bore on the *Lydia's* stern. The wind caught the smoke and whipped it round Hornblower, blinding him. He felt the deck leap as the shots struck home, heard a scream from Clay's party beside him, felt a splinter scream past his cheek, and then, just as annihilation seemed about to engulf him, the frightful succession of shots ended, the smoke was borne away, the *Natividad* had gone by, and he was still alive and could look round him. The slide of the aftermost carronade had been smashed, and one of Clay's men was lying screaming on the deck with the gun across his thighs and two or three of his mates striving futilely to prize it off him.

"Stop that!" screamed Hornblower — the necessity of having to give such an order sent his voice up to the same pitch as that of the miserable wretch in his agony — "Cut that bloody wreckage away! Mr. Clay, keep them at work!"

A cable's length away, over the grey topped waves the *Natividad* was slowly wearing round to return and deal a fresh blow at her helpless opponent. It was lucky that the *Natividad* was an unhandy ship, like all those stumpy fourth rates — it gave Hornblower more time between the broadsides to try and get the *Lydia* into a condition so that she could face her enemy again.

"Foretop, there! Mr. Galbraith! Get the headsails in."

"Aye aye, sir."

The absence of the fore-topmast-staysail and storm jib would balance to some extent the loss of the mizzen topsail and driver. He might, by juggling with the helm, get the *Lydia* to lie to the wind a trifle then, and hit back at his big opponent. But there was no hope of doing so while all this wreckage was trailing astern like a vast sea anchor. Until that was cut away she could only lie helpless, dead before the wind, suffering her enemy's blows in silence. A glance showed him that the *Natividad* had worn round now, and was heading to cross their stern again.

"Hurry up!" he screamed to the axe men. "You, there, Holroyd, Tooms, get down into the mizzen chains."

He suddenly realised how high-pitched and hysterical his voice had become. At all costs he must preserve before Clay and the men his reputation for imperturbability. He forced himself, convulsively, to look casually at the *Natividad* as she came plunging down on them again, wicked with menace; he made himself grin, and shrug his shoulders, and speak in his normal voice.

"Don't mind about her, my lads. One thing at a time. Cut this wreckage away first, and we'll give the Dagoes their bellyful after."

The men hacked with renewed force at the tough tangles of cordage. Something gave way, and a new extravagant plunge on the part of the *Lydia,* as a huge wave lifted her stern, caused the wreckage to run out a little farther before catching again, this time on the mizzen stay, which, sweeping the deck, tumbled three men off their feet. Hornblower seized one of the fallen axes, and fell desperately on the rope as it sawed back and forth with the roll of the ship. From the tail of his eye he saw the *Natividad* looming up, but he could spare no attention for her. For the moment she represented merely a tiresome interruption to his work, not a menace to his life.

Then once more he was engulfed in the smoke and din of the *Natividad's* broadside. He felt the wind of shot round him, and heard the scream of splinters. The cries of the man under the carronade ceased abruptly, and beneath his feet he could feel the crash as the shot struck home in the *Lydia's* vitals. But he was mesmerised by the necessity of completing his task. The mizzen stay parted under his axe; he saw another rope draw up taut, and cut that as well — the pattern of the seams of the deck planking at that point caught his notice — felt another severed and flick past him, and then knew that the *Lydia* was free from the wreckage. Almost at his feet lay young Clay, sprawled upon the deck, but Clay had no head. He noted that as an interesting phenomenon, like the pattern of the deck seams.

A sudden breaking wave drenched him with spray; he swept the water from his eyes and looked about him. Most of the men who had been on the quarterdeck with him were dead, marines, seamen, officers. Simmonds had what was left of the marines lined up against the taffrail, ready to reply with musketry to the *Natividad's* twenty-four pounders. Bush was in the main top, and Hornblower suddenly realised that to him was due the cutting of the mizzen top mast stay which had finally freed the ship. At the wheel stood the two quartermasters, rigid, unmoving, gazing straight ahead; they were not the same as the men who had stood there when the action began, but the iron discipline of the Navy and its unbending routine had kept the wheel manned through the vicissitudes of the battle.

Out on the starboard quarter the *Natividad* was wearing round again. Hornblower realised with a little thrill that this time he need not submit meekly to the punishment she was determined to administer. It called for an effort to make himself work out the problem of how to work the ship round, but he forced his mind to concentrate on it, comparing the proportional leverages of the fore and main topsails, and visualising in his mind the relative positions of the centre of the ship and the mainmast — luckily this latter was stepped a little aft.

"Man the braces, there!" he called. "Mr. Bush, we'll try and bring her to the wind."

"Aye aye, sir."

He looked back at the *Natividad*, plunging and heaving towards them.

"Hard-a-starboard!" he snapped at the quartermasters. "Stand to your guns, men."

The crew of the *Natividad*, looking along their guns, suddenly saw the *Lydia's* battered stern slowly turn from them. For a fleeting half minute, while the English frigate held her way, the quartermasters straining at her wheel were able to bring the wind abeam of her as the *Natividad* swept by.

"Fire!" yelled Gerard — his voice, too, was cracking with excitement.

The *Lydia* heaved again with the recoil of the guns, and the smoke billowed over her deck, and through the smoke came the iron hail of the *Natividad's* broadside.

"Give it her again, lads!" screamed Gerard. "There goes her foremast! Well done, lads."

The guns' crews cheered madly, even though their two hundred voices sounded feeble against the gale. In that sudden flurry of action the enemy had been hard hit. Through the smoke Hornblower saw the *Natividad's* foremast shrouds suddenly slacken, tauten again, slacken once more, and then her whole foremast bowed forward; her main topmast whipped and then followed it, and the whole vanished over the side. The *Natividad* turned, turned instantly up into the wind, while at the same time the *Lydia's* head fell off as she turned downward despite the efforts of the men at the wheel. The gale screamed past Hornblower's ears as the strip of grey sea which divided the ships widened more and more. One last gun went off on the main deck, and then the two ships lay pitching upon the turbulent sea, each unable to harm the other.

Hornblower wiped the spray slowly from his eyes again. This battle was like some long drawn nightmare, where one situation of fantastic unreality merged into the next. He felt as if he were in a nightmare, too — he could think clearly, but only by compelling himself to do so, as though it were unnatural to him.

The gap between the ships had widened to a full half mile, and was widening further. Through his glass he could see the *Natividad's* forecastle black with men struggling with the wreck of the foremast. The ship which was first ready for action again would win. He snapped the glass shut and turned to face all the problems which he knew were awaiting his immediate solution.

Chapter XV

THE Captain of the *Lydia* stood on his quarterdeck while his ship, hove to under main staysail and three-reefed main topsail, pitched and wallowed in the fantastic sea. It was raining now, with such violence that nothing could be seen a hundred yards away, and there were deluges of spray sweeping the deck, too, so that he and his clothes were as wet as if he had been swimming in the sea, but he was not aware of it. Everyone was appealing to him for orders — first lieutenant, gunner, boatswain, carpenter, surgeon, purser. The ship had to be made fit to fight again, even though there was every doubt as to whether she would even live through the storm which shrieked round her. It was the acting-surgeon who was appealing to him at the moment.

"But what am I to *do,* sir?" he said pathetically, white faced, wringing his hands. This was Laurie, the purser's steward who had been appointed acting-surgeon when Hankey the surgeon died. He had fifty wounded down in the grim, dark cockpit, maddened with pain, some with limbs torn off, and all of them begging for the assistance which he had no idea of how to give.

"What are you to *do,* sir?" mimicked Hornblower scornfully, beside himself with exasperation at this incompetence. "After two months in which to study your duties you have to ask what to do!"

Laurie only blenched a little more at this, and Hornblower had to make himself be a little helpful and put some heart in this lily-livered incompetent.

"See here, Laurie," he said, in more kindly fashion. "Nobody expects miracles of you. Do what you can. Those who are going to die you must make easy. You have my orders to reckon every man who has lost a limb as one of those. Give them laudanum — twenty five drops a man, or more if that won't ease them. Pretend to bandage 'em. Tell 'em they're certain to get better and draw a pension for the next fifty years. As for the others, surely your mother wit can guide you. Bandage 'em until the bleeding stops. You have rags enough to bandage the whole ship's crew. Put splints on the broken bones. Don't move any man more than is necessary. Keep every man quiet. A tot of rum to every wounded man, and promise 'em another at eight bells if they lie still. I never knew a Jack yet who wouldn't go through hell fire for a tot of rum. Get below, man, and see to it."

"Aye aye, sir."

Laurie could only think of his own responsibility and duty; he scuttled away below without a thought for the hell-turned-loose on the main deck. Here one of the twelve pounders had come adrift, its breechings shot away by the *Natividad's* last broadside. With every roll of the ship it was rumbling back and forth across the deck, a ton and a half of insensate weight, threatening at any moment to burst through the ship's side. Galbraith with twenty men trailing ropes, and fifty men carrying mats and hammocks, was trailing it cautiously from point to point in the hope of tying it or smothering it into helplessness. As Hornblower watched them, a fresh heave of the ship canted it round and sent it thundering in a mad charge straight at them. They parted wildly before it, and it charged through them, its trucks squealing like a forest of pigs, and brought up with a shattering crash against the mainmast.

"Now's your chance, lads! Jump to it!" yelled Hornblower.

Galbraith, running forward, risked limb and life to pass a rope's end through an eye tackle. Yet he had no sooner done it than a new movement of the ship swung the gun round and threatened to waste his effort.

"Hammocks, there!" shouted Hornblower. "Pile them quick! Mr. Galbraith, take a turn with that line round the mainmast. Whipple, put your rope through the breeching ring. Quick, man! Now take a turn!"

Hornblower had accomplished what Galbraith had failed to do — had correlated the efforts of the men in the nick of time so that now the gun was bound and helpless. There only remained the ticklish job of manœuvring it back to its gun port and securing it with fresh breechings. Howell the carpenter was at his elbow now, waiting until he could spare a moment's attention from this business with the gun.

"Four feet an' more in the well, sir," said Howell, knuckling his forehead. "Nearer five, an' making fast as well as I could tell. Can I have some more men for the pumps, sir?"

"Not until that gun's in place," said Hornblower, grimly. "What damage have you found?"

"Seven shot holes, sir, below water line. There's no pluggin' of 'em, not with this sea runnin', sir."

"I know that," snapped Hornblower. "Where are they?"

"All of 'em for'rard, somehow, sir. One clean through the third frame timber, starboard side. Two more —— "

"I'll have a sail fothered under the bottom as soon as there are enough men to spare. Your men at the pumps will have to continue pumping. Report to the first lieutenant's party with your mates now."

The first lieutenant and the boatswain were busily engaged upon the duty of erecting a jury mizzenmast. Already the boatswain had come ruefully to the captain with the information that half the spare spars secured between the gangways had been damaged by shot, but there was a main topsail yard left which would serve. But to sway up its fifty-five foot length into a vertical position was going to be a tricky business — hard enough in a smooth sea, dangerous and prolonged out here with the Pacific running mad. In harbour an old ship — a sheer hulk — would be brought alongside, and would employ the two immense spars which constituted her sheers as a crane in which to lift the new mast vertically into the ship. Here there was nothing of the sort available, and the problem of raising the spar might seem insoluble, but Bush and Harrison between them were tackling it with all the resource and energy the Navy could display.

Happily there was that stump of the old mizzenmast left — its nine feet of length relieved them of the tiresome complication of stepping the new mast, which they proposed instead merely to fish to the stump. The after part of the ship was alive with working parties each intent on its own contribution to the work in hand. With tackles and rollers the spar had been eased aft until its butt was solidly against the stump of the mizzenmast. Harrison was now supervising the task of noosing shrouds to the new masthead; after that he would have to prepare the masthead to receive the cap and the trussel trees which the carpenter and his mates would now have to make.

In the mizzen chains on either side Harrison's mates were supervising the efforts of two other parties engaged upon attaching the other ends of the shrouds to the channels, where with dead eyes and lanyards the shrouds could be kept taut as the mast rose. Bush was attending to the preparation of the jears and tackle at the mainmast which would help to accomplish a great part of the lift; the sailmaker and his mates were rousing out and adapting sails to fit the new mast, gaff, and yards. Another party of men under the gunner was engaged on the difficult task of remounting the dismounted quarterdeck carronade, while Gerard was aloft with the topmen attending to the repair of the damage done to the standing and running rigging of the remaining masts. All this was in the rain, with the wind shrieking round them; and yet the rain and the wind seemed warm to the touch, so oppressively hot was it. The half-naked seamen, slaving at their task, were running wet with sweat as well as with rainwater and spray. The ship was a nightmare of insane yet ordered activity.

A sudden flurry of rain heralded the arrival of a clear spell. Braced upon the heaving deck Hornblower set his glass to his eye; the *Natividad* was visible again, hull down now, across the tossing grey flecked sea. She was hove-to as well, looking queerly lopsided in her partially dismasted condition. Hornblower's glass could discover no sign of any immediate replacement of the missing spars; he thought it extremely probable that there was nothing left in the ship to serve as jury masts. In that case as soon as the *Lydia* could carry enough sail aft to enable her to beat to windward he would have the *Natividad* at his mercy — as long as the sea was not running high enough to make gunnery impossible.

He glowered round the horizon; at present there was no sign of the storm abating, and it was long past noon. With the coming of night he might lose the *Natividad* altogether, and nightfall would give his enemy a further respite in which to achieve repairs.

"How much longer, Mr. Harrison?" he rasped.

"Not long now, sir. Nearly ready, sir."

"You've had long enough and to spare for a simple piece of work like that. Keep the men moving, there."

"Aye aye, sir."

Hornblower knew that the men were cursing him under their breath; he did not know they admired him as well, as men will admire a hard master despite themselves.

Now it was the cook come to report to him — the cook and his mates had been the only men in the ship who could be spared for the grisly work allotted to them.

"All ready, sir," he said.

Without a word Hornblower strode forward down the starboard side gangway, taking his prayer book from his pocket. The fourteen dead were there, shrouded in their hammocks, two to a grating, a roundshot sewn into the foot of each hammock. Hornblower blew a long blast upon his silver whistle, and activity ceased on board while he read, compromising between haste and solemnity, the office for the burial of the dead at sea.

"We therefore commit their bodies to the deep —— "

The cook and his mates tilted each grating in turn, and the bodies fell with sullen splashes overside while Hornblower read the concluding words of the service. As soon as the last words were said he blew his whistle again and all the bustle and activity recommenced. He grudged those few minutes taken from the work bitterly, but he knew that any unceremonious pitching overboard of the dead would be resented by his men, who set all the store by forms and ceremonies to be expected of the uneducated.

And now there was something else to plague him. Picking her way across the main deck below him came Lady Barbara, the little negress clinging to her skirts.

"My orders were for you to stay below, ma'am," he shouted to her. "This deck is no place for you."

Lady Barbara looked round the seething deck and then tilted her chin to answer him.

"I can see that without having it pointed out to me," she said, and then, softening her manner, "I have no intention of obstructing, Captain. I was going to shut myself in my cabin."

"Your cabin?"

Hornblower laughed. Four broadsides from the *Natividad* had blasted their way through that cabin. The idea of Lady Barbara shutting herself up there struck him as being intensely funny. He laughed again, and then again, before checking himself in hurried mistrust as an abyss of hysteria opened itself before him. He controlled himself.

"There is no cabin left for you, ma'am. I regret that the only course open to you is to go back whence you have come. There is no other place in the ship that can accommodate you at present."

Lady Barbara, looking up at him, thought of the cable tier she had just left. Pitch dark, with only room to sit hunched up on the slimy cable, rats squeaking and scampering over her legs; the ship pitching and rolling madly, and Hebe howling with fright beside her; the tremendous din of the guns, and the thunderous rumble of the gun trucks immediately over her head as the guns were run in and out; the tearing crash which had echoed through the ship when the mizzenmast fell; the ignorance of how the battle was progressing — at this very moment she was still unaware whether it had been lost or won or merely suspended; the stench of the bilge, the hunger and the thirst.

The thought of going back there appalled her. But she saw the captain's face, white with fatigue and strain under its tan, and she had noted that laugh with its hysterical pitch, abruptly cut off, and the grim effort that had been made to speak to her reasonably. The captain's coat was torn across the breast, and his white trousers were stained — with blood, she suddenly realised. She felt pity for him, then. She knew now that to speak to him of rats and stinks and baseless fears would be ridiculous.

"Very good, Captain," she said quietly, and turned to retrace her steps.

The little negress set up a howl, and was promptly shaken into silence as Lady Barbara dragged her along.

Chapter XVI

"READY now, sir," said Bush.

The crew of the *Lydia* had worked marvellously. The guns were all secured now, and the main deck cleared of most of the traces of the fight. A sail stretched over the bottom of the ship had done much to check the inflow of water, so that now only twenty men were at work upon the pumps and the level in the well was measurably sinking. The sailmaster had his new sails ready, the boatswain his rigging, the carpenter his accessories. Already Harrison had his men at the windlass, and the mast lay ready for hoisting.

Hornblower looked round him. All the mad effort put into the work to get it done speedily was wasted, for the gale still showed no signs of abating and with this present wind blowing it would be hopeless to try to beat over to the *Natividad*. He had driven his men hard — overdriven them — to lose no time, and now it was obvious that they might have done it all at their leisure. But the work might as well be completed now. He ran his eye over the waiting groups of men; each knew their duty, and there was an officer at each strategic point to see that orders were carried out.

"Very good, Mr. Bush," he said.

"Hoist away, there!" yelled Bush to the windlass crew.

The windlass began to turn, the rope began to groan through the jears, and the mast rose, little by little, watched by every eye. The mad plunges of the ship threatened to ruin everything. There was danger of the masthead escaping from the ropes that held it; there was danger of the butt slipping away from the stump of the mizzenmast against which it rested. Everything had to be watched, every precaution taken, to see that neither of these possibilities developed. Bush watched the jears, while Gerard at the main masthead attended to the slings. Galbraith was in the mizzen chains on one side, Rayner on the other. Boatswain and carpenter stood with ropes and spars at the butt end of the mast, but it was the captain, leaning on the quarterdeck rail, whose duty it was to see that every part of the cumbrous machine did its work in its proper relation to the others. It was he whom the crew would blame for failure.

He knew it, too. He watched the dizzy heave and pitch of the ship, and the masthead wavering in the slings, and he heard the butt end grinding upon the deck as it moved uneasily between the two spars lashed as buttresses against the stump of the mizzenmast. It was an effort to think clearly, and he could only compel his mind to it by an exertion of all his will. He was sick and tired and nervous.

It was of vital importance that the hands at the shrouds and backstays only took up as much slack as was won for them by the jears, and refrained from tightening up when a roll of the ship swung the mast over on their side a trifle. Yet this was just what they persisted in doing, maddeningly, so obsessed were they with the necessity of keeping all taut to prevent the swaying mast from taking charge. Twice the grip of the slings on the masthead was imperilled in this way, and Hornblower had to key himself up to his highest pitch for several seconds, watching the roll of the ship, so as to time precisely the next heave which would obviate the danger. His voice was hoarse with shouting.

Slowly the mast left the horizontal and swayed up towards the perpendicular. Hornblower's calculating eye, measuring stresses and reactions, saw that the crisis was now come — the moment when the jears could raise the masthead no more and the final lifting must be accomplished by the pull of the backstays aft. The next few moments were tricky ones, because the masthead would now be deprived of the positive support of the slings. The jears had to be disconnected from the windlass and their work done by the backstays. Two lengths of cable had to be passed round the sloping jury mast and the vertical stump, with gangs of men ready to tighten them, tourniquet fashion, with capstan bars as each gain was made. Yet in these first seconds the backstays were at a mechanical disadvantage and would certainly not bear the strain which would be imposed on them if the windlass were employed in an endeavour to drag the mast upright by brute force.

The motion of the ship must be utilised to help. Hornblower had to watch the motion carefully, calling to the men to wait as the ship rolled and plunged, and then, as the bow slowly emerged from the creaming sea and climbed steadily skywards, he had to set windlass men and tourniquet men and lanyard men all in action at once, and then check them all instantly as the bow began to sink again and full strain came onto the rigging. Twice he managed it successfully, and then three times — although the third time an unexpected wave lifted the *Lydia's* stern at the wrong moment and nearly wrecked everything.

Then the fourth heave settled it all. The mast was now so nearly vertical that shrouds and backstays were at a mechanical advantage, and everything could be hove taut regardless of the ship's motion. Shrouds and backstays could be set up now in normal fashion, the jury mast adequately fished to the stump — in fact all the difficult part of the work was completed. Hornblower leaned against the rail, sick with weariness, wondering dully how these iron-framed men of his could find the strength to cheer as they put the finishing touches to their work.

He found Bush beside him — Bush had a rag round his head, bloodstained because of the cut in his forehead inflicted by the falling block.

"A magnificent piece of work, if I may say so, sir," he said.

Hornblower eyed him sharply, suspicious as ever of congratulation, knowing his own weakness so well. But Bush, surprisingly, seemed to mean in all sincerity what he said.

"Thank you," said Hornblower, grudgingly.

"Shall I send up the topmast and yards, sir?"

Hornblower looked round the horizon once more. The gale was blowing as madly as ever, and only a grey smudge on the distant horizon marked where the *Natividad* was battling with it. Hornblower could see that there was no chance of showing any more canvas at present, no chance of renewing the fight while the *Natividad* was still unprepared. It was a bitter pill to swallow. He could imagine what would be said in service circles when he sent in his report to the Admiralty. His statement that the weather was too bad to renew the action, after having received such a severe handling, would be received with pitying smiles and knowing wags of the head. It was a hackneyed excuse, like the uncharted rock which explained faulty navigation. Cowardice, moral or even perhaps physical, would be the unspoken comment on every side — at ten thousand miles distance no one could judge of the strength of a storm. He could divest himself of some of his responsibility by asking Bush his opinion, and requesting him to go through the formality of putting it in writing; but he turned irritably from the thought of displaying weakness before his inferior.

"No," he said, without expression. "We shall stay hove-to until the weather moderates."

There was a gleam of admiration in Bush's bloodshot eyes — Bush could well admire a captain who could make with such small debate a decision so nearly touching his professional reputation. Hornblower noticed it, but his cursed temperament forbade him to interpret it correctly.

"Aye aye, sir," said Bush, warned by the scowl on his captain's forehead not to enlarge on the subject. But his affection for his captain compelled him to open a fresh one. "If that's the case, sir, why not take a rest? You look mortally tired, sir, indeed you do. Let me send and have a berth screened off for you in the wardroom."

Bush found his hand twitching — he had been about to commit the enormity of patting his captain's shoulder, and restrained himself just in time.

"Fiddlesticks!" snapped Hornblower. As if a captain of a frigate could publicly admit that he was tired! And Hornblower could not trust himself to show any weakness at all — he always remembered how on his first commission his second-in-command had taken advantage of lapses on his part.

"It is rather you who need a rest," said Hornblower. "Dismiss the starboard watch, and go below and turn in. Have someone attend to that forehead of yours, first. With the enemy in sight I shall stay on deck."

After that it was Polwheal who came to plague him — Hornblower wondered ineffectively whether he came of his own initiative or whether Bush sent him up.

"I've been to attend to the lady, sir," said Polwheal; Hornblower's tired mind was just beginning to grapple with the problem of what to do with Lady Barbara in a damaged ship cleared for action. "I've screened off a bit of the orlop for her, sir. The wounded's mostly quiet by now, sir. I slung a 'ammock for her — nipped into it like a bird, she did, sir. She's taken food, too, sir — what was left of that cold chicken an' a glass of wine. Not that she wanted to, sir, but I persuaded her, like."

"Very good, Polwheal," said Hornblower. It was an enormous relief to hear that one responsibility at least was lifted from his shoulders.

"An' now about you, sir," went on Polwheal. "I've got you up some dry clothes from your chest in your storeroom, sir — I'm afraid that last broadside spoilt everything in your cabin, sir. An' I've got your boat cloak, sir, all warm an' dry. Do you care to shift your clothes up here or down below, sir?"

Polwheal could take much for granted and could wheedle the rest. Hornblower had anticipated dragging his weary form in his water logged clothes up and down the quarterdeck all through the night, his nervous irritation not permitting him to contemplate any other course. Polwheal unearthed Lady Barbara's hammock chair from somewhere and lashed it to the rail and persuaded Hornblower to sit in it and consume a supper of biscuit and rum. Polwheal wrapped the boat cloak about him and airily took it for granted that he would continue to sit there, since his determination was fixed not to turn in while the enemy was still close at hand.

And marvellously, as he sat there, with the spray wetting his face and the ship leaping and rolling under him, his head drooped upon his breast and he slept. It was only a broken and fitful sleep, but astonishingly restorative. He woke every few minutes. Twice it was the sound of his own snores which roused him. At other times he woke with a start to see whether the weather was moderating; at other times still the thoughts which went running on through his mind despite his dozing called him out of his unconsciousness when they reached some fresh startling conclusion regarding what opinion England and his crew would hold of him after this battle.

Soon after midnight his sailor's instincts called him definitely into complete wakefulness. Something was happening to the weather. He scrambled stiffly to his feet. The ship was rolling more wildly than ever, but as he sniffed round him he knew that there was an improvement. He walked across to the binnacle, and Bush loomed vastly out of the darkness beside him.

"Wind's shifting southerly an' moderating, sir," said Bush.

The shift of the wind was breaking up the long Pacific waves into steeper seas, as the *Lydia's* antics displayed well enough.

"Black as the Earl of Hell's riding boots, all the same, sir," grumbled Bush, peering into the darkness.

Somewhere, perhaps twenty miles from them, perhaps only two hundred yards, the *Natividad* was combating the same gale. If the moon were to break through the scurrying clouds they might be at grips with her at any moment, yet while they were talking it was so dark that they could hardly make out the loom of the main topsail from the quarterdeck.

"She was going away to leeward much faster than us when we saw her last," said Bush meditatively.

"I happened to notice that myself," snapped Hornblower.

In this present darkness, however much the gale might moderate, there was nothing they could do. Hornblower could foresee, awaiting them, another of those long intervals of time with nothing to do and everything ready which punctuate the life of a naval officer and which were so liable to irritate him if he allowed them to. He realised that here was another opportunity to show himself as an iron-nerved man whom no tension could disturb. He yawned elaborately.

"I think I shall go to sleep again," he said, speaking with the utmost unconcern. "See that the lookouts keep awake, if you please, Mr. Bush. And have me called as soon as it grows lighter."

"Aye aye, sir," said Bush, and Hornblower went back to his boat cloak and his hammock chair.

He lay there for the rest of the night, unsleeping, and yet staying rigidly still so that the quarterdeck officers might think him asleep and admire the steadiness of his nerves. His mind was busy on the task of guessing what Crespo might be planning in the *Natividad.*

The latter was so badly crippled that probably he would be able to make no effective repairs while at sea. It would be much to his advantage to make for the Gulf of Fonseca again. There he could step a new foremast and send up a new main topmast. If the *Lydia* tried to interfere with her there she could overwhelm her by her superior weight in those confined waters; and besides, she would have the assistance of shore boats and possibly even of shore batteries. Moreover he could land his wounded and refill the gaps in his crew caused by the recent action — even landsmen would be of use in a fight to a finish. Crespo was a man of sufficient flexibility of mind not to scorn a retreat if it were to his advantage. The doubtful point was whether Crespo would dare to face El Supremo after an unsuccessful action.

Hornblower lay considering the matter, balancing his estimate of Crespo's character against what he knew of El Supremo. He remembered Crespo's glibness of tongue; that man would be able to convince even El Supremo that his return to his base with the *Lydia* undefeated was all part of a cunning plan for the more certain destruction of the enemy. Certainly his best course would be to return, and probably that would be the course he would adopt, and that course implied an attempted evasion of the *Lydia.* In that case he would — Hornblower's mind began feverish calculations of the *Natividad's* present position and future course. In consequence of her bigger bulk, and her two decks, she would have made far more leeway during the night — she was far to leeward at nightfall, for that matter. With the wind shifting and moderating as it was doing at present she would soon be able to make what sail her crippled condition would permit. The wind would be nearly foul for a run to the Gulf of Fonseca. Making for the mainland would be dangerous in Crespo's opinion, for the *Lydia* could hem her in between sea and shore and compel her to fight. Most likely he would reach far out to sea, clawing southward at the same time as much as he could, and make for the Gulf of Fonseca by a long detour out of sight of land. In that case

Hornblower must guess at what would be his position at dawn. He plunged into further tortuous mental calculations.

Eight bells sounded; the watch was called; he heard Gerard come to take over the deck from Bush. The wind was dropping fast, although the sea showed no sign of moderating as yet. The sky as he looked up at it was perceptibly lighter — here and there he could see stars between the clouds. Crespo would certainly be able to make sail now and attempt his escape. It was time for Hornblower to come to a decision. He climbed out of the hammock chair and walked across to the wheel.

"We will make sail, if you please, Mr. Bush."

"Aye aye, sir."

Hornblower gave the course, and he knew as he gave it that it might be quite the wrong one. He might have completely miscalculated. Every yard that the *Lydia* was sailing now might be in a direction away from the *Natividad*. Crespo might at this very moment be heading past him to safety. He might never destroy the *Natividad* at all if she fortified herself in the Gulf of Fonseca. There would be some who would attribute his failure to incompetence, and there would be not a few who would call it cowardice.

Chapter XVII

FROM the *Lydia's* masthead, in the clear daylight of the Pacific, a ship might be seen at a distance of as much as twenty miles, perhaps. A circle of twenty miles' radius, therefore, covered the extent of sea over which she had observation. It kept Hornblower occupied, during the remaining hours of darkness, to calculate the size of the circle in which the *Natividad* would necessarily be found next morning. She might be close at hand; she might be as much as a hundred and fifty miles away. That meant that if pure chance dictated the positions of the ships at dawn, it was almost exactly fifty to one against the *Natividad* being in sight; fifty to one on the ruin of Hornblower's professional reputation and only his professional abilities to counterbalance those odds. Only if he had guessed his enemy's plans correctly would he stand justified, and his officers knew it as well as he. Hornblower was conscious that Gerard was looking at him with interest through the darkness, and that consciousness caused him to hold himself rigid and immobile on the deck, neither walking up and down nor fidgeting, even though he could feel his heart beating faster each time he realised that dawn was approaching.

The blackness turned to grey. Now the outlines of the ship could be ascertained. The main topsail could be seen clearly. So could the fore topsail. Astern of them now the faintest hint of pink began to show in the greyness of the sky. Now the bulk of the grey waves overside could be seen as well as their white edges. Overhead by now the stars were invisible. The accustomed eye could pierce the greyness for a mile about the ship. And then astern, to the eastward, as the *Lydia* lifted on a wave, a grain of gold showed over the horizon, vanished, returned, and grew. Soon it became a great slice of the sun, sucking up greedily the faint mist which hung over the sea. Then the whole disc lifted clear, and the miracle of the dawn was accomplished.

"Sail ho!" came pealing down from the masthead; Hornblower had calculated aright.

Dead ahead, and ten miles distant, she was wallowing along, her appearance oddly at contrast with the one she had presented yesterday morning. Something had been done to give her a jury rig. A stumpy topmast had been erected where her foremast had stood, raked far back in clumsy fashion; her main topmast had been replaced by a slight spar — a royal mast, presumably — and on this jury rig she carried a queer collection of jibs and foresails and spritsails all badly set — "Like old Mother Brown's washing on the line" said Bush — to enable her to keep away from the wind with main course and mizzen topsail and driver set.

At sight of the *Lydia* she put her helm over and came round until her masts were line, heading away from the frigate.

"Making a stern chase of it," said Gerard, his glass to his eye. "He had enough yesterday, I fancy."

Hornblower heard the remark. He could understand Crespo's psychology better than that. If it were profitable to him to postpone action, and it undoubtedly was, he was quite right to continue doing so, even at the eleventh hour. At sea nothing was certain. Something might prevent the *Lydia's* coming into action; a squall of wind, the accidental carrying away of a spar, an opportune descent of mist — any one of the myriad things which might happen at sea. There was still a chance that the *Natividad* might get clear away, and Crespo was exploiting that chance to the last of his ability. That was logical though unheroic, exactly as one might expect of Crespo.

It was Hornblower's duty to see that the chance did not occur. He examined the *Natividad* closely, ran his eyes over the *Lydia's* sails to see that every one was drawing, and bethought himself of his crew.

"Send the hands to breakfast," he said — every captain of a King's ship took his men into action with full bellies if possible.

He remained, pacing up and down the quarterdeck, unable to keep himself still any longer. The *Natividad* might be running away, but he knew well that she would fight hard enough when he caught her up. Those smashing twenty-four pounders which she carried on her lower deck were heavy metal against which to oppose the frail timbers of a frigate. They had wrought enough damage yesterday — he could hear the melancholy clanking of the pumps keeping down the water which leaked through the holes they had made; that clanking sound had continued without a break since yesterday. With a jury mizzenmast, and leaking like a sieve despite the sail under her bottom, with sixty four of her attenuated crew hors de combat, the *Lydia* was in no condition to fight a severe battle. Defeat for her and death for him might be awaiting them across that strip of blue sea.

Polwheal suddenly appeared beside him on the quarterdeck, a tray in his hand.

"Your breakfast, sir," he said, "seeing as how we'll be in action when your usual time comes."

As he proffered the tray Hornblower suddenly realised how much he wanted that steaming cup of coffee. He took it eagerly and drank thirstily before he remembered that he must not display human weakness of appetite before his servant.

"Thank you, Polwheal," he said, sipping discreetly.

"An' 'er la'ship's compliments, sir, an' please may she stay where she is in the orlop when the action is renooed."

"Ha — h'm," said Hornblower, staring at him, thrown out of his stride by this unexpected question. All through the night he had been trying to forget the problem of Lady Barbara, as a man tries to forget an aching tooth. The orlop meant that Lady Barbara would be next to the wounded, separated from them only by a canvas screen — no place for a woman. But for that matter neither was the cable tier. The obvious truth was that there was no place for a woman in a frigate about to fight a battle.

"Put her wherever you like as long as she is out of reach of shot," he said, irritably.

"Aye aye, sir. An' 'er la'ship told me to say that she wished you the best of good fortune today, sir, an' — an' — she was confident that you would meet with the success you — you deserve, sir."

Polwheal stumbled over this long speech in a manner which

revealed that he had not been quite as successful in learning it fluently as he wished.

"Thank you, Polwheal," said Hornblower, gravely. He remembered Lady Barbara's face as she looked up at him from the main deck yesterday. It was clean cut and eager — like a sword, was the absurd simile which came up in his mind.

"Ha — h'm," said Hornblower angrily. He was aware that his expression had softened, and he feared lest Polwheal should have noticed it, at a moment when he knew about whom he was thinking. "Get below and see that her ladyship is comfortable."

The hands were pouring up from breakfast now; the pumps were clanking with a faster rhythm now that a fresh crew was at work upon them. The guns' crews were gathered about their guns, and the few idlers were crowded on the forecastle eagerly watching the progress of the chase.

"Do you think the wind's going to hold, sir?" asked Bush, coming onto the quarterdeck like a bird of ill omen. "Seems to me as if the sun's swallowing it."

There was no doubting the fact that as the sun climbed higher in the sky the wind was diminishing in force. The sea was still short, steep, and rough, but the *Lydia's* motion over it was no longer light and graceful. She was pitching and jerking inelegantly, deprived of the steady pressure of a good sailing wind. The sky overhead was fast becoming of a hard metallic blue.

"We're overhauling 'em fast," said Hornblower, staring fixedly at the chase so as to ignore these portents of the elements.

"Three hours and we're up to 'em," said Bush. "If the wind only holds."

It was fast growing hot. The heat which the sun was pouring down on them was intensified by its contrast with the comparative coolness of the night before. The crew had begun to seek the strips of shade under the gangways, and were lying there wearily. The steady clanging of the pumps seemed to sound louder now that the wind was losing its force. Hornblower suddenly realised that he would feel intensely weary if he permitted himself to think about it. He stood stubborn on the quarterdeck with the sun beating on his back, every few moments raising his telescope to stare at the *Natividad,* while Bush fussed about the trimming of the sails as the breeze began to waver.

"Steer small, blast you," he growled at the quartermaster at the wheel as the ship's head fell away in the trough of a wave.

"I can't, sir, begging your pardon," was the reply. "There aren't enough wind."

It was true enough. The wind had died away so that the *Lydia* could not maintain the two knot speed which was sufficient to give her rudder power to act.

"We'll have to wet the sails. Mr. Bush, see to it, if you please," said Hornblower.

One division of one watch was roused up to this duty. A soaking wet sail will hold air which would escape it if it were dry. Whips were rove through the blocks on the yards, and sea water hoisted up and poured over the canvas. So hot was the sun and so rapid the evaporation that the buckets had to be kept continually in action. To the clanging of the pumps was now added the shrilling of the sheaves in the blocks. The *Lydia* crept, still plunging madly, over the tossing sea and under the glaring sky.

"She's boxing the compass now," said Bush with a jerk of his thumb at the distant *Natividad.* "She can't compare with this beauty. She won't find that new rig of hers any help, neither."

The *Natividad* was turning idly backwards and forwards on the waves, showing sometimes her broadside and sometimes her three masts in line, unable to steer any course in the light air prevailing. Bush looked complacently up at his new mizzenmast, a pyramid of canvas, and then across at the swaying *Natividad,* less than five miles away. The minutes crept by, their passage marked only by the monotonous noises of the ship. Hornblower stood in the scorching sunlight, fingering his telescope.

"Here comes the wind again, by God!" said Bush, suddenly. It was sufficient wind to make the ship heel a little, and to summon a faint harping from the rigging. " 'Vast heaving with those buckets, there."

The *Lydia* crept steadily forward, heaving and plunging to the music of the water under her bows, while the *Natividad* grew perceptibly nearer.

"It will reach him quickly enough. There! What did I say?"

The *Natividad's* sails filled as the breeze came down to her. She straightened upon her course.

" 'Twon't help him as much as it helps us. God, if it only holds!" commented Bush.

The breeze wavered and then renewed itself. The *Natividad* was hull-up now across the water when a wave lifted her. Another hour — less than an hour — and she would be in range.

"We'll be trying long shots at her soon," said Bush.

"Mr. Bush," said Hornblower, spitefully, "I can judge of the situation without the assistance of your comments, profound though they be."

"I beg your pardon, sir," said Bush, hurt. He flushed angrily for a moment until he noticed the anxiety in Hornblower's tired eyes, and then stumped away to the opposite rail to forget his rage.

As if by way of comment the big main-course flapped loudly, once, like a gun. The breeze was dying away as motivelessly as it had begun. And the *Natividad* still held it; she was holding her course steadily, drawing away once more, helped by the fluky wind. Here in the tropical Pacific one ship can have a fair wind while another two miles away lies becalmed, just as the heavy sea in which they were rolling indicated that last night's gale was still blowing, over the horizon, at the farther side of the Gulf of Tehuantepec. Hornblower stirred uneasily in the blazing sun. He feared lest he should see the *Natividad* sail clean away from him; the wind had died away so much that there was no point in wetting the sails, and the *Lydia* was rolling and sagging about aimlessly now to the send of the waves. Ten minutes passed before he was reassured by the sight of the *Natividad's* similar behaviour.

There was not a breath of wind now. The *Lydia* rolled wildly, to the accompaniment of a spasmodic creaking of woodwork, flapping of sails, and clattering of blocks. Only the clangour of the pumps sounded steadily through the hot air. The *Natividad* was four miles away now — a mile and a half beyond the farthest range of any of the *Lydia's* guns.

"Mr. Bush," said Hornblower. "We will tow with the boats. Have the launch and the cutter hoisted out."

Bush looked doubtful for a moment. He feared that two could play at that game. But he realised — as Hornblower had realised before him — that the *Lydia's* graceful hull would be more amenable to towing than the *Natividad's* ungainly bulk, even without counting the possibility that yesterday's action might have left her with no boat left that would swim. It was Hornblower's duty to try every course that might bring his ship into action with the enemy.

"Boats away!" roared Harrison. "Cutter's crew, launch's crew."

The pipes of his mates endorsed the orders. The hands tailed on to the tackles, and each boat in turn was swayed up into the air, and lowered outboard, the boats' crews fending off as the *Lydia* rolled in the swell.

There began for the boats' crews a period of the most exhausting and exasperating labour. They would tug and strain at the oars, moving the ponderous boats over the heaving waves, until the tow ropes tightened with a jerk as the strain came upon them. Then, tug as they would, they would seem to make no progress at all, the oar blades foaming impotently through the blue water, until the *Lydia* consented to crawl forward a little and the whole operation could be repeated. The heaving waves were a hindrance to them — sometimes every man on one side of a boat would catch a simultaneous crab so that the boat would spin round and become a nuisance to the other one — and the *Lydia,* so graceful and willing when under sail, was a perfect bitch when being towed.

She yawed and she sagged, falling away in the trough on occasions so much that the launch and the cutter were dragged, with much splashing from the oars, stern first after her wavering bows, and then changing her mind and heaving forward so fast after the two ropes that the men, flinging their weight upon the oar looms in expectation of a profitless pull, were precipitated backwards with the ease of progression while in imminent danger of being run down.

They sat naked on the thwarts while the sweat ran in streams down their faces and chests, unable — unlike their comrades at the pumps — to forget their fatigues in the numbness of monotonous work when every moment called for vigilance and attention, tugging painfully away, their agonies of thirst hardly relieved by the allowance of water doled out to them by the petty officers in the sternsheets, tugging away until even hands calloused by years of pulling and hauling cracked and blistered so that the oars were agony to touch.

Hornblower knew well enough the hardship they were undergoing. He went forward and looked down at the toiling seamen, knowing perfectly well that his own body would not be able to endure that labour for more than half an hour at most. He gave orders for an hourly relief at the oars, and he did his best to cheer the men on. He felt an uneasy sympathy for them — three quarters of them had never been sailors until this commission, and had no desire to be sailors either, but had been swept up by the all-embracing press seven months ago. Hornblower was always able (rather against his will) to do what most of his officers failed to do — he saw his crew not as topmen or hands, but as what they had been before the press caught them, stevedores, wherry men, porters.

He had waggoners and potters — he had even two draper's assistants and a printer among his crew; men snatched without notice from their families and their employment and forced into this sort of labour, on wretched food, in hideous working conditions, haunted always by the fear of the cat or of Harrison's rattan, and with the chance of death by drowning or by hostile action to seal the bargain. So imaginative an individualist as Hornblower was bound to feel sympathy with them even when he felt he ought not, especially as he (in common with a few other liberals) found himself growing more and more liberal minded with the progress of years. But to counterbalance this weakness of his there was his restless nervous anxiety to finish off well any task he had set himself to do. With the *Natividad* in sight he could not rest until he had engaged her, and when a captain of a ship cannot rest his crew certainly cannot — aching backs or bleeding hands notwithstanding.

By careful measurement with his sextant of the subtended angles he was able to say with certainty at the end of an hour that the efforts of the boats' crews had dragged the *Lydia* a little nearer to the *Natividad*, and Bush, who had taken the same measurements, was in agreement. The sun rose higher and the *Lydia* crept inch by inch towards her enemy.

"*Natividad's* hoisting out a boat, sir," hailed Knyvett from the foretop.

"How many oars?"

"Twelve, sir, I think. They're taking the ship in tow."

"And they're welcome," scoffed Bush. "Twelve oars won't move that old tub of a *Natividad* very far."

Hornblower glared at him and Bush retired to his own side of the quarterdeck again; he had forgotten his captain was in this unconversational mood. Hornblower was fretting himself into a fever. He stood in the glaring sun while the heat was reflected up into his face from the deck under his feet. His shirt chafed him where he sweated. He felt caged, like a captive beast, within the limitations of practical details. The endless clanking of the pumps, the rolling of the ship, the rattle of the rigging, the noise of the oars in the rowlocks, were driving him mad, as though he could scream (or weep) at the slightest additional provocation.

At noon he changed the men at the oars and pumps, and sent the crew to dinner — he remembered bitterly that he had already made them breakfast in anticipation of immediate action. At two bells he began to wonder whether the *Natividad* might be within extreme long range, but the mere fact of wondering told him that it was not the case — he knew his own sanguine temperament too well, and he fought down the temptation to waste powder and shot. And then, as he looked for the thousandth time through his telescope, he suddenly saw a disc of white appear on the high stern of the *Natividad*. The disc spread and expanded into a thin cloud, and six seconds after its first appearance the dull thud of the shot reached his ears. The *Natividad* was evidently willing to try the range.

"*Natividad* carries two long eighteens aft on the quarterdeck," said Gerard to Bush in Hornblower's hearing. "Heavy metal for stern chasers."

Hornblower knew it already. He would have to run the gauntlet of those two guns for an hour, possibly, before he could bring the brass nine-pounder on his forecastle into action. Another puff of smoke from the *Natividad,* and this time Hornblower saw a spout of water rise from the breast of a wave half a mile ahead. But at that long range and on that tossing sea it did not mean that the *Lydia* was still half a mile beyond the *Natividad's* reach. Hornblower heard the next shot arrive, and saw a brief fountain of water rise no more than fifty yards from the *Lydia's* starboard quarter.

"Mr. Gerard," said Hornblower. "Send for Mr. Marsh and see what he can do with the long nine forward."

It would cheer the men up to have a gun banging away occasionally instead of being merely shot at without making any reply. Marsh came waddling up from the darkness of the magazine, and blinked in the blinding sunshine. He shook his head doubtfully as he eyed the distance between the ships, but he had the gun cleared away, and he loaded it with his own hands, lovingly. He measured out the powder charge on the fullest scale, and he spent several seconds selecting the roundest and truest shot from the locker. He trained the gun with care, and then stood aside, lanyard in hand, watching the heave of the ship and the send of the bows, while a dozen telescopes were trained on the *Natividad* and every eye watched for the fall of the shot. Suddenly he jerked the lanyard and the cannon roared out, its report sounding flat in the heated motionless air.

"Two cables' lengths astern of her!" yelled Knyvett from the foretop. Hornblower had missed the splash — another proof, to his mind, of his own incompetence, but he concealed the fact under a mask of imperturbability.

"Try again, Mr. Marsh," he said.

The *Natividad* was firing both stern chasers together now. As Hornblower spoke there came a crash forward as one of the eighteen-pounder balls struck home close above the water line. Hornblower could hear young Savage, down in the launch, hurling shrill blasphemies at the men at the oars to urge them on — that shot must have passed just over his head. Marsh stroked his beard and addressed himself to the task of reloading the long nine-pounder. While he was so engaged, Hornblower was deep in the calculation of the chances of battle.

That long nine, although of smaller calibre, was of longer range than his shorter main deck guns, while the carronades which comprised half of the *Lydia's* armament were useless at anything longer than close range. The *Lydia* would have to draw up close to her enemy before she could attack her with effect. There would be a long and damaging interval between the moment when the *Natividad* should be able to bring all her guns into action and the moment when the *Lydia* could hit back at her. There would be casualties, guns dismounted perhaps, serious losses. Hornblower balanced the arguments for and against continuing to try and close with the enemy while Mr. Marsh was squinting along the sights of the nine-pounder. Then Hornblower scowled to himself, and ceased tugging at his chin, his mind made up. He had started the action; he would go through it to the end, cost what it might. His flexibility of mind could crystallise into sullen obstinacy.

The nine-pounder went off as though to signal this decision.

"Just alongside her!" screamed Knyvett triumphantly from the foretop.

"Well done, Mr. Marsh," said Hornblower, and Marsh wagged his beard complacently.

The *Natividad* was firing faster now. Three times a splintering crash told of a shot which had been aimed true. Then suddenly a thrust as if from an invisible hand made Hornblower reel on the quarterdeck, and his ears were filled with a brief rending noise. A skimming shot had ploughed a channel along the planking of the quarterdeck. A marine was sitting near the taffrail stupidly contemplating his left leg, which no longer had a foot on the end of it; another marine dropped his musket with a clatter and clapped his hands to his face, which a splinter had torn open, with blood spouting between his fingers.

"Are you hurt, sir?" cried Bush, leaping across to Hornblower.

"No."

Hornblower turned back to stare through his glass at the *Natividad* while the wounded were being dragged away. He saw a dark dot appear alongside the *Natividad*, and lengthen and diverge. It was the boat with which they had been trying to tow — perhaps they were giving up the attempt. But the boat was not being hoisted in. For a second Hornblower was puzzled. The *Natividad's* stumpy foremast and mainmast came into view. The boat was pulling the ship laboriously round so that her whole broadside would bear. Not two, but twenty five guns would soon be opening their fire on the *Lydia.*

Hornblower felt his breath come a little quicker, unexpectedly, so that he had to swallow in order to regulate things again. His pulse was faster, too. He made himself keep the glass to his eye until he was certain of the enemy's manœuvre, and then walked forward leisurely to the gangway. He was compelling himself to appear lighthearted and carefree; he knew that the fools of men whom he commanded would fight more diligently for a captain like that.

"They're waiting for us now, lads," he said. "We shall have some pebbles about our ears before long. Let's show 'em that Englishmen don't care."

They cheered him for that, as he expected and hoped they would do. He looked through his glass again at the *Natividad.* She was still turning, very slowly — it was a lengthy process to turn a clumsy two-decker in a dead calm. But her three masts were fully separate from each other now, and he could see a hint of the broad white stripes which ornamented her side.

"Ha — h'm," he said.

Forward he could hear the oars grinding away as the men in the boats laboured to drag the *Lydia* to grips with her enemy. Across the deck a little group of officers — Bush and Crystal among them — were academically discussing what percentage of hits might be expected from a Spanish broadside at a range of a mile. They were coldblooded about it in a fashion he could never hope to imitate with sincerity. He did not fear death so much — not nearly as much — as defeat and the pitying contempt of his colleagues. The chiefest dread at the back of his mind was the fear of mutilation. An ex-naval officer stumping about on two wooden legs might be an object of condolence, might receive lip service as one of Britain's heroic defenders, but he was a figure of fun nevertheless. Hornblower dreaded the thought of being a figure of fun. He might lose his nose or his cheek and be so mutilated that people would not be able to bear to look at him. It was a horrible thought which set him shuddering while he looked through the telescope, so horrible that he did not stop to think of the associated details, of the agonies he would have to bear down there in the dark cockpit at the mercy of Laurie's incompetence.

The *Natividad* was suddenly engulfed in smoke, and some seconds later the air and the water around the *Lydia,* and the ship herself, were torn by the hurtling broadside.

"Not more than two hits," said Bush, gleefully.

"Just what I said," said Crystal. "That captain of theirs ought to go round and train every gun himself."

"How do you know he did not?" argued Bush.

As punctuation the nine-pounder forward banged out its defiance. Hornblower fancied that his straining eyes saw splinters fly amidships of the *Natividad,* unlikely though it was at that distance.

"Well aimed, Mr. Marsh!" he called. "You hit him squarely."

Another broadside came from the *Natividad,* and another followed it, and another after that. Time after time the *Lydia's* decks were swept from end to end with shot. There were dead men laid out again on the deck, and the groaning wounded were dragged below.

"It is obvious to anyone of a mathematical turn of mind," said Crystal, "that those guns are all laid by different hands. The shots are too scattered for it to be otherwise."

"Nonsense!" maintained Bush sturdily. "See how long it is between broadsides. Time enough for one man to train each gun. What would they be doing in that time otherwise?"

"A Dago crew —— " began Crystal, but a sudden shriek of cannon balls over his head silenced him for a moment.

"Mr. Galbraith!" shouted Bush. "Have that main t'gallant stay spliced directly." Then he turned triumphantly on Crystal. "Did you notice," he asked, "how every shot from that broadside went high? How does the mathematical mind explain that?"

"They fired on the upward roll, Mr. Bush. Really, Mr. Bush, I think that after Trafalgar —— "

Hornblower longed to order them to cease the argument which was lacerating his nerves, but he could not be such a tyrant as that.

In the still air the smoke from the *Natividad's* firing had banked up round about her so that she showed ghostly through the cloud, her solitary mizzen topmast protruding above it into the clear air.

"Mr. Bush," he asked, "at what distance do you think she is now?"

Bush gauged the distance carefully.

"Three parts of a mile, I should say, sir."

"Two thirds, more likely, sir," said Crystal.

"Your opinion was not asked, Mr. Crystal," snapped Hornblower.

At three quarters of a mile, even at two thirds, the *Lydia's* carronades would be ineffective. She must continue running the gauntlet. Bush was evidently of the same opinion, to judge by his next orders.

"Time for the men at the oars to be relieved," he said, and went forward to attend to it. Hornblower heard him bustling the new crews down into the boats, anxious that the pulling should be resumed before the *Lydia* had time to lose what little way she carried.

It was terribly hot under the blazing sun, even though it was now long past noon. The smell of the blood which had been spilt on the decks mingled with the smell of the hot deck seams and of the powder smoke from the nine-pounder with which Marsh was still steadily bombarding the enemy. Hornblower felt sick — so sick that he began to fear lest he should disgrace himself eternally by vomiting in full view of his men. When fatigue and anxiety had weakened him thus he was far more conscious of the pitching and rolling of the ship under his feet. The men at the guns were silent now, he noticed — for long they had laughed and joked at their posts, but now they were beginning to sulk under the punishment. That was a bad sign.

"Pass the word for Sullivan and his fiddle," he ordered.

The red-haired Irish madman came aft, and knuckled his forehead, his fiddle and bow under his arm.

"Give us a tune, Sullivan," he ordered. "Hey there, men, who is there among you who dances the best hornpipe?"

There was a difference of opinion about that apparently.

"Benskin, sir," said some voices.

"Hall, sir," said others.

"No, MacEvoy, sir."

"Then we'll have a tournament," said Hornblower. "Here, Benskin, Hall, MacEvoy. A hornpipe from each of you, and a guinea for the man who does it best."

In later years it was a tale told and retold, how the *Lydia* towed into action with hornpipes being danced on her main deck. It was quoted as an example of Hornblower's cool courage, and only Hornblower knew how little truth there was in the attribution. It kept the men happy, which was why he did it. No one guessed how nearly he came to vomiting when a shot came in through a forward gunport and spattered Hall with a seaman's brains without causing him to miss a step.

Then later in that dreadful afternoon there came a crash from forward, followed by a chorus of shouts and screams overside.

"Launch sunk, sir!" hailed Galbraith from the forecastle, but Hornblower was there as soon as he had uttered the words.

A round shot had dashed the launch practically into its component planks, and the men were scrambling in the water, leaping up for the bobstay or struggling to climb into the cutter, all of them who survived wild with the fear of sharks.

"The Dagoes have saved us the trouble of hoisting her in," he said, loudly. "We're close enough now for them to feel our teeth."

The men who heard him cheered.

"Mr. Hooker!" he called to the midshipman in the cutter. "When you have picked up those men, kindly starboard your helm. We are going to open fire."

He came aft to the quarterdeck again.

"Hard a-starboard," he growled at the quartermaster. "Mr. Gerard, you may open fire when your guns bear."

Very slowly the *Lydia* swung round. Another broadside from

the *Natividad* came crashing into her before she had completed the turn, but Hornblower actually did not notice it. The period of inaction was over now. He had brought his ship within four hundred yards of the enemy, and all his duty now was to walk the deck as an example to his men. There were no more decisions to make.

"Cock your locks!" shouted Gerard in the waist.

"Easy, Mr. Hooker. Way enough!" roared Hornblower.

The *Lydia* turned, inch by inch, with Gerard squinting along one of the starboard guns to judge of the moment when it would first bear.

"Take your aim!" he yelled, and stood back, timing the roll of the ship in the heavy swell. "Fire!"

The smoke billowed out amid the thunder of the discharge, and the *Lydia* heaved to the recoil of the guns.

"Give him another, lads!" shouted Hornblower through the din. Now that action was joined he found himself exalted and happy, the dreadful fears of mutilation forgotten. In thirty seconds the guns were reloaded, run out, and fired. Again and again and again, with Gerard watching the roll of the ship and giving the word. Counting back in his mind, Hornblower reckoned five broadsides from the *Lydia,* and he could only remember two from the *Natividad* in that time. At that rate of firing the *Natividad's* superiority in numbers of guns and weight of metal would be more than counterbalanced. At the sixth broadside a gun went off prematurely, a second before Gerard gave the word. Hornblower sprang forward to detect the guilty crew — it was easy enough from their furtive look and suspicious appearance of busyness. He shook his finger at them.

"Steady, there!" he shouted. "I'll flog the next man who fires out of turn."

It was very necessary to keep the men in hand while the range was as long as at present, because in the heat and excitement of the action the gun captains could not be trusted to judge the motion of the ship while preoccupied with loading and laying.

"Good old Horny!" piped up some unknown voice forward,

and there was a burst of laughter and cheering, cut short by Gerard's next order to fire.

The smoke was banked thick about the ship already — as thick as a London fog, so that from the quarterdeck it was impossible to see individuals on the forecastle, and in the unnatural darkness which it brought with it one could see the long orange flashes of the guns despite the vivid sunshine outside. Of the *Natividad* all that could be seen was her high smoke cloud and the single topmast jutting out from it. The thick smoke, trailing about the ship in greasy wreaths, made the eyes smart and irritated the lungs, and affected the skin like thundery weather until it pricked uncomfortably.

Hornblower found Bush beside him.

"*Natividad's* feeling our fire, sir," he roared through the racket. "She's firing very wild. Look at that, sir."

Of the broadside fired only one or two shots struck home. Half a dozen plunged together into the sea astern of the *Lydia* so that the spray from the fountains which they struck up splashed round them on the quarterdeck. Hornblower nodded happily. This was his justification for closing to that range and for running the risks involved in the approach. To maintain a rapid fire, well aimed, amid the din and the smoke and the losses and the confusion of a naval battle called for discipline and practice of a sort that he knew the *Natividad's* crew could not boast.

He looked down through the smoke at the *Lydia's* main deck. The inexperienced eye, observing the hurry and bustle of the boys with the cartridge buckets, the mad efforts of the gun crews, the dead and the wounded, the darkness and the din, might well think it a scene of confusion, but Hornblower knew better. Everything that was being done there, every single action, was part of the scheme worked out by Hornblower seven months before when he commissioned the *Lydia,* and grained into the minds of all on board during the long and painful drills since. He could see Gerard standing by the mainmast, looking almost saintly in his ecstasy — gunnery was as much Gerard's ruling passion as women; he could see the midshipmen and other warrant officers each by his sub-division of guns, each looking to Gerard for his orders and keeping his guns working rhythmically, the loaders with their rammers, the cleaners with their sponges, the gun captains crouching over the breeches, right hands raised.

The port side battery was already depleted of most of its men; there were only two men to a gun there, standing idle yet ready to spring into action if a shift of the fight should bring their guns to bear. The remainder were on duty round the ship — replacing casualties on the starboard side, manning the pumps whose doleful clanking continued steadily through the fearful din, resting on their oars in the cutter, hard at work aloft repairing damages. Hornblower found time to be thankful that he had been granted seven months in which to bring his crew into its present state of training and discipline.

Something — the concussion of the guns, a faint breath of air, or the send of the sea — was causing the *Lydia* to turn away a trifle from her enemy. Hornblower could see that the guns were having to be trained round farther and farther so that the rate of firing was being slowed down. He raced forward, running out along the bowsprit until he was over the cutter where Hooker and his men sat staring at the fight.

"Mr. Hooker, bring her head round two points to starboard."

"Aye aye, sir."

The men bent to their oars and headed their boat towards the *Natividad;* the towrope tightened while another badly aimed broadside tore the water all round them into foam. Tugging and straining at the oars they would work the ship round in time. Hornblower left them and ran back to the quarterdeck. There was a white-faced ship's boy seeking him there.

"Mr. Howell sent me, sir. Starboard side chain pump's knocked all to pieces."

"Yes?" Hornblower knew that Howell the ship's carpenter would not merely send a message of despair.

"He's rigging another one, sir, but it will be an hour before it works, sir. He told me to tell you the water's gaining a little, sir."

"Ha — h'm," said Hornblower. The infant addressing him

grew round-eyed and confidential now that the first strangeness of speaking to his captain had worn off.

"There was fourteen men all knocked into smash at the pump, sir. 'Orrible, sir."

"Very good. Run back to Mr. Howell and tell him the captain is sure he will do his best to get the new pump rigged."

"Aye aye, sir."

The boy dived down to the main deck, and Hornblower watched him running forward, dodging the hurrying individuals in the crowded space there. He had to explain himself to the marine sentry at the fore hatchway — no one could go below without being able to show that it was his duty which was calling him there. Hornblower felt as if the message Howell had sent did not matter at all. It called for no decision on his part. All there was to do was to go on fighting, whether the ship was sinking under their feet or not. There was a comfort in being free of all responsibility in this way.

"One hour and a half already," said Bush, coming up rubbing his hands. "Glorious, sir. Glorious."

It might have been no more than ten minutes for all Hornblower could tell, but Bush had in duty bound been watching the sand glass by the binnacle.

"I've never known Dagoes stick to their guns like this before," commented Bush. "Their aim's poor, but they're firing as fast as ever. And it's my belief we've hit them hard, sir."

He tried to look through the eddying smoke, even fanning ridiculously with his hands in the attempt — a gesture which, by showing that he was not quite as calm as he appeared to be, gave Hornblower an absurd pleasure. Crystal came up as well as he spoke.

"The smoke's thinning a little, sir. It's my belief that there's a light air of wind blowing."

He held up a wetted finger.

"There is indeed, sir. A trifle of breeze over the port quarter. Ah!"

There came a stronger puff as he spoke, which rolled away the smoke in a solid mass over the starboard bow and revealed the scene as if a theatre curtain had been raised. There was the *Natividad,* looking like a wreck. Her jury foremast had gone the way of its predecessor, and her mainmast had followed it. Only her mizzenmast stood now, and she was rolling wildly in the swell with a huge tangle of rigging trailing over her disengaged side. Abreast her foremast three ports had been battered into one; the gap looked like a missing tooth.

"She's low in the water," said Bush, but on the instant a fresh broadside vomited smoke from her battered side, and this time by some chance every shot told in the *Lydia,* as the crash below well indicated. The smoke billowed round the *Natividad,* and as it cleared the watchers saw her swinging round head to wind, helpless in the light air. The *Lydia* had felt the breeze. Hornblower could tell by the feel of her that she had steerage way again; the quartermaster at the wheel was twirling the spokes to hold her steady. He saw his chance on the instant.

"Starboard a point," he ordered. "Forward, there! Cast off the cutter."

The *Lydia* steadied across her enemy's bows and raked her with thunder and flame.

"Back the main tops'l," ordered Hornblower.

The men were cheering again on the main deck through the roar of the guns. Astern the red sun was dipping to the water's edge in a glory of scarlet and gold. Soon it would be night.

"She must strike soon. Christ! Why don't she strike?" Bush was saying, as at close range the broadsides tore into the helpless enemy, raking her from bow to stern. Hornblower knew better. No ship under Crespo's command and flying El Supremo's flag would strike her colours. He could see the golden star on a blue ground fluttering through the smoke.

"Pound him, lads, pound him!" shouted Gerard.

With the shortening range he could rely on his gun captains to fire independently now. Every gun's crew was loading and firing as rapidly as possible. So hot were the guns that at each discharge they leaped high in their carriages, and the dripping sponges thrust down their bores sizzled and steamed at the touch of the scorching hot metal. It was growing darker, too. The flashes of the guns could be seen again now, leaping in long orange tongues from the gun muzzles. High above the fast fading sunset could be seen the first star, shining out brilliantly.

The *Natividad's* bowsprit was gone, splintered and broken and hanging under her forefoot, and then in the dwindling light the mizzenmast fell as well, cut through by shots which had ripped their way down the whole length of the ship.

"She must strike now, by God!" said Bush.

At Trafalgar Bush had been sent as prize master into a captured Spanish ship, and his mind was full of busy memories of what a beaten ship looked like — the dismounted guns, the dead and wounded heaped on the deck and rolling back and forth as the dismasted ship rolled on the swell, the misery, the pain, the helplessness. As if in reply to him there came a sudden flash and report from the *Natividad's* bows. Some devoted souls with tackles and hand-spikes had contrived to slew a gun round so that it would bear right forward, and were firing into the looming bulk of the *Lydia.*

"Pound him, lads, pound him!" screamed Gerard, half mad with fatigue and strain.

The *Lydia* by virtue of her top hamper was going down to leeward fast upon the rolling hulk. At every second the range was shortening. Through the darkness, when their eyes were not blinded with gun flashes, Hornblower and Bush could see figures moving about on the *Natividad's* deck. They were firing muskets now, as well. The flashes pricked the darkness and Hornblower heard a bullet thud into the rail beside him. He did not care. He was conscious now of his overmastering weariness.

The wind was fluky, coming in sudden puffs and veering unexpectedly. It was hard, especially in the darkness, to judge exactly how the two ships were nearing each other.

"The closer we are, the quicker we'll finish it," said Bush.

"Yes, but we'll run on board of her soon," said Hornblower.

He roused himself for a further effort.

"Call the hands to stand by to repel boarders," he said, and he walked across to where the two starboard side quarterdeck carronades were thundering away. So intent were their crews on their work, so hypnotised by the monotony of loading and firing, that it took him several seconds to attract their notice. Then they stood still, sweating, while Hornblower gave his orders. The two carronades were loaded with canister brought from the reserve locker beside the taffrail. They waited, crouching beside the guns, while the two ships drifted closer and closer together, the *Lydia's* main deck guns still blazing away. There were shouts and yells of defiance from the *Natividad*, and the musket flashes from her bows showed a dark mass of men crowding there waiting for the ships to come together. Yet the actual contact was unexpected, as a sudden combination of wind and sea closed the gap with a rush. The *Natividad's* bow hit the *Lydia* amidships, just forward of the mizzenmast, with a jarring crash. There was a pandemonium of yells from the *Natividad* as they swarmed forward to board, and the captains of the carronades sprang to their lanyards.

"Wait!" shouted Hornblower.

His mind was like a calculating machine, judging wind and sea, time and distance, as the *Lydia* slowly swung round. With hand spikes and the brute strength of the men he trained one carronade round and the other followed his example, while the mob on the *Natividad's* forecastle surged along the bulwarks waiting for the moment to board. The two carronades came right up against them.

"Fire!"

A thousand musket balls were vomited from the carronades straight into the packed crowd. There was a moment of silence, and then the pandemonium of shouts and cheers was replaced by a thin chorus of screams and cries — the blast of musket balls had swept the *Natividad's* forecastle clear from side to side.

For a space the two ships clung together in this position; the *Lydia* still had a dozen guns that would bear, and these pounded away with their muzzles almost touching the *Natividad's* bow. Then wind and sea parted them again, the *Lydia* to leeward now, drifting away from the rolling hulk; in the English ship every gun was in action, while from the *Natividad* came not a gun, not even a musket shot.

Hornblower fought off his weariness again.

"Cease firing," he shouted to Gerard on the main deck, and the guns fell silent.

Hornblower stared through the darkness at the vague mass of the *Natividad*, wallowing in the waves.

"Surrender!" he shouted.

"Never!" came the reply — Crespo's voice, he could have sworn to it, thin and high-pitched. It added two or three words of obscene insult.

Hornblower could afford to smile at that, even through his weariness. He had fought his battle and won it.

"You have done all that brave men could do," he shouted.

"Not all, yet, Captain," wailed the voice in the darkness.

Then something caught Hornblower's eye — a wavering glow of red round about the *Natividad's* vague bows.

"Crespo, you fool!" he shouted. "Your ship's on fire! Surrender, while you can."

"Never!"

The *Lydia's* guns, hard against the *Natividad's* side, had flung their flaming wads in amongst the splintered timbers. The tinder-dry wood of the old ship had taken fire from them, and the fire was spreading fast. It was brighter already than when Hornblower had noticed it; the ship would be a mass of flames soon. Hornblower's first duty was to his own ship — when the fire should reach the powder charges on the *Natividad's* decks, or when it should attain the magazine, the ship would become a volcano of flaming fragments, imperilling the *Lydia*.

"We must haul off from her, Mr. Bush," said Hornblower, speaking formally to conceal the tremor in his voice. "Man the braces, there."

The *Lydia* swung away, closehauled, clawing her way up to windward of the flaming wreck. Bush and Hornblower gazed back at her. There were bright flames now to be seen, spouting from the shattered bows — the red glow was reflected in the heaving sea around her. And then, as they looked, they saw the flames vanish abruptly, like an extinguished candle. There was nothing to be seen at all, nothing save darkness and the faint glimmer of the wave crests. The sea had swallowed the *Natividad* before the flames could destroy her.

"Sunk, by God!" exclaimed Bush, leaning out over the rail.

Hornblower still seemed to hear that last wailing "Never!" during the seconds of silence that followed. Yet he was perhaps the first of all his ship's company to recover from the shock. He put his ship about and ran down to the scene of the *Natividad's* sinking. He sent off Hooker and the cutter to search for survivors — the cutter was the only boat left, for gig and jolly boat had been shattered by the *Natividad's* fire, and the planks of the launch were floating five miles away. They picked up a few men — two were hauled out of the water by men in the *Lydia's* chains, and the cutter found half a dozen swimmers; that was all. The *Lydia's* crew tried to be kind to them, as they stood on her deck in the lantern light with the water streaming from their ragged clothes and their lank black hair, but they were sullen and silent; there was even one who struggled for a moment, as if to continue the battle which the *Natividad* had fought so desperately.

"Never mind, we'll make topmen of them yet," said Hornblower, trying to speak lightly.

Fatigue had reached such a pitch now that he was speaking as if out of a dream, as if all these solid surroundings of his, the ship, her guns and masts and sails, Bush's burly figure, were unreal and ghostlike, and only his weariness and the ache inside his skull were existing things. He heard his voice as though he were speaking from a yard away.

"Aye aye, sir," said the boatswain.

Anything was grist that came to the Royal Navy's mill — Harrison was prepared to make seamen out of the strangest human material; he had done so all his life, for that matter.

"What course shall I set, sir?" asked Bush, as Hornblower turned back to the quarterdeck.

"Course?" said Hornblower, vaguely. "Course?"

It was terribly hard to realise that the battle was over, the *Natividad* sunk, that there was no enemy afloat within thousands of miles of sea. It was hard to realise that the *Lydia* was in acute danger, too; that the pumps, clanking away monotonously, were not quite able to keep the leaks under, that the *Lydia* still had a sail stretched under her bottom, and stood in the acutest need of a complete refit.

Hornblower came by degrees to realise that now he had to start a new chapter in the history of the *Lydia,* to make fresh plans. And there was a long line of people waiting for immediate orders, too — Bush, here, and the boatswain and the carpenter and the gunner and that fool Laurie. He had to force his tired brain to think again. He estimated the wind's force and direction, as though it were an academic exercise and not a mental process which for twenty years had been second nature to him. He went wearily down to his cabin and found the shattered chart cases amid the indescribable wreckage, and he pored over the torn chart.

He must report his success at Panama as soon as he could; that was obvious to him now. Perhaps he could refit there, although he saw small chance of it in that inhospitable roadstead, especially with yellow fever in the town. So he must carry the shattered *Lydia* to Panama. He laid off a course for Cape Mala, by a supreme effort compelled his mind to realise that he had a fair wind, and came up again with his orders to find that the mass of people who were clamouring for his attention had miraculously vanished. Bush had chased them all away, although he never discovered it. He gave the course to Bush, and then Polwheal materialised himself at his elbow, with boat cloak and hammock chair. Hornblower had no protest left in him. He allowed himself to be wrapped in the cloak, and he fell half fainting into the chair. It was twenty one hours since he had last sat down. Polwheal had brought food, too, but he merely ignored that. He wanted no food; all he wanted was rest.

Then for a second he was wide awake again. He had remembered Lady Barbara, battened down below with the wounded in the dark and stifling bowels of the ship. But he relaxed at once. The blasted woman could look after herself — she was quite capable of doing so. Nothing mattered now. His head sank on his breast again. The next thing to disturb him was the sound of his own snores, and that did not disturb him long. He slept and he snored through all the din which the crew made in their endeavour to get the *Lydia* shipshape again.

Chapter XVIII

WHAT awoke Hornblower was the sun, which lifted itself over the horizon and shone straight into his eyes. He stirred and blinked, and for a space he tried, like a child, to shield his eyes with his hands and to return to sleep. He did not know where he was, and for that time he did not care. Then he began to remember the events of yesterday, and he ceased trying to sleep and instead tried to wake up. Oddly, at first he remembered the details of the fighting and could not recall the sinking of the *Natividad*. When that recollection shot into his brain he was fully awake.

He rose from his chair, stretching himself painfully, for all his joints ached with the fatigues of yesterday. Bush was standing by the wheel, his face grey and lined and strangely old in the hard light. Hornblower nodded to him and received his salute in return; Bush was wearing his cocked hat over the dirty white bandage round his forehead. Hornblower would have spoken to him, but all his attention was caught up immediately in looking round the ship. There was a good breeze blowing which must have backed round during the night, for the *Lydia* could only just hold her course closehauled. She was under all plain sail; Hornblower's rapid inspection revealed to him innumerable splices both in standing and running rigging; the jury mizzenmast seemed to be standing up well to its work, but every sail that was spread seemed to have at least one shot hole in it — some of them a dozen or more. They gave the ship a little of the appearance of a tattered vagabond. The first part of today's work would be spreading a new suit of sails; new rigging could wait for a space.

It was only then, after weather and course and sail set had been noted, that Hornblower's sailor's eye came down to the decks. From forward came the monotonous clangour of the pumps; the clear white water which was gushing from them was the surest indication that the ship was making so much water that it could only just be kept in check. On the lee side gangway was a long,

long row of corpses, each in its hammock. Hornblower flinched when he saw the length of the row, and it called for all his will to count them. There were twenty four dead men along the gangway; and fourteen had been buried yesterday. Some of these dead might be — probably were — the mortally wounded of yesterday, but thirty eight dead seemed certainly to indicate at least seventy wounded down below. Rather more than one third of the *Lydia's* company were casualties, then. He wondered who they were, wondered whose distorted faces were concealed beneath those hammocks.

The dead on deck outnumbered the living. Bush seemed to have sent below every man save for a dozen men to hand and steer, which was sensible of him, seeing that everyone must be worn out with yesterday's toil while one man out of every seven on board would have to be employed at the pumps until the shot holes could be got at and plugged. The rest of the crew, at first glance, were all asleep, sprawled on the main deck under the gangways. Hardly anyone had had the strength to sling a hammock (if their hammocks had survived the battle); all the rest lay as they had dropped, lying tangled here and there, heads pillowed on each other or on more unsympathetic objects like ringbolts and the hind axletrees of the guns.

There were still evident many signs of yesterday's battle, quite apart from the sheeted corpses and the dark stains, not thoroughly swabbed, which disfigured the white planking. The decks were furrowed and grooved in all directions, with jagged splinters still standing up here and there. There were shot holes in the ship's sides with canvas roughly stretched over them. The port sills were stained black with powder; on one of them an eighteen-pounder shot stood out, half buried in the tough oak. But on the other hand an immense amount of work had been done, from laying out the dead to securing the guns and frapping the breechings. Apart from the weariness of her crew, the *Lydia* was ready to fight another battle at two minutes' notice.

Hornblower felt a prick of shame that so much should have been done while he slept lazily in his hammock chair. He forced himself to feel no illwill on that account. Although to praise Bush's work was to admit his own deficiencies he felt that he must be generous.

"Very good indeed, Mr. Bush," he said, walking over to him; yet his natural shyness combined with his feeling of shame to make his speech stilted. "I am both astonished and pleased at the work you have accomplished."

"Today is Sunday, sir," said Bush, simply.

So it was. Sunday was the day of the captain's inspection, when he went round every part of the ship examining everything, to see that the first lieutenant was doing his duty in keeping the ship efficient. On Sunday the ship had to be swept and garnished, all the falls of rope flemished down, the hands fallen in by divisions in their best clothes, divine service held, the Articles of War read — Sunday was the day when the professional ability of every first lieutenant in His Britannic Majesty's Navy was tried in the balance.

Hornblower could not fight down a smile at this ingenuous explanation.

"Sunday or no Sunday," he said, "you have done magnificently, Mr. Bush."

"Thank you, sir."

"And I shall remember to say so in my report to the Admiralty."

"I know you'll do that, sir."

Bush's weary face was illuminated by a gleam of pleasure. A successful single ship action was usually rewarded by promotion to Commander of the first lieutenant, and for a man like Bush, with no family and no connections, it was his only hope of making that vitally important step. But a captain who was anxious to enhance his own glory could word his report so that it appeared that he had won his victory despite of, instead of by the aid of, his first lieutenant — instances were known.

"They may make much of this in England, when eventually they hear about it," said Hornblower.

"I'm certain of it, sir. It isn't every day of the week that a frigate sinks a ship of the line."

It was stretching a point to call the *Natividad* that — sixty years ago when she was built she may have been considered just fit to lie in the line, but times had changed since then. But it was a very notable feat that the *Lydia* had accomplished, all the same. It was only now that Hornblower began to appreciate how notable it was, and his spirits rose in proportion. There was another criterion which the British public was prone to apply in estimating the merit of a naval action, and the Board of Admiralty itself not infrequently used the same standard.

"What's the butcher's bill?" demanded Hornblower, brutally, voicing the thoughts of both of them — brutally because otherwise he might be thought guilty of sentiment.

"Thirty eight killed, sir," said Bush, taking a dirty scrap of paper from his pocket. "Seventy five wounded. Four missing. The missing are Harper, Dauson, North, and Chump the negro, sir — they were lost when the launch was sunk. Clay was killed in the first day's action —— "

Hornblower nodded; he remembered Clay's headless body sprawled on the quarterdeck.

" — and John Summers, master's mate, Henry Vincent and James Clifton, boatswain's mates, killed yesterday, and Donald Scott Galbraith, third lieutenant, Lieutenant Samuel Simmonds of the Marines, Midshipman Howard Savage, and four other warrant officers wounded."

"Galbraith?" said Hornblower. That piece of news prevented him from beginning to wonder what would be the reward of a casualty list of a hundred and seventeen, when frigate captains had been knighted before this for a total of eighty killed and wounded.

"Badly, sir. Both legs smashed below the knees."

Galbraith had met the fate which Hornblower had dreaded for himself. The shock recalled Hornblower to his duty.

"I shall go down and visit the wounded at once," he said, and checked himself and looked searchingly at his first lieutenant. "What about you, Bush? You don't look fit for duty."

"I am perfectly fit, sir," protested Bush. "I shall take an hour's rest when Gerard comes up to take over the deck from me."

"As you will, then."

Down below decks in the orlop it was like some canto in the *Inferno*. It was dark; the four oil lamps whose flickering, reddish yellow glimmer wavered from the deck beams above seemed to serve only to cast shadows. The atmosphere was stifling. To the normal stenches of bilge and of ship's stores was added the stinks of sick men crowded together, of the sooty lamps, of the bitter powder smell which had drifted in yesterday and had not yet succeeded in making its way out again. It was appallingly hot; the heat and the stink hit Hornblower in the face as he entered, and within five seconds of his entry his face was as wet as if it had been dipped in water, so hot was it and so laden was the atmosphere with moisture.

As complex as the air was the noise. There were the ordinary ship noises — the creaking and groaning of timber, the vibration of the rigging transmitted downward from the chains, the sound of the sea outside, the wash of the bilge below, and the monotonous clangour of the pumps forward intensified by the ship-timbers acting as sounding boards. But all the noises acted only as accompaniment to the din in the cockpit, where seventy five wounded men, crammed together, were groaning and sobbing and screaming, blaspheming and vomiting. Lost souls in hell could hardly have had a more hideous environment, or be suffering more.

Hornblower found Laurie, standing aimlessly in the gloom.

"Thank God you've come, sir," he said. His tone implied that he cast all responsibility, gladly, from that moment on the shoulders of his captain.

"Come round with me and make your report," snapped Hornblower. He hated this business, and yet, although he was completely omnipotent on board, he could not turn and fly as his instincts told him to do. The work had to be done, and Hornblower knew that now Laurie had proved his incompetence he himself was the best man to deal with it. He approached the last man in the row, and drew back with a start of surprise. Lady Barbara was there; the wavering light caught her classic features as she knelt beside the wounded man. She was sponging his face and his throat as he writhed on the deck.

It was a shock to Hornblower to see her engaged thus. The day was yet to come when Florence Nightingale was to make nursing a profession in which women could engage. No man of taste could bear the thought of a woman occupied with the filthy work of a hospital. Sisters of Mercy might labour there for the good of their souls; boozy old women might attend to women in labour and occasionally take a hand at sick nursing, but to look after wounded men was entirely men's work — the work of men who deserved nothing better, either, and who were ordered to it on account of their incapacity or their bad record like men ordered to clean out latrines. Hornblower's stomach revolted at the sight of Lady Barbara here in contact with dirty bodies, with blood and pus and vomit.

"Don't do that!" he said, hoarsely. "Go away from here. Go on deck."

"I have begun this work now," said Lady Barbara, indifferently. "I am not going to leave it unfinished."

Her tone admitted no possibility of argument; she was apparently talking of the inevitable — much as she might say that she had caught a cold and would have to bear with it until it had run its course.

"The gentleman in charge here," she went on, "knows nothing of his duties."

Lady Barbara had no belief in the nobility of nursing; to her mind it was a more degrading occupation than cooking or mending clothes (work which had only occasionally, when the exigencies of travel demanded it, engaged her capable fingers) but she had found a job which was being inefficiently done when there was no one save herself to do it better, at a time when the King's service depended in part on its being done well. She had set herself to the work with the same wholehearted attention to detail and neglect of personal comfort with which one of her brothers had governed India and another had fought the Mahrattas.

"This man," went on Lady Barbara, "has a splinter of wood under his skin here. It ought to be extracted at once."

She displayed the man's bare chest, hairy and tattooed. Under the tattooing there was a horrible black bruise, stretching from the breast bone to the right armpit, and in the muscles of the armpit was a jagged projection under the skin; when Lady Barbara laid her fingers on it the man writhed and groaned with pain. In fighting between wooden ships splinter wounds constituted a high proportion of the casualties, and the hurtling pieces of wood could never be extracted by the route by which they entered, because their shape gave them natural barbs. In this case the splinter had been deflected by the ribs so as to pass round under the skin, bruising and lacerating, to its present place in the armpit.

"Are you ready to do it now?" asked Lady Barbara of the unhappy Laurie.

"Well, madam —— "

"If you will not, then I will. Don't be a fool, man."

"I will see that it is done, Lady Barbara," interposed Hornblower. He would promise anything to get this finished and done with.

"Very well, then, Captain."

Lady Barbara rose from her knees, but she showed no sign of any intention of retiring in a decent female fashion. Hornblower and Laurie looked at each other.

"Now, Laurie," said Hornblower, harshly. "Where are your instruments? Here, you, Wilcox, Hudson. Bring him a good stiff tot of rum. Now, Williams, we're going to get that splinter out of you. It is going to hurt you."

Hornblower had to struggle hard to keep his face from writhing in disgust and fear of the task before him. He spoke harshly to stop his voice from trembling; he hated the whole business. And it was a painful and bloody business, too. Although Williams tried hard to show no weakness, he writhed as the incision was made, and Wilcox and Hudson had to catch his hands and force his shoulders back. He gave a horrible cry as the long dark strip of wood was dragged out, and then fell limp, fainting, so that he uttered no protest at the prick of the needle as the edges of the wound were clumsily sewn together.

Lady Barbara's lips were firmly compressed. She watched Laurie's muddled attempts at bandaging, and then she stooped without a word and took the rags from him. The men watched her fascinated as with one hand firmly behind Williams' spine she passed the roll dexterously round his body and bound the fast-reddening waste firmly to the wound.

"He will do now," said Lady Barbara, rising.

Hornblower spent two stifling hours down there in the cockpit going the round with Laurie and Lady Barbara, but they were not nearly such agonising hours as they might have been. One of the main reasons for his feeling so unhappy regarding the care of the wounded had been his consciousness of his own incompetence. Insensibly he came to shift some of his responsibility onto Lady Barbara's shoulders; she was so obviously capable and so unintimidated that she was the person most fitted of all in the ship to be given the supervision of the wounded. When Hornblower had gone round every bed, when the five newly dead men had been dragged out, he faced her under the wavering light of the last lamp in the row.

"I don't know how I can thank you, ma'am," he said. "I am as grateful to you as any of these wounded men."

"There is no gratitude needed," said Lady Barbara, shrugging her slim shoulders, "for work which had to be done."

A good many years later her ducal brother was to say "The King's government must be carried on" in exactly the same tone. The man in the bed beside them waved a bandaged arm.

"Three cheers for her leddyship!" he croaked. "Hip hip, hurrah!"

Some of the shattered invalids joined him in his cheers — a melancholy chorus, blended with the wheezing and groaning of the delirious men around them. Lady Barbara waved a deprecating hand and turned back to the captain.

"We must have air down here," she said. "Can that be arranged? I remember my brother telling me how the mortality in the hospital at Bombay declined as soon as they began to give the patients air. Perhaps those men who can be moved can be brought on deck?"

"I will arrange it, ma'am," said Hornblower.

Lady Barbara's request was strongly accented by the contrast which Hornblower noticed when he went on deck — the fresh Pacific air, despite the scorching sunshine, was like champagne after the solid stink of the orlop. He gave orders for the immediate reestablishment of the canvas ventilating shafts which had been removed when the decks were cleared for action.

"And there are certain of the wounded, Mr. Rayner," he went on, "who would do better if brought up on deck. You must find Lady Barbara Wellesley and ask her which men are to be moved."

"Lady Barbara Wellesley, sir?" said Rayner, surprised and tactless, because he knew nothing of the last development.

"You heard what I said," snapped Hornblower.

"Aye aye, sir," said Rayner hurriedly, and dived away below in fear lest he should say anything further to annoy his captain.

So that on board H.M.S. *Lydia* that morning divisions were held and divine service conducted a little late, after the burial of the dead, with a row of wounded swaying in hammocks on each side of the main deck, and with the faint echo of the horrible sounds below floating up through the air shafts.

Chapter XIX

ONCE more the *Lydia* held her course along the Pacific coast of Central America. The grey volcanic peaks, tinged with pink, slid past her to the eastward, with the lush green of the coastal strip sometimes just visible at their feet. The sea was blue and the sky was blue; the flying fish skimmed the surface, leaving their fleeting furrows behind them. But every minute of the day and night twenty men toiled at the pumps to keep her from sinking, and the rest of the able bodied crew worked all their waking hours at the task of refitting.

The fortnight which elapsed before she rounded Cape Mala went far to reduce her list of wounded. Some of the men were by then already convalescent — the hard physical condition which they had enjoyed, thanks to months of heavy work at sea, enabled them to make light of wounds which would have been fatal to men of soft physique. Shock and exhaustion had relieved the ship of others, and now gangrene, the grim Nemesis which awaited so many men with open wounds in those pre-antiseptic days, was relieving her of still more. Every morning there was the same ceremony at the ship's side, when two or three or six hammock-wrapped bundles were slid over into the blue Pacific.

Galbraith went that way. He had borne the shock of his wound, he had even survived the torture to which Laurie submitted him when, goaded by Lady Barbara's urgent representations, he had set to work with knife and saw upon the smashed tangles of flesh and bone which had been his legs. He had bade fair to make a good recovery, lying blanched and feeble in his cot, so that Laurie had been heard to boast of his surgical skill and of the fine stumps he had made and of the neatness with which he had tied the arteries. Then, suddenly, the fatal symptoms had shown themselves, and Galbraith had died five days later after a fortunate delirium.

Hornblower and Lady Barbara drew nearer to each other during these days. Lady Barbara had fought a losing battle for Galbraith's life to the very end, had fought hard and without sparing herself, and yet seemingly without emotion as if she were merely applying herself to a job which had to be done. Hornblower would have thought this was the case if he had not seen her face on the occasion when Galbraith was holding her hands and talking to her under the impression that she was his mother. The dying boy was babbling feverishly in the broad Scots into which he had lapsed as soon as delirium overcame him, clutching her hands and refusing to let her go, while she sat with him talking calmly and quietly in an effort to soothe him. So still was her voice, so calm and unmoved was her attitude, that Hornblower would have been deceived had he not seen the torment in her face.

And for Hornblower it was unexpectedly painful when Galbraith died. Hornblower always looked upon himself as a man content to make use of others, pleasingly devoid of human weaknesses. It was a surprise to him to find how hurt and sorry he was at Galbraith's death, and to find his voice trembling and tears in his eyes as he read the service, and to feel a shudder of distress at the thought of what the sharks were doing to Galbraith's body, down there below the blue surface of the Pacific. He told himself that he was being weak, and then hastened to assure himself that he was merely annoyed at the loss of a useful subordinate, but he could not convince himself. In a fury of reaction he flung himself into the business of driving his men harder in their task of refitting the *Lydia,* and yet now when his eyes met Lady Barbara's, on deck or across the dinner table, it was not with the complete lack of sympathy which had previously prevailed. There was a hint of understanding between them now.

Hornblower saw little enough of Lady Barbara. They dined together on some afternoons, always with at least one other officer present, but for the most part he was busy with his professional duties and she with her care of the sick. They neither of them had the time, and he at least had not the superfluous energy to spare for the flirtations that those mild tropic nights should have brought in their train. And Hornblower, as soon as they entered the Gulf of Panama, had sufficient additional worries for the moment to drive away all possibility of a flirtation.

The Pearl Islands were just in view over the port bow, and the *Lydia,* closehauled, was heading for Panama one day's sail ahead when the guarda-costa lugger which had encountered them before hove up over the horizon to windward. At sight of the *Lydia* she altered course and came running down wind towards her, while Hornblower kept steadily on his course. He was a little elated with the prospect of making even such a fever-ridden port as badly equipped as Panama, because the strain of keeping the *Lydia* afloat was beginning to tell on him.

The lugger hove-to a couple of cables' lengths away, and a few minutes later the same smart officer in the brilliant uniform came clambering up onto the Lydia's deck as had boarded from her once before.

"Good morning, Captain," he said, bowing profoundly. "I trust Your Excellency is enjoying the best of health?"

"Thank you," said Hornblower.

The Spanish officer was looking curiously about him; the *Lydia* still bore many marks of her recent battle — the row of wounded in hammocks told a good part of the story. Hornblower saw that the Spaniard seemed to be on his guard, as though determined to be noncommittal at present until something unknown had revealed itself.

"I see," said the Spaniard, "that your fine ship has been recently in action. I hope that Your Excellency had good fortune in the encounter?"

"We sank the *Natividad* if that is what you mean," said Hornblower, brutally.

"You sank her, Captain?"

"I did."

"She is destroyed?"

"She is."

The Spaniard's expression hardened — Hornblower was led for a moment to think that it was a bitter blow to him to hear that for the second time the Spanish ship had been beaten by an English ship of half her force.

"Then, sir," said the Spaniard, "I have a letter to give you."

He felt in his breast pocket, but with a curious gesture of hesitation — Hornblower realised later that he must have had two letters, one in one pocket and one in another, of different import, one to be delivered if the *Natividad* were destroyed and the other if she were still able to do damage. The letter which he handed over when he was quite certain which was which was not very brief, but was worded with a terseness that implied (having regard to the ornateness of the Spanish official style) absolute rudeness, as Hornblower was quick to realise when he tore open the wrapper and read the contents.

It was a formal prohibition from the Viceroy of Peru for the *Lydia* to drop anchor in, or to enter into, any port of Spanish America, in the Viceroyalty of Peru, or the Viceroyalty of Mexico, or the Captain-Generalcy of New Granada.

Hornblower re-read the letter, and while he did so the dismal clangour of the pumps, drifting aft to his ears, made more acute the worries which instantly leaped upon him. He thought of his battered, leaking ship, his sick and wounded, his weary crew and his attenuated stores, of the rounding of the Horn and the four thousand miles of the Atlantic which lay between him and England. And more than that; he remembered the supplementary orders which had been given him when he left England, regarding the effort he was to make to open Spanish America to British trade and to establish an Isthmian canal.

"You are aware of the contents of this letter, sir?" he asked.

"Yes, sir."

The Spaniard was haughty, even brazen about it.

"Can you explain this most unfriendly behaviour on the part of the Viceroy?"

"I would not presume to explain my master's actions, sir."

"And yet they are in sore need of explanation. I cannot understand how any civilised man could abandon an ally who has fought his battles for him and is in need of help solely because of those battles."

"You came unasked into these seas, sir. There would have been no battle for you to fight if you had stayed in those parts of the world where your King rules. The South Sea is the property of His Most Catholic Majesty, who will tolerate no intruder upon it."

"I understand," said Hornblower.

He guessed that new orders had come out to Spanish America now that the government of Spain had heard of the presence of an English frigate in the Pacific. The retention of the American monopoly was to the Spanish mind as dear as life itself. There was no length to which the Spanish government would not go to retain it, even though it meant offending an ally while in the midst of a life and death struggle with the most powerful despot in Europe. To the Spaniards in Madrid the *Lydia's* presence in the Pacific hinted at the coming of a flood of British traders, at the drying up of the constant stream of gold and silver on which the Spanish government depended, at — worse still — the introduction of heresy into a part of the world which had been kept faithful to the Pope through three centuries. It did not matter if Spanish America were poor, misgoverned, disease ridden, nor if the rest of the world felt the pinch of being shut out at a time when the Continental System had ruined European trade.

In a clear-sighted moment Hornblower foresaw that the world could not long tolerate selfishness carried to these lengths, and that soon, amid general approval, Spanish America would throw off the Spanish yoke. Later, if neither Spain nor New Granada would cut that canal, someone else would step in and do it for them. He was minded to say so, but his innate caution restrained him. However badly he had been treated, there was nothing to be gained by causing an open breach. There was a sweeter revenge in keeping his thoughts to himself.

"Very good, sir," he said. "My compliments to your master. I will call at no port on the Spanish Main. Please convey His Excellency my lively sense of gratitude at the courtesy with which I have been treated, and my pleasure at this further proof of the good relations between the governments of which we have the good fortune to be subjects."

The Spanish officer looked at him sharply, but Hornblower kept his face immobile while bending his spine with studied courtesy.

"And now, sir," went on Hornblower dryly, "I must, much to my regret, wish you goodday and a pleasant journey. I have much to attend to."

It was irksome to the Spaniard to be dismissed in this cavalier fashion, but he could take no open exception to anything Hornblower had said. He could only return Hornblower's bow and walk back to the ship's side. No sooner was he back in his boat than Hornblower turned to Bush.

"Keep the ship hove-to, if you please, Mr. Bush," he said.

The *Lydia* rolled heavily, hove-to, on the swell, while her captain resumed his interrupted pacing of the quarterdeck, eyed furtively by those officers and men who had guessed at the bad news this latest despatch contained. Up and down, up and down, walked Hornblower, between the carronade slides on the one hand and the ringbolts on the other, while the clanking of the pumps, floating drearily on the heavy air, told him at every second how urgent it was that he should form some new decision.

First of all, however, before even the question of the condition of the ship arose, he must decide about stores and water — every ship's captain had to consider that problem first. Six weeks back he had filled his storerooms and his water barrels. But since that time he had lost a quarter of his crew. At a pinch, even allowing for a long time to refit, there was enough food to last them back to England, therefore; especially as the easterly rounding of the Horn was never as prolonged as the westerly one, and (now that all need of secrecy had disappeared) if necessary St. Helena or Sierra Leone or Gibraltar would be open to him to replenish.

That was intensely satisfactory. He could devote his whole mind now to his ship. Refit he must. The *Lydia* could not hope to survive the storms of Cape Horn in her present condition, leaking like a sieve, jury rigged, and with a sail fothered under her bottom. The work could not be done at sea, and the harbours were barred to him. He must do as old buccaneers did — as Drake and Anson and Dampier had done in these very waters — find some secluded cove where he could careen his ship. It would not be easy on the mainland for the Spaniards had settled round every navigable bay. It would have to be an island, therefore.

Those Pearl Islands on the horizon would not be suitable, for Hornblower knew them to be inhabited and to be frequently visited from Panama — besides, the lugger was still in sight and watching his movements. Hornblower went down below and got out his charts; there was the island of Coiba which the *Lydia* had passed yesterday. His charts told him nothing of it save its position, but it was clearly the place to investigate first. Hornblower laid off his course and then went on deck again.

"We will put the ship about, if you please, Mr. Bush," he said.

Chapter XX

INCH by inch His Britannic Majesty's frigate *Lydia* crept into the bay. The cutter was out ahead, with Rayner sounding industriously, while with a dying breath of air behind her and a shred of sail set the *Lydia* felt her way between the two headlands into the tortuous channel. Those capes, one each side of the entrance, were steep rocky cliffs, and the one overlapped the other a trifle so that only an eye sharpened by necessity, and which had made the most of its recent opportunities of learning the typical rock formations of that coast, could have guessed at the possibility of an expanse of water behind them.

Hornblower took his eye from the ship's course as she crawled round the corner to study the bay before him. There were mountains all round it, but on the farther side the slope down to the water was not nearly so steep, and on the water's edge there, at the foot of the dazzling green which clothed the banks all round, was a hint of golden sand which told of the sort of bottom which he sought. It would be shelving there, without a doubt, and free from rock.

"This seems very suitable," said Hornblower to Bush.

"Aye aye, sir. Made for the job," said Bush.

"Then you may drop anchor. We shall start work at once."

It was terribly hot in that little bay in the island of Coiba. The lofty mountains all about cut off any wind that might be blowing, and at the same time reflected the heat to a focus in the bay. As the cable rasped out through the hawsehole Hornblower felt the heat descend upon him. He was wet with sweat even while he stood still on the quarterdeck; he longed for a bath and for a little leisure, to rest until the cool of the evening, but he could not allow himself any such luxury. Time was, as ever, of vital importance. He must make himself secure before the Spaniards could discover where he had hidden himself.

"Call back the cutter," he said.

On land it was even hotter than on the water. Hornblower had himself rowed to the sandy beach, sounding as he went, and examining with care the sample of the bottom which the tallow on the bottom of the lead brought up for his inspection. It was sand without a doubt — he could beach the *Lydia* safely there. He landed in the breathless jungle; there was clearly no human life here, to judge by the pathlessness of the close-packed vegetation. Tall trees and scrub, creepers and parasites, were all tangled together in their silent struggle for life. Strange birds with strange cries flitted through the twilight of the branches; Hornblower's nostrils were assailed by the reek of the decaying matter beneath his feet. With a sweating escort, musket in hand, about him, he cut his way through the forest. He emerged where the rock was too steep for vegetation ever to have gained a foothold, into the blinding sunlight at the mouth of the bay. He climbed, sweating and exhausted, up the steep ledges. The *Lydia* floated idly on the dazzling blue of the little bay. The opposite headland frowned down upon him across the mouth, and he studied its soaring ledges through his glass. Then he went back to his ship, to goad his men into frantic activity.

Before she could be beached, before the carpenter and his men could set to work upon her bottom, the *Lydia* must be lightened. And also, before she could be laid defenceless on her side, this bay must be made secure from all aggressors. Tackles were rigged, and the two-ton eighteen-pounders were swayed up from the main deck. With careful management and exact balancing the cutter could just carry one of these monsters. One at a time they were ferried to the headlands, where Rayner and Gerard were already at work with parties preparing emplacements. Toiling gangs were set to work preparing rough paths up the faces of the cliffs, and no sooner were these complete than the men were turned on with tackles and ropes to drag the guns up the paths. Powder and shot for the guns followed them, and then food and water for the garrisons. At the end of thirty six hours of exacting labour the *Lydia* was a hundred tons lighter, and the entrance to the bay was so defended that any vessel attempting it would have to brave the plunging fire of twenty guns.

In the meanwhile another party had been working like furies on shore above the sandy beach. Here they cleared away a section of forest, and dragged the fallen trees into a rough breastwork, and into the rude fort so delimited, among the tree stumps, another party brought up beef barrels, and flour bags, and spars, and guns, and shot, and powder barrels, until the *Lydia* was a mere empty shell rolling in the tiny waves of the bay. The men stretched canvas shelters for themselves as protection against the frequent tropical showers which deluged on them, and for their officers they built rude timber huts — and one for the women as well.

In giving that order Hornblower made his sole acknowledgement of the women's existence. During this flurry of work, and under the strain of the responsibility which he bore, he had neither the time nor the surplus energy to spare for conversation with Lady Barbara. He was tired, and the steamy heat drained his energies, but his natural reaction to these conditions, having in mind the need for haste, was to flog himself into working harder and harder, obstinately and unreasonably, so that the days passed in a nightmare of fatigue, during which the minutes he passed with Lady Barbara were like the glimpses a man has of a beautiful woman during delirium.

He drove his men hard from earliest dawn as long as daylight lasted, keeping them slaving away in the crushing heat until they shook their heads over him in rueful admiration. They did not grudge him the efforts he called for; that would have been impossible for British sailors led by a man who was so little prepared to spare himself. And besides, the men displayed the constant characteristic of British crews of working the more cheerfully the more unusual the conditions. Sleeping on beds of sand instead of in their far more comfortable hammocks, working on solid earth instead of on board ship, hemmed in by dense forest instead of engirdled by a distant horizon — all this was stimulating and cheering.

The fireflies in the forest, the strange fruits which were found for them by their impressed prisoners from the *Natividad*, the very mosquitoes which plagued them, helped at the same time to keep them happy. Down the cliff face beside one of the entrance batteries there tumbled a constant stream of clear water, so that for once in their lives the men were allowed as much fresh water as they could use, and to men who for months at a time had to submit to having a sentry standing guard over their drinking water this was an inexpressible luxury.

Soon, on the sandy shore, and as far as possible from the stored powder barrels, canvas-covered and sentry-guarded, there were fires lit over which was melted the pitch brought from the boatswain's store. There had not been enough defaulters during those days to pick all the oakum required — some of the ship's company had to work at oakum picking while the *Lydia* was hove over and the carpenter applied himself to the task of setting her bottom to rights. The shot holes were plugged, the strained seams caulked and pitched, the missing sheets of copper were replaced by the last few sheets which the *Lydia* carried in reserve. For four days the tiny bay was filled with the sound of the caulking hammers at work, and the reek of melting pitch drifted over the still water as the smoking cauldrons were carried across to the working parties.

At the end of that time the carpenter expressed himself as satisfied, and Hornblower, anxiously going over every foot of the ship's bottom, grudgingly agreed with him. The *Lydia* was hove off, and, still empty, was kedged and towed across the bay until she lay at the foot of the high cliff where one of the batteries was established — the shore was steep enough at this point to allow her to lie close in here when empty of guns and stores. At this point Lieutenant Bush had been busy setting up a projecting gallows, a hundred feet above, and vertically over, the ship's deck. Painfully, and after many trials, the *Lydia* was manœuvred until she could be moored so that the stump of her mizzenmast stood against the plumb line which Bush dropped from the tackles high above. Then the wedges were knocked out, the tackles set to work, and the stump was drawn out of her like a decayed tooth.

That part of the work was easy compared with the next step. The seventy five foot main yard had to be swayed up to the gallows, and then hung vertically down from them; if it had slipped it would have shot down like some monstrous arrow and would have sunk her for certain. When the yard was exactly vertical and exactly above the mizzenmast step it was lowered down, inch by inch, until its solid butt could be coaxed by anxious gangs through the main deck and through the orlop until it came at last solidly to rest in its step upon the keelson. It only remained then to wedge it firmly in, to set up new shrouds, and the *Lydia* had once more a mizzenmast which could face the gales of the Horn.

Back at her anchorage, the *Lydia* could be ballasted once more, with her beef barrels and water barrels, her guns and her shot, save for what was left in the entrance batteries. Ballasted and steady upon her keel, she could be re-rigged and her topmasts set up again. Every rope was re-rove, her standing rigging newly set up, replacements effected until she was as efficient a ship as when she had left Portsmouth newly commissioned.

It was then that Hornblower could allow himself time to draw breath and relax. The captain of a ship that is no ship, but only a mere hulk helpless in a landlocked inlet, cannot feel a moment's peace. A heretic in an Inquisitor's dungeon is happy compared with him. There is the menacing land all about him, the torment of helplessness as a perpetual goad, the fear of an ignominious siege to wake him in the night. Hornblower was like a man released from a sentence of death when he trod the *Lydia's* deck once more and allowed his eye to rove contentedly upward and ever upward through the aspiring rigging, with the clangour of the pumps which had echoed in his ears during the last fortnight's cruise completely stilled, happy in the consciousness of a staunch ship under his feet, comfortable in the knowledge that there would be no more campaigns to plan until he reached England.

At this very moment they were dismantling one of the entrance batteries, and the guns were being ferried out to the *Lydia* one by one. Already he had a broadside battery which could fire, a ship which could manœuvre, and he could snap his fingers at every Spaniard in the Pacific. It was a glorious sensation. He turned and found Lady Barbara on the quarterdeck beside him, and he smiled at her dazzlingly.

"Good morning, ma'am," he said. "I trust you found your cabin comfortable again?"

Lady Barbara smiled back at him — in fact she almost laughed, so comical was the contrast between this greeting and the scowls she had encountered from him during the last eleven days.

"Thank you, Captain," she said. "It is marvellously comfortable. Your crew has worked wonders to have done so much in such little time."

Quite unconsciously he had reached out and taken both her hands in his, and was standing there holding them, smiling all over his face in the sunshine. Lady Barbara felt that it would only need a word from her to set him dancing.

"We shall be at sea before nightfall," he said, ecstatically.

She could not be dignified with him, any more than she could have been dignified with a baby; she knew enough of men and affairs not to resent his previous preoccupation. Truth to tell, she was a trifle fond of him because of it.

"You are a very fine sailor, sir," she said to him, suddenly. "I doubt if there is another officer in the King's service who could have done all you have done on this voyage."

"I am glad you think so, ma'am," he said, but the spell was broken. He had been reminded of himself, and his cursed self-consciousness closed in upon him again. He dropped her hands, awkwardly, and there was a hint of a blush in his tanned cheeks.

"I have only done my duty," he mumbled, looking away.

"Many men can do that," said Lady Barbara, "but few can do it well. The country is your debtor — my sincerest hope is that England will acknowledge the debt."

The words started a sudden train of thought in Hornblower's mind; it was a train he had followed up often before. England would only remember that his battle with the *Natividad* had been unnecessary; that a more fortunate captain would have heard of the new alliance between Spain and England before he had handed the *Natividad* over to the rebels, and would have saved all the trouble and friction and loss which had resulted. A frigate action with a hundred casualties might be glorious, but an unnecessary action with a hundred casualties was quite inglorious. No one would stop to think that it was his careful obedience to orders and skill in carrying them out which had been the reason of it. He would be blamed for his own merits, and life was suddenly full of bitterness again.

"Your pardon, ma'am," he said, and he turned away from her and walked forward to bawl orders at the men engaged in swaying an eighteen-pounder up from the launch.

Lady Barbara shook her head at his back.

"Bless the man!" she said to herself, softly. "He was almost human for a while."

Lady Barbara was fast acquiring, in her forced loneliness, the habit of talking to herself like the sole inhabitant of a desert island. She checked herself as soon as she found herself doing so, and went below and rated Hebe soundly for some minor sin of omission in the unpacking of her wardrobe.

Chapter XXI

THE rumour had gone round the crew that the *Lydia* was at last homeward bound. The men had fought and worked, first on the one side and then on the other, without understanding the trend of high politics which had decided whom they should fight and for whom they should work. That Spaniards should be first enemies, and then friends, and then almost hostile neutrals, had hardly caused one of them a single thought. They had been content to obey orders unthinkingly; but now, it seemed certain, so solidly based was the rumour, that the *Lydia* was on her way home. To the scatter-brained crew it seemed as if England was just over the horizon. They gave no thought to the five thousand stormy miles of sea that lay before them. Their heads were full of England. The pressed men thought of their wives; the volunteers thought of the women of the ports and of the joys of paying off. The sun of their rapture was not even overcast by any cloud of doubt as to the chances of their being turned over to another ship and sent off half round the world again before ever they could set foot on English soil.

They had flung themselves with a will into the labour of warping out of the bay, and not one of them looked back with regret to the refuge which alone had made their homeward voyage possible. They had chattered and played antics like a crew of monkeys when they dashed aloft to set sail, and the watch below had danced and set to partners through the warm evening while the *Lydia* bowled along with a favourable breeze over the blue Pacific. Then during the night the wind died away with its usual tropical freakishness, from a good breeze to a faint air, and from a faint air to a slow succession of fluky puffs which set the sails slatting and the rigging creaking and kept the watch continually at work at the braces trimming the sails.

Hornblower awoke in his cot in the cool hour before dawn. It was still too dark to see the tell-tale compass in the deck over his head, but he could guess from the long roll of the ship and the intermittent noises overhead that calm weather had overtaken them. It was almost time for him to start his morning walk on the quarterdeck, and he rested, blissfully free of all feeling of responsibility, until Polwheal came in to get out his clothes. He was putting on his trousers when a hail from the masthead lookout came echoing down through the scuttle.

"Sail ho! Broad on the larboard beam. It's that there lugger again, sir."

That feeling of freedom from worry vanished on the instant. Twice had that ill-omened lugger been seen in this very Gulf of Panama, and twice she had been the bearer of bad news. Hornblower wondered, with a twinge of superstition, what this third encounter would bring forth. He snatched his coat from Polwheal's hands and put it on as he dashed up the companionway.

The lugger was there, sure enough, lying becalmed some two miles away; there were half a dozen glasses trained on her — apparently Hornblower's officers shared his superstition.

"There's something about that craft's rig which gives me the horrors," grumbled Gerard.

"She's just a plain Spanish guarda-costa," said Crystal. "I've seen 'em in dozens. I remember off Havana —— "

"Who hasn't seen 'em?" snapped Gerard. "I was saying — hullo! There's a boat putting off."

He glanced round and saw his captain appearing on the deck.

"Lugger's sending a boat, sir."

Hornblower did his best to make his expression one of sturdy indifference. He told himself that commanding, as he did, the fastest and most powerful ship on the Pacific coast, he need fear nothing. He was equipped and ready to sail half round the world, to fight any ship up to fifty guns. The sight of the lugger ought to cause him no uneasiness — but it did.

For long minutes they watched the boat come bobbing towards them over the swell. At first it was only a black speck showing occasionally on the crests. Then the flash of the oar blades could be seen, as they reflected the rays of the nearly level sun, and then the oars themselves, as the boat grew like some great black water beetle creeping over the surface, and at last she was within hail, and a few minutes after for the third time the young Spanish officer in his brilliant uniform mounted to the *Lydia's* deck and received Hornblower's bow.

He made no attempt to conceal his curiosity, nor the admiration which blended with it. He saw that the jury mizzenmast had disappeared and had been replaced by a new spar as trim and as efficient as any set up in a navy yard; he saw that the shot holes had been expertly patched; he noticed that the pumps were no longer at work — that in fact during the sixteen days since he last saw her the ship had been entirely refitted, and, to his certain knowledge, without any aid from the shore and in no harbour save perhaps for some deserted inlet.

"It surprises me to see you here again, sir," he said.

"To me," said Hornblower, with perfect courtesy, "it is a pleasure as well as a surprise."

"To me also it is a pleasure," said the Spaniard quickly, "but I had thought you were far on your way home by now."

"I am on my way home," said Hornblower, determined to give no cause for offence if possible, "but as you see, sir, I have not progressed far as yet. However, I have effected, as perhaps you may notice, the repairs that were necessary, and now nothing will delay me from proceeding to England with the utmost despatch — unless, sir, there is some new development which makes it advisable, for the sake of the common cause of our two countries, for me to remain longer in these waters."

Hornblower said these last words anxiously, and he was already devising in his mind excuses to free himself from the consequences of this offer if it were accepted. But the Spaniard's reply reassured him.

"Thank you, sir," he said, "but there is no need for me to take advantage of your kindness. His Most Catholic Majesty's dominions are well able to guard themselves. I am sure that His Britannic Majesty will be glad to see such a fine frigate returning to forward his cause."

The two captains bowed to each other profoundly at this exchange of compliments before the Spaniard resumed his speech.

"I was thinking, sir," he went on, "that perhaps if you would do me the great honour of visiting my ship for a moment, taking advantage of this prevailing calm, I should be able to show Your Excellency something which would be of interest and which would demonstrate our ability to continue without your kind assistance."

"What is it?" asked Hornblower, suspiciously.

The Spaniard smiled.

"It would give me pleasure if I could show it to you as a surprise. Please, sir, would you not oblige me?"

Hornblower looked automatically round the horizon. He studied the Spaniard's face. The Spaniard was no fool; and only a fool could meditate treachery when almost within range of a frigate which could sink his ship in a single broadside. And mad though most Spaniards were, they were not mad enough to offer violence to a British captain. Besides, he was pleased with the thought of how his officers would receive his announcement that he was going on board the lugger.

"Thank you, sir," he said. "It will give me great pleasure to accompany you."

The Spaniard bowed again, and Hornblower turned to his first lieutenant.

"I am going to visit the lugger, Mr. Bush," he said. "I shall only be gone a short time. Call away the cutter and send her after me to bring me back."

Hornblower was delighted to see how Bush struggled to conceal his consternation at the news.

"Aye aye, sir," he said. He opened his mouth and shut it again; he wanted to expostulate and yet did not dare, and finally repeated feebly, "Aye aye, sir."

In the small boat rowing back to the lugger the Spaniard was the mirror of courtesy. He chatted politely about weather conditions. He mentioned the latest news of the war in Spain — it was quite undoubted that a French army had surrendered to the Spaniards in Andalusia, and that Spanish and British armies were assembling for a march into France. He described the ravages of yellow fever on the mainland. He contrived, all the same, to allow no single hint to drop as to the nature of the surprise which he was going to show Hornblower in the lugger.

The two captains were received with Spanish ceremony as they swung themselves up into the lugger's waist. There was a great deal of bustle and parade, and two bugles and two drums sounded a resounding march horribly out of tune.

"All in this ship is yours, sir," said the Spaniard with Castilian courtesy, and seeing no incongruity in his next sentence, "Your Excellency will take some refreshment? A cup of chocolate?"

"Thank you," said Hornblower. He was not going to imperil his dignity by asking what was the nature of the surprise in store for him. He could wait — especially as he could see the launch already half way towards the lugger.

The Spaniard was in no hurry to make the revelation. He was evidently savouring in anticipation the Englishman's certain astonishment. He pointed out certain peculiarities in the lugger's rig; he called up his officers to present to Hornblower; he discussed the merits of his crew — nearly all native Indians as on board the *Natividad*. In the end Hornblower won; the Spaniard could wait no longer to be asked.

"Would you please to come this way, sir?" he said. He led the way onto the foredeck, and there, chained by the waist to a ring-bolt, with irons on his wrists and ankles, was El Supremo.

He was in rags — half naked in fact, and his beard and hair were matted and tangled, and his own filth lay on the deck about him.

"I think," said the Spanish captain, "that you have already had the pleasure, sir, of meeting His Excellency Don Julian María de Jesús de Alvarado y Moctezuma, who calls himself the Almighty?"

El Supremo showed no sign of being disconcerted by the gibe.

"Captain Hornblower has indeed been presented to me already," he said loftily. "He has worked for me long and devotedly. I trust you are enjoying the best of health, Captain?"

"Thank you, sir," said Hornblower.

Despite his rags, and his filth, and his chains, El Supremo bore himself with the same elaborate dignity as Hornblower remembered so well those many weeks ago.

"I too," he said, "am as well as the world could desire. It is a source of continual satisfaction to me to see my affairs progressing so well."

A negro servant appeared on the deck at that moment with a tray of chocolate; another followed him with a couple of chairs. Hornblower, at the invitation of his host, sat down. He was glad to do so, as his knees seemed suddenly weak under him, but he had no desire at all for his chocolate. The Spanish captain drank noisily, and El Supremo eyed him as he did so. There came a gleam of appetite in his face. His lips moistened and smacked softly together, his eyes brightened, his hand came out; and then next moment he was calm and indifferent again.

"I trust that the chocolate is to your liking, sirs," he said. "I ordered it specially for you. My own appetite for chocolate has long since disappeared."

"That is just as well," said the Spanish captain. He laughed loudly and drank again, smacking his lips.

El Supremo ignored him, and turned to Hornblower.

"You see I wear these chains," he said. "It is a strange whim on the part of myself and my servants that I should do so. I hope you agree with me that they set off my figure quite admirably?"

"Y-yes, sir," stammered Hornblower.

"We are on our way to Panama, where I shall mount the throne of the world. They talk of hanging; these fellows here say that there is a gallows awaiting us on the bastion of the Citadel. That will be the framework of my golden throne. Golden, it will be, with diamond stars and a great turquoise moon. It will be from there that I shall issue my next decrees to the world."

The Spanish captain guffawed again, but El Supremo still stood in quiet dignity, hugging his chains, with the sun blazing down on his tangled head.

"He will not last long in this mood," said the Spanish captain to Hornblower behind his hand. "I can see signs of the change coming. It gives me great felicity that you have had the opportunity of seeing him in both his moods."

"The sun grows in his splendour every day," said El Supremo. "He is magnificent and terrible, as I am. He can kill — kill — kill, as he killed the men I exposed to him — when was it? And Moctezuma is dead, and all his line save me, in the hundreds of years ago. I alone remain. And Hernandez is dead, but it was not the sun that killed him. They hanged Hernandez even while the blood dripped from his wounds. They hanged him in my city of San Salvador, and as they hanged him he still called upon the name of El Supremo. They hanged the men and they hanged the women, in long rows at San Salvador. Only El Supremo is left, to govern from his golden throne. His throne! His throne!"

El Supremo was staring about him now. There was a hint of bewildered realisation in his face as he jangled his chains. He peered at them stupidly.

"Chains! These are chains!"

He was bawling and shouting. He laughed madly, and then he wept and he cursed, flinging himself about on the deck and biting at his chains. His words were no longer articulate as he slobbered and writhed.

"It is interesting, is it not?" said the Spanish captain. "He will struggle and shout sometimes for twenty four hours without a stop."

"Bah!" said Hornblower, and his chair fell with a clatter to the deck as he got to his feet. He was on the verge of vomiting. The Spaniard saw his white face and trembling lips, and was faintly amused, and made no attempt to conceal it.

But Hornblower could give no vent to the flood of protest which was welling up within him. His cautious mind told him that a madman in a ship as small as the lugger must of necessity be chained to the deck, and his conscience reminded him uneasily of the torments he had seen El Supremo inflict without expostulation. This Spanish way of making a show out of insanity and greatness was repulsive enough, but could be paralleled often enough in English history. One of the greatest writers of the English language, and a dignitary of the Church to boot, had once been shown in his dotage for a fee. There was only one line of argument which he could adopt.

"You are going to hang him, mad as he is?" he asked. "With no chance of making his peace with God?"

The Spaniard shrugged.

"Mad or sane, rebels must hang. Your Excellency must know that as well as I do."

Hornblower did know it. He was left without any argument at all, and was reduced to stammering inarticulation, even while he boiled with contempt for himself on that account. All that was left for him to do, having lost all his dignity in his own eyes, was to try and retain some few shreds of it in the eyes of his audience. He braced himself up, conscious of the hollowness of the fraud.

"I must thank you very much, sir," he said, "for having given me the opportunity of witnessing a most interesting spectacle. And now, repeating my thanks, I fear that I must regretfully take my departure. There seems to be a breath of wind blowing."

He went down the side of the lugger as stiffly as he might, and took his seat in the sternsheets of the launch. He had to brace himself again to give the word to cast off, and then he sat silent and gloomy as he was rowed back to the *Lydia*. Bush and Gerard and Lady Barbara watched him as he came on deck. It was as if there was death in his face. He looked round him, unseeing and unhearing, and then hurried below to hide his misery. He even sobbed, with his face in his cot, for a second, before he was able to take hold of himself and curse himself for a weak fool. But it was days before he lost that deathly look, and during that time he kept himself solitary in his cabin, unable to bring himself to join the merry parties on the quarterdeck whose gay chatter drifted down to him through the skylight. To him it was a further proof of his weakness and folly that he should allow himself to be so upset by the sight of a criminal madman going to meet the fate he richly deserved.

Chapter XXII

Lady Barbara and Lieutenant Bush were sitting talking in the warm moonlight night beside the taffrail. It was the first time that Bush had happened to share a tête-à-tête with her, and he had only drifted into it by chance — presumably if he had foreseen it he would have avoided it, but now that he had drifted into conversation with her he was enjoying himself to the exclusion of any disquietude. He was sitting on a pile of the oakum-filled cushions which Harrison had had made for Lady Barbara, and he nursed his knees while Lady Barbara leaned back in her hammock chair. The *Lydia* was rising and falling softly to the gentle music of the waves and the harping of the rigging in the breeze. The white sails glimmered in the brilliant moon; overhead the stars shone with strange brightness. But Bush was not talking of himself, as any sensible man would do under a tropic moon with a young woman beside him.

"Aye, ma'am," he was saying. "He's like Nelson. He's nervous, just as Nelson was, and for the same reason. He's thinking all the time — you'd be surprised, ma'am, to know how much he thinks about."

"I don't think it would surprise me," said Lady Barbara.

"That's because you think, too, ma'am. It's us stupid ones who'd be surprised, I meant to say. He has more brains than all the rest of us in this ship put together, excepting you, ma'am. He's mighty clever, I do assure you."

"I can well believe it."

"And he's the best seaman of us all, and as for navigation — well, Crystal's a fool compared with him, ma'am."

"Yes?"

"Of course, he's short with me sometimes, the same as he is with everyone else, but bless you, ma'am, that's only to be expected. I know how much he has to worry him, and he's not strong, the same as Nelson wasn't strong. I am concerned about him sometimes, ma'am."

"You are fond of him."

"Fond, ma'am?" Bush's sturdy English mind grappled with the word and its sentimental implications, and he laughed a trifle self-consciously. "If you say so I suppose I must be. I hadn't ever thought of being fond of him before. I like him, ma'am, indeed I do."

"That is what I meant."

"The men worship him, ma'am. They would do anything for him. Look how much he has done this commission, and the lash not in use once in a week, ma'am. That is why he is like Nelson. They love him not for anything he does or says, but for what he is."

"He's handsome, in a way," said Lady Barbara — she was woman enough to give that matter consideration.

"I suppose he is, ma'am, now you come to mention it. But it wouldn't matter if he were as ugly as sin as far as we was concerned."

"Of course not."

"But he's shy, ma'am. He never can guess how clever he is. It's that which always surprises me about him. You'd hardly believe it, ma'am, but he has no more faith in himself than — than I have in myself, ma'am, to put it that way. Less, ma'am, if anything."

"How strange!" said Lady Barbara. She was accustomed to the sturdy self-reliance of her brothers, unloved and unlovable leaders of men, but her insight made her comment only one of politeness — it was not really strange to her.

"Look, ma'am," said Bush, suddenly, dropping his voice.

Hornblower had come up on deck. They could see his face, white in the moonlight, as he looked round to assure himself that all was well with his ship, and they could read in it the torment which was obsessing him. He looked like a lost soul during the few seconds he was on deck.

"I wish to God I knew," said Bush as Hornblower retreated again to the solitude of his cabin, "what those devils did to him or said to him when he went on board the lugger. Hooker who was in the cutter said he heard someone on board howling like a madman. The torturing devils! It was some of their beastliness, I suppose. You could see how it has upset him, ma'am."

"Yes," said Lady Barbara, softly.

"I should be grateful if you could try to take him out of himself a little, ma'am, begging your pardon. He is in need of distraction, I suspicion. Perhaps you could — if you'll forgive me, ma'am."

"I'll try," said Lady Barbara, "but I don't think I shall succeed where you have failed. Captain Hornblower has never taken a great deal of notice of me, Mr. Bush."

Yet fortunately the formal invitation to dine with Lady Barbara, which Hebe conveyed to Polwheal and he to his captain, arrived at a moment when Hornblower was just trying to emerge from the black fit which had engulfed him. He read the words as carefully as Lady Barbara had written them — and she had devoted much care to the composition of the note. Hornblower read Lady Barbara's pretty little apology for breaking in upon him at a time when he was obviously engrossed in his work, and he went on to read how Lady Barbara had been informed by Mr. Bush that the *Lydia* was about to cross the Equator, and that she thought such an occasion merited some mild celebration. If Captain Hornblower, therefore, would give Lady Barbara the pleasure of his company at dinner and would indicate to her which of his officers he considered should be invited at the same time, Lady Barbara would be delighted. Hornblower wrote back to say that Captain Hornblower had much pleasure in accepting Lady Barbara's kind invitation to dinner, and hoped that Lady Barbara would invite whomever she pleased in addition.

Yet even in the pleasure of returning to society there was some alloy. Hornblower had always been a poor man, and at the time when he commissioned the *Lydia* he had been at his wits' end about where to turn for money in the need for leaving Maria comfortably provided for. In consequence he had not outfitted himself satisfactorily, and now, all these months later, his clothes were in the last stages of decay. The coats were all patched and darned; the epaulettes betrayed in their brassy sheen the fact that they had begun life merely coated with bullion; the cocked hats were all wrecks; he had neither breeches nor stockings fit to be seen; his once white scarves were all coarsened now, and could never be mistaken again for silk. Only the sword "of fifty guineas' value" retained its good appearance, and he could not wear that at a dinner party.

He was conscious that his white duck trousers, made on board the *Lydia*, had none of the fashionable appearance to which Lady Barbara was accustomed. He looked shabby and he felt shabby, and as he peered at himself in his little mirror he was certain that Lady Barbara would sneer at him. There were grey hairs in his brown curls, too, and then, to his horror, as he straightened his parting, he caught a glimpse of pink scalp — his baldness had increased beyond all measure of late. He eyed himself with complete disgust, and yet he felt that he would gladly give a limb or his remaining hair in exchange for a ribbon and star with which to dazzle Lady Barbara; yet even that would be of no avail, for Lady Barbara had lived all her life in an atmosphere of Garters and Thistles, orders which he could never hope to wear.

He was on the verge of sending a message to Lady Barbara to say that he had changed his mind and would not dine with her that evening, until he thought that if he did so, after all these preparations, Polwheal would guess that it was the result of his realisation of his shabbiness and would laugh at him (and his shabbiness) in consequence. He went in to dinner and had his revenge upon the world by sitting silent and preoccupied at the head of the table, blighting with his gloomy presence all attempts at conversation, so that the function began as a frigid failure. It was a poor sort of revenge, but there was a slight gratification to be found in observing Lady Barbara looking down the table at him in concern. In the end he was deprived even of that, for Lady Barbara suddenly smiled and began talking lightly and captivatingly, and led Bush into describing his experiences at Trafalgar — a tale she had heard, to Hornblower's certain knowledge, twice at least already.

The conversation became general, and then animated, for Gerard could not bear to leave all the talking to Bush, and he had to break in with the story of his encounter with an Algerine corsair off Cape Spartel in his old slaving days. It was more than Hornblower's flesh and blood could stand, to stay silent with everyone talking in this fashion. Against his will he found himself entering into the conversation, and an artless question from Lady Barbara about Sir Edward Pellew inveigled him still further in, for Hornblower had been both midshipman and lieutenant in Pellew's ship, and was proud of it. Not until the end of dinner was he able to steady himself, and decline, after the drinking of the King's health, Lady Barbara's invitation to a rubber of whist. That at least, he thought, would make an impression on her — it certainly did upon his officers, for he saw Bush and Gerard exchange startled glances on hearing their captain refuse to play whist. Back in his cabin again he listened through the bulkhead to the uproarious game of *vingt-et-un* which Lady Barbara had suggested instead. He almost wished he were playing too, even though in his opinion *vingt-et-un* was a game for the feeble-minded.

The dinner had served its purpose, however, in making it possible to meet Lady Barbara's eye again on deck. He could converse with her, too, discussing with her the condition of the few wounded who remained upon the sick list, and after a few morning encounters it was easy to fall into conversation with her during the breathless afternoons and the magic tropical nights as the *Lydia* held her course over the calm Pacific. He had grown hardened again to his shabby coats and his shapeless trousers; he was forgetting the resentful plans he had once turned over in his mind to confine Lady Barbara to her cabin; and, mercifully, his memory was no longer being so acutely troubled by pictures of El Supremo chained to the deck, of Galbraith dying, and of poor little Clay's body sprawled headless on the bloody planks — and when those memories lapsed he could no longer accuse himself of being a coward for being worried by them.

Those were happy days indeed. The routine of the *Lydia* progressed like clockwork. Almost every hour of every day there was enough wind to give her steerage way, and sometimes it blew just hard enough to relieve the monotony. There were no storms during that endless succession of golden days, and the mind could contemplate its endlessness with tranquillity, for 50 degrees South

Latitude seemed impossibly far away; they could enjoy the blissfulness of eternity, disregarding the constant warning conveyed to them as every noontide showed the sun lower in the sky and every midnight showed the Southern Cross higher.

They could be friends during those heavenly nights when the ship's wake showed as a long trail of fire on the faintly luminous water. They learned to talk together, endlessly. She could chatter about the frivolities of the Vice-Regal court at Dublin, and of the intrigues which could enmesh a Governor-General of India; of penniless French émigrés putting purse-proud northern ironmasters in their places; of Lord Byron's extravagances and of the Royal Dukes' stupidities; and Hornblower learned to listen without a twinge of envy.

He could tell, in return, of months spent on blockade, combating storms off the ironbound Biscay coast, of how Pellew took his frigates into the very surf to sink the *Droits-de-l'homme* with two thousand men on board, of hardship and cruelty and privation — a monotonous toilsome life as fantastic to her as hers appeared to him. He could even tell her, as his self-consciousness dwindled, of the ambitions which he knew would seem to her as trivial as those of a child yearning for a hobby horse; of the two thousand pounds in prize money which he had decided would be all that he would require to eke out his half-pay, the few acres and the cottage and the shelves and shelves of books.

And yet she heard this without a smile, with even a trace of envy in her calm face as the moon shone down on them; for her own ambitions were far more vague and far less likely to be realised. She hardly knew what it was that she wanted, and she knew that whatever it was, she could only hope to attain it by ensnaring a husband. That an earl's daughter could envy a penniless frigate captain moved Hornblower inexpressibly, as he watched her face in the moonlight; he was glad even while he was unhappy that Lady Barbara should have to envy anything of anyone.

They could talk of books and of poetry, and Hornblower championed the cause of the classical school which looked back to the days of Queen Anne against the barbarous leaders of the revolt who seemed to delight in setting every established rule at defiance.

She heard him with patience, even with approval, as he talked of Gibbon (the object of his sincerest admiration) and Johnson and Swift, when he quoted from Pope and Gray, but she could approve of the barbarians as well. There was a madman called Wordsworth of whose revolutionary opinions in literature Hornblower had heard with vague horror; Lady Barbara thought there was something to be said for him. She turned the tables neatly on Hornblower by claiming Gray as a precursor of the same school; she quoted Campbell and that Gothic innovator, Scott, and she won Hornblower's grudging approval of an ungainly poem called "The Rime of the Ancient Mariner," although he maintained sturdily, in the last ditch, that its only merit lay in its content, and that it would have been infinitely better had Pope dealt with the theme in heroic couplets — especially if Pope had been assisted by someone who knew more about navigation and seamanship than did this Coleridge fellow.

Lady Barbara now wondered vaguely, sometimes, whether it was not strange that a naval officer should be so earnest a student of literature, but she was learning rapidly. Sea captains were not all of a class, as the uninitiated might carelessly decide. From Bush and Gerard and Crystal as well as from Hornblower she heard of captains who wrote Greek elegiacs, of captains who cluttered up their cabins with marbles looted from the Greek islands, captains who classified sea-urchins and corresponded with Cuvier — these on the one hand, just as there were captains who delighted in seeing human backs lacerated with the cat-o'-nine-tails, captains who drank themselves insensible every night and who raised hell in their ships during bouts of delirium tremens, captains who starved their crews and captains who turned up all hands at every bell, night and day. She found that she was sure, all the same, that Hornblower was an outstanding member of a class which people on shore tended not to credit with nearly so much ability as they actually possessed.

She had, from the time of her first arrival on board, found pleasure in Hornblower's society. Now they had formed a habit of each other, as though they were insidious drugs, and were vaguely uneasy when out of sight of each other. The voyage had been monotonous enough, as the *Lydia* held steadily southward, for habits to be easily formed; it had become a habit to exchange a smile when they met on the quarterdeck in the morning — a smile illumined by secret memories of the intimacy of the conversation of the night before. It was a habit now for Hornblower to discuss the ship's progress with Lady Barbara after he had taken the noon sights, a habit now for him to drink coffee with her in the afternoons, and especially was it a habit for them to meet at sunset by the taffrail, although no appointment had been made and no hint of their meeting had ever been suggested, and to lounge in the warm darkness while conversation grew up, seemingly from no roots at all, and blossomed and flowered exotically, under the magic brilliance of the stars until with a reluctance of which they were hardly conscious they drifted off to bed, hours after midnight.

They could even sit silent together now, watching, wordlessly, the mastheads circling amid the stars with the rolling of the ship, listening to the faint orchestra of the ship's fabric, and their thoughts paralleling each other's so that when eventually one of them spoke it was to harmonise completely with what was in the other's mind. At those times Lady Barbara's hand, like a healthy young woman's, was at her side where it could be touched without too great effort. When she had not wanted them to do so men had taken her hand often before, at London balls and Governor-Generals' receptions, but now, conscious though she was of how reckless and imprudent it would be to encourage the slightest physical intimacy on this voyage with months more to last, she still was reckless and imprudent enough to risk it without attempting to analyse her motives. But Hornblower seemed unconscious of that hand. She would see his face lifted to the stars, peaceful and immobile, and she found pleasure in giving herself credit for the change in it from the evening when she had talked with Bush and seen Hornblower's torment.

For happy weeks that phase of the voyage lasted, while the *Lydia* ran steadily south and still more south, until the evenings grew chill and the mornings misty, until the blue sky changed to grey and the first rain they had known for three weeks wetted the

Lydia's decks, and the west wind blew more blustering and searching, so that Lady Barbara had to wrap herself in a boat cloak to be able to sit on deck at all. Those evenings by the taffrail came to an imperceptible end, and the *Lydia* thrashed along through half a gale, and it grew steadily colder even though this was the Antipodean summer. For the first time in her life Lady Barbara saw Hornblower dressed in tarpaulins and sou'wester, and she thought oddly, how well those hideous garments suited him. There were times when he would come sauntering into the cabin, his eyes bright and his cheeks flushed with the wind, and she felt her pulses leap in sympathy with his.

She knew she was being foolish. She told herself that this weakness of hers only arose because Hornblower was the one man with any culture or any trace of eligibility on board the *Lydia,* and because life in close contact with him for four continuous months was bound to make her either love him or hate him — and as there was no room for hatred in her system the other thing was inevitable. She told herself, too, that as soon as she returned to civilisation, as soon as she could see Hornblower against that usual background of hers which had faded with the passage of the months almost out of her memory, he would lose his interest and his charm.

On board ship one saw things in a false perspective, she informed herself. Salt beef and salt pork, weevilly bread and dried peas, with a glass of lemon juice twice a week; that meant monotony. Trifles assumed an exaggerated importance when leading a life like that. Just as toothache tended to disappear when something occurred to distract the mind, so would this heartache of hers disappear when she had other things to think about. It was all very true; but strangely it made not the least difference to her present feelings.

They had reached the region of westerly trade winds now. Every day they roared harder and harder, and every day the sea rose higher and higher. The *Lydia* was thrashing along magnificently now; there were two or three days when she logged over two hundred and forty nautical miles as her day's run from noon to noon. It was cold, and it rained in torrents, and the main deck was often knee deep in water. There were days when all Lady

Barbara could do was to brace herself in her cot while the ship tossed and rolled as though at any moment she would turn completely over, while Hebe (who never succeeded quite in overcoming her seasickness) moaned in her blankets on the deck and her teeth chattered with the cold. No fire could be kept alight; nothing could be cooked, while the groaning of the ship's timbers swelled into a volume of sound comparable to that of an organ in a church.

At the very climax of the voyage, at their farthest south, the freakishness of Cape Horn weather displayed itself, when Lady Barbara awoke one morning to find the ship rising and swooping once more in orderly fashion, and Polwheal knocked at the cabin door with a message from the captain to the effect that this morning Lady Barbara might, if she wished, take advantage of the break in the weather to take the air on deck. She found the sky blue and the air clear though keen enough to make the duffle coat which Gerard had lent her grateful. The wind had died away to a mere fresh breeze, before which the *Lydia* was careening gaily along under all sail to the royals, and there was a bright sun shining all around them. It was a joy to walk the deck once more. It was if anything an even greater joy to drink hot coffee, steaming hot, again, served by a grinning Polwheal to Lady Barbara and the officers on the quarterdeck. There was an excruciating pleasure in filling her lungs with pure air after days of breathing the mephitic vapours of below decks. She caught Hornblower's eyes and they exchanged smiles of delight. In all the rigging the sailors' clothes, spread hastily to dry, were gesticulating as though with joy, waving a thousand glad arms and legs in the sparkling air.

Cape Horn allowed them just that one pleasurable morning; before noon a thin cloud had spread itself over the sun, and the wind was increasing in force again, and to windward there were solid banks of black cloud coming up and overhauling them rapidly.

"Get the royals in, Mr. Bush," growled Hornblower, glowering aft. "Lady Barbara, I am afraid that you will have to retire to your cabin again."

The gale fell on them with a shriek when Lady Barbara had

hardly reached her cabin; they ran before it all the afternoon, and at evening Lady Barbara could tell by the motion of the ship (so experienced a sailor had she become) that Hornblower had been compelled to heave her to. For thirty six hours the *Lydia* remained hove-to, while the heavens tore themselves to pieces around her, but there was comfort in the knowledge that on her easterly course all her drift to leeward helped her on her way. Lady Barbara found it hard to believe that men had ever succeeded in sailing a ship westward round the Horn. It helped her to agree with Hornblower that before very long, at the latest as soon as a general peace was concluded, the whole world would arise and write in the demand for the cutting of a canal through the Isthmus of Panama. Meanwhile there was nothing to do except to wait for the happy day when they would reach St. Helena, and could enjoy fresh meat again, and vegetables, even — impossibly Utopian though it might seem — milk and fruit.

Chapter XXIII

On that voyage the change in conditions after rounding the Horn was most dramatic. It seemed to Lady Barbara almost as if one day they were labouring along over grey seas before the southwesterly gales, cold and uncomfortable, with waves running as high as the yard arms, and the next they were enjoying blue skies and gentle breezes from the southeast. They had in fact been fortunate, for the last thundering gale from the southwest had carried them well into the region of the southerly trades. They were leaving the Antipodean autumn behind them, and the northern spring was coming down in the track of the sun to meet them. The sea was blue again, as blue as any blue well could be, in its usual marvellous contrast with the white foam. There were flying fish furrowing the enamelled surface. In a flash the privations and discomforts of the Horn were forgotten.

It seemed the most natural thing in the world that as night fell Lady Barbara should find herself seated as ever by the taffrail, and just as natural that Hornblower should loom up in the half light beside her and should accept her unvaryingly polite invitation to a seat beside her. It was perfectly natural that the officers should accept this state of affairs as one which had long existed, and that the officer of the watch should confine his walk to the forward part of the quarterdeck. At eight bells when Gerard came up to relieve Rayner the latter with a jerk of his thumb and a cock of his head called the former's attention to the little dark group by the taffrail. Gerard grinned, his white teeth in his swarthy face gleaming in the starlight.

He had made his trial of the lady's virtue in the long ago, before the captain had noticed her existence. He did not think that Hornblower would succeed where he had failed, and in any case Gerard prided himself on having sufficient sense not to try to compete with his own captain. Gerard had conquests enough to think about during the silent night watches, and he was philosopher enough to wish his captain good luck while keeping his back turned squarely to them as they talked quietly, only just out of earshot of him.

Yet to Hornblower — and to Lady Barbara — things were not the same here in the Atlantic as they had been in the Pacific. Hornblower seemed to feel a tension he had not felt before. Perhaps the rounding of the Horn had forced it home upon him that even sailing ship voyages must end sometime, that even the three thousand odd miles that lay between them and Portsmouth would not last for ever. In the Pacific, appropriately enough, he had found peace in Lady Barbara's company. Here in the Atlantic he was conscious of uneasiness, as he might be if the barometer were falling rapidly in a glassy calm in West Indian waters.

For some reason — perhaps merely because he had been thinking of England — the image of Maria had been much before his eyes of late; Maria, short and tubby, with a tendency to spots in her complexion, with the black silk parasol which she affected; or Maria in her flannel nightshift and curl papers with a loving note sounding hoarsely in her voice; Maria arguing with a lodging house keeper, and Maria on board the ship at Portsmouth, her poor opinion of common sailors evident in her expression. It was disloyal to think of Maria like that; rather should he think of her as she was that feverish night in the Southsea lodgings, her eyes red with weeping, struggling bravely to keep her lips from trembling while little Horatio died of the smallpox in her arms and little Maria lay dead in the next room.

"Ha — h'm," said Hornblower, harshly, and he stirred uneasily in his seat.

Lady Barbara looked at his face in the starlight. It bore that bleak, lonely expression which she had come to dread.

"Can you tell me what is the matter, Captain?" she asked, gently.

Hornblower sat silent for some seconds before he shook his head. No, he could not tell her. For that matter he did not know himself; introspective though he was, he had not dared to admit to himself that he had been making comparisons between someone short and stout and someone tall and slender, between someone with apple cheeks and someone with a classic profile.

Hornblower slept badly that night, and his morning walk which followed was not devoted to the purpose for which it had originally been destined. He could not keep his mind at work upon the problems of stores and water, of how to keep the crew busy and out of mischief, of winds and courses, which he was accustomed to solve at this time so as to appear a man of decision the rest of the day. Part of the time he was too unhappy to think connectedly, and for the rest his mind was busy wrestling with suppositions so monstrous that they appalled him. He was tempted to make advances to Lady Barbara; that, at least, he could admit to himself. He wanted to do so so badly. There was an ache in his breast, a most painful yearning as he thought of it.

What was monstrous about his thoughts was the suspicion that possibly Lady Barbara would not repulse him. It seemed inconceivable and yet possible, like something in a nightmare. He might even put his hot hand on her cool bosom — a thought which made him writhe in strange anguish. His longing to taste her sweetness was excruciating. He had been nearly a year cooped up in the *Lydia* now, and a year of unnatural living breeds strange fancies. Somewhere just over the gloomy horizon of Hornblower's mind there lurked fancies stranger yet; dark phantoms of rape and murder.

Yet even while Hornblower thus toyed with madness his cursed analytical powers were at work upon other pros and cons. Whether he offended Lady Barbara, or whether he seduced her, he was playing with fire. The Wellesley family could blast him at their whim. They could snatch him from his command and leave him to rot for ever on half-pay; even worse, they could find, somewhere in his actions of the past year, if their animosity were sufficient, grounds for a courtmartial, and a courtmartial under Wellesley pressure could strip him of his commission and leave him a pauper dependent on parish relief. That was the worst that could happen — save perhaps for a duel with a result fatal to himself — and the very best was not much better. Supposing, as was just conceivable, the Wellesleys could tolerate the seduction of their sister — supposing that, confronted with a *fait accompli,* they resolved to try to make the best of things. No, that was not conceivable at all. He would have to procure a divorce from Maria, and that would involve an act of parliament and the expenditure of five thousand pounds.

To meddle with Lady Barbara would mean risking utter ruin — professional, social, and financial. And he knew he could not trust himself where risks were concerned. When he had had the *Lydia* towed into range of the *Natividad* and had fought it out with her gun to gun he had run such appalling risks that to this day he felt a little chill down his spine on recalling them. Risk and danger lured him even while he knew he was a fool to expose himself to them, and he knew that no risk would deter him once he had embarked on a course of action. Even at this moment, thinking about it in cold blood, there was something dangerously fascinating in the thought of wiping the eye of the whole Wellesley family and then daring them to do their worst.

And then all these cold blooded considerations were swept away to nothing again in a white hot wave of passion as he thought of her, slim and lovely, understanding and sweet. He was trembling with passion, the hot blood running under his skin, and muddled images streamed through his mind in a fantastic panorama. He stood by the rail staring unseeing over the blue sea with its patches of golden weed, conscious of nothing save the riot in his own body and mind. When his heart had at last slowed down to normal, and he turned to look round over the ship, everything was oddly sharp and clear. He could see the smallest details of the complicated splicing which one of the hands was engaged upon on the forecastle a hundred and twenty feet away. Immediately afterwards he was heartily glad that he had regained his self control, for Lady Barbara came on deck, smiling as she always did when the sun shone on her face on emerging from the deck cabin, and soon he was in conversation with her.

"I spent last night dreaming dreams," said Lady Barbara.

"Indeed?" said Hornblower, awkwardly. He, too, had been dreaming.

"Yes," said Lady Barbara, "I was dreaming mostly of eggs.

Fried eggs, and buttered eggs. And slices of white bread spread thick with butter. And café au lait with plenty of cream. And cabbage — plain boiled cabbage. My dreams were not extravagant enough to run to a purée of spinach, but I almost attained to a dish of young carrots. And behold, this morning Hebe brings me my black coffee and my weevilly maize bread, and Polwheal sends in to ask me if I will be pleased to take beef or pork for my dinner. Today I think I start on the seventh brother of the pig whose chops I first tasted at Panama. I know his breed by now."

Lady Barbara could still laugh and show her white teeth in her brown face, as she made this speech, and her laugh whisked away Hornblower's passion for a space. He was in sympathy with her — months of ship's fare set everyone literally dreaming of fresh food — but her fine naturalness acted upon Hornblower's state of mind like an open window on a stuffy room. It was that talk about food which staved off the crisis for a few more days — golden days, during which the *Lydia* kept the southeast trades on her beam and reached steadily across the south Atlantic for St. Helena.

The wind did not fail her until the very evening when the look-out at the masthead, the setting of the sun in a golden glory having enabled him to gaze ahead once more, caught sight of the tip of the mountain top just as the light was fading from the sky, and his cry of "Land ho!" told Hornblower that once more he had made a perfect landfall. All day long the wind had been dying away, and with the setting of the sun it dwindled to nothing, tantalisingly, just when a few more hours of it would have carried the *Lydia* to the island. From the deck there was still no sign of land, and as Gerard pointed out to Lady Barbara, she would have to take its proximity on trust until the wind condescended to blow again. Her disappointment at this postponement of her promised buttered eggs was so appealing that Crystal hastened forward and stuck his open claspknife in the mainmast. That was a sure way of raising a wind, he said — and if by any mishap it should fail on this occasion he would set all the ship's boys whistling in unison and chance the tempests such imprudence might summon from the deep.

It may have been the mere fact of this respite working on Hornblower's subconscious mind which precipitated the crisis; for undoubtedly Hornblower had a lurking fear that the call at St. Helena might well bring about some undesired alteration in affairs on board the *Lydia.* On the other hand, the thing was bound to happen, and perhaps coincidence merely allotted that evening for it. It was coincidence that Hornblower should come into the main cabin in the half light at a moment when he thought Lady Barbara was on deck, and it was coincidence that his hand should brush against her bare arm as they stood cramped between the table and the locker and he apologised for his intrusion. She was in his arms then, and they kissed, and kissed again. She put one hand behind his shoulder and touched the back of his neck, and they were giddy with passion. Then a roll of the ship forced him to let her go, and she sank down upon the locker, and she smiled at him as she sat so that he came down on his knees beside her, his head on her breast, and she stroked his curls, and they kissed again as if they would never tire. She spoke to him with the endearments which her nurse had used to her when she was a child — she had never learned yet to use endearments.

"My dear," she whispered. "My sweet. My poppet."

It was hard to find words that would tell him of her love for him.

"Your hands are beautiful," she said, spreading one of them on her own palm, and playing with the long slender fingers. "I have loved them ever since Panama."

Hornblower had always thought his hands bony and ugly, and the left one bore the ingrained powder stain he had acquired at the boarding of the *Castilla.* He looked at her to see if she were teasing him, and when he saw that she was not he could only kiss her again — her lips were so ready for his kisses. It was like a miracle that she should want to be kissed. Passion carried them away once more.

Hebe's entrance made them part; at least it made Hornblower spring up, to sit bolt upright and self-conscious, while Hebe grinned at them with sly eyes. To Hornblower it was a dreadful thing for a captain to be caught toying with a woman on board his ship actually in commission. It was contrary to the Articles of

War — worse, it was undignified, subversive of discipline, dangerous. Lady Barbara remained quite unruffled.

"Go away, Hebe," she said calmly. "I shall not need you yet."

And she turned back to Hornblower, but the spell was broken. He had seen himself in a new light, grovelling furtively on a couch with a passenger. He was blushing hotly, angry with himself, and already wondering how much the officer of the watch and the man at the wheel had heard of their murmurings through the open skylight.

"What are we to do?" he asked feebly.

"Do?" she replied. "We are lovers, and the world is ours. We do as we will."

"But — " he said, and again, "but —— "

He wanted to explain to her in half a dozen words the complications he could see hedging him in. There was a cold fit on him; he wanted to tell her of how he dreaded the ill concealed amusement of Gerard, the utterly tactless tactfulness of Bush, and how the captain of a ship was not nearly as much his own master as she apparently thought, but it was hopeless. He could only stammer, and his hands flapped feebly, and his face was averted. He had forgotten all these practical details in those mad dreams of his. She put her hand on his chin and made him turn to her.

"Dear," she asked. "What is troubling you? Tell me, dear."

"I am a married man," he said, taking the coward's way out.

"I know that. Are you going to allow that to interfere with — us?"

"Besides — " he said, and his hands flapped again in the hopeless effort to express all the doubts which consumed him.

She condescended to sink her pride a little farther.

"Hebe is safe," she said, softly. "She worships me. Nor would she dare to be indiscreet."

She saw the look in his face, and rose abruptly. Her blood and lineage were outraged at this. However veiled her offer had been, it had been refused. She was in a cold rage now.

"Please have the kindness, Captain," she said, "to open that door for me."

She swept out of the cabin with all the dignity of an earl's daughter, and if she wept when in the privacy of her own cabin Hornblower knew nothing of it. He was pacing the deck above, up and down, up and down, endlessly. This was the end of his fine dreams. This was how he showed himself a man to whom danger and risk only made a plan more attractive. He was a fine lady-killer, a devil of a buck. He cursed himself in his shame, he jeered at himself as a man who could face the wrath of the Wellesleys in imagination and who flinched from the amusement of Gerard in practice.

It all might have come right in the end. If the calm had persisted for two or three days, so that Lady Barbara could have forgotten her wrath and Hornblower his doubts, more might have happened. There might have been an echoing scandal in high life. But as it was, at midnight a little wind began to blow — perhaps it was Crystal's claspknife which had summoned it — and Gerard came to him for orders. Again he could not flout public opinion. He could not face the thought of the suspicions which would arise and the secret questions which would be asked if he gave orders for the ship to be put about and to head away from St. Helena at a time when the wind held fair.

Chapter XXIV

"THERE's the devil of a lot of shipping there," said Bush, his glass to his eye, as they opened up the roadstead in the dawn. "The devil of a lot. Men o' war, sir. No, Indiamen. Men o' war *and* Indiamen, sir. There's a three-decker! It's the old *Téméraire,* sir, or I'm a Dutchman, with a rear admiral's flag. Must be the rendezvous for the homeward bound convoy, sir."

"Pass the word for Mr. Marsh," said Hornblower.

There would be salutes to be fired, calls to be paid — he was caught up in the irresistible current of naval routine, and he would be too busy now for hours to have a word with Lady Barbara even if she condescended to allow him one. He did not know whether to be glad or sorry.

The *Lydia* made her number, and the sound of the salutes began to roll slowly round the bay. Hornblower was in his shabby full dress — the faded blue coat with the brassy epaulettes, the worn white breeches, the silk stockings with the innumerable ladders which Polwheal had cobbled roughly together. The port officer came up the side to receive his certificate of the absence of infectious disease on board. A moment later the anchor roared out overside, then Hornblower called for the cutter to take him over to the Admiral. He was actually going over the side when Lady Barbara came on deck — he saw her, just for a second, gazing with pleasure up the green mountain slopes, and looking with surprise at the massed shipping inshore. He longed to stop and speak to her, but once more the dignity expected of a captain checked him. Nor could he take her with him — no captain starting on an official round of calls could go round in his boat with a woman in the sternsheets beside him, not even when subsequent explanation would reveal her to be a Wellesley.

The cutter pulled steadily over to the *Téméraire.*

"*Lydia,*" shouted the coxswain in reply to the hail from her deck, and he held up the four fingers which indicated the presence in the boat of a captain as a warning for them to prepare the correct ceremonial.

Sir James Saumarez received Hornblower in the quarter gallery of his flagship. He was tall and spare, of youthful appearance until he took off his hat and revealed his snow-white hair. He listened courteously to Hornblower's brief explanation of his presence; after forty years at sea and sixteen years of continuous warfare he could guess at the wild adventures which remained undescribed in Hornblower's verbal report. There was a gleam of approval in his fierce blue eyes when he heard that the *Lydia* had sunk a fifty-gun two-decker in a ship to ship duel.

"You can accompany me and the convoy," he said, at the end. "I have no more than two ships of the line and not a single frigate to escort the whole East Indian convoy. One would have thought that the Government would have learnt the need of frigates since the war started in 'ninety three, don't you think? I will send you written orders this morning. And now, sir, perhaps you will give me the pleasure of your company at the breakfast party at which I am about to be host?"

Hornblower pointed out that it was his duty to call upon the governor.

"His Excellency is breakfasting with me," said the Admiral.

Hornblower knew that it was ill to continue to raise a series of objections to a suggestion by an Admiral, but he had to raise a fresh one.

"There is a lady on board the *Lydia*, sir," he said, and when the Admiral's eyebrows went up he hurriedly began to explain Lady Barbara's presence to him.

The Admiral whistled.

"A Wellesley!" he said. "And you brought her round the Horn? Here, we must tell Lady Manningtree of this."

He led the way unceremoniously into the lofty Admiral's cabin. There was a long table with a snowy cloth, glittering with crystal and silver, and by the table there stood chatting a little group of men and women, beautifully dressed. The Admiral made hurried introductions — His Excellency the Governor, and Her Excellency; the Earl and Countess of Manningtree, Sir Charles and Lady Wheeler.

Lady Manningtree was a short and dumpy woman with good humour in every line of her face. She showed no sign of the dignity and reserve which might be expected of the wife of an ex-governor general returning from his term of office.

"Captain Hornblower has brought Lady Barbara Wellesley with him from Darien," said Sir James, and plunged into rapid explanation. Lady Manningtree listened in perfect horror.

"And you have left her there? On that little ship?" she said. "The poor lamb! She must not stay there another moment! I shall go and bring her away this very instant! Sir James, you must excuse me. I will not have a moment's peace until she is comfortably in the cabin next to mine on board the *Hanbury Castle*. Sir James, would you be so good as to order a boat for me?"

She left in a whirl of apologies and explanations, a fluttering of petticoats and a perfect torrent of objurgations, mainly directed at Hornblower.

"When women take charge," said Sir James philosophically, after she had departed, "it is best for the men to stand from under. Will you sit here, Captain?"

Curiously, Hornblower could eat almost nothing of that delicious breakfast. There were heavenly mutton cutlets. There was coffee with fresh milk. There was new wheaten bread. There was butter, there were fruits, there were vegetables, all the things Hornblower had dreamed about when his thoughts had not been occupied with Lady Barbara, and now he could only eat a mouthful here and there. Fortunately his lack of appetite went unnoticed because he was kept so busy answering the questions which were rained on him, about Lady Barbara, about his adventures in the Pacific, about his passage round the Horn, and then back to Lady Barbara again.

"Her brother is doing great things in Spain," said Sir James. "Not the eldest one, the Marquis, but Arthur — the one who won the battle of Assaye. He came well out of that court of inquiry after Vimiero. Now he has bundled Soult out of Portugal, and when I left Lisbon he was in full march on Madrid. Since Moore was killed he is the most promising soldier in the army."

"Humph," said Lady Wheeler. The name of Wellesley was still anathema to a certain section of Anglo-Indians. "This Lady Barbara is a good deal younger than he is, I fancy? I remember her as quite a child in Madras."

Eyes were turned toward Hornblower, but Lord Manningtree in the kindness of his heart spared him the embarrassment of having to explain Lady Barbara's age.

"She's no child," he said, bluffly. "She's a very talented young woman. Declined a dozen good offers in India, too, and God knows how many since then."

"Humph," said Lady Wheeler again.

That breakfast began to seem interminable to Hornblower, and he was glad when the party showed signs of breaking up. The governor seized the opportunity to discuss with him the matter of the stores for which the *Lydia* would have to indent — naval routine still claimed him for her own. There was urgent need for him to return to his ship; he made his excuses to Sir James and said goodbye to the rest of the company.

The Admiral's barge was still hooked on to the *Lydia's* chains when he returned to her; her crew were dressed in crimson coats with gold-laced hats. Hornblower had known frigate captains who dressed their gig's crews in fancy costumes in this fashion too, but they were wealthy men who had been fortunate in the matter of prize money, not penniless fellows like himself. He went on board; Lady Barbara's baggage was piled on the gangway waiting to be swung down into the barge. Down in the main cabin could be heard a continuous chatter of female voices. Lady Manningtree and Lady Barbara were sitting there deep in conversation; obviously there had been so much to say that they could not wait until they had reached the *Hanbury Castle*. One topic had led to another so enthralling that they had forgotten the barge, forgotten the waiting baggage, forgotten even about breakfast.

Apparently Lady Barbara had taken the opportunity, when her baggage had been brought up from the storeroom, to unpack some new clothes. She was wearing a new gown which Hornblower had not seen before, and a new turban and veil. She was very obviously the great lady now. To Hornblower's startled mind she seemed as she stood up to be six inches taller than when he saw her last. And clearly Hornblower's arrival, breaking the thread of their conversation, constituted for them a signal for their departure.

"Lady Barbara has been telling me all about your voyage," said Lady Manningtree, buttoning her gloves. "I think you deserve a world of thanks for the care you have taken of her."

The kind hearted old lady was one of those people who can never think evil. She looked round the tiny ugly cabin.

"Nevertheless," she went on, "I think that it is high time that she enjoyed a little more comfort than you can offer her here."

Hornblower managed to gulp out a few words regarding the superior arrangements for passengers on board a luxurious Indiaman.

"I don't mean to imply that it is your fault, Captain," protested Lady Manningtree, hastily. "I'm sure your ship is a very beautiful ship. A frigate, isn't it? But frigates were never made to carry females, and that's all one can say. And now we must say goodbye, Captain. I hope we may have the pleasure of receiving you on the *Hanbury Castle* later. There will be sure to be opportunities during this very tedious voyage home. Goodbye, Captain."

Hornblower bowed and allowed her to pass before him. Lady Barbara followed.

"Goodbye," she said. Hornblower bowed again as she went down in a curtsey. He was looking straight at her, but somehow he could see no detail of her face — only a white blur.

"Thank you for all your kindness," said Lady Barbara.

The barge left the ship's side, and rowed steadily away. She was all blurred, too, a vague patch of red and gold. Hornblower found Bush beside him.

"The victualling officer's signalling, sir," he said.

Hornblower's duties were clamouring for his attention. As he turned away from the ship's side to plunge into them he found himself, idiotically, remembering that in two months' time or so he would be seeing Maria again. He felt vaguely glad about that before it passed out of his mind again. He felt he would be happy with Maria. Overhead the sun was shining brightly, and before him rose the steep green slopes of St. Helena.

Ship of the Line

The *Sutherland*–Ship of the Line

Chapter I

CAPTAIN HORATIO HORNBLOWER was reading a smudgy proof which the printers had just sent round to his lodgings.

"To all Young Men of *Spirit*," he read. "Seamen, Landsmen, and Boys, who wish to strike a Blow for Freedom and to cause the Corsican Tyrant to wish that he had never dared the Wrath of these British Isles. His Majesty's Ship *Sutherland* of two decks and seventy four guns is at present commissioning at Plymouth, and a few *Vacancies* still exist to complete her Crew. Captain *Horatio Hornblower* in command has lately returned from a Cruize in the *South Sea* during which in command of the Frigate *Lydia* of thirty six guns, he engaged and *sank* the Spanish vessel *Natividad* of two decks and more than *twice the force*. The Officers, Petty Officers, and Men of the *Lydia* have all joined him in the *Sutherland*. What Heart of Oak can resist this Appeal to Join this Band of Heroes and Share with them the new Glories which await them? Who will teach Monsieur *Jean Crapaud* that the Seas are *Britannia's* where no Frog-eating *Frenchman* can show his Face? Who wishes for a Hatful of Golden Louis d'or for *Prize money?* There will be *Fiddlers* and *Dancing* every evening, and Provision at *sixteen* ounces to the Pound, the Best of Beef, the Best of Bread, and *Grog* at midday every Day of the Week and *Sundays*, all in addition to the *Pay* under the *Warrant* of His Most Gracious Majesty King *George!* In the *Place* where this notice is read can be found an Officer of His Majesty's Ship *Sutherland* who will enlist any *Willing Hearts* who Thirst for Glory."

Captain Hornblower struggled against hopelessness as he read the proof. Appeals of this sort were to be read in dozens in every market town. It hardly seemed likely that he could attract recruits to a humdrum ship of the line when dashing frigate captains of twice his reputation were scouring the country and able to produce figures of prize money actually won in previous voyages. To send four lieutenants, each with half a dozen men, round the southern counties to gather recruits in accordance with this poster was going to cost him practically all the pay he had accumulated last commission, and he feared lest it should be money thrown away.

Yet something had to be done. The *Lydia* had supplied him with two hundred able-bodied seamen (his placard said nothing of the fact that they had been compulsorily transferred without a chance of setting foot on English soil after a commission of two years' duration) but to complete his crew he needed another fifty seamen and two hundred landsmen and boys. The guardship had found him none at all. Failure to complete his crew might mean the loss of his command, and from that would result unemployment and half-pay — eight shillings a day — for the rest of his life. He could form no estimate at all of with how much favour he was regarded at the Admiralty, and in the absence of data it was natural to him to believe that his employment hung precariously in the balance.

Anxiety and strain brought oaths to his lips as he tapped on the proof with his pencil — silly blasphemies of whose senselessness he was quite well aware even as he mouthed them. But he was careful to speak softly; Maria was resting in the bedroom through the double doors behind him, and he did not want to rouse her. Maria (although it was too early to be certain) believed herself to be pregnant, and Hornblower was sated with her cloying tenderness. His irritation increased at the thought of it; he hated the land, the necessity of recruiting, the stuffy sitting-room, the loss of the independence he had enjoyed during the months of his last commission. Irritably he took his hat and stole quietly out. The printer's messenger was waiting, hat in hand, in the hall. To him Hornblower abruptly handed back the proof with a curt order for one gross of placards to be struck off, and then he made his way into the noisy streets.

The toll keeper at the Halfpenny Gate Bridge at sight of his uniform let him through without payment; a dozen watermen at the ferry knew him as the Captain of the *Sutherland* and competed to catch his eye — they could expect an ample fee for rowing a Captain to his ship up the long length of the Hamoaze. Hornblower took his seat in a pair-oared wherry; it gave him some satisfaction to say no word at all as they shoved off and began the long pull through the tangle of shipping. Stroke oar shifted his quid and was about to utter some commonplace or other to his passenger, but at sight of his black brow and ill-tempered frown he thought better of it and changed his opening word to a self-conscious cough — Hornblower, acutely aware of the byplay although he had spared the man no open glance, lost some of his ill temper as a result. He noticed the play of muscles in the brown forearms as the man strained at his oar; there was tattooing on the wrist, and a thin gold ring gleamed in the man's left ear. He must have been a seaman before he became a waterman — Hornblower longed inexpressibly to have him haled on board when they should reach the *Sutherland;* if he could only lay his hands on a few dozen prime seamen his anxiety would be at an end. But the fellow of course would have a certificate of exemption, else he would never be able to ply his trade here in a part where a quarter of the British Navy came seeking for men.

The victualling yard and the dockyard as they rowed past were swarming with men, too, all of them able-bodied, and half of them seamen — shipwrights and riggers — at whom Hornblower stared as longingly and as helplessly as a cat at goldfish in a bowl. The rope walk and the mast house, the sheer hulk and the smoking chimneys of the biscuit bakery went slowly by. There was the *Sutherland,* riding to her moorings off Bull Point; Hornblower, as he gazed at her across the choppy water, was conscious of a queer admixture of conservative dislike in the natural pride which he felt in his new command. Her round bow looked odd at a time when every British-built ship of the line had the beak head to which his eye had long grown accustomed; her lines were ungainly and told their tale (as Hornblower noticed every time he looked at her) of more desirable qualities sacrificed for shallow draught. Everything about her — save for the lower masts which were of English origin — proved that she was Dutch-built, planned to negotiate the mud banks and shallow estuaries of the Dutch coast. The *Sutherland,* in fact, had once been the Dutch

74 *Eendracht,* captured off the Texel, and, now rearmed, the ugliest and least desirable two-decker in the Navy List.

God help him, thought Hornblower, eyeing her with a distaste accentuated by his lack of men to man her, if ever he should find himself trying to claw off a lee shore in her. She would drift off to leeward like a cocked-hat paper boat. And at the subsequent courtmartial nobody would believe a word of the evidence regarding her unweatherly qualities.

"Easy!" he snapped at the wherrymen, and the oars ceased to grind in the rowlocks as the men rested; the sound of the waves slapping the sides of the boat became suddenly more apparent.

As they drifted over the dancing water Hornblower continued his discontented examination. She was newly painted, but in as niggardly a fashion as the dockyard authorities could manage — the dull yellow and black was unrelieved by any white or red. A wealthy captain and first lieutenant would have supplied the deficiency out of their own pockets, and would have shown a lick of gold leaf here and there, but Hornblower had no money to spare for gold leaf, and he knew that Bush, who kept four sisters and a mother on his pay, had none either — not even though his professional future depended in some part on the appearance of the *Sutherland.* Some captains would by hook or by crook have cozened more paint — gold leaf too, for that matter — out of the dockyard, as Hornblower ruefully told himself. But he was not good at cozening; not the prospect of all the gold leaf in the world could lead him to slap a dockyard clerk on the back and win his favour with flattery and false bonhomie; not that his conscience would stop him, but his self-consciousness would.

Someone on deck had spied him now. He could hear the pipes twittering as preparations were made to receive him. Let 'em wait a bit longer; he was not going to be hurried today. The *Sutherland*, riding high without her stores in her, was showing a wide streak of her copper. That copper was new, thank God. Before the wind the ugly old ship might show a pretty turn of speed. As the wind swung her across the tide she revealed her run to him. Looking over her lines, Hornblower occupied his mind with estimates of how to get the best performance out of her.

Twenty two years of seagoing experience helped him. Before his mind's eye he called up a composite diagram of all the forces that would be at work on her at sea — the pressure of the wind on her sails, the rudder balancing the headsails, the lateral resistance of the keel, the friction of the skin, the impact of waves against her bows. Hornblower sketched out a preliminary trial arrangement, deciding just how (until practical tests gave him more data) he would have the masts raked and the ship trimmed. But next moment he remembered bitterly that at present he had no crew to man her, and that unless he could find one all these plans would be useless.

"Give way," he growled to the wherrymen, and they threw their weight on the oars again.

"Easy, Jake," said bow oar to stroke, looking over his shoulder.

The wherry swung round under the *Sutherland's* stern — trust those men to know how a boat should be laid alongside a ship of war — giving Hornblower a sight of the stern gallery which constituted to Hornblower one of the most attractive points about the ship. He was glad that the dockyard had not done away with it, as they had done in so many ships of the line. Up in that gallery he would be able to enjoy wind and sea and sun, in a privacy unattainable on deck. He would have a hammock chair made for use there. He could even take his exercise there, with no man's eye upon him — the gallery was eighteen feet long, and he would only have to stoop a little under the overhanging cove. Hornblower yearned inexpressibly for the time when he would be out at sea, away from all the harassing troubles of the land, walking his stern gallery in the solitude in which alone he could relax nowadays. Yet without a crew all this blissful prospect was withheld from him indefinitely. He must find men somewhere.

He felt in his pockets for silver to pay the boatmen, and although silver was woefully short his self-consciousness drove him into overpaying the men in the fashion he attributed to his fellow captains of ships of the line.

"Thank 'ee, sir. Thank 'ee," said stroke oar, knuckling his forehead.

Hornblower went up the ladder and came in through the entry

port with its drab paint where in the Dutchmen's time gilding had blazed bravely. The pipes of the boatswain's mates twittered wildly, the marine guard presented arms, the side boys stood rigidly at attention. Gray, master's mate, — lieutenants kept no watch in harbour, — was officer of the watch and saluted as Hornblower touched his hat to the quarterdeck. Hornblower did not condescend to speak to him, although Gray was a favourite of his; the rigid guard he kept on himself for fear of unnecessary loquacity forbade. Instead he looked round him silently.

The decks were tangled with gear as the work of rigging the ship proceeded, but the tangle, as Hornblower was careful to note, carried under its surface the framework of orderliness. The coils of rope, the groups at work on the deck, the sailmaker's party sewing at a topsail on the forecastle, gave an impression of confusion, but it was disciplined confusion. The severe orders which he had issued to his officers had borne fruit. The crew of the *Lydia*, when they had heard that they were to be transferred bodily to the *Sutherland* without even a day on shore, had nearly mutinied. They were in hand again now.

"Master-at-arms wishes to report, sir," said Gray.

"Send for him, then," answered Hornblower.

The master-at-arms was the warrant officer responsible for enforcing discipline, and was a man new to Hornblower, named Price. Hornblower concluded that he had allegations of indiscipline to lodge, and he sighed even while he set his face in an expression of merciless rigidity. Probably it would be a matter of flogging, and he hated the thought of the blood and the agony. But, at the beginning of a commission like this, with a restive crew under his orders, he must not hesitate to flog if necessary — to have the skin and flesh stripped from the offender's backbone.

Price was coming along the gangway now at the head of the strangest procession. Two by two behind him came a column of thirty men, each one handcuffed to his neighbour, save for the last two who clanked drearily along with leg irons at their ankles. Nearly all of them were in rags, and the rags had no sort of nautical flavour about them at all. The rags of a great many of them were sacking, some had corduroy, and Hornblower, peering closer, saw that one wore the wrecks of a pair of moleskin breeches. Yet another wore the remains of what had once been a respectable black broadcloth suit — white skin showed through a rent in the shoulder. All of them had stubbly beards, black, brown, golden, and grey, and those who were not bald had great mops of tangled hair. The two ship's corporals brought up the rear.

" 'Alt," ordered Price. "Orf 'ats."

The procession shuffled to a halt, and the men stood sullenly on the quarterdeck. Some of them kept their eyes on the deck, while the others gaped sheepishly round them.

"What the devil's all this?" demanded Hornblower, sharply.

"New 'ands, sir," said Price. "I signed a receipt to the sodgers what brought 'em, sir."

"Where did they bring them from?" rasped Hornblower.

"Exeter assizes, sir," said Price, producing a list. "Poachers, four of 'em. Waites, that's 'im in the moleskin breeches, sir, 'e was found guilty of sheepstealing. That 'un in black, 'is crime's bigamy, sir — 'e was a brewer's manager before this 'appened to 'im. The others is larceny mostly, sir, 'cept for them two in front what's in for rick burning and t'other two in irons. Robbery with violence is what they done."

"Ha — h'm," said Hornblower, wordless for the moment. The new hands blinked at him, some with hope in their eyes, some with hatred, some with indifference. They had chosen service at sea rather than the gallows, or transportation, or the gaol. Months in prison awaiting trial accounted for their dilapidated appearance. Here was a fine addition to the ship's company, thought Hornblower, bitterly — budding mutineers, sullen skulkers, half-witted yokels. But hands they were and he must make the most of them. They were frightened, sullen, resentful. It would be worth trying to win their affection. His naturally humanitarian instincts dictated the course he decided to pursue after a moment's quick thinking.

"Why are they still handcuffed?" he demanded, loud enough for them all to hear. "Release them at once."

"Begging your pardon, sir," apologised Price. "I didn't want to without orders, sir, seeing what they are and 'ow they come 'ere."

"That's nothing to do with it," snapped Hornblower. "They're enlisted in the King's service now. And I'll have no man in irons in *my* ship unless he's given *me* cause to order it."

Hornblower kept his gaze from wavering towards the new hands, and steadily addressed his declamation to Price — it was more effective delivered that way, he knew, even while he despised himself for using such rhetorical tricks.

"I never want to see new hands in the charge of the master-at-arms again," he continued, hotly. "They are recruits in an honourable service, with an honourable future before them. I'll thank you to see to it another time. Now find one of the purser's mates and see that each of these men is properly dressed in accordance with my orders."

Normally it might be harmful to discipline to rate a subordinate officer in front of the men, but in the case of the master-at-arms Hornblower knew that little damage was being done. The men would come to hate the master-at-arms anyway sooner or later — his privileges of rank and pay were given him so that he might be a whipping boy for the crew's discontent. Hornblower could drop the rasp from his voice and address the hands directly, now.

"A man who does his duty as best he can," he said, kindly, "has nothing to fear in this ship, and everything to hope for. Now I want to see how smart you can look in your new clothes, and with the dirt of the place you have come from washed off you. Dismiss."

He had won over some of the poor fools, at least, he told himself. Some of the faces which had been sullen with despair were shining with hope now, after this experience of being treated as men and not as brutes — for the first time for months, if not the first time in their lives. He watched them off the gangway. Poor devils; in Hornblower's opinion they had made a bad bargain in exchanging the gaol for the navy. But at least they represented thirty out of the two hundred and fifty additional human bodies which he needed to drag at ropes and to heave at capstan bars so as to take this old *Sutherland* out to sea.

Lieutenant Bush came hastening onto the quarterdeck, and touched his hat to his captain. The stern swarthy face with its incongruous blue eyes broke into a smile just as incongruous. It gave Hornblower a queer twinge, almost of conscience, to see the evident pleasure which Bush experienced at sight of him. It was odd to know that he was admired — it might even be said that he was loved — by this very capable sailor, this splendid disciplinarian and fearless fighter who boasted so many of the good qualities in which Hornblower felt himself to be lacking.

"Good morning, Bush," he said. "Have you seen the new draft?"

"No, sir. I was rowing guard for the middle watch and I've only just turned out. Where do they hail from, sir?"

Hornblower told him, and Bush rubbed his hands with pleasure.

"Thirty!" he said. "That's rare. I never hoped for more than a dozen from Exeter assizes. And Bodmin assizes open today. Please God we get another thirty there."

"We won't get topmen from Bodmin assizes," said Hornblower, comforted beyond measure at the equanimity with which Bush regarded the introduction of gaolbirds into the *Sutherland's* crew.

"No, sir. But the West India convoy's due this week. The guards ought to nab two hundred there. We'll get twenty if we get our rights."

"M'm," said Hornblower, and turned away uneasily. He was not the sort of captain — neither the distinguished kind nor the wheedling kind — who could be sure of favours from the Port Admiral. "I must look round below."

That changed the subject effectively enough.

"The women are restless," said Bush. "I'd better come too, sir, if you don't object."

The lower gun deck offered a strange spectacle, lit vaguely by the light which came through half a dozen open gun ports. There were fifty women there. Three or four were still in their hammocks, lying on their sides looking out on the others. Some were sitting in groups on the deck, chattering loud-voiced. One or two were chaffering for food through the gun ports with the occupants of shore boats floating just outside; the netting which impeded desertion had a broad enough mesh to allow a hand to pass through. Two more, each backed by a supporting group, were quarrelling violently. They were in odd contrast — one was tall and dark, so tall as to have to crouch round-shouldered under the five-foot deck beams, while the other, short, broad, and fair, was standing up boldly before her menacing advance.

"That's what I said," she maintained stoutly. "And I'll say it again. I ain't afeared o' *you*, Mrs. Dawson, as you call yourself."

"A-ah," screamed the dark one at this crowning insult. She swooped forward, and with greedy hands she seized the other by the hair, shaking her head from side to side as if she would soon shake it off. In return her face was scratched and her shins were kicked by her stout-hearted opponent. They whirled round in a flurry of petticoats, when one of the women in the hammocks screamed warning to them.

"Stop it, you mad bitches! 'Ere's the cap'n."

They fell apart, panting and tousled. Every eye was turned towards Hornblower as he walked forward in the patchy light, his head bowed under the deck above.

"The next woman fighting will be put ashore instantly," growled Hornblower.

The dark woman swept her hair from her eyes and sniffed with disdain.

"You needn't put *me* ashore, cap'n," she said. "I'm goin'. There ain't a farden to be had out o' this starvation ship."

She was apparently expressing a sentiment which was shared by a good many of the women, for the speech was followed by a little buzz of approval.

"Ain't the men *never* goin' to get their pay notes?" piped up the woman in the hammock.

"Enough o' that," roared Bush, suddenly. He pushed forward, anxious to save his captain from the insults to which he was exposed, thanks to a government which left its men still unpaid after a month in port. "You there, what are you doing in your hammock after eight bells?"

But this attempt to assume a counter offensive met with disaster.

"I'll come out if you like, Mr. Lieutenant," said she, flicking off her blanket and sliding to the deck. "I parted with my gown to buy my Tom a sausage, and my petticoat's bought him a soop o'

West Country ale. Would you have me on deck in my shift, Mr. Lieutenant?"

A titter went round the deck.

"Get back and be decent," spluttered Bush, on fire with embarrassment.

Hornblower was laughing too — perhaps it was because he was married that the sight of a half-naked woman alarmed him not nearly as much as it did his first lieutenant.

"Never will I be decent now," said the woman, swinging her legs up into the hammock and composedly draping the blanket over herself, "until my Tom gets his pay warrant."

"An' when he gets it," sneered the fair woman, "what can he do with it without shore leave? Sell it to a bumboat shark for a quarter!"

"Fi' pound for twenty three months' pay!" added another. "An' me a month gone a'ready."

"Avast, there," said Bush.

Hornblower beat a retreat, abandoning — forgetting, rather — the object of his visit of inspection below. He could not face those women when the question of pay came up again. The men had been scandalously badly treated, imprisoned in the ship within sight of land, and their wives (some of them certainly were wives, although by Admiralty regulation a simple verbal declaration of the existence of a marriage was sufficient to allow them on board) had just cause of complaint. No one, not even Bush, knew that the few guineas which had been doled out among the crew represented a large part of Hornblower's accumulated pay — all he could spare, in fact, except for the necessary money to pay his officers' expenses when they should start on their recruiting journeys.

His vivid imagination and absurd sensitiveness between them perhaps exaggerated part of the men's hardships. The thought of the promiscuity of life below decks, where a man was allotted eighteen inches' width in which to swing his hammock, while his wife was allowed the eighteen inches next to him, all in a long row, husbands, wives, and single men, appalled him. So did the thought of women having to live on the revolting lower-deck food. Possibly he made insufficient allowance for the hardening effect of long habit.

He emerged through the fore hatchway onto the main deck a little unexpectedly. Thompson, one of the captains of the forecastle, was dealing with the new hands.

"P'raps we'll make sailors of you," he was saying, "and p'raps we won't. Overside with a shot at your feet, more likely, before we sight Ushant. And a waste o' good shot, too. Come on wi' that pump, there. Let's see the colour o' your hides, gaolbirds. When the cat gets at you we'll see the colour o' your backbones, too, you ——"

"Enough of that, Thompson," roared Hornblower, furious.

In accordance with his standing orders the new hands were being treated to rid them of vermin. Naked and shivering, they were grouped about the deck. Two of them were having their heads shorn down to the bare skin; a dozen of them, who had already submitted to this treatment (and looking strangely sickly and out of place with the prison pallor still on them), were being herded by Thompson towards the wash-deck pump which a couple of grinning hands were working. Fright was making them shiver as much as cold — not one of them, probably, had ever had a bath before, and what with that prospect, and Thompson's blood-curdling remarks, and the strange surroundings, they were pitiful to see.

It enraged Hornblower, who somehow or other had never forgotten the misery of his early days at sea. Bullying was abhorrent to him like any other sort of wanton cruelty, and he had no sympathy whatever with the aim of so many of his brother officers, to break the spirit of the men under them. One of these days his professional reputation and his future might depend on these very men risking their lives cheerfully and willingly — sacrificing them, if need be — and he could not imagine cowed and broken-spirited men doing that. The shearing and the bath were necessary, if the ship was to be kept clear of the fleas and bugs and lice which could make life a misery on board, but he was not going to have his precious men cowed more than was unavoidable. It was curious that Hornblower, who never could believe himself to be a leader of men, would always lead rather than drive.

"Under the pump with you, men," he said, kindly, and when they still hesitated, "When we get to sea you'll see *me* under that pump, every morning at seven bells. Isn't that so, there?"

"Aye aye, sir," chorused the hands at the pump — their captain's strange habit of having cold sea water pumped over him every morning had been a source of much discussion on board the *Lydia*.

"So under with you, and perhaps you'll all be captains one of these days. You, there, Waites, show these others you're not afraid."

It was blessed good fortune that Hornblower was able not only to remember the name, but to recognise in his new guise Waites, the sheepstealer with the moleskin breeches. They blinked at this resplendent captain in his gold lace, whose tone was cheerful and whose dignity still admitted taking a daily bath. Waites steeled himself to dive under the spouting hose, and, gasping, rotated heroically under the cold water. Someone threw him a lump of holystone with which to scrub himself, while the others jostled for their turn; the poor fools were like sheep — it was only necessary to set one moving to make all the rest eager to follow.

Hornblower caught sight of a red angry welt across one white shoulder. He beckoned Thompson out of earshot.

"You've been free with that starter of yours, Thompson," he said.

Thompson grinned uneasily, fingering the two-foot length of rope knotted at the end, with which petty officers were universally accustomed to stimulate the activity of the men under them.

"I won't have a petty officer in my ship," said Hornblower, "who doesn't know when to use a starter and when not to. These men haven't got their wits about 'em yet, and hitting 'em won't remedy it. Make another mistake like that, Thompson, and I'll disrate you. And then you'll clean out the heads of this ship every day of this commission. That'll do."

Thompson shrank away, abashed by the genuine anger which Hornblower had displayed.

"Keep your eye on him, Mr. Bush, if you please," added Hornblower. "Sometimes a reprimand makes a petty officer take it out of the men more than ever to pay himself back. And I won't have it."

"Aye aye, sir," said Bush, philosophically.

Hornblower was the only captain he had ever heard of who bothered his head about the use of starters. Starters were as much part of Navy life as bad food and eighteen inches per hammock and peril at sea. Bush could never understand Hornblower's disciplinary methods. He had been positively horrified when he had heard his captain's public admission that he too had baths under the wash-deck pump — it seemed madness for a captain to allow his men to guess that they were of the same flesh as his. But two years under Hornblower's command had taught him that Hornblower's strange ways sometimes attained surprising results. He was ready to obey him, loyally though blindly, resigned and yet admiring.

Chapter II

"THE boy from the Angel has brought a note, sir," said the landlady, when Hornblower called her in in reply to her knock at the sitting-room door. "He waits an answer."

Hornblower felt a shock as he read the address — the clear feminine handwriting which he recognised although it was months since he saw it last meant so much to him. He tried to disguise his feelings as he spoke to his wife.

"It is addressed to both of us, my dear," he said. "Shall I open it?"

"As you please," said Maria.

Hornblower broke the wafer and unfolded the note.

The Angel Inn,
Plymouth.
Fourth May 1810.

Rear Admiral Sir Percy and Lady Barbara Leighton would esteem it an Honour if Captain and Mrs. Horatio Hornblower would dine with them at this address Tomorrow, the Fifth, at four o'clock.

"The Admiral is at the Angel. He wants us to dine with him tomorrow," said Hornblower, as casually as his beating heart would allow. "Lady Barbara is with him. I think we must accept, my dear."

He passed the note over to his wife.

"I have only my blue sack gown," said Maria, looking up from reading it.

The first thing a woman ever thought about on receiving an invitation was what she should wear. Hornblower tried to bend his mind to the consideration of the blue sack gown, when all the time his heart was singing songs at the knowledge that Lady Barbara was only two hundred yards away.

"It looks perfect on you, my dear," he said. "You know how much I have always liked it."

It would call for a far better gown to look well on Maria's dumpy figure. But Hornblower knew that they must — they *must* — accept the invitation, and it would be a kindness to reassure Maria. It did not matter what clothes Maria wore as long as she thought she looked well in them. Maria smiled happily at the compliment, giving Hornblower a prick of conscience. He felt like Judas. Maria would look coarse and badly dressed and stupid beside Lady Barbara, and yet he knew that as long as he pretended to be in love with her she would be happy and unconscious.

He wrote a careful acceptance, and rang the bell for it to be given to the messenger. Then he buttoned his uniform coat.

"I must go down to the ship," he said.

Maria's reproachful look hurt him. He knew that she had been looking forward to spending the afternoon with him, and indeed he had not intended to visit the ship that day. It was only an excuse to gain privacy for himself. He could not bear the thought of being mewed up in that sitting-room with Maria and her platitudes. He wanted to be alone, to hug to himself the thought that Lady Barbara was in the same town, that he was going to see her tomorrow. He could not sit still with those thoughts bubbling within him. He could have sung for joy as he walked briskly down to the ferry, thrusting aside all remembrance of Maria's dutiful acquiescence in his departure — well she knew how great were the demands made upon a captain by the commissioning of a ship of the line.

In his yearning for solitude he urged the rowers of his boat until they sweated. On deck he gave the briefest of salutes to the quarterdeck and to the officer of the watch, before plunging below to the security and peace for which he had been yearning. There were a hundred matters to which he could have devoted his attention but he would not stay for one of them. He strode across his cabin — littered with the preparations made for when he should come on board — and out through the stern window into the great stern gallery. There, sheltered from all interruption, he could lean against the rail, and stare across the water.

The ebb was running, and with the wind light from the north-east the *Sutherland's* stern gallery looked southward down the length of the Hamoaze. To his left lay the dockyard, as busy as a beehive. Before him the glittering water was studded with shipping, with shore boats rowing hither and thither. In the distance beyond the roofs of the victualling yard he could see Mount Edgecumbe — Plymouth was out of his sight, round the corner from the Devil's Point; he would not have the satisfaction of gazing upon the roof that sheltered Lady Barbara.

Still, she was there, and he would see her tomorrow. He gripped the rail in his ecstasy until his fingers hurt him. He turned away and began to walk up and down the gallery, his hands behind his back to counterbalance the stoop necessitated by the cove above. The pain he had felt at first, three weeks back, when he had heard of Lady Barbara's marriage to Admiral Leighton was gone by now. There was only the joy in the thought that she still remembered him. Hornblower dallied with the idea that she might have travelled down to Plymouth with her husband in the expectation of seeing him. It was possible — Hornblower would not stop to think that she might have been influenced by the desire to spend a few more days with her new husband. She must have cajoled Sir Percy into sending this invitation on the moment of his arrival; Hornblower would not make allowance for the fact that any admiral must be anxious for an early opportunity to study an unknown captain placed under his command. She must have made Sir Percy ask at the Admiralty for his services — that would explain why they had found for him a new ship and a new command without a single month's interval of half-pay. It was to Lady Barbara that he owed the very comforting addition of ten shillings a day to his pay which went with the command of a ship of the line.

He was a quarter of the way up the captains' list now. In less than twenty years' time — long before he was sixty — if he continued to obtain commands in this fashion he would hoist his flag as an admiral. Then they might yellow him if they wanted to; he would be satisfied with admiral's rank. On admiral's half-pay he could live in London, find a patron who would nominate him to a seat in Parliament. He would know power, and dignity, and security. All this was possible — and Lady Barbara still remembered him, cherished a kindly thought of him, was anxious to see him again despite the ludicrous way in which he had behaved towards her. High spirits bubbled within him again.

A sea gull, wheeling motionless up wind, suddenly flapped its wings until it hovered stationary, and screamed raucously in his face. It flapped and screamed aimlessly along the gallery, and then, equally aimlessly, wheeled away again. Hornblower followed it with his eyes, and when he resumed his walk the thread of his thoughts was broken. Instantly there loomed up again into his consciousness the knowledge of the frightful need of men under which he laboured. Tomorrow he would have to confess miserably to his admiral that the *Sutherland* was still a hundred and fifty men short of complement; he would be found wanting in the very first of a captain's duties. An officer might be the finest possible seaman, the most fearless fighter (and Hornblower did not think himself either), and yet his talents were useless if he could not man his ship.

Probably Leighton had never asked for his services at all, and he had been allotted to Leighton's squadron by some trick of fate. Leighton would suspect him of having been his wife's lover, would be consumed with jealousy, and would watch for every opportunity to achieve his ruin. He would make his life a misery to him, would plague him to madness, and would finally have him broken and dismissed the service — any admiral could break any captain if he set his mind to it. Perhaps Lady Barbara had planned to put him thus in Leighton's power, and was working his ruin in revenge for his treatment of her. That seemed much more likely than his earlier wild imaginings, thought Hornblower, the cold fit working on him.

She must have guessed just what Maria was like, and must have sent the invitation so as to have the pleasure of gloating over her weaknesses. The dinner tomorrow would be one long humiliation for him. He could not venture to draw on his next quarter's pay for another ten days at least; otherwise he would have taken Maria out to buy her the finest gown in Plymouth — although what would a Plymouth gown avail in the sight of an earl's daughter who would undoubtedly buy all her clothes from Paris? He had not twenty pounds in the whole world now, having sent Bush and Gerard and Rayner and Hooker, his four lieutenants, out to drum up recruits. They had taken thirty men with them, the only trustworthy men in the whole ship, too. Probably there would be trouble on the lower deck in consequence — probably reaching a head tomorrow while he was dining with his admiral.

Gloomy anticipation could go no farther than that. He jerked his head up with irritation, and hit it hard against one of the beams of the cove above. Then he clenched his fists and cursed the service, as he had cursed it a thousand times before. That made him laugh at himself — if Hornblower had never been able to laugh at himself he would have been, long ago, another of the mad captains in the Navy List. He took a firmer grip on his emotions and set himself to thinking seriously about the future.

The orders which had attached him to Admiral Leighton's squadron had stated briefly that he was destined for service in the Western Mediterranean, and it was an uncovenanted mercy on the part of the lords of the Admiralty to give him that much warning. He had known of captains who had laid in personal stores in the expectation of service in the West Indies only to find that they had been allotted to the Baltic convoy. The Western Mediterranean meant the Toulon blockade, the protection of Sicily, harassing the Genoese coasters, and, presumably, taking a hand in the war in Spain. It meant a more variegated life than the blockade of Brest, at least, although now that Spain was England's ally there would be far less chance of prize money.

His ability to speak Spanish seemed to make it certain that the *Sutherland* would be employed on the coast of Catalonia in concert with the Spanish army. Lord Cochrane had distinguished himself there, but Cochrane was under a cloud now. The courts-martial which had followed the action in the Basque Roads were still echoing through the service, and Cochrane would be lucky if he ever got another ship — he was the standing example of the folly of an officer on the active list taking part in politics. Perhaps, thought Hornblower, trying to combat both optimism and pessimism simultaneously, he was intended by the Admiralty to supply Cochrane's place. If that were the case, it meant that his professional reputation was far higher than he dared believe. Hornblower had to battle sternly with his feelings at that thought; he found himself grinning when he warned himself that excess of emotion only resulted in his hitting his head on the beams above.

That quieted him, and he began to tell himself, philosophically, that all this anticipation was merely waste of effort; he would know sooner or later anyway, and all the worrying in the world would not alter his destiny a ha'p'orth. There were a hundred and twenty British ships of the line at sea, and nearly two hundred frigates, and in every one of these three hundred and twenty ships there was a port captain, each one a god to his crew, and presumably each one a puppet to the Admiralty. He must act like a sensible man, empty his mind of all these imaginings, and go home and spend a quiet evening with his wife untroubled by thoughts of the future.

Yet even as he left the stern gallery to pass the word for his gig to take him back a new wave of delirious anticipation surged through him at the thought of seeing Lady Barbara tomorrow.

Chapter III

"Do I look well?" asked Maria, her toilet completed.

Hornblower was buttoning his full-dress coat as he stood and looked at her; he made himself smile admiringly at her.

"Admirable, my dear," he said. "That gown sets off your figure better than any you have ever worn."

His tact was rewarded by a smile. It was no use speaking the truth to Maria, telling her that that particular shade of blue revolted against the heavy red of her cheeks. With her thick figure and coarse black hair and bad complexion Maria could never appear well dressed. At best she looked like a shopkeeper's wife; at worst like some scrub woman dressed in finery cast off by her mistress. Those stubby red hands of hers, thought Hornblower, looking at them, were very like a scrub woman's.

"I have my Paris gloves," said Maria, noting the direction of his glance. It was the very devil, the way in which she was eager to anticipate every wish of his. It was in his power to hurt her horribly, and the knowledge made him uncomfortable.

"Better and better," he said, gallantly. He stood before the mirror and twitched his coat into position.

"Full dress suits you well," said Maria, admiringly.

Hornblower's first act when he had returned to England in the *Lydia* had been to buy himself new uniforms — there had been humiliating incidents last commission as a result of the poverty of his wardrobe. He eyed himself tolerantly in the glass. This coat was of the finest blue broadcloth. The heavy epaulettes that hung at the shoulders were of real bullion, and so was the broad gold lace round the edges and the buttonholes. Buttons and cuffs flashed as he moved; it was pleasant to see the heavy gold stripes on his cuffs that marked him as a captain with more than three years' seniority. His cravat was of thick China silk. He approved the cut of his white Kerseymere breeches. The thick white silk stockings were the best that he could find — he remembered with a twinge of conscience as he gloated over them that Maria wore concealed under her skirt only cheap cotton stockings at four shillings a pair. From the crown of his head to his ankles he was dressed as a gentleman should be dressed; only about his shoes was he doubtful. Their buckles were merely pinchbeck, and he feared lest their brassiness should be accentuated by contrast with the genuine gold everywhere else — funds had begun to run low when he bought them, and he had not dared spend twenty guineas on gold buckles. He must take care this evening to do nothing to call attention to his feet. It was a pity that the sword of one hundred guineas' value voted him by the Patriotic Fund for his fight with the *Natividad* had not yet reached him. He still had to wear the fifty-guinea sword which had been awarded him eight years ago after the capture of the *Castilla* as a mere lieutenant.

He took up his cocked hat — the button and lace on it were real gold, too — and his gloves.

"Are you ready, my dear?" he asked.

"Quite ready, Horatio," said Maria. She had early learned how he hated unpunctuality, and dutifully took care never to offend in this respect.

The afternoon sunlight in the street sparkled on his gold; a militia subaltern whom they passed saluted him respectfully. Hornblower noted that the lady who hung on the subaltern's arm looked more keenly at Maria than at him, and he thought he read in her glance the pitying amusement he expected. Maria was undoubtedly not the sort of wife one would expect to see on the arm of a distinguished officer. But she was his wife all the same, the friend of his childhood, and the self-indulgent soft-heartedness which had moved him to marry her had to be paid for now. Little Horatio and little Maria had died of the smallpox in a Southsea lodging — he owed her his devotion on account of that if for nothing else. And she thought she was carrying another child of his now. That had been madness, of course, but madness excusable in a man whose heart was torn with jealousy at the news that Lady Barbara was married. Still, it had to be paid for in more devotion to Maria; all his decent instincts as well as his soft-heartedness and irresolution compelled him to remain faithful to her, to give her pleasure, to act as if he were her truly devoted husband.

Nor was that all. His pride would never permit him to make public acknowledgment that he had made a mistake, a silly blunder worthy of any foolish boy. On that account alone, even if he could steel himself to break Maria's heart, he would never come to an open breach with her. Hornblower could remember the lewd comments of the Navy over Nelson's matrimonial affairs, and there were Bowen's and Samson's after that. As long as he held loyally to his wife that kind of thing would never be said about him. People were tolerant of eccentricity while they laughed at weakness. They might marvel at his devotion, but that was all. While he carried himself as if Maria was the only woman in the world for him people would be forced to assume that there was more in her constitution than was apparent to an onlooker.

"It is the Angel to which we are bidden, is it not, my dear?" asked Maria, breaking in on his thoughts.

"Why, yes."

"We have walked straight past it. You did not hear me when I spoke before."

They retraced their steps, and a jolly Devon servant maid led them through into the cool dark depths at the back of the inn. There were several persons in the oak-panelled room into which they were ushered, but for Hornblower there was only one. Lady Barbara was there in a blue silk dress, blue-grey, the exact colour of her eyes. From a gold chain round her neck hung a sapphire pendant, but the sapphires seemed lifeless compared with her glance. Hornblower made his bow, and mumbled as he presented Maria. The fringes of the room seemed to be deep in mist; only Lady Barbara could be clearly seen. The golden sunburn which Hornblower had last seen in her cheeks had disappeared now; her complexion was as creamy white as any great lady's should be.

Hornblower became aware that someone else was speaking to him — had been speaking for some time.

"A most pleasurable occasion, Captain Hornblower," he was saying. "May I present you? Captain Hornblower, Mrs. Elliott. Captain Hornblower, Mrs. Bolton. My flag-captain, Captain

Elliott, of the *Pluto.* And Captain Bolton of the *Caligula,* who tells me he was shipmates with you in the old *Indefatigable.*"

The mists were clearing a little from Hornblower's eyes. He was able to stammer a few words, but fortunately the entrance of the innkeeper with the announcement of dinner gave him a little longer in which to collect himself. It was a circular table at which they were seated. Opposite him sat Bolton, with his ruddy cheeks and open, honest face. Hornblower still felt Bolton's grip lingering on his palm and remembered the horniness of his hand. There was nothing of the elegant world about Bolton, then. Nor was there about Mrs. Bolton, who sat on Hornblower's right, between him and the Admiral. She was as plain and as dowdy as Maria herself — to Hornblower's infinite relief.

"I must congratulate you, Captain, on your appointment to the *Sutherland,*" said Lady Barbara on his left. A breath of perfume was wafted from her as she spoke, and Hornblower's head swam. To smell the scent of her, and to hear her voice again, was like some romantic drug to him. He did not know what he said in reply.

"The innkeeper here," announced the Admiral to the table at large, dipping a ladle into the silver tureen before him, "swore to me that he knew the art of turtle soup, and I entrusted a turtle to his care. God send he spoke the truth. The sherry wine — George, the sherry — I trust you will find tolerable."

Hornblower incautiously took a mouthful of soup far too hot, and the pain he experienced while swallowing it helped to bring him back into reality. He turned his head to study this admiral to whom he would owe obedience for the next two or three years, who had won Lady Barbara's hand in marriage after a courtship that could not have endured more than three weeks. He was tall and heavily built and darkly handsome. The star of the Bath and the red ribbon set off his glittering uniform. In age he could hardly be much over forty — only a year or two older than Hornblower — so that he must have attained to post rank at the earliest age family influence could contrive it. But the perceptible fullness about his jowl indicated to Hornblower's mind either self-indulgence or stupidity; both, perhaps.

So much Hornblower saw in a few seconds' inspection. Then he forced himself to think of his manners, although between Lady Barbara and the Admiral it was hard to think clearly.

"I trust you are enjoying the best of health, Lady Barbara?" he said. A quaint quarterdeck rasp of formality crept into his voice as he tried to hit the exact tone he thought the complicated situation demanded. He saw Maria, on the other side of Captain Elliott beyond Lady Barbara, raise her eyebrows a little — Maria was always sensitive to his reactions.

"Indeed, yes," said Lady Barbara, lightly. "And you, Captain?"

"I have never known Horatio better," said Maria, interposing.

"That is good news," said Lady Barbara, turning towards her. "Poor Captain Elliott here is still shaken sometimes with the ague he acquired at Flushing."

It was deftly done; Maria and Lady Barbara and Elliott were at once engaged in a conversation which left no room for Hornblower. He listened for a moment, and then forced himself to turn to Mrs. Bolton. She had no fund of small talk. "Yes" and "No" were all she could say, seemingly, and the Admiral on her other side was deep in talk with Mrs. Elliott. Hornblower lapsed into gloomy silence. Maria and Lady Barbara continued a conversation from which Elliott soon dropped out, and which was continued across his unresisting body with a constancy which not even the arrival of the next course could interrupt.

"Can I carve you some of this beef, Mrs. Elliott?" asked the Admiral. "Hornblower, perhaps you will be good enough to attend to those ducks before you. Those are neats' tongues, Bolton, a local delicacy — as you know, of course. Will you try them, unless this beef claims your allegiance? Elliott, tempt the ladies with that ragout. They may be partial to foreign kickshaws — made dishes are not to my taste. On the sideboard there is a cold beefsteak pie which the landlord assures me is exactly like those on which his reputation is founded, and a mutton ham such as one only finds in Devonshire. Mrs. Hornblower? Barbara, my dear?"

Hornblower, carving the ducks, felt a real pain in his breast at this casual use of the Christian name which was sacred to him.

For a moment it impeded his neat dissection of long strips from the ducks' breasts. With an effort he completed his task, and, as no one else at table seemed to want roast duck, he took for himself the plateful he had carved. It saved him from having to meet anyone's eyes. Lady Barbara and Maria were still talking together. It seemed to his heated imagination as if there was something specially pointed about the way Lady Barbara turned her shoulder to him. Perhaps Lady Barbara had decided that it was a poor compliment to her that he should have loved her, now that she had discovered the crudity of his taste from his choice of a wife. He hoped Maria was not being too stupid and gauche — he could overhear very little of their conversation. He could eat little of the food with which the table was covered — his appetite, always finicking, had quite disappeared. He drank thirstily of the wine which was poured for him until he realised what he was doing, and checked himself; he disliked being drunk even more than overeating. Then he sat and fiddled with his food on his plate, making a pretence at eating; fortunately Mrs. Bolton beside him had a good appetite and was content to be silent while indulging it, as otherwise they would have made a dull pair.

Then the table was swept clear to make room for cheese and dessert.

"Pineapples not as good as we enjoyed at Panama, Captain Hornblower," said Lady Barbara, turning back to him unexpectedly. "But perhaps you will make a trial of them?"

He was almost too flustered to cut the thing with the silver knife, so much was he taken off his guard. He helped her eventually, awkwardly. Now that he had her attention again he longed to talk to her, but the words would not come — or rather, seeing that what he found he wanted to ask her was whether she liked married life, while he just had enough sense not to blurt out that question, he did not have enough to substitute another for it.

"Captain Elliott and Captain Bolton," she said, "have been plying me incessantly with questions about the battle between the *Lydia* and the *Natividad*. Most of them were of too technical a nature for me to answer, especially, as I told them, since you kept me immured in the orlop where I could see nothing of the fight. But everyone seems to envy me even that experience."

"Her ladyship's right," roared Bolton, across the table — his voice was even louder than when Hornblower had known him as a young lieutenant. "Tell us about it, Hornblower."

Hornblower flushed and fingered his neckcloth, conscious of every eye upon him.

"Spit it out, man," persisted Bolton; no lady's man, and oppressed by the company, he had said hardly a word so far, but the prospect of having the battle described found his tongue for him.

"The Dons put up a better fight than usual?" asked Elliott.

"Well —— " began Hornblower, lured into explaining the conditions in which he had fought. Everybody listened; apt questions from one or other of the men drew him on, bit by bit. Gradually the story unfolded itself, and the loquaciousness against which Hornblower was usually on his guard led him into eloquence. He told of the long duel in the lonely Pacific, the labour and slaughter and agony, up to the moment when, leaning weakly against the quarterdeck rail, he had known triumph at the sight of his beaten enemy sinking in the darkness.

He stopped self-consciously there, hot with the realisation that he had been guilty of the unforgivable sin of boasting of his own achievements. He looked round the table from face to face, expecting to read in them awkwardness or downright disapproval, pity or contempt. It was with amazement that instead he saw expressions which he could only consider admiring. Bolton, over there, who was at least five years his senior as a captain and ten in age, was eyeing him with something like hero worship. Elliott, who had commanded a ship of the line under Nelson, was nodding his massive head with intense appreciation. The admiral, when Hornblower could bring himself to steal a glance at him, was still sitting transfixed. There might possibly be a shade of regret in his dark handsome face that his lifetime in the Navy had brought him no similar opportunity for glory. But the simple heroism of Hornblower's tale had fascinated him too; he stirred himself and met Hornblower's gaze admiringly.

"Here's a toast for us," he said, lifting his glass. "May the captain of the *Sutherland* rival the exploits of the captain of the *Lydia*."

The toast was drunk with a murmur of approval while Hornblower blushed and stammered. The admiration of men whose approval he valued was overwhelming; more especially as now he was beginning to realise that he had won it under false pretences. Only now was the memory returning to him of the sick fear with which he had awaited the *Natividad's* broadsides, the horror of mutilation which had haunted him during the battle. He was one of the contemptible few, not like Leighton and Elliott and Bolton, who had never known fear in their lives. If he had told the whole truth, told of his emotions as well as of the mere manœuvres and incidents of the fight, they would be sorry for him, as for a cripple, and the glory of the *Lydia's* victory would evaporate. His embarrassment was relieved by Lady Barbara's arising from the table and the other women following her example.

"Do not sit too long over your wine," said Lady Barbara, as the men stood for them. "Captain Hornblower is a whist player of renown, and there are cards waiting for us."

Chapter IV

WHEN they walked away from the Angel through the pitch-dark street Maria clung eagerly to Hornblower's arm.

"A delightful evening, my dear," she said. "Lady Barbara seems to be a very genteel person."

"I'm glad you have enjoyed yourself," said Hornblower. He knew only too well that Maria after any party to which he accompanied her delighted in discussing the others who had been present. He shrank from the inevitable dissection of Lady Barbara which was bound to come.

"She has breeding," said Maria, inexorably, "far beyond what I was led to expect by what you had told me about her."

Searching back in his memory Hornblower realised that he had only laid stress on her fine courage and her ability to mix with men without embarrassment. At that time it had pleased Maria to think of an earl's daughter as a masculine hoyden; now she was just as pleased to revert to the traditional attitude, admiring her for her breeding, and being gratified at her condescension.

"She is a very charming woman," he said, cautiously falling in with Maria's mood.

"She asked me if I were going to accompany you on your approaching voyage, and I explained that with the hopes of the future which we were beginning to cherish it was inadvisable."

"You told her *that?*" asked Hornblower sharply. At the last moment he was able to keep the anguish out of his voice.

"She wished me joy," said Maria, "and asked me to give you her fe-felicitations."

It irked Hornblower inexpressibly to think of Maria discussing her pregnancy with Lady Barbara. He would not allow himself to think why. But the thought of Lady Barbara's knowledge was one more complexity in the whirl of thoughts in his mind, and there was no chance of straightening anything out in the course of the short walk to their lodgings.

"Oh," said Maria when they were in their bedroom. "How tight those shoes were!"

She chafed her feet in the white cotton stockings as she sat in the low chair; from the candle on the dressing table her shadow danced on the opposite wall. The shadow of the bed tester lay in a grim black rectangle on the ceiling.

"Hang up that best coat of yours carefully," said Maria, beginning to take the pins out of her hair.

"I'm not ready for sleep," said Hornblower, despairingly.

He felt that no price would be too great to pay at the moment to be able to slip away to the solitude of his ship. But he certainly could not do that; the hour would make such a thing odd and the full dress uniform he wore would make it preposterous.

"Not ready for sleep?" It was so like Maria to repeat his words. "How strange, after this tiring evening! Did you eat too much roast duck?"

"No," said Hornblower. It was hopeless to try to explain a too rapidly working mind to Maria, hopeless to try to escape. Any attempt to do so would only hurt her feelings, and he knew by experience he could never make himself do that. With a sigh he began to unbuckle his sword.

"You have only to compose yourself in bed and you will sleep," said Maria, from her own constant experience. "We have few enough nights together left to us now, darling."

That was so; Admiral Leighton had told them that the *Pluto, Caligula,* and *Sutherland* were ordered to escort as far as the Tagus the East India convoy which was even then assembling. And that raised once more the cursed question of the shortage of men — how the devil was he to complete his crew in time? Bodmin assizes might send him a few more criminals. His lieutenants, due to return any day now, might bring in a few volunteers. But he needed fifty more topmen, and topmen could not be picked up in gaols, nor in market squares.

"It is a hard service," said Maria, thinking of the approaching separation.

"Better than counters at eightpence a week," replied Hornblower, forcing himself to speak lightly.

Before their marriage Maria had taught in a school with graduated fees — readers paid fourpence, writers sixpence, and counters eightpence.

"Indeed, yes," said Maria. "I owe much to you, Horatio. Here's your nightshirt, ready for you. The torment I went through when Miss Wentworth found I had taught Alice Stone the multiplication table although her parents only paid fourpence! And then the ungrateful minx egged that little Hopper boy to let those mice loose in the schoolroom. But I'd suffer it all again, darling, if — if that would keep you near me."

"Not while duty calls, my dear," said Hornblower, diving into his nightshirt. "But I'll be back with a bagful of guineas for prize money before two years are up. Mark my words."

"Two years!" said Maria, pitifully.

Hornblower yawned elaborately, and Maria rose to the bait thus deftly cast, just as Hornblower had been sure she would.

"And you said you were not ready for sleep!" she said.

"It has come upon me now," said Hornblower. "Perhaps the Admiral's port is beginning to take effect. I can hardly keep my eyes open. I shall say 'good night' now, my love."

He kissed her as she sat before the dressing table, and, turning hastily away, he climbed up into the big bed. There, lying on the farthest edge, keeping rigidly still, he lay until Maria had blown out the candle and climbed up beside him, until her breathing grew quiet and regular. Only then could he relax and change position and give rein to the galloping thoughts coursing through his mind.

He remembered what Bolton had said to him with a wink and a nod when they had found themselves together at one time during the evening in a corner where they could not be overheard.

"He means six votes to the Government," said Bolton, jerking his head towards the Admiral.

Bolton was as stupid as a good seaman could be, but he had been in London recently and attended a levee and had heard the gossip. The poor old King was going mad again, a Regency was imminent, and with the Regency the Tories might go out and the Whigs might come in — the six votes of the Leighton interests were valuable. With the Marquis Wellesley as Foreign Secretary, and Henry Wellesley as Ambassador in Spain, and Sir Arthur Wellesley — what was his new title? Lord Wellington of course — as Commander in Chief in the Peninsula it was not surprising to find Lady Barbara Wellesley married to Sir Percy Leighton, and still less to find the latter given a command in the Mediterranean. The virulence of the Opposition was growing day by day, and the history of the world hung in the balance.

Hornblower shifted restlessly in bed at the thought, but a slight movement by Maria in reply fixed him rigid again. It was only a small party of men — the Wellesleys chief among them — who still had the resolution to continue the struggle against the Corsican's dominion. The smallest check, on land, at sea, or in Parliament, might pull them from their high positions, bring their heads perilously near the block, and tumble all Europe into ruin.

Sometime during the evening Lady Barbara had been pouring tea, and Hornblower had found himself standing alone beside her, waiting for his refilled cup.

"It gave me pleasure," she had murmured, "when my husband told me you had been given the *Sutherland*. England needs all her best captains at present."

She must have meant more than she said then. Probably she was hinting at the necessity for maintaining Leighton in his command. It had been no indication, all the same, that she had exerted herself to obtain the appointment for Hornblower. But it was satisfactory to be able to think that she had married Sir Percy for some other reason than love. Hornblower hated the thought of Lady Barbara being in love with anyone. He began to remember every word she had said to her husband, every look she had given him. Certainly she did not seem in the least like an adoring bride. But the fact remained that she was Leighton's wife — that she was in bed with him at this very minute. Hornblower writhed in fresh anguish at the thought.

Then he checked himself. He told himself very sensibly that only misery and madness lay before him if he allowed himself to think about that, and, grasping resolutely at the tail of the first train of thought which recurred to him, he began to analyse the whist he had been playing. If he had not taken that unsuccessful finesse against that lead of Elliott's he would have saved the rubber. His play had been correct — the chances were three to two — but a gambler would not have stopped to consider that. He would have gone baldheaded for results and in this case would have achieved them. But only a gambler could risk a king being unguarded. He prided himself on the precision and science of his play. Nevertheless, he was two guineas the poorer as a result of this evening, and the loss of two guineas was a devilish serious matter at present.

He wanted to buy a litter of pigs and two dozen fowls — a couple of sheep as well, for that matter — before weighing anchor in the *Sutherland*. There was the wine he needed, too. Some he could buy later and more advantageously in the Mediterranean, but it would be well to have five or six dozen on board at the start. The effect on the officers and men might be bad for discipline if he were not provided with every luxury as a captain should be; and if the voyage out were long and lazy he would have to entertain his brother captains — the Admiral, too, most likely — and they would look at him askance if he offered them the ship's fare on which he was content to live. The list of things he needed stretched longer and longer in his imagination. Port, sherry, and Madeira. Apples and cigars. Raisins and cheeses. A dozen at least of shirts. Four more pairs of silk stockings if there was to be much shore-going formality, as seemed likely. A chest of tea. Pepper and cloves and allspice. Prunes and figs. Wax candles. All these things were necessary to his dignity as captain — and to his own pride, for he hated the idea of people thinking him poor.

He could spend all the next quarter's pay on these things and still not have bought too much. Maria would feel the pinch during the next three months, but Maria, fortunately, was used to poverty and to staving off creditors. It was hard on Maria, but if ever he became an admiral he would repay her loyalty with luxury. There were books which he wanted to buy as well; not for entertainment — he had a chest of books, including Gibbon's *Decline and Fall of the Roman Empire* for bedside reading, all old friends — but to fit him for the coming campaign. In the *Morning Chronicle* yesterday there had been a notice of *An Account of the Present*

War in Spain which he would like to have, and there were half a dozen others. The more he knew about the peninsula on whose coast he was going to fight, and of the leaders of the nation he was to help, the better. But books cost money, and he did not know where to turn for money.

He rolled over again and thought of the ill fortune which had always dogged him in the matter of prize money. The Admiralty had refused to pay out a penny on account of the sunk *Natividad*. Since the capture of the *Castilla* when he was a young lieutenant he had never had a windfall, while frigate captains whom he knew had made thousands of pounds. It was maddening — especially as in his present poverty-stricken condition he was hampered in his exertions to complete the *Sutherland's* crew. That shortage of men was the most harassing of all his worries — that and the thought of Lady Barbara in Leighton's arms. Hornblower's thoughts had gone full circle now, and were starting all over again. There was plenty to keep him restless and wakeful all through the weary night, until the dawn began to creep through the curtains; fantastic theories about Lady Barbara's state of mind, and hard-headed plans for making the *Sutherland* efficient for sea.

Chapter V

CAPTAIN HORNBLOWER was walking up and down his quarter-deck amid all the last-minute bustle of getting ready for sea. He was raging to himself at the length of time necessary for these final preparations, although he knew quite well that every factor causing delay was susceptible to a reasonable explanation. Two thirds of the men scurrying about the decks, urged on by the cane of Harrison the boatswain and the rope's ends of the petty officers, were landsmen most of whom until lately had never seen the sea, let alone been in a ship. The simplest order left them merely bewildered, and they had to be led to their tasks and the ropes actually put into their hands; even then they were far more inefficient than trained seamen, because they had not learned the knack of throwing all their weight simultaneously on the rope and walking away with it. And having once set them heaving, it was hard for a petty officer to remember that a shout of "Avast" or "Belay" meant nothing to them. More than once the few trained seamen among them, obeying promptly, were thrown off their feet and trampled upon by the rush of landsmen still heaving away. On one occasion of this sort a water butt while being hove up by a whip to the main yard-arm had simply gone away with a run again, and only the mercy of Providence had saved it from going clean through the bottom of the longboat overside.

It was owing to Hornblower's own orders that the water was so late in being brought aboard. Water left months in cask became so foul and so crawling with living things that he had put off bringing it aboard until the last possible moment. Even a gain of a day or two was desirable. That twelve tons of biscuit had also been delayed was the result of the usual incompetence of the victualling yard, whose officials seemed incapable of reading or writing or figuring. The complication due to the fact that a shore boat with captain's stores was having to be unloaded at the same time, and its precious cargo passed carefully down the after hatchway, was due to the Patriotic Fund's delay in sending down to him the sword value one hundred guineas which he had been awarded for his fight with the *Natividad*. No shopkeeper or ship chandler would give credit to a captain about to sail on a new commission. The sword had only arrived yesterday, barely in time for him to pledge it with Duddingstone the chandler, and Duddingstone had only grudgingly given him credit on it, forcing him to promise faithfully to redeem it at the earliest opportunity.

"A sight too much writing on this for me," said Duddingstone, pointing with a stubby forefinger at the wordy legend which the Patriotic Fund had had engraved, at vast expense, upon the blue steel of the blade.

Only the gold on hilt and scabbard and the seed pearls on the pommel had any intrinsic value. Duddingstone, to give him his due, had been quite right in saying that it was hardly worth forty guineas' credit at his shop, even allowing for his profit and the chance of its being redeemed. But he had kept his word and had sent off the stores at dawn next morning — one more complication in the business of preparing for sea.

Along the gangway Wood the purser was dancing with rage and anxiety.

"God damn and blast all you ham-fisted yokels!" he was saying. "And you, sir, down there. Take that grin off your face and be more careful, or I'll have you clapped under hatches to sail with us today. Easy, there, easy! Christ, rum at seven guineas an anker isn't meant to be dropped like pig iron!"

Wood was supervising the loading of the rum. The old hands were doing their best to make sure that the clumsiness of the new ones would result in the staving of a keg or two, so as to swill from the leaks, and the grinning lightermen overside were abetting them. Hornblower could see by the red faces and uncontrollable hilarity that some of the men had succeeded in getting at the spirits, despite Wood's eagle eye and the marine sentries on guard; but he had no intention of interfering. It would merely compromise his dignity to try to keep sailors from stealing rum if they had the barest opportunity — no one had ever yet succeeded in that task.

From his position of vantage beside the quarterdeck rail he looked down upon a curious bit of byplay on the main deck. A bewildered young giant — a tin miner, Hornblower guessed, from his biceps — had rounded upon Harrison, apparently driven frantic by the volley of orders and blasphemy hurled at him. But Harrison at forty five had fought his way up to boatswain's rank through hundreds of such encounters, and in his prime might have contested for the highest honours of the prize ring. He slipped the Cornishman's clumsy punch and felled him with a crashing blow on the jaw. Then without ceremony he seized him by the scruff of the neck and kicked him across the deck to the tackle which was waiting. Dazed, the Cornishman took hold with the others and heaved with them, while Hornblower nodded approvingly.

The Cornishman had made himself liable to "death, or such less penalty," as the Articles of War said, by raising his hand to his superior officer. But it was not the moment to invoke the Articles of War, even though they had been read over to the Cornishman last night on his compulsory enlistment. Gerard had sailed round with the longboat and had raided Redruth and Camborne and St. Ives, taking each place by surprise and returning with fifty stout Cornishmen who could hardly be expected yet to appreciate the administrative machinery of the service which they had joined. In a month's time, perhaps, when everyone on board would have learnt the heinousness of such an offence, a courtmartial might be needed and a flogging — death, perhaps — but at the present time it was best to do what Harrison had just done, and crack the man on the jaw and set him to work again. Hornblower found time to thank God he was a captain and out of the hurly-burly, for any attempt on his part at cracking men on the jaw would be a lamentable failure, he knew.

He shifted his weight from one leg to the other, and was reminded of the fact that he was horribly tired. Night after night now he had not slept, and his days had been spent in all the numerous activities necessitated by commissioning a ship of the line. The nervous tension induced by his worrying about Lady Barbara and Maria, by money troubles and manning troubles, had prevented him from leaving the details to Bush and Gerard even though he knew they were perfectly capable of dealing with everything. Worry and anxiety would not allow him to rest, and had goaded him into activity. He felt sick and stupid and weary. Day after day he had longed for the moment when he should get to sea, and could settle down into the comfortable solitude which surrounds a ship's captain, leaving all his shore worries behind him, even leaving Lady Barbara behind him.

He had the sense to realise that this new meeting with her had thoroughly upset him. He had given up as insoluble the problem of whether or not she had secured his nomination to the *Sutherland;* he had tried his hardest to combat his consuming jealousy of her husband. He had persuaded himself in the end that what he wanted more than anything else was to escape from her, just as he wanted to escape from Maria's cloying sweetness and lovable stupidity, from all the complex misery of life on land. He had yearned for the sea as a castaway yearns for a drink of water. Two days ago the prospect of thus standing on the deck in the final bustle of departure seemed marvellously desirable to him. Now, he realised with a gulp, he was not quite so sure. It was like having a limb torn out by the roots to be leaving Lady Barbara like this. And, oddly enough, he was distressed at leaving Maria, too. There would be a child born before he could be home again, a child well over a year old, running about, perhaps even saying its first few words. Maria would have to go through her pregnancy and confinement without his moral support; and he knew, despite the brave way in which she had dismissed the subject, and despite her stout-hearted good-bye, how much she would miss him. It was that which made it so painful to leave her.

With all her courage her lips had trembled and her eyes had been wet when she lifted her face to him, in the sitting-room of their lodgings; they had agreed long ago that it was foolish to prolong the pangs of parting by her accompanying him on board. Even then the urge to be off had still been strong enough to take him from her arms without a pang, but it was different now. Hornblower mentally spurned himself as a sentimental fool, and glanced impatiently up at the masthead vane. Without a doubt, the wind was backing northerly. If it should come round to north or nor'east the admiral would be anxious to start. The convoy, and the *Pluto* and *Caligula,* were assembled now, or pretty nearly, in Cawsand Bay; if the admiral decided not to wait for the stragglers he would be irritated at the *Sutherland's* delay, be it never so unavoidable.

"Keep the men to it, Mr. Bush," shouted Hornblower.

"Aye aye, sir," answered Bush, patiently.

That patience in his voice irritated Hornblower further. It implied a slight rebuke, a rebuke only apparent to Bush and Hornblower. Hornblower knew that Bush was working as hard as he could, and that he was working the men as hard as he could, too. Hornblower's order had been a mere manifestation of impatience, and Bush knew it. Hornblower was annoyed with himself for having so unguardedly broken his rule of never saying an unnecessary word to his officers, and by way of advancing a reason for having spoken he went down below to his cabin, as he had not intended to do.

The sentry stood aside for him as he entered the door of his sleeping cabin on the half deck. There was plenty of room here; even the presence of a twelve-pounder left ample space for his cot and his desk and his chest. Polwheal had set everything to rights here already; Hornblower passed through into the main cabin. Here there was ample room, too; the Dutchmen who designed the *Sutherland* had lofty ideas regarding the comfort of the captain. The cabin extended across the whole width of the stern, and the great stern windows gave plenty of light. The stone-coloured paint made the cabin sunny and cheerful, and the black bulks of a twelve-pounder on each side made an effective colour scheme. A couple of hands were standing by Polwheal in here while he lay on his stomach packing away cases of wine into the lockers. Hornblower glared at them, realising that he could not yet retire to the solitude of the stern gallery while he should be under their observation through the stern windows.

He went back to the sleeping gallery and threw himself with a sigh on his cot, but his restlessness brought him to his feet again and across to his desk. He took out a crackling document and sat down to look through it again.

Orders to the Inshore Squadron, Western Mediterranean, by Sir Percy Gilbert Leighton, K.B., Rear Admiral of the Red, Commanding.

There was nothing unusual about them at all — night signals, private signals, British, Spanish and Portuguese; rendezvous in case of separation; a line or two regarding the tactics to be adopted in the event of encountering while with the convoy a hostile squadron of any force. The flagship would accompany the Lisbon convoy of transports into the Tagus — calling for orders, presumably; the *Caligula* was to take the storeships *Harriet* and *Nancy* to Port Mahon; the *Sutherland* was to escort the East Indiamen as far as Latitude 35° before heading for the Straits, to the final rendezvous off Palamos Point. Captains of His Britannic Majesty's ships were informed that the coast of Andalusia, with the exception of Cadiz and Tarifa, was in the hands of the French, and so also was the coast of Catalonia from the frontier to Tarragona. At the same time captains entering any Spanish port whatever must take the most careful precautions lest the French should be in occupation there. The attached schedule of instructions to masters of ships in the convoy was mostly repetition of all this.

But to Hornblower, musing over these orders, they told a very full and complicated story. They told how, although Trafalgar had been fought five years back, and although England was maintaining at sea the greatest fleet the world had ever seen, she was still having to strain every nerve in the struggle. The Corsican was still building fleets in nearly every port in Europe, Hamburg, Antwerp, Brest, Toulon, Venice, Trieste, and a score of places in between, so that outside every port storm-beaten squadrons of English battleships had to maintain an unceasing watch — a hundred and twenty ships of the line could be found employment, if they could have been spared, on the blockade alone, without regard to the other duties. And at the same time every creek and fishing harbour along half the coasts of Europe maintained privateers, even if hardly better than big rowboats full of men, always ready to dash out and capture the helpless British merchant ships to be found in every sea. To guard against these depredations British frigates had to maintain unceasing patrol, and no King's ship could be despatched on any mission whatever without taking advantage of the opportunity given to convoy merchant shipping on part of their journey at least. In this war against the world only the most careful and scientific distribution of force could prevail, and now, mustering all her strength, England was taking the offensive. Her armies were on the march in Spain, and three ships of the line, scraped together from other duties from which they might just be spared, were being sent to attack the vulnerable flank which Bonaparte had incautiously exposed by his advance into the Peninsula. The *Sutherland* was destined to be the point of the spearhead which was making the thrust against the tyranny which dominated all Europe.

All very well, said Hornblower to himself. Automatically he was pacing up and down again, his head bent under the deck beams, and his walk limited to four strides between the twelve-pounder and the door. It was an honourable and responsible position, and yet he had not the men to man his ship. To make or set sail in the way it should be done in a King's ship—or rather, with the rapidity and facility which might make the difference between defeat and victory — called for two hundred and fifty trained seamen. And if all the trained men were aloft at once there would be none at the guns. To serve the guns, if both broadsides were in action at once, called for four hundred and fifty men — two hundred of them, he admitted, might be untrained — and nearly a hundred more carrying powder and engaged upon necessary duties about the ship.

He had a hundred and ninety trained men from the *Lydia* and a hundred and ninety raw landsmen. During the commissioning of the *Sutherland* only twenty old *Lydias* had deserted, abandoning two years' pay and risking the penalty of a thousand lashes, and he knew he was lucky at that. Some captains would have lost two thirds of their crews during as long a stay as this in a home port. But those twenty missing men would have been desperately useful now. He was a hundred and seventy men — a hundred and seventy *trained* men — short of complement. In six weeks he might drill his landsmen, all except that proportion of hopeless ones, diseased, crippled, or idiotic whom he could expect to find among them, into passable seamen and gunners. But in less than six weeks, possibly in less than three, he would be in action on the coast of Spain. By tomorrow night, even, he might be at grips with the enemy — the wind was backing towards the east and might bring out a French squadron of ships of the line from Brest, evading the blockading squadron, and crammed with men, to fall upon such a tempting prize as the East India convoy. What chance would the *Sutherland* stand, yard-arm to yard-arm with a French first rate, with only two thirds of her proper crew, and half of them seasick?

Hornblower clenched his fists again, boiling with exasperation at the thought. It was he who would be held responsible for any disaster, who would have to sustain the contempt or the pity — either alternative horrible to contemplate — of his brother captains. He yearned and hungered for men, more passionately than ever miser desired gold, or a lover his mistress. And now he had no more chance of finding any. Gerard's raid upon St. Ives and Redruth had been his last effort; he knew that he had been fortunate to get as many as fifty men from there. There would be no chance of obtaining any from the convoy. Government transports to Lisbon, Government storeships to Port Mahon, East India Company's ships — he could not take a man from any of those. He felt like a man in a cage.

He went across to his desk again and took out his private duplicate of the ship's watch bill, which he and Bush had sat up through most of the night to draw up. It was largely upon that watch bill that the efficiency of the ship would depend in her short-handed condition; the trained men had to be distributed evenly over every strategic point, with just the right proportion of landsmen to facilitate training and yet not to impede the working of the ship. Foretop, maintop, and mizzen top; forecastle and afterguard; every man had to be assigned a duty, so that whatever evolution out of the thousand possible was being carried out, in fair weather or foul, in daylight or darkness, he would go to his position without confusion or waste of time, knowing exactly what he had to do. He had to have his place at the guns allotted him under the command of the officer of his division.

Hornblower looked through the watch bill again. It was satisfactory as far as it went. It had a kind of card-castle stability — adequate enough at first sight, but incapable of standing any strain or alteration. Casualties or disease would bring the whole thing down in ruins. He flung the watch bill down as he remembered that, if the cruise were a healthy one, he might expect one death every ten days from accident or natural causes without regard to hostile action. Fortunately it was the unseasoned men who were the more likely to die.

Hornblower cocked his ear at the din on the main deck. The hoarse orders, the pipes of the boatswain's mates, and the stamp-and-go of many feet told him that they were heaving up the long-boat from overside. A strange squeaking, unlike that of the sheaves in the blocks, which had reached him for some time and which he had been unable to identify so far, he suddenly realised was the noise of the various families of pigs — captain's stores and ward-room stores — at last come on board. He heard a sheep bleating and then a cock crowing to the accompaniment of a roar of laughter. He had brought no cock along with his hens; it must belong to someone in the wardroom or the midshipmen's berth.

Someone thumped on the cabin door, and Hornblower snatched up his papers and dropped into his chair. Not for worlds would he be seen standing up and obviously awaiting the hour of departure with discomposure.

"Come in!" he roared.

A scared young midshipman put his head round the door — it was Longley, Gerard's nephew, newly come to sea.

"Mr. Bush says the last of the stores are just coming on board, sir," he piped.

Hornblower eyed him with a stony indifference which was the only alternative to grinning at the frightened little imp.

"Very good," he growled, and busied himself with his papers.

"Yes, sir," said the boy, after a moment's hesitation, withdrawing.

"Mr. Longley!" roared Hornblower.

The child's face, more terrified than ever, reappeared round the door.

"Come inside, boy," said Hornblower, testily. "Come in and stand still. What was it you said last?"

"Er — sir — I said — Mr. Bush —— "

"No, nothing of the sort. What was it you said *last?*"

The child's face wrinkled into the extreme of puzzlement, and then cleared as he realised the point of the question.

"I said, 'Yes sir,' " he piped.

"And what ought you to have said?"

"Aye aye, sir."

"Right. Very good."

"Aye aye, sir."

That boy had a certain amount of quickness of wit, and did not allow fright to bereave him entirely of his senses. If he learned quickly how to handle the men he would make a useful warrant officer. Hornblower put away his papers and locked his desk; he took a few more turns up and down his cabin, and then, a sufficient interval having elapsed to conserve his dignity, he went up to the quarterdeck.

"Make sail when you're ready, Mr. Bush," he said.

"Aye aye, sir. Easy with those falls there, you — you —— "

Even Bush had reached the condition when there was no more savour in oaths. The ship was in a horrible state of muddle, the decks were filthy, the crew exhausted. Hornblower stood with his hands behind him in a careful attitude of Olympian detachment as the order was given for all hands to make sail, and the petty officers drove the crew, stupid with weariness, to their stations. Savage, the senior midshipman, whom Hornblower had seen grow from boyhood to manhood under his eye, came shouting for the afterguard to man the main topsail halliards. Savage was wan and his eyes were bloodshot; a night of debauchery in some foul haunt in Plymouth had not left him in the best of condition. As he shouted he put his hand to his temple, where clearly the din he was making was causing him agony. Hornblower smiled to himself at the sight — the next few days would sweat him clean again.

"Captain of the afterguard!" yelled Savage, his voice cracking. "I don't see the afterguard coming aft! Quicker than that, you men! Clap on to the main topsail halliards, there! I say, you master-at-arms. Send the idlers aft. D'ye hear, there!"

A boatswain's mate headed a rush to the mizzen rigging at Hornblower's elbow. Hornblower saw young Longley standing hesitating for a second, looking up at the men preceding him, and then, with a grimace of determination, the boy leaped for the ratlines and scrambled up after them. Hornblower appreciated the influences at work upon him — his fear of the towering height above him, and then his stoical decision that he could follow wherever the other men could venture. Something might be made of that boy.

Bush was looking at his watch and fuming to the master.

"Nine minutes already! God, look at them! The marines are more like sailors!"

The marines were farther aft, at the mizzen topsail halliards. Their booted feet went clump-clump-clump on the deck. They did their work like soldiers, with soldierly rigidity, as if at drill. Sailors always laughed at that, but there was no denying that at the present moment it was the marines who were the more efficient.

The hands scurried from halliards to braces. A roar from Harrison forward told that the mooring was slipped, and Hornblower, casting a final glance up at the wind vane, saw that the wind had backed so far easterly that rounding Devil's Point was not going to be simple. With the yards braced round the *Sutherland* turned on her keel and slowly gathered way. Women's screeches and a fluttering of handkerchiefs from the shore boats told how some of the wives whom Hornblower had turned out twenty four hours ago had put off to say good-bye. Close overside he saw a woman in the stern sheets of a boat blubbering unashamed, her mouth wide open and the tears running like rivers. It was no more than an even chance that she would ever see her man again.

"Keep your eyes inboard, there!" yelled Harrison, who had detected some member of the crew waving farewell. Every man's attention must be kept strictly to the business in hand now.

Hornblower felt the ship heel as Bush directed her course as near to the wind as she would lie; with Devil's Point ahead, and an unfamiliar ship to handle, it was clearly as well to get as far to windward as possible. That heeling of the ship awakened a storm of memories. It was not until one was in a ship under sail, with the deck unstable under one's feet, and the familiar rattle of the blocks and piping of the rigging in one's ears, that the thousand and one details of life at sea became vivid and recognisable again. Hornblower found himself swallowing hard with excitement.

They were shaving the Dockyard Point as closely as possible. Most of the dockyard hands left their work to stare at them, stolidly, but not a soul among them raised a cheer. In seventeen years of warfare they had seen too many King's ships putting out to sea to be excited about this one. Hornblower knew that he ought to have a band on board, to strike up "Britons, Strike Home" or "Come cheer up, my lads, 'tis to glory we steer," but he had no band; he had not the money for one, and he was not going to call on the marine fifer or the ship's fiddler to make a tinny little noise at this moment. Stonehouse Pool was opening up before them now, and beyond it lay the roofs of Plymouth. Maria was there somewhere; perhaps she could see the white topsails, close-hauled to the wind. Perhaps Lady Barbara was there, looking out at the *Sutherland*. Hornblower gulped again.

A little flaw of wind, blowing down Stonehouse Pool, took the ship nearly aback. She staggered until the helmsman allowed her to pay off. Hornblower looked round to starboard. They were coming dangerously close in to Cremyll — he had been correct in his surmise that the *Sutherland* would make plenty of leeway. He watched the wind, and the set of the tide off the point. He looked ahead at Devil's Point on the starboard bow. It might be necessary at any moment to put the ship about and beat up to northward again before breasting the tide once more. At the very moment when he saw that they would weather the point he saw Bush raise his head to bark the orders to go about.

"Keep her steady as she goes, Mr. Bush," he said; the quiet order was an announcement that he had taken charge, and Bush closed the mouth which had opened to give the order.

They cleared the buoy a bare fifty yards from any danger, with the water creaming under the lee now as she lay over to the fresh breeze. Hornblower had not interfered to demonstrate the superiority of his seamanship and judgment, but merely because he could not stand by and watch something being done a little less artistically than was possible. In the cold-blooded calculation of chances he was superior to his lieutenant, as his ability at whist proved. Hornblower stood sublimely unconscious of his motives; in fact he hardly realised what he had done — he never gave a thought to his good seamanship.

They were heading straight for the Devil's Point now; Hornblower kept his eye on it as they opened up the Sound.

"You can put the helm aport now," he said. "And set the t'gallant sails, Mr. Bush."

With the wind abeam they headed into the Sound, the rugged Staddon Heights to port and Mount Edgecumbe to starboard. At every yard they advanced towards the open sea the wind blew fresher, calling a keener note from the rigging. The *Sutherland* was feeling the sea a little now, heaving perceptibly to the waves under her bows. With the motion, the creaking of the wooden hull became audible — noticeable on deck, loud below until the ear grew indifferent to the noise.

"God blast these bloody farmers!" groaned Bush, watching the way in which the topgallant sails were being set.

Drake's Island passed away to windward; the *Sutherland* turned her stern to it as with the wind on her port quarter she headed down the Sound. Before the topgallant sails were set they were abreast of Picklecomb Point and opening up Cawsand Bay. There was the convoy — six East Indiamen with their painted ports like men of war, all flying the gridiron flag of the Honourable Company and one sporting a broad pendant for all the world like a king's commodore; the two naval storeships and the four transports destined for Lisbon. The three-decker *Pluto* and the *Caligula* were rolling to their anchors to seaward of them.

"Flagship's signalling, sir," said Bush, his glass to his eye. "You ought to have reported it a minute ago, Mr. Vincent."

The *Pluto* had not been in sight more than thirty seconds, but there was need for promptness in acknowledging this, the first signal made by the Admiral.

"*Sutherland's* pendant, sir," said the unfortunate signal midshipman, staring through his glass. "Negative. No. 7. Number Seven is 'Anchor,' sir."

"Acknowledge," snapped Hornblower. "Get those t'gallants in again and back the main topsail, Mr. Bush."

With his telescope Hornblower could see men racing up the rigging of the ships. In five minutes both the *Pluto* and the *Caligula* had a cloud of canvas set.

"They commissioned at the Nore, blast 'em," growled Bush.

At the Nore, the gateway of the busiest port in the world, ships of the Royal Navy had the best opportunity of completing their crews with prime seamen taken from incoming merchant vessels, in which it was not necessary to leave more than half a dozen hands to navigate their ships up to London river. In addition, the *Pluto* and *Caligula* had enjoyed the advantage of having been able to drill their crews during the voyage down channel. Already they were standing out of the bay. Signals were soaring up the flagship's halliards.

"To the convoy, sir," said Vincent. "Make haste. Up anchor. Make all sail con-conformable with the weather, sir. Jesus, there's a gun."

An angry report and a puff of smoke indicated that the admiral was calling pointed attention to his signals. The Indiamen, with their heavy crews and man-o'-war routine, were already under weigh. The storeships and transports were slower, as was only to be expected. The other ships were backing and filling outside for what seemed an interminable time before the last of them came creeping out.

" 'Nother signal from the flagship, sir," said Vincent, reading the flags and then hurriedly referring to the signal book. "Take up stations as previously ordered."

That would be to windward of the convoy, and, with the wind abaft as it was, in the rear. Then the ships of war could always dash down to the rescue if a Frenchman tried to cut off one of the convoy under their noses. Hornblower felt the freshening breeze on his cheek. The flagship's topgallants were set, and, as he looked, he saw her royals being spread as well. He would have to conform, but with the wind increasing as it was he fancied that it would not be long before they would have to come in again. Before nightfall they would be reefing topsails. He gave the order to Bush, and watched while the crew gathered at Harrison's bellow of "All hands make sail." He could see the landsmen flinch, not unnaturally — the *Sutherland's* main royal yard was a hundred and ninety feet above the deck and swaying in a dizzy circle now that the ship was beginning to pitch to the Channel rollers.

Hornblower turned his attention to the flagship and the convoy; he could not bear the sight of frightened men being hounded up the rigging by petty officers with rope's ends. It was necessary, he knew. The Navy did not — of necessity could not — admit the existence of the sentences "I cannot" and "I am afraid." No exceptions could be made, and this was the right moment to grain it into men who had never known compulsion before that every order must be obeyed. If his officers were to start with leniency, leniency would always be expected, and leniency, in a service which might at any moment demand of a man the willing sacrifice of his life, could only be employed in a disciplined crew which had had time to acquire understanding. But Hornblower knew, and sympathised with, the sick terror of a man driven up to the masthead of a ship of the line when previously he had never been higher than the top of a haystack. It was a pitiless, cruel service.

"Peace'll be signed," grumbled Bush to Crystal, the master, "before we make sailors out of these clodhoppers."

A good many of the clodhoppers in question had three days before been living peacefully in their cottages with never a thought of going to sea. And here they were under a grey sky, pitching over a grey sea, with a keener breeze than ever they had known blowing round them, overhead the terrifying heights of the rigging, and underfoot the groaning timbers of a reeling ship.

They were well out to sea now, with the Eddystone in sight from the deck, and under the pressure of the increased sail the *Sutherland* was growing lively. She met her first big roller, and heaved as it reached her bow, rolled, corkscrew fashion, as it passed under her, and then pitched dizzily as it went away astern. There was a wail of despair from the waist.

"Off the decks, there, blast you!" raved Harrison. "Keep it off the decks!"

Men were being seasick already, with the freedom of men taken completely by surprise. Hornblower saw a dozen pale forms staggering and lurching towards the lee rails. One or two men had sat down abruptly on the deck, their hands to their temples. The ship heaved and corkscrewed again, soaring up and then sinking down again as if she would never stop, and the shuddering wail from the waist was repeated. With fixed and fascinated eyes Hornblower watched a wretched yokel vomiting into the scuppers. His stomach heaved in sympathy, and he found himself swallowing hard. There was sweat on his face although he suddenly felt bitterly cold.

He was going to be sick, too, and that very soon. He wanted to be alone, to vomit in discreet privacy, away from the amused glances of the crowd on the quarterdeck. He braced himself to speak with his usual stern indifference, but his ear told him that he was only achieving an unsuccessful perkiness.

"Carry on, Mr. Bush," he said. "Call me if necessary."

He had lost his sea legs, too, during this stay in harbour — he reeled as he crossed the deck, and he had to cling with both hands to the rail of the companion. He reached the half deck safely and lurched to the after-cabin door, stumbling over the coaming. Polwheal was laying dinner at the table.

"Get out!" snarled Hornblower, breathlessly. "Get out!"

Polwheal vanished, and Hornblower reeled out into the stern gallery, fetching up against the rail, leaning his head over towards the foaming wake. He hated the indignity of seasickness as much as he hated the misery of it. It was of no avail to tell himself, as he did, despairingly, while he clutched the rail, that Nelson was always seasick, too, at the beginning of a voyage. Nor was it any help to point out to himself the unfortunate coincidence that voyages always began when he was so tired with excitement and mental and physical exertion that he was ready to be sick anyway. It was true, but he found no comfort in it as he leaned groaning against the rail with the wind whipping round him.

He was shivering with cold now as the nor'easter blew; his heavy jacket was in his sleeping cabin, but he felt he could neither face the effort of going to fetch it, nor call Polwheal to bring it. And this, he told himself with bitter irony, was the calm solitude for which he had been yearning while entangled in the complications of the shore. Beneath him the pintles of the rudder were groaning in the gudgeons, and the sea was seething yeastily in white foam under the counter. The glass had been falling since yesterday, he remembered, and the weather was obviously working up into a nor'easterly gale. Hounded before it, across the Bay of Biscay, he could see no respite before him for days, at this moment when he felt he could give everything he had in the world for the calm of the Hamoaze again.

His officers were never sick, he thought resentfully, or if they were they were just sick and did not experience this agonising misery. And forward two hundred seasick landsmen were being driven pitilessly to their tasks by overbearing petty officers. It did a man good to be driven to work despite his seasickness, always provided that discipline was not imperilled thereby as it would be in his case. And he was quite, quite sure that not a soul on board felt as miserable as he did, or even half as miserable. He leaned against the rail again, moaning and blaspheming. Experience told him that in three days he would be over all this and feeling as well as ever in his life, but at the moment the prospect of three days of this was just the same as the prospect of an eternity of it. And the timbers creaked and the rudder groaned and the wind whistled and the sea hissed, everything blending into an inferno of noise as he clung shuddering to the rail.

Chapter VI

WHEN the first paroxysm was over Hornblower was able to note that the breeze was undoubtedly freshening. It was gusty, too, sudden squalls bringing flurries of rain which beat into the stern gallery where he was standing. He was suddenly consumed with anxiety as to what would happen aloft if the *Sutherland* were caught in a wilder squall than usual with a crew unhandy at getting in sail. The thought of the disgrace involved in losing spars or canvas in sight of the whole convoy drove all thought of seasickness out of his head. Quite automatically he went forward to his cabin, put on his pilot coat, and ran up on deck. Gerard had taken over from Bush.

"Flagship's shortening sail, sir," he said, touching his hat.

"Very good. Get the royals in," said Hornblower, turning to look round the horizon through his glass.

The convoy was behaving exactly as convoys always did, scattering before the wind as if they really wanted to be snapped up by a privateer. The Indiamen were in a fairly regular group a mile ahead to leeward, but the six other ships were hull down and spread out far beyond them.

"Flagship's been signalling to the convoy, sir," said Gerard.

Hornblower nearly replied, "I expect she has," but restrained himself in time and limited himself to the single word "Yes." As he spoke a fresh series of flag hoists soared up the *Pluto's* halliards.

"*Caligula's* pendant," read off the signal midshipman. "Make more sail. Take station ahead of convoy."

So Bolton was being sent ahead to enforce the orders which the transports had disregarded. Hornblower watched the *Caligula* reset her royals and go plunging forward over the grey sea in pursuit of the transports. She would have to run down within hailing distance and possibly have to fire a gun or two before she could achieve anything; masters of merchant ships invariably paid no attention at all to flag signals even if they could read them. The

Indiamen were getting in their topgallants as well — they had the comfortable habit of shortening sail at nightfall. Happy in the possession of a monopoly of the Eastern trade, and with passengers on board who demanded every luxury, they had no need to worry about slow passages and could take care that their passengers ran no risk of being disturbed in their sleep by the stamping and bustle of taking off sail if the weather changed. But from all appearances it might have been deliberately planned to spread the convoy out still farther. Hornblower wondered how the admiral would respond, and he turned his glass upon the *Pluto*.

Sure enough, she burst into hoist after hoist of signals, hurling frantic instructions at the Indiamen.

"I'll lay he wishes he could courtmartial 'em," chuckled one midshipman to the other.

"Five thousand pounds, those India captains make out of a round voyage," was the reply. "What do they care about admirals? God, who'd be in the Navy?"

With night approaching and the wind freshening there was every chance of the convoy being scattered right at the very start of its voyage. Hornblower began to feel that his admiral was not showing to the best advantage. The convoy should have been kept together; in a service which accepted no excuses Sir Percy Leighton stood already condemned. He wondered what he would have done in the admiral's place, and left the question unanswered, vaguely telling himself the profound truth that discipline did not depend on the power to send before a courtmartial; he did not think that he could have done better.

"*Sutherland's* pendant," said the signal midshipman, breaking in on his reverie. "Take — night — station."

"Acknowledge," said Hornblower.

That was an order easy to obey. His night station was a quarter of a mile to windward of the convoy. Here he was drawing up fast upon the Indiamen to his correct position. He watched the *Pluto* go down past the Indiamen in the wake of the *Caligula;* apparently the admiral had decided to make use of his flagship as a connecting link between the halves of the convoy. Night was coming down fast and the wind was still freshening.

He tried to walk up and down the reeling deck so as to get some warmth back into his shivering body; his stomach was causing him terrible misgivings again now with this period of waiting. He fetched up against the rail, hanging on while he fought down his weakness. Of all his officers, Gerard, handsome, sarcastic, and able, was the one before whom he was least desirous of vomiting. His head was spinning with seasickness and fatigue, and he thought that if he could only lie down he might perhaps sleep, and in sleep he could forget the heaving misery of his interior. The prospect of being warm and snug in his cot grew more and more urgent and appealing.

Hornblower held on grimly until his eye told him, in the fast fading light, that he was in his correct station. Then he turned to Gerard.

"Get the t'gallants in, Mr. Gerard."

He took the signal slate and wrote on it, painfully, while warring with his insurgent stomach, the strictest orders his mind could devise to the officer of the watch with regard to keeping in sight, and to windward, of the convoy.

"There are your orders, Mr. Gerard," he said. He quavered on the last word, and he did not hear Gerard's "Aye aye, sir," as he fled below.

This time it was agony to vomit, for his stomach was completely empty. Polwheal showed up in the cabin as he came staggering back, and Hornblower cursed him savagely and sent him away again. In his sleeping cabin he fell across his cot, and lay there for twenty minutes before he could rouse himself to sit up. Then he dragged off his two coats, and, still wearing his shirt and waistcoat and breeches, he got under the blankets with a groan. The ship was pitching remorselessly as she ran before the wind, and all the timbers complained in spasmodic chorus. Hornblower set his teeth at every heave, while the cot in which he lay soared upward twenty feet or more and then sank hideously downward under the influence of each successive wave. Nevertheless, with no possibility of consecutive thinking, it was easy for exhaustion to step in. He was so tired that with his mind empty he fell asleep in a few minutes, motion and noise and seasickness notwithstanding.

So deeply did he sleep that when he awoke he had to think for a moment before he realised where he was. The heaving and tossing, of which he first became conscious, was familiar and yet unexpected. The door into the after cabin, hooked open, admitted a tiny amount of grey light, in which he blinked round him. Then, simultaneously with the return of recollection, his stomach heaved again. He got precariously to his feet, staggered across the after cabin to the rail of the stern gallery, and then peered miserably across the grey sea in the first faint light of dawn, with the wind whipping round him. There was no sail in sight from there, and the consequent apprehension helped him to recover himself. Putting on coat and greatcoat again, he walked up to the quarterdeck.

Gerard was in charge of the deck, so that the middle watch was not yet ended. Hornblower gave a surly nod in reply to Gerard's salute, and stood looking forward over the grey sea, flecked with white. The breeze was shrilling in the rigging, just strong enough for it to be unnecessary to reef topsails, and right aft, blowing round Hornblower's ears as he stood with his hands on the carved rail. Ahead lay four of the Indiamen, in a straggling line ahead, and then he saw the fifth and sixth not more than a mile beyond them. Of the flagship, of the transports, of the storeships, of the *Caligula*, there was nothing to be seen at all. Hornblower picked up the speaking trumpet.

"Masthead, there! What do you see of the flagship?"

"Northin', sir. Northin' in sight nowhere, sir, 'cepting for the Indiamen, sir."

And that was that, thought Hornblower, replacing the speaking trumpet. A rare beginning to a voyage. The traverse board showed that the *Sutherland* had held steadily on her course through the night, and the deck log on the slate showed speeds of eight and nine knots. Before long Ushant should be in sight in this clear weather; he had done all his duty in keeping the Indiamen under his eye, on their course, and under canvas conformable with the weather. He only wished that the queasiness of his stomach would permit him to be quite confident about it, for the gloomy depression of seasickness filled him with foreboding. If a victim had to be found, it would be he, he felt sure. He gauged the strength of the wind and decided that it would be inadvisable to set more sail in the hope of overtaking the rest of the convoy. And with that, having reached the satisfactory conclusion that he could do nothing to avert blame if blame were coming to him, he felt more cheerful. Life at sea had taught him to accept the inevitable philosophically.

Eight bells sounded, and he heard the call for the watch below. Bush arrived on the quarterdeck to relieve Gerard. Hornblower felt Bush's keen glance directed at him, and ignored it in surly silence. He had made it a rule never to speak unnecessarily, and he had found so much satisfaction in it that he was never going to break it. There was satisfaction to be found now, in paying no attention to Bush, who kept stealing anxious glances at him, ready to respond the moment he was spoken to, like a dog with his master. Then it occurred to Hornblower that he must be cutting a very undignified figure, unshaved and tousled, and probably pale green with seasickness. He went off below in a pet again.

In the cabin where he sat with his head in his hands all the hanging fitments were swaying in the slow time set by the creaking of the timbers. But as long as he did not look at them he was not uncontrollably sick. When Ushant had been sighted he would lie down and close his eyes. Then Polwheal came in, balancing a tray like a conjuror.

"Breakfast, sir," said Polwheal in a flood of garrulity. "I didn't know you was up, sir, not till the port watch told me when they came below. Coffee, sir. Soft bread, sir. Galley fire's bright an' I could have it toasted for you in two twos, sir, if you 'uld like it that way."

Hornblower looked at Polwheal in a sudden flood of suspicion. Polwheal was making no attempt to offer him any of the fresh food, except for bread, which he had sent on board; not a chop or a steak, nor rashers of bacon, nor any of the other delicacies he had bought so recklessly. Yet Polwheal knew he had eaten no dinner yesterday, and Polwheal was usually insistent that he should eat and overeat. He wondered why, therefore, Polwheal should be offering him a Frenchman's breakfast like this. Polwheal's stony composure wavered a little under Hornblower's stare, confirming Hornblower's suspicions. Polwheal had guessed the secret of his captain's seasickness.

"Put it down," he rasped, quite unable to say more at the moment. Polwheal put the tray on the table and still lingered.

"I'll pass the word when I want you," said Hornblower sternly.

With his head between his hands he reviewed all of what he could remember of yesterday. Not merely Polwheal, he realised now, but Bush and Gerard — the whole ship's company, for that matter — knew that he suffered from seasickness. Subtle hints in their bearing proved it, now that he came to think about it. At first the thought merely depressed him, so that he groaned again. Then it irritated him. And finally his sense of humour asserted itself and he smiled. While he smiled, the pleasant aroma of the coffee reached his nostrils, and he sniffed at it wondering, reacting to the scent in two opposite ways at once, conscious both of the urge of hunger and thirst and of the revulsion of his stomach. Hunger and thirst won in the end. He poured coffee for himself and sipped it, keeping his eyes rigidly from the swaying of the cabin fitments. With the blessed warmth of the strong sweet coffee inside him he instinctively began to eat the bread, and it was only when he had cleared the tray that he began to feel qualms of doubt as to the wisdom of what he had done. Even then his luck held, for before the waves of seasickness could overcome him a knock on the cabin door heralded the news that land was in sight, and he could forget them in the activity the news demanded of him.

Ushant was not in sight from the deck, but only from the masthead, and Hornblower made no attempt to climb the rigging to see it. But as he stood with the wind whipping round him and the rigging harping over his head he looked over the grey sea eastward to where France lay beyond the horizon. Of all landfalls perhaps this one loomed largest in English naval history. Drake and Blake, Shovel and Rooke, Hawke and Boscawen, Rodney and Jervis and Nelson had all of them stood as he was standing, looking eastward as he was doing. Three quarters of the British mercantile marine rounded Ushant, outward and homeward. As a lieutenant under Pellew in the *Indefatigable* he had beaten about in sight of Ushant for many weary days during the blockade of Brest. It was in these very waters that the *Indefatigable* and the *Amazon* had driven the *Droits de l'Homme* into the breakers, and a thousand men to their deaths. The details of that wild fight thirteen years ago were as distinct in his memory as those of the battle with the *Natividad* only nine months back; that was a symptom of approaching old age.

Hornblower shook off the meditative gloom which was descending on him, and applied himself to the business of laying a fresh course for Finisterre and directing the Indiamen upon it — the first was a far easier task than the second. It called for an hour of signalling and gunfire before every one of his flock had satisfactorily repeated his signals; it appeared to Hornblower as if the masters of the convoy took pleasure in misunderstanding him, in ignoring him, in repeating incorrectly. The *Lord Mornington* flew the signal for ten minutes at the dip, as if to indicate that it was not understood; it was only when the *Sutherland* had borne down almost within hail of her, Hornblower boiling with fury, that she was able to clear the jammed signal halliards and hoist the signal properly.

Bush chuckled sardonically at the sight, and began some remark to his captain to the effect that even Indiamen were as inefficient as men of war at the beginning of a commission, but Hornblower stamped away angrily out of earshot, leaving Bush staring after him. The ridiculous incident had annoyed Hornblower on account of his fear lest he himself should appear ridiculous; but it had its effect in prolonging his forgetfulness of his seasickness. It was only after a spell of standing solitary on the starboard side while Bush gave the orders that brought the *Sutherland* up to windward of the convoy again that he calmed down and began to experience internal misgivings once more. He was on the point of retiring below when a sudden cry from Bush recalled him to the quarterdeck.

"*Walmer Castle's* hauled her wind, sir."

Hornblower put his glass to his eye. The *Walmer Castle* was the leading ship of the convoy, and the farthest to port. She was about three miles away, and there was no mistaking the fact that she had spun round on her heel and was now clawing frantically up to windward towards them.

"She's signalling, sir," said Vincent, "but I can't read it. It might be No. 29, but that's 'Discontinue the action' and she can't mean that."

"Masthead!" bellowed Bush. "What can you see on the port bow?"

"Northin', sir."

"She's hauled it down now, sir," went on Vincent. "There goes another one! No. 11, sir. 'Enemy in sight.' "

"Here, Savage," said Bush. "Take your glass and up with you."

The next ship in the straggling line had come up into the wind too; Savage was halfway up the rigging when the masthead look-out hailed.

"I can see 'em now, sir. Two luggers, sir, on the port bow."

Luggers off Ushant could only mean French privateers. Swift, handy, and full of men, with a length of experience at sea only equalled by that of the British Navy, they would court any danger to make a prize of a fat East Indiaman. Such a capture would make their captains wealthy men. Bush, Vincent, everyone on the quarterdeck looked at Hornblower. If he were to lose such a ship entrusted to his charge he would forfeit every bit of credit at the Admiralty that he possessed.

"Turn up the hands, Mr. Bush," said Hornblower. In the excitement of instant action he had no thought for the dramatic aspect of affairs, forgot the need to pose, and made no attempt to impress his subordinates with his calm; and the calculations which came flooding up into his mind had so rapidly engrossed him that he betrayed no excitement whatever, as they saw.

The Indiamen all carried guns — the *Lord Mornington* actually had eighteen ports a side — and could beat off any long-range attack by a small privateer. The luggers' tactics would be to swoop alongside and board; no boarding nettings manned by an Indiaman's crew would keep out a hundred Frenchmen mad for gold. They would manœuvre so as to cut off a ship to windward of him

— while he was beating up against the wind they could rush her in three minutes and carry her off under his very eyes. He must not allow such a situation to arise, and yet the Indiamen were slow, his crew was undrilled, and French luggers were as quick as lightning in stays — there were two of them, as well, and he would have to parry two thrusts at once.

They were in sight now from the deck, their dark sails lifting above the horizon, two-masted and close-hauled. The dark squares of their sails were urgent with menace, and Hornblower's eye could read more than the mere drama of the silhouettes against the clear horizon. They were small, with not more than twenty guns apiece, and no more than nine-pounders at that — the *Sutherland* could sink them with a couple of broadsides if they were ever foolish enough to come within close range. But they were fast; already they were hull up, and Hornblower could see the white water under their bows. And they were lying at least a point nearer the wind than ever he could induce the *Sutherland* to lie. Each would have at least a hundred and fifty men on board, because French privateers had little thought for the comfort of their crews, nor needed to when they only intended to dash out of port, snap up a prize, and dash back again.

"Shall I clear for action, sir?" asked Bush, greatly daring.

"No," snapped Hornblower. "Send the men to quarters and put out the fires."

There was no need to knock down bulkheads and risk spoiling his property and imperil the livestock on board, because there was no chance of a stand-up fight. But a stray nine-pounder ball into the galley fire might set the whole ship ablaze. The men went to their stations, were pushed there, or led there — some of the men were still confused between port and starboard sides — to the accompaniment of the low-voiced threats and curses of the petty officers.

"I'll have the guns loaded and run out, too, if you please, Mr. Bush."

More than half the men had never seen a cannon fired in their lives. This was the first time they had even heard the strange mad music of the gun trucks rumbling over the planking. Hornblower heard it with a catch in his breath — it called up many memories. The privateers gave no sign of flinching when the *Sutherland* showed her teeth, as Hornblower, watching them closely, saw. They held steadily on their course, heading close-hauled to meet the convoy. But their appearance, Hornblower was glad to see, had done more to herd the merchantmen together than his orders had done. They were huddled together in a mass, each ship closer aboard its neighbour than any merchant captain could be induced to steer save under the impulse of fear. He could see boarding nettings being run up on board them, and they were running out their guns. The defence they could offer would only be feeble, but the fact that they could defend themselves at all was important in the present state of affairs.

A puff of smoke and a dull report from the leading privateer showed that she had opened fire; where the shot went Hornblower could not see, but the tricolour flag soared up each of the luggers' mainmasts, and at a word from Hornblower the red ensign rose to the *Sutherland's* peak in reply to this jaunty challenge. Next moment the luggers neared the *Walmer Castle,* the leading ship to port, with the evident intention of running alongside.

"Set the t'gallants, Mr. Bush," said Hornblower. "Helm a-starboard. Meet her. Steady."

The *Walmer Castle* had sheered off in fright, almost running on board her starboard-side neighbour, who had been forced to put her helm over as well. Then, in the nick of time, the *Sutherland* came dashing down. The luggers put up their helms and bore away to avoid the menace of her broadside, and their first clumsy rush had been beaten off.

"Main tops'l aback!" roared Hornblower.

It was of supreme importance to preserve his position of advantage to windward of the convoy, whence he could dash forward to the threatened point of danger. The convoy drew slowly ahead, with the luggers leading them. Hornblower watched them steadily, the practice of years enabling him to keep them in the focus of his telescope as he stood on the heaving deck. They spun round suddenly on the starboard tack again, moving like clockwork, leaping to meet the *Lord Mornington* on the starboard wing like hounds at the throat of a stag. The *Lord Mornington* sheered out of her course, the *Sutherland* came tearing down upon her, and the luggers went about, instantly, heading for the *Walmer Castle* again.

"Hard-a-starboard!" rasped Hornblower. The *Walmer Castle*, to his vast relief, managed to throw her topsails aback, and the *Sutherland* reached her just in time. She swept across her stern; Hornblower could see her whiskered captain in his formal blue frock coat beside her wheel, and half a dozen Lascar sailors leaping hysterically over her deck. The luggers wore away, just out of gunshot of the *Sutherland*. There was smoke eddying round one of the other Indiamen; apparently she had loosed off her broadside straight into the blue.

"They're wasting powder there, sir," volunteered Bush, but Hornblower made no reply, being too busy with his mental calculations.

"As long as they have the sense not to scatter — " said Crystal.

That was an important consideration; if the convoy once divided he could not hope to defend every portion of it. There was neither honour nor glory to be won in this contest between a ship of the line and two small privateers — if he beat them off the world would think nothing of it, while if any one of the convoy was lost he could imagine only too well the ensuing public outcry. He had thought of signalling to his charges that they should keep together, but he had rejected the idea. Signalling would only confuse them, and half of them would probably misread the signal. It was better to rely on their natural instinct of self-preservation.

The privateers had come up into the wind again, and were working to windward directly astern of the *Sutherland*. From the very look of them, of their sharp black hulls and far-raked masts, Hornblower could guess that they had concerted some new move. He faced aft, watching them closely. Next moment the plan revealed itself. He saw the bows of the leader swing to starboard, those of the second one to port. They were diverging, and each with the wind on her quarter came racing down, white water foaming at their bows, lying over to the stiff breeze, each of them a picture of malignant efficiency. As soon as they were clear of the *Sutherland* they would converge again attacking opposite wings of the convoy. He would hardly have time to beat off first one and then return to chase the other away.

He thought wildly for a moment of trying to bring the whole convoy to the wind together, and rejected the plan at once. They would probably spread out in the attempt, if they did not fall foul of each other, and in either case, scattered or crippled, they would fall easy victims to their enemies. All he could do was to attempt to tackle both ships in succession. It might seem hopeless, but there was nothing to be gained in abandoning the only plan possible. He would play it out to the last second.

He dropped his telescope on the deck, and sprang up onto the rail, hanging on by the mizzen rigging. He stared at his enemies, turning his head from side to side, calculating their speeds and observing their courses, his face set rigid in an intensity of concentration. The lugger to starboard was slightly nearer, and consequently would arrive at the convoy first. He would have a minute or so more in hand to get back to deal with the second if he turned on this one. Another glance confirmed his decision, and he risked his reputation upon it — without a thought now, in the excitement of action, for that reputation of his.

"Starboard two points!" he called.

"Starboard two points!" echoed the quartermaster.

The *Sutherland* swung round, out of the wake of the convoy, and headed to cross the bows of the starboard-side lugger. In turn, to avoid the ponderous broadside which was menacing her, the latter edged away, farther and farther as the *Sutherland* moved down upon her. By virtue of her vastly superior speed she was forereaching both upon the convoy and the escort; and the *Sutherland* in her effort to keep between the privateer and the merchantmen was being lured farther and farther away from her proper position to interfere with the designs of the other lugger. Hornblower was aware of that, but it was risk he was compelled to take, and he knew, despairingly, that if the Frenchmen played the right game he would be beaten. He could never drive the first lugger so far away and to leeward as to render her innocuous and still have time enough to get back and deal with the other. Already he was dangerously astray, but he held on his course, almost abreast now both of the convoy and of the lugger to starboard. Then he saw the other lugger turn to make its dash in upon the convoy.

"Hands to the braces, Mr. Bush!" he called. "Hard-a-starboard!"

The *Sutherland* came round, heeling over with the wind abeam and a trifle more canvas than was safe. She seemed to tear through the water as she raced for the convoy, which was wheeling in confusion away from the attack. As if through a forest of masts and sails Hornblower could see the dark sails of the lugger swooping down upon the helpless *Walmer Castle,* which must have responded slowly to her helm, or been badly commanded, and was being left astern by the others. A dozen simultaneous calculations raced through Hornblower's mind. He was thinking like a highly complex machine, forecasting the course of the lugger, and of the six Indiamen, and making allowances for the possible variations resulting from their captains' personal traits. He had to bear in mind the speed of the *Sutherland*, and the rate at which she was drifting to leeward under her press of canvas. To circumnavigate the scattering convoy would take too much time and would deprive him of any opportunity of surprise. He called his orders quietly down to the helmsman, steering for the narrowing gap between two ships. The *Lord Mornington* saw the two-decker rushing down upon her, and swerved as Hornblower had anticipated.

"Stand to your guns, there!" he bellowed. "Mr. Gerard! Give the lugger a broadside as we pass her!"

The *Lord Mornington* was past and gone in a flash; beyond her was the *Europe* — she had worn round a little and seemed to be heading straight for a collision.

"God blast her!" roared Bush. "God —— " The *Sutherland* had shaved across her bows, her jib boom almost brushing the *Sutherland's* mizzen rigging. Next moment the *Sutherland* had dashed through the narrowing gap between two more ships. Beyond was the *Walmer Castle,* and alongside her the lugger, taken completely by surprise at this unexpected appearance. In the stillness which prevailed on board the *Sutherland* they could hear the pop-popping of small arms — the Frenchmen were scrambling up to the lofty deck of the Indiaman. But as the big two-decker came hurtling down upon him the French captain tried for safety. Hornblower could see the French boarders leaping down again to the lugger, and her vast mainsail rose ponderously under the united effort of two hundred frantic arms. She had boomed off from the Indiaman and came round like a top, but she was five seconds too late.

"Back the mizzen tops'l!" snapped Hornblower to Bush. "Mr. Gerard!"

The *Sutherland* steadied herself for a crushing blow.

"Take your aim!" screamed Gerard, mad with excitement. He was by the forward section of guns on the main deck, which would bear first. "Wait till your guns bear! Fire!"

The rolling broadside which followed, as the ship slowly swung round, seemed to Hornblower's tense mind to last for at least five minutes. The intervals between the shots were ragged, and some of the guns were clearly fired before they bore. Elevation was faulty, too, as the splashes both this side of, and far beyond, the lugger bore witness. Nevertheless, some of the shots told. He saw splinters flying in the lugger, a couple of shrouds part. Two sudden swirls in the crowd on her deck showed where cannon balls had ploughed through it.

The brisk breeze blew the smoke of the straggling broadside clear instantly, so that his view of the lugger a hundred yards away was uninterrupted. She had still a chance of getting away. Her sails were filled, and she was slipping fast through the water. He gave the orders to the helmsman which would cause the *Sutherland* to yaw again and bring her broadside to bear. As he did so nine puffs of smoke from the lugger's side gave warning that she was firing her six-pounder popguns. The Frenchmen were game enough. A musical tone like a brief expiring note on an organ sang in his ear as a shot passed close overhead, and a double crash below told him that the *Sutherland* was hit. Her thick timbers ought to keep out six-pounder shot at that range.

He heard the rumble of the trucks as the *Sutherland's* guns were run out again, and he leaned over the rail to shout to the men on the main deck.

"Take your aim well!" he shouted. "Wait till your sights bear!"

The guns went off in ones and twos down the *Sutherland's* side as she yawed. There was only one old hand at each of the *Sutherland's* seventy four guns, and although the officers in charge of the port-side battery had sent over some of their men to help on the starboard side they would naturally keep the trained layers in case the port-side guns had to be worked suddenly. And there were not seventy four good gun layers left over from the *Lydia's* old crew — he remembered the difficulty he had experienced in drawing up the watch bill.

"Stop your vents!" shouted Gerard, and then his voice went up into a scream of excitement. "There it goes! Well done, men!"

The big mainmast of the lugger, with the mainsail and topmast and shrouds and all, was leaning over to one side. It seemed to hang there naturally, for a whole breathing space, before it fell with a sudden swoop. Even then a single shot fired from her aftermost gun proclaimed the Frenchman's defiance. Hornblower turned back to the helmsman to give the orders that would take the *Sutherland* within pistol shot and complete the little ship's destruction. He was aflame with excitement. Just in time he remembered his duty; he was granting the other lugger time to get in among the convoy, and every second was of value. He noted his excitement as a curious and interesting phenomenon, while his orders brought the *Sutherland* round on the other tack. As she squared away a long shout of defiance rose from the lugger, lying rolling madly in the heavy sea, her black hull resembling some crippled water beetle. Someone was waving a tricolour flag from the deck.

"Good-bye, Mongseer Crapaud," said Bush. "You've a long day's work ahead of you before you see Brest again."

The *Sutherland* thrashed away on her new course; the convoy had all turned and were beating up towards her, the lugger on their heels like a dog after a flock of sheep. At the sight of the *Sutherland* rushing down upon her she sheered off again. Obstinately, she worked round to make a dash at the *Walmer Castle* —

steering wide as usual — but Hornblower swung the *Sutherland* round and the *Walmer Castle* scuttled towards her for protection. It was easy enough, even in a clumsy ship like the *Sutherland,* to fend off the attacks of a single enemy. The Frenchman realised this after a few minutes more, and bore away to the help of her crippled consort.

Hornblower watched the big lugsail come round and fill, and the lugger lying over as she thrashed her way to windward; already the dismasted Frenchman was out of sight from the *Sutherland's* quarterdeck. It was a relief to see the Frenchman go — if he had been in command of her he would have left the other to look after herself and hung onto the convoy until nightfall; it would have been strange if he had not been able to snap up a straggler in the darkness.

"You can secure the guns, Mr. Bush," he said, at length.

Someone on the main deck started to cheer, and the cheering was taken up by the rest of the crew. They were waving their hands or their hats as if a Trafalgar had just been won.

"Stop that noise," shouted Hornblower, hot with rage. "Mr. Bush, send the hands aft here to me."

They came, all of them, grinning with excitement, pushing and playing like schoolboys; even the rawest of them had forgotten his seasickness in the excitement of the battle. Hornblower's blood boiled as he looked down at them, the silly fools.

"No more of that!" he rasped. "What have you done? Frightened off a couple of luggers not much bigger than our long boat! Two broadsides from a seventy four, and you're pleased with yourselves for knocking away a single spar! God, you ought to have blown the Frenchie out of the water! Two broadsides, you pitiful baby school! You must lay your guns better than that when it comes to real fighting, and I'll see you learn how — me and the cat between us. And how d'you make sail? I've seen it done better by Portuguese niggers!"

There was no denying the fact that words spoken from a full heart carry more weight than all the artifices of rhetoric. Hornblower's genuine rage and sincerity had made a deep impression, so stirred up had he been at the sight of botched and bungling work. The men were hanging their heads now, and shifting uneasily from one foot to the other, as they realised that what they had done had not been so marvellous after all. And to do them justice, half their exhilaration arose from the mad excitement of the *Sutherland's* rush through the convoy, with ships close on either hand. In later years, when they were spinning yarns of past commissions, the story would be embroidered until they began to affirm that Hornblower had steered a two-decker in a howling storm through a fleet of two hundred sail all on opposing courses.

"You can pipe down now, Mr. Bush," said Hornblower. "And when the hands have had their breakfasts you can exercise them aloft."

In the reaction following his excitement he was yearning to get away to the solitude of the stern gallery again. But here came Walsh the surgeon, trotting up to the quarterdeck and touching his hat.

"Surgeon's report, sir," he said. "One warrant officer killed. No officers and no seamen wounded."

"Killed?" said Hornblower, his jaw dropping. "Who's killed?"

"John Hart, midshipman," answered Walsh.

Hart had been a promising seaman in the *Lydia,* and it was Hornblower himself who had promoted him to the quarterdeck and obtained his warrant for him.

"Killed?" said Hornblower again.

"I can mark him 'mortally wounded,' sir, if you prefer it," said Walsh. "He lost a leg when a six-pounder ball came in through No. 11 gun port on the lower deck. He was alive when they got him down to the cockpit, but he died the next minute. Popliteal artery."

Walsh was a new appointment, who had not served under Hornblower before. Otherwise he might have known better than to indulge in details of this sort with so much professional relish.

"Get out of my road, blast you," snarled Hornblower.

His prospect of solitude was spoiled now. There would have to be a burial later in the day, with flag half-mast and yards a-cockbill. That in itself was irksome. And it was Hart who was dead — a big gangling young man with a wide, pleasant smile. The thought of it robbed him of all pleasure in his achievements this morning. Bush was there on the quarterdeck, smiling happily both at the thought of what had been done today and at the thought of four solid hours' exercise aloft for the hands. He would have liked to talk, and Gerard was there, eager to discuss the working of his beloved guns. Hornblower glared at them, daring them to address one single word to him; but they had served with him for years, and knew better.

He turned and went below; the ships of the convoy were sending up flags — the sort of silly signals of congratulation one might expect of Indiamen, probably half of them misspelled. He could rely on Bush to hoist "Not understood" until the silly fools got it right, and then to make a mere acknowledgment. He wanted nothing to do with them, or with anybody else. The one shred of comfort in a world which he hated was that, with a following wind and the convoy to leeward, he would be private in his stern gallery, concealed even from inquisitive telescopes in the other ships.

Chapter VII

HORNBLOWER took a last pull at his cigar when he heard the drum beating to divisions. He exhaled a lungful of smoke, his head thrown back, looking out from under the cove of the stern gallery up at the blissful blue sky, and then down at the blue water beneath, with the dazzling white foam surging from under the *Sutherland's* counter into her wake. Overhead he heard the measured tramp of the marines as they formed up across the poop deck, and then a brief shuffle of heavy boots as they dressed their line in obedience to the captain's order. The patter of hundreds of pairs of feet acted as a subdued accompaniment as the crew formed up round the decks. When everything had fallen still again Hornblower pitched his cigar overboard, hitched his full-dress coat into position, settled his cocked hat on his head, and walked with dignity, his left hand on his swordhilt, forward to the half deck and up the companion ladder to the quarterdeck. Bush was there, and Crystal, and the midshipmen of the watch. They saluted him, and from farther aft came the snick-snack-snick of the marines presenting arms.

Hornblower stood and looked round him in leisurely fashion; on this Sunday morning it was his duty to inspect the ship, and he could take advantage of the fact to drink in all the beauty and the artistry of the scene. Overhead the pyramids of white canvas described slow cones against the blue sky with the gentle roll of the ship. The decks were snowy white — Bush had succeeded in that in ten days' labour — and the intense orderliness of a ship of war was still more intense on this morning of Sunday inspection. Hornblower shot a searching glance from under lowered eyelids at the crew ranged in long single lines along the gangways and on the main deck. They were standing still, smart enough in their duck frocks and trousers. It was their bearing that he wished to study, and that could be done more effectively in a sweeping glance from the quarterdeck than at the close range of the inspection. There could be a certain hint of insolence in the way a restive crew stood to attention, and one could perceive lassitude in a dispirited crew. He could see neither now, for which he was thankful.

Ten days of hard work, of constant drill, of unsleeping supervision, of justice tempered by good humour, had done much to settle the hands to their duty. He had had to order five floggings three days ago, forcing himself to stand apparently unmoved while the whistle and crack of the cat-o'-nine-tails sickened his stomach. One of those floggings might do a little good to the recipient — an old hand who had apparently forgotten what he had learned and needed a sharp reminder of it. The other four would do none to the men whose backs had been lacerated; they would never make good sailors and were mere brutes whom brutal treatment could at least make no worse. He had sacrificed them to show the wilder spirits what might happen as a result of inattention to orders — it was only by an actual demonstration that one could work on the minds of uneducated men. The dose had to be prescribed with the utmost accuracy, neither too great nor too small. He seemed, so his sweeping glance told him, to have hit it off exactly.

Once more he looked round to enjoy the beauty of it all — the orderly ship, the white sails, the blue sky; the scarlet and pipeclay of the marines, the blue and gold of the officers; and there was consummate artistry in the subtle indications that despite the inspection the real pulsating life of the ship was going on beneath it. Where four hundred and more men stood at attention awaiting his lightest word, the quartermaster at the wheel with his mind on the binnacle and the leach of the main course, the lookouts at the masthead, and the officer of the watch with his telescope were living demonstrations of the fact the ship must still be sailed and the King's service carried on.

Hornblower turned aside to begin his inspection. He walked up and down the quadruple ranks of the marines, but although he ran his eye mechanically over the men he took notice of nothing. Captain Morris and his sergeants could be relied upon to attend to details like the pipeclaying of belts and the polishing of buttons. Marines could be drilled and disciplined into machines in a way sailors could not be; he could take the marines for granted and he was not interested in them. Even now, after ten days, he hardly knew the faces and names of six out of the ninety marines on board.

He passed on to the lines of seamen, the officers of each division standing rigidly in front. This was more interesting. The men were trim and smart in their whites — Hornblower wondered how many of them ever realised that the cost of their clothing was deducted from the meagre pay they received when they were paid off. Some of the new hands were horribly sunburned, as a result of unwise exposure to the sudden blazing sun of yesterday. A blond burly figure here had lost the skin from his forearms as well as from his neck and forehead. Hornblower recognised him as Waites, condemned for sheepstealing at Exeter assizes — that explained the sunburn, for Waites had been blanched by months of imprisonment awaiting trial. The raw areas looked abominably painful.

"See that this man Waites," said Hornblower to the petty officer of the division, "attends the surgeon this afternoon. He is to have goose grease for those burns, and whatever lotions the surgeon prescribes."

"Aye aye, sir," said the petty officer.

Hornblower passed on down the line, scanning each man closely. Faces well remembered, faces it was still an effort to put a name to. Faces that he had studied two years back in the far Pacific on board the *Lydia,* faces he had first seen when Gerard brought back his boatload of bewildered captives from St. Ives. Swarthy faces and pale, boys and elderly men, blue eyes, brown eyes, grey eyes. A host of tiny impressions were collecting in Hornblower's mind; they would be digested together later during his solitary walks in the stern gallery, to form the raw material for the plans he would make to further the efficiency of his crew.

"That man Simms ought to be rated captain of the mizzen-top. He's old enough now. What's this man's name? Dawson? No, Dawkins. He's looking sulky. One of Goddard's gang — it looks as if he's still resenting Goddard's flogging. I must remember that."

The sun blazed down upon them, while the ship lifted and swooped over the gentle sea. From the crew he turned his attention to the ship — the breechings of the guns, the way the falls were flemished down, the cleanliness of the decks, the galley and the forecastle. At all this he need only pretend to look — the skies would fall before Bush neglected his duty. But he had to go through with it, with a show of solemnity. Men were oddly influenced — the poor fools would work better for Bush if they thought Hornblower was keeping an eye on him, and they would work better for Hornblower if they thought he inspected the ship thoroughly. This wretched business of capturing men's devotion set Hornblower smiling cynically when he was unobserved.

"A good inspection, Mr. Bush," said Hornblower, returning to the quarterdeck. "The ship is in better order than I hoped for. I shall expect the improvement to continue. You may rig the church now."

It was a God-fearing Admiralty who ordered church service every Sunday morning, otherwise Hornblower would have dispensed with it, as befitted a profound student of Gibbon. As it was, he had managed to evade having a chaplain on board — Hornblower hated parsons. He watched the men dragging up mess stools for themselves, and chairs for the officers. They were working diligently and cheerfully, although not with quite that disciplined purposefulness which characterised a fully trained crew. His coxswain Brown covered the compass box on the quarterdeck with a cloth, and laid on it, with due solemnity, Hornblower's Bible and prayer book. Hornblower disliked these services; there was always the chance that some devout member of his compulsory congregation might raise objections to having to attend — Catholic or Nonconformist. Religion was the only power which could ever pit itself against the bonds of discipline; Hornblower remembered a theologically minded master's mate who had once protested against his reading the benediction, as though he, the King's representative at sea — God's representative, when all was said and done — could not read a benediction if he chose!

He glowered at the men as they settled down, and began to read. As the thing had to be done, it might as well be done well, and, as ever, while he read he was struck once more by the beauty of Cranmer's prose and the deftness of his adaptation. Cranmer had been burned alive two hundred and fifty years before — did it benefit him at all to have his prayer book read now?

Bush read the lessons in a tuneless bellow as if he were hailing the foretop. Then Hornblower read the opening lines of the hymn, and Sullivan the fiddler played the first bars of the tune. Bush gave the signal for the singing to start — Hornblower could never bring himself to do that; he told himself he was neither a mountebank nor an Italian opera conductor — and the crew opened their throats and roared it out.

But even hymn singing had its advantages. A captain could often discover a good deal about the spirits of his crew by the way they sang their hymns. This morning either the hymn chosen was specially popular or the crew were happy in the new sunshine, for they were singing lustily, with Sullivan sawing away at an ecstatic obligato on his fiddle. The Cornishmen among the crew apparently knew the hymn well, and fell upon it with a will, singing in parts to add a leavening of harmony to the tuneless bellowings of the others. It all meant nothing to Hornblower — one tune was the same as another to his tone-deaf ear, and the most beautiful music was to him no more than comparable to the noise of a cart along a gravel road. As he listened to the unmeaning din, and gazed at the hundreds of gaping mouths, he found himself wondering as usual whether or not there was any basis of fact in this legend of music — whether other people actually heard something more than mere noise, or whether he was the only person on board not guilty of willful self-deception.

Then he saw a ship's boy in the front row. The hymn meant something to him, at least. He was weeping broken-heartedly, even while he tried to keep his back straight and to conceal his emotions, with the big tears running down his cheeks and his nose all beslobbered. The poor little devil had been touched in one way or another — some chord of memory had been struck. Perhaps the last time he had heard that hymn was in the little church at home, beside his mother and brothers. He was homesick and heartbroken now. Hornblower was glad for his sake as well as for his own when the hymn came to an end; the next ceremony would steady the boy again.

He took up the Articles of War and began to read them, as the Lords Commissioners of the Admiralty had ordained should be done each Sunday in every one of His Britannic Majesty's ships. He knew the solemn sentences by heart at this, his five hundredth reading, every cadence, every turn of phrase, and he read them well. This was better than any vague religious service or Thirty Nine Articles. Here was a code in black and white, a stern, unemotional call to duty pure and simple. Some Admiralty clerk or pettifogging lawyer had had a gift of phrasing just as felicitous as Cranmer's. There was no trumpet call about it, no claptrap appeal to sentiment; there was merely the cold logic of the code which kept the British Navy at sea, and which had guarded England during seventeen years of a struggle for life. He could tell by the deathlike stillness of his audience as he read that their attention had been caught and held, and when he folded the paper away and looked up he could see solemn, set faces. The ship's boy in the front row had forgotten his tears. There was a faraway look in his eyes; obviously he was making good resolutions to attend more strictly to his duty in future. Or perhaps he was dreaming wild dreams of the time to come when he would be a captain in a gold-laced coat commanding a seventy four, or of brave deeds which he would do.

In a sudden revulsion of feeling Hornblower wondered if lofty sentiment would armour the boy against cannon shot — he remembered another ship's boy who had been smashed into a red jam before his eyes by a shot from the *Natividad.*

Chapter VIII

In the afternoon Hornblower was walking his quarterdeck; the problem before him was so difficult that he had quitted his stern gallery — he could not walk fast enough there, owing to his having to bend his head, to set his thoughts going. The people on the quarterdeck saw his mood, and kept warily over to the lee side, leaving the whole weather side, nearly thirty yards of quarterdeck and gangway, to him. Up and down he walked, up and down, trying to nerve himself to make the decision he hankered after. The *Sutherland* was slipping slowly through the water with a westerly breeze abeam; the convoy were clustered together only a few cables' lengths to leeward.

Gerard shut his telescope with a snap.

"Boat pulling towards us from *Lord Mornington*, sir," he said. He wanted to warn his captain of the approach of visitors, so that if he thought fit he could make himself unapproachable in his cabin; but he knew, as well as Hornblower did, that it might be unwise for a captain to act in too cavalier a fashion towards the notabilities on board the East India convoy.

Hornblower looked across at the boat creeping beetlelike towards him. Ten days of a strong northeasterly wind had not merely hurried the convoy to the latitude of North Africa where he was to leave them to their own devices, but had prevented all intercourse and visiting between ships until yesterday. Yesterday there had been a good deal of coming and going between the ships of the convoy; it was only natural that today he should receive formal calls, which he could not well refuse. In another two hours they would be parting company — it could not be a prolonged ordeal.

The boat ran alongside, and Hornblower walked forward to receive his two guests — Captain Osborn of the *Lord Mornington*, in his formal frock coat, and someone else, tall and bony, resplendent in civilian full dress with ribbon and star.

"Good afternoon, Captain," said Osborn. "I wish to present you to Lord Eastlake, Governor-designate of Bombay."

Hornblower bowed; so did Lord Eastlake.

"I have come," said Lord Eastlake, clearing his throat, "to beg of you, Captain Hornblower, to receive on behalf of your ship's company this purse of four hundred guineas. It has been subscribed by the passengers of the East India convoy in recognition of the skill and courage displayed by the *Sutherland* in the action with the two French privateers off Ushant."

"In the name of my ship's company I thank your lordship," said Hornblower.

It was a very handsome gesture, and as he took the purse he felt like Judas, knowing what designs he was cherishing against the East India convoy.

"And I," said Osborn, "am the bearer of a most cordial invitation to you and to your first lieutenant to join us at dinner in the *Lord Mornington*."

At that Hornblower shook his head with apparent regret.

"We part company in two hours," he said. "I was about to hang out a signal to that effect. I am deeply hurt by the necessity of having to refuse."

"We shall all be sorry on board the *Lord Mornington*," said Lord Eastlake. "Ten days of bad weather have deprived us of the pleasure of the company of any of the officers of the Navy. Cannot you be persuaded to alter your decision?"

"This has been the quickest passage I have made to these latitudes," said Osborn. "I begin to regret it now that it appears to have prevented our seeing anything of you."

"I am on the King's service, my lord, and under the most explicit orders from the admiral."

That was an excuse against which the Governor-designate of Bombay could not argue.

"I understand," said Lord Eastlake. "At least, can I have the pleasure of making the acquaintance of your officers?"

Once more that was a handsome gesture; Hornblower called them up and presented them one by one; horny-handed Bush, and Gerard handsome and elegant, Captain Morris of the marines and his two gawky subalterns, the other lieutenants and the master, down to the junior midshipman, all of them delighted and embarrassed at this encounter with a lord.

At last Lord Eastlake turned to go.

"Good-bye, Captain," he said, proffering his hand. "A prosperous voyage in the Mediterranean to you."

"Thank you, my lord. And a good passage to Bombay to you. And a successful and historic term of office."

Hornblower stood weighing the purse — an embroidered canvas bag at which someone had laboured hard recently — in his hand. He felt the weight of the gold, and under his fingers he felt the crackle of the bank notes. He would have liked to treat it as prize money, and take his share under prize-money rules, but he knew he could not accept that sort of reward from civilians. Still, his crew must show full appreciation.

"Mr. Bush," he said, as the boat shoved off. "Man the yards. Have the men give three cheers."

Lord Eastlake and Captain Osborn acknowledged the compliment as they pulled away; Hornblower watched the boat creep back to the *Lord Mornington.* Four hundred guineas. It was a lot of money, but he was not going to be bought off with four hundred guineas. In that very moment he came to his decision, after twenty four hours of vacillation. He would display to the East India convoy the independence of Captain Hornblower.

"Mr. Rayner," he said. "Clear away the launch and the longboat. Have the helm put up and run down to leeward of the convoy. I want those boats in the water by the time we reach them. Mr. Bush. Mr. Gerard. Your attention, please."

Amid the bustle and hurry of wearing the ship, and tailing on at the stay tackles, Hornblower gave his orders briefly. For once in his life Bush ventured to demur when he realised what Hornblower had in mind.

"They're John Company's ships, sir," he said.

"I had myself fancied that such was the case," said Hornblower with elaborate irony. He knew perfectly well the risk he was running in taking men from ships of the East India Company — he would be both offending the most powerful corporation in

England and contravening Admiralty orders. But he needed the men, needed them desperately, and the ships from whom he was taking them would sight no land until they reached St. Helena. It would be three or four months before any protest could reach England, and six months before any censure could reach him in the Mediterranean. A crime six months old might not be prosecuted with extreme severity; and perhaps in six months' time he would be dead.

"Give the boats' crews pistols and cutlasses," he said, "just to show that I'll stand no nonsense. I want twenty men from each of those ships."

"Twenty!" said Bush, gaping with admiration. This was flouting the law on the grand scale.

"Twenty from each. And mark you, I'll have only white men. No Lascars. And able seamen every one of them, men who can hand, reef, and steer. And find out who their quarter gunners are, and bring them. You can use some trained gunners, Gerard?"

"By God I can, sir."

"Very good."

Hornblower turned away. He had reached his decision unaided, and he did not want to discuss it further. The *Sutherland* had run down to the convoy. First the launch and then the cutter dropped into the water and pulled over to the clustered ships, while the *Sutherland* dropped farther down to leeward to await their return, hove to with main topsail to the mast. Through his glass Hornblower saw the flash of steel as Gerard with his boarding party ran up onto the deck of the *Lord Mornington* — he was displaying his armed force early so as to overawe any thought of resistance. Hornblower was in a fever of anxiety which he had to struggle hard to conceal. He shut his glass with a snap and began to pace the deck.

"Boat pulling towards us from *Lord Mornington*, sir," said Rayner, who was as excited as his captain, and far more obviously.

"Very good," said Hornblower with careful unconcern.

That was a comfort. If Osborn had given Gerard a point-blank refusal, had called his men to arms and defied him, it might give rise to a nasty situation. A court of law might call it murder if someone got killed in a scuffle while illegal demands were being enforced. But he had counted on Osborn being taken completely by surprise when the boarding party ran onto his deck. He would be able to offer no real resistance. Now Hornblower's calculations were proving correct; Osborn was sending a protest, and he was prepared to deal with any number of protests — especially as the rest of the convoy would wait on their Commodore's example and could be relieved of their men while the protesting was going on.

It was Osborn himself who came in through the entry port, scarlet with rage and offended dignity.

"Captain Hornblower!" he said, as he set foot on the deck. "This is an outrage! I must protest against it, sir. At this very moment your lieutenant is parading my crew with a view to impressment."

"He is acting by my orders, sir," said Hornblower.

"I could hardly believe it when he told me so. Are you aware, sir, that what you propose to do is contrary to the law? It is a flagrant violation of Admiralty regulations. A perfect outrage, sir. The ships of the Honourable East India Company are exempt from impressment, and I, as Commodore, must protest to the last breath of my body against any contravention of the law."

"I shall be glad to receive your protest when you make it, sir."

"But — but —— " spluttered Osborn. "I have delivered it. I have *made* my protest, sir."

"Oh, I understand," said Hornblower. "I thought these were only remarks preliminary to a protest."

"Nothing of the sort," raved Osborn, his portly form almost dancing on the deck. "I have protested, sir, and I shall continue to protest. I shall call the attention of the highest in the land to this outrage. I shall come from the ends of the earth, gladly, sir, to bear witness at your courtmartial. I shall not rest — I shall leave no stone unturned — I shall exert all my influence to have this crime punished as it deserves. I'll have you cast in damages, sir, as well as broke."

"But, Captain Osborn —— " began Hornblower, changing his tune just in time to delay the dramatic departure which Osborn was about to make. From the tail of his eye Hornblower had seen the *Sutherland's* boats pulling towards two more victims, having presumably stripped the first two of all possible recruits. As Hornblower began to hint at a possible change of mind on his part, Osborn rapidly lost his ill temper.

"If you restore the men, sir, I will gladly retract all I have said," said Osborn. "Nothing more will be heard of the incident, I assure you."

"But will you not allow me to ask for volunteers from among your crews, Captain?" pleaded Hornblower. "There may be a few men who would like to join the King's service."

"Well — yes, I will even agree to that. As you say, sir, you may find a few restless spirits."

That was the height of magnanimity on Osborn's part, although he was safe in assuming that there would be few men in his fleet foolish enough to exchange the comparative comfort of the East India Company's service for the rigours of life in the Royal Navy.

"Your seamanship in that affair with the privateers, sir, was so admirable that I find it hard to refuse you anything," said Osborn, pacifically. The *Sutherland's* boats were alongside the last of the convoy now.

"That is very good of you, sir," said Hornblower, bowing. "Allow me, then, to escort you into your gig. I will recall my boats. Since they will have taken volunteers first, we can rely upon it that they will have all the willing ones on board, and I shall return the unwilling ones. Thank you, Captain Osborn. Thank you."

He saw Captain Osborn over the side and walked back to the quarterdeck. Rayner was eyeing him with amazement on account of his sudden volte-face, which gave him pleasure, for Rayner would be still more amazed soon. The cutter and launch, both of them as full of men as they well could be, were running down now to rejoin, passing Osborn's gig as it was making its slow course to windward. Through his glass Hornblower could see Osborn wave his arm as he sat in his gig; presumably he was shouting something to the boats as they went by. Bush and Gerard very properly paid him no attention. In two minutes they were alongside, and the men came pouring on deck, a hundred and twenty men laden with their small possessions, escorted by thirty of the *Sutherland's* hands. They were made welcome by the rest of the crew, all with broad grins. It was a peculiarity of the British pressed sailor that he was always glad to see other men pressed — in the same way, thought Hornblower, as the fox who lost his brush wanted all the other foxes to lose theirs.

Bush and Gerard had certainly secured a fine body of men; Hornblower looked them over as they stood in apathy, or bewilderment, or sullen rage, upon the *Sutherland's* main deck. At no warning they had been snatched from the comfort of an Indiaman, with regular pay, ample food, and easy discipline, into the hardships of the King's service, where the pay was problematic, the food bad, and where their backs were liable to be flogged to the bones at a simple order from their new captain. Even a sailor before the mast could look forward with pleasure to his visit to India, with all its possibilities; but these men were destined instead now to two years of monotony only varied by danger, where disease and the cannon balls of the enemy lay in wait for them.

"I'll have those boats hoisted in, Mr. Rayner," said Hornblower.

Rayner's eyelids flickered for a second — he had heard Hornblower's promise to Captain Osborn, and he knew that more than a hundred of the new arrivals would refuse to volunteer. The boats would only have to be hoisted out again to take them back. But if Hornblower's wooden expression indicated anything at all, it was that he meant what he said.

"Aye aye, sir," said Rayner.

Bush was approaching now, paper in hand, having agreed his figures regarding the recruits with Gerard.

"A hundred and twenty, total, sir, as you ordered," said Bush. "One cooper's mate — he was a volunteer, one hundred and nine able seamen — two of 'em volunteered; six quarter gunners; four landsmen, all volunteers."

"Excellent, Mr. Bush. Read 'em in. Mr. Rayner, square away as soon as those boats are inboard. Mr. Vincent! Signal to the convoy. 'All-men-have-volunteered. Thank you. Good-bye.' You'll have to spell out 'volunteered,' but it's worth it."

Hornblower's high spirits had lured him into saying an unnecessary sentence. But when he took himself to task for it he could readily excuse himself. He had a hundred and twenty new hands, nearly all of them able seamen — the *Sutherland* had nearly her full complement now. More than that, he had guarded himself against the wrath to come. When the inevitable chiding letter arrived from the Admiralty he would be able to write back and say that he had taken the men with the East India Company's Commodore's permission; with any good fortune he could keep the ball rolling for another six months. That would give him a year altogether in which to convince the new hands that they had volunteered — by that time some of them at least might be sufficiently enamoured of their new life to swear to that; enough of them to befog the issue, and to afford to an Admiralty, prepared of necessity to look with indulgence on breaches of the pressing regulations, a loophole of excuse not to prosecute him too hard.

"*Lord Mornington* replying, sir," said Vincent. " 'Do not understand the signal. Await boat'!"

"Signal 'Good-bye' again," said Hornblower.

Down on the main deck Bush had nearly finished reading through the Articles of War to the new hands — the necessary formality to make them servants of the King, submissive to the hangman and the cat.

Chapter IX

THE *Sutherland* had reached her rendezvous off Palamos Point, apparently the first of the squadron, for there was no sign as yet of the flagship or of the *Caligula.* As she beat slowly up under easy sail against the gentle southeasterly wind Gerard was taking advantage of this period of idleness to exercise the crew at the guns. Bush had too long had his way in drilling the crew aloft; it was time for practice with the big guns, as Hornblower had agreed. Under the scorching sun of a Mediterranean midsummer the men, naked to the waist, had sweated rivers running the guns out and in again, training round with handspikes, each man of the crew learning the knack of the flexible rammer — all the mechanical drill which every man at the guns had to learn until he could be trusted to run up, fire, clean, and reload, and to go on doing so for hour after hour, in thick powder smoke and with death all round him. Drill first, marksmanship a long way second, but all the same it was policy to allow the men to fire off the guns a few times — they found compensation in that for the arduous toil at the guns.

A thousand yards to port the quarter boat was bobbing over the glittering sea. There was a splash, and then they could see the black dot of the cask she had thrown overboard before pulling hastily out of the line of fire.

"No. 1 gun!" bellowed Gerard. "Take your aim! Cock your locks! Fire — stop your vents!"

The foremost eighteen-pounder roared out briefly while a dozen glasses looked for the splash.

"Over and to the right!" announced Gerard. "No. 2 gun!"

The main-deck eighteen-pounders, the lower-deck twenty-four-pounders, spoke each in turn. Even with experienced gun layers it would have been too much to expect to hit a cask at such a long range in thirty seven shots; the cask still bobbed unharmed. Every gun of the port battery tried again, and still the cask survived.

"We'll shorten the range. Mr. Bush, have the helm put up and run the ship past the cask a cable's length away. Now, Mr. Gerard."

Two hundred yards was a short enough range even for carronades; the forecastle and quarterdeck carronades' crews stood to their weapons as the *Sutherland* ran down to the cask. The guns went off nearly simultaneously as they bore, the ship trembling to the concussions, while the thick smoke eddied upwards round the naked men. The water boiled all round the cask, as half a ton of iron tore it up in fountains, and in the midst of the splashes the cask suddenly leaped clear of the water, dissolving into its constituent staves as it did so. All the guns' crews cheered while Hornblower's silver whistle split the din as a signal to cease fire, and the men clapped each other on the shoulder exultantly. They were heartily pleased with themselves. As Hornblower knew, the fun of knocking a cask to pieces was full compensation for two hours' hard work at gun drill.

The quarter boat dropped another cask; the starboard-side battery prepared to bombard it, while Hornblower stood blinking gratefully in the sunshine on the quarterdeck, feeling glad to be alive. He had as full a crew as any captain could hope for, and more trained topmen than he could ever have dared to expect. So far everyone was healthy; his landsmen were fast becoming seamen, and he would train them into gunners even quicker than that. This blessed midsummer sunshine, hot and dry, suited his health admirably. He had left off fretting over Lady Barbara, thanks to the intense pleasure which it gave him to see his crew settling down into a single efficient unit. He was glad to be alive, with high spirits bubbling up within him.

"Good shot, there!" said Hornblower. An extraordinarily lucky shot from one of the lower-deck guns had smashed the second cask to fragments. "Mr. Bush, see that every man of that gun's crew gets a tot of rum tonight."

"Aye aye, sir."

"Sail ho!" came from the masthead. "Deck, there. Sail right to wind'ard, an' comin' down fast."

"Mr. Bush, have the quarter boat recalled. Heave the ship to on the starboard tack, if you please."

"Aye aye, sir."

Even here, no more than fifty miles from France, and not more than twenty from a corner of Spain under French domination, there was very small chance of any sail being French, especially on the course this one was steering — any French vessel crept along the coast without venturing a mile to sea.

"Masthead! What do you make of the sail?"

"She's a ship, sir, wi' all sail set. I can see her royals an' t'garn stuns'ls."

"Belay!" roared the boatswain's mate to the hands hoisting in the quarter boat.

The fact that the approaching vessel was a full-rigged ship made it more unlikely still that she was French — French commerce was confined to small craft, luggers and brigs and tartans, now. Probably she was one of the ships the *Sutherland* had come to meet. A moment later the suspicion was confirmed from the masthead.

"Deck, there! Sail looks like *Caligula* to me, sir. I can see her torps'ls now, sir."

So she was; Captain Bolton must have completed his task of escorting the storeships into Port Mahon. Within an hour the *Caligula* was within gunshot.

"*Caligula* signalling, sir," said Vincent. "Captain to captain. 'Delighted to see you. Will you dine with me now?' "

"Hoist the assent," replied Hornblower.

The pipes of the boatswain's mates twittered into one last weird wail as Hornblower went up the side of the *Caligula;* the side boys stood at attention; the marines presented arms; and Captain Bolton came forward, his hand held out and his craggy face wreathed in smiles.

"First at the rendezvous!" said Bolton. "Come this way, sir. It does my heart good to see you again. I've twelve dozen sherry here I'll be glad to hear your opinion of. Where are those glasses, steward? Your very good health, sir!"

Captain Bolton's after cabin was furnished with a luxury which contrasted oddly to Hornblower's. There were satin cushions on the lockers; the swinging lamps were of silver, and so were the table appointments on the white linen cloth on the table. Bolton had been lucky in the matter of prize money when in command of a frigate — a single cruise had won him five thousand pounds — and Bolton had started life before the mast. The momentary jealousy which Hornblower experienced evaporated as he noted the poor taste of the cabin fittings, and remembered how dowdy Mrs. Bolton had looked when he saw her last. More than anything else, Bolton's obvious pleasure at seeing him, and the genuine respect he evinced in his attitude towards him, combined to give Hornblower a better opinion of himself.

"From the rapidity with which you reached the rendezvous, it appears that your passage was even quicker than ours," said Bolton, and the conversation lapsed into technicalities, which endured even after dinner was served.

And clearly Bolton had little idea of what kind of dinner to offer in this scorching heat. There was pea soup, excellent, but heavy. Red mullet — a last-minute purchase in Port Mahon at the moment of sailing. A saddle of mutton. Boiled cabbage. A Stilton cheese, now a little past its best. A syrupy port which was not to Hornblower's taste. No salad, no fruit, not one of the more desirable products of the Minorca Bolton had just left.

"Minorquin mutton, I fear," said Bolton, carvers in hand. "My last English sheep died mysteriously at Gibraltar and provided dinner for the gunroom. But you will take a little more, sir?"

"Thank you, no," said Hornblower. He had eaten manfully through a vast helping, and, gorged with mutton fat, was sitting sweating now in the sweltering cabin. Bolton pushed the wine back to him, and Hornblower poured a few drops into his half-empty glass. A lifetime of practice had made him adept at appearing to drink level with his host while actually drinking one glass to three. Bolton emptied his own glass and refilled it.

"And now," said Bolton, "we must await in idleness the arrival of Sir Mucho Pomposo, Rear Admiral of the Red."

Hornblower looked at Bolton quite startled. He himself would never have risked speaking of his superior officer as Mucho Pomposo to anyone. Moreover, it had not occurred to him to think of Sir Percy Leighton in that fashion. Criticism of a superior who had yet to demonstrate to him his capacity one way or the other was not Hornblower's habit; and possibly he was specially slow to criticise a superior who was Lady Barbara's husband.

"Mucho Pomposo, I said," repeated Bolton. He had drunk one glass more of port than was quite wise, and was pouring himself out another one. "We can sit and polish our backsides while he works that old tub of a *Pluto* round from Lisbon. Wind's sou'-easterly. So it was yesterday, too. If he didn't pass the Straits two days back it'll be a week or more before he appears. And if he doesn't leave all the navigation to Elliott he'll never arrive at all."

Hornblower looked up anxiously at the skylight. If any report of this conversation were to reach higher quarters it would do Bolton no good. The latter interpreted the gesture correctly.

"Oh, never fear," he said. "I can trust my officers. They don't respect an admiral who's no seaman any more than I do. Well, what have you to say?"

Hornblower proffered the suggestion that one of the two ships might push to the northward and begin the task of harassing the French and Spanish coast while the other stayed on the rendezvous awaiting the admiral.

"That's a worthy suggestion," said Bolton.

Hornblower shook off the lassitude occasioned by the heat and the vast meal inside him. He wanted the *Sutherland* to be despatched on this duty. The prospect of immediate action was stimulating. He could feel his pulse quickening at the thought, and the more he considered it the more anxious he was that the choice would fall on him. Days of dreary beating about on and off the rendezvous made no appeal to him at all. He could bear it if necessary — twenty years in the Navy would harden anyone to waiting — but he did not want to have to. He did not want to.

"Who shall it be?" said Bolton. "You or me?"

Hornblower took a grip of his eagerness.

"You are the senior officer on the station, sir," he said. "It is for you to say."

"Yes," said Bolton, meditatively. "Yes."

He looked at Hornblower with a considering eye.

"You'd give three fingers to go," he said suddenly, "and you know it. You're the same restless devil that you were in the *Indefatigable*. I remember beating you for it, in '93, or was it '94?"

Hornblower flushed hotly at the reminder. The bitter humiliation of being bent over a gun and beaten by the lieutenant of the midshipmen's berth rankled to this day when it was recalled to him. But he swallowed his resentment; he had no wish to quarrel with Bolton, especially at this juncture, and he knew he was exceptional in regarding a beating as an outrage.

"In '93," he said. "I'd just joined."

"And now you're a post captain, and the most noteworthy one in the bottom half of the list," said Bolton. "God, how time flies. I'd let you go, Hornblower, for old times' sake, if I didn't want to go myself."

"Oh," said Hornblower. His evident disappointment made his expression ludicrous. Bolton laughed.

"Fair's fair," he said. "I'll spin a coin for it. Agreed?"

"Yes, sir," said Hornblower, eagerly. Better an even chance than no chance at all.

"You'll bear me no malice if I win?"

"No, sir. None."

With maddening slowness Bolton reached into his fob and brought out his purse. He took out a guinea and laid it on the table, and then, with the same deliberation, while Hornblower wrestled with his eagerness, he replaced the purse. Then he took up the guinea, and poised it on his gnarled thumb and forefinger.

"King or spade?" he asked, looking across at Hornblower.

"Spade," said Hornblower, swallowing hard.

The coin rang as Bolton spun it into the air; he caught it, and crashed it onto the table.

"Spade it is," he said, lifting his hand.

Bolton went through all the motions once more of taking out his purse, putting the guinea back, and thrusting the purse into his fob, while Hornblower forced himself to sit still and watch him. He was cool again now, with the immediate prospect of action.

"Damn it, Hornblower," he said. "I'm glad you won. You can speak the Dago's lingo, which is more than I can. You've had experience with 'em in the South Sea. It's the sort of duty just made for you. Don't be gone more than three days. I ought to put that in writing, in case his High Mightiness comes back. But I won't trouble. Good luck to you, Hornblower, and fill your glass."

Hornblower filled it two thirds full — if he left a little in the bottom he would only have drunk half a glass more than he wanted then. He sipped, and leaned back in his chair, restraining his eagerness as long as possible. But it overcame him at last, and he rose.

"God damn it, man, you're not going?" said Bolton. Hornblower's attitude was unmistakable, but he could not believe the evidence of his eyes.

"If you would permit me, sir," said Hornblower. "There's a fair wind —— "

Hornblower was actually stammering as he tried to make all his explanations at once. The wind might change; if it was worth while separating it was better to go now than later; if the *Sutherland* were to stand in towards the coast during the dark hours there was a chance that she might snap up a prize at dawn — every sort of explanation except the true one that he could not bear to sit still any longer with immediate action awaiting him just over the horizon.

"Have it your own way then," grumbled Bolton. "If you must, you must. You're leaving me with a half-empty bottle. Does that mean you don't like my port?"

"No, sir," said Hornblower, hastily.

"Another glass, then, while your boat's crew is making ready. Pass the word for Captain Hornblower's gig."

The last sentence was bellowed towards the closed door of the cabin, and was immediately repeated by the sentry outside.

Boatswain's pipes twittered as Hornblower went down the *Caligula's* side, officers stood to attention, side boys held the lines.

The gig rowed rapidly over the silver water in the fading evening; Coxswain Brown looked sidelong, anxiously, at his captain, trying to guess what this hurried and early departure meant. In the *Sutherland* there was similar anxiety; Bush and Gerard and Crystal and Rayner were all on the quarterdeck awaiting him — Bush had obviously turned out of bed at the news that the captain was returning.

Hornblower paid no attention to their expectant glances. He had made it a rule to offer no explanations — and there was a pleasurable selfish thrill in keeping his subordinates in ignorance of their future. Even as the gig came leaping up to the tackles he gave the orders which squared the ship away before the wind, heading back to the Spanish coast where adventure awaited them.

"*Caligula's* signalling, sir," said Vincent. "Good luck."

"Acknowledge," said Hornblower.

The officers on the quarterdeck looked at each other, wondering what the future held in store for them for the commodore to wish them good luck. Hornblower noted the interchange of glances without appearing to see them.

"Ha — h'm," he said, and walked with dignity below, to pore over his charts and plan his campaign. The timbers creaked faintly as the gentle wind urged the ship over the almost placid sea.

Chapter X

"Two bells, sir," said Polwheal, waking Hornblower from an ecstatic dream. "Wind east by south, course nor' by east, an' all sail set to the royal, sir. An' Mr. Gerard says to say land in sight on the larboard beam."

This last sentence jerked Hornblower from his cot without a moment's more meditation. He stripped off his nightshirt and put on the clothes Polwheal held ready for him. Unshaved and uncombed he hurried up to the quarterdeck. It was full daylight now, with the sun half clear of the horizon and looking over the starboard quarter, and just abaft the port beam a grey mountain shape reflecting its light. That was Cape Creus, where a spur of the Pyrenees came jutting down to the Mediterranean, carrying the Spanish coast line out to its farthest easterly point.

"Sail ho!" yelled the lookout at the masthead. "Nearly right ahead. A brig, sir, standing out from the land on the starboard tack."

It was what Hornblower had been hoping for; it was for this reason that he had laid his course so as to be on this spot at this moment. All the seaboard of Catalonia, as far south as Barcelona and beyond, was in the hands of the French, and a tumultuous French army — the *Account of the Present War in Spain* estimated it at nearly eighty thousand men — was endeavouring to extend its conquests southwards and inland.

But they had Spanish roads to contend against as well as Spanish armies. To supply an army eighty thousand strong, and a large civilian population as well, was impossible by land over the Pyrenean passes, even though Gerona had surrendered last December after a heroic defence. Food and siege materials and ammunition had to be sent by sea, in small craft which crept along the coast, from shore battery to shore battery, through the lagoons and the shallows off the coast of the Gulf of the Lion, past the rocky capes of Spain, as far as Barcelona.

Since Cochrane's recall, this traffic had met with hardly any interference from the British in the Mediterranean. When Hornblower first reached his rendezvous off Palamos Point he had been careful to disappear again over the horizon immediately, so as to give no warning of the approach of a British squadron. He had hoped that the French might grow careless. With the wind nearly in the east, and Cape Creus running out almost directly eastwards, there was a chance that some supply ship or other, compelled to stand far out from the land to weather the point, might be caught at dawn out of range of the shore batteries, having neglected to make this dangerous passage at night. And so it had proved.

"Hoist the colours, Mr. Gerard," said Hornblower. "And call all hands."

"The brig has wore, sir," hailed the lookout. "She's running before the wind."

"Head so as to cut her off, Mr. Gerard. Set stuns'ls both sides."

Before the wind, and with only the lightest of breezes blowing, was the *Sutherland's* best point of sailing, as might be expected of her shallow build and clumsy beam. In these ideal conditions she might easily have the heels of a deep-laden coasting brig.

"Deck, there!" hailed the lookout. "The brig's come to the wind again, sir. She's on her old course."

That was something very strange. If the chase had been a ship of the line, she might have been challenging battle. But a mere brig, even a brig of war, would be expected to fly to the shelter of the shore batteries. Possibly she might be an English brig.

"Here, Savage. Take your glass and tell me what you can see."

Savage dashed up the main rigging at the word.

"Quite right, sir. She's close-hauled again on the starboard tack. We'll pass her to leeward on this course. She's wearing French national colours, sir. And she's signalling now, sir. Can't read the flags yet, sir, and she's nearly dead to leeward, now."

What the devil was the brig up to? She had settled her own fate by standing to windward again; if she had dashed for the land the moment she had sighted the *Sutherland* she might possibly have escaped. Now she was a certain capture — but why was a French brig signalling to a British ship of the line? Hornblower sprang up onto the rail; from there he could see the brig's topsails over the horizon, as she held her windward course.

"I can read the signal now, sir. MV."

"What the devil does MV mean?" snapped Hornblower to Vincent, and then regretted that he had said it. A look would have done as well.

"I don't know, sir," said Vincent, turning the pages of the signal book. "It's not in the code."

"We'll know soon enough," said Bush. "We're coming up to her fast. Hullo! She's wearing round again. She's come before the wind. But it's no use now, Mongseer. You're ours. A handsome bit of prize money there for us, my lads."

The excited chatter of the quarterdeck reached Hornblower's ears to be unheard. This last attempt at flight on the Frenchman's part had explained his previous movements. Bush, Gerard, Vincent, Crystal, were all too careless to have thought about it, too excited at the prospect of prize money. Hornblower could guess now what had happened. At first sight of the *Sutherland*, the brig had turned to fly. Then she had seen the red ensign which the *Sutherland* had hoisted, and misread it as the French colours — both sides had made the same mistake before this; the red fly both of tricolour and of red ensign led easily to confusion.

It was fortunate this time that Leighton had been Rear-Admiral of the Red, so that the *Sutherland* had worn his colours. What was more, the *Sutherland* had the round bow given her by her Dutch builders, the same as nearly every French ship of the line, and unlike every English ship save three or four. So the brig had taken the *Sutherland* to be French, and as soon as she was sure of this had held to the wind again, anxious to make her offing so as to weather Cape Creus. Then the MV signal which she had flown had been the private French recognition signal — that was something well worth knowing. It was only when the *Sutherland* did not make the expected conventional reply that the French captain had realised his mistake, and made one last dash for liberty.

A quite unavailing dash, for the *Sutherland* had cut her off from all chance of escape to leeward. The ships were only two miles apart now, and converging. Once more the brig came round, this time with the very faint hope of clawing away out of range to windward. But the *Sutherland* was hurtling close upon her.

"Fire a shot near him," snapped Hornblower.

At that threat the French captain yielded. The brig hove to, and the tricolour came down from her peak. A cheer went up from the *Sutherland's* main deck.

"Silence, there!" roared Hornblower. "Mr. Bush, take a boat and board her. Mr. Clarke, you're prize-master. Take six hands with you and navigate her to Port Mahon."

Bush was all smiles on his return.

"Brig *Amelie,* sir. Six days out from Marseilles for Barcelona. General cargo of military stores. Twenty five tons of powder. One hundred and twenty five tons of biscuit. Beef and pork in casks. Brandy. Admiralty agent at Port Mahon'll buy her, sure as a gun, ship, stores, and all." Bush rubbed his hands. "And we the only ship in sight!"

If any other British ship had been in sight she would have shared the prize money. As it was the only shares to be given away were those of the admiral commanding in the Mediterranean and of Admiral Leighton commanding the squadron. Between them they would have one third of the value, so that Hornblower's share would be about two ninths — several hundred pounds at least.

"Bring the ship before the wind," said Hornblower. Not for worlds would he give any sign of his delight at being several hundred pounds richer. "We've no time to lose."

He went below to shave, and as he scraped the lather from his cheeks and contemplated the melancholy face in the glass he meditated once more on the superiority of sea over land. The *Amelie* was a small vessel, almost inconsiderable in size. But she carried between two and three hundred tons of stores; and if the French had tried to send that amount overland to Barcelona it would have called for a first-class military convoy — a hundred or more waggons, hundreds of horses, taking up a mile or more of road and needing a guard of thousands of troops to protect it from the attacks of the Spanish partisans. Troops and horses would have needed food, too, and that would call for more waggons still, all crawling along at fifteen miles a day at most over the Spanish roads. Small wonder, then, that the French preferred to run the risk of sending their stores by sea. And what a blow it would be for the harassed French army to find a British squadron on their flank, and their best route of communication broken.

Walking forward to take his bath with Polwheal in attendance, a new idea struck him.

"Pass the word for the sailmaker," he said.

Potter the sailmaker came aft and stood at attention while Hornblower rotated himself under the jet of the wash-deck pump.

"I want a French ensign, Potter," said Hornblower. "There's not one on board?"

"French ensign, sir? No, sir."

"Then make one. I'll give you twenty minutes, Potter."

Hornblower continued to rotate under the jet of the pump, rejoicing in its refreshing impact on this hot morning. The chances were that no Frenchman had observed the capture of the *Amelie* from Cape Creus, and that was the only land in sight at the time. Even if someone had done so, it would take many hours to warn all the coast line of the presence of a British ship of the line. Having taken the French by surprise, the right game to play was to go on exploiting that surprise to the utmost, making use of every device that would make the blow effective. He went back to his cabin and put on refreshing clean linen, still turning over in his mind the details of his plans which were now losing their nebulousness of the night before and growing more and more clear-cut.

"Breakfast, sir?" asked Polwheal, tentatively.

"Bring me some coffee on the quarterdeck," said Hornblower. He could not bear the thought of food — perhaps because of his present excitement, perhaps because of his enormous dinner of the night before.

From the quarterdeck could be seen shadowy blue masses on the horizon right ahead — the peaks of the Pyrenees; between them and the sea crawled the road from France to Spain. The sailmaker's mate came running aft with his arms full of a vast bundle.

"Mr. Vincent," said Hornblower. "I'll have this flag hoisted instead of our own."

The officers on the quarterdeck eyed the strange tricolour as it rose to the peak, and they looked from the flag to their captain, whispering among themselves. Grouped on the lee side, not one of them dared to try to open a conversation with Hornblower on the weather side. Hornblower exulted both in their excitement and in their silence.

"Send the hands to quarters as soon as they have breakfasted, Mr. Bush," said Hornblower. "Clear for action, but keep the ports shut. I want the longboat and launch ready to be hoisted out at a moment's notice."

The hands came tumbling up from breakfast in a perfect babble of sound — the order to clear for action, the tricolour at the peak, the mountains of Spain ahead, the morning's capture, all combining to work them up into wild excitement.

"Keep those men silent on the main deck, there!" bellowed Hornblower. "It sounds like Bedlam turned loose."

The noise dwindled abruptly, the men creeping about like children in a house with an irascible father. The bulkheads came down, the galley fire was tipped overside. The boys were running up with powder for the guns; the shot garlands between the guns were filled with the black iron spheres ready for instant use.

"Cleared for action, sir," said Bush.

"Ha — h'm," said Hornblower. "Captain Morris, if I send away the longboat and launch, I want twenty marines in each. Have your men told off ready."

Hornblower took his glass and studied once more the rapidly nearing coast line. There were cliffs here, and the coast road wound at the foot of them, at the water's edge, and the shore was steep-to, according to his charts. But it would be a sensible precaution to start the lead going soon. He was taking a risk in approaching a lee shore guarded by heavy batteries — the *Sutherland* might be badly knocked about before she could beat to windward out of range again. Hornblower was counting not merely on the disguise he had adopted, but on the very fact that the French would not believe that an English ship could take that risk.

To the French in the batteries the presence of a French ship of the line off that coast was susceptible of explanation — she might have ventured forth from Toulon, or have come in from the Atlantic, or she might be a refugee from some Ionian island attacked by the British, seeking refuge after long wanderings. He could not believe that they would open fire without allowing time for explanation.

At a word from Hornblower the *Sutherland* turned on a course parallel with the shore, heading northward with the wind abeam. She was creeping along now, in the light breeze, only just out of gunshot of the shore. The sun was blazing down upon them, the crew standing silently at their stations, the officers grouped on the quarterdeck, Hornblower with the sweat running down his face, sweeping the coast with his glass in search of an objective. The little wind was calling forth only the faintest piping from the rigging; the rattle of the blocks to the gentle roll of the ship sounded unnaturally loud in the silence as did the monotonous calling of the man at the lead. Suddenly Savage hailed from the foretop.

"There's a lot of small craft, sir, at anchor round the point, there. I can just see 'em from here, sir."

A dark speck danced in the object glass of Hornblower's telescope. He lowered the instrument to rest his aching eye, and then raised it again. The speck was still there; it was a tricolour flag waving lazily in the wind from a flagstaff on the point. That was what Hornblower had been seeking. A French battery perched on the top of the cliff. Forty-two-pounders, probably, sited with a good command, probably with furnaces for heating the shot — no ship that floated could fight them. Clustered underneath, a little coasting fleet, huddling there for shelter at the sight of a strange sail.

"Tell your men to lie down," said Hornblower to Morris. He did not want the red coats of the marines drawn up on the quarterdeck to reveal his ship prematurely for what she was.

The *Sutherland* crept along, the grey cliffs growing more clearly defined as at Hornblower's order she was edged closer inshore. Beyond the cliffs mountain peaks were revealing themselves with startling suddenness whenever Hornblower's rigid concentration on the battery relaxed. He could see the parapets now in his glass, and he almost thought he could see the big guns peeping over them. At any moment now the battery might burst into thunder and flame and smoke, and in that case he would have to turn and fly, baffled. They were well within gunshot now. Perhaps the French had guessed the *Sutherland's* identity, and were merely waiting to have her well within range. Every minute that the *Sutherland* approached meant another minute under fire when she tried to escape. The loss of a mast might mean in the end the loss of the ship.

"Mr. Vincent," said Hornblower, without shifting his gaze from the battery. "Hoist MV."

The words sent a stir through the group of officers. They could be certain now of what plan Hornblower had in mind. The trick increased the risk of detection at the same time as, if it were successful, it gave them more opportunity of approaching the battery. If MV were the French recognition signal, and was being correctly employed, well and good. If not — the battery would soon tell them so. Hornblower, his heart thumping in his breast, judged that at any rate it might confuse the issue for the officer in the battery and induce him to delay a little longer. The signal rose up the halliards, and the battery still stayed silent. Now a signal hoist soared up the battery's flagstaff.

"I can't read that, sir," said Vincent. "One of 'em's a swallow-tail we don't use."

But the mere fact of the battery's signalling in reply meant that they were at least doubtful of the *Sutherland's* identity — unless it were part of the plan to lure her closer in. Yet if the battery delayed much longer it would be too late.

"Mr. Bush, do you see the battery?"

"Yes, sir."

"You will take the longboat. Mr. Rayner will take the launch, and you will land and storm the battery."

"Aye aye, sir."

"I will give you the word when to hoist out."

"Aye aye, sir."

"Quarter less eight," droned the leadsman — Hornblower had listened to each cast subconsciously; now that the water was shoaling he was compelled to give half his attention up to the leadsman's cries while still scrutinising the battery. A bare quarter of a mile from it now; it was time to strike.

"Very good, Mr. Bush. You can go now."

"Aye aye, sir."

"Back the main tops'l, Mr. Gerard."

At Bush's orders the dormant ship sprang to life. The shrilling of the pipes brought the boats' crews to the falls at the run. This was the time when the painful drill would reveal its worth; the more quickly those boats were swung out, manned, and away, the less would be the danger and the greater the chance of success. Longboat and launch dropped to the water, the hands swarming down the falls.

"Throw the guns down the cliff, Mr. Bush. Wreck the battery if you can. But don't stay a moment longer than necessary."

"Aye aye, sir."

They were off, the men tugging like maniacs at the oars.

"Helm a-lee! Mr. Gerard, put the ship about. And down with that flag, and send up our own. Ah!"

The air was torn with the passage of cannon shot overhead. The whole ship shook as something struck her a tremendous blow forward. Hornblower saw the smoke billow up round the battery — it had opened fire at last. And thank God it was firing at the ship; if one of those shots hit a boat he would be in a pretty scrape. So pleased was he at the thought that it never occurred to him to wonder about his own personal safety.

"Mr. Gerard, see if the guns can reach the battery. See that every shot is properly aimed. It is no use unless the embrasures can be swept."

Another salvo from the battery, and too high again, the shots howling overhead. Little Longley, strutting the quarterdeck with his dirk at his hip, checked in his stride to duck, instinctively, and then, with a side glance at his captain, walked on with his neck as stiff as a ramrod. Hornblower grinned.

"Mr. Longley, have that main topgallant halliard spliced at once."

It was a kindness to keep the boy busy so that he would have no time to be afraid. Now the *Sutherland's* starboard broadside began to open fire, irregularly, as the gun captains fancied their weapons bore. Flying jets of dust from the face of the cliff showed that most of the shots were hitting thirty feet too low. But if even one or two shots got in through the embrasures and killed someone working the guns it would be a valuable help in unsettling the artillery men. Another salvo. This time they had fired at the boats. The launch almost vanished under the jets of water flung up by the plunging fire, and Hornblower gulped with anxiety. But next moment the launch reappeared, limping along crabwise — a shot must have smashed some of the oars on one side. But the boats were safe now; close up to the cliffs as they were the guns above could surely not be depressed sufficiently to hit them. The long-boat was in the very surf now, with the launch at her heels. Now the men were tumbling out and splashing up to the beach.

For a moment Hornblower wished that, contrary to etiquette, he had taken command of the landing party, fearing lest a disorderly and piecemeal attack should waste all the advantages gained. No, Bush was safe enough. He could see him through his glass, leaping up onto the road and then turning to face the landing party. Hornblower could see Bush's arms wave as he gave his orders. Someone led off a party of seamen to the right — that was Rayner, for Hornblower's straining eyes could perceive his bald head and unmistakable round-shouldered gait. Morris was taking the marines — a solid block of scarlet — off to the left. Bush was forming up the remainder in the centre — Bush was clearheaded enough. There were three gullies in the face of the cliff, marked with straggling greenery, and indicating the easiest points of ascent. As the flanking parties reached the bottom of their paths, Hornblower saw Bush's sword flash as he called his men on. They were breasting the cliffs now, all three parties simultaneously. A tiny faint cheer crept out over the water to the ship.

One or two of the main-deck guns were making better practice now. Twice Hornblower thought he saw earth flying from the embrasures as shots struck them; so much the better, but the firing must stop now that the men were mounting the cliff. He pealed on his whistle and bellowed the order. In dead silence the ship slid on through the water while every eye watched the landing party. They were pouring over the top now. Sudden gusts of smoke showed that the guns were firing again — canister or grape, probably. Any of those parties caught in a whirlwind of canister from a forty-two-pounder might well be wiped out. Weapons were sparkling on the parapet; little pin pricks of smoke indicated small-arm fire. Now out on the left the red coats of the marines were on the very top of the parapet, and a white-clad sailor was waving from the centre. They were pouring over, although red dots and white dots littered the face of the parapet to mark where men had fallen. One anxious minute with nothing to see seemed to last for hours. And then the tricolour flag came slowly down its staff, and the hands on the main deck burst into a storm of cheering. Hornblower shut his glass with a snap.

"Mr. Gerard, put the ship about. Send in the quarter boats to take possession of the craft in the bay."

There were four tartans, a felucca, and two cutter-rigged boats clustered at anchor in the tiny bay below the battery — a fine haul, especially if they were fully laden. Hornblower saw the dinghies pulling madly from them for the shore on the side away from the battery, as the crews fled to escape captivity. Hornblower was glad to see them go; he did not want to be burdened with prisoners, and he had been a prisoner himself for two weary years in Ferrol. Something fell in an avalanche down the cliff, crashing onto the road at its foot in a cloud of dust and debris. It was a forty-two-pounder heaved up by brute force over the parapet; Bush had got to work quickly enough at dismantling the battery — if Bush were still alive. Another gun followed at an interval, and another after that.

The small craft, two of them towing the quarter boats, were beating out towards the *Sutherland* where she lay hove to awaiting them, and the landing party was coming down the cliff face again and forming up on the beach. Lingering groups indicated that the wounded were being brought down. All these necessary delays seemed to stretch the anticlimax into an eternity. A bellowing roar from the battery, and a fountain of earth and smoke — momentarily like those volcanoes at whose foot the *Lydia* had anchored last commission — told that the magazine had been fired. Now at last the launch and longboat were pulling back to the ship, and Hornblower's telescope, trained on the stern sheets of the longboat, revealed Bush sitting there, alive and apparently well. Even then, it was a relief to see him come rolling aft, his big craggy face wreathed in smiles, to make his report.

"The Frogs bolted out of the back door as we came in at the front," he said. "They hardly lost a man. We lost ——"

Hornblower had to nerve himself to listen to the pitiful list. Now that the excitement was over he felt weak and ill, and it was only by an effort that he was able to keep his hands from trembling. And it was only by an effort that he could make himself smile and mouth out words of commendation first to the men whom Bush singled out for special mention and then to the whole crew drawn up on the main deck. For hours he had been walking the quarterdeck pretending to be imperturbable, and now he was in the throes of the reaction. He left it to Bush to deal with the prizes, to allot them skeleton crews and send them off to Port Mahon, while without a word of excuse he escaped below to his cabin. He had even forgotten that the ship had been cleared for action, so that in his search for privacy he had to sit in his hammock chair at the end of the stern gallery, just out of sight from the stern windows, while the men were replacing the bulkheads and securing the guns. He lay back, his arms hanging and his eyes closed, with the water bubbling under the counter below him and the rudder pintles groaning at his side. Each time the ship went about as Bush worked her out to make an offing his head sagged over to the opposite shoulder.

What affected him most was the memory of the risks he had run; at the thought of them little cold waves ran down his back and his legs. He had been horribly reckless in his handling of the ship — only by the greatest good fortune was she not now a dismasted wreck, with half her crew killed and wounded, drifting onto a lee shore with an exultant enemy awaiting her. It was Hornblower's nature to discount his achievements to himself, to make no allowance for the careful precautions he had taken to ensure success, for his ingenuity in making the best of circumstances. He cursed himself for a reckless fool, and for his habit of plunging into danger and only counting the risk afterwards.

A rattle of cutlery and crockery in the cabin recalled him to himself, and he sat up and resumed his unmoved countenance just in time as Polwheal came out into the stern gallery.

"I've got you a mouthful to eat, sir," he said. "You've had nought since yesterday."

Hornblower suddenly knew that he was horribly hungry, and at the same time he realised that he had forgotten the coffee Polwheal had brought him, hours ago, to the quarterdeck. Presumably that had stayed there to grow cold until Polwheal fetched it away. With real pleasure he got up and walked into the cabin; so tempting was the prospect of food and drink that he felt hardly a twinge of irritation at having Polwheal thus fussing over him and trying to mother him and probably getting ready to take overmuch advantage of his position. The cold tongue was delicious, and Polwheal with uncanny intuition had put out a half bottle of claret — not one day a month did Hornblower drink anything stronger than water when by himself, yet today he drank three glasses of claret, knowing that he wanted them, and enjoying every drop.

And as the food and the wine strengthened him, and his fatigue dropped away, his mind began to busy itself with new plans, devising, without his conscious volition, fresh methods of harassing the enemy. As he drank his coffee the ideas began to stir within him, and yet he was not conscious of them. All he knew was the cabin was suddenly stuffy and cramped, and that he was yearning again for the fresh air and fierce sunshine outside. Polwheal, returning to clear the table, saw his captain through the stern windows pacing the gallery, and years of service under Hornblower had taught him to make the correct deductions from Hornblower's bent, thoughtful head, and the hands which, although clasped behind him, yet twisted and turned one within the other as he worked out each prospective development.

In consequence of what Polwheal had to tell, the lower deck all knew that another move was imminent, fully two hours before Hornblower appeared on the quarterdeck and gave the orders which precipitated it.

Chapter XI

"THEY'RE shooting well, sir," said Bush, as a fountain of water leaped suddenly and mysteriously into brief life a hundred yards from the port beam.

"Who couldn't shoot well with their advantages?" answered Gerard. "Forty-two-pounders, on permanent mounts fifty feet above the water, and soldiers to serve 'em ten years in the ranks?"

"I've seen 'em shoot worse, all the same," said Crystal.

"It's a mile an' a half if it's a yard," said Bush.

"More than that," said Crystal.

"A scant mile," said Gerard.

"Nonsense," said Bush.

Hornblower broke into their wrangling.

"Your attention, please, gentlemen. And I shall want Rayner and Hooker — pass the word, there, for Mr. Rayner and Mr. Hooker. Now, study the place with care."

A dozen telescopes trained on Port Vendres, with the sunset reddening behind. In the background Mount Canigou stood out with a startling illusion of towering height; to the left the spurs of the Pyrenees ran clean down into the sea at Cape Cerbera, marking where Spain had ended and France begun. In the centre the white houses of Port Vendres showed pink under the sunset, clustering round the head of the little bay. In front of them a vessel swung at anchor, under the protection of the batteries on either side of the bay which were marked by occasional puffs of smoke as the guns there tried repeatedly, at extreme long range, to hit this insolent ship which was flaunting British colours within sight of the Empire's coasts.

"Mark that battery to the left, Mr. Gerard," said Hornblower. "Mr. Rayner, you see the battery to the right — there goes a gun. Mark it well. I want no mistake made. Mr. Hooker, you see how the bay curves? You must be able to take a boat straight up to the ship there tonight."

"Aye aye, sir," said Hooker, while the other officers exchanged glances.

"Put the ship upon the port tack, Mr. Bush. We must stand out to sea, now. These are your orders, gentlemen."

Turning from one officer to another, Hornblower ran briefly through their instructions. The ship sheltering in Port Vendres was to be cut out and taken that night, as a climax to the twenty four hours which had begun with the capture of the *Amelie* and continued with the storming of the battery at Llanza.

"The moon rises at one o'clock. I shall take care to be back in our present position here at midnight," said Hornblower.

With good fortune, the garrison of Port Vendres might be lured into tranquillity by the sight of the *Sutherland* sailing away now, and she could return unobserved after nightfall. An hour of darkness would suffice to effect a surprise, and the rising moon would give sufficient light for the captured ship to be brought out if successful, and for the attackers to rally and escape if unsuccessful.

"Mr. Bush will remain in command of the ship," said Hornblower.

"Sir!" protested Bush. "Please, sir —— "

"You've won sufficient distinction today, Mr. Bush," said Hornblower.

Hornblower was going in with the attack. He knew that he would not be able to bear the anxiety of waiting outside with the firing and the fighting going on inside — he was in a fever already, now that he was allowing his mind to dwell on the prospective action, although he was taking care not to show it.

"Every man in the boarding party must be a seaman," said Hornblower. "Mr. Gerard and Mr. Rayner can divide the marines between them."

His listeners nodded, understanding. To set sail in a strange ship and get her under way in darkness would call for seamanship.

"You all understand what is expected of you?" asked Hornblower, and they nodded again. "Mr. Hooker, repeat your orders."

Hooker repeated them accurately. He was a good officer, as

Hornblower had known when he had recommended him for promotion to lieutenant on the *Lydia's* return.

"Good," said Hornblower. "Then, gentlemen, you will please set your watches with mine. There will be enough light from the stars to read them. What, no watch, Mr. Hooker? Perhaps Mr. Bush will be good enough to lend you his."

Hornblower could see, from his officers' expressions, that this synchronisation of the watches had impressed upon them the necessity for accurately conforming to the time-table which he had laid down, in a fashion nothing else could have done. Otherwise they would have paid only casual attention to the intervals of "five minutes" and "ten minutes" which he had given, and he could appreciate in a manner they could not the necessity for exact adherence to schedule in a complex operation carried out in the darkness.

"You are all agreed now? Then perhaps all you gentlemen with the exception of the officer of the watch will give me the pleasure of your company at dinner."

Again the officers interchanged glances; those dinners in Hornblower's cabin on the eve of action were famous. Savage could remember one on board the *Lydia* before the duel with the *Natividad*. The other two present then had been Galbraith, the lieutenant of his division, and Clay, his best friend. And Galbraith had died of gangrene in the far Pacific, and Clay's head had been smashed by a cannon ball.

"There'll be no whist tonight, Savage," smiled Hornblower, reading his thoughts. "There will be too much to do before midnight."

Often before Hornblower had insisted on whist before action, and had concealed his own nervousness by criticism of the play of his preoccupied fellow players. Now he was forcing himself to be smiling, genial, and hospitable as he led the way into the cabin. His nervous tension inclined to make him talkative, and this evening, when his guests were more tongue-tied even than usual, he could for once give rein to his inclinations, and chat freely in an attempt to keep conversation going. The others eyed him wondering as he smiled and gossiped. They never saw him in this mood except on the eve of action, and they had forgotten how human and fascinating he could be when he employed all his wiles to captivate them. For him it was a convenient way to keep his mind off the approaching action, thus to exercise himself in fascination while still drawing the rigid line which divided the captain from his subordinates.

"I am afraid," said Hornblower in the end, crumpling his napkin and tossing it onto the table, "it is time for us to go on deck again, gentlemen. What a mortal pity to break up this gathering!"

They left the lamp-lit brilliance of the cabin for the darkness of the deck. The stars were glowing in the dark sky, and the *Sutherland* was stealing ghostlike over the sea which reflected them; her pyramids of canvas soared up to invisibility, and the only sounds to be heard were the rattle of the rigging and the periodic music of the water under her forefoot as she rode over the tiny invisible waves. The crew was resting on the gangways and the main deck, conversing in whispers, and when the subdued voices of their officers called them to duty they mustered silently, each division assembling for its particular duty. Hornblower checked the position of the ship with Bush, and strained his eye through his night glass towards the invisible shore.

"Longboat crew here!" called Gerard softly.

"Launch crew here!" echoed Rayner, and their allotted parties formed up quietly abreast of the mainmast.

The cutters' crews were assembling on the quarterdeck; Hornblower was taking two hundred and fifty men altogether—if the expedition were a complete disaster Bush would hardly have sufficient men to navigate the *Sutherland* back to the rendezvous.

"You can heave-to, Mr. Bush," he said.

One by one the boats were hoisted out, and lay on their oars a few yards off. Last of all, Hornblower went down the side and seated himself beside Brown and Longley in the stern of the barge; the men at the oars pushed off at a growl from Brown, and the flotilla, with muffled oars, began to pull steadily away from the ship. The darkness was intense, and, by the usual optical illusion, seemed still more intense close to the surface of the sea than up on the deck of the *Sutherland*. Slowly the barge drew ahead, and as the longboat and launch diverged out on each quarter they were rapidly lost to sight. The oars seemed to touch the velvety blackness of the sea without a sound.

Hornblower made himself sit still, his hand resting on the hilt of his fifty-guinea sword. He wanted to crane his neck round and look at the other boats; with every minute's inaction he grew more nervous. Some fool of a marine might fiddle with the lock of his musket, or someone's pistol, carelessly left at full cock, might go off as its owner tugged at his oar. The slightest warning given on shore would ruin the whole attack; might mean the loss of hundreds of lives, and call down upon his head — if he survived — a withering rebuke from his admiral. Grimly he made himself sit still for five more minutes before taking up his night glass.

Then at last he caught the faintest possible glimpse of grey cliff. With his hand on the tiller he altered course until they were almost in the mouth of the inlet.

"Easy!" he breathed, and the boat glided silently forward under the stars. Close astern two tiny nuclei of greater darkness indicated where the two cutters rested on their oars. Holding his watch under his nose he could just see the time — he must wait three full minutes.

A distant sound reached his ear; there were oars pulling in the harbour. He heard them splashing two hundred yards ahead; he fancied he could even see the splashes. The French were, as he expected, rowing guard round their precious ship. Yet her captain had not realised that a guard boat rowing with muffled oars, creeping very slowly along, would be a far more dangerous obstacle to a cutting-out expedition than any boat merely busily rowing up and down across the entrance. He looked at his watch again.

"Oars," he whispered, and the men braced themselves ready to pull. "There's the guard boat ahead. Remember, men, cold steel. If any man fires before I do I'll shoot him with my own hand. Give way!"

The barge crept forward again, stealing into the harbour. In a few more seconds she would be at the point where the batteries' fire crossed, the point which sentries would have under constant observation, upon which the guns would be laid at nightfall so that a salvo would blow any approaching boat out of the water. For a horrible second Hornblower wondered whether launch and longboat had gone astray. Then he heard it. A loud challenge on his right, heard clearly across the water, followed by another on his left, and both instantly drowned in a wild rattle of musketry fire. Rayner and Gerard were leading their parties against the batteries, and both of them, as their orders had dictated, were making an infernal noise about it so as to distract the gunners at the vital moment.

His eye caught the splashes of the guard boat's oars, more noticeable than ever with the crew pulling wildly as they paid attention to the din on shore instead of to their own business. The barge shot silently and unnoticeably towards it. She was only fifty yards from the guard boat when someone at last caught sight of her.

"*Qui va là?*" cried someone, sharply, but before any answer could be expected the barge came crashing up against the guard boat's side, as Hornblower dragged the tiller round.

His quick order had got the oars in a second before the collision, while the impact of the barge swept the oars of the guard boat away, tumbling half her crew in a tangle into the bottom of the boat. Hornblower's sword was out, and at the instant of contact he leaped madly from the barge to the guard boat, choking with excitement and nervousness as he did so. He landed with both feet on someone in the stern, trod him down, and miraculously kept his own footing. There was a white face visible down by his knee, and he kicked at it, wildly, felt a jar up his leg as the kick went home, and at the same moment he cut with all his strength at another head before him. He felt the sword bite into bone; the boat rolled frightfully under him as more of the barge's crew came tumbling into the guard boat. Someone was heaving himself upright before him — someone with a black gash of a moustache across his face in the starlight, and therefore no Englishman. Hornblower lunged fiercely as he reeled in the rocking boat, and he and his opponent came down together upon the men under their feet. When he scrambled up the struggle was over, without a shot being fired. The guard boat's crew was dead, or overboard, or knocked unconscious. Hornblower felt his neck and his wrist wet and sticky — with blood, presumably, but he did not have time to think about that.

"Into the barge, men," he said. "Give way."

The whole fight had hardly taken more than a few seconds. At the batteries the racket of the attack was still continuing, and even as the barge pushed away from the derelict guard boat there came a sudden splutter of musketry fire from higher up the bay. The two cutters had reached the anchored ship without impediment, rowing, as Hornblower's orders had dictated, past the two locked boats straight for her. With his hand on the tiller he set a course for the musket flashes. Apparently the cutter's crews had not succeeded in carrying the ship at the first rush, for the sparkle of the firing stayed steady along the ship's bulwark — she must have had her boarding nettings rigged and her crew fairly wide awake.

The child Longley at his side was leaping about in his seat with excitement.

"Sit still, boy," growled Hornblower.

He put the tiller over and the barge swept under the ship's stern towards the disengaged side of the ship.

"Oars!" hissed Hornblower. "Take hold, there, bowman. Now, all together, men, and give a cheer."

It was a hard scramble up the side of the ship, and her boarding nettings were rigged, sure enough. Hornblower found foothold on the bulwark through the netting, swaying perilously, leaning far out over the water, for the nettings were rigged from the yard-arms and sloped sharply outwards. He struggled in them like a fly in a web. Beside him he saw Longley, writhing similarly. The boy had his dirk between his teeth in the fashion he had heard about in sailors' yarns. He looked so foolish hanging in the netting with the great clumsy weapon in his mouth that Hornblower giggled insanely on his insecure foothold. He snatched his sword from his sheath, clutching with the other hand, and slashed at the tarry cordage. The whole net was heaving and tossing as the barge's crew wrenched at it; he was almost jerked from his hold.

But everyone around him was cheering madly. This surprise

attack on the unguarded side must be shaking the nerve of the defenders trying to beat off the cutters' crews. The fifty-guinea sword was of the finest steel and had a razor edge; it was cutting through strand after strand of the netting. Suddenly something parted with a rush. For one horrible second Hornblower lost his footing and nearly fell outwards, but with a convulsive effort he recovered and swung himself forward, falling through the net on his hands and knees, the sword clattering on the deck before him. A Frenchman was rushing at him; his eye caught a glimpse of the steel head of a levelled pike. He snatched hold of the shaft, twisting onto his back, guiding the weapon clear. The Frenchman's knee crashed into the back of his head, and his neck was badly wrenched as the Frenchman tumbled over on top of him. He kicked himself clear, found his sword, miraculously, and stood to face the other dark shapes rushing at him.

A pistol banged off at his ear, half deafening him, and it seemed as if the whole mass of those attacking him melted away into nothing at the flash. Those others crossing the deck now were English; they were cheering.

"Mr. Crystal!"

"Sir!"

"Cut the cable. Is Mr. Hooker there?"

"Aye aye, sir."

"Get aloft with your boat's crew and set sail."

There was no time for self-congratulation yet. Boats might come dashing out from the shore with reinforcements for the ship's crew; and Rayner and Gerard might be repulsed by the garrisons of the batteries so that he would have to run the gantlet of the guns.

"Brown!"

"Sir!"

"Send up that rocket."

"Aye aye, sir."

The rocket which Brown had brought with him at Hornblower's orders was to be the signal to the landing parties that the ship was taken. And there was a decided breath of air coming off the land which would carry the ship out of the bay; Hornblower had counted on that — after the scorching heat of the day a land breeze was only to be expected.

"Cable's parted, sir!" hailed Crystal from forward.

Hooker had loosed the main topsail, and the ship was already gathering sternway.

"Hands to the braces, there, barge's crew, first cutter's crew. Benskin! Ledly! Take the wheel. Hard-a-starboard."

Brown's flint and steel were clicking and flashing as he crouched on the deck. The rocket rose in an upward torrent of sparks and burst high above into stars. As the fore staysail was set the ship's head came round, and as she steadied on her course down the bay with the wind abaft the moon cleared the horizon right ahead — a gibbous, waning moon, giving just enough light for Hornblower to be able to con the ship easily out of the bay between the batteries. Hornblower could hear whistles blowing, piercing the sound of the musketry which was still popping round the batteries. Rayner and Gerard were calling off their men now.

Two splashes overside indicated that a couple of the ship's crew were swimming for the shore rather than face captivity. It had been a well-timed and successful operation.

Chapter XII

THIS Gulf of the Lion was not likely to be a very profitable cruising ground, so Hornblower decided as he scanned the French coast through his telescope. It was so deeply embayed that any wind from north to west through south would find his ship with land under her lee; it was shallow, treacherous, and liable to be whipped by storms into a tremendous sea. Navigational risks were worth taking if a suitable prize offered, but, thought Hornblower looking at the coast, there was small chance of any prize. From Port Vendres as far round as Marseilles — the limit of the Inshore Squadron's sector — the flat shore was bordered by vast dreary lagoons which were separated from the sea by long spits of sand and even by peninsulas of cultivated land. There were batteries here and there upon the sand spits, and regular forts to support them, and the little towns, Cette, Aigues-Mortes, and so on, were encompassed by mediæval fortifications which could defy any effort he could make against them.

But the main factor was that chain of lagoons, linked together since Roman times by a series of canals. Vessels up to two hundred tons could creep along inside the coast line — he could actually see through his glass, at this very moment, brown sails apparently sailing over the green vineyards. The entrances to the chain were all defended by solid works, and if he were to try to surprise one of these it would involve running all the risk of taking his ship in through the tortuous channels between the sand banks, under gunfire. Even if he should succeed he could still hardly attack the shipping in the lagoons.

The blue Mediterranean under the glaring blue sky shaded to green and even to yellow as it shoaled here and there in patches, a constant reminder to Hornblower as he walked his deck of the treacherous water he was navigating. Forward, the ship was a hive of industry. Bush, watch in hand, had fifty men whom he was drilling aloft — they had set and furled the fore-topgallant sail a dozen times in the last hour and a half, which must be puzzling the numerous telescopes trained on the ship from the shore. Harrison the boatswain, down on the main deck, was squatting on a stool with two of his mates and twenty landsmen cross-legged in a ring round him — he was teaching the advanced class some of the refinements of knotting and splicing. From the lower gun deck the squeal and rumble of gun trucks told how Gerard was exercising embryo gun layers at the six forward twenty-four-pounders — Gerard's ambition was to have six trained gun captains at every gun, and he was a long way yet from achieving it. On the poop Crystal with his sextant was patiently trying to instruct the midshipmen in the elements of navigation — the young devils were fidgety as Crystal droned on. Hornblower was sorry for them. He had delighted in mathematics since his boyhood; logarithms had been playthings to him at little Longley's age, and a problem in spherical trigonometry was to him a source of pleasure, analogous, he realised, to the pleasure some of those lads found in the music which was so incomprehensible to him.

A monotonous hammering below indicated that the carpenter and his mates were putting the finishing touches to their repair of the big hole which had been made yesterday morning — incredible that it was hardly more than twenty four hours ago — by the forty-two-pounder at Llanza, while the clanking of the pumps showed that the petty criminals of the ship were pumping her out. The *Sutherland*, thanks to her recent docking, leaked extraordinarily little, less than an inch a day in calm weather, and Hornblower was able to deal with this small amount by an hour's pumping every morning, allotting to it the miscreants who had found themselves in Bush's or Harrison's black books by being last up the hatchway, or lashing up their hammocks with four and a half turns, or by committing any of the numerous crimes of omission or commission which annoy boatswains and first lieutenants. A turn at pumping — the most monotonous and uninviting work in the ship — was a far more economical punishment than the cat, and Hornblower believed it to be more deterrent, rather to Bush's amusement.

Smoke was pouring from the galley chimney, and even on the

quarterdeck Hornblower could smell the cooking that was going on. The men were going to have a good dinner today, with duff; yesterday they had eaten and drunk nothing save biscuit and cold water, thanks to the ship having been engaged three times in twenty four hours. They did not mind that as long as they were successful — it was amazing how beneficial a little success was to discipline. Today, with eleven dead and sixteen wounded, with thirty four men away in prizes — less two prisoners who had elected to serve the King of England rather than face one of his prisons — the *Sutherland* was more effective as a fighting unit than the day before yesterday with practically a full complement. Hornblower could see, from the quarterdeck, the cheerfulness and high spirits of everyone in sight.

He was cheerful and in high spirits himself. For once his self-depreciation was in abeyance. He had forgotten his fears of yesterday, and three successful actions in a day had re-established his self-confidence. He was at least a thousand pounds the richer by his captures, and that was good to think about. He had never before in his life had a thousand pounds. He remembered how Lady Barbara had tactfully looked away after a single glance at the pinchbeck buckles on his shoes. Next time he dined with Lady Barbara he would be wearing solid gold buckles, with diamonds set in them if he chose, and by some inconspicuous gesture he would call her attention to them. Maria would have bracelets and rings to flaunt his success before the eyes of the world.

Hornblower remembered with pride that he had not known a moment's fear last night in Port Vendres, not when he leaped on board the guard boat, not even when he had found himself in the nightmare embrace of the boarding netting. Just as he now had the wealth for which he had longed, so he had proved to himself to his own surprise that he possessed the brute physical courage which he had envied in his subordinates. Even though, characteristically, he attached no importance to the moral courage and organising ability and ingenuity he had displayed, he was on the crest of a wave of optimism and self-confidence. With high spirits bubbling inside him he turned once more to scan the flat repulsive coast on his left hand, applying himself to the problem of how to stir up confusion there. Down below there were the captured French charts with which the Admiralty had supplied him — as they had the *Pluto* and *Caligula* as well, presumably. Hornblower spent the earliest hours of daylight in poring over them. He called up their details before his mind's eye as he looked across the shallows at the green bar of coast, and the brown sails beyond. He was as close in as he dared, and yet that sail was half a mile beyond cannon shot.

Over to the left was Cette, perched up on the top of a little hill prominent above the surrounding flat land. Hornblower was reminded of Rye overlooking Romney Marsh, but Cette was a gloomy little town of a prevailing black colour, unlike Rye's cheerful greys and reds. And Cette, he knew, was a walled town, with a garrison, against which he could attempt nothing. Behind Cette was the big lagoon called the Etang de Thau, which constituted a major link in the chain of inland waterways which offered shelter and protection to French shipping all the way from Marseilles and the Rhone Valley to the foot of the Pyrenees. Cette was invulnerable as far as he was concerned, and vessels on the Etang de Thau were safe from him.

Of all the whole inland route he was opposite the most vulnerable part, this short section where the navigable channel from Aigues-Mortes to the Etang de Thau was only divided from the sea by a narrow spit of land. If a blow were to be struck, it was here that he must strike it; moreover, at this very moment he could see something at which to strike — that brown sail no more than two miles away. That must be one of the French coasters, plying between Port Vendres and Marseilles with wine and oil. It would be madness to attempt anything against her, and yet — and yet — he felt mad today.

"Pass the word for the captain's coxswain," he said to the midshipman of the watch. He heard the cry echo down the main deck, and in two minutes Brown was scurrying towards him along the gangway, halting breathless for orders.

"Can you swim, Brown?"

"Swim, sir? Yes, sir."

Hornblower looked at Brown's burly shoulders and thick neck.

There was a mat of black hair visible through the opening of his shirt.

"How many of the barge's crew can swim?"

Brown looked first one way and then the other before he made the confession which he knew would excite contempt. Yet he dared not lie, not to Hornblower.

"I dunno, sir."

Hornblower refraining from the obvious rejoinder was more scathing than Hornblower saying "You ought to know."

"I want a crew for the barge," said Hornblower. "Everyone a good swimmer, and everyone a volunteer. It's for a dangerous service, and, mark you, Brown, they must be true volunteers — none of your press-gang ways."

"Aye aye, sir," said Brown, and after a moment's hesitation, "Everyone'll volunteer, sir. It'll be hard to pick 'em. Are you going, sir?"

"Yes. A cutlass for every man. And a packet of combustibles for every man."

"Com-combustibles, sir?"

"Yes. Flint and steel. A couple of port-fires, oily rags, and a bit of slow match, in a watertight packet for each man. Go to the sailmaker and get oilskin for them. And a lanyard each to carry it if we swim."

"Aye aye, sir."

"And give Mr. Bush my compliments. Ask him to step this way, and then get your crew ready."

Bush came rolling aft, his face alight with excitement; and before he had reached the quarterdeck the ship was abuzz with rumours — the wildest tales about what the captain had decided to do next were circulating among the crew, who had spent the morning with one eye on their duties and the other on the coast of France.

"Mr. Bush," said Hornblower, "I am going ashore to burn that coaster over there."

"Aye aye, sir. Are you going in person, sir?"

"Yes," snapped Hornblower. He could not explain to Bush that he was constitutionally unable to send men away on a task for which volunteers were necessary and not go himself. He eyed Bush defiantly, and Bush eyed him back, opened his mouth to protest, thought better of it, and changed what he was going to say.

"Longboat and launch, sir?"

"No. They'd take the ground half a mile from the shore."

That was obvious; four successive lines of foam showed where the feeble waves were breaking, far out from the water's edge.

"I'm taking my barge and a volunteer crew."

Still Hornblower, by his expression, dared Bush to make any protest at all, but this time Bush actually ventured to make one.

"Yes, sir. Can't I go, sir?"

"No."

There was no chance of further dispute in the face of that blank negative. Bush had the queer feeling — he had known it before — as he looked at Hornblower's haughty expression, that he was a father dealing with a high-spirited son; he loved his captain as he would have loved a son if ever he had had one.

"And mark this, too, Bush. No rescue parties. If we're lost, we're lost. You understand? Shall I give you that in writing?"

"No need, sir. I understand."

Bush said the words sadly. When it came to the supreme test of practice, Hornblower, however much he respected Bush's qualities and abilities, had no opinion whatever of his first lieutenant's capacity to make original plans. The thought of Bush blundering about on the mainland of France throwing away valuable lives in a hopeless attempt to rescue his captain frightened him.

"Right. Heave the ship to, Mr. Bush. We'll be back in half an hour if all goes well. Stand off and on to wait for us."

The barge pulled eight oars; as Hornblower gave the word he had high hopes that her launching had passed unobserved from the shore. Bush's morning sail drill must have accustomed the French to seemingly purposeless manœuvres by the *Sutherland;* her brief backing of her topsails might be unnoticed. He sat at Brown's side while the men bent to their oars. The boat danced quickly and lightly over the sea; he set a course so as to reach the shore a little ahead of the brown sail which was showing just over the green strip of coast. Then he looked back at the *Sutherland*, stately under her pyramids of sails, and dwindling with extraordinary rapidity as the barge shot away from her. Even at that moment Hornblower's busy mind set to work scanning her lines and the rake of her masts, debating how he could improve her sailing qualities.

They had passed the first line of breakers without taking ground — breakers they could hardly be called, so sluggish was the sea — and darted in towards the golden beach. A moment later the boat balked as she slid over the sand, moved on a few yards, and grounded once more.

"Over with you, men," said Hornblower.

He threw his legs over the side and dropped thigh deep into the water. The crew were as quick as he, and seizing the gunwales, they ran the lightened boat up until the water was no higher than their ankles. Hornblower's first instinct was to allow excitement to carry him away and head a wild rush inland, but he checked himself.

"Cutlasses?" he asked, sternly. "Fire packets?"

Running his eye over his nine men he saw that every one was armed and equipped, and then he started his little expedition steadily up the beach. The distance was too great to expect them to run all the way and swim afterwards. The sandy beach was topped by a low shingle bank where samphire grew. They leaped over this and found themselves among green vines; not twenty yards away an old, bent man and two old women were hoeing along the rows. They looked up in blank surprise at this sudden apparition, standing and staring voiceless at the chattering group of seamen. A quarter of a mile away, across the level vineyard, was the brown spritsail. A small mizzen was visible now behind it. Hornblower picked out a narrow path leading roughly in that direction.

"Come along, men," he said, and broke into a dog trot. The old man shouted something as the seamen trampled the vines; they laughed like children at hearing French spoken for the first time in their lives. To most of them this was their first sight of a vineyard, too — Hornblower could hear them chattering behind him in amazement at the orderly rows of seemingly worthless stumps, and the tiny bunches of immature grapes.

They crossed the vineyard; a sharp drop on the farther side brought them onto a rough towpath along the canal. Here the lagoon was no more than two hundred yards wide, and the navigable channel was evidently close up to the towpath, for a sparse line of beacons a hundred yards out presumably marked the shallows. Two hundred yards away the coaster was creeping slowly towards them, still unconscious of her danger. The men uttered a wild cheer and began tearing off their jackets.

"Quiet, you fools," growled Hornblower. He unbuckled his sword belt and stripped off his coat.

At the sound of the men's shouting the crew of the coaster came tumbling forward. There were three men, and a moment later they were joined by two sturdy women, looking at them from under their hands. It was one of the women, quicker witted, who guessed what the group of men stripping on the bank implied. Hornblower, tearing off his breeches, heard one of them give a shriek and saw her running aft again. The coaster still crept over the water towards them, but when it was nearly opposite the big spritsail came down with a run and she swung away from the towpath as her helm was put over. It was too late to save her, though. She passed through the line of beacons and grounded with a jerk in the shallows beyond. Hornblower saw the man at the wheel quit his charge and turn and stare at them, with the other men and the women grouped round them. He buckled his sword about his naked body. Brown was naked, too, and was fastening his belt round his waist, and against his bare skin lay a naked cutlass.

"Come along, men," said Hornblower; the quicker the better. He put his hands together and dropped into the lagoon in an ungainly dive; the men followed him, shouting and splashing. The water was as warm as milk, but Hornblower swam as slowly and as steadily as he could. He was a poor swimmer, and the coaster a hundred and fifty yards away seemed very distant. The sword dangling from his waist already seemed heavy. Brown came surging past him, swimming a lusty overarm stroke, with the lanyard of his packet of combustibles between his white teeth, and his thick black hair sleek with water. The other men followed; by the time they neared the coaster Hornblower was a long way last. They all scrambled up before him into the low waist of the vessel, but then discipline reasserted itself and they turned and stooped to haul him on board. He pressed aft, with sword drawn. Women and men were there in a sullen group, and for a moment he was puzzled to know what to do with them. French and English faced each other in the dazzling sunlight, the water streaming from the naked men, but in the tenseness of that meeting no one thought of the nakedness. Hornblower remembered with relief the dinghy towing behind; he pointed to it and tried to remember his French.

"*Au bateau,*" he said. "*Dans le bateau.*"

The French hesitated. There were four middle-aged men and one old one; one old woman and one middle-aged. The English seamen closed up behind their captain, drawing their cutlasses from their belts.

"*Entrez dans le bateau,*" said Hornblower. "Hobson, pull that dinghy up alongside."

The middle-aged woman broke into a storm of invective, screeching, high-pitched, her hands gesticulating wildly and her wooden shoes clattering on the deck.

"I'll do it, sir," interposed Brown. " 'Ere, you, 'op in there."

He took one of the men by the collar, flourished his cutlass and dragged him across the deck to the side. The man yielded, and lowered himself over the side, and, once the example was set, the others followed it. Brown cast off the painter and the crowded dinghy drifted away, the woman still shrieking curses in her Catalan French.

"Set the ship on fire," said Hornblower. "Brown, take three men below and see what you can do there."

The late crew had got out a couple of oars and were paddling cautiously over to the towpath, the dinghy laden down to within an inch of the water's edge. Hornblower watched them as they crawled across, and climbed the bank to the path.

His picked crew did their work quickly and neatly. A mighty crashing from below showed that Brown's party was bursting into the cargo to make a nest for a fire. Smoke emerged almost at once from the cabin skylight; one of the men had piled the furniture there together, soused it in oil from the lamps, and got the whole thing into a blaze at once.

"Cargo is oil in barr'ls and grain in sacks, sir," reported Brown. "We stove in some barr'ls an' ripped some sacks open, sir. That'll burn. Look, sir."

From the main hatchway a thin ghost of black smoke was already rising, and the heat pouring up from the hatch made all the forward part of the ship appear to dance and shimmer in the sunshine. There was a fire in the dry timberwork of the deck just forward of the hatch, too. It was crackling and banging explosively, although this fire was hardly visible thanks to the strong sunlight and the absence of smoke, and there was fire in the forecastle — smoke was billowing out of the bulkhead door and rolling towards them in a sullen wave.

"Get some of the deck planks up," said Hornblower, hoarsely.

The splintering crash of the work was followed by a contrasting silence — and yet no silence, for Hornblower's ear caught a muffled, continuous roaring. It was the noise of the flames devouring the cargo, as the increased draught caused by the piercing of the decks set the flames racing through the inflammable stuff.

"God! There's a sight!" exclaimed Brown.

The whole waist of the ship seemed to open as the fire poured up through the deck. The heat was suddenly unbearable.

"We can go back now," said Hornblower. "Come along, men."

He set the example by diving once more into the lagoon, and the little naked band began to swim slowly back to the towpath. Slowly, this time; the high spirits of the attack had evaporated. The awful sight of the red fire glowing under the deck had sobered every man. They swam slowly, clustered round their captain, while he set a pace limited by his fatigue and unscientific breaststroke. He was glad when he was able at last to stretch out a hand and grasp the weeds growing on the towpath bank. The others scrambled out before him; Brown offered him a wet hand and helped him up to the top.

"Holy Mary!" said one of the men. "Will ye look at th' old bitch?"

They were thirty yards from where they had left their clothes, and at that spot the coaster's crew had landed. At the moment when the Irishman called their attention to them the old woman who had reviled them cast one last garment into the lagoon. There was nothing left lying on the bank. One or two derelict shirts still floated in the lagoon, buoyed up by the air they contained, but practically all their clothes were at the bottom.

"What did you do that for, damn you?" raved Brown — all the seamen had rushed up to the coaster's crew and were dancing and gesticulating naked round them. The old woman pointed across at the coaster. It was ablaze from end to end, with heavy black smoke pouring from her sides. They saw the rigging of the mainmast whisk away in smouldering fragments, and the mast suddenly sag to one side, barely-visible flames licking along it.

"I'll get your shirt back for you, sir," said one of the men to Hornblower, tearing himself free from the fascination of the sight.

"No. Come along," snapped Hornblower.

"Would you like the old man's trousers, sir?" asked Brown. "I'll take 'em off him and be damned to him, sir. 'Tisn't fit —— "

"No!" said Hornblower again.

Naked, they climbed up to the vineyard. One last glance down showed that the two women were weeping, heartbroken, now. Hornblower saw one of the men patting one of the women on the shoulder; the others watched with despairing apathy the burning of their ship — their all. Hornblower led the way over the vines. A horseman was galloping towards them; his blue uniform and cocked hat showed that he was one of Bonaparte's gendarmes. He reined up in front of them, reaching for his sabre, but at the same time, not too sure of himself, he looked to right and to left for the help which was not in sight.

"Ah, would you!" said Brown, dashing to the front waving his cutlass.

The other seamen closed up beside him, their weapons ready, and the gendarme hastily wheeled his horse out of harm's way; a gleam of white teeth showed under his black moustache. They hurried past him; he had dismounted when Hornblower looked back, and was trying, as well as his restless horse would allow, to take his carbine out of the boot beside his saddle. At the top of the beach stood the old man and the two women who had been hoeing; the old man brandished his hoe and threatened them, but the two women stood smiling shamefaced, looking up under lowered eyelids at their nakedness. There lay the barge, just in the water, and far out there was the *Sutherland* — the men cheered at the sight of her.

Lustily they ran the boat out over the sand, paused while Hornblower climbed in, pushed her out farther, and then came tumbling in over the side and took the oars. One man yelped with pain as a splinter in a thwart pricked his bare posterior; Hornblower grinned automatically, but the man was instantly reduced to silence by a shocked Brown.

" 'Ere 'e comes, sir," said stroke oar, pointing aft over Hornblower's shoulder.

The gendarme was leaping clumsily down the beach in his long boots, his carbine in his hand. Hornblower, craning round, saw him kneel and take aim; for a second Hornblower wondered, sickly, whether his career was going to be ended by the bullet of a French gendarme, but the puff of smoke from the carbine brought not even the sound of the bullet — a man who had ridden far, and run fast in heavy boots, could hardly be expected to hit a ship's boat at two hundred yards with a single shot.

Over the spit of land between sea and lagoon they could see a vast cloud of smoke. The coaster was destroyed beyond any chance of repair. It had been a wicked waste to destroy a fine ship like that, but war and waste were synonymous terms. It meant misery and poverty for the owners; but at the same time it would mean that the length of England's arm had been demonstrated now to the people of this enemy land whom the war had not affected during these eighteen years save through Bonaparte's conscription. More than that; it meant that the authorities responsible for coast defence would be alarmed about this section of the route from Marseilles to Spain, the very section which they had thought safest.

That would mean detaching troops and guns to defend it against future raids, stretching the available forces thinner still along the two hundred miles of coast. A thin screen of that sort could easily be pierced at a selected spot by a heavy blow struck without warning — the sort of blow a squadron of ships of the line, appearing and disappearing at will over the horizon, could easily strike. If the game were played properly, the whole coast from Barcelona to Marseilles could be kept in a constant state of alarm. That was the way to wear down the strength of the Corsican colossus; and a ship favoured by the weather could travel ten, fifteen times as fast as troops could march, as fast even as a well-mounted messenger could carry a warning. He had struck at the French centre, he had struck at the French left wing. Now he must hasten and strike at the French right wing on his way back to the rendezvous. He uncrossed and recrossed his knees as he sat in the stern sheets of the barge, his desire for instant action filling him with restlessness while the boat drew closer to the *Sutherland*.

He heard Gerard's voice saying "What the devil — ?" come clearly over the water to him; apparently Gerard had just detected the nakedness of everyone in the approaching boat. The pipes had twittered to call the watch's attention to the arrival of the ship's captain. He would have to come in naked through the entry port, receiving the salutes of the officers and marines, but keyed up as he was he gave no thought to his dignity. He ran up to the deck with his sword hanging from his naked waist — it was an ordeal which could not be avoided, and he had learned in twenty years in the Navy to accept the inevitable without lamentation. The faces of the side boys and of the marines were wooden in their effort not to smile, but Hornblower did not care. The black pall of smoke over the land marked an achievement of which any man might be proud. He stayed naked on the deck until he had given Bush the order to put the ship about which would take the *Sutherland* southward again in search of fresh adventure. The wind would just serve for a southwesterly course, and he was not going to waste a minute of a favourable wind.

Chapter XIII

THE *Sutherland* had seen nothing of the *Caligula* during her long sweep southwestward. Hornblower had not wanted to, and, more, had been anxious not to. For it was just possible that the *Pluto* had reached the rendezvous, and in that case the Admiral's orders would override Captain Bolton's, and he would be deprived of this further opportunity before his time limit had elapsed. It was during the hours of darkness that the *Sutherland* had crossed the latitude of Cape Bagur — the Palamos Point of the rendezvous — and morning found the *Sutherland* far to the southwestward, with the mountains of Catalonia a blue streak on the horizon over the starboard bow.

Hornblower had been on deck since dawn, a full hour before the land was sighted; at his orders the ship wore round and stood close-hauled to the northeastward again, edging in to the shore as she did so until the details of the hilly country were plainly visible. Bush was on deck, standing with a group of other officers; Hornblower, pacing up and down, was conscious of the glances they were darting at him, but he did his best not to notice them, as he kept his telescope steadily directed at the land. He knew that Bush and all the others thought he had come hither with a set purpose in mind, and that they were awaiting the orders which would plunge the ship again into the same kind of adventures which had punctuated the last two days. They credited him with diabolical foresight and ingenuity; he was not going to admit to them how great a part good fortune had played, nor was he going to admit that he had brought the *Sutherland* down here, close in to Barcelona, merely on general principles and in the hope that something might turn up.

It was stifling hot already; the blue sky glared with a brassy tint to the eastward, and the easterly breeze seemed not to have been cooled at all by its passage across four hundred miles of the Mediterranean from Italy. It was like breathing the air of a brick kiln;

Hornblower found himself running with sweat within a quarter of an hour of cooling himself off under the wash-deck pump. The land slipping by along their larboard beam seemed to be devoid of all life. There were lofty grey-green hills, many of them capped with a flat table top of stone with precipitous rocky slopes; there were grey cliffs and brown cliffs, and occasional dazzling beaches of golden sand. Between the sea and those hills ran the most important highroad in Catalonia, that connecting Barcelona with France. Surely, thought Hornblower, something ought to show up somewhere along here. He knew there was a bad mountain road running parallel ten miles inland, but the French would hardly use it of their own free will. One of the reasons why he had come here was to force them to abandon the highroad in favour of the byroad where the Spanish partisans would have a better chance of cutting up their convoys; he might achieve that merely by flaunting the British flag here within gunshot of the beach, but he would rather bring it about by administering a sharp lesson. He did not want this blow of his against the French right flank to be merely a blow in the air.

The hands were skylarking and laughing as they washed the decks; it was comforting to see their high spirits, and peculiarly comforting to allow oneself to think that those high spirits were due to the recent successes. Hornblower felt a glow of achievement as he looked forward, and then, as was typical of him, began to feel doubts as to whether he could continue to keep his men in such good order. A long, dreary cruise on blockade service might soon wear down their spirits. Then he spurned away his doubts with determined optimism. Everything had gone so well so far; it would continue to go well. This very day, even though the chances were a hundred to one against it, something was certain to happen. He told himself defiantly that the vein of good fortune was not yet exhausted. A hundred to one against or a thousand to one, something was going to happen again today, some further chance of distinction.

On the shore over there was a little cluster of white cottages above a golden beach. And drawn up on the beach were a few boats — Spanish fishing boats, presumably. There would be no sense in risking a landing party, for there was always the chance that the village would have a French garrison. Those fishing boats would be used to supply fish to the French army, too, but he could do nothing against them, despite that. The poor devils of fishermen had to live: if he were to capture or burn those boats he would set the people against the alliance with England — and it was only in the Peninsula, out of the whole world, that England had any allies.

There were black dots running on the beach now. One of the fishing boats was being run out into the sea. Perhaps this was the beginning of today's adventure; he felt hope, even certainty, springing up within him. He put his glass under his arm and turned away, walking the deck apparently deep in thought, his head bent and his hands clasped behind him.

"Boat putting off from the shore, sir," said Bush, touching his hat.

"Yes," said Hornblower carelessly.

He was endeavouring to show no excitement at all. He hoped that his officers believed that he had not yet seen the boat and was so strong-minded as not to step out of his way to look at her.

"She's pulling for us, sir," added Bush.

"Yes," said Hornblower, still apparently unconcerned. It would be at least ten minutes before the boat could near the ship — and the boat must be intending to approach the *Sutherland,* or else why should she put off so hurriedly as soon as the *Sutherland* came in sight? The other officers could train their glasses on the boat, could chatter in loud speculation as to why she was approaching. Captain Hornblower could walk his deck in lofty indifference, awaiting the inevitable hail. No one save himself knew that his heart was beating faster. Now the hail came, high-pitched, across the glittering water.

"Heave to, Mr. Bush," said Hornblower, and stepped with elaborate calm to the other side to hail back.

It was Catalan which was being shouted to him; his wide and exact knowledge of Spanish — during his two years as a prisoner on parole when a young man he had learned the language thoroughly to keep himself from fretting into insanity — and his rough and ready French enabled him to understand what was being spoken, but he could not speak Catalan. He hailed back in Spanish.

"Yes," he said. "This is a British ship."

At the sound of his voice someone else stood up in the boat. The men at the oars were Catalans in ragged civilian dress; this man wore a brilliant yellow uniform and a lofty hat with a plume.

"May I be permitted to come on board?" he shouted in Spanish. "I have important news."

"You will be very welcome," said Hornblower, and then, turning to Bush, "A Spanish officer is coming on board, Mr. Bush. See that he is received with honours."

The man who stepped onto the deck and looked curiously about him, as the marines saluted and the pipes twittered, was obviously a hussar. He wore a yellow tunic elaborately frogged in black, and yellow breeches with broad stripes of gold braid. Up to his knees he wore shiny riding boots with dangling gold tassels in front and jingling spurs on the heels; a silver-grey coat trimmed with black astrakhan, its sleeves empty, was slung across his shoulders. On his head was a hussar busby, of black astrakhan with a silver-grey bag hanging out of the top behind an ostrich plume, and gold cords from the back of it round his neck, and he trailed a broad curved sabre along the deck as he advanced to where Hornblower awaited him.

"Good day, sir," he said, saluting. "I am Colonel José Gonzales de Villena y Danvila, of His Most Catholic Majesty's Olivenza Hussars."

"I am delighted to meet you," said Hornblower. "And I am Captain Horatio Hornblower, of His Britannic Majesty's ship *Sutherland*."

"How fluently your excellency speaks Spanish!"

"Your excellency is too kind. I am fortunate in my ability to speak Spanish, since it enables me to make you welcome on board my ship."

"Thank you. It was only with difficulty that I was able to reach you. I had to exert all my authority to make those fishermen row me out. They were afraid lest the French should discover that they had been communicating with an English ship. Look! They are rowing home already for dear life."

"There is no French garrison in that village at present, then?"

"No, sir, none."

A peculiar expression played over Villena's face as he said this. He was a youngish man of fair complexion, though much sunburned, with a Hapsburg lip (which seemed to indicate that he might owe his high position in the Spanish army to some indiscretion on the part of one of his female ancestors) and hazel eyes with drooping lids. Those eyes met Hornblower's without a hint of shiftiness. They merely seemed to be pleading with him not to continue his questioning, but Hornblower ignored the appeal — he was far too anxious for data.

"There are Spanish troops there?" he asked.

"No, sir."

"But your regiment, Colonel?"

"It is not there, Captain," said Villena, and continued hastily. "The news I have to give you is that a French army — Italian, I should say — is marching along the coast road there, three leagues to the north of us."

"Ha!" said Hornblower. That was the news he wanted.

"They were at Malgret last night, on their way to Barcelona. Ten thousand of them — Pino's and Lecchi's divisions of the Italian army."

"How do you know this?"

"It is my duty to know it, as an officer of light cavalry," said Villena with dignity.

Hornblower looked at Villena and pondered. For three years now, he knew, Bonaparte's armies had been marching up and down the length and breadth of Catalonia. They had beaten the Spaniards in innumerable battles, had captured their fortresses after desperate sieges, and yet were no nearer subjecting the country than when they had first treacherously invaded the province. The Catalans had not been able to overcome in the field even the motley hordes Bonaparte had used on this side of Spain — Italians, Germans, Swiss, Poles, all the sweepings of his army — but at the same time they had fought on nobly, raising fresh forces in every unoccupied scrap of territory, and wearing out their opponents by the incessant marches and counter-marches they imposed on them. Yet that did not explain how a Spanish colonel of hussars found himself quite alone near the heart of the Barcelona district where the French were supposed to be in full control.

"How did you come to be there?" he demanded, sharply.

"In accordance with my duty, sir," said Villena, with lofty dignity.

"I regret very much that I still do not understand, Don José. Where is your regiment?"

"Captain —— "

"Where is it?"

"I do not know, sir."

All the jauntiness was gone from the young hussar now. He looked at Hornblower with big pleading eyes as he was made to confess his shame.

"Where did you see it last?"

"At Tordera. We — we fought Pino there."

"And you were beaten?"

"Yes. Yesterday. They were on the march back from Gerona and we came down from the mountains to cut them off. Their cuirassiers broke us, and we were scattered. My — my horse died at Arens de Mar there."

The pitiful words enabled Hornblower to understand the whole story in a wave of intuition. Hornblower could visualise it all — the undisciplined hordes drawn up on some hillside, the mad charges which dashed them into fragments, and the helter-skelter flight. In every village for miles round there would be lurking fugitives today. Everyone had fled in panic. Villena had ridden his horse until it dropped, and being the best mounted, had come farther than anyone else — if his horse had not died he might have been riding now. The concentration of the French forces to put ten thousand men in the field had led to their evacuation of the smaller villages, so that Villena had been able to avoid capture, even though he was between the French field army and its base at Barcelona.

Now that he knew what had happened there was no advantage

to be gained from dwelling on Villena's misfortunes; indeed it was better to hearten him up, as he would be more useful that way.

"Defeat," said Hornblower, "is a misfortune which every fighting man encounters sooner or later. Let us hope we shall gain our revenge for yesterday today."

"There is more than yesterday to be revenged," said Villena.

He put his hand in the breast of his tunic and brought out a folded wad of paper; unfolded it was a printed poster, which he handed over to Hornblower who glanced at it and took in as much of the sense as a brief perusal of the Catalan in which it was printed permitted. It began, "We, Luciano Gaetano Pino, Knight of the Legion of Honour, Knight of the Order of the Iron Crown of Lombardy, General of Division, commanding the forces of His Imperial and Royal Majesty Napoleon, Emperor of the French and King of Italy in the district of Gerona hereby decree —— " There were numbered paragraphs after that, dealing with all the offences anyone could imagine against His Imperial and Royal Majesty. And each paragraph ended — Hornblower ran his eye down them — "will be shot"; "penalty of death"; "will be hanged"; "will be burned" — it was a momentary relief to discover that this last referred to villages sheltering rebels.

"They have burned every village in the uplands," said Villena. "The road from Figueras to Gerona — ten leagues long, sir — is lined with gallows, and upon every gallows is a corpse."

"Horrible!" said Hornblower, but he did not encourage the conversation. He fancied that if any Spaniard began to talk about the woes of Spain he would never stop. "And this Pino is marching back along the coast road, you say?"

"Yes."

"Is there deep water close into the shore at any spot?"

The Spaniard raised his eyebrows in protest at that question, and Hornblower realised that it was hardly fair to ask a colonel of hussars about soundings.

"Are there batteries protecting the road from the sea?" he asked, instead.

"Oh, yes," said Villena. "Yes, I have heard so."

"Where?"

"I do not know exactly, sir."

Hornblower realised that Villena was probably incapable of giving exact topographical information about anywhere, which was what he would expect of a Spanish colonel of light cavalry.

"Well, we shall go and see," he said.

Chapter XIV

HORNBLOWER had shaken himself free from the company of Colonel Villena, who showed, now that he had told of his defeat, a hysterical loquacity and a pathetic unwillingness to allow him out of his sight. He had established him in a chair by the taffrail out of the way, and escaped below to the security of his cabin, to pore once more over the charts. There were batteries marked there — most of them apparently dated from the time, not so long ago, when Spain had been at war with England, and they had been erected to protect coasting vessels which crept along the shore from battery to battery. In consequence they were established at points where there was not merely deep water close in, but also a bit of shelter given by projecting points of land in which the fugitives could anchor. There had never been any thought in men's minds then that marching columns might in the future be attacked from the sea, and exposed sections of coast — like this twenty miles between Malgret and Arens de Mar — which offered no anchorage might surely be neglected. Since Cochrane was here a year ago in the *Impérieuse* no British ship had been spared to harass the French in this quarter.

The French since then had had too many troubles on their hands to have time to think of mere possibilities. The chances were that they had neglected to take precautions — and in any case they could not have enough heavy guns and trained gunners to guard the whole coast. The *Sutherland* was seeking a spot a mile and a half at least from any battery, where the water was deep enough close in for her to sweep the road with her guns. She had already hauled out of range of one battery, and that was marked on his chart and, moreover, was the only one marked along the stretch. It was most unlikely that the French had constructed others since the chart was last brought up to date. If Pino's column had left Malgret at dawn the *Sutherland* must be nearly up level with it now. Hornblower marked the spot which his instinct told him would be the most suitable, and ran up on deck to give the orders which would head the *Sutherland* in towards it.

Villena climbed hastily out of his chair at sight of him, and clinked loudly across the deck towards him, but Hornblower contrived to ignore him politely by acting as if his whole attention was taken up by giving instructions to Bush.

"I'll have the guns loaded and run out, too, if you please, Mr. Bush," he concluded.

"Aye aye, sir," said Bush.

Bush looked at him pleadingly. This last order, with its hint of immediate action, set the pinnacle on his curiosity. All he knew was that a Dago colonel had come on board. What they were here for, what Hornblower had in mind, he had no means of guessing. Hornblower always kept his projected plans to himself, because then if he should fail his subordinates would not be able to guess the extent of the failure. But Bush felt sometimes that his life was being shortened by his captain's reticence. He was pleasantly surprised this time when Hornblower condescended to make explanations, and he was never to know that Hornblower's unusual loquaciousness was the result of a desire to be saved from having to make polite conversation with Villena.

"There's a French column expected along the road over there," he said. "I want to see if we can get in a few shots at them."

"Aye aye, sir."

"Put a good man in the chains with the lead."

"Aye aye, sir."

Now that Hornblower actually wanted to be conversational he found it impossible — for nearly three years he had checked every impulse to say an unnecessary word to his second in command; and Bush's stolid "Aye aye sirs" were not much help. Hornblower took refuge from Villena by glueing his eye to his telescope and scanning the nearing shore with the utmost diligence. Here there were bold grey-green hills running almost to the water's edge, and looping along the foot of them, now ten feet up, and now a hundred feet, ran the road.

As Hornblower looked at it, his glass revealed a dark tiny speck on the road far ahead. He looked away, rested his eye, and looked again. It was a horseman, riding towards them. A moment later he saw a moving smudge behind, which fixed his attention by an occasional sparkle and flash from the midst of it. That was a body of horsemen; presumably the advanced guard of Pino's army. It would not be long before the *Sutherland* was up opposite to them. Hornblower gauged the distance of the ship from the road. Half a mile, or a little more — easy cannon shot, though not as easy as he would like.

"By the deep nine!" chanted the man at the lead. He could edge in a good deal closer at this point, if, when he turned the ship about and followed Pino along the shore, they came as far as here. It was worth remembering. As the *Sutherland* proceeded to meet the advancing army, Hornblower's brain was busy noting landmarks on the shore and the corresponding soundings opposite them. The leading squadron of cavalry could be seen distinctly now — men riding cautiously, their sabres drawn, looking searchingly on all sides as they rode; in a war where every rock and hedge might conceal a musketeer determined on killing one enemy at least their caution was understandable.

Some distance behind the leading squadron Hornblower could make out a longer column of cavalry, and beyond that again a long, long line of white dots, which puzzled him for a moment with its odd resemblance to the legs of a caterpillar all moving together. Then he smiled. They were the white breeches of a column of infantry marching in unison; by some trick of optics their blue coats as yet showed up not at all against their grey background.

"And a half ten!" called the leadsman.

He could take the *Sutherland* much closer in here when he wanted to. But at present it was better to stay out at half gunshot. His ship would not appear nearly as menacing to the enemy at that distance. Hornblower's mind was hard at work analysing the reactions of the enemy to the appearance of the *Sutherland* — friendly hat-waving by the cavalry of the advanced guard, now opposite him, gave him valuable additional data. Pino and his men had never yet been cannonaded from the sea, and had had no experience so far of the destructive effect of a ship's heavy broadside against a suitable target. The graceful two-decker, with her pyramids of white sails, would be something outside their experience. Put an army in the field against them, and they could estimate its potentialities instantly, but they had never encountered ships before. His reading told him that Bonaparte's generals tended to be careless of the lives of their men; and any steps taken to avoid the *Sutherland's* fire would involve grave inconvenience — marching back to Malgret to take the inland road, or crossing the pathless hills to it direct. Hornblower guessed that Pino, somewhere back in that long column and studying the *Sutherland* through his glass, would make up his mind to chance the *Sutherland's* fire and would march on hoping to get through without serious loss. Pino would be disappointed, thought Hornblower.

The cavalry at the head of the main column were opposite them. The second regiment twinkled and sparkled in the flaming sunlight like a river of fire.

"Those are the cuirassiers!" said Villena, gesticulating wildly at Hornblower's elbow. "Why do you not fire, Captain?"

Hornblower realised that Villena had probably been gabbling Spanish to him for the last quarter of an hour, and he had not heard a word he had said. He was not going to waste his surprise attack on cavalry who could gallop away out of range. This opening broadside must be reserved for slow-moving infantry.

"Send the men to the guns, Mr. Bush," he said, forgetting all about Villena again in a flash, and to the man at the wheel, "Starboard a point."

"And a half nine," called the leadsman.

The *Sutherland* headed closer into shore.

"Mr. Gerard!" hailed Hornblower. "Train the guns on the road, and only fire when I give you the signal."

A horse artillery battery had followed the cavalry — popgun six-pounders whose jolting and lurching showed well how bad was the surface of the road, one of the great highways of Spain. The men perched on the limbers waved their hands in friendly fashion to the beautiful ship close in upon them.

"By the mark six!" from the leadsman.

He dared not stand closer in.

"Port a point. Steady!"

The ship crept on through the water; not a sound from the crew, standing tense at their guns — only the faint sweet music of the breeze in the rigging, and the lapping of the water overside. Now they were level with the infantry column, a long dense mass of blue-coated and white-breeched soldiers, stepping out manfully, a little unreal in the haze of dust. Above the blue coats could be seen the white lines of their faces — every face was turned towards the pretty white-sailed ship creeping over the blue-enamel water. It was a welcome diversion in a weary march, during a war when every day demanded its march. Gerard was giving no orders for change of elevation at the moment — here the road ran level for half a mile, fifty feet above the sea. Hornblower put his silver whistle to his lips. Gerard had seen the gesture. Before Hornblower could blow, the centre main-deck gun had exploded, and a moment later the whole broadside followed with a hideous crash. The *Sutherland* heeled to the recoil, and the white, bitter-tasting smoke came billowing up.

"God, look at that!" exclaimed Bush.

The forty one balls from the *Sutherland's* broadside and cannonades had swept the road from side to side. Fifty yards of the column had been cut to fragments. Whole files had been swept away; the survivors stood dazed and stupid. The gun trucks roared as the guns were run out again, and the *Sutherland* lurched once more at the second broadside. There was another gap in the column now, just behind the first.

"Give it 'em again, boys!" yelled Gerard.

The whole column was standing stock still and silly to receive the third broadside; the smoke from the firing had drifted to the shore now, and was scattering over the rocks in thin wreaths.

"Quarter less nine!" called the leadsman.

In the deepening water Hornblower could close nearer in. The next section of the column, seeing the terrible ship moving down upon them implacably, about to blast them into death, was seized with panic and bolted wildly down the road.

"Grape, Mr. Gerard!" shouted Hornblower. "Starboard a point!"

Farther down the road the column had not fled. Those who stood firm and those who ran jammed the road with a struggling mass of men, and the *Sutherland* under the orders of her captain closed in upon them pitilessly, like a machine, steadied again, brought her guns to bear upon the crowd, and then swept the road clear with her tempest of grapeshot as though with a broom.

"God blast me!" raved Bush. "That'll show 'em."

Villena was snapping his fingers and dancing about the deck like a clown, dolman flying, plume nodding, spurs jangling.

"By the deep seven!" chanted the leadsman. But Hornblower's eye had caught sight of the little point jutting out from the shore close ahead, and its hint of jagged rock at its foot.

"Stand by to go about!" he rasped.

His mind was working at a feverish pace — there was water enough here, but that point indicated a reef — a ridge of harder rock which had not been ground away like the rest of the shore, and remained as a trap below the surface on which the *Sutherland* might run without warning between two casts of the lead. The *Sutherland* came up to the wind, and stood out from the shore. Looking aft, they could see the stretch of road which she had swept with her fire. There were dead and wounded in heaps along it. One or two men stood among the wreck; a few were bending over the wounded, but most of the survivors were on the hillside above the road, scattered on the steep slopes, their white breeches silhouetted against the grey background.

Hornblower scanned the shore. Beyond the little point there would be deep water close in again, as there had been on the other side of it.

"We will wear ship again, Mr. Bush," he said.

At the sight of the *Sutherland* heading for them the infantry on the road scattered wildly up the hillside, but the battery of artillery beyond had no such means of escape open to it. Hornblower saw drivers and gunners sitting helplessly for an instant; then he saw the officer in command, his plume tossing, gallop along the line, calling the men to action with urgent gesticulations. The drivers wheeled their horses in the road, swinging their guns across it, the gunners leaping down from the limbers, unhooking the gun trails, and bending over their guns as they worked frantically to bring them into action. Could a battery of nine-pounder field pieces effect anything against the *Sutherland's* broadside?

"Reserve your fire for the battery, Mr. Gerard," shouted Hornblower.

Gerard waved his hat in acknowledgment. The *Sutherland* swung slowly and ponderously round. One gun went off prematurely — Hornblower was glad to see Gerard noting the fact so as to punish the gun's crew later — and then the whole broadside was delivered with a crash, at the moment when the Italian artillerymen were still at work with their rammers loading their guns. The rush of smoke obscured the view from the quarterdeck; it did not clear until already one or two well-served guns were rumbling up into firing position again. By that time the wind had rolled it away in a solid bank, and they could see the hard-hit battery. One gun had had a wheel smashed, and was leaning drunkenly over to one side; another, apparently hit full on the muzzle, had been flung back from its carriage and was pointing up to the sky. There were dead men lying round the guns, and the living were standing dazed by the torrent of shot which had delayed them. The mounted officer had just flung himself from his saddle and let his horse go free while he ran to the nearest gun. Hornblower could see him calling the men about him, determined on firing one shot at least in defiance of the thundering tormentor.

"Give 'em another, men!" shouted Gerard, and the *Sutherland* heeled once more to the broadside.

By the time the smoke cleared away the *Sutherland* had passed on, leaving the battery behind. Hornblower could see it wrecked and ruined, another of its guns dismounted, and not a man visible on his feet near the guns. Now the *Sutherland* was opposite more infantry — the second division of the column, presumably — which shredded away in panic up the hillside section by section as the *Sutherland* neared them. Hornblower saw them scattering. He knew that it was as damaging to an army to be scattered and broken up like this as for it to be decimated by fire; he would as soon not kill the poor devils, except that his own men would be more delighted at casualties among the enemy than at a mere demoralisation whose importance they could not appreciate.

There was a group of horsemen on the hillside above the road. Through his telescope he could see that they were all splendidly mounted, and dressed in a variety of uniforms flashing with gold and diversified with plumes. Hornblower guessed them to be the staff of the army; they would serve well as a target in the absence of larger bodies of formed troops. He attracted Gerard's notice and pointed. Gerard waved back. His two midshipmen-messengers went running below to point out the new target to the officers on the lower gun deck; Gerard himself bent over the nearest gun and squinted along it, while the gun captains set the tangent sights in accordance with the orders he bellowed through his speaking trumpet. Gerard stood aside and jerked the lanyard, and the whole broadside followed the shot he fired.

The blast of shot reached the group of horsemen. Men and horses went down together; there was hardly a rider left in his saddle. So universal was the destruction that Hornblower guessed that close under the surface soil must be rock, flying chips of which had scattered like grapeshot. He wondered if Pino were among those hit, and found himself to his surprise hoping that Pino had had both legs shot off. He told himself that until that morning he had not even heard Pino's name, and he felt a momentary scorn for himself, for feeling a blind animosity towards a man merely because he was his opponent.

Some officer a little farther down the road had kept his men together, drawn up stubbornly in a mass along the road, refusing to allow them to scatter. It was small advantage that his stern discipline brought his men. Hornblower brought his ship steadily round until the guns bore, and then tore the steady regiment to fragments with a fresh broadside. As the smoke eddied round him a sharp rap on the rail at his side made him look down. There was a musket ball stuck there — someone had fired at long range, two hundred yards or more, and succeeded in hitting the ship. The ball must have been nearly spent when it arrived, for it was embedded to half its depth and had retained its shape. It was just too hot to touch; he picked it out with his handkerchief over his fingers, and juggled with it idly, as he had done, he told himself, with hot chestnuts when he was a boy.

The clearing smoke revealed the new destruction he had wrought, the slaughtered files and heaped-up dead; he fancied that he could even hear the screaming of the wounded. He was glad that the troops were scattering up the hillside and presenting no target, for he was sick of slaughter although Bush was still blaspheming with excitement and Villena still capering at his side. Surely he must reach the rear of the column soon — from advanced guard to rearguard the army could not occupy more than eight or nine miles of road. As the thought came into his head he saw the road here was full of stationary waggons — the baggage train of the army. Those squat vehicles with four horses apiece must be ammunition caissons; beyond was a string of country carts, each with its half dozen patient oxen, dun-coloured, with sheepskins hanging over their foreheads. Filling the rest of the road beside the carts were pack mules, hundreds of them, looking grotesquely malformed with their ungainly burdens on their backs. There was no sign of a human being — the drivers were mere dots climbing the hillside, having abandoned their charges.

The *Account of the Present War in the Peninsula* which Hornblower had so attentively studied had laid great stress on the difficulties of transport in Spain. A mule or horse was as valuable — several times as valuable, for that matter — as any soldier. Hornblower set his expression hard.

"Mr. Gerard!" he shouted. "Load with grape. I want those baggage animals killed."

A little wail went up from the men at the guns who heard the words. It was just like those sentimental fools to cheer when they killed men and yet to object to killing animals. Half of them would deliberately miss if they had the chance.

"Target practice. Single guns only," bellowed Hornblower to Gerard.

The patient brutes would stand to be shot at, unlike their masters, and the gun layers would have no opportunity to waste ammunition. As the *Sutherland* drifted slowly along the shore her guns spoke out one by one, each one in turn hurling a hatful of grape, at extreme grapeshot range, onto the road. Hornblower watched horses and mules go down, kicking and plunging. One or two of the pack mules, maddened with fear, managed to leap the bank out of the road and scramble up the hill, scattering their burdens as they did so. Six oxen attached to a cart all went down together, dead simultaneously. Held together by their yokes they stayed, two by two, on their knees and bellies, their heads stretched forward, as if in prayer. The main deck murmured again in pity as the men saw the result of the good shot.

"Silence there!" roared Gerard, who could guess at the importance of the work in hand.

Bush plucked at his captain's sleeve, daring greatly in thus breaking in on his preoccupation with a suggestion.

"If you please, sir. If I took a boat's crew ashore I could burn all those waggons, destroy everything there."

Hornblower shook his head. It was like Bush not to see the objections to such a plan. The enemy might fly before guns to which they had no chance of replying, but if a landing party were put within their reach they would fall upon it fiercely enough — more fiercely than ever as a result of their recent losses. It was one thing to land a small party to attack fifty artillerymen in a battery taken completely by surprise, but it was quite another to land in the face of a disciplined army ten thousand strong. The words with which Hornblower tried to soften his refusal were blown into inaudibility by the explosion of the quarterdeck carronade beside them, and when Hornblower again opened his mouth to speak there was a fresh distraction on the shore to interrupt him.

Someone was standing up in the next cart destined to receive fire, waving a white handkerchief frantically. Hornblower looked through his glass; the man appeared to be an officer of some sort, in his blue uniform with red epaulettes. But if he were trying to surrender he must know that his surrender could not be accepted in that it could not be put into effect. He must take his chance of the next shot. The officer suddenly seemed to realise it. He stooped down in the cart and rose again still waving his handkerchief and supporting someone who had been lying at his feet. Hornblower could see that the man hung limp in his arms; there was a white bandage round his head and another round his arm, and Hornblower suddenly realised that these carts were the ambulance vehicles of the army, full of the sick and of the wounded from yesterday's skirmish. The officer with the handkerchief must be a surgeon.

"Cease fire!" bellowed Hornblower, shrilling on his whistle. He was too late to prevent the next shot being fired, but luckily it was badly sighted and merely raised a cloud of dust from the cliff face below the road. It was illogical to spare draught animals which might be invaluable to the French for fear of hitting wounded men who might recover and again be active enemies, but it was the convention of war, deriving its absurdity from war itself.

Beyond the waggon train was the rearguard, but that was scattered over the hillside sparsely enough not to be worth powder and shot. It was time to go back and harass the main body once more.

"Put the ship about, Mr. Bush," said Hornblower. "I want to retrace our course."

It was not so easy on a course diametrically opposite to the previous one. The wind had been on the *Sutherland's* quarter before; now it was on her bow and she could only keep parallel to the shore by lying as close-hauled as she would sail. To make any offing at all when they reached the little capes which ran out from the shore the ship would have to go about, and the leeway she made might drift her into danger unless the situation were carefully watched. But the utmost must be done to harass the Italians and to demonstrate to them that they could never use the coast road again; Bush was delighted — as Hornblower could see from the fierce light in his eyes — that his captain was going to stick to his task and not sail tamely off after defiling once along the column, and the men at the starboard-side guns rubbed their hands with pleasure at the prospect of action as they bent over the weapons that had stood unused so far.

It took time for the *Sutherland* to go about and work into position again for her guns to command the road; Hornblower was pleased to see the regiments which had reformed break up again as their tormentor neared them and take to the hillside once more.

But close-hauled the *Sutherland* could hardly make three knots past the land, allowing for the vagaries of the coast line and the wind; troops stepping out as hard as they could go along the road could keep their distance from her if necessary, and perhaps the Italian officers might realise this soon enough. He must do what damage he could now.

"Mr. Gerard!" he called, and Gerard came running to his beckoning, standing with face uplifted to hear his orders from the quarterdeck. "You may fire single shots at any group large enough to be worth it. See that every shot is well aimed."

"Aye aye, sir."

There was a body of a hundred men or so massed on the hillside opposite them now. Gerard himself laid the gun and estimated the range, squatting on his heels to look along the dispart sights with the gun at full elevation. The ball struck the rock in front of them and ricochetted into the group; Hornblower saw a sudden swirl in the crowd, which scattered abruptly leaving two or three white-breeched figures stretched on the ground behind it. The crew cheered at the sight. Marsh the gunner had been hurriedly sent for by Gerard to take part in this accurate shooting; the gun he was training killed more men in another group, over which flashed something on a pole which Hornblower, straining his eye through his telescope, decided must be one of the imperial eagles which Bonaparte's bulletins so often mentioned and at which British cartoonists so often jeered.

Shot after shot crashed out from the *Sutherland's* starboard battery as she made her slow way along the coast. Sometimes the crew cheered when some of the scrambling midgets on the hillside were knocked over; sometimes the shot was received in chill silence when no effect could be noted. It was a valuable demonstration to the gunners on the importance of being able to lay their guns truly, to estimate range and deflection, even though it was traditional in a ship of the line that all the gunners had to do was to serve their guns as fast as possible with no necessity for taking aim with their ship laid close alongside the enemy.

Now that the ear was not deafened by the thunder of a full broadside, it could detect after each shot the flattened echo thrown back by the hills, returning from the land with its quality oddly altered in the heated air. For it was frightfully hot; Hornblower, watching the men drinking eagerly at the scuttle butt as their petty officers released them in turns for the purpose, wondered if those poor devils scrambling over the rocky hillsides in the glaring sun were suffering from thirst. He feared they were. He had no inclination to drink himself — he was too preoccupied listening to the chant of the men at the lead, with watching the effect of the firing and with seeing that the *Sutherland* was running into no danger.

Whoever was in command of the shattered field-artillery battery farther along the road was a man who knew his duty. Midshipman Savage in the foretop attracted Hornblower's attention to it with a hail. The three serviceable guns had been slewed round to point diagonally across the road straight at the ship, and they fired the moment Hornblower trained his glass on them. Wirra-wirra-wirra; one of the balls passed high over Hornblower's head, and a hole appeared in the *Sutherland's* main topsail. At the same time a crash forward told where another shot had struck home. It would be ten minutes before the *Sutherland's* broadside could bear on the battery.

"Mr. Marsh," said Hornblower. "Turn the starboard bow chasers on that battery."

"Aye aye, sir."

"Carry on with your target practice, Mr. Gerard."

"Aye aye, sir."

As part of the programme for training his men into fighting machines it would be invaluable to give them firing practice while actually under fire from the enemy — no one knew better than Hornblower the difference between being fired at and not being fired at. He found himself in the act of thinking that one or two unimportant casualties might be worth receiving in these circumstances as part of the crew's necessary experience, and then he drew back in horror from the thought that he was casually condemning some of his own men to mutilation or death — and he might himself be one of those casualties. It was intolerably easy to separate mentally the academic theories of war from the human side of it, even when one was engaged in it oneself. To his men down below the little uniformed figures scrambling over the hillside were not human beings suffering agonies from heat and thirst and fatigue; and the still figures which littered the road here were not disembowelled corpses, lately fathers or lovers. They might as well be tin soldiers for all his men thought about them. It was mad that at that moment, irrelevantly in the heat, and the din of firing, he should start thinking about Lady Barbara and her pendant of sapphires, and Maria, who must now be growing ungainly with her child within her. He shook himself free from such thoughts — while they had filled his mind the battery had fired another salvo whose effect he actually had not noticed.

The bow chasers were banging away at the battery; their fire might unsteady the men at the field guns. Meanwhile the broadside guns were finding few targets offered them, for the Italian division opposite them had scattered widely all over the hillside in groups of no more than half a dozen at the most — some of them were right up on the skyline. Their officers would have a difficult time reassembling them, and any who wished to desert — the *Account of the Present War in the Peninsula* had laid stress on the tendency of the Italians to desert — would have ample opportunity today.

A crash and a cry below told that a shot from the battery had caused one at least of the casualties Hornblower had been thinking about — from the highpitched scream of agony it must have been one of the ship's boys who had been hit; he set his lips firm as he measured the distance the ship still had to sail before bringing her broadside to bear. He would have to receive two more salvos; it was the tiniest bit difficult to wait for them. Here came one — it passed close overhead with a sound like an infinity of bees on an urgent mission; apparently the gunners had made inadequate allowance for the rapidly decreasing range. The main topgallant backstay parted with a crack, and a gesture from Bush sent a party to splice it. The *Sutherland* would have to swing out now in readiness to weather the point and reef ahead.

"Mr. Gerard! I am going to put the ship about. Be ready to open fire on the battery when the guns bear."

"Aye aye, sir."

Bush sent the hands to the braces. Hooker was forward in charge of the headsail sheets. The *Sutherland* came beautifully up into the wind as her helm was put down, and Hornblower watched the field guns, now less than a quarter of a mile away, through his glass. The gunners saw the *Sutherland* swinging round — they had seen that before, and knew the tempest of shot that would follow. Hornblower saw one man run from the guns, and saw others follow him, clawing their way desperately up the bank onto the hillside. Others flung themselves flat on their faces — only one man was left standing, raving and gesticulating beside the guns. Then the *Sutherland* heaved to the recoil of her guns once more, the acrid smoke came billowing up, and the battery was blotted out of sight. Even when the smoke cleared the battery could not be seen. There were only fragments — shattered wheels, an axle tree pointing upwards, the guns themselves lying tumbled on the ground. That had been a well-aimed broadside; the men must have behaved as steadily as veterans.

Hornblower took his ship out round the reef and stood in again for the shore. On the road just ahead was the rear of an infantry column; the leading division must have been formed up again on the road while the *Sutherland* was dealing with the second one. Now it was marching off down the road at a great pace, embanked in a low, heavy cloud of dust.

"Mr. Bush! We must try and catch that column."

"Aye aye, sir."

But the *Sutherland* was a poor sailor close-hauled, and time and again when she was on the point of overtaking the rear of the column she had to go about and head out from the shore in order to weather a projecting point of land. Sometimes she was so close to the hurrying infantry that Hornblower could see through his glass the white faces above the blue tunics of the men looking back over their shoulders. And here and there along the road in the track of the division he saw men who had fallen out — men sitting by the roadside with their heads in their hands, men leaning exhausted on their muskets staring at the ship gliding by, sometimes men lying motionless and unconscious on their faces where they had fallen, overwhelmed by fatigue and heat.

Bush was fretting and fuming as he hastened about the ship trying to coax a little more speed out of her, setting every spare man to work carrying hammocks laden with shot from the lee side to the weather side, trimming the sails to the nicest possible degree of accuracy, blaspheming wildly whenever the gap between ship and men showed signs of lengthening.

But Hornblower was well content. An infantry division which had been knocked about as badly as this one, and then sent flying helter-skelter in panic for miles, dropping stragglers by the score, and pursued by a relentless enemy, would have such a blow to its self-respect as to be vastly weakened as a fighting force for weeks. Before he came into range of the big coastal battery on the farther side of Arens de Mar he gave over the pursuit — he did not want the flying enemy to recover any of its lost spirit by seeing the *Sutherland* driven off by the fire of the heavy guns there, and to circle round out of range would consume so much time that night would be upon them before they could be back on the coast again.

"Very good, Mr. Bush. You can put the ship on the starboard tack and secure the guns."

The *Sutherland* steadied to an even keel, and then heeled over again as she paid off on the other tack.

"Three cheers for the cap'n," yelled someone on the main deck — Hornblower could not be sure who it was, or he would have punished him. The storm of cheering that instantly followed drowned his voice and prevented him from checking the men, who shouted until they were tired, all grinning with enthusiasm for the captain who had led them to victory five times in three days. Bush was grinning too, and Gerard, beside him on the quarterdeck. Little Longley was dancing and yelling with an utter disregard for an officer's dignity, while Hornblower stood sullenly glowering down at the men below. Later he might be delighted at the recollection of this spontaneous proof of the men's affection and devotion, but at present it merely irritated and embarrassed him.

As the cheering died away the voice of the leadsman made itself heard again.

"No bottom! No bottom with this line!"

He was still doing the duty to which he had been assigned, and would continue to do it until he received orders to rest — a most vivid example of the discipline of the Navy.

"Have that man taken out of the chains at once, Mr. Bush!" snapped Hornblower, annoyed at the omission to relieve the man.

"Aye aye, sir," said Bush, chagrined at having been for once remiss in his work.

The sun was dipping in purple and red into the mountains of Spain, in a wild debauch of colour that made Hornblower catch his breath as he looked at the extravagant beauty of it. He was mazed and stupid now, in reaction from his exalted quickness of thought of the preceding hours; too stupid as yet even to be conscious of any fatigue. Yet he must still wait to receive the surgeon's report. Someone had been killed or wounded today — he remembered vividly the crash and the cry when the shot from the field guns hit the ship.

The gunroom steward had come up on the quarterdeck and touched his forehead to Gerard.

"Begging your pardon, sir," he said. "But Tom Cribb's been killed."

"What?"

"Yes indeed, sir. Knocked 'is 'ead clean off. Dretful, 'e looks, laying there, sir."

"What's this you say?" interrupted Hornblower. He could remember no man on board of the name of Tom Cribb — which was the name of the heavyweight champion of England — nor any reason why the gunroom steward should report a casualty to a lieutenant.

"Tom Cribb's been killed, sir," explained the steward. "And Mrs. Siddons, she's got a splinter in 'er — in 'er backside, begging your pardon, sir. You could 'ave 'eard 'er squeak from 'ere, sir."

"I did," said Hornblower.

Tom Cribb and Mrs. Siddons must be a pig and a sow belonging to the gunroom mess. It was a comfort to realise that.

"She's all right now, sir. The butcher clapped a 'andful o' tar on the place."

Here came Walsh the surgeon with his report that there had been no casualties in the action.

"Excepting among the pigs in the manger, sir," added Walsh, with a deprecating deference of one who proffers a joke to his superior officer.

"I've just heard about them," said Hornblower.

Gerard was addressing the gunroom steward.

"Right!" he was saying. "We'll have his chitterlings, fried. And you can roast the loin. See that you get the crackling crisp. If it's leathery like the last time we killed a pig, I'll have your grog stopped. There's onions and there's sage — yes, and there's a few apples left. Sage and onions and apple sauce — and mark you this, Loughton, don't put any cloves in that sauce. No matter what the other officers say, I won't have 'em. In an apple pie, yes, but not with roast pork. Get started on that at once. You can take a leg to the bos'n's mess with my compliments, and roast the other one — it'll serve cold for breakfast."

Gerard was striking the fingers of one hand into the palm of the other to accentuate his points; the light of appetite was in his face — Hornblower fancied that when there were no women available Gerard gave all the thought he could spare from his guns to his belly. A man whose eyes could go moist with appetite at the thought of fried chitterlings and roast pork for dinner on a scorching July afternoon in the Mediterranean, and who could look forward with pleasure to cold leg of pork for breakfast next day should by rights have been fat like a pig himself, but Gerard was lean and handsome and elegant. Hornblower thought of the developing paunch within his own waistband with momentary jealousy.

But Colonel Villena was wandering about the quarterdeck like a lost soul. Clearly he was simply living for the moment when he would be able to start talking again — and Hornblower was the only soul on board with enough Spanish to maintain a conversation. Moreover, as a colonel he ranked with a post captain, and could expect to share the hospitality of the captain's cabin. Hornblower decided that he would rather be overfed with hot roast pork than have to endure Villena's conversation.

"You seem to have planned a feast for tonight, Mr. Gerard," he said.

"Yes, sir."

"Would my presence be unwelcome in the gunroom to share it?"

"Oh no, sir. Of course not, sir. We would be delighted if you would honour us, sir."

Gerard's face lit with genuine pleasure at the prospect of acting as host to his captain. It was such a sincere tribute that Hornblower's heart was warmed, even while his conscience pricked him at the memory of why he had invited himself.

"Thank you, Mr. Gerard. Then Colonel Villena and myself will be guests of the gunroom tonight."

With any luck, Villena would be seated far enough from him to save him from the necessity for Spanish conversation.

The marine sergeant drummer had brought out all that the ship could boast of a band — the four marine fifers and the four drummers. They were marching up and down the gangway to the thunder and the rumble of the drums while the fifes squealed away bravely at the illimitable horizon.

"Hearts of oak are our ships
Jolly tars are our men —— "

The bald words and the trite sentiments seemed to please the crew, although every man jack of it would have been infuriated if he had been called a "jolly tar."

Up and down went the smart red coats, and the jaunty beat of the drums thrilled so that the crushing heat was forgotten. In the west the marvellous sky still flamed in glory, even while in the east the night was creeping up over the purple sea.

Chapter XV

"EIGHT bells, sir," said Polwheal.

Hornblower woke with a start. It seemed to him as if he could not have been asleep more than five minutes, while actually it had been well over an hour. He lay on his cot in his nightshirt, for he had thrown off his coverings during the sweltering heat of the night; his head ached and his mouth had a foul taste. He had retired to bed at midnight, but — thanks to roast pork for supper — he had tossed and turned in the frightful heat for two or three hours before going to sleep, and now here he was awakened at four o'clock in the morning, simply because he had to prepare his report to Captain Bolton or to the admiral (if the latter had arrived) for delivery that morning at the rendezvous. He groaned miserably with fatigue, and his joints ached as he put his feet to the deck and sat up. His eyes were gummy and hard to open, and they felt sore when he rubbed them.

He would have groaned again except for the need to appear in Polwheal's eyes superior to human weaknesses — at the thought of that he stood up abruptly and posed as somebody feeling perfectly wide awake. A bath under the wash-deck pump, and a shave made the pose almost a reality, and then, with dawn creeping up over the misty horizon, he sat down at his desk and cut himself a new pen, licked its point meditatively before dipping it into the ink, and began to write.

"I have the honour to report that in accordance with the orders of Captain Bolton, on the 20th inst., I proceeded —— "

Polwheal came in with his breakfast, and Hornblower turned to the steaming hot coffee for a spur to his already flagging energies. He flipped the pages of the ship's log to refresh his memory — so much had happened lately that he was actually vague already about the details of the capture of the *Amelie*. The report had to be written badly, avoiding Gibbonesque antitheses or high-flying sentiment, yet at the same time Hornblower disliked the use of the kind of phrasing which was customary in captain's reports. When listing the prizes taken from beside the battery at Llanza he was careful to write "as named in the margin" instead of the irritating phrase "as per margin" which had become stereotyped in the Navy since its classic use by an unlettered captain nearly a hundred years before the War of Jenkins' Ear. He was compelled to use the word "proceed" even though he hated it — in official reports the Navy never set sail, nor went, nor put to sea, nor journeyed, but always proceeded, just as in the same way captains never suggested or advised or recommended, but always respectfully submitted. Hornblower had respectfully to submit that until the French battery was reestablished at Llanza the coastal route from France to Spain was now most vulnerable between Port Vendres and Rosas Bay.

While he struggled with the wording of his description of the raid on the Etang de Thau near Cette he was interrupted by a knock on his door. Longley entered in response to his call.

"Mr. Gerard sent me, sir. The squadron's in sight on the starboard bow."

"The flagship's there, is she?"

"Yes, sir."

"Right. My compliments to Mr. Gerard, and will he please alter course to close her."

"Aye aye, sir."

His report would have to be addressed to the admiral, then, and not to Captain Bolton, and it would have to be finished within the next half hour. He dashed his pen into the ink and began to scribble feverishly, describing the harassing of the divisions of Pino and Lecchi on the coast road between Malgret and Arens de Mar. It came as a shock to him when he computed the casualties inflicted on the Italians — they must have numbered five or six hundred, exclusive of stragglers. He had to word that carefully, otherwise he would probably be suspected of gross exaggeration, a serious crime in the eyes of authority. Yesterday five or six hundred men were killed or mutilated who today would have been alive and well if he had not been an active and enterprising officer. The mental eyes with which Hornblower viewed his exploit saw a double image — on the one hand he saw corpses, widows and orphans, misery and pain, while on the other he saw white-breeched figurines motionless on a hillside, tin soldiers knocked over, arithmetical digits recorded on paper. He cursed his analytical mind at the same time as he cursed the heat and the need for writing the report. He was even vaguely conscious of his own cross-grainedness, which always plunged him into depression after a success.

He dashed off his signature to the document, and shouted for Polwheal to bring a candle to melt the sealing wax while he peppered sand over the wet ink. Thanks to the heat his hands stuck clammily to the limp paper. When he came to address the report — "Rear Admiral Sir P. G. Leighton, K.B." — the ink spread and ran on the smeared surface as though on blotting paper. But at any rate the thing was done; he went on deck, where already the sunshine was oppressive. The brassiness of the sky, noticeable yesterday, was far more marked today, and Hornblower had noticed that the barometer in his cabin indicated a steady fall which had begun three days ago. There was a storm coming, without a doubt, and moreover a storm which had so long been foretold would be all the more violent when it did come. He turned to Gerard with orders to keep a sharp eye on the weather and to be ready to shorten sail at the first hint of trouble.

"Aye aye, sir," said Gerard.

Over there rolled the two other ships of the squadron, the *Pluto* with her three tiers of ports, and the red ensign at the mizzen masthead indicating the presence on board of a rear admiral of the Red, and the *Caligula* astern of her.

"Pass the word to Mr. Marsh to salute the admiral's flag," said Hornblower.

While the salute was being returned a hoist of flags ran up the *Pluto's* rigging.

"*Sutherland's* pendant," read off Vincent. "Take station astern."

"Acknowledge."

The hoist was succeeded by another.

"*Sutherland's* pendant," said Vincent again. "Flag to captain. Come on board and report."

"Acknowledge. Mr. Gerard, clear away my barge. Where's Colonel Villena?"

"Not seen him yet this morning, sir."

"Here, Mr. Savage, Mr. Longley. Run down and get Colonel Villena out of bed. I want him ready as soon as my barge is cleared away."

"Aye aye, sir."

It took two and a half minutes before the captain's barge was in the water with Hornblower seated in the stern, and at the very last second Villena made his appearance at the ship's side. He looked as disagreeable as might be expected, at having been routed out of bed by two brusque midshipmen who could speak no word of his language and dressed with their clumsy and hurried aid. His busby was awry and his coat incorrectly hooked, and his sabre and pelisse still hung over his arm. He was hauled down into the boat by the impatient boat's crew, who did not want to imperil their ship's reputation for smartness by waiting for him after the admiral had signalled for them.

Villena lurched miserably to his thwart beside Hornblower. He was unshaven and bedraggled, and his eyes were as gummy as Hornblower's had been on his awakening. He sat down muttering and grumbling, still half asleep, trying in dazed fashion to complete his dressing, while the men bent to their oars and sent the barge skimming over the water. It was only as they neared the flagship that Villena was able to open his eyes fully and begin to talk, and for the short remaining period Hornblower felt no need for elaborate politeness. He was full of hope that the admiral would invite Villena to be his guest for the sake of any information he could give regarding conditions ashore.

Captain Elliott was at the ship's side to greet him as they came on board.

"Glad to see you, Hornblower," he said, and then in response to Hornblower's introduction he mumbled incoherently to Villena, eyeing the latter's gaudy uniform and unshaven chin in blank astonishment. He was obviously relieved when the formality was over and he could address himself to Hornblower again. "The admiral's in his cabin. This way, gentlemen, if you please."

The flag lieutenant in the admiral's cabin along with the admiral was young Sylvester, whom Hornblower had heard of as a capable young officer even though he was — as might have been expected — a sprig of the nobility. Leighton himself was ponderous and slow of speech this morning; in the stifling heat the sweat was visible in little rivers running down the sides of his heavy chin. He and Sylvester made a brave attempt to welcome Villena. They both of them spoke French fairly well and Italian badly, and by amalgamating what they knew of those two languages with what remained of their schoolboy Latin they were able to make themselves understood, but it was heavy going. Obviously with relief Leighton turned to Hornblower.

"I want to hear your report, Hornblower," he said.

"I have it here in writing, sir."

"Thank you. But let us hear a little about your doings verbally. Captain Bolton tells me he spoke a prize you had taken. Where did you go?"

Hornblower began his account — he was glad that events had moved so fast that he was able to omit all reference to the circumstances in which he had parted company from the East India convoy. He told of his capture of the *Amelie* and of the little fleet of small vessels at Llanza. The admiral's heavy face showed a gleam of extra animation when he heard that he was a thousand pounds the richer as a result of Hornblower's activity, and he nodded sympathetically when Hornblower explained the necessity of burning the last prize he had taken — the coaster near Cette. Cautiously Hornblower put forward the suggestion that the squadron might be most profitably employed in watching between Port Vendres and Rosas, on which stretch, thanks to the destruction of the battery at Llanza, there was now no refuge for French shipping. A hint of a groove appeared between the admiral's eyebrows at that, and Hornblower swerved away from the subject. Clearly Leighton was not the sort of admiral to welcome suggestions from his inferiors.

Hornblower hurriedly began to deal with the next day's action to the southwestward.

"One moment, Captain," said Leighton. "You mean you went southward the night before last?"

"Yes, sir."

"You must have passed close to this rendezvous during the darkness?"

"Yes, sir."

"You made no attempt to ascertain whether the flagship had arrived?"

"I gave orders for a specially good lookout to be kept, sir."

The groove between Leighton's eyebrows was very noticeable now. Admirals were always plagued by the tendency of their captains, when on blockade service, to make excuses to get away and act independently — if only because it increased their share of prize money — and obviously Leighton was not merely determined to deal drastically with any such tendency but also he guessed that Hornblower had been careful to arrange his cruise so as to pass the rendezvous at night.

"I am extremely annoyed, Captain Hornblower, that you should have acted in such a fashion. I have already admonished Captain Bolton for allowing you to go, and now that I find you were within ten miles of here two nights ago I find it difficult to express my displeasure. I reached the rendezvous that very evening, as it happened, and as a result of your behaviour two of His Majesty's ships of the line have been kept idle here for nearly forty eight hours until you should see fit to rejoin. Please understand, Captain Hornblower, that I am very annoyed indeed, and I shall have to report my annoyance to the admiral commanding in the Mediterranean, for him to take any action he thinks necessary."

"Yes, sir," said Hornblower. He tried to look as contrite as he could, but his judgment told him that it was not a court-martial matter — he was covered by Bolton's orders — and it was doubtful if Leighton would really carry out his threat of reporting to higher authority.

"Please continue," said Leighton.

Hornblower began to describe the action against the Italian

divisions. He could see by Leighton's expression that he attached little importance to the moral effect achieved, and that his imagination was not powerful enough to allow him to gauge the effect on the Italians of an ignominious retreat before an invulnerable enemy. At Hornblower's suggestion that they had lost five hundred men at least Leighton moved restlessly and exchanged glances with Sylvester — he clearly did not believe him. Hornblower decided discreetly not to put forward his estimate that the Italians had lost at least another five hundred men through straggling and desertion.

"Very interesting," said Leighton, a trifle insincerely.

A knock at the cabin door and the entrance of Elliott eased the situation.

"The weather's looking very nasty, sir," he said. "I was thinking that if Captain Hornblower wishes to rejoin his ship —— "

"Yes, of course," said Leighton, rising.

From the deck they could see black clouds to leeward, rising rapidly against the wind.

"You'll only just have time," said Elliott, looking at the sky as Hornblower prepared to go down into his barge.

"Yes indeed," said Hornblower. His main anxiety was to get away from the *Pluto* before anyone noticed that he was leaving Villena behind — the latter, with no understanding of the English conversation, was hanging back on the quarterdeck, and Hornblower was able to scramble down into the boat without anyone thinking of him.

"Give way," said Hornblower, before he was fairly seated, and the barge shot away from the *Pluto's* side.

With an admiral and his staff on board, the accommodation, three-decker though she was, must already be strained. The presence of a Spanish colonel would mean that some unfortunate lieutenant would be rendered extremely uncomfortable. But Hornblower could harden his heart to the troubles of the unknown lieutenant.

Chapter XVI

The thunder was already rolling on the horizon when Hornblower set foot on the *Sutherland's* deck again, although the heat showed no signs of diminishing at present and the wind had dropped away almost to nothing. The black clouds had stretched over the sky nearly overhead, and what blue was left was of a hard metallic tint.

"It'll be coming soon, sir," said Bush. He looked complacently upwards; the *Sutherland's* sail had already been reduced by his orders to topsails only, and now the crew were busy taking a reef in them. "But where it'll come from, God only knows."

He mopped his sweating forehead; the heat was frightful, and the ship, with no wind to steady her, was heaving painfully on the uneasy sea. The blocks were chattering loudly as she rolled.

"Oh, come *on,* blast you," grumbled Bush.

A breath of air, hot as though from a brick kiln, stole upon them, and the *Sutherland* steadied for a moment. Then came another, hotter and stronger.

"There it comes!" said Bush, pointing.

The black sky was suddenly split by dazzling lightning, followed almost instantaneously by a tremendous crash of thunder, and the squall came racing down upon them; they could see its hard, metallic line on the surface of the grey sea. Almost taken aback, the *Sutherland* shuddered and plunged. Hornblower bellowed orders to the helmsman, and she paid off before it, steadying again. The shrieking wind brought hail with it — hailstones as big as cherries, which bit and blinded and stung, rattling with an infernal din on the decks, and whipping the sea into a yeasty foam whose hiss was audible even through the other noises. Bush held the big collar of his tarpaulin coat up round his face, and tried to shield his eyes with the brim of his sou'wester, but Hornblower found the keen wind so delicious that he was unconscious of the pain the hailstones caused him. Polwheal, who came running up on deck with his tarpaulin and sou'wester, had positively to jog his elbow to attract his attention and get him to put them on.

The *Pluto,* hove to, came drifting down two cables' lengths clear of the *Sutherland's* starboard bow; the big three-decker was even more unhandy and made more leeway than the *Sutherland* herself. Hornblower watched her and wondered how Villena was feeling now, battened down below with the timbers groaning round him. He was commending himself to the saints, presumably. The *Caligula* was still up to windward under reefed topsails, her man-o'-war pendant blown out stiff and straight as a pole. She was the most weatherly of the three ships, for her British designers had had in mind as principal object the building of a ship to contend with storms — not, as in the case of the *Pluto,* of cramming the utmost artillery into a given length and beam, nor, as the Dutch designers had been compelled to do in the case of the *Sutherland,* to give the minimum of draught compatible with a maximum of seaworthiness.

Almost without warning the wind whipped round four whole points, and the *Sutherland* lurched and plunged, her storm canvas slatting like a discharge of guns, before she paid off again. The hail had given place to torrential rain now, driven along almost horizontally by the howling wind, and the sudden change in the wind called up a short, lumpy sea over which the *Sutherland* bucked and plunged in ungainly fashion. He looked over to the *Pluto* — she had been caught nearly aback, but Elliott was handling her well and she had paid off in time. Hornblower felt that he would rather command the flat-bottomed old *Sutherland* than a clumsy three-decker, ninety eight guns and thirty-two-pounders and first-rate's pay notwithstanding.

The wind shrieked at him again, nearly tearing his tarpaulin from his back. The *Sutherland* trying to lie over on her side in a gale like this was like a cow trying to waltz. Bush was yelling something at him. Hornblower caught the words "relieving tackles" and nodded, and Bush vanished below. Four men at the wheel, aided by the powerful leverage of the barrel of the wheel, might possibly manage to control it despite the *Sutherland's* frantic behaviour, but the strain thrown on the tiller ropes would be enormous, and as precautionary measure it would be better to place six or eight men at relieving tackles in the gunroom, to share the strain both on the men at the wheel and on the tiller ropes. A petty officer would have to be posted at the grating nearest the wheel to shout down instructions to the men at the relieving tackles — all highly skilled work, the thought of which made Hornblower bless his own resolution in stripping the East India convoy of seamen.

To windward the horizon was concealed in a pearly mistiness of rare beauty, but to leeward it was clearer, and reaching up to the sky in that direction there was a bar of blue — the mountains of Spain. In that direction there was Rosas Bay, poor shelter with the present southeasterly gale blowing, and closed to British ships in any case because of the French guns mounted there; Rosas was a fortress whose siege and capture by the French had provided Cochrane with opportunities for distinguishing himself a year ago. The northern extremity of Rosas Bay was Cape Creus — the *Sutherland* had captured the *Amelie* while the latter was endeavouring to weather this point. Beyond Cape Creus the coast trended away again northwesterly, giving them ample sea room in which to ride out the gale, for these summer storms in the Mediterranean never lasted long, violent though they were.

"Flagship's signalling, sir," yelled the midshipman of the watch. "No. 35, make all sail conformable with the weather."

The *Pluto* was showing storm staysails as well as her close-reefed topsails; apparently the admiral had decided that Cape Creus was dangerously near, and wished to claw out a little farther to windward in case of emergencies. It was a sensible precaution; Hornblower gave the necessary orders to set the *Sutherland* on the same course, although it was all that the men at the wheel and relieving tackles could do to keep her from coming up into the wind. The guns' crews were busy double-breeching the guns lest the heavings of the ship should cause any to break loose, and there was already a party of men at work on the two chain pumps. The working of the ship was not causing her to take in much water as yet, but Hornblower believed in keeping the well as clear as possible in case the time should come when pumping would be urgently necessary. The *Caligula* was far to windward already — Bolton was making the fullest use of the weatherly qualities of his ship and was keeping, very properly, as far as possible out of harm's way. But the *Sutherland* and the *Pluto* were safe enough, always excepting accidents. The loss of a spar, a gun breaking loose, a sudden leak developing, and the situation might be dramatically changed, but at present they were safe enough.

Overhead the thunder was rolling so unceasingly that Hornblower noticed it no longer. The play of the lightning among the black clouds was dazzling and beautiful. At this rate the storm could not last much longer; equilibrium was restoring itself fast. But there would be some flurries yet, and the wind had already kicked up a heavy sea, here in this shallow corner of the Mediterranean; there was plenty of water washing over the main deck as the *Sutherland* rolled. The air, even the deluges of rain and spray, were exhilarating after the stifling heat of the past few days, and the wind screaming in the rigging made a music which even Hornblower's tone-deaf ear could appreciate. He was surprised that so much time had passed when Polwheal came to tell him his dinner was ready — what dinner there was, with the galley fire extinguished.

When he came on deck again the wind had sensibly diminished, and over to windward there were patches of clear sky to be seen, of a steely green-blue, and the rain had ceased, although the sea was wilder than ever.

"It's blown itself out quick enough, sir," said Bush.

"Yes," answered Hornblower, but with mental reservation. That steely sky was not the blue of returning calm, and he never yet had known one of these Mediterranean storms die away without at least one expiring effort. And he was still very conscious of Cape Creus on the horizon to leeward. He looked keenly round him, at the *Pluto* to leeward, veiled in spray, and the *Caligula* far to windward and her canvas only rarely visible across the tossing grey water.

Then it happened — a sudden howling squall, which laid the

Sutherland over and then veered round with astonishing quickness. Hornblower clung to the mizzen weather rigging, bellowing orders. It was wild while it lasted; for a moment it felt as if the *Sutherland* would never rise again, and then as if she might be driven under stern-foremost as the wind took her aback. It howled and shrieked round them with a violence which it had not yet displayed. Only after a long struggle was the ship brought to the wind again and hove to; the shift in the wind had made the sea lumpier and more erratic than ever, so that she was bucking and plunging in a senseless fashion which made it hard even for those who had spent a lifetime at sea to keep their footing. But not a spar had carried away, and not a rope had parted — clear proof of the efficient work of Plymouth Dockyard and of the seamanship of Bush and Harrison.

Bush was shouting something now, and pointing away over the quarter, and Hornblower followed the gesture with his eyes. The *Pluto* had vanished, and for a moment Hornblower thought she must have sunk with all hands. Then a breaking wave revealed her, right over on her beam ends, the grey waves breaking clean over her exposed bottom, her yards pointing to the sky, sails and rigging showing momentarily black through the white foam in the lee of her.

"Jesus Christ!" yelled Bush. "The poor devils have gone!"

"Set the main topmast stays'l again!" yelled Hornblower back.

She had not sunk yet; there might possibly be some survivors, who might live long enough in the wild sea to grab a rope's end from the *Sutherland's* deck and who might be hauled on board without being beaten to death; it had to be tried even though it was a hundred to one against one of the thousand men on board being saved. Hornblower worked the *Sutherland* slowly over towards the *Pluto*. Still the latter lived, with the waves breaking over her as if she were a half-tide rock. Hornblower's imagination pictured what was happening on board — the decks nearly vertical, with everything carrying away and smashing which could. On the weather side the guns would be hanging by their breechings; the least unsoundness there and they would fall straight down the decks, to smash holes on the opposite side which would sink her in a flash. Men would be crawling about in the darkness below decks; on the main deck the men who had not been washed away would be clinging on like flies on a windowpane, soused under as the waves broke.

Through his levelled glass he caught sight of a speck on the exposed upper side of the *Pluto,* a speck that moved, a speck which survived the breach of a wave over it. There were other specks, too, and there was a gleam of something in swift regular movement. Some gallant soul had got a party together to hack at the weather shrouds of the main mast, and as the *Sutherland* closed he saw the shrouds part, and the foremast shrouds as well. With a shuddering roll the Pluto heaved herself out of the water like a whale, water cascading from her scuppers, and as she rolled towards the *Sutherland* her mizzen mast went as well, on the opposite side. Freed from the overpowering leverage of her top hamper she had managed to recover — naval discipline and courage had won her a further chance of life during the few seconds which had been granted her while she lay on her beam ends. Hornblower could see men still hard at work, hacking madly at the uncut shrouds to free the ship from the wreckage thrashing alongside.

But she was in poor case. Her masts had gone, a few feet from the deck; even her bowsprit had disappeared. And with the loss of their steadying weight the bare hull was rolling insanely, heaving right over until her bottom copper was exposed on one side, and then rolling equally far back again, taking only a few seconds to accomplish a roll which extended through far more than a right angle. The wonder was that she did not roll over and over, as a wooden ninepin might do, floating on its side. Inside the ship it must be like an inferno, like a madman's nightmare; and yet she lived, she floated, with some at least of her crew alive on her decks. Overhead the thunder pealed a final roll. Even westward, to leeward, there was a gap visible through the clouds, and the Spanish sun was trying to break through. The wind was no more now than a strong gale. It was the last hurricane effort of the storm which had done the damage.

And yet that last effort must have endured longer than Hornblower could have guessed. He was suddenly conscious of Cape Creus large upon the horizon, and the wind was driving nearly straight from the ships towards it. It would only be a matter of an hour or two before the dismasted hulk was in the shallows at the foot of the cape where certain destruction awaited her — and to make it doubly certain there were French guns on Cape Creus ready to pound a helpless target.

"Mr. Vincent," said Hornblower. "Make this signal, '*Sutherland* to flagship. Am about to give assistance.' "

That made Bush jump. In that boiling sea, on a lee shore, the *Sutherland* would find it difficult to give assistance to a mastless hulk twice her size. Hornblower turned upon him.

"Mr. Bush, I want the bower cable got out through a stern port. As quickly as you can, if you please. I am going to tow the flagship off."

Bush could only look his expostulations — he knew his captain too well to demur openly. But anyone could see that for the *Sutherland* to attempt the task was to take her into danger probably uselessly. The scheme would be practically impossible from the start, owing to the difficulty of getting the cable to the *Pluto* as she rolled and lunged, wildly and aimlessly, in the trough. Nevertheless, Bush was gone before Hornblower could do more than read his expression. With that wind steadily thrusting them towards the land every second was of value.

With her flat bottom and with all her top hamper exposed to the wind the *Sutherland* was going off to leeward a good deal faster than the *Pluto*. Hornblower had to work his ship with the utmost care, fighting his way to windward close-hauled before heaving-to and allowing her to drop back again; there was only the smallest margin to spare. The gale was still blowing strongly, and the least clumsiness in handling, the slightest accident to sail or spar, meant danger. Despite the chill of the wind and the steady rain the *Sutherland's* topmen were sweating freely soon, thanks to the constant active exertion demanded of them by their captain, as he backed and filled, worked up to windward and went about, keeping his ship hovering round the dismasted *Pluto* like a seagull round a bit of wreckage. And Cape Creus was growing nearer and nearer. From below came a steady tramp and thumps and dragging noises as Bush's party slaved away to haul the ponderous twenty-inch cable aft along the lower gun deck.

Now Hornblower was measuring distances with his eye, and gauging the direction of the wind with the utmost care. He could not hope to haul the *Pluto* bodily out to sea — it was as much as the *Sutherland* could do to work herself to windward — and all he intended was to tow her aside a trifle to gain advantage of the respite, the additional sea room which would be afforded by avoiding the cape. Postponement of disaster was always a gain. The wind might drop — probably would — or change, and given time the *Pluto's* crew would be able to set up jury masts and get their ship under some sort of control. Cape Creus was nearly due west, and the wind was a little north of east, the tiniest trifle north. It would be best from that point of view to drag the *Pluto* away southerly; in that case they stood a better chance of weathering the cape. But southwards from Cape Creus stretched Rosas Bay, limited southward by Cape Bagur, and such a course might drift them under the guns of Rosas, expose them to the annoyance of the gunboats which were probably stationed there, and end in worse disaster than before. Northwards there would be no such danger; the guns at Llanza could not be remounted yet, and there were twenty miles of clear water from the tip of the cape to Llanza anyway. Northwards was safer — if only he could be sure of weathering the cape. Hornblower's imagination was hard at work trying to calculate, on quite insufficient data, the rate of drift he could expect and the possible distance the *Sutherland* would be able to tow the dismasted three-decker in the time granted. With the data insufficient, imagination was all he had to go upon. He had decided on a northward course when a young seaman came running breathless up to the quarterdeck.

"Mr. Bush says the cable'll be ready in five minutes, sir," he said.

"Right," answered Hornblower. "Mr. Vincent, signal to the flagship 'Stand by to receive a line.' Mr. Morkell, pass the word for my coxswain."

A line! The quarterdeck officers stared at each other. The *Pluto* was plunging and lunging quite irrationally in the trough of the sea. She was still heeling over so as to show her copper before rolling back to bury the white streaks between her gunports, but in addition, in the irregular sea, she was lunging now forward, now aft, as incalculable whim took her. She was as dangerous to approach as a gun loose on a rolling deck. Any sort of collision between the ships might well, in that sea, send them both incontinently to the bottom.

Hornblower ran his eyes over Brown's bulging muscles as he stood before him.

"Brown," he said. "I've selected you to heave a line to the flagship as we go down past her. D'you know anyone in the ship who could do it better? Frankly, now."

"No, sir. Can't say as I do, sir."

Brown's cheerful self-confidence was like a tonic.

"What are you going to use, then?"

"One o' them belayin' pins, sir, an' a lead line, if I can have one, sir."

Brown was a man of instant decision — Hornblower's heart warmed to him, not for the first time.

"Make ready, then. I shall lay our stern as close to the flagship's bows as is safe."

At the moment the *Sutherland* was forging slowly ahead under storm jib and close-reefed topsails, two hundred yards to windward of the *Pluto*. Hornblower's mind became a calculating machine again, estimating the *Sutherland's* relative drift down upon the *Pluto*, the latter's drunken reelings and plungings, the *Sutherland's* present headway, the send of the waves and the chances of a cross-wave intervening. He had to wait for two long minutes before the moment for which he was planning should arrive, his eyes glued upon the *Pluto* until their relative positions should be exactly what he wanted.

"Mr. Gerard," said Hornblower — his mind was too busy for him to be afraid. "Back the main tops'l."

The *Sutherland's* way was checked. At once the gap between the two ships began to narrow, as the *Sutherland* drifted down upon the *Pluto* — a gap of grey angry water with bearded waves.

Fortunately the *Pluto* was lying fairly constantly in the trough without yawing, only surging forward or back as some unexpected sea struck her. Brown was standing statuesquely on the taffrail, balancing superbly. The lead line was coiled on the deck at his side, attached to the belaying pin which he swung pendulum fashion, idly, from his fist. He made a magnificent picture there against the sky, with no hint of nervousness as he watched the distance dwindle. Even at that moment Hornblower felt a hint of envy of Brown's physique and robust self-confidence. The *Sutherland* was coming down fast upon the *Pluto* — upon the latter's wave-swept forecastle Hornblower could see a group of men waiting anxiously to catch the line. He looked to make sure that Brown's assistants were ready with a stouter line to bend on the lead line.

"We'll do it, by God!" said Gerard to Crystal.

Gerard was wrong — at the present relative rates of drift the ships would pass at least ten yards further apart than Brown could be expected to throw the belaying pin and its hampering trailer of line.

"Mr. Gerard," said Hornblower coldly, "back the mizzen tops'l."

The hands were ready at the braces; the order was hardly given before it was executed. The *Sutherland* was making a tiny trifle of sternway now, and the gap was closing farther still. The *Pluto*'s towering bow, lifting to a wave, seemed right upon them. Gerard and Crystal were swearing softly in unison, without the slightest idea of what they were saying, as they watched, fascinated. Hornblower felt the wind blowing cold about his shoulders. He wanted to call to Brown to throw, and with difficulty checked himself. Brown was the better judge of what he could do. Then he threw, with the *Sutherland*'s stern lifting to a wave. The belaying pin flew with the line wavering behind it in the wind. It just reached the *Pluto*'s beak-head bows and caught round a remnant of the standing rigging of the bowsprit, where a ragged sailor astride the spar seized it with a wave of his arm. Next moment a wave broke clean over him, but he held on, and they saw him pass the end of the line up to the waiting group on the forecastle.

"Done it!" shrieked Gerard. "Done it, done it, done it!"

"Mr. Gerard," said Hornblower. "Brace the mizzen tops'l sharp up."

The line was uncoiling fast from the deck as the *Pluto* hauled it in; soon the heavier line was on its way out to the dismasted ship. But they had not long to spare; with their different rates of drift it was impossible for Hornblower in that gale to keep the two ships that same distance apart — impossible and dangerous. The *Sutherland* hove-to and went to leeward faster than the *Pluto*, close-hauled she forged ahead, and it was Hornblower's task to combine these two factors so that the increasing distance between the ships was kept down to a minimum — a nice algebraic problem in convergent series which Hornblower had to convert into mental arithmetic and solve in his head.

When suddenly the *Pluto* decided irrationally to rush forward upon the *Sutherland* he found himself recasting his estimates at the very moment when everyone else was holding his breath and waiting for the collision. Gerard had a couple of parties standing by with spars to try to bear the *Pluto* off — not that they could have achieved much against her three thousand tons dead weight — and the bight of an old sail filled with hammocks as a fend-off, and there was wild activity on the forecastle of the *Pluto* as well, but at the very last moment, with blasphemy crackling all round, the dismasted ship suddenly sheered off and everyone breathed again more freely, except Hornblower. If the *Pluto* could surge in that fashion towards the *Sutherland,* she could surge away from her also, and if she were to do so while the line was hauling in the twenty-three-inch cable she would part the line for certain and leave the whole business to be done again — and Cape Creus was looming very near now.

"*Caligula* signalling, sir," said Vincent. " 'How can I help?' "

"Reply 'Wait,' " said Hornblower over his shoulder to him; he had actually forgotten the *Caligula's* existence. Bolton would be a fool if he came down unnecessarily to leeward, towards a hostile lee shore.

A mighty splash over the stern indicated that Bush down below was paying out some of the hawser through the after port so as to provide some slack if the *Pluto* surged away, but the process might be overdone — it was a hemp cable, which sank in water, and to have out too much would imperil the line which was drawing it in. Hornblower leaned over the heaving stern.

"Mr. Bush!" he bellowed.

"Sir!" said Bush's voice from below through the open port.

"Avast there, now!"

"Aye aye, sir."

The line was taking the strain now, and the cable was creeping slowly out towards the *Pluto* like some sea worm. Hornblower watched as it straightened — this was a business demanding calculation as close as any so far. He had to shout his orders for Bush to pay out more cable, or to wait, his eyes on the ships, on the sea, on the wind. The cable was two hundred yards long, but fifty of those lay in the *Sutherland* herself — the job had to be completed before the ships were a hundred and fifty yards apart. Hornblower only began to feel relieved when he saw the end of the cable curve up out of the sea onto the *Pluto's* bows, and a waving of flags told him that the end had been taken inboard and made fast.

Hornblower looked at the nearing land, felt the wind on his cheek. His earlier calculations were proving correct, and if they held on this tack they would be drifted into Rosas Bay even if they cleared the land.

"Mr. Vincent," he said. "Signal to the flagship 'I am preparing to go about on the other tack.' "

Gerard looked his amazement. It appeared to him that Hornblower was going to unnecessary trouble and imperilling both ships by this manœuvre — he could see no farther than Cape Creus, only the friendly sea and the dangerous land. With a seaman's instinct he wanted to get both ships comfortably under control with sea room under their lee, and he did not stop to consider beyond that. He could see the land and feel the wind, and his reaction to these circumstances was instinctive.

"Mr. Gerard," said Hornblower. "Go to the wheel. When the strain comes on the hawser —— "

Gerard did not need to be told about that. With three thousand tons trailing on her stern the *Sutherland* would behave unlike any ship the quartermasters had ever steered, and extraordinary and unexpected measures would have to be taken to keep her from flying up into the wind. The hawser was tightening already. The bight of it rose slowly out of the sea, straightening like a bar, the water spouting out of it in fountains, while a thunderous creaking below told how the bitts were feeling the strain. Then the cable slackened a trifle, the creaking diminished, and the *Sutherland* had got the *Pluto* under way. With every yard they went, and every bit of way the *Pluto* received, the latter sagged less and less to leeward. As soon as she could answer the helm the strain on the *Sutherland's* quartermasters would be eased.

Bush came up on the quarterdeck again, his task below completed.

"I want you to work the ship, Mr. Bush, when we go about."

"Aye aye, sir," said Bush. He looked at the land, and felt the wind, and his thoughts followed an exact parallel to Gerard's, but Bush by now never dreamed of doubting his captain's judgment in a matter of seamanship. His mental state was now that if Hornblower thought it right, it must be so, and there was no need to wonder about it.

"Send the hands to the braces. It must be like lightning when I give the word."

"Aye aye, sir."

The *Pluto* was gathering way, and every yard after this that they made in a southerly direction would be a dead loss when they turned northerly.

"Back the mizzen tops'l," said Hornblower.

The *Sutherland* lost way, and the *Pluto* came steadily forging down upon her. Hornblower could actually see Captain Elliott come running forward to see for himself what was happening. He could not guess what Hornblower was intending.

"Have the signal 'Tack' bent and ready to send up, Mr. Vincent."

The *Pluto* was very near now.

"Brace the mizzen tops'l up, Mr. Bush."

The *Sutherland* gathered speed again — she had just the distance allowed by the slackening of the hawser in which to gather way and go about before the tow began to interfere. Hornblower watched the cable and estimated the speed of the ship through the water.

"Now, Mr. Bush! That signal, Mr. Vincent!"

The helm was put down, the yards braced up, with Rayner forward attending to the fore topmast staysail. She was coming round, her canvas volleying as she came into the wind; on board the *Pluto* as they read the signal they had the sense to put their own helm down too, and with steerageway upon her she began to come round a little and allow Hornblower a little more room for his manœuvres. Now the *Sutherland* was over on the opposite tack, and gathering way, but the *Pluto* was only halfway round. There would be a terrific jerk in a moment. Hornblower watched the tightening cable rising from the sea.

"Stand by, Mr. Gerard!"

The jerk came, and the *Sutherland* shuddered. The drag of the cable across her stern was doing the most fantastic things to her — Hornblower could hear Gerard volleying orders to the quartermasters at the wheel and down the grating to the men at the relieving tackles below. For one palpitating second it seemed as if she must be dragged back and thrown in irons, but Gerard at the wheel and Bush at the braces and Rayner forward fought her tooth and nail. Shuddering, she paid off again, and the *Pluto* followed her round. They were over on the other tack at last heading northwards towards the comparative security of the Gulf of the Lion.

Hornblower looked at green-topped Cape Creus, close in now, and a little forward of the port beam. It was going to be a very near-run thing, for besides her own natural leeway the *Sutherland* was being dragged to leeward by the dead weight of the *Pluto*, and her speed through the water towards safety was diminished by the same dead weight. It was going to be a very near thing indeed. Hornblower stood with the wind howling round him, his busy mind plunged into calculations of drift and distance again. He looked back at the *Pluto*, not rolling so badly now that she had way on her. The towrope was at an angle to the length of the *Sutherland*, and the *Pluto* was at a further angle to the towrope.

He could rely on Elliott to make the most economical use of his helm, but the drag on the *Sutherland* must be tremendous. He ought to try to get a little more speed out of the *Sutherland*, but with a full gale blowing it was dangerous to spread any more canvas. If a sail were to split or a spar carry away they would be on the shore in no time.

He looked towards the land again, to measure the diminishing distance, and as he looked a warning rose like a ghost out of the sea a cable's length away. It was a pillar of water six feet high, which rose from the breast of a wave and vanished as quickly and as mysteriously as it had risen. Hornblower could hardly believe he had seen it, but a glance at Crystal's and Bush's faces, intentionally immobile, assured him that he had. A cannon ball had plunged into the water there, calling up that splash, although in the high wind he had neither heard the shot nor seen the smoke from the land. The battery on Cape Creus was firing at him, and he was nearly in range. Soon there would be forty-two-pounder balls coming about his ears.

"Flagship's signalling, sir," said Vincent.

On board the *Pluto* they had managed to attach a block to the top of the stump of the foremast and send up a signal; the fluttering flags could be seen clearly from the *Sutherland's* quarterdeck.

" 'Flag to *Sutherland*,' " read Vincent. " 'Cast off — tow — if necessary.' "

"Reply 'Submit not necessary.' "

They must make more speed through the water, there was no doubt about that. It was an interesting problem in chances, but more of the sort to appeal to a player of hazard than a whist player. To set more sail increased the danger to both ships at the same time as it gave them a greater chance of reaching safety. Yet if he set more sail and lost a spar he still might possibly struggle with the *Sutherland* out of danger, and the *Pluto* would be no more lost than she would be if he cast her off ignominiously now.

"Mr. Bush, I'll have the reefs shaken out of the fore tops'l."

"Aye aye, sir," said Bush. He had anticipated the necessity for it, and he had guessed that his captain would choose the bolder course — he was learning fast, even at his age, was Bush.

The topmen went running up the rigging and out along the fore-topsail yard; standing on the swaying foot ropes with the gale howling round them, holding on by their elbows over the yard, they struggled with the reef points. The sail shook itself out with a loud flap, and the *Sutherland* heeled sharply over under the increased pressure. Hornblower noticed the flat catenary curve of the heavy cable astern flatten itself a trifle more, but the rope gave no sign of breaking under the strain. Despite the increased heel of the ship the men at the wheel were actually finding their task a little easier, for the leverage of the big fore topsail forward tended to balance the eternal drag of the tow aft.

He glanced at the land just in time to see a puff of smoke from the summit of Cape Creus, blown instantly into invisibility by the gale. Where the shots fell he could not tell at all, for he neither saw nor heard them; the sea was too rough for the splashes to be easily seen. But the fact that the battery was firing showed that they must at least be almost in range — they were circling on the very edge of ruin. Nevertheless, the *Sutherland* was making better speed through the water, and looking aft he could see preparations advancing on the *Pluto's* deck for setting up a jury main mast. Any fragment of sail which the *Pluto* could carry would ease the *Sutherland's* task enormously, and in an hour they might have the work completed. Yet in an hour darkness would be come to shield them from the fire of the battery; in an hour their fate would be decided one way or another. Everything depended on the occurrences of the next hour.

The sun had broken through the westerly clouds now, changing the hills and mountains of Spain from grey to gold. Hornblower nerved himself to endure the waiting during the next hour, and the *Sutherland* and the *Pluto* came through that hour successfully. At the end of that time they had weathered Cape Creus, and had drawn so far to the northward that the land under their lee had dropped away abruptly from a mile and a half distant to fifteen miles. Night found them safe, and Hornblower very weary.

Chapter XVII

"CAPTAIN HORNBLOWER will command the landing party," said Admiral Leighton, finally.

Elliott and Bolton both nodded in entire agreement as they sat round the council table in the *Pluto's* cabin. A landing party six hundred strong, contributed by three ships of the line, was certainly a captain's command, and Hornblower was equally certainly the best captain to command it. They had been expecting some such move as this ever since the *Pluto* had returned refitted from Port Mahon, and Leighton had shifted his flag back into her from the *Caligula*. The coming and going of Colonel Villena from the shore had heralded it, too. For three weeks the *Caligula* and the *Sutherland* had ranged along the coast of Catalonia, and the *Pluto* returning had brought back welcome fresh provisions, the *Sutherland's* prize crews, and even a dozen new hands for each ship. With the ships at full strength they might well strike a heavy blow, and the capture of Rosas, if it could be effected, would undoubtedly throw the whole of the French arrangements for the subjection of Catalonia into confusion.

"Now, are there any comments?" asked the admiral. "Captain Hornblower?"

Hornblower looked round the big cabin, the cushioned lockers, the silver on the table, Elliott and Bolton gorged with the vast dinner they had consumed, Sylvester with paper and ink before him, Villena in his gawdy yellow uniform staring idly about while the English conversation which he did not understand went on round him. On the bulkhead opposite him hung a portrait of Lady Barbara, a likeness so good as to be startling — Hornblower felt as if he might hear her voice at any moment. He caught himself wondering what they did with it when they cleared for action, tore his thoughts away from Lady Barbara with an effort, and tried as tactfully as he could to show his distaste for the whole scheme.

"I think," he said at length, "that it might be unwise to trust so entirely to the cooperation of the Spanish army."

"There are seven thousand men ready to march," said Leighton. "From Olot to Rosas is no more than thirty miles."

"But Cerona lies between."

"Colonel Villena assures me that there are byroads round the town passable to an army without cannon. He himself, as you know, has made the journey four times."

"Yes," said Hornblower. Sending a single horseman was a different proposition entirely from marching seven thousand men by mountain paths. "But can we be certain of seven thousand men? And can we be sure that they will come?"

"Four thousand men would suffice for the siege," said Leighton. "And I have General Rovira's definite promise to march."

"Still they might not come," said Hornblower. He realised it was hopeless to try to argue with a man who had not had personal experience of Spanish promises, and who had not imagination enough to visualise the difficulties of arranging combined action between forces separated by thirty miles of mountainous country. The telltale groove had appeared between Leighton's eyebrows.

"What alternative do you suggest, then, Captain Hornblower?" he asked, impatience evident at having thus to reopen the whole question.

"I should suggest that the squadron confine itself to actions within its own strength, without having to depend on Spanish help. The coast battery at Llanza has been reestablished. Why not try that? Six hundred men ought to be able to storm it."

"My instructions," said Leighton ponderously, "are to the effect that I must act in the closest cooperation with the Spanish forces. Rosas has a garrison of no more than two thousand men, and Rovira has seven thousand only thirty miles away. The main body of the French Seventh Corps is to the southward of Barcelona — we have a week at least in which to effect something against Rosas. From the squadron we can supply heavy guns, men to work them, and more men to head a storming column when we have effected a breach. It appears to me to be an eminently suitable opportunity for combined action, and I quite fail to understand your objections, Captain Hornblower. But perhaps they are not so cogent, now?"

"I did no more than to state them at your request, sir."

"I did not ask for objections, but for comments, or helpful suggestions. I looked for more loyalty from you, Captain Hornblower."

That made the whole argument pointless. If Leighton only wanted servile agreement there was no sense in continuing. He had clearly made up his mind, and on the face of it he had a very strong case. Hornblower knew that his objections were more instinctive than reasoned, and a captain could not very well put forward the plea of greater experience to an admiral.

"I can assure you of my loyalty, sir."

"Very well. Captain Bolton? Captain Elliott? No comments? Then we can start work at once. Mr. Sylvester will let you have your orders in writing. I trust that we are on the eve of the most resounding success the east coast of Spain has seen since this Spanish war began."

The fall of Rosas would indeed be a resounding success if it could be achieved. As a town with practicable communication with the sea it could hardly be retaken by the French now that there was a strong English squadron on the spot to sustain it. It would be a constant threat to the French communications, a base where Spanish armies from anywhere in the Peninsula could be thrown on shore, of such importance that the Seventh Corps would be bound to cease their attempts at the conquest of Catalonia and concentrate all their strength on the task of retaking it or observing it. But it was Spanish information that there was no French field army within reach. It was a Spanish promise to bring Rovira down from Olot to effect a siege, and a Spanish promise to have transport animals ready to drag the siege train from the landing point.

But with Leighton set upon it, there was nothing for it but to go through with the affair wholeheartedly. If everything went right, they would win a great success, and although Hornblower had never yet heard of a combined operation of war in which everything went right, he could still hope for one, and draft his arrangements for the landing of the siege train from the fleet in accordance with that hope.

Two nights later the squadron came gliding in the early darkness, with the hills and cliffs of the Cape Creus peninsula looming faintly in the distance, to drop anchor together off the sandy cove beside Selva de Mar which had been agreed upon as the best place for landing. Four miles to the westward was the battery at Llanza; five miles to the east was the battery on the end of Cape Creus, and six miles due southward, across the root of the long peninsula of which Cape Creus forms the tip, lay the town of Rosas.

"Good luck, sir," said Bush, looming up in the darkness of the quarterdeck as Hornblower made ready to go down into his barge.

"Thank you, Bush," answered Hornblower. The punctilious "Mr." could be dropped occasionally in unofficial speeches of this sort. But the fact that he found his hand sought and gripped by Bush's large horny one was an indication that Bush took the most serious view of the impending operation.

The barge took him quickly over the placid water which reflected the numberless stars overhead; soon the noise of the gentle waves breaking on the sandy beach was louder than the subdued rumbling of the landing force in process of embarkation. A sharp challenge came from the beach to the approaching boat; it was pleasant to hear that it was worded in Spanish, which made it appear much less likely that it was a French force posted there to oppose a landing, and probable that it was the party of guerrilleros who had been promised. Hornblower stepped ashore, and a group of cloaked figures, just visible in the starlight, came down the beach towards him.

"The English captain?" asked one of them in Spanish.

"Captain Horatio Hornblower, at your service."

"I am Colonel Juan Claros, of the third tercio of Catalan migueletes. I bid you welcome in the name of Colonel Rovira."

"Thank you. How many men have you here?"

"My tercio. That is to say a thousand men."

"How many animals?"

"Fifty horses and a hundred mules."

Villena had promised that all northern Catalonia would be swept for draught animals for the siege train. There were four miles of hill paths and a mile of flat plain to be covered between here and Rosas — it would take fifty horses to drag one of the two and a half ton twenty-four-pounders over rough country. Had there been fewer animals than this Hornblower would have refused to move, but the Spaniards had provided the barest minimum necessary.

"Take the barge back," said Hornblower to Longley. "The landing can proceed."

Then he turned again to Claros.

"Where is Colonel Rovira?"

"He is over beyond Castellon, closing in on Rosas."

"What is his force?"

"He has every Spaniard able to carry arms in northern Catalonia, Captain, except for my tercio. Seven thousand men at least."

"H'm."

That was exactly according to plan. The army was to be under the walls at dawn, and to be joined as quickly as possible by the siege train, so that the battering could start without delay immediately upon the alarm being given. There was only the barest minimum of time available to reduce Rosas before the main French army could come up from Barcelona. Hornblower felt that he must make every effort to carry out his part of the programme, since the Spaniards were adhering so closely to theirs.

"Have you any patrol watching Rosas?" asked Hornblower.

"A squadron of regular cavalry. They will give the alarm if any sortie comes from the fortress."

"Excellent."

He would not be able to get the guns far from the beach before dawn, and by that time Rovira would have hemmed Rosas in, while any hitch would be reported by the cavalry. It was a good piece of organisation. Hornblower felt he had misjudged the Spaniards, or perhaps these Catalan irregulars were better soldiers than the ordinary Spanish army — which was not unlikely.

The steady splash of oars heralded the approach of the boats of the squadron; the leading ones were up to the beach and the men in them came tumbling out, stirring up a faint phosphorescence in the water. The white cross-belts of the marines showed up in startling contrast with their red coats, which appeared black in the faint light.

"Major Laird!"

"Sir!"

"Take a party to the top of the cliff. Post your pickets where you think best, but remember your orders. Allow nobody out of earshot."

Hornblower wanted to have a solid disciplined force out as a screen in front of him, not trusting Spanish precautions against surprise, but in darkness, with three languages — Spanish, Catalan, and English — in use, he did not want to risk any muddle or misunderstanding. It was the sort of minor technical difficulty which could not be appreciated by an admiral without experience. The longboats with the guns were grounding far out in the shallows. Men were already hauling into position the rough landing pontoon of spars lashed into rafts, the outer sections buoyed up by casks, which Hornblower had had prepared. Cavendish, the first lieutenant of the *Pluto*, was doing this part of the work thoroughly well and without troubling Hornblower for orders.

"Where are the horses and mules, Colonel?"

"Up above."

"I shall want them down here shortly."

It was only a matter of minutes for most of the material to be brought ashore, even though a thousand rounds of shot for the twenty-four-pounders — a hundred rounds per gun, one day's consumption — weighed over ten tons. Three hundred seamen and three hundred marines, working under naval discipline, could land ten tons of shot, and the necessary powder barrels, and the beef and bread for one day's rations, in no time worth mentioning. It was the guns which presented the greatest difficulty. The first of the ten twenty-four-pounders was only now being coaxed onto the pontoon, for it was a desperate business to run it up the brief ramp from the platform built on the thwarts, where it had been precariously perched during its passage from the ship, over the boat's gunwale. The pontoon sank under its ponderous weight until its surface was awash. Two hundred men, thigh-deep in water, tailed onto the dragropes which were attached to the gun, and, floundering and splashing, their feet seeking foothold in the soft sand below and finding none, they gradually hauled the thing towards the beach.

Like all guns Hornblower had ever seen, it behaved with a pigheaded obstinacy that might have been instigated by infernal powers with a perverted sense of humour. Although it had been fitted, by Hornblower's orders, with specially large trucks to make it more easy to surmount inequalities of surface, it caught and stuck, over and over again, in its passage over the spars. Handspikes and crowbars were handled diligently in the dark by Cavendish and his men to coax it over the inequalities. And then it would slew round, with Cavendish bellowing to the men to avast, for fear lest the maddening thing should run clean off the platform into the water alongside; only when it had been pushed and heaved straight again could the men tail onto the dragropes once more. There were ten of these guns, Hornblower reflected, and four miles of paths, uphill and down, over which they had to be dragged.

He had had the base of the pier prolonged over the sand by further rafts of timber laid out there, right up to where the sand gave place to the rocky bottom of the steep combe which seamed the cliff here and led to the summit. The horses and mules, each with a man at its head whose rags were obvious in the darkness, were waiting here in a great herd, but of course the Spaniards, although they knew they had come to drag guns, had provided no sort of harness for the operation.

"Here, you men," said Hornblower, turning to a waiting group of sailors. "There's plenty of line over there. Harness up these horses to the gun. You can find some spare canvas if you look for it."

"Aye aye, sir."

It was quite fantastic to see what seamen could turn their hands to. They fell to work with a will, knotting and tying. The English words they used may have sounded strange to the Spanish horses' ears as they wheeled the animals into position, but they seemed to be effective enough. Even the horse-holders, gabbling Catalan, pushed and shoved until they were more help than hindrance. Whinnying and clattering in the darkness — barely relieved by the light of a dozen lanterns — the puzzled brutes were got into line. Rope collars padded with canvas were slipped over their heads, rope traces were passed back to the eyebolts in the gun carriage.

"Avast!" roared one of the sailors just as the strain was beginning to come on. "This beggar's got his starboard leg over the line!"

By the time the second gun had reached the water's edge they were ready to start hauling up the first. Whips cracked and sailors shouted. The horses plunged as they sought foothold in the sand, but the gun began to move, with a vast creaking and crackling of timber under the trucks. The movement was spasmodic and jerky, and when they began to breast the steep slope of the combe it died away altogether. Twenty Spanish horses, underfed and undersized, could not haul that gun up the slope.

"Mr. Moore," said Hornblower, irritably. "See that that gun is hauled up."

"Aye aye, sir."

A hundred men on dragropes as well as twenty horses managed it, aided by a party behind with crowbars to help over the worst inequalities and to sprag the wheels with rocks at moments when neither men nor horses could pull for another second. Hornblower felt he had really accomplished a great deal when he stood on the summit, with dawn creeping out of the sea, and looked at the line of ten guns, and the mountain of stores, which had been all dragged up in the course of the night.

The gradual coming of the light enabled him to look about him. Down below was the golden beach, dotted with details of the landing party, and beyond that the blue sea, with the ships of the squadron rolling to their anchors. On his own level the summit of the peninsula stretched in a rocky uneven expanse before him. Over to his right the rock broke completely through in a vast table-topped hill, but southward, in the direction of Rosas, which he would have to follow, a narrow goat path wound through the low scrub of arbutus bushes. Claros beside him was revealed as a lean man, sunburnt to the colour of tobacco, with a long black moustache above an excellent set of white teeth, which he displayed in a smile.

"I have a horse for you, Captain."

"Thank you, Colonel. That is very kind of you."

There were a few brown figures creeping dispiritedly about the rocks; in the dips between the low crests there were brown masses which were just beginning to disintegrate in the sunlight from huddles of sleeping men into sleepy groups, who, still clutching their blankets about them, moved aimlessly here and there. Hornblower regarded his allies with a disfavour which was not diminished by the fact that it was exactly what he had anticipated, and which was intensified by his sleepless night.

"Would you be so kind," he said, "as to send a message to Colonel Rovira, telling him that we are about to march on Rosas, and that I hope to reach there with at least some of the guns at noon?"

"Certainly, Captain."

"And I must ask you for the help of your men in the transport of my guns and stores."

Claros looked more dubious at that, and more dubious still when he was told that of his men four hundred would be needed to help with the guns while another four hundred would have to carry a twenty-four-pound cannon ball each all the way to Rosas. Hornblower overrode his objections a little crossly.

"And after that, Colonel," he said, "they will have to return here for more. I was promised a sufficiency of pack animals; if you do not supply me with four-legged ones, I must use those with two. Now, if you please, I want to get the column started."

Ten horses or mules to every gun, with a hundred men at the dragropes. A hundred men ahead to labour on the task of improving the path, rolling rocks out of the way and filling up holes. Four hundred men carrying cannon balls, some of them leading the pack mules with gunpowder kegs slung over their backs. Claros looked still more askance when it became apparent that every man of his tercio would be at work, while Hornblower proposed to leave two hundred of his marines free of any labouring duty.

"That is how I wish it arranged, Colonel. If you do not like it, you can try to find a Spanish battering train."

Hornblower was determined upon keeping a substantial portion of his disciplined force closed up and ready for an emergency, and his determination was obvious enough to silence Claros' protests.

There was already an outcry behind them when the mules were being loaded up. Hornblower strode over with Claros at his heels, to find a Spanish officer threatening Gray with a drawn sword, his ragged guerrilleros behind him handling their muskets.

"What's all this? What is happening here?" demanded Hornblower, first in English and then in Spanish. Everybody turned to him all speaking at once, like schoolboys in a playground dispute. The officer's explosive Catalan was almost incomprehensible to him, and he turned to listen to Gray.

"It's like this, sir," said the master's mate, displaying a lighted cigar in his hand. "This Dago lieutenant here, sir, he was a-smoking this while we was loading up the mules. I says to him, very respectful, sir, 'No smoking in the magazine, sir,' but he didn't take no notice, not understanding, maybe. So I says to him, I says, 'No smokingo, magazino, senor,' an' he just blew out a puff of smoke and turned his back on me. So I took away his cigar, an' he drew his sword, sir."

Claros had at the same time heard his officer's explanation, and Claros and Hornblower faced each other.

"Your sailor has insulted my officer," said Claros.

"Your officer has been very foolish," said Hornblower.

It seemed like an impasse.

"Look, sir," said Gray, suddenly. He pointed to one of the barrels swinging against the ribs of the patient mule who bore it. It was slightly stove, and a thin black trickle of powder had run from it. There was powder on the mule's flank, powder on the ground. The danger of fire was obvious, must be obvious even to a Catalan. Claros could not suppress a half smile as he looked.

"My sailor acted hastily," said Hornblower, "but I think you will admit, Colonel, that he was in part justified. He will tender a profound apology, and then, perhaps, you will issue strict orders against smoking near the powder."

"Very well," said Claros.

Hornblower turned to Gray.

"Say to the officer, 'God save our gracious King, senor.' Say it humbly."

Gray looked startled.

"Go on, man," said Hornblower, testily. "Do what I say."

"God save our gracious king, senor," said Gray, in a tone that was at least unnatural, if not humble.

"The man wishes to express to you his profound regret for his rudeness," explained Hornblower to the officer, and Claros nodded approvingly, spat out a couple of brief orders, and turned away. The crisis was over, and no feelings hurt on either side. The sailors were grinning and cheerful, while the Catalans looked proudly down upon the lighthearted barbarians.

Chapter XVIII

CAPTAIN HORNBLOWER checked his horse on the top of the last of the hitherto interminable rocky undulations. The August sun was blazing overhead, and innumerable flies plagued him and his horse and his companions. At his side rode Claros, behind them Longley and Brown sat uneasily their rawboned Rosinantes along with the three Spanish staff officers. Far back along the path was a solid block of scarlet, where Major Laird had his marines formed up as an advanced guard, while here and there on the grey-green hills scarlet dots showed where he had posted pickets as a precaution against surprise. Farther back still could be seen a caterpillar of men, naked to the waist, labouring at their task of improving the path for the guns, and beyond that a sort of multiple caterpillar with a black dot at the end showed where the first gun had reached. In five hours it had travelled little more than three miles. Hornblower, looking up at the sun, saw that he had an hour and a half left in which to keep his appointment — in which to haul his guns over a mile of rock and over a mile of the plain which lay below him. He felt a twinge of conscience at the thought that he would probably be a little late with the first of the guns, and he certainly would not be able to open fire against the walls before five or six o'clock in the evening.

There below him, a mile away but seemingly much nearer in the clear air, lay the town of Rosas. Hornblower could recognise all the features of the place which his map indicated. To the right was the citadel — from his elevated position Hornblower could see the pentagonal outline of its grey ramparts, with the blue sea behind. In the centre was the town itself, a single long street lying close to the shore, with a line of earthworks guarding it on the landward side. To the left was the high tower of Fort Trinidad on the other flank. The weakest point was undoubtedly the centre, but it would be of little use assailing that, as the citadel and the Trinidad could hold out independently. The best course would be to take the bull by the horns and breach and storm the citadel by an attack delivered from close by the water's edge. The town could not be held if the citadel fell, although the Trinidad might cause further trouble.

Hornblower had allowed his thoughts to run away with him. He had been so busy planning the reduction of Rosas that he had not even noticed the general peacefulness of the scene. The tricoloured flags flapped idly from the flagstaffs in the citadel and the Trinidad, and they were the most warlike things in sight. There was no sign on the bare plain of any besieging army. Meanwhile it could only be a question of hours before the garrison discovered how near to them lay a valuable convoy, and how weak was the force guarding it.

"Where is the army of Catalonia?" Hornblower demanded angrily, of Claros. He received a deprecatory shrug of the shoulders.

"I do not know, Captain."

To Hornblower it meant that his precious convoy, and his far more precious landing party, were strung out over three miles of country within easy reach of any column which the governor of Rosas might send out.

"You told me Colonel Rovira was marching on Rosas last night!"

"He seems to have been delayed."

"The messenger — the one you said you would send at dawn — has he returned?"

Claros, by a raising of his eyebrows and a jerk of the head, passed this question on to the chief of staff.

"He did not go," said this officer.

"*What?*" said Hornblower in English. He had to fight down his bewilderment and struggle with his dazed senses in order to speak Spanish again. "Why not?"

"It would have put the officer to unnecessary trouble," said the chief of staff. "If Colonel Rovira comes, he comes. If he cannot, no message of ours will bring him."

Hornblower pointed over to the right. In a fold of the hills a line of some fifty picketed horses and a few groups of seated men indicated the position of the squadron of cavalry which had been watching the town since yesterday.

"Why did they not report that Colonel Rovira had not arrived?" he demanded.

"The officer commanding had my orders to report when he *did* arrive," answered Claros.

He was showing no signs of indignation at the barely concealed contempt in Hornblower's expression, but Hornblower kept his rage in hand for a little longer in his endeavour to keep the enterprise alive.

"We are in a very considerable danger here," he said.

Claros shrugged his shoulders again at the Englishman's timidity.

"My men are used to the mountains. If the garrison comes out to attack us we can get away by goat paths over there," he answered, pointing away to the precipitous sides of the mesa in the distance. "They will never dare to follow us there, and if they did they would never catch us."

"But my guns? My men?"

"In war there is always danger," said Claros, loftily.

Hornblower's answer was to turn to Longley.

"Ride back at once," he said to the boy. "Halt the guns. Halt the convoy. Halt every man on the path. Nothing is to move a yard farther without orders from me."

"Aye aye, sir."

Longley wheeled his horse round and clattered off; the boy had somewhere learned to ride well before coming to sea. Claros and his staff, Hornblower and Brown, all watched him go, and then turned back to face each other. The Spaniards could guess what were the orders that had been given him.

"Not a gun or a man of mine will stir," said Hornblower, "until I see Colonel Rovira's army on the plain there. Will you be good enough to send a message to him now?"

Claros tugged at his long moustache and then gave the order to his staff; his junior officers argued sulkily with each other before one of them took the note written by the chief of staff and set off with it. Clearly no one relished the prospect of a ride of perhaps twenty miles under a hot sun in search of Rovira's column.

"It is nearly the hour for dinner," said Claros. "Will you have my men's food served out to them, Captain?"

Hornblower's jaw dropped at that. He had thought nothing more could surprise him, and he was proved wrong. Claros' tobacco-brown face gave no indication that he thought there was anything other than what was strictly ordinary in his assumption that his thousand men were to feed on the stores laboriously landed from the squadron. It was on the tip of Hornblower's tongue to refuse pointblank, but he stopped to consider. He guessed that if they were not fed, Claros' men would simply melt away in search of food, and there was still a faint chance that Rovira might arrive and the siege be taken in hand. For the sake of that chance, it was as well to make this concession and make the most of the few hours granted them before their presence should be discovered.

"I will give orders for it," he said, and the dignified colonel's expression showed no change at either demanding or receiving favours from the Englishman with whom he had just been on the verge of quarrelling.

Soon sailors and Catalans were all of them eating heartily. Even the squadron of cavalry smelt food from afar, like vultures, and rode hastily back to join in the feast, leaving only an unhappy half dozen to continue the watch over Rosas. Claros and his staff seated themselves in a group ministered to by orderlies. And as was to be expected, *comida* was followed by siesta — after a vast meal every Spaniard stretched himself in the shade which the scrub afforded, and snored, flat on his back, with a Peninsular disregard for the flies which buzzed over his open mouth.

Hornblower neither ate nor slept. He dismounted and gave his horse over into Brown's charge, and then hobbled up and down on his hilltop looking down at Rosas, with his heart full of bitterness. He had written carefully to the admiral to explain the reason of his halt — carefully, because he did not want to appear to belong to the type of officer who sees difficulties at every turn — and the answer had simply enraged him. Was it not possible, Leighton had asked in his reply, to attempt something against the fortress with the fifteen hundred men he had in hand? Where was General

Rovira? The tone of that question indicated that Hornblower was somehow at fault regarding Rovira's nonarrival. Captain Hornblower must remember the need to work in the closest and most cordial cooperation with England's allies. The squadron could not possibly continue to supply Claros' force with food for long; Hornblower must tactfully call Colonel Claros' attention to the need for drawing upon his own sources of supplies. It was highly important that the arrival of the British squadron should be signalised by a great success, but on no account was any operation to be undertaken which might imperil the safety of the landing party. Leighton's letter was a completely futile piece of writing, having regard for the present facts, but a Court of Inquiry who knew none of them would consider it eminently sane and sensible.

"Begging your pardon, sir," said Brown, suddenly. "The Froggies down there is on the move."

Startled, Hornblower looked down at Rosas. There were three serpents issuing out of the fortress — three long narrow columns of troops creeping out onto the plain, one each from the citadel, the village, and the Trinidad. A hoarse shout from the Spanish cavalry picket proclaimed that they had seen the same phenomenon; the little party left their post and rode headlong back to the scattered Spanish army. Hornblower went on staring for two more minutes; the columns showed no sign of ending, but wound on interminably out of the fortifications. Two were heading towards him, while the one from the citadel was taking a different route, off to his right, with the clear intention of cutting off the Spanish retreat to the mainland. Hornblower's eye caught the flash of musket barrels in the sunlight; still the columns were winding out — there must be a thousand men at least in each. The Spanish information which had estimated the garrison's strength as two thousand as a maximum must be as faulty as all the rest.

Claros came clattering up with his staff to gaze out over the plain. He paused only for an instant to take in the significance of what he saw — every man with him pointed simultaneously to the outflanking column — and then he wheeled about and spurred back again. As he wheeled his eyes met Hornblower's; they were expressionless as ever, but Hornblower knew what he intended.

If he abandoned the convoy and marched his men with all haste for the mesa, he could just get away in time, and he was set upon it. Hornblower knew in that instant that there was not the least use appealing to him to cover the retreat of the convoy, even if the Catalans were steady enough to fight a rearguard action against greatly superior numbers.

The safety of the landing party was dependent solely on its own exertions, and there was not a moment to be lost. Hornblower scrambled onto his horse — the heads of the French columns were well out onto the plain now, and some would be soon ascending the steep escarpment of the plateau — and dashed back after Claros. Then, as he neared the place where Major Laird had his marines already drawn up into line, he checked the pace of his weary horse to a sober trot. It would never do to display too much haste or anxiety. That would only unsteady the men.

And he had a difficult problem to decide, too. The obvious best course was to abandon everything, guns, stores, and all, and march his men back to the ships headlong. The lives of trained seamen were too valuable to be lightly thrown away, and if he did as common sense directed he would have every man safely on board before the French column caught them up; in any matter-of-fact scale of relative values even a few seamen were worth more than ten twenty-four-pounders, and their ammunition and whatever foodstuffs had been landed. Yet in war the matter-of-fact frequently held only second place. A headlong flight to the ships, and abandonment of guns and stores, would depress the spirits of the men inordinately; a fighting retreat with next to no loss would raise them. He made up his mind as he halted his horse beside Major Laird.

"We'll have three thousand French on us in an hour, Laird," he said quietly. "You'll have to hold them back while we get the stores on board again."

Laird nodded. He was a tall red-faced Scot, red-haired and inclined to stoutness; his cocked hat was tilted back off his forehead and he mopped his face with a lilac-coloured silk handkerchief which clashed dreadfully in the sunlight with his red coat and sash.

"Aye," he said. "We'll do that."

Hornblower spared a second to glance down the double lines of marines, the homely brown faces under the shakos, and the white cross belts in Euclidean line. The disciplined composure the marines displayed was comforting and reassuring. He kicked his heels into the shaggy sides of his horse and trotted down the path. Here came Longley, tearing back on his pony.

"Ride to the beach, Longley. Tell the admiral it is necessary to reembark the men and stores, and ask that all the boats of the squadron should be ready to take us off."

A column of Spaniards was already hurrying off in disorderly fashion up a cross path towards the mainland. A Spanish officer was collecting the remainder of his men; a British petty officer was looking on in puzzled fashion as they unhitched a team of horses from one of the guns and began to lead them away.

"Stop!" shouted Hornblower, riding up in the nick of time and delving hurriedly into his mind for adequate Spanish. "We shall keep those horses. Here, Shelton, Drake, bring those horses back. Brown, ride on. Tell every officer that the Spaniards can go, but they're not to take a mule or horse with them."

There were sullen looks among the Spaniards. In a country in whose every corner war had raged bitterly for two years draught and pack animals were of the utmost imaginable value. The meanest Spanish peasant in the ranks knew it, knew that the loss of those animals would mean an empty belly for him in some new campaign a month off. But the British sailors were equally determined. They handled their pistols and cutlasses with every intention of using them if necessary, and the Spaniards remembered the French column which was marching to cut off their retreat. All down the path they abandoned the animals and drew off, sulkily, while Hornblower kicked his weary horse into renewed activity, as he rode along, turning back towards the beach all the guns and material which had been dragged so far with such exertion. He reached the head of the steep gully and rode down it to the beach. On that tranquil afternoon the sea was blue and smooth like enamel; far out the squadron rode peacefully at anchor, and below him lay the golden sand of the beach, while over the enamelled surface plied the boats of the squadron like huge beetles. All round him grasshoppers were singing deafeningly. The beach party was already hard at work reembarking the beef barrels and bread bags piled there. He could safely leave this part of the work to Cavendish, and he turned back again and rode up the gully. At the top a party of seamen arrived with the first of the mule train. He left orders for the animals to be brought back to the guns as soon as their loads were taken off, and rode on.

The nearest gun was within half a mile of the gully, men and horses labouring to drag it up the path — for this half mile the land sloped away fairly steeply inland from the top of the cliffs. The men gave him a cheer, and he waved his hand and tried to sit his horse as if he were an accomplished rider; it was comforting to think that Brown behind him was an even worse horseman, so that the contrast might help. Then a distant pop-pop-popping, its tone unnatural in the heated air, told him that Laird's rearguard was in action.

He rode hastily along the path, Brown and Longley at his heels, past the other gun teams labouring on the steep hillsides, towards the firing. At one point along the path there was a long line of cannon balls, lying where the Spanish carrying party had dropped them when the alarm came. Those would have to be lost — there was no chance at all of getting them back to the ships. He arrived unexpectedly at the scene of the firing. Here the country was a succession of short steep ups and downs, the rocky soil covered with a dense undergrowth, amid which grasshoppers were still singing loudly through the musketry. Laird had his men strung out along the summit of one of the major ridges; Hornblower came upon him standing on a lump of rock overlooking the path, the lilac handkerchief still in one hand and his sword in the other, and muskets banging away all along the ridge on either side of him. He had the air of a man completely enjoying himself, and he looked down at Hornblower with the irritation of a man disturbed while composing a work of art.

"All well?" asked Hornblower.

"Aye," said Laird, and then, grudgingly, "come up and see for yourself."

Hornblower got off his horse and scrambled up the rock, balancing precariously on its slippery summit beside the major.

"Ye'll observe," said Laird, academically, and rolling his r's, "that formed troops must keep to the paths in this terrain. Moreover, detached skirmishes lose their sense of direction rapidly, and this thorny vegetation is admirably adapted to hinder free movement."

From the rock Hornblower looked down upon a sea of green — the nearly impenetrable maquis which clothes the stony hillsides of Mediterranean Spain — through which the red coats of the marines, shoulder-deep in the scrub, were hardly visible. Here and there puffs of white smoke, drifting over the surface, marked where recently there had been firing. On the opposite hillside there were other puffs of smoke and faint stirrings among the undergrowth. Hornblower saw white faces, and blue coats, and sometimes even white breeches over there where the French struggled through the thorny scrub. Much farther back he could see part of a column of troops waiting on a section of the path. Two or three musket bullets came buzzing through the air close over his head.

"We are quite safe here," said Laird, "until the enemy turns our flank. If ye look over there to the right, ye'll observe a French regiment advancing along a path roughly parallel to this one. As soon as it reaches that thorn tree there, we shall have to retreat and take up a fresh position and leave them all their work to do again. Fortunately that path is only a sheep track of uncertain direction. It may never reach that thorn tree."

Hornblower could see a long line of French shakos bobbing along above the maquis as he followed Laird's pointing finger; its loops and winds showed that the path must be, as Laird had suggested, a mere chance sheep track. Another bullet buzzed past them.

"The French standard of musketry," said Laird, "is lower now even than it was at Maida, where I had the honour of being engaged as an officer on Sir John Stuart's staff. Those fellows have been firing at me for half an hour now without hitting me, nor even with the remotest chance of hitting me. But with two of us up here the possibility is doubled. I would recommend you, sir, to descend and devote your attention to accelerating the march of the convoy."

They looked at each other keenly. Hornblower knew quite well that the command of the rearguard was Laird's duty, in which he should not interfere as long as it was properly performed. It was the fear of being thought afraid which made him hesitate to descend. As he stood, he felt his cocked hat struck a violent blow which twisted it on his head so that it toppled off; with an instinctive grab he caught it as it fell.

"That outflanking column," said Laird, steadily, "is about to reach the thorn tree. I must ask you officially, sir" — he dragged out the long word into "offeeecially" — "to go back before I call on my men to retreat. Our retirement will necessarily be hurried."

"Very well, Major," said Hornblower, grinning despite himself, and slipping down from the rock with all the dignity he could muster. He got on his horse and trotted down the path again; he examined his hat with a little thrill of pride to see that the bullet had hit the gold loop at the front, passing within two inches of his head, and he had felt no fear. Where the path crossed the summit of the next ridge he drew rein again; the musketry in the rear had suddenly became more intense. He waited, and then a detachment of marines came running along the path with Captain Morris at their head. They had no attention to spare for him as they turned aside and plunged into the undergrowth on either side of the path, seeking points of vantage from which their fire would cover the retreat of their comrades. The musketry fire spluttered out abruptly, and then up the path they came, Laird at their head, half a dozen men under a young lieutenant bringing up the rear and turning to keep back the nearest enemy with warning shots.

Confident that the rearguard was under efficient direction, Hornblower was able to ride on to where the rearmost gun was standing stubbornly at the foot of a slope. The weary horses were plunging and slipping on the rocky surface as they strove to drag the thing up under the urgings of the sailors, but now there were only half a dozen seamen in place of the fifty Spaniards who had helped to drag it from the beach. They were reduced to heaving the gun up the slope foot by foot with crowbars; their naked ribs — most of them had thrown off their shirts — were glistening with sweat. Hornblower racked his brains for the appropriate thing to say.

"Heave away, my lads. Boney hasn't any guns as good as these. Don't let the Dagoes give him a birthday present."

The column of Spaniards could now be seen like a long worm ascending the precipitous sides of the mesa. They had made their escape. Hornblower, looking after them, felt a sudden feeling of hatred for them and the race they represented. They were a proud nation, yet never so proud as to disdain favours from others, hating foreigners only a little more than they hated each other, ignorant, misgoverned, misusing the wealth with which nature had endowed their country; Spain was a natural prey to any stronger nation. France had made this attempt at conquest, and it was only England's jealousy which was defeating it. Sometime in the future the country would be torn to pieces in the strife between Liberals and Conservatives, and at some period in that struggle the European powers would find sufficient accord to seize upon the fragments. Civil war and foreign aggression, centuries of them, perhaps, constituted the future of Spain unless the Spaniards set their house in order.

He brought back his mind with an effort from profitless speculation on the future to deal with the petty problems in hand — detailing the returning mule teams to assist in dragging the guns, portioning out the failing strength of his men so as to make the best speed with the mass of material yet remaining; the spluttering musketry to the rear told how men were suffering wounds and death for the sake of preserving it from the enemy. He sternly cast out the doubts which assailed him as to whether the gesture were worth the price, and kicked his exhausted horse into a last effort as he clattered along the path.

Half the guns were on the beach at last — for the final run down the steep gully to the sand little exertion was needed — and the remainder was fast nearing the head of the gully. The beach was cleared of all the stores that had been landed, and the first gun was even now being dragged along the landing pier for transfer to the ships. Cavendish, in command at the beach, came up to Hornblower.

"What about the horses and mules, sir?"

Shipping a hundred and fifty animals would be as difficult a task as shipping the guns, and they would be an intolerable nuisance on board. Certainly they must not be allowed to fall into the hands of the French; in Spain at the present time they were the most valuable form of booty. The sensible thing to do would be to cut the brutes' throats on the beach. Yet they were enormously valuable. If only they could be got away, and kept alive on board for a few days, they might be landed again and handed back to the Spaniards. To slaughter the wretched beasts would have as bad a moral effect on the men as losing the guns. Crushed biscuit would feed them on board — from the look of them it would be better fare than they had experienced for some time — and the fresh-water problem was hardly insurmountable. In the rear Laird was still fighting his successful rearguard action, and the sun was fast setting over the mesa.

"Send them on board with the other stores," said Hornblower, at last.

"Aye aye, sir," said Cavendish, allowing no shade of expression in his face to hint at his conviction that mules were far more trouble than guns to coax into small boats and to heave up into the ships.

The work went on. One of the guns, with the malicious ingenuity of all its tribe, fell over and dismounted itself during its passage down the gully, but the men did not allow the accident to delay them long. With crowbars they heaved the huge mass of iron down the slope and over the sand, rolling it, like a barrel, along the pier and into the longboat awaiting it. The ships had tackle which would make light of its weight and would remount it in no time. Hornblower gave up his horse to be led to the water's edge and to be coaxed into a boat, while he walked away along the summit of the cliff to take his stand on a high point from which he could overlook both the beach and the head of the gully where Laird would make his final stand.

"Run to Major Laird," he said to Brown. "Tell him everything is on the beach now."

Ten minutes later events suddenly moved with a rush. Brown must have met the marines in their final movement of retreat, for the scarlet uniforms came pouring back up the path, to take up their position along the summit of the cliff, their line reaching nearly to where Hornblower was standing. The French were hard on their heels; Hornblower could see their uniforms moving through the scrub, and the musketry popped furiously along the line.

"Look out, sir!" called Longley, suddenly. He pushed his captain violently in the ribs, jostling him off the flat rock on which he was standing. Hornblower heard two or three bullets pass over his head as he struggled to keep his footing, and at the same moment a group of French infantry, fifty or more, came bursting out of the bush, running hard for them. They were between Hornblower and the nearest marines; the only way of escape was down the steep face of the cliff, and he had no more than a second in which to make up his mind to take it.

"This way, sir!" squeaked Longley. "Down here!"

Longley dropped like a monkey to a narrow ledge below, beckoning him down with waving arms. Two blue-coated infantrymen were close upon him, their bayonets levelled; one of them was shouting something which Hornblower could not understand. He turned and jumped after Longley, his feet just reaching the ledge a dozen feet below; and he swayed there with a vertical drop of over a hundred feet below him. Longley caught his arm, and, leaning outwards, scanned the descent keenly and yet with a nightmare coolness.

"This is the best way, sir. You see that bush? If we can reach that, we ought to get over there. There's a bit of a gully there joining the big one. Shall I go first, sir?"

"Yes," said Hornblower.

A musket banged over his head and he felt the wind of the bullet — the French were leaning over the top of the cliff firing down at them. Longley braced himself, and then leaped wildly along the face of the cliff, slid down it in a cloud of dust and fragments, and caught the stout bush he had pointed out to Hornblower. Then, moving cautiously away from it, he found an inequality on which to rest, and from there beckoned again to his captain. Hornblower tried to nerve himself for the leap, and then drew back. Another bullet — it actually struck the ledge close to his feet. Hornblower plunged heavily from the end of the ledge, turning his face to the cliff. He felt the rock tearing at his clothes as he slid. Then he crashed into the bush and grasped it madly, his feet seeking foothold.

"Now, over here, sir. Catch hold of that lump with your hands. Put your foot into that crack, sir. No! Not that foot! T'other one!"

Longley's voice went up into a squeak like a bat's in the excitement as he edged himself along the cliff and at the same time instructed his captain where to put his hands and feet. Hornblower clung to the cliff face like a fly on a windowpane. His hands and arms were aching already — the activities of two days and a night had already drained his strength. A bullet whacked into the rock between him and the midshipman, a chip which it displaced struck his knee a sharp tap. He looked down, and his head swam at the sight of the drop below him. In his exhausted state he felt he would gladly loose his hold and drop down to the quick death awaiting him.

"Come on, sir!" said Longley. "Not much more now, sir. Don't look down!"

He recalled himself to sanity. Changing foothold and handhold inch by inch, he shuffled along in accordance with Longley's instructions.

"Just a minute," said Longley. "Are you all right, sir? Wait here while I go and have a look."

Hornblower clung on with aching arms and legs. He kept his face against the cliff, stupid with fatigue and fear. Then he heard Longley beside him again.

"It's all right, sir. There's only one nasty bit. Get your feet down onto that knob, there. Where that bit of grass is."

They had to get past a projecting boss in the face of the cliff;

there was one awful second when Hornblower had no foothold, and with his legs dangling had to stretch to a new handhold.

"They can't see us here, sir. You can rest a bit, if you'd like to," said Longley solicitously.

Hornblower lay on his face in the shallow depression which grooved the cliff, conscious for a space of nothing save the cessation of strain. Then with a rush he remembered everything — his dignity, the work on the beach, the fighting on the summit. He sat up and looked down; with a solid lump of the cliff under him his head would stand that. The beach was clear of guns now, in the darkening evening, and only a few animals stood waiting their turn to be coaxed into the boats. Up above the firing seemed to have died down for a space; either the French had begun to despair of achieving anything further or they were gathering for a last effort.

"Come on," said Hornblower, abruptly.

The rest of the descent was easy; they could slide and scramble all the way until he felt the welcome sand under his feet. A worried-looking Brown materialised here, his face clearing as he caught sight of his captain. Cavendish was standing supervising the despatch of the last cutter.

"Very good, Mr. Cavendish. The seamen can go next. Are the armed boats ready?"

"Yes, sir."

It was nearly dark now, and the sky gave only a faint light when the marines began to pour down the gully and over the sand. The last shots in the long retreat were fired by the four-pounders mounted in the bows of the two longboats which lay nosing the sand while the final section of marines splashed out into the water to them. The long red tongues of flame lit up the dark masses of Frenchmen swarming down onto the beach, and the blast of grape which they had hurled was followed by a gratifying chorus of screams and cries from the stricken masses.

"A very handsome operation indeed," said Major Laird from his seat in the stern of the longboat beside Hornblower.

Hornblower dropping in weariness was inclined to agree with him, although he was shivering with the chill of his soaked breeches, and his hands smarted from cuts and abrasions, and other parts of him pained him with saddle soreness as if they were being held before a fierce fire. They rowed out over the silent sea to a ship strange with the whinnying of horses and smelling stable-like already.

Hornblower staggered on board; he saw the boatswain's mate who held the lantern for him glance curiously at his ragged clothes and white face. He walked blindly past the dark line of horses and mules, picketed head and heel to the deck ringbolts, to the security of his cabin. He ought to make his report to the admiral — surely he could leave that until daylight. The deck seemed to be heaving under him rhythmically. Polwheal was there, and food was laid on the candle-lighted table, but Hornblower later could never remember eating any. Faintly he could remember Polwheal helping him into bed, and a vivid, clear-cut memory always abode with him of hearing Polwheal, through the closed cabin door, arguing with the sentry outside.

" 'Twarn't Horny's fault," said Polwheal, didactically.

Then sleep swooped down upon Hornblower, sleep which held him fast, even though he was conscious through it of the aches and pains which assailed him, of the perils he had encountered that day, of the fear which had tortured him on the cliff.

Chapter XIX

THE *Sutherland* was wallowing through the stormy waters of the Gulf of the Lion, under a grey sky, with white-flecked wave tops all round her, while her captain stood on his heaving quarter-deck enjoying the cold blast of the mistral round his ears. The nightmare adventure on the Spanish mainland was three weeks past now; for over a fortnight the ship had been clear of horses and mules, the stable smell had nearly disappeared, and the decks were white once more. Much more important, the *Sutherland* had been sent away on detached duty with orders to examine the French coast line all the way along to Toulon; he was free from the clogging authority of the admiral again, and he breathed the keen air with the delight of someone released from slavery. Lady Barbara's husband was not a man whom it was a pleasure to serve.

The whole ship seemed to be infected with this feeling of freedom — unless it was pleasure in the contrast between the present weather and the tranquil skies and calm seas which had prevailed so long. Here came Bush, rubbing his hands and grinning like a gargoyle.

"Blowing a little, sir," said Bush, "and it'll blow harder than this before it's over."

"Very likely," said Hornblower.

He grinned back, lightheartedly, with a bubbling of high spirits within him. It was quite fantastic how stimulating it was to be thrashing to windward again against a stiff breeze, especially with the nearest admiral a hundred miles away. In southern France that same wind would be causing grumbling and complaints, and the French would be going about hugging their cloaks to them, but here at sea it was perfectly delightful.

"You can put the hands to any work you please, Mr. Bush," said Hornblower magnanimously, as discretion returned to him and he evaded the tempting snares of falling into idle conversation.

"Aye aye, sir."

Young Longley came aft with the sandglass to attend to the hourly heaving of the log, and Hornblower watched him from the corner of his eye. The boy was carrying himself with assurance now, and gave his orders easily. He was the only one of all the midshipmen whose calculations of the day's work made any pretence at accuracy, and the incident on the cliff had shown him to be a lad of quick decision. Towards the end of this commission, and at a suitable opportunity, Hornblower decided, he would appoint him acting lieutenant; he watched him bending over the traverse board marking up the hour's run with a queer wonder as to whether he was observing a future Nelson, an admiral who would some day rule forty ships of the line.

He was an ugly little fellow, with his stubbly hair and monkey face, yet it was hard not to feel a surge of affection for him. If little Horatio, the child whom smallpox had killed on the third day in those Southsea lodgings, had grown up in this fashion Hornblower would have been proud of him. Perhaps he might have done — but it was not a good thing to think himself into gloom on a fresh morning like this about the little boy he had loved. There would be another child by the time he reached home. Hornblower hoped it might be a boy; and he was nearly sure that Maria hoped the same. Not that any little boy could quite take the place of Horatio — Hornblower felt a new flood of depression when he remembered how Horatio had said, "Papa! Want papa!" and had rested his face against his shoulder that evening when the first malaise of the illness was creeping over him. He shook his depression off; if his return to England was at the earliest moment he could hope for the child would be crawling about the floor with all a baby's misdirected zeal. He might even be talking a little, and would hang his head with shyness when his strange papa arrived, so that Hornblower would have the task of winning his confidence and affection. It would be a pleasant task.

Maria was going to ask Lady Barbara to be godmother to the child — it would be delightful if Lady Barbara agreed. Any child with the influence of the Wellesley family behind it could contemplate a secure future. Without a doubt it was the Wellesley influence which had put Leighton in command of the squadron he was mismanaging. And by this time Hornblower was sure that it was the Wellesley influence which had put him in command of one of the ships of that squadron and retained him in employment without a single day of half-pay. He was still in doubt about what had been Lady Barbara's motive, but on a stimulating morning like this he could almost venture to believe that it was because she loved him; he would far rather it were that than it should merely be because she admired his professional ability. Or it might be just an amused and tolerant kindliness towards an inferior whom she knew to love her.

That thought called up a surge of revolt. She had been his for the asking, once. He had kissed her, clasped her. No matter that he had been afraid to take her — he slurred that memory over in his present indignation — she had offered, and he had declined. As a suppliant once, she had no right to pose to herself now as his patroness. He stamped his feet with mortification as he paced the deck.

But his clairvoyance was instantly blurred by his idealism. His memory of a cool and self-collected Lady Barbara, the perfect hostess, the dignified wife of an admiral, was overlaid by mental pictures of a tender Lady Barbara, a loving Lady Barbara, with a beauty which would take a man's breath away. His heart was torn with longing for her; he felt sick and sad and lonely in his rush of desire for her, for the angel of goodness and sweetness and kindliness he thought her to be. His pulse beat faster as he remembered her white bosom with the sapphire pendant resting on it, and animal desire came to reinforce the boyish affection he bore her.

"Sail ho!" bellowed the masthead lookout, and Hornblower's dreaminess was stripped from him in a flash, like the straw wrapping from a bottle.

"Where away?"

"Right in the wind's eye, sir, an' comin' up fast."

A brisk nor'easterly wind like the present meant ideal weather conditions for French ships which wished to escape from the blockade of Marseilles and Toulon. It was a fair wind for the escaping ship, enabling her to get out of harbour and cover a long distance during the first night, while at the same time it pushed the blockading squadron away to leeward. This might well be a ship engaged on breaking the blockade, and if such were the case she would have small chance to escape with the *Sutherland* right to leeward of her. It would be consistent with the good fortune he had enjoyed on detached service during the present commission if this were to be another prize for him.

"Keep her steady as she goes," said Hornblower, in reply to Bush's look of inquiry. "And turn the hands up, if you please, Mr. Bush."

"Deck, there!" hailed the lookout. "She's a frigate, an' British by the look of her."

That was a disappointment. There were fifty possible explanations of a British frigate's presence here and on her present course which offered no chance of action as opposed to one which might involve the proximity of an enemy. Her topsails were in sight already, white against the grey sky.

"Begging your pardon, sir," said the gunlayer of one of the port-side quarterdeck carronades. "Stebbings here thinks he knows who she is."

Stebbings was one of the hands taken from the East India convoy, a middle-aged man with grey hairs in his beard.

"*Cassandra,* sir, thirty two, seems to me. She convoyed us last v'yage."

"Captain Frederick Cooke, sir," added Vincent, flipping hastily over the pages of the printed list.

"Ask her number and make sure," ordered Hornblower.

Cooke had been posted six months later than he had; in the event of any combined operations he would be the senior officer.

"Yes, she's the *Cassandra,* sir," said Vincent, his eye to his telescope, as a hoist of flags went up to the frigate's fore-topsail yard-arm.

"She's letting fly her sheets," said Bush, with a hint of excitement in his voice. "Queer, that is, sir."

From time immemorial, dating back long before a practical

flag-signalling system had been devised, letting fly the sheets had been a conventional warning all the world over of the approach of a fleet.

"She's signalling again, sir," said Vincent. "It's hard to read with the flags blowing straight towards us."

"Damn it, sir," blazed Bush. "Use your eyes, or I'll know the reason why not."

"Numeral. Four. Literal. Seventeen ——" began Vincent slowly.

"Four — hostile — ships of the line — astern — to windward — course — sou'west," translated Longley with the signal book.

"Beat to quarters, if you please, Mr. Bush. And wear the ship directly."

It was not the *Sutherland's* task to fight odds of four to one. If there were any British ships in pursuit he could throw himself in the enemy's path and rely on crippling at least two Frenchmen so as to ensure their capture, but until he knew more about the situation he must keep as clear as was possible.

"Ask, 'Are any British ships at hand?' " he said to Vincent, while the *Sutherland* first lay over on her side and then rose to an even keel as Bush brought her before the wind.

"Reply negative, sir," said Vincent, a minute later, through the din of clearing for action.

It was as he expected, then. The four French ships of the line had broken out of Toulon during the darkness and while the blockading squadron had been blown away to leeward. Only the *Cassandra,* the inshore lookout, had caught sight of them, and had run before them so as to keep them under observation.

"Ask, 'Where is the enemy?' " said Hornblower. It was an interesting exercise, calling for familiarity with the signal book, to frame a message so as to use the fewest number of flags.

"Six — miles — astern — bearing — nor'east," Longley translated from the code book as Vincent read out the numbers.

So the French were lying right before the wind. That might merely be because they wanted to put as great a distance as possible between them and the blockading squadron off Toulon, but it was not likely that the officer in command would run wastefully direct to leeward unless that was the course most suited to his plan. It ruled out completely any thought of Sicily or the Adriatic or the Eastern Mediterranean as objective, and it pointed directly to the Spanish coast near Barcelona and beyond that to the Straits of Gibraltar.

Hornblower on his quarterdeck set himself to try to think the thoughts of Bonaparte at the Tuileries. Beyond the Straits lay the Atlantic and the whole world. Yet it was hard to imagine any useful objective for four French ships of the line out there; the French West Indies had been nearly all reduced by English expeditions, the Cape of Good Hope was in English hands, Mauritius was about to fall. The French squadron might be intended for a mere commerce-destroying raid, but in that case an equal number of frigates would be both cheaper and more effective. That was not like Bonaparte. And on the other hand exactly enough time had elapsed for the appearance of Leighton's squadron on the Catalan coast and the resultant dearth of supplies to have been reported to the Tuileries, and for orders to have been transmitted thence to Toulon. Those orders would bear the Bonaparte stamp. Three British ships on the Catalan coast? Then send four French ones against them. Man them with crews picked from all the ships rotting in Toulon harbour. Load them with all the stores for which the Barcelona garrison is clamouring. Let them slip out one dark night, hack their way through to Barcelona, crush the British squadron if they can, and return if they are lucky. In a week they might be back safe and sound, and if not — every omelette demands the breaking of eggs.

That must be the French plan, and he would glady bet all he had that he was right. It only remained to decide how to defeat the French aims, and the opening moves were obvious. First, he must keep between the French and their objective, and second, it would be desirable to keep out of sight of the French, over their horizon, as long as possible — it would be a surprise to them to find a ship of considerable force, and not a mere frigate, in their path; and surprise was half a battle. In that case his first instinctive move had been correct, and the *Sutherland* was on the right course to achieve both these ends — Hornblower wondered uneasily whether his unthinking mind had jumped at once to the conclusions which his thinking mind had only just reached. All that remained to be done was to call down the *Pluto* and the *Caligula*. Three British ships of the line, and a frigate could fight four French ships, picked crews or not, and Bonaparte's opinion notwithstanding.

"Cleared for action, sir," said Bush, touching his hat. His eyes were bright with the anticipation of action. Hornblower saw in him a fighting man of the type to which he regretted he did not belong — a man who relished the prospect of a battle for its own sake, who loved physical danger, who would never stop to count the odds against him.

"Dismiss the watch below, if you please," said Hornblower.

There was no object in keeping every man at his station when action was far distant, and Hornblower saw Bush's expression alter when he heard the words. They meant that the *Sutherland* was not going to plunge immediately into action against odds of four to one.

"Aye aye, sir," he said, reluctantly.

There was something to be said for Bush's point of view, for the *Sutherland* well handled might knock away so many French spars as to leave two or three at least of the French so crippled as to fall a certain prey into British hands sooner or later. It would be at the cost of her own destruction, however, and he could think about it again later. A fair wind today might still mean a foul wind tomorrow; there might still be time for the *Pluto* and the *Caligula* to come up if only they could be informed of the proximity of their prey.

"Give me that signal book," said Hornblower to Longley.

He turned its pages, refreshing his memory regarding the wording of some of the arbitrary signals. In sending a long message there was always danger of misunderstanding. And he pulled at his chin while he composed his message. Like every British officer retreating, he was running the risk of having his motives misunderstood, even though, as he told himself petulantly, not even the mad British public, gorged with past victories, could condemn him for refusing action against odds of four to one. But if everything went wrong the Wellesley faction might seek a scapegoat; and the order he was about to transmit might mean the difference between success and failure, between a court of inquiry and the thanks of Parliament.

"Send this message," he said abruptly to Vincent.

Hoist after hoist the flags crept up the mast. The *Cassandra* was to set all sail she could carry, and to make use of her frigate's turn of speed to turn westward, seek out the *Pluto* and *Caligula* — Hornblower could not be exact in his description of their position — and bring them down to Barcelona. Phrase by phrase the *Cassandra* acknowledged the signal. Then there was a pause after its completion, before Vincent, glass to eye, reported.

"*Cassandra* signalling, sir. 'Submit —— ' "

It was the first time Hornblower had ever had that word addressed to him. He had used it so often in signals to admirals and senior captains, had included it so often in reports, and now another officer was beginning a signal to him with the word "Submit." It was a clear, definite proof of his growing seniority, and gave him a thrill keener even than he had known when a ship had first piped the side for him on his being posted. Yet naturally that word "submit" ushered in a protest. Cooke of the *Cassandra* was not in the least anxious to be thus summarily dismissed from the scene of a promising action. He submitted that it would be better for the *Cassandra* to stay in sight of the French.

"Signal 'Carry out orders acknowledged,' " said Hornblower, tersely.

Cooke was wrong and he was right — Cooke's protest helped his decision to crystallise. A frigate's whole function, what she was built for, was to enable the ships of the line to come into action. The *Cassandra* could not face a single broadside from one of the ships rolling along after her; if she could bring the *Pluto* and the *Caligula* into action she would have multiplied her own value an infinity of times. It was heart-warming to Hornblower to be not only convinced that he was right, but to be able to enforce the course of action he had decided upon. That six months' difference in seniority made Cooke obedient to him, and would make him obedient all their lives — if ever Cooke and he flew their flags together as admirals he would still be the senior and Cooke the junior. He watched the *Cassandra* shake out the reefs from her topsails and bear away westwards, with all her five knots' superiority of speed being put to its best use now.

"Shorten sail, Mr. Bush," said Hornblower.

The French would see the *Cassandra* vanish over their horizon; there was a chance that the *Sutherland* might keep them under observation without being seen. He stuck his telescope into his pocket and set himself to climb the mizzen rigging, sedately — even a little laboriously; it was imperilling his dignity to do so, when every hand in the ship could climb the mast quicker than he, but he had to see with his own eyes the enemy astern of him. The ship was plunging heavily in the following sea, and the wind blew keenly about his ears. It called for resolution to continue his ascent without undignified pauses, so as to appear merely as leisurely as a captain had a right to be, and yet neither timid nor awkward.

At last he found a secure perch on the mizzen-topmast crosstrees, and could train his glass on the heaving horizon. With her main topsail taken in the *Sutherland's* speed was considerably reduced, and it could not be long before the French appeared. He saw them soon enough — a tiny rectangle of white just lifting over the horizon, then another beside it, and another, and another.

"Mr. Bush!" he roared. "Set the main tops'l again, if you please. And send Mr. Savage up here."

The four French ships were rolling along in lubberly French fashion in a wide line abreast, half a mile apart — presumably their captains were afraid of collision if they drew closer — and it was a hundred to one that their lookouts would never notice the tiny dot which would be all they could see of the *Sutherland*. Savage came tumbling up beside him, hardly out of breath after his lightning scramble up the ratlines.

"Take this glass," said Hornblower. "You see the French squadron? I want to hear instantly if they alter course, or if they head-reach upon us, or we on them."

"Aye aye, sir," said Savage.

He had done all he could do now, when he reached the deck

again. It only remained to wait, patiently, until tomorrow. Tomorrow would see some sort of battle, hopeless or even — or if there were no battle it would mean that the French had disappeared and he would go before a court-martial. He was careful to keep his expression quite composed, and to try to appear as if he did not feel the tension of waiting in the least. It would be in the old tradition if he invited his officers to dinner and whist tonight.

Chapter XX

THE situation was one likely to disturb any captain's sleep, with four hostile ships of the line to windward needing to be kept under observation, and with calculations continually bobbing up from the subconscious to the conscious regarding the chances of the *Cassandra* bringing down Admiral Leighton in time to cut off the enemy. The weather conditions were unsettling, too — the wind, having worked up nearly to gale force towards evening, diminished until midnight, increased again, and then, with the inconsequence of Mediterranean winds, began to die away steadily.

Certainly Hornblower never expected to sleep. He was too excited, and his mind was too active. When the watch was changed in the evening he lay down on his cot to have a rest, and, being quite convinced that he had no chance of sleeping, he naturally fell into a deep dreamless sleep so heavy that Polwheal had to shake him by the shoulder at midnight to awaken him. He came on deck to find Bush standing by the binnacle.

"Too dark for anything to be seen, sir," said Bush, and then, excitement and exasperation getting the better of his formality, he growled, "Black as Newgate Knocker."

"Have you seen anything of the enemy?"

"I thought I did, sir, half an hour back, but nothing to be sure of. Wind's dropped a lot, too."

"Yes," said Hornblower.

As so often was the case at sea, there was nothing to do but wait. Two screened lanterns swayed down on the main deck, where the watch lay at their stations by the guns; the keen wind harped in the rigging, and the ship rose and plunged in the following sea with a lightness and grace no one would expect of her who had only seen her with the wind abeam. Nothing to do but to wait; if he stayed on deck he would only fidget and display his nervousness, so he might as well go and conceal his nervousness in his screened-off cot.

"Send for me at once if you catch sight of the enemy," he said, with elaborate carelessness, and went back again below.

He lay on his cot with his mind busy, for he knew that having slept once there was no chance whatever of sleeping again. So perfect was this conviction that sleep ambushed him once more, leaped upon him unawares, as he lay thinking about the *Cassandra,* so that it only seemed two minutes later that he heard Polwheal speaking to him as if from another world.

"Mr. Gerard's compliments, sir, an' it's beginnin' to get lighter, sir."

It called for quite an effort to rouse himself and get up from his cot; only when he was drowsily on his feet did he begin to feel pleased at having been genuinely asleep each time that Polwheal came to call him. He could picture Polwheal telling his cronies about the iron nerves of the captain, who could sleep like a child on a night when the ship was aboil with the prospect of action.

"Anything to report, Mr. Gerard?" he said, as he reached the quarterdeck.

"No, sir. I had to reef down for an hour at two bells, it blew so hard. But it's dropping fast now, sir, and backing sou'easterly."

"H'm," said Hornblower.

The faintest hint of light was beginning to tinge the gloomy sky, but nothing could be seen yet more than a cable's length away. A southeasterly wind would be nearly foul for the French on their course to Barcelona; it would be dead foul for the *Pluto* and *Caligula.*

"Thought I felt the loom o' the land, sir, before the light came," said Gerard.

"Yes," said Hornblower. Their course during the night would bring them close into Cape Creus of hated memory; he picked up the slate beside the binnacle, and, calculating from the hourly readings of the log, he made their position to be some fifteen miles off the cape. If the French had held the same course during the night they would soon have Rosas Bay and comparative security under their lee — of course, if they had not, if they had evaded him in the darkness, the consequence to him did not bear thinking about.

The light was broadening fast. Eastwards the watery clouds seemed to be thinning just above the horizon. Undoubtedly they were thinning; for a second they parted, and a speck of gold could be seen through them, just where the white-flecked sea met the sky, and a long beam of sunlight shone level over the sea.

"Land-ho!" yelled the masthead lookout, and westward they could see a bluish smudge on the horizon where the mountains of Spain loomed faintly over the curve of the world.

And Gerard glanced anxiously at his captain, took a turn or two up and down the deck, gnawed at his knuckles, and then could restrain his impatience no longer.

"Masthead, there! What do you see of the enemy?"

The pause that followed seemed ages long before the reply came.

"Northin', sir. Northin' in sight barrin' the land to looard."

Gerard renewed his anxious glance at his captain, but Hornblower, during that pause, had set his face sternly so that his expression was unmoved. Bush was coming onto the quarterdeck now; anyone could see that he was wild with anxiety. If four French ships of the line had evaded action it would mean half-pay for Hornblower for life, if nothing worse. Hornblower retained his stony expression; he was proud of being able to do so.

"Put the ship about, Mr. Gerard, if you please, and lay her on the starboard tack."

The French might perhaps have altered course in the darkness, and might now be lost in the centre of the Western Mediterranean, but Hornblower still did not think it likely. His officers had made insufficient allowance for the lubberliness of the unpracticed French. If Gerard had had to reef topsails in the night they might well have had to heave to; and both Bush and Gerard were overeager — during the night the *Sutherland* might have gained twenty miles on the French. By retracing his course he was confident that he would sight them again.

Confident as far as the whist-playing part of his mind was concerned, that is to say. He could not control the sick despair in his breast, nor the acceleration of his heart beats; he could only conceal them, keeping his face a mask and forcing himself to stand still instead of pacing about in his anxiety. Then he thought of an activity which would help to occupy his mind and yet not betray his nervousness.

"Pass the word for my steward," he said.

His hands were just steady enough to permit him to shave, and a chill bath under the wash-deck pump gave him new vigour. He put on clean clothes and parted his lessening hair with elaborate exactitude, for under the wash-deck pump he had told himself that they would sight the French again before he had completed his toilet. It was with a sense of acute disappointment that he laid down the comb when he had no more smallest excuse to continue its use, and turned to put on his coat, with no news of the French. And then, with his foot on the companion, there came a wild yell from Midshipman Parker at the masthead.

"Sail in sight! Two — three of 'em, sir. Four! It's the enemy!"

Hornblower continued his progress up the companion without faltering in his step, and he hoped people noticed it. Bush was halfway up the rigging with his glass, and Gerard was pacing — almost prancing — about the quarterdeck in his delight. Observing them, Hornblower was glad he had had no childish doubts about the correctness of his actions.

"Wear the ship, if you please, Mr. Bush. Lay her on the port tack."

A talkative captain might supplement the order with a brief explanation of the necessity for keeping the ship between the French and Spain, but Hornblower bit off the explanation as it rose to his lips. No unnecessary words would escape him.

"The wind's still working round southerly, sir," said Gerard.

"Yes," said Hornblower.

And it would drop, a good deal, too, as the day progressed, he decided. The sun was fast breaking through the clouds, with every prospect of a warm day — a Mediterranean autumn day, with a rising barometer and only the faintest of breezes. The hammocks had been piled in the netting, and the watch not at their stations were clattering onto the deck with buckets and holystones. The routine of the Navy had to be maintained, even though there was every chance that the decks they were swabbing would be running with blood before the day was over. The men were skylarking and joking — Hornblower felt a little thrill of pride as he looked at them and remembered the sullen despondent crowd with which he had sailed. Consciousness of real achievement was some compensation for the thankless service which employed him; and it helped him to forget, too, the uneasy feeling that today or tomorrow — soon, anyway — he would know again, as the whirl of battle eddied round him, the physical fear of which he was so intolerably ashamed.

As the sun climbed up the sky the wind dropped steadily, moving round even more southerly, and the mountains of Spain came nearer and nearer and grew more and more defined as their course brought them closer to the land. Hornblower held on as long as he could, bracing up his yards as the wind veered, and then finally heaving to while the French squadron crept up over the horizon. The shift in the wind had deprived them of the windward position; if they moved down to attack him he could escape northward so that if they pursued him they would be running towards the *Pluto* and *Caligula,* but he had no hope that they would. French ships of the line who had evaded the blockading squadron would race to accomplish their mission first, and would only fight afterwards, however tempting the bait dangled before them. If the wind shifted no farther round they could just hold their course for Barcelona, and he had not the least doubt that they would do so if not prevented. He would hang on to them and try to attack some isolated ship during the night if no help arrived.

"They're signalling a lot, sir," said Bush, his glass to his eye.

They had been signalling all day, for that matter — the first flurry of bunting, Hornblower shrewdly surmised, had been occasioned by their catching sight of the *Sutherland,* unaware that she had been keeping company with them for fifteen hours. Frenchmen retained their talkative habits at sea, and no French captain was happy without messages passing back and forth along the squadron.

The *Sutherland* was clear of the Cape Creus peninsula now, and Rosas Bay was opening out on her beam. It was in these very waters, but in very different weather conditions, that the *Pluto* had lost her masts and had been towed to safety by the *Sutherland;* over there, on those green-grey slopes, had occurred the fiasco of the attack on Rosas; through his glass Hornblower thought he could discern the precipitous face of the mesa up which Colonel Claros had led his fugitive Catalans. If the wind came farther round now, the French had a refuge open to them under the guns of Rosas, where they would be safe until the British could bring up fireships and explosion vessels to drive them out again; actually it would be a more secure refuge for them than the anchorage at Barcelona.

He looked up at the pendant flapping at the masthead — the wind was certainly southerly. It was growing doubtful whether the French would weather Palamos Point on their present tack, while he would certainly have to go about soon and stand out into the Frenchmen's wake, with all his advantage of position lost by the inconstancy of the weather. And the wind was beginning to come in irregular puffs now — a sure sign of its diminishing force. He turned his glass on the French squadron again to see how they were behaving. There was a fresh series of signals fluttering at their yard-arms.

"Deck, there!" yelled Savage from the masthead.

Then there was a pause. Savage was not too sure of what he could see.

"What is it, Mr. Savage?"

"I think — I'm not quite sure, sir — there's another sail, right on the horizon, sir, abaft the enemy's beam."

Another sail! It might be a stray merchant ship. Otherwise it would only be Leighton's ships or the *Cassandra.*

"Keep your eye on her, Mr. Savage."

It was impossible to wait for news. Hornblower swung himself up into the shrouds and climbed upwards. At Savage's side he trained his glass in the direction indicated. For a second the French squadron danced in the object glass, disregarded, as he searched.

"A bit farther round, sir. About there, I think, sir."

It was the tiniest fleck of white, too permanent for a wave

crest, of a different shade from the few clouds against the blue. Hornblower nearly spoke, but succeeded in limiting himself to "Ha — h'm."

"It's nearer now, sir," said Savage, telescope to eye. "I should say, sir, it's a ship's fore-royal."

There could be no doubt about it. Some ship under full sail was out there beyond the Frenchmen, and standing in to cross their wake.

"Ha — h'm," said Hornblower. He said no more, but snapped his telescope shut and addressed himself to the descent.

Bush dropped to the deck to meet him from the shrouds he had ascended; Gerard, Crystal, they were all on the quarterdeck eyeing him anxiously.

"The *Cassandra,*" said Hornblower, "standing in towards us."

By saying that, he was risking his dignity to demonstrate his good sight. No one could guess the new arrival to be the *Cassandra* from just that glimpse of her royals. But it could only be the *Cassandra* who would be on that course, unless his judgment were sadly at fault. Should she be revealed not to be, he would appear ridiculous — but the temptation to appear to recognise her when Savage was not even sure whether she was a ship or a cloud was too strong.

All the implications of the *Cassandra's* appearance were evident to the officers' minds at once.

"Where's the flagship and *Caligula?*" demanded Bush, of no one in particular.

"Maybe coming up, too," said Gerard.

"The Frogs are cut off if they are," said Crystal.

With the *Pluto* and *Caligula* to seaward of them, and the *Sutherland* to landward, Palamos Point to windward, and a fluky wind veering foul, it would be only by good fortune they could escape a battle. Every eye turned towards the French squadron; they were nearly hull-up now, heading south-by-west close-hauled, a three-decker in the van followed by three two-deckers, admiral's flags flying at the foremasts of the first and third ships. The broad white stripes which decorated their sides stood out sharp and clear in the pure air. If the *Pluto* and *Caligula* were far astern of the *Cassandra* the Frenchmen would still be as much in ignorance of their proximity as was the *Sutherland*, which would explain why they were still holding their course.

"Deck there!" hailed Savage. "The strange sail's *Cassandra*. I can see her tops'ls now, sir."

Bush and Gerard and Crystal looked at Hornblower with a strange respect for his penetrating vision; it had been well worth risking his dignity for that.

The sails suddenly flapped loudly; a puff of wind had followed a comparative lull, and from a more southerly point than before. Bush turned to shout orders for the trimming of the sails, and the others turned instantly to watch the French reaction.

"They're going about!" said Gerard, loudly.

Undoubtedly they were doing so; on the new tack they would weather Palamos Point but would be standing out to sea nearer to the British squadron — if the British were there.

"Mr. Bush," said Hornblower. "Put the ship about, if you please."

"*Cassandra's* signalling, sir," yelled Savage.

"Up with you!" snapped Hornblower to Vincent and Longley. Telescope and signal book in hand, they raced for the masthead; everyone on the quarterdeck watched their progress anxiously.

"*Cassandra's* signalling to the flagship, sir!" yelled Vincent.

So Leighton was out there, over the horizon — over the Frenchmen's horizon, too, judging from their actions. Bonaparte might send out four French ships to fight three English ones, but no French admiral, safely at sea and knowing the capacity of his crews far better than his emperor, would obey those orders if he could help it.

"What's she saying, boy?" hailed Hornblower.

"She's too far off to be sure, sir, but I think she's reporting the enemy's new course."

Let the Frenchmen hold that course for an hour, and they were lost, cut off from Rosas and certain to be overhauled before they reached Barcelona.

"They're going about again, by God!" said Gerard, suddenly.

Wordless, they watched the four French ships come up into

the wind, and come over onto the other tack. Then they came round, farther and farther still, until in all four ships their three masts were in line; every one of them was heading straight for the *Sutherland*.

"Ha — h'm," said Hornblower, watching his fate bearing down upon him; and again, "Ha — h'm."

The French lookouts must have glimpsed Leighton's mastheads. With Rosas Bay six miles under his lee and Barcelona a hundred miles almost to windward the French admiral could have taken little time to reach a decision in face of those strange sails on his horizon. He was dashing instantly for shelter; the single ship of the line which lay directly in his path must be destroyed if she could not be evaded.

The sick waves of excitement and apprehension which Hornblower experienced did not prevent calculations pouring into his mind. The French had six miles to go with a fair wind. He still did not know whereabouts on the circumference of the possible circle whose centre was the French flagship Leighton was at the moment. But he would have twenty miles, perhaps a little more, to sail for certain, and with the wind — such wind as there was — abeam, if he were in the most advantageous position, and on his port bow if he were far astern. And, shifting as it was, it would be dead foul for him in two hours. Twenty to one, Hornblower estimated the odds against the admiral being able to catch the French before they reached the protection of the guns at Rosas. Only unheard-of flukes of wind would do it, and only then if the *Sutherland* were able to knock away a good many spars before she was beaten into helplessness. So keenly had Hornblower been calculating that it was only then that he remembered, with a gulp of excitement, that the *Sutherland* was his ship, and the responsibility his, as well.

Longley came sliding down the backstay, the whole height from topmast head to the deck, his face white with excitement.

"Vincent sent me, sir. *Cassandra's* signalling, and he thinks it's 'Flag to *Sutherland*, No. 21.' Twenty one's 'Engage the enemy,' sir. But it's hard to read the flags."

"Very good. Acknowledge."

So Leighton at least had the moral courage to assume the responsibility for sending one ship against four. In that respect he was worthy of being Lady Barbara's husband.

"Mr. Bush," he said. "We've a quarter of an hour. See that the men get a bite to eat in that time."

"Aye aye, sir."

He looked again at the four ships all steering slowly down upon him. He could not hope to turn them back, but he could only hope to accompany them in their race to Rosas Bay. Any ship that he could totally dismast would fall prey to Leighton; the others he must damage so sorely that they could not repair themselves in Rosas, which had not the smallest dockyard facilities. Then they would stay there until fireships, or a large-scale cutting-out expedition, or a properly organised attack by land on the fortress, should result in their destruction. He thought he ought to succeed in that, but he could not bring himself to visualise what would happen to the *Sutherland* meanwhile. He swallowed hard, and set himself to plan the manœuvres of the first encounter. The leading French ship mounted eighty guns — they were run out and grinning at him through her open ports, while each of the Frenchmen had, as though in bravado, at least four tricolour flags floating in the rigging. He looked up at the battered red ensign hanging from the peak against the blue of the sky, and then he plunged into realities.

"Hands to the braces, Mr. Bush. I want the ship handled like lightning when the time comes. Mr. Gerard! I'll have every gun captain flogged tomorrow who fires before his gun bears."

The men at the guns grinned; they would give of their best for him without any threat of flogging, and they knew he knew it.

Bow to bow the *Sutherland* was approaching the eighty-gun ship, unwavering; if both captains held their courses steadily there would be a collision which might sink both ships. Hornblower kept his eye on the Frenchman to detect the first signs of irresolution; the *Sutherland* was lying as near to the wind as she could, with her sails on the point of flapping. If the French captain had the sense to bring his ship to the wind the *Sutherland* could do nothing decisive against her, but the chances were he would leave his decision to the last moment and then instinctively put his ship before the wind as the easiest course with an unhandy crew. At half a mile smoke suddenly eddied round the Frenchman's bows, and a shot came humming overhead. She was firing her bow chasers, but there was no need to warn Gerard not to reply — he knew the value of that first unhurried broadside too well. With the distance halved two holes appeared in the *Sutherland's* main topsail; Hornblower did not hear the passage of the shot, so intent was he on noting the Frenchman's actions.

"Which way will he go?" said Bush, beating one hand with the other. "Which way? He's holding on farther than I thought."

The farther the better; the more hurried the Frenchman's manœuvre the more helpless he would be. The bowsprits were only a hundred yards apart now, and Hornblower set his teeth so as not to give the instinctive order to up helm. Then he saw a flurry on the Frenchman's decks, and her bow swung away from him — to leeward.

"Hold your fire!" Hornblower shouted to Gerard, fearful lest a premature broadside should waste the opportunity. Gerard waved his hat in reply, with a flash of white teeth in his brown face. The two ships were overlapping now, not thirty yards apart, and the Frenchman's guns were beginning to bear. In the bright sunlight Hornblower could see the flash of the epaulettes of the officers on the quarterdeck, the men at the forecastle carronades stooping to look along the sights. This was the moment.

"Helm a-weather, slow," he said to the helmsman. A glance at Bush was enough — he was anticipating this order. The *Sutherland* began to wear round slowly, beginning her turn to cross the Frenchman's stern before the two ships were alongside. Bush began to bellow the orders to the men at the braces and the headsail sheets, and as he did so the Frenchman's broadside burst into thunder and flame and smoke. The *Sutherland* shook and jarred with the impact of the shot; one of the mizzen shrouds above Hornblower's head parted with a twang at the same moment as a hole appeared in the quarterdeck bulwark near him amid a shower of splinters. But the *Sutherland's* bow was already almost touching the Frenchman's stern. Hornblower could see an eddy of panic on her quarterdeck.

"Keep her at that!" he shouted to the helmsman.

Then with a series of heavy crashes, one following another as the *Sutherland* crossed her enemy's stern and each section of guns bore in turn, she fired her broadside into her, heeling slightly at each discharge, with every shot tearing its destructive course from end to end of the ship. Gerard came leaping onto the quarterdeck, having run down the whole length of the main deck, keeping pace with the firing. He bent eagerly over the nearest carronade, altered its elevation with a quick twist of the screw, and jerked the lanyard, with a wave of the hand to the other gun captains to do the same. The carronades roared out, sweeping the Frenchman's quarterdeck with grape on top of the roundshot. Hornblower saw the officers there dashed to the deck like lead soldiers, saw rigging parting, and the big stern windows of the French ship disappear like a curtain jerked from its pole.

"That's given him a bellyful," said Bush.

That was the sort of broadside which won battles. That single discharge had probably knocked half the fight out of the Frenchman, killing and wounding a hundred men or more, dismounting half a dozen guns. In a single-ship duel she would strike her flag in less than an hour. But now she had drawn ahead while the *Sutherland* was completing her turn, and the second Frenchman, the one with the rear admiral's flag, was close on the weather quarter. She had all plain sail set, and was overhauling them fast; in a moment she would be able to rake the *Sutherland* as the *Sutherland* had raked her consort.

"Starboard!" said Hornblower to the helmsman. "Stand to your guns on the port side!" His voice rang uncannily loud in the stillness following the firing.

The Frenchman came on undeviating, not disdaining a broadside to broadside duel, but not attempting to manœuvre, especially against an enemy who had proved himself alert, at a time when manœuvring meant delay in gaining the shelter of Rosas. The ships inclined together, growing nearer and nearer as the Frenchman head-reached upon the *Sutherland* and the *Suther-*

land's course approached hers. From the *Sutherland's* deck they could hear the excited orders which the French officers were shouting to their men, trying to restrain their eagerness until the decisive moment.

They were not entirely successful all the same, as first one gun and then another went off as excitable gunners let fly — where the shots went Heaven alone knew. A word from Hornblower swung the *Sutherland* round until she lay parallel to her opponent, and as she steadied on her new course Hornblower waved his hand to Gerard as a signal to open fire. There was not more than half a second between the two broadsides; the *Sutherland,* heaving up her side to the recoil of her guns, heaved over farther still to the impact of the shot. As the smoke came billowing up round her the air was filled with the splintering crash of the shot striking her sides; there were screams and cries from below in proof of the damage received.

"Keep at it now, lads! Fire as you will!" shouted Gerard.

Those hours of drill bore fruit now. The sponges were thrust into the reeking gun muzzles, and the moment they were withdrawn the powder and the rammer and the shot were ready for insertion. Almost simultaneously the gun trucks rumbled as the crews flung themselves on the tackles and ran the guns up; almost simultaneously the guns roared out. This time there was a perceptible and measurable interval before the Frenchman replied in a straggling and irregular salvo. The gentle wind blowing on the engaged quarter kept the ship engulfed in the smoke; the gunners labouring on the main deck were as vague as in a dense fog to Hornblower, but the masts and sails of the Frenchman still stood out clear against the blue sky. The *Sutherland's* third broadside followed close on the heels of the Frenchman's second.

"Three to her two, as usual," said Bush, coolly. A shot struck the mizzen-mast bitts and sprayed the deck with splinters. "She's still drawing ahead, sir."

It was hard to think clearly in this frightful din, with death all round. Captain Morris had his marines all along the port-side gangway firing away at everyone visible on the other ship's decks; the two ships were within easy musket shot. The *Sutherland's* broadsides were growing irregular now, as the most efficient crews worked their guns faster than the others, while the Frenchman was delivering a running fire in which there were occasional louder explosions to be heard when several guns went off together. It was like the clattering of the hoofs of four coach horses on a hard road, sometimes in unison for a space, and then spreading out again.

"I fancy his fire's slackening, sir," said Bush. "It doesn't surprise me."

The *Sutherland* had not suffered mortally yet, judging by the number of dead on the main deck. She could still fight for a long time yet.

"See his mainmast, sir!" yelled Bush.

His main topmast was bowing forward, slow and dignified, with the topgallant mast bowing further forward still. Through the smoke they could see the mainmast inclining aft. Then all dignity left the soaring mass of spar and canvas. It hung S-shaped in the air for a breathless second, and then tumbled down with a rush, fore and mizzen topmasts falling with it. Hornblower felt a grim satisfaction at the sight — there were no spare mainmasts to be had in Rosas. The *Sutherland's* crew cheered piercingly, and hastened to fire in a few last shots as their ship drew ahead of her crippled opponent. A minute later the din of the firing ceased, the tiny breeze blew away the smoke, and the sun came shining through upon the littered deck again.

Aft lay their late antagonist, a great mass of wreckage trailing alongside, the second lower-deck gun from the bow pointing out of its port at an impossible angle of elevation to show she had one gun at least knocked useless. A quarter of a mile ahead was the first ship they had fired into; she had paid no attention to the duel behind her but had continued under all sail for the safety of Rosas Bay, just like a Frenchman. And beyond her, sweeping round the horizon, were the cruel mountains of Spain, and the white roofs of Rosas were clearly visible above the golden shore. The *Sutherland* was close to the wide mouth of the bay; halfway between her and Rosas lay two gigantic beetles on the flat blue surface — gunboats coming out of Rosas under sweeps.

And close astern of the crippled ship came the other two ships of the French squadron, the three-decker with the vice admiral's flag and a two-decker in her wake. It was the moment for decision.

"Masthead there!" hailed Hornblower. "Can you see anything of the flagship?"

"No, sir. Nothing but *Cassandra*."

Hornblower could see the *Cassandra's* royals himself, from the deck, pearly white on the horizon; the *Pluto* and *Caligula* must still be nearly twenty miles away — possibly becalmed. The tiny breeze which was urging the *Sutherland* into the bay was probably a sea breeze; the day was hot enough for that. Leighton would hardly arrive in time to take part in this battle. Hornblower could put his ship about now, and tack into safety, beating off the two other enemies if they interfered with him, or he could throw himself into their path; and with every second carrying him a yard nearer Rosas he must decide quickly. If he fought, there was the faintest possible chance that Leighton might be brought up in time to pick up the cripples, but so faint a chance as to be negligible.

The *Sutherland* would be destroyed, but her enemies would be so knocked about as to be detained in Rosas for days or even weeks. And that was desirable, because it would be several days before preparations could be made to attack them in their anchorage, and during those days there would always be the chance of their escaping — three of them, at least — from Rosas as they had escaped from Toulon.

Hornblower balanced in his mind the loss of a seventy four to England against the certain loss of four ships of the line to France. And then he knew, suddenly, that his cogitation had been wasted. If he withdrew, he would all the rest of his life suspect himself of having done so out of cowardice, and he foresaw with clarity the years of mental uneasiness it would bring. He would fight whether it was the right thing or not, and as he reached that decision he realised with relief that it was the correct course as well. One more second he wasted, looking up at the blue sky which he loved, and then he gulped down his muddled emotions.

"Lay the ship on the port tack, if you please, Mr. Bush," he said.

The crew cheered again, the poor fools, when they saw that they were about to face the rest of the French, even though it meant the certain death of half of them at least. Hornblower felt pity — or was it contempt? — for them and their fighting madness or thirst for glory. Bush was as bad as any of them, judging by the way his face had lit up at the order. He wanted the Frenchmen's blood just because they were Frenchmen, and thought nothing of the chance of being a legless cripple if he were granted the chance of smashing a few French legs first.

The crippled two-decker with the rear admiral's flag came drifting down on them — this sea breeze would push all wrecks into Rosas Bay under the guns of the fortress — and the men working lackadaisically at clearing the wreckage ran from their work when they looked up and saw the *Sutherland's* guns swinging round towards them. The *Sutherland* fired three broadsides into her with hardly a gun in reply before she drifted clear — another fifty or so dead Frenchmen for Bush, thought Hornblower, viciously, as the rumble of the gun trucks died away and the men stood waiting once more, silent now, beside their guns. Here came the three-decker, now, beautiful with her towering canvas, hideous with her grinning guns. Even at that moment Hornblower marked, with professional interest, the decided tumble-home of her sides, much greater than English shipwrights allowed.

"Let her pay off slowly, Mr. Bush," he said. He was going to set his teeth into the three-decker like a bulldog.

Round came the *Sutherland*, slowly, slowly. Hornblower saw that his last manœuvre with the *Sutherland* was going to be as well timed as ever he could wish. She was on the same course as the three-decker at exactly the moment the latter drew up opposite to her; the guns of both ships bore simultaneously, a hundred yards apart, and burst simultaneously into thunder and smoke.

In the earlier encounters time had seemed to pass slowly. Now it seemed to be passing fast, the infernal din of the broadsides seeming almost unintermitting, the figures hurrying about in the smoke seeming to be moving twice as fast as normally.

"Edge in closer on her," said Hornblower to the helmsman, and then, his last order given, he could abandon himself to the mad inconsequence of it all. Shots seemed to be tearing up the deck all round him, smashing great gashes in the planking. With the clear unreality of a nightmare he saw Bush fall, with blood running from the stump of his leg where a foot was missing. Two men of the surgeon's crew bent over him to carry him below.

"Leave me on deck," said Bush. "Let got of me, you dogs."

"Take him away," said Hornblower. The harshness of his voice was of a piece with the madness of everything else, for he was glad to be able to order Bush into a place of safety where he might yet live.

The mizzen topmast fell, and spars and blocks and tackle came raining all round him — death falling from the heavens as well as hurtling in from overside, but still he lived. Now the fore-topsail yard was shot through in the slings; dimly through the smoke he could see Hooker leading a party aloft to repair it. Out of the tail of his eye he saw something new and strange looming through the smoke — it was the fourth French ship, coming up on the *Sutherland's* disengaged side. He found himself waving his hat and shrieking some nonsense or other to his men, who cheered him back as they brought the starboard-side guns into action. The smoke was thicker, and the din more tremendous, and the whole ship throbbing with every gun in action.

Little Longley was at his side now, white-faced, miraculously alive after the fall of the mizzen topmast.

"I'm *not* frightened. I'm *not* frightened," the boy said; his jacket was torn clean across the breast and he was trying to hold it together as he denied the evidence of the tears in his eyes.

"No, sonny, of course you're not," said Hornblower.

Then Longley was dead, hands and breast smashed into pulp. There was a main-deck gun not run out, he saw as he looked away from Longley's body. He was about to call attention to the abandoned gun, when he noticed its slaughtered crew lying in fragments round it, and he saw that there were no longer any men to spare to get it into action again. Soon there would be more guns than one out of action. The very carronade beside him had but three men to man it — so had the next one, and the next. Down on the maindeck there were marines carrying powder and shot; Gerard must have set them to that work, and the powder boys must be mostly dead. If only this din would stop, and allow him to think!

It seemed to him as if at that the din redoubled. Foremast and mainmast came down together with a splintering crash audible high above the gunfire, the mass of wreckage tumbling over the starboard side. He ran forward, to find Hooker there already hard at work with a group of men drawn from the blinded guns hacking away at the rigging to cut it clear. The three-foot-thick end of the broken mainmast had smashed a gun carriage and killed the crew during its fall. Shots from the two-decker on that side were smashing through the men at work, and already smoke was pouring up from the canvas hanging over the side where the flame of the guns had set it on fire. Hornblower took an axe from the hand of a dead man and fell to work hacking and cutting along with the others. When the last rope was cut, and the flaring mass had dropped overside, and a hasty inspection showed that the timber of the ship had not caught fire, he swept the sweat from his forehead and looked round the ship from his new point of view.

The whole deck was heaped and littered with dead men and fragments of dead men. The wheel was gone, the masts, the bulwarks were beaten flat, the hatch coamings a mere fringe of splinters. But the guns which could still be worked were still firing, each manned by its attenuated crew. On either side the enemy loomed through the smoke, but the three-decker had lost two topmasts and the two-decker her mizzen mast, and their sails were in shreds and their rigging hanging in festoons, seen dimly in the smoke. The firing was as fierce as ever. He wondered dully by what miracle he survived to walk through the tempest of shot back to his post on the quarterdeck.

Some puff of wind was altering the relative position of the

ships. The three-decker was swinging round, coming closer; Hornblower was already running forward down the port side, with seeming feet of lead, when the three-decker's starboard bow came with a grinding bump against the *Sutherland's* port bow. Frenchmen were gathering to leap down onto the *Sutherland's* deck, and Hornblower drew his sword as he ran.

"Boarders!" he yelled. "All hands repel boarders! Boom them off, there, Hooker, Crystal."

High above his head towered the three-decker. Musketry was spattering along her bulwarks, and Hornblower heard bullets rapping into the deck round him. Men with swords and pikes in their hands were scrambling down the three-decker's sides, and more were spewing out of the middle-deck gunport onto the *Sutherland's* gangway. Hornblower found himself caught up in a wave of British sailors with cutlasses and pikes, rammers and handspikes, men naked to the waist and grey with powder smoke. Everyone was jostling and slipping and struggling. He was flung up against a dapper little French lieutenant with his hat rakishly awry. For the moment his arms were pinned to his sides by the press, and the Frenchman was struggling to pull a pistol from his waistband.

"*Rends-toi*," he spluttered, as the weapon came free, but Hornblower brought up his knee and the Frenchman's head went back in agony and he dropped the pistol.

And the three-decker was swinging away clear again, urged by the puff of wind and the thrust of the spar Crystal and Hooker and their party were pushing against her side. Some of the Frenchmen leaped back to the ship. Some leaped into the sea. A dozen who were left dropped their weapons — one of them too late to check the pike which was thrust into his stomach. The puff of wind was still blowing, drifting the French ships away from the dismasted *Sutherland* and rolling away the smoke. The sun came out and shone upon them and the hideous decks as though from behind a cloud, and the din of the firing ended magically as the guns ceased to bear.

Sword in hand, Hornblower stood while the men about him secured the prisoners. The cessation of the noise had not brought him the relief he had hoped for — on the contrary, he was mazed and stupid, and in his weariness he found it a desperate effort to think clearly. The wind had drifted the *Sutherland* well inside the bay, and there was no sign at all of the *Pluto* or *Caligula* — only the *Cassandra,* hull down over the horizon, a helpless spectator of the fight. The two battered French ships, almost as helpless as the *Sutherland,* thanks to the damage they had received aloft, were floating a short distance off; down the side of the three-decker, dribbling from the scuppers, Hornblower noticed a dark streak — human blood.

The two-decker was still swinging round; her shattered side was out of sight, now she was presenting her stern, and now her other side to the *Sutherland's* bow. Hornblower watched her stupidly. And then — a bellowing roar, and her broadside came tearing into the *Sutherland.* A cloud of splinters flew from the shattered stump of the foremast, and the gun beside Hornblower rang like a bell to a glancing shot.

"Oh, stop!" muttered Hornblower. "For God's sake!"

The men on the *Sutherland's* deck were dragging themselves to the guns again. Gerard was nowhere to be seen, but Hooker — a good boy, that — was walking along the main deck apportioning the men to the guns so that some at least might be worked. But the men were faint with fatigue, and at present no gun would bear, while the dismasted *Sutherland* could do nothing to save herself. Another broadside, ripping and tearing through the ship. Hornblower became conscious of a faint undercurrent of noise — the feeble chorus of the wounded men huddled in every corner of the ship. The gunboats were working round cautiously with their sweeps to take up a position under the *Sutherland's* stern; soon they would be firing their forty-two-pounders into her on the water line. Sun and blue sea and blue sky; the grey-green mountains of Spain, the golden beach and white houses of Rosas — Hornblower looked round him at them all, despairingly, and it was agony to look.

Another broadside; Hornblower saw two men knocked into a bloody mess at Hooker's side.

"Strike," he said to himself. "We must strike."

But the *Sutherland* had no colours flying that she could strike, and Hornblower's dazed mind wrestled with this problem as he walked aft. The forty-two-pounder in one of the gunboats boomed out loudly, and Hornblower felt the jar as the shot smashed into the ship's side below him. Hooker was on the quarterdeck now, and Crystal, and Howell the carpenter.

"There's four feet of water in the well, sir," said this last, "an' no pump left."

"Yes," said Hornblower, dully. "I shall surrender."

He read agreement in the grey faces of his officers, but they said nothing. If only the *Sutherland* would sink under them the problem would solve itself but that would be too much to hope for. She would only grow more and more waterlogged, sinking as each deck in turn was submerged, while the pitiless cannonade would continue. It might be as much as twenty four hours before she sank completely and in that time the little wind would have drifted her aground under the guns of Rosas. All he could do was to surrender. He thought of the other British captains who had found themselves in similar positions — Thompson of the *Leander* and the captain of the *Swiftsure* and the unfortunate man under Saumarez in Algeciras Bay; they, too, had hauled down their flags after a long fight against heavy odds.

Somebody was hailing from the two-decker; he could not understand what was said, but it must be a demand to surrender.

"*Oui,*" he shouted back. "*Oui.*"

For answer there came another broadside, smashing home with a splintering of timber and to the accompaniment of a shriek from below.

"Oh God!" said Hooker.

Hornblower realised that he must have misunderstood the question, and with the realisation came a solution of the difficulty. He ran as fast as his stiff legs would carry him, down to the indescribable chaos which represented what was left of his cabin. Hurriedly he turned over the litter there, while the men at the guns watched him expressionless as animals. He found what he sought at last, and came up on the quarterdeck with his arms full of it.

"Here," he said, giving it to Crystal and Howell. "Hang that over the side."

It was the tricolour flag he had had made to deceive the batteries at Llanza. At sight of it the men in the gunboats bent to their oars to propel their craft alongside, while Hornblower stood with the sun shining on his bare head waiting for them. They would take his sword of honour away from him. And the other sword of honour was still in pawn to Duddingstone the ship chandler, and he would never be able to redeem it now, with his career wrecked. And the shattered hull of the *Sutherland* would be towed in triumph under the guns of Rosas — how long would it be before the Mediterranean fleet came down to avenge her, to retake her from her captors, or burn her in one vast pyre along with her shattered conquerors? And Maria was going to bear him a child, whom he would never see during all the years of his captivity. And Lady Barbara would read of his capture in the newspapers — what would she think of his surrendering? But the sun was hot on his head, and he was very weary.

Flying Colours

The Cutter—*Witch of Endor*

Chapter I

CAPTAIN HORNBLOWER was walking up and down along that sector of the ramparts of Rosas, delimited by two sentries with loaded muskets, which the commandant had granted to him for exercise. Overhead shone the bright autumn sun of the Mediterranean, hanging in a blue Mediterranean sky and shining on the Mediterranean blue of Rosas Bay — the blue water fringed with white where the little waves broke against the shore of golden sand and grey-green cliff. Black against the sun above his head there flapped the tricolour flag of France, proclaiming to the world that Rosas was in the hands of the French, that Captain Hornblower was a prisoner. Not half a mile from where he walked lay the dismasted wreck of his ship the *Sutherland*, beached to prevent her from sinking, and in line beyond her there swung at their anchors the four ships of the line which had fought her. Hornblower, narrowing his eyes and with a twinge of regret for his lost telescope, could see even at that distance that they were not ready for sea again, nor were likely to be. Even the two-decker which had emerged from the fight with all her masts intact still had her pumps at work every two hours to keep her afloat, and the other three had not yet succeeded in setting up masts to replace the ones lost in the battle. The French were a lubberly lot of non-seamen, as might be expected after seventeen years of defeat at sea and six of continuous blockade.

They had been all honey to him, in their French fashion, praising him for his "glorious defence" after his "bold initiative" in dashing in with his ship to interpose between their four and their refuge at Rosas. They had expressed the liveliest pleasure at discovering that he had miraculously emerged unhurt from a battle which had left two thirds of his men killed and wounded. But they had plundered in the fashion which had made the armed forces of the Empire hated throughout Europe. They had searched the pockets even of the wounded who had cumbered the *Sutherland's* decks in moaning heaps. Their admiral, on his first encounter with Hornblower, had expressed surprise that the latter was not wearing the sword which the admiral had sent back to him in recognition of his gallantry, and on Hornblower's denial that he had ever seen the weapon again after giving it up had instituted a search which discovered the sword cast aside somewhere in his flagship, the glorious inscription still engraved upon the blade, but with the gold stripped from hilt and guard and scabbard. And the admiral had merely laughed at that and had not dreamed of instituting a search for the thief; the Patriotic Fund's gift still hung at Hornblower's side, the tang of the blade protruding nakedly from the scabbard without the gold and ivory and seed pearls which had adorned it.

The French soldiers and sailors who had swarmed over the captured ship had torn away even the brasswork in the same fashion; they had gorged upon the unappetising provisions in a way which proved how miserable were the rations provided for the men who fought for the Empire — but it was only a few who had swilled themselves into insensibility from the rum casks. In face of similar temptation (to which no British officer would have exposed his men) British seamen would have drunk until nine tenths of them were incapable or fighting mad. The French officers had made the usual appeal to their prisoners to join the French ranks, making the usual tempting offers of good treatment and regular pay to anyone who cared to enlist either in the army or the navy. Hornblower was proud that no single man had succumbed to the temptation.

As a consequence the few sound men now languished in strict confinement in one of the empty storerooms of the fortress, deprived of the tobacco and rum and fresh air which for most of them represented the difference between heaven and hell. The wounded — the hundred and forty-five wounded — were rotting in a dank casemate where gangrene and fever would soon make an end of them. To the logical French mind the poverty-stricken Army of Catalonia, which could do little even for its own wounded, would be mad to expend any of its resources on attention to wounded who would be intolerable nuisances should they survive.

A little moan escaped Hornblower's lips as he paced the ramparts. He had a room of his own, a servant to wait on him, fresh air and sunshine, while the poor devils he had commanded were suffering all the miseries of confinement — even the three or four other unwounded officers were lodged in the town gaol. True, he suspected that he was being reserved for another fate. During those glorious days when, in command of the *Sutherland*, he had won for himself, unknowing, the nickname of "the Terror of the Mediterranean," he had managed to storm the battery at Llanza by bringing his ship up close to it flying the tricolour flag. That had been a legitimate *ruse de guerre* for which historical precedents without number could be quoted, but the French Government had apparently deemed it a violation of the laws of war. The next convoy to France or Barcelona would bear him with it as a prisoner to be tried by a military commission. Bonaparte was quite capable of shooting him, both from personal rancour and as a proof of the most convincing sort to Europe of British duplicity and wickedness, and during the last day or two Hornblower thought he had read as much in the eyes of his gaolers.

Just enough time had elapsed for the news of the *Sutherland's* capture to have reached Paris and for Bonaparte's subsequent orders to have been transmitted to Rosas. The *Moniteur Universel* would have blazed out in a pæan of triumph, declaring to the continent that this loss of a ship of the line was clear proof that England was tottering to her fall like ancient Carthage; in a month or two's time presumably there would be another announcement to the effect that a traitorous servant of perfidious Albion had met his just deserts against a wall in Vincennes or Montjuich.

Hornblower cleared his throat nervously as he walked; he expected to feel afraid and was surprised that he did not. The thought of an abrupt and inevitable end of that sort did not alarm him as much as did his shapeless imaginings when he was going into action on his quarterdeck. In fact he could almost view it with relief, as putting an end to his worries about his wife Maria whom he had left pregnant, and to his jealous torments of longing for Lady Barbara who had married his admiral; in the eyes of England he would be regarded as a martyr whose widow deserved a pension. It would be an honourable end, then, which a man ought to welcome — especially a man like Hornblower whose persistent and unfounded disbelief in his own capacity left him continually frightened of professional disgrace and ruin.

And it would be an end of captivity, too. Hornblower had been a prisoner once before, for two heartbreaking years in Ferrol, but with the passing of time he had forgotten the misery of it until this new experience. In those days, too, he had never known the freedom of his own quarterdeck, and had never tasted the unbounded liberty — the widest freedom on earth — of being a captain of a ship. It was torture now to be a prisoner, even with the liberty to look upon the sky and the sea. A caged lion must fret behind his bars in the same way as Hornblower fretted against his confinement. He felt suddenly sick and ill through restraint. He clenched his fists and only by an effort prevented himself from raising them above his head in a gesture of despair.

Then he took hold of himself again, with an inward sneer at his childish weakness. To distract himself he looked out again to the blue sea which he loved, the row of black cormorants silhouetted against the grey cliff, the gulls wheeling against the blue sky. Five miles out he could see the topsails of His Majesty's frigate *Cassandra,* keeping sleepless watch over the four French ships huddled for shelter under the guns of Rosas, and beyond them he could see the royals of the *Pluto* and the *Caligula* — Admiral Leighton, the unworthy husband of his beloved Lady Barbara, was flying his flag in the *Pluto,* but he refused to let that thought worry him — where they awaited an accession of strength from the Mediterranean fleet before coming in to destroy the ships which had captured him. He could rely upon the British to avenge his defeat. Martin, the vice-admiral with the Toulon blockading squadron, would see to it that Leighton did not make a hash of this attack, powerful as might be the guns of Rosas.

He looked along the ramparts at the massive twenty-four-pounders mounted there. The bastions at the angles carried forty-two-pounders — colossal pieces. He leaned over the parapet and looked down; it was a sheer drop from there of twenty five feet to the bottom of the ditch, and along the bottom of the ditch itself ran a line of stout palisades, which no besieging army could damage until he had sapped right up to the lip of the ditch. No hurried, extemporised attack could carry the citadel of Rosas. A score of sentries paced the ramparts, even as did he; in the opposite face he could see the massive gates, with the portcullis down, where a hundred men of the grand guard were always ready to beat back any surprise attack which might elude the vigilance of the twenty sentinels.

Down there, in the body of the place, a company of infantry was being put through its drill — the shrill words of command were clearly audible to him up here. It was Italian which was being spoken; Bonaparte had attempted his conquest of Catalonia mainly with the foreign auxiliaries of his empire, Italians, Neapolitans, Germans, Swiss, Poles. The uniforms of the infantry down there were as ragged as the lines they were forming; the men were in tatters, and even the tatters were not homogeneous — the men wore white or blue or grey or brown according to the resources of the depots which had originally sent them out. They were half-starved, poor devils, as well. Of the five or six thousand men based on Rosas the ones he could see were all that could be spared for military duty; the others were all out scouring the countryside for food — Bonaparte never dreamed of trying to feed the men whom he compelled to serve him, just as he only paid them, as an afterthought, a year or two in arrears. It was amazing that his ramshackle Empire had endured so long — that was the clearest proof of the incompetence of the various kingdoms which had pitted their strengths against it. Over on the other side of the Peninsula the French Empire was at this very minute putting out all its strength against a man of real ability and an army which knew what discipline was. On the issue of that struggle depended the fate of Europe. Hornblower was convinced that the redcoats with Wellington to lead them would be successful; he would have been just as certain even if Wellington were not his beloved Lady Barbara's brother.

Then he shrugged his shoulders. Not even Wellington would destroy the French Empire quickly enough to save him from trial and execution. Moreover, the time allowed him for his day's exercise was over now. The next items in his monotonous programme would be to visit the sick in the casemate, and then the prisoners in the storeroom — by the courtesy of the commandant he was allowed ten minutes for each, before being shut up again in his room, drearily to attempt to reread the half-dozen books which were all that the garrison of Rosas possessed, or to pace up and down, three steps each way, or to lie huddled on his bed wondering about Maria and the child that was to be born in the New Year, and torturing himself with thoughts of Lady Barbara.

Chapter II

HORNBLOWER awoke that night with a start, wondering what it was that had awakened him. A moment later he knew, when the sound was repeated. It was the dull thud of a gun fired on the ramparts above his head. He leaped from his bed with his heart pounding, and before his feet touched the floor the whole fortress was in a turmoil. Overhead there were guns firing. Somewhere else, outside the body of the fortress, there were hundreds of guns firing; through the barred windows of his room came a faint flickering as the flashes were reflected down from the sky. Immediately outside his door drums were beating and bugles were pealing as the garrison was called to arms — the courtyard was full of the sounds of nailed boots clashing on the cobbles.

That tremendous pulsation of artillery which he could hear could mean only one thing. The fleet must have come gliding into the bay in the darkness, and now he could hear the rolling of its broadsides as it battered the anchored ships. There was a great naval battle in progress within half a mile of him, and he could see nothing of it. It was utterly maddening. He tried to light his candle, but his trembling fingers could do nothing with his flint and steel. He dashed the tinderbox to the floor, and, fumbling in the darkness, he dragged on his coat and trousers and shoes and then beat upon the door madly with his fists. The sentry outside was Italian, he knew, and he spoke no Italian — only fluent Spanish and bad French.

"*Officier! Officier!*" he shouted, and then he heard the sentry call for the sergeant of the guard, and the measured step of the sergeant as he came up. The clatter of the garrison's falling in under arms had already died away.

"What do you want?" asked the sergeant's voice — at least so Hornblower fancied, for he could not understand what was said.

"*Officier! Officier!*" raved Hornblower, beating still on the heavy door. The artillery was still rolling terrifically outside. Hornblower went on pounding on the door even until he heard the key in the lock. The door swung open and he blinked at the light of a torch which shone into his eyes. A young subaltern in a neat white uniform stood there between the sergeant and the sentry.

"*Qu'est-ce-que monsieur désire?*" he asked — he at least understood French, even if he spoke it badly. Hornblower fumbled to express himself in an unfamiliar tongue.

"I want to see!" he stammered. "I want to see the battle! Let me go on to the walls."

The young officer shook his head reluctantly; like the other officers of the garrison, he felt a kindly feeling towards the English captain who — so rumour said — was so shortly to be conducted to Paris and shot.

"It is forbidden," he said.

"I will not escape," said Hornblower; desperate excitement was loosening his tongue now. "Word of honour — I swear it! Come with me, but let me see! I want to see!"

The officer hesitated.

"I cannot leave my post here," he said.

"Then let me go alone. I swear I will stay on the walls. I will not try to escape."

"Word of honour?" asked the subaltern.

"Word of honour. Thank you, sir."

The subaltern stood aside, and Hornblower dashed out of his room, down the short corridor to the courtyard, and up the ramp which led to the seaward bastion. As he reached it, the forty-two-pounder mounted there went off with a deafening roar, and the long tongue of orange flame nearly blinded him. In the darkness the bitter powder-smoke engulfed him. Nobody in the groups bending over the guns noticed him, and he ran down the steep staircase to the curtain wall, where, away from the guns, he could see without being blinded.

Rosas Bay was all a-sparkle with gun flashes. Then, five times in regular succession, came the brilliant red glow of a broadside, and each glow lit up a stately ship gliding in rigid line ahead past the anchored French ships. The *Pluto* was there; Hornblower saw her three decks, her ensign at the peak, her admiral's flag at the mizzen, her topsails set and her other canvas furled. Leighton would be there, walking his quarterdeck — thinking of Barbara, perhaps. And that next astern was the *Caligula*. Bolton would be stumping about her deck, revelling in the crash of her broadsides. She was firing rapidly and well — Bolton was a good captain, although a badly educated man. The words *Oderint dum metuant*, — the Cæsar Caligula's maxim, — picked out in letters of gold across the *Caligula's* stern had meant nothing to Bolton until Hornblower translated and explained them to him. At this very moment, perhaps, those letters were being defaced and battered by the French shot.

But the French squadron was firing back badly and irregularly. There was no sudden glow of broadsides where they lay anchored, but only an irregular and intermittent sparkle as the guns were loosed off anyhow. In a night action like this, and after a sudden surprise, Hornblower would not have trusted even English seamen with independent fire. He doubted if as many as one-tenth of the French guns were being properly served and pointed. As for the heavy guns pealing away beside him from the fortress, he was quite certain they were doing no good to the French cause and possibly some harm. Firing at half a mile in the darkness, even from a steady platform and with large-calibre guns, they were as likely to hit friend as foe. It had well repaid Admiral Martin to send in Leighton and his ships in the moonless hours of the night, risking all the navigational perils of the bay.

Hornblower choked with emotion and excitement as his imagination called up the details of what would be going on in the English ships — the leadsmen chanting the soundings with disciplined steadiness, the heave of the ship to the deafening crash of the broadside, the battle lanterns glowing dimly in the smoke of the lower decks, the squeal and rattle of the gun trucks as the guns were run up again, the steady orders of the officers in charge of sections of guns, the quiet voice of the captain addressing the helmsmen. He leaned far over the parapet in the darkness, peering down into the bay.

A whiff of wood smoke came to his nostrils, sharply distinct from the acrid powder smoke which was drifting by from the guns. They had lit the furnaces for heating shot, but the commandant would be a fool if he allowed his guns to fire red-hot shot in these conditions. French ships were as inflammable as English ones, and just as likely to be hit in a close battle like this. Then his grip tightened on the stonework of the parapet, and he stared and stared again with aching eyes towards what had attracted his notice. It was the tiniest, most subdued little red glow in the distance. The English had brought in fire ships in the wake of their fighting squadron. A squadron at anchor like this was the best possible target for a fire ship, and Martin had planned his attack well in sending in his ships of the line first to clear away guard boats and beat down the French fire and occupy the attention of the crews. The red glow suddenly increased, grew brighter and brighter still, revealing the hull and masts and rigging of a small brig; still brighter it grew as the few daring spirits who remained on board flung open hatches and gunports to increase the draught. The tongues of flame which soared up were visible even to Hornblower on the ramparts, and they revealed to him, too, the form of the *Turenne* alongside her — the one French ship which had emerged from the previous battle with all her masts. Whoever the young officer in command of the fire ship might be, he was a man with a cool head and determined will, thus to select the most profitable target of all.

Hornblower saw points of fire begin to ascend the rigging of the *Turenne* until she was outlined in red like some set-piece in a firework display. Sudden jets of flame showed where powder charges on her deck were taking fire; and then the whole set-piece suddenly swung round and began to drift before the gentle wind as the burnt cables gave way. A mast fell in an upward torrent of sparks, strangely reflected in the black water all round. At once the sparkle of gunfire in the other French ships began to die away as the crews were called from their guns to deal with the drifting menace, and a slow movement of the shadowy forms lit by the flames revealed that their cables had been cut by officers terrified of death by fire.

Then suddenly Hornblower's attention was distracted to a point closer in to shore, where the abandoned wreck of the *Sutherland* lay beached. There, too, a red glow could be seen, growing and spreading momentarily. Some daring party from the British squadron had boarded her and set her on fire too, determined not to leave even so poor a trophy in the hands of the French. Farther out in the bay three red dots of light were soaring upwards slowly, and Hornblower gulped in sudden nervousness lest an English ship should have caught fire as well, but he realised next moment that it was only a signal — three vertical red lanterns — which was apparently the prearranged recall, for with their appearance the firing abruptly ceased. The blazing wrecks lit up now the whole of this corner of the bay with a lurid red in whose light could be distinctly seen the other French ships, drifting without masts or anchors, towards the shore. Next came a blinding flash and a stunning explosion as the magazine of the *Turenne* took fire. For several seconds after the twenty tons of gunpowder had exploded Hornblower's eyes could not see nor his mind think; the blast of it had shaken him, like a child in the hands of an angry nurse, even where he stood.

He became aware that daylight was creeping into the bay, revealing the ramparts of Rosas in hard outlines, and dulling the flames from the wreck of the *Sutherland*. Far out in the bay, already beyond gunshot of the fortress, the five British ships of the line were standing out to sea in their rigid line-ahead. There was something strange about the appearance of the *Pluto;* it was only at his second glance that Hornblower realised that she had lost her main topmast — clear proof that one French shot at least had done damage. The other ships revealed no sign of having received any injury during one of the best-managed affairs in the long history of the British Navy. Hornblower tore his gaze from his vanishing friends to study the field of battle. Of the *Turenne* and the fire ship there was no sign at all; of the *Sutherland* there only remained a few blackened timbers emerging from the water, with a wisp of smoke suspended above them. Two ships of the line were on the rocks to the westward of the fortress, and French seamanship would never make them seaworthy again. Only the three-decker was left, battered and mastless, swinging to the anchor which had checked her on the very edge of the surf. The next easterly gale would see her, too, flung ashore and useless. The British Mediterranean Fleet would in the future have to dissipate none of its energies in a blockade of Rosas.

Here came General Vidal, the Governor of the fortress, making his rounds with his staff at his heels, and just in time to save Hornblower from falling into a passion of despair at watching the English squadron disappear over the horizon.

"What are you doing here?" demanded the general, checking at the sight of him. Under the sternness of his expression could be read the kindly pity which Hornblower had noticed in the faces of all his enemies when they began to suspect that a firing party awaited him.

"The officer of the grand guard allowed me to come up here," explained Hornblower in his halting French. "I gave him my parole of honour not to try to escape. I will withdraw it again now, if you please."

"He had no business to accept it, in any case," snapped the general, but with that fateful kindliness still apparent. "You wanted to see the battle, I suppose?"

"Yes, General."

"A fine piece of work your compatriots have done." The general shook his head sadly. "It will not make the government in Paris feel any better disposed towards you, I fear, Captain."

Hornblower shrugged his shoulders; he had already caught the infection of that gesture during his few days' sojourn among Frenchmen. He noted, with a lack of personal interest which seemed odd to him even then, that this was the first time the governor had hinted openly at danger threatening him from Paris.

"I have done nothing to make me afraid," he said.

"No, no, of course not," said the governor hastily and out of countenance, like a parent denying to a child that a prospective dose of medicine would be unpleasant.

He looked round for some way of changing the subject, and fortunate chance brought one. From far below in the bowels of the fortress came a muffled sound of cheering — English cheers, not Italian screeches.

"That must be those men of yours, Captain," said the general, smiling again. "I fancy the new prisoner must have told them by now the story of last night's affair."

"The new prisoner?" demanded Hornblower.

"Yes, indeed. A man who fell overboard from the admiral's ship — the *Pluto,* is it not? — and had to swim ashore. Ah, I suspected you would be interested, Captain. Yes, off you go and talk to him. Here, Dupont, take charge of the captain and escort him to the prison."

Hornblower could hardly spare the time in which to thank his captor, so eager was he to interview the new arrival and hear what he had to say. Two weeks as a prisoner had already had their effect in giving him a thirst for news. He ran down the ramp, Dupont puffing beside him, across the cobbled court, in through the door which a sentry opened for him at a gesture from his escort, down the dark stairway to the ironstudded door where stood two sentries on duty. With a great clattering of keys the doors were opened for him and he walked into the room.

It was a wide low room — a disused storeroom, in fact — lit and ventilated only by a few heavily barred apertures opening into the fortress ditch. It stank of closely confined humanity and it was at present filled with a babel of sound as what was left of the crew of the *Sutherland* plied questions at someone hidden in the middle of the crowd. At Hornblower's entrance the crowd fell apart and the new prisoner came forward; he was naked save for his duck trousers, and a long pigtail hung down his back.

"Who are you?" demanded Hornblower.

"Phillips, sir. Maintopman in the *Pluto.*"

His honest blue eyes met Hornblower's gaze without a sign of flinching. Hornblower could guess that he was neither a deserter nor a spy — he had borne both possibilities in mind.

"How did you come here?"

"We was settin' sail, sir, to beat out o' the bay. We'd just seen the old *Sutherland* take fire, an' Cap'n Elliott he says to us, he says, sir, 'Now's the time, my lads. Tops'ls and to'gar'ns.' So up we went aloft, sir, an' I'd just taken the earring o' the main to'gar'n when down came the mast, sir, an' I was pitched off into the water. So was a lot o' my mates, sir, but just then the Frenchy which was burnin' blew up, an' I think the wreckage killed a lot of 'em, sir, 'cos then I found I was alone, an' *Pluto* was gone away, an' so I swum for the shore, an' there was a lot of Frenchies what I think had swum from the burning Frenchy an' they took me to some sojers an' the sojers brought me here, sir. There was a orficer what arst me questions — it'd 'a made you laugh, sir, to hear him trying to speak English — but I wasn't sayin' nothin', sir. An' when they see that, they puts me in here along with the others, sir. I was just telling 'em about the fight, sir. There was the old *Pluto,* an' *Caligula,* sir, an' —— "

"Yes, I saw it," said Hornblower, shortly. "I saw that *Pluto* had lost her main topmast. Was she knocked about much?"

"Lor' bless you, sir, no, sir. We hadn't had half a dozen shot come aboard, an' they didn't do no damage, barrin' the one what wounded the admiral."

"The admiral!" Hornblower reeled a little as he stood, as though he had been struck. "Admiral Leighton, d'you mean?"

"Admiral Leighton, sir."

"Was — was he badly hurt?"

"I dunno, sir. I didn't see it meself, o' course, sir, seein' as how I was on the main deck at the time. Sailmaker's mate, he told me, sir, that the admiral had been hit by a splinter. Cooper's mate told *him,* sir, what helped to carry him below."

Hornblower could say no more for the present. He could only stare at the kindly stupid face of the sailor before him. Yet even in that moment he could take note of the fact that the sailor was not in the least moved by the wounding of his admiral. Nelson's death had put the whole fleet into mourning, and he knew of half a dozen other flag officers whose death or whose wounding would have brought tears into the eyes of the men serving under him. If it had been one of those, the man would have told of the accident to him before mentioning his own misadventures. Hornblower had known before that Leighton was not beloved by his officers, and here was a clear proof that he was not beloved by his men either. But perhaps Barbara had loved him. She had at least married him. Hornblower forced himself to speak, to bear himself naturally.

"That will do," he said, curtly, and then looked round to catch his coxswain's eye. "Anything to report, Brown?"

"No, sir. All well, sir."

Hornblower rapped on the door behind him to be let out of prison, to be conducted by his guard back to his room again, where he could walk up and down, three steps each way, his brain seething like a pot on a fire. He knew only enough to unsettle him, to make him anxious. Leighton had been wounded, but that did not mean that he would die. A splinter wound — that might mean much or little. Yet he had been carried below. No admiral would have allowed that, if he had been able to resist — not in the heat of a fight, at any rate. His face might be lacerated or his belly torn open — Hornblower, shuddering, shook his mind free from the memories of all the horrible wounds he had seen received on shipboard during twenty years' service. But, cold-bloodedly, it was an even chance that Leighton would die — Hornblower had signed too many casualty lists to be unaware of the chances of a wounded man's recovery.

If Leighton were to die, Barbara would be free again. But what had that to do with him, a married man — a married man whose wife was pregnant? She would be no nearer to him, not while Maria lived. And yet it assuaged his jealousy to think of her as a widow. But then perhaps she would marry again, and he would have to go once more through all the torment he had endured when he had first heard of her marriage to Leighton. In that case he would rather Leighton lived — a cripple, perhaps, mutilated or impotent; the implications of that train of thought drove him into a paroxysm of too-rapid thinking from which he emerged only after a desperate struggle for sanity.

In the cold reaction which followed he sneered at himself for a fool. He was the prisoner of a man whose empire extended from the Baltic to Gibraltar. He told himself he would be an old man, that his child and Maria's would be grown up before he regained his liberty. And then with a sudden shock he remembered that he might soon be dead — shot for violation of the laws of war. Strange how he could forget that possibility. Sneering, he told himself that he had a coward's mind which could leave the imminence of death out of its calculations because the possibility was too monstrous to bear contemplation.

There was something else he had not reckoned upon lately, too. If Bonaparte did not have him shot, if he regained his freedom, even then he still had to run the gauntlet of a court-martial for the loss of the *Sutherland*. A court-martial might decree for him death or disgrace or ruin; the British public would not hear lightly of a British ship of the line surrendering, however great the odds against her. He would have liked to ask Phillips, the seaman from the *Pluto*, about what had been said in the fleet regarding the *Sutherland's* action, whether the general verdict had been one of approval or not. But of course it would be impossible to ask; no captain could ask a seaman what the fleet thought of him, even if there was a chance of hearing the truth — which, too, was doubtful. He was compassed about with uncertainties — the uncertainties of his imprisonment, of the possibility of his trial by the French, of his future court-martial, of Leighton's wound. There was even an uncertainty regarding Maria; she was pregnant — would the child be a girl or a boy, would he ever see it, would anyone raise a finger to help her, would she be able to educate the child properly without his supervision?

Once more the misery of imprisonment was borne in upon him. He grew sick with longing for his liberty, for his freedom, for Barbara and for Maria.

Chapter III

HORNBLOWER was walking next day upon the ramparts again; the sentries with their loaded muskets stood one at each end of the sector allotted to him, and the subaltern allotted to guard him sat discreetly against the parapet so as not to break in upon the thoughts which preoccupied him. But he was too tired to think much now — all day and nearly all night yesterday he had paced his room, three paces up and three paces back, with his mind in a turmoil. Exhaustion was saving him now, and he could think no more.

He welcomed as a distraction a bustle at the main gate, the turning out of the guard, the opening of the gate, and the jingling entrance of a coach drawn by six fine horses. He stood and watched the proceedings with all the interest of a captive. There was an escort of fifty mounted men in the cocked hats and blue-and-red uniforms of Bonaparte's gendarmerie, coachman and servants on the box, an officer dismounting hurriedly to open the door. Clearly the new arrival must be a man of importance. Hornblower experienced a faint feeling of disappointment when there climbed out of the coach not a Marshal with plumes and feathers, but just another officer of gendarmerie. A youngish man with a bullet-black head, which he revealed as he held his cocked hat in his hand while stooping to descend; the star of the Legion of Honour on his breast; high black boots with spurs. Hornblower wondered idly why a colonel of gendarmerie who was obviously not crippled should arrive in a coach instead of on horseback. He watched him go clinking across to the governor's headquarters.

Hornblower's walk was nearly finished when one of the young French aides-de-camp of the governor approached him on the ramparts and saluted.

"His Excellency sends you his compliments, sir, and he would be glad if you could spare him a few minutes of your time as soon as it is convenient to you."

Addressed to a prisoner, as Hornblower told himself bitterly, these words might as well have been "Come at once."

"I will come now, with the greatest pleasure," said Hornblower, maintaining the solemn farce.

Down in the governor's office the same colonel of gendarmerie was standing conversing alone with His Excellency; the governor's expression was sad.

"I have the honour of presenting to you, Captain," he said, turning, "Colonel Jean-Baptiste Caillard, Grand Eagle of the Legion of Honour, and one of His Imperial Majesty's personal aides-de-camp. Colonel, this is Captain Horatio Hornblower, of His Britannic Majesty's Navy."

The governor was clearly worried and upset. His hands were fluttering and he stammered a little as he spoke, and he had made a pitiful muddle of his attempt on the aspirates of Hornblower's name. Hornblower bowed, but as the colonel remained unbending he stiffened to attention. He could recognize that type of man at once — the servant of a tyrant, and in close personal association with him, modelling his conduct not on the tyrant's, but on what he fancied should be the correct behaviour of a tyrant, far out-Heroding Herod in arbitrariness and cruelty. It might be merely a pose — the man might be a kind husband and the loving father of a family — but it was a pose which might have unpleasant results for anyone in his power. His victims would suffer in his attempt to prove, to himself as well as to others, that he could be more stern, more unrelenting — and therefore naturally more able — than the man who employed him.

Caillard ran a cold eye over Hornblower's appearance.

"What is he doing with that sword at his side?" he asked of the governor.

"The admiral returned it to him on the day of the battle," explained the governor hastily. "He said —— "

"It doesn't matter what he said," interrupted Caillard. "No criminal as guilty as he can be allowed a weapon. And a sword is the emblem of a gentleman of honour, which he most decidedly is not. Take off that sword, sir."

Hornblower stood appalled, hardly believing he had understood. Caillard's face wore a fixed mirthless smile which showed white teeth, below the black moustache which lay like a gash across his olive face.

"Take off that sword," repeated Caillard; and then, as Hornblower made no movement, "If Your Excellency will permit me to call in one of my gendarmes, I will have the sword removed."

At the threat Hornblower unbuckled his belt and allowed the weapon to fall to the ground; the clatter rang loud in the silence. The sword of honour which the Patriotic Fund had awarded him ten years ago for his heading of the boarding party which took the *Castilla* lay on the floor, jerked half out of its scabbard. The hiltless tang and the battered places on the sheath where the gold had been torn off bore mute witness to the lust for gold of the Empire's servants.

"Good!" said Caillard. "Now will Your Excellency have the goodness to warn this man of his approaching departure?"

"Colonel Caillard," said the governor, "has come to take you and your first lieutenant, Mistaire — Mistaire Bush, to Paris."

"Bush?" blazed out Hornblower, moved as not even the loss of his sword could move him. "Bush? That is impossible. Lieutenant Bush is seriously wounded. It might easily be fatal to take him on a long journey at present."

"The journey will be fatal to him in any case," said Caillard, still with the mirthless smile and the gleam of white teeth.

The governor wrung his hands.

"You cannot say that, Colonel. These gentlemen have still to be tried. The Military Commission has yet to give its verdict."

"These gentlemen, as you call them, Your Excellency, stand condemned out of their own mouths."

Hornblower remembered that he had made no attempt to deny, while the admiral was questioning him and preparing his report, that he had been in command of the *Sutherland* the day she wore French colours and her landing party stormed the battery at Llanza. He had known the ruse to be legitimate enough, but he had not reckoned on a French emperor determined upon convincing European opinion of the perfidy of England and cunning enough to know that a couple of resounding executions might well be considered evidence of guilt.

"The colonel," said the governor to Hornblower, "has brought his coach. You may rely upon it that Mistaire Bush will have every possible comfort. Please tell me which of your men you would like to accompany you as your servant. And if there is anything which I can provide which will make the journey more comfortable I will do so with the greatest pleasure."

Hornblower debated internally the question of the servant. Polwheal, who had served him for years, was among the wounded in the casemate. Nor, he fancied, would he have selected him in any case; Polwheal was not the man for an emergency — and it was just possible that there might be an emergency. Latude had escaped from the Bastille. Was not there a faint chance that Hornblower might escape from Vincennes? Hornblower thought of Brown's bulging muscles and cheerful devotion.

"I would like to take my coxswain, Brown, if you please," he said.

"Certainly. I will send for him and have your present servant pack your things with him. And with regard to your needs for the journey?"

"I need nothing," said Hornblower. At the same time as he spoke he cursed himself for his pride. If he were ever to save himself and Bush from the firing party in the ditch at Vincennes, he would need gold.

"Oh, I cannot allow you to say that," protested the governor. "There may be some few comforts you would like to buy when you are in France. Besides, you cannot deprive me of the pleasure of being of assistance to a brave man. Please do me the favour of accepting my purse. I beg you to, sir."

Hornblower fought down his pride and took the proffered wallet. It was of surprising weight and gave out a musical chink as he took it.

"I must thank you for your kindness," he said. "And for all your courtesy while I have been your prisoner."

"It has been a pleasure to me, as I said," replied the governor. "I want to wish you the — the very best of good luck on your arrival in Paris."

"Enough of this," said Caillard. "My orders from His Majesty call for the utmost expedition. Is the wounded man in the courtyard?"

The governor led the way out, and the gendarmes closed up round Hornblower as they walked towards the coach. Bush was lying there on a stretcher, strangely pale and strangely wasted out there in the bright light. He was feebly trying to shield his eyes from the sun; Hornblower ran and knelt beside him.

"They're going to take us to Paris, Bush," he said.

"What, you and me, sir?"

"Yes."

"It's a place I've often wanted to see."

The Italian surgeon who had amputated Bush's foot was plucking at Hornblower's sleeve and fluttering some sheets of paper. These were instructions, he explained in faulty Italian French, for the further treatment of the stump. Any surgeon in France would understand them. As soon as the ligatures came away the wound would heal at once. He had put a parcel of dressings into the coach for use on the journey. Hornblower tried to thank him, but was interrupted when the surgeon turned away to supervise the lifting of Bush, stretcher and all, into the coach. It was an immensely long vehicle, and the stretcher just fitted in across one door, its ends on the two seats.

Brown was there now, with Hornblower's valise in his hand. The coachman showed him how to put it into the boot. Then a gendarme opened the other door and stood waiting for Hornblower to enter. Hornblower looked up at the ramparts towering above him; no more than half an hour ago he had been walking there, worn out with doubt. At least one doubt was settled now. In a fortnight's time perhaps they would all be settled, after he had faced the firing party at Vincennes. A spurt of fear welled up within him at the thought, destroying the first momentary feeling almost of pleasure. He did not want to be taken to Paris and shot; he wanted to resist. Then he realised that resistance would be both vain and undignified, and he forced himself to climb into the coach, hoping that no one had noticed his slight hesitation.

A gesture from the sergeant of gendarmerie brought Brown to the door as well, and he came climbing in to sit apologetically with his officers. Caillard was mounting a big black horse, a spirited, restless creature which champed at its bit and passaged feverishly about. When he had settled himself in the saddle the word was given, and the horses were led round the courtyard, the coach jolting and heaving over the cobbles, out through the gate and down to the road which wound under the guns of the fortress. The mounted gendarmerie closed up round the coach, a whip cracked, and they were off at a slow trot, to the jingling of the harness and the clattering of the hoofs and the creaking of the leatherwork.

Hornblower would have liked to have looked out of the windows at the houses of Rosas village going by — after three weeks' captivity the change of scene allured him — but first he had to attend to his wounded lieutenant.

"How is it going, Bush?" he asked, bending over him.

"Very well, thank you, sir," said Bush.

There was sunlight streaming in through the coach windows now, and here a succession of tall trees by the roadside threw flickering shadows over Bush's face. Fever and loss of blood had made Bush's face less craggy and gnarled, drawing the flesh tight over the bones so that he looked unnaturally younger, and he was pale instead of being the mahogany brown to which Hornblower was accustomed. Hornblower thought he saw a twinge of pain cross Bush's expression as the coach lurched on the abominable road.

"Is there anything I can do?" he asked, trying hard to keep the helplessness out of his voice.

"Nothing, thank you, sir," whispered Bush.

"Try and sleep," said Hornblower.

Bush's hand which lay outside the blanket twitched and stirred and moved towards him; he took it and he felt a gentle pressure.

For a few brief seconds Bush's hand stroked his, feebly, caressing it as though it were a woman's. There was a glimmer of a smile on Bush's drawn face with its closed eyes. During all the years they had served together it was the first sign of affection either had shown for the other. Bush's head turned on the pillow, and he lay quite still, while Hornblower sat not daring to move for fear of disturbing him.

The coach had slowed to a walk — it must be breasting the long climb which carried the road across the roots of the peninsula of Cape Creus. Yet even at that speed the coach lurched and rolled horribly; the surface of the road must be utterly uncared for. The sharp ringing of the hoofs of the escort's horses told that they were travelling over rock, and the irregularity of the sound was a clear indication of the way the horses were picking their way among the holes. Framed in the windows Hornblower could see the gendarmes in their blue uniforms and cocked hats jerking and swaying about with the rolling of the coach. The presence of fifty gendarmes as an escort was not a real indication of the political importance of himself and Bush, but only a proof that even here, only twenty miles from France, the road was unsafe for small parties — a little band of Spanish *guerilleros* was to be found on every inaccessible hill-top.

But there was always a chance that Claros or Rovira with their Catalan *miqueletes* a thousand strong might come swooping down on the road from their Pyrenean fastnesses. Hornblower felt hope surging up within him at the thought that at any moment, in that case, he might find himself a free man again. His pulse beat faster and he crossed and uncrossed his knees restlessly — with the utmost caution so as not to disturb Bush. He did not want to be taken to Paris to face a mockery of a trial. He did not want to die. He was beginning to fret himself into a fever, when common sense came to his rescue and he compelled himself to sink into a stolid indifference.

Brown was sitting opposite him, primly upright with his arms folded. Hornblower almost grinned, sympathetically, at sight of him. Brown was actually self-conscious. He had never in his life before, presumably, had to be at such close quarters with a couple of officers. Certainly he must be feeling awkward at having to sit in the presence of two such lofty individuals as a captain and a first lieutenant. For that matter, it was at least a thousand to one that Brown had never been inside a coach before, had never sat on leather upholstery with a carpet under his feet. Nor had he had any experience in gentlemen's service, his duties as captain's coxswain being mainly disciplinary and executive. There was something comic about seeing Brown, with the proverbial adaptability of the British seaman, aping what he thought should be the manners of the gentleman's gentleman, and sitting there as if butter would not melt in his mouth.

The coach lurched again, quickening its pace, and the horses broke from a walk into a trot. They must be at the top of the long hill now, with a long descent before them, which would bring them back to the seashore somewhere near Llanza, where he had stormed the battery under protection of the tricolour flag. It was an exploit he had been proud of — still was, for that matter. He had never dreamed for one moment that it would lead him to Paris and a firing party. Through the window on Bush's side he could see the rounded brown slopes of the Pyrenees soaring upwards; on the other side, as the coach swung sickeningly round a bend, he caught a glimpse of the sea far below, sparkling in the rays of the afternoon sun. He craned his neck to look at it, the sea which had played him so many scurvy tricks and which he loved. He thought, with a little catch in his throat, that this would be the last day on which he would ever see it. Tonight they would cross the frontier; tomorrow they would plunge into France; and in ten days, a fortnight, he would be rotting in his grave at Vincennes. It would be hard to leave this life, even with all its doubts and uncertainties, to lose the sea with its whims and its treacheries, Maria and the child, Lady Barbara . . .

Those were white cottages drifting past the windows; and on the side towards the sea, perched on the grassy cliff, was the battery of Llanza. He could see a sentry dressed in blue and white; stooping and looking upwards he could see the French flag at the top of the flagstaff — Bush, here, had hauled it down not so many weeks ago. He heard the coachman's whip crack and the horses quickened their pace; it was still eight miles or so to the frontier and Caillard must be anxious to cross before dark. The mountains, bristling here with pines, were hemming the road in close between them and the sea. Why did not Claros or Rovira come to save him? At every turn of the road there was an ideal site for an ambush. Soon they would be in France and it would be too late. He had to struggle again to remain impassive. The prospect of crossing into France seemed to make his fate far more certain and imminent.

It was growing dark fast — they could not be far now from the frontier. Hornblower tried to visualise the charts he had often handled, so as to remember the name of the French frontier town, but his mind was not sufficiently under control to allow it. The coach was coming to a standstill; he heard footsteps outside, heard Caillard's metallic voice saying "In the name of the Emperor" and an unknown voice say "*Passez, passez, monsieur.*" The coach lurched and accelerated again; they were in France now. Now the horses' hoofs were ringing on cobblestones. There were houses; one or two lights to be seen. Outside the houses there were men in all kinds of uniforms, and a few women picking their way among them, dressed in pretty costumes with caps on their heads. He could hear laughter and joking. Then abruptly the coach swerved to the right and drew up in the courtyard of an inn. Lights were appearing in plenty in the fading twilight. Someone opened the door of the coach and drew down the steps for him to descend.

Chapter IV

HORNBLOWER looked round the room to which the innkeeper and the sergeant of gendarmerie had jointly conducted them. He was glad to see a fire burning there, for he was stiff and chilled with his long inactivity in the coach. There was a truckle bed against one wall, a table with a white cloth already spread. A gendarme appeared at the door, stepping slowly and heavily — he was the first of the two who were carrying the stretcher. He looked round to see where to lay it down, turned too abruptly, and jarred it against the jamb of the wall.

"Careful with that stretcher!" snapped Hornblower; and then, remembering he had to speak French, "*Attention! Mettez le brancard là. Doucement!*"

Brown came and knelt over the stretcher.

"What is the name of this place?" asked Hornblower of the innkeeper.

"Cerbère. Hotel Iéna, monsieur," answered the innkeeper, fingering his leather apron.

"Monsieur is allowed no speech with anyone whatever," interposed the sergeant. "He will be served, but he must address no speech to the inn servants. If he has any wishes, he will speak to the sentry outside his door. There will be another sentry outside his window."

A gesture of his hand called attention to the cocked hat and the musket barrel of a gendarme, darkly visible through the glass.

"You are too amiable, monsieur," said Hornblower.

"I have my orders. Supper will be served in half an hour."

"I would be obliged if Colonel Caillard would give orders for a surgeon to attend Lieutenant Bush's wounds at once."

"I will ask him, sir," said the sergeant, escorting the innkeeper from the room.

Bush, when Hornblower bent over him, seemed somehow a

little better than in the morning. There was a little colour in his cheeks and more strength in his movements.

"Is there anything I can do, Bush?" asked Hornblower.

"Yes . . ."

Bush explained the needs of sick-room nursing. Hornblower looked up at Brown, a little helplessly.

"I am afraid it'll call for two of you, sir, because I'm a heavy man," said Bush apologetically. It was the apology in his tone which brought Hornblower to the point of action.

"Of course," he said with all the cheerfulness he could bring into his voice. "Come on, Brown. Lift him from the other side."

After the business was finished, with no more than a single half-stifled groan from Bush, Brown displayed more of the astonishing versatility of the British seaman.

"I'll wash you, sir, shall I? An' you haven't had your shave today, have you, sir?"

Hornblower sat and watched in helpless admiration the deft movements of the burly sailor as he washed and shaved his first lieutenant. The towels were so well arranged that no single drop of water fell on the bedding.

"Thank 'ee, Brown, thank 'ee," said Bush, sinking back on his pillow.

The door opened to admit a little bearded man in a semi-military uniform carrying a leather case.

"Good evening, gentlemen," he said, sounding all his consonants in the manner which Hornblower was yet to discover was characteristic of the Midi. "I am the surgeon, if you please. And this is the wounded officer? And these are the hospital notes of my confrère at Rosas? Excellent. Yes, exactly. And how are you feeling, sir?"

Hornblower had to translate, limpingly, the surgeon's questions to Bush, and the latter's replies. Bush put out his tongue, and submitted to having his pulse felt, and his temperature gauged by a hand thrust into his shirt.

"So," said the surgeon. "And now let us see the stump. Will you hold the candle for me here, if you please, sir?"

He turned back the blankets from the foot of the stretcher,

revealing the little basket which guarded the stump, laid the basket on the floor and began to remove the dressings.

"Would you tell him, sir," asked Bush, "that my foot which isn't there tickles most abominably and I don't know how to scratch it?"

The translation taxed Hornblower's French to the utmost, but the surgeon listened sympathetically.

"That is not at all unusual," he said. "And the itchings will come to a natural end in course of time. Ah, now here is the stump. A beautiful stump. A lovely stump."

Hornblower, compelling himself to look, was vaguely reminded of the knuckle end of a roast leg of mutton; the irregular folds of flesh were caught in by half-healed scars, but out of the scars hung two ends of black thread.

"When *Monsieur le Lieutenant* begins to walk again," explained the surgeon, "he will be glad of an ample pad of flesh at the end of the stump. The end of the bone will not chafe — "

"Yes, exactly," said Hornblower, fighting down his squeamishness.

"A very beautiful piece of work," said the surgeon. "As long as it heals properly and gangrene does not set in. At this stage the surgeon has to depend on his nose for his diagnosis."

Suiting the action to the word the surgeon sniffed at the dressings and at the raw stump.

"Smell, monsieur," he said, holding the dressings to Hornblower's face. Hornblower was conscious of the faintest whiff of corruption.

"Beautiful, is it not?" said the surgeon. "A fine healthy wound and yet every evidence that the ligatures will soon free themselves."

Hornblower realised that the two threads hanging out of the scars were attached to the ends of the two main arteries. When corruption inside was complete the threads could be drawn out and the wounds allowed to heal; it was a race between the rotting of the arteries and the onset of gangrene.

"I will see if the ligatures are free now. Warn your friend that I shall hurt him a little."

Hornblower looked towards Bush to convey the message, and was shocked to see that Bush's face was distorted with apprehension.

"I know," said Bush. "I know what he's going to do — sir."

Only as an afterthought did he say that "sir," which was the clearest proof of his mental preoccupation. He grasped the bedclothes in his two fists, his jaw set and his eyes shut.

"I'm ready," he said through his clenched teeth.

The surgeon drew firmly on one of the threads and Bush writhed a little. He drew on the other.

"A-ah," gasped Bush, with sweat on his face.

"Nearly free," commented the surgeon. "I could tell by the feeling of the threads. Your friend will soon be well. Now let us replace the dressings. So. And so." His dexterous plump fingers rebandaged the stump, replaced the wicker basket, and drew down the bed coverings.

"Thank you, gentlemen," said the surgeon, rising to his feet and brushing his hands one against the other. "I will return in the morning."

"Hadn't you better sit down, sir?" came Brown's voice to Hornblower's ears as though from a million miles away, after the surgeon had withdrawn. The room was veiled in grey mist which gradually cleared away as he sat, to reveal Bush lying back on his pillow and trying to smile, and Brown's homely honest face wearing an expression of acute concern.

"Rare bad you looked for a minute, sir. You must be hungry, I expect, sir, not having eaten nothing since breakfast, like."

It was tactful of Brown to attribute this faintness to hunger, to which all flesh might be subject without shame, and not merely to weakness in face of wounds and suffering.

"That sounds like supper coming now," croaked Bush from the stretcher, as though one of a conspiracy to ignore their captain's feebleness.

The sergeant of gendarmerie came clanking in, two women behind him bearing trays. The women set the table deftly and quickly, their eyes downcast, and withdrew without looking up, although one of them smiled at the corner of her mouth in response to a meaning cough from Brown, which drew a gesture of irritation from the sergeant. The latter cast one searching glance round the room before shutting and locking the door with a clashing of keys.

"Soup," said Hornblower, peering into the tureen which steamed deliciously. "And I fancy this is stewed veal."

The discovery confirmed him in his notion that Frenchmen lived exclusively on soup and stewed veal — he put no faith in the more vulgar notions regarding frogs and snails.

"You will have some of this broth, I suppose, Bush?" he continued. He was talking desperately hard now to conceal the feeling of depression and unhappiness which was overwhelming him. "And a glass of this wine? It has no label — let's hope for the best."

"Some of their rotgut claret, I suppose," grunted Bush. Eighteen years of war with France had given most Englishmen the notion that the only wines fit for men to drink were port and sherry and Madeira, and that Frenchmen only drank thin claret, which gave an unaccustomed drinker the bellyache.

"We'll see," said Hornblower as cheerfully as he could. "Let's get you propped up first."

With his hand behind Bush's shoulders he heaved him up a little; as he looked round helplessly, Brown came to his rescue with pillows taken from the bed, and between them they settled Bush with his head raised and his arms free and a napkin under his chin. Hornblower brought him a plate of soup and a piece of bread.

"*M'm,*" said Bush, tasting. "Might be worse. Please, sir, don't let yours get cold."

Brown brought a chair for his captain to sit at the table, and stood in an attitude of attention beside it; there was another place laid, but his action proclaimed as loudly as words how far it was from his mind to sit with his captain. Hornblower ate, at first with distaste and then with increasing appetite.

"Some more of that soup, Brown," said Bush. "And my glass of wine, if you please."

The stewed veal was extraordinarily good, even to a man who was accustomed to meat he could set his teeth in.

"Dash my wig," said Bush from the bed. "Do you think I could have some of that stewed veal, sir? This travelling has given me an appetite."

Hornblower had to think about that. A man in a fever should be kept on a low diet, but Bush could not be said to be in a fever now, and he had lost a great deal of blood which he had to make up. The yearning look on Bush's face decided him.

"A little will do you no harm," he said. "Take this plate to Mr. Bush, Brown."

Good food and good wine — the fare in the *Sutherland* had been repulsive, and at Rosas scanty — tended to loosen their tongues and make them more cheerful. Yet it was hard to unbend beyond a certain unstated limit. The awful majesty surrounding a captain of a ship of the line lingered even after the ship had been destroyed; more than that, the memory of the very strict reserve which Hornblower had maintained during his command acted as a constraint. And to Brown a first lieutenant was in a position nearly as astronomically lofty as a captain; it was awesome to be in the same room as the two of them, even with the help of making-believe to be their old servant. Hornblower had finished his cheese by now, and the moment which Brown had been dreading had arrived.

"Here, Brown," he said rising, "sit down and eat your supper while it's still hot."

Brown, now at the age of twenty-eight, had served His Majesty in His Majesty's ships from the age of eleven, and during that time he had never made use at table of other instruments than his sheath knife and his fingers; he had never eaten off china, nor had he drunk from a wineglass. He experienced a nightmare sensation as if his officers were watching him with four eyes as large as footballs the while he nervously picked up a spoon and addressed himself to this unaccustomed task. Hornblower realised his embarrassment in a clairvoyant flash. Brown had thews and sinews which Hornblower had often envied; he had a stolid courage in action which Hornblower could never hope to rival. He could knot and splice, hand, reef, and steer, cast the lead or pull an oar, all of them far better than his captain. He could go aloft on a black night in a howling storm without thinking twice about it, but the sight of a knife and fork made his hands tremble. Hornblower thought about how Gibbon would have pointed the moral epigrammatically in two vivid antithetical sentences.

Humiliation and nervousness never did any good to a man — Hornblower knew that if anyone ever did. He took a chair unobtrusively over beside Bush's stretcher and sat down with his back almost turned to the table, and he plunged desperately into conversation with his first lieutenant while the crockery clattered behind him.

"Would you like to be moved into the bed?" he asked, saying the first thing which came into his head.

"No thank you, sir," said Bush. "Two weeks now I've slept in the stretcher. I'm comfortable enough, sir, and it'd be painful to move me, even if — if —— "

Words failed Bush to describe his utter determination not to sleep in the only bed and leave his captain without one.

"What are we going to Paris for, sir?" asked Bush.

"God knows," said Hornblower. "But I have a notion that Boney himself wants to ask us questions."

That was the answer he had decided upon hours before in readiness for this inevitable question; it would not help Bush's convalescence to know the fate awaiting him.

"Much good will our answers do him," said Bush, grimly. "Perhaps we'll drink a dish of tea in the Tuileries with Maria Louisa."

"Maybe," answered Hornblower. "And maybe he wants lessons in navigation from you. I've heard he's weak at mathematics."

That brought a smile. Bush notoriously was no good with figures and suffered agonies when confronted with a simple problem in spherical trigonometry. Hornblower's acute ears heard Brown's chair scrape a little; presumably his meal had progressed satisfactorily.

"Help yourself to the wine, Brown," he said, without turning round.

"Aye aye, sir," said Brown cheerfully.

There was a whole bottle of wine left as well as some in the other. This would be a good moment for ascertaining if Brown could be trusted with liquor. Hornblower kept his back turned to him and struggled on with his conversation with Bush. Five minutes later Brown's chair scraped again more definitely, and Hornblower looked round.

"Had enough, Brown?"

"Aye aye, sir. A right good supper."

The soup tureen and the dish of stew were both empty; the bread had disappeared all save the heel of the loaf; there was only a morsel of cheese left. But one bottle of wine was still two thirds full — Brown had contented himself with a half bottle at most, and the fact that he had drunk that much and no more was the clearest proof that he was safe as regards alcohol.

"Pull the bellrope, then."

The distant jangling brought in time the rattling of keys to the door, and in came the sergeant and the two maids; the latter set about clearing the tables under the former's eye.

"I must get something for you to sleep on, Brown," said Hornblower.

"I can sleep on the floor, sir."

"No, you can't."

Hornblower had decided opinions about that; there had been occasions as a young officer when he had slept on the bare planks of a ship's deck, and he knew their unyielding discomfort.

"I want a bed for my servant," he said to the sergeant.

"He can sleep on the floor."

"I will not allow anything of the kind. You must find a mattress for him."

Hornblower was surprised to find how quickly he was acquiring the ability to talk French; the quickness of his mind enabled him to make the best use of his limited vocabulary and his retentive memory had stored up all sorts of words, once heard, and was ready to produce them from the subconscious part of his mind as soon as the stimulus of necessity was applied.

The sergeant had shrugged his shoulders and rudely turned his back.

"I shall report your insolence to Colonel Caillard tomorrow morning," said Hornblower, hotly. "Find a mattress immediately."

It was not so much the threat that carried the day as long-ingrained habits of discipline. Even a sergeant of French gendarmerie was accustomed to yielding deference to gold lace and epaulettes and an authoritative manner. Possibly the obvious indignation of the maids at the suggestion that so fine a man should be left to sleep on the floor may have weighed with him too. He called to the sentry at the door and told him to bring a mattress from the stables where the escort were billeted. It was only a palliasse of straw when it came, but it was something infinitely more comfortable than bare and draughty boards, all the same. Brown looked his gratitude to Hornblower as the mattress was spread out in the corner of the room.

"Time to turn in," said Hornblower, ignoring it, as the door was locked behind the sergeant. "Let's make you comfortable, first, Bush."

It was some obscure self-conscious motive which made Hornblower select from his valise the embroidered nightshirt over which Maria's busy fingers had laboured lovingly — the nightshirt which he had brought with him from England for use should he dine and sleep at a governor's or on board the flagship. All the years he had been a captain he had never shared a room with anyone save Maria, and it was a novel experience for him to prepare for bed in sight of Bush and Brown, and he was ridiculously self-conscious about it, regardless of the fact that Bush, white and exhausted, was already lying back on his pillow with drooping eyelids, while Brown modestly stripped off his trousers with downcast eyes, wrapped himself in the cloak which Hornblower insisted on his using, and curled himself up on his palliasse without a glance at his superior.

Hornblower got into bed.

"Ready?" he asked, and blew out the candle; the fire had died down to embers which gave only the faintest red glow in the room. It was the beginning of one of those wakeful nights which Hornblower had grown by now able to recognise in advance. The moment he blew out the candle and settled his head on the pillow he knew he would not be able to sleep until just before dawn. In his ship he would have gone up on deck or walked his stern gallery; here he could only lie grimly immobile. Sometimes a subdued crackling told how Brown was turning over on his straw mattress; once or twice Bush moaned a little in his feverish sleep.

Today was Wednesday. Only sixteen days ago and Hornblower had been captain of a seventy-four, and absolute master of the happiness of five hundred seamen. His least word directed the operations of a gigantic engine of war; the blows it had dealt had caused an imperial throne to totter. He thought regretfully of night-time aboard his ship, the creaking of the timbers and the singing of the rigging, the impassive quartermaster at the wheel in the faint light of the binnacle and the officer of the watch pacing the quarterdeck.

Now he was a nobody; where once he had minutely regulated five hundred men's lives he was reduced to chaffering for a single mattress for the only seaman left to him; police sergeants could insult him with impunity; he had to come and to go at the bidding of someone he despised. Worse than that — Hornblower felt the hot blood running under his skin as the full realisation broke upon him again — he was being taken to Paris as a criminal. Very soon indeed, in some cold dawn, he would be led out into the ditch at Vincennes to face a firing party. Then he would be dead. Hornblower's vivid imagination pictured the impact of the musket bullets upon his breast, and he wondered how long the pain would last before oblivion came upon him. It was not the oblivion that he feared, he told himself — indeed in his present misery he almost looked forward to it. Perhaps it was the finality of death, the irrevocableness of it.

No, that was only a minor factor. Mostly it was instinctive fear of a sudden and drastic change to something completely unknown. He remembered the night he had spent as a child in the inn at Andover, when he was going to join his ship next day and enter upon the unknown life of the Navy. That was the nearest comparison — he had been frightened then, he remembered, so frightened he had been unable to sleep; and yet "frightened" was too strong a word to describe the state of mind of someone who was quite prepared to face the future and could not be really blamed for this sudden acceleration of heartbeat and prickling of sweat!

A moaning sigh from Bush, loud in the stillness of the room, distracted him from his analysis of his fear. They were going to shoot Bush, too. Presumably they would lash him to a stake to have a fair shot at him — curious how, while it was easy to order a party to shoot an upright figure, however helpless, every instinct revolted against shooting a helpless man prostrate on a stretcher. It would be a monstrous crime to shoot Bush, who, even supposing his captain were guilty, could have done nothing except obey orders. But Bonaparte would do it. The necessity of rallying Europe round him in his struggle against England was growing ever more pressing. The blockade was strangling the Empire of the French as Antæus had been strangled by Hercules. Bonaparte's unwilling allies — all Europe, that was to say, save Portugal and Sicily — were growing restive and thinking about defection; the French people themselves, Hornblower shrewdly guessed, were by now none too enamoured of this King Stork whom they had imposed on themselves. It would not be sufficient for Bonaparte merely to say that the British fleet was the criminal instrument of a perfidious tyranny; he had said that for a dozen years. The mere announcement that British naval officers had violated the laws of war would carry small enough weight, too. But to try a couple of officers and shoot them would be a convincing gesture, and the perverted statement of facts issued from Paris might help to sustain French public opinion — European public opinion as well — for another year or two in its opposition to England.

But it was bad luck that the victims should be Bush and he. Bonaparte had had a dozen British naval captains in his hands during the last few years, and he could have trumped up charges against half of them. Presumably it was destiny which had selected Hornblower and Bush to suffer. Hornblower told himself that for twenty years he had been aware of a premonition of sudden death. It was certain and inevitable now. He hoped he would meet it bravely, go down with colours flying; but he mistrusted his own weak body. He feared that his cheeks would be pale and his teeth would chatter, or worse still that his heart would weaken so that he would faint before the firing party had done their work. That would be a fine opportunity for a mordant couple of lines in the *Moniteur Universel* — fine reading for Lady Barbara and Maria.

If he had been alone in the room he would have groaned aloud in his misery and turned over restlessly. But as it was he lay grimly rigid and silent. If his subordinates were awake they would never be allowed to guess that he was awake, too. To divert his mind from his approaching execution he cast round in search of something else to think about, and new subjects presented themselves in swarms. Whether Admiral Leighton were alive or dead, and whether, if the latter were the case, Lady Barbara Leighton would think more often or less often about Hornblower, her lover; how Maria's pregnancy was progressing; what was the state of British public opinion regarding the loss of the *Sutherland*, and, more especially, what Lady Barbara thought about his surrendering — there were endless things to think and worry about; there was endless flotsam bobbing about in the racing torrent of his mind. And the horses stamped in the stable, and every two hours he heard the sentries being changed outside window and door.

Chapter V

DAWN was not fully come, the room was only faintly illuminated by the grey light, when a clash of keys and a stamping of booted feet outside the door heralded the entrance of the sergeant of gendarmerie.

"The coach will leave in an hour's time," he announced. "The surgeon will be here in half an hour. You gentlemen will please be ready."

Bush was obviously feverish; Hornblower could see that at his first glance as he bent over him, still in his embroidered silk nightshirt. Yet Bush stoutly affirmed that he was not ill.

"I'm well enough, thank you, sir," he said; but his face was flushed and yet apprehensive, and his hands gripped his bed-clothes. Hornblower suspected that the mere vibration of the floor as he and Brown walked about the room was causing pain to the unhealed stump of his leg.

"I'm ready to do anything you want done," said Hornblower.

"No, thank you, sir. Let's wait till the doctor comes, if you don't mind, sir."

Hornblower washed and shaved in the cold water in the wash-hand-stand jug; during the time which had elapsed since he had left the *Sutherland* he had never been allowed hot. But he yearned for the cold shower bath he had been accustomed to take under the jet of the wash-deck pump; his skin seemed to creep when he stopped to consider it, and it was a ghoulish business to make shift with washing glove and soap, wetting a few inches at a time. Brown dressed himself unobtrusively in his own corner of the room, scurrying out like a mouse to wash when his captain had finished.

The doctor arrived with his leather satchel.

"And how is he this morning?" he asked, briskly; Hornblower saw a shade of concern pass over his face as he observed Bush's evident fever.

He knelt down and exposed the stump, Hornblower beside him. The limb jerked nervously as it was grasped with firm fingers; the doctor took Hornblower's hand and laid it on the skin above the wound.

"A little warm," said the doctor. It was hot to Hornblower's touch. "That may be a good sign. We shall know now."

He took hold of one of the ligatures and pulled at it. The thing came gliding out of the wound like a snake.

"Good!" said the doctor. "Excellent!"

He peered closely at the debris entangled in the knot, and then bent to examine the trickle of pus which had followed the ligature out of the wound.

"Excellent," repeated the doctor.

Hornblower went back in his mind through the numerous reports which surgeons had made to him regarding wounded men, and the verbal comments with which they had amplified them. The words "laudable pus" came up in his mind; it was important to distinguish between the drainage from a wound struggling to heal itself and the stinking ooze of a poisoned limb. This was clearly "laudable pus," judging by the doctor's comments.

"Now for the other one," said the doctor. He pulled at the remaining ligature, but all he got was a cry of pain from Bush — which seemed to go clean through Hornblower's heart — and a convulsive writhing of Bush's tortured body.

"Not quite ready," said the doctor. "I should judge that it will only be a matter of hours, though. Is your friend proposing to continue his journey today?"

"He is under orders to continue it," said Hornblower in his limping French. "You would consider such a course unwise?"

"Most unwise," said the doctor. "It will cause him a great deal of pain and may imperil the healing of the wound."

He felt Bush's pulse and rested his hand on his forehead.

"Most unwise," he repeated.

The door opened behind him to reveal the gendarmerie sergeant.

"The carriage is ready."

"It must wait until I have bandaged this wound. Get outside," said the doctor testily.

"I will go and speak to the colonel," said Hornblower.

He brushed past the sergeant, who tried too late to intercept him, into the main corridor of the inn, and out into the courtyard where stood the coach. The horses were being harnessed up, and a group of gendarmes were saddling their mounts on the farther side. Chance dictated that Colonel Caillard should be crossing the courtyard, too, in his blue-and-red uniform and his gleaming high boots, the star of the Legion of Honour dancing on his breast.

"Sir," said Hornblower.

"What is it now?" demanded Caillard.

"Lieutenant Bush must not be moved. He is very badly wounded and a crisis approaches."

The broken French came tumbling disjointedly from Hornblower's lips.

"I can do nothing in contravention of my orders," said Caillard. His eyes were cold and his mouth hard.

"You were not ordered to kill him," protested Hornblower.

"I was ordered to bring you and him to Paris with the utmost dispatch. We shall start in five minutes."

"But, sir . . . Cannot you wait even today?"

"Even as a pirate you must be aware of the impossibility of disobeying orders," said Caillard.

"I protest against those orders in the name of humanity."

That was a melodramatic speech, but it was a melodramatic moment, and in his ignorance of French Hornblower could not pick and choose his words. A sympathetic murmur in his ear attracted his notice, and, looking round, he saw the two aproned maids and a fat woman and the innkeeper all listening to the conversation with obvious disapproval of Caillard's point of view. They shut themselves away behind the kitchen door as Caillard turned a terrible eye upon them, but they had granted Hornblower a first momentary insight into the personal unpopularity which imperial harshness was causing in France.

"Sergeant," said Caillard abruptly. "Put the prisoners into the coach."

There was no hope of resistance. The gendarmes carried Bush's stretcher out into the courtyard and perched it upon the seats, with Brown and Hornblower running round it to protect it from unnecessary jerks. The surgeon was scribbling notes hurriedly at the foot of the sheaf of notes regarding Bush's case which Hornblower had brought from Rosas. One of the maids came clattering across the courtyard with a steaming tray, which she passed in to Hornblower through the open window. There was a platter of bread and three bowls of a black liquid which Hornblower was later to come to recognise as coffee — what blockaded France had come to call coffee. It was no pleasanter than the infusion of burnt crusts which Hornblower had sometimes drunk on shipboard during a long cruise without the opportunity of renewing cabin stores, but it was warm and stimulating at that time in the morning.

"We have no sugar, sir," said the maid apologetically.

"It doesn't matter," answered Hornblower, sipping thirstily.

"It is a pity the poor wounded officer has to travel," she went on. "These wars are terrible."

She had a snub nose and a wide mouth and big black eyes — no one could call her attractive, but the sympathy in her voice was grateful to a man who was a prisoner. Brown was propping up Bush's shoulders and holding a bowl to his lips. He took two or three sips and turned his head away. The coach rocked as two men scrambled up on to the box.

"Stand away, there!" roared the sergeant.

The coach lurched and rolled and wheeled round out of the gates, the horses' hoofs clattering loud on the cobbles, and the last Hornblower saw of the maid was the slight look of consternation on her face as she realised that she had lost the breakfast tray for good.

The road was bad, judging by the way the coach lurched; Hornblower heard a sharp intake of breath from Bush at one jerk. He remembered what the swollen and inflamed stump of

Bush's leg looked like; every jar must be causing him agony. He moved up the seat to the stretcher and caught Bush's hand.

"Don't you worry yourself, sir," said Bush. "I'm all right."

Even while he spoke Hornblower felt him grip tighter as another jolt caught him unexpectedly.

"I'm sorry, Bush," was all he could say; it was hard for the captain to speak at length to the lieutenant on such personal matters as his regret and unhappiness.

"We can't help it, sir," said Bush, forcing his peaked features into a smile.

That was the main trouble, their complete helplessness. Hornblower realised that there was nothing he could say, nothing he could do. The leather-scented stuffiness of the coach was already oppressing him, and he realised with horror that they would have to endure this jolting prison of theirs for another twenty days, perhaps, before they should reach Paris. He was restless and fidgety at the thought of it, and perhaps his restlessness communicated itself by contact to Bush, who gently withdrew his hand and turned his head to one side leaving his captain free to fidget within the narrow confines of the coach.

Still there were glimpses of the sea to be caught on one side, and of the Pyrenees on the other. Putting his head out of the window Hornblower ascertained that their escort was diminished today. Only two troopers rode ahead of the coach, and four clattered behind at the heels of Caillard's horse. Presumably their entry into France made any possibility of a rescue far less likely. Standing thus, his head awkwardly protruding through the window, was less irksome than sitting in the stuffiness of the carriage. There were the vineyards and the stubble fields to be seen, and the swelling heights of the Pyrenees receding into the blue distance. There were people, too — nearly all women, Hornblower noted — who hardly looked up from their hoeing to watch the coach and its escort bowling along the road. Now they were passing a party of uniformed soldiers — recruits and convalescents, Hornblower guessed, on their way to their units in Catalonia — shambling along the road more like sheep than soldiers. The young officer at their head saluted the glitter of the star on

Caillard's chest and eyed the coach curiously at the same time.

Strange prisoners had passed along that road before him; Alvarez, the heroic defender of Gerona, who died on a wheelbarrow — the only bed granted him — in a dungeon on his way to trial, and Toussaint l'Ouverture, the Negro hero of Haiti, kidnapped from his sunny island and sent to die, inevitably, of pneumonia in a rocky fortress in the Jura; Palafox of Zaragoza, young Mina from Navarre — all victims of the tyrant's Corsican rancour. He and Bush would only be two more items in a list already notable. D'Enghien, who had been shot in Vincennes six years ago, was of the blood-royal, and his death had caused a European sensation; but Bonaparte had murdered plenty more. Thinking of all those who had preceded him made Hornblower gaze more yearningly from the carriage window, and breathe more deeply of the free air.

Still in sight of sea and hills — Mount Canigou still dominating the background — they halted at a posting inn beside the road to change horses. Caillard and the escort took new mounts; four new horses were harnessed up to the coach, and in less than a quarter of an hour they were off again, breasting the steep slope before them with renewed strength. They must be averaging six miles to the hour at least, thought Hornblower, his mind beginning to make calculations. How far Paris might be he could only guess — five or six hundred miles, he fancied. From seventy to ninety hours of travel would bring them to the capital, and they might travel eight, twelve, fifteen hours a day. It might be five days, it might be twelve days, before they reached Paris — vague enough figures. He might be dead in a week's time, or he might be still alive in three weeks. Still alive! As Hornblower thought those words he realised how greatly he desired to live; it was one of those moments when the Hornblower whom he observed so dispassionately and with a faint contempt suddenly blended with the Hornblower who was himself, the most important and vital person in the whole world. He envied the bent old shepherd in the distance with the plaid rug over his shoulders, hobbling over the hillside bent over his stick.

Here was a town coming — there were ramparts, a frowning

citadel, a lofty cathedral. They passed through a gateway and the horses' hoofs rang loudly on cobblestones as the coach threaded its way through narrow streets. Plenty of soldiers here, too; the streets were filled with variegated uniforms. This must be Perpignan, of course, the French base for the invasion of Catalonia. The coach stopped with a jerk in a wider street where an avenue of plane trees and a flagged quay bordered a little river, and, looking upward, Hornblower read the sign "Hotel de la Poste et du Perdrix. Route Nationale 9. Paris 849." With a rush and bustle the horses were changed, Brown and Hornblower were grudgingly allowed to descend and stretch their stiff legs before returning to attend to Bush's wants — they were few enough in his present fever. Caillard and the gendarmes were snatching a hasty meal — the latter at tables outside the inn, the former visible through the windows of the front room. Someone brought the prisoners a tray with slices of cold meat, bread, wine, and cheese. It had hardly been handed into the coach when the escort climbed upon their horses again, the whip cracked, and they were off. The coach heaved and dipped like a ship at sea as it mounted first one hump-backed bridge and then another, before the horses settled into a steady trot along the wide straight road bordered with poplars.

"They waste no time," said Hornblower, grimly.

"No sir, that they don't," agreed Brown.

Bush would eat nothing, shaking his head feebly at the offer of bread and meat. All they could do for him was to moisten his lips with wine, for he was parched and thirsty; Hornblower made a mental note to remember to ask for water at the next posting house, and cursed himself for forgetting anything so obvious up to now. He and Brown shared the food, eating with their fingers and drinking turn and turn about from the bottle of wine, Brown apologetically wiping the bottle's mouth with the napkin after drinking. And as soon as the food was finished Hornblower was on his feet again, craning through the carriage window, watching the countryside drifting by. A thin chill rain began, soaking his scanty hair as he stood there, wetting his face and even running in trickles down his neck, but still he stood there, staring out at freedom.

The sign of the inn where they stopped at nightfall read "Hotel de la Poste de Sigean. Route Nationale 9. Paris 805. Perpignan 44." This place Sigean was no more than a sparse village, straggling for miles along the high road, and the inn was a tiny affair, smaller than the posting stables round the other three sides of the courtyard. The staircase to the upper rooms was too narrow and winding for the stretcher to be carried up them; it was only with difficulty that the bearers were able to turn with it into the salon which the innkeeper reluctantly yielded to them. Hornblower saw Bush wincing as the stretcher jarred against the sides of the door.

"We must have a surgeon at once for the lieutenant," he said to the sergeant.

"I will inquire for one."

The innkeeper here was a surly brute with a squint; he was ungracious about clearing his best sitting-room of its spindly furniture, and bringing in beds for Hornblower and Brown, and producing the various articles they asked for to help make Bush comfortable. There were no wax candles nor lamps; only tallow dips which stank atrociously.

"How's the leg feeling?" asked Hornblower, bending over Bush.

"All right, sir," said Bush, stubbornly, but he was so obviously feverish and in such obvious pain that Hornblower was anxious about him.

When the sergeant escorted in the maid with the dinner he asked, sharply:

"Why has the surgeon not come?"

"There is no surgeon in this village."

"No surgeon? The lieutenant is seriously ill. Is there no — no apothecary?"

Hornblower used the English word in default of French.

"The cow-doctor went across the hills this afternoon and will not be back tonight. There is no one to be found."

The sergeant went out of the room, leaving Hornblower to explain the situation to Bush.

"All right," said the latter, turning his head on the pillow with the feeble gesture which Hornblower dreaded. Hornblower nerved himself.

"I'd better dress that wound of yours myself," he said. "We might try cold vinegar on it, as they do in our service."

"Something cold," said Bush, eagerly.

Hornblower pealed at the bell, and when it was eventually answered he asked for vinegar and obtained it. Not one of the three had a thought for their dinner cooling on the side table.

"Now," said Hornblower.

He had a saucer of vinegar beside him, in which lay the soaking lint, and the clean bandages which the surgeon at Rosas had supplied were at hand. He turned back the bedclothes and revealed the bandaged stump. The leg twitched nervously as he removed the bandages; it was red and swollen and inflamed, hot to the touch for several inches above the point of amputation.

"It's pretty swollen here, too, sir," whispered Bush. The glands in his groin were huge.

"Yes," said Hornblower.

He peered at the scarred end, examined the dressings he had removed, with Brown holding the light. There had been a slight oozing from the point where the ligature had been withdrawn yesterday; much of the rest of the scar was healed and obviously healthy. There was only the other ligature which could be causing this trouble; Hornblower knew that if it were ready to come out it was dangerous to leave it in. Cautiously he took hold of the silken thread. The first gentle touch of it conveyed to his sensitive fingers a suggestion that it was free. It moved distinctly for a quarter of an inch, and, judging by Bush's quiescence, it caused him no sudden spasm of pain. Hornblower set his teeth and pulled; the thread yielded very slowly, but it was obviously free, and no longer attached to the elastic artery. He pulled steadily against a yielding resistance. The ligature came slowly out of the wound, knot and all. Pus followed it in a steady trickle, only slightly tinged with blood. The thing was done.

The artery had not burst, and clearly the wound was in need of the free drainage open to it now with the withdrawal of the ligature.

"I think you're going to start getting well now," he said, aloud, making himself speak cheerfully. "How does it feel?"

"Better," said Bush. "I think it's better, sir."

Hornblower applied the soaking lint to the scarred surface. He found his hands trembling, but he steadied them with an effort as he bandaged the stump — not an easy job, this last, but one which he managed to complete in adequate fashion. He put back the wicker shield, tucked in the bedclothes, and rose to his feet. The trembling was worse than ever now, and he was shaken and sick, which surprised him.

"Supper, sir?" asked Brown. "I'll give Mr. Bush his."

Hornblower's stomach registered a protest at the suggestion of food. He would have liked to refuse, but that would have been too obvious a confession of weakness in front of a subordinate.

"When I've washed my hands," he said loftily.

It was easier to eat than he had expected, when he sat down to force himself. He managed to choke down enough mouthfuls to make it appear as if he had eaten well, and with the passage of the minutes the memory of the revolting task on which he had been engaged became rapidly less clear. Bush displayed none of the appetite nor any of the cheerfulness which had been so noticeable last night; that was the obvious result of his fever. But with free drainage to his wound it could be hoped that he would soon recover. Hornblower was tired now, as a result of his sleepless night the night before, and his emotions had been jarred into a muddle by what he had had to do; it was easier to sleep tonight, waking only at intervals to listen to Bush's breathing, and to sleep again reassured by the steadiness and tranquillity of the sound.

Chapter VI

AFTER that day the details of the journey became more blurred and indistinct — up to that day they had had all the unnatural sharpness of a landscape just before rain. Looking back at the journey, what was easiest to remember was Bush's convalescence — his steady progress back to health from the moment that the ligature was withdrawn from his wound. His strength began to come back fast, so fast that it would have been astonishing to anyone who did not know of his iron constitution and of the Spartan life he had always led. The transition was rapid between the time when his head had to be supported to allow him to drink and the time when he could sit himself up by his own unaided strength.

Hornblower could remember those details when he tried to, but all the rest was muddled and vague. There were memories of long hours spent at the carriage window, when it always seemed to be raining, and the rain wetted his face and hair. Those were hours spent in a sort of melancholy; Hornblower came to look back on them afterwards in the same way as someone recovered from insanity must look back on the blank days in the asylum. All the inns at which they stayed and the doctors who had attended to Bush were confused in his mind. He could remember the relentless regularity with which the kilometre figures displayed at the posting stations indicated the dwindling distance between them and Paris — Paris 525, Paris 383, Paris 287; somewhere at that point they changed from Route Nationale No. 9 to Route Nationale No. 7. Each day was bringing them nearer to Paris and death, and each day he sank farther into apathetic melancholy. Issoire, Clermont-Ferrand, Moulins; he read the names of the towns through which they passed without remembering them.

Autumn was gone now, left far behind down by the Pyrenees. Here winter had begun. Cold winds blew in melancholy fashion through the long avenues of leafless trees, and the fields were brown and desolate. At night he was sleeping heavily, tormented by dreams which he could not remember in the morning; his days he spent standing at the carriage window staring with sightless eyes over a dreary landscape where the chill rain fell. It seemed as if he had spent years consecutively in the leathery atmosphere of the coach, with the clatter of the horses' hoofs in his ears, and, visible in the tail of his eye, the burly figure of Caillard riding at the head of the escort close to the offside hind wheel.

During the bleakest afternoon they had yet experienced it did not seem as if Hornblower would be roused from his stupor even by the sudden unexpected stop which to a bored traveller might provide a welcome break in the monotony of travel. Dully, he watched Caillard ride up to ask the reason; dully, he gathered from the conversation that one of the coach horses had lost a shoe and had gone dead lame. He watched with indifference the unharnessing of the unfortunate brute, and heard without interest the unhelpful answers of a passing travelling salesman with a pack-mule of whom Caillard demanded the whereabouts of the nearest smith. Two gendarmes went off at a snail's pace down a side track, leading the crippled animal; with only three horses the coach started off again towards Paris.

Progress was slow, and the stage was a long one. Only rarely before had they travelled after dark, but here it seemed that night would overtake them long before they could reach the next town. Bush and Brown were talking quite excitedly about this remarkable mishap — Hornblower heard their cackle without noticing it, as a man long resident beside a waterfall no longer hears the noise of the fall. The darkness which was engulfing them was premature. Low black clouds covered the whole sky, and the note of the wind in the trees carried with it something of menace. Even Hornblower noted that, nor was it long before he noticed something else: that the rain beating upon his face was changing to sleet, and then from sleet to snow; he felt the big flakes upon his lips, and tasted them with his tongue. The gendarme who lit the lamps beside the driver's box revealed to them through the windows the front of his cloak caked thick with snow, shining faintly in the feeble light of the lamp. Soon the sound of the horses' feet was muffled and dull, the wheels could hardly be heard, and the pace of the coach diminished still further as it ploughed through the snow piling in the road. Hornblower could hear the coachman using his whip mercilessly upon his weary animals — they were heading straight into the piercing wind, and were inclined to take every opportunity to flinch away from it.

Hornblower turned back from the window to his subordinates inside the coach — the faint light which the glass front panel allowed to enter from the lamps was no more than enough to enable him just to make out their shadowy forms. Bush was lying huddled under all his blankets; Brown was clutching his cloak round him, and Hornblower for the first time noticed the bitter cold. He shut the coach window without a word, resigning himself to the leathery stuffiness of the interior. His dazed melancholy was leaving him without his being aware of it.

"God help sailors," he said, cheerfully, "on a night like this."

That drew a laugh from the others in the darkness — Hornblower just caught the note of pleased surprise in it which told him that they had noticed and regretted the black mood which had gripped him during the last few days, and were pleased with this first sign of his recovery. Resentfully he asked himself what they expected of him. They did not know, as he did, that death awaited him and Bush in Paris. What was the use of thinking and worrying, guarded as they were by Caillard and six gendarmes? With Bush a hopeless cripple, what chance was there of escape? They did not know that Hornblower had put aside all thought of escaping by himself. If by a miracle he had succeeded, what would they think of him in England when he arrived there with the news that he had left his lieutenant to die? They might sympathise with him, pity him, understand his motive — he hated the thought of any of that; better to face a firing party at Bush's side, never to see Lady Barbara again, never to see his child. And better to spend his last few days in apathy than in fretting. Yet the present circumstances, so different from the monotony of the rest of the journey, had stimulated him. He laughed and chatted with the others as he had not done since they left Béziers.

The coach crawled on through the darkness with the wind shrieking overhead. Already the windows on one side were opaque with the snow which was plastered upon them — there was not warmth enough within the coach to melt it. More than once the coach halted, and Hornblower, putting his head out, saw that they were having to clear the horses' hoofs of the snow balled into ice under their shoes.

"If we're more than two miles from the next posthouse," he announced, sitting back again, "we won't reach it until next week."

Now they must have topped a small rise, for the horses were moving quicker, almost trotting, with the coach swaying and lurching over the inequalities of the road. Suddenly from outside they heard an explosion of shouts and yells.

"*Hé, hé, hé!*"

The coach swung round without warning, lurching frightfully, and came to a halt leaning perilously over to one side. Hornblower sprang to the window and looked out. The coach was poised perilously on the brink of a river; Hornblower could see the black water sliding along almost under his nose. Two yards away a small rowing boat, moored to a post, swayed about under the influence of wind and stream. Otherwise there was nothing to be seen in the blackness. Some of the gendarmes had run to the coach horses' heads; the animals were plunging and rearing in their fright at the sudden apparition of the river before them.

Somehow in the darkness the coach must have got off the road and gone down some side track leading to the river here; the coachman had reined his horses round only a fraction of a second before disaster threatened. Caillard was sitting his horse blaring sarcasms at the others.

"A fine coachman you are, God knows. Why didn't you drive straight into the river and save me the trouble of reporting you to the sous-chef of the administration? Come along, you men. Do you want to stay here all night? Get the coach back to the road, you fools."

The snow came driving down in the darkness, the hot lamps sizzling continuously as the flakes lighted on them. The coachman got his horses under control again, the gendarmes stood back, and the whip cracked. The horses plunged and slipped, pawing for a footing, and the coach trembled without stirring from the spot.

"Come along, now!" shouted Caillard. "Sergeant, and you, Pellaton, take the horses. You other men get to the wheels! Now, altogether. Heave! Heave!"

The coach lurched a scant yard before halting again. Caillard cursed wildly.

"If the gentlemen in the coach would descend and help," suggested one of the gendarmes, "it would be better."

"They can, unless they would rather spend the night in the snow," said Caillard; he did not condescend to address Hornblower directly. For a moment Hornblower thought of telling him that he would see him damned first — there would be some satisfaction in that — but on the other hand he did not want to condemn Bush to a night of discomfort merely for an intangible self-gratification.

"Come on, Brown," he said, swallowing his resentment, and he opened the door and they jumped down into the snow.

Even with the coach thus lightened, and with five men straining at the spokes of the wheels, they could make no progress. The snow had piled up against the steep descent to the river, and the exhausted horses plunged uselessly in the deep mass.

"God, what a set of useless cripples!" raved Caillard. "Coachman, how far is it to Nevers?"

"Six kilometres, sir."

"You mean you think it's six kilometres. Ten minutes ago you thought you were on the high road and you were not. Sergeant, ride into Nevers for help. Find the mayor, and bring every able-bodied man in the name of the Emperor. You, Ramel, ride with the sergeant as far as the high road, and wait there until he returns. Otherwise they'll never find us. Go on, sergeant, what are you waiting for? And you others, tether your horses and put your cloaks on their backs. You can keep warm digging the snow away from that bank. Coachman, come off that box and help them."

The night was incredibly dark. Two yards from the carriage

lamps nothing was visible at all, and with the wind whistling by they could not hear, as they stood by the coach, the movement of the men in the snow. Hornblower stamped about beside the coach and flogged himself with his arms to get his circulation back. Yet this snow and this icy wind were strangely refreshing. He felt no desire at the moment for the cramped stuffiness of the coach. And as he swung his arms an idea came to him, which checked him suddenly in his movements, until, ridiculously afraid of his thoughts being guessed, he went on stamping and swinging more industriously than ever. The blood was running hot under his skin now, as it always did when he was making plans — when he had outmanœuvred the *Natividad*, for instance, and when he had saved the *Pluto* in the storm off Cape Creus.

There had been no hope of escape without the means of transporting a hopeless cripple; now, not twenty feet from him, there was the ideal means — the boat which rocked at its moorings at the river bank. On a night like this it was easy to lose one's way altogether — except in a boat on a river; in a boat one had only to keep shoving off from shore to allow the current to carry one away faster than any horse could travel in these conditions. Even so, the scheme was utterly harebrained. For how many days would they be able to preserve their liberty in the heart of France, two ablebodied men and one on a stretcher? They would freeze, starve — possibly even drown. But it was a chance, and nothing nearly as good would present itself (as far as Hornblower could judge from his past observations) between now and the time when the firing party at Vincennes would await them. Hornblower observed with mild interest that his fever was abating as he formed his resolve; and he was sufficiently amused at finding his jaw set in an expression of fierce resolution to allow his features to relax into a grim smile. There was always something laughable to him in being involved in heroics.

Brown came stamping round the coach and Hornblower addressed him, contriving with a great effort to keep his voice low and yet matter-of-fact.

"We're going to escape down the river in that boat, Brown," he said.

"Aye aye, sir," said Brown, with no more excitement in his voice than if Hornblower had been speaking of the cold. Hornblower saw his head in the darkness turn towards the nearly invisible figure of Caillard, pacing restlessly in the snow beside the coach.

"That man must be silenced," said Hornblower.

"Aye aye, sir." Brown meditated for a second before continuing. "Better let me do that, sir."

"Very good."

"Now, sir?"

"Yes."

Brown took two steps towards the unsuspecting figure.

"Here," he said. "Here, you."

Caillard turned and faced him, and as he turned he received Brown's fist full on his jaw, in a punch which had all Brown's mighty fourteen stone behind it. He dropped in the snow, with Brown leaping upon him like a tiger, Hornblower behind him.

"Tie him up in his cloak," whispered Hornblower. "Hold on to his throat while I get it unbuttoned. Wait. Here's his scarf. Tie his head up in that first."

The sash of the Legion of Honour was wound round and round the wretched man's head. Brown rolled the writhing figure over and with his knee in the small of his back tied his arms behind him with his neckcloth. Hornblower's handkerchief sufficed for his ankles — Brown strained the knot tight. They doubled the man in two and bundled him into his cloak, tying it about him with his swordbelt. Bush, lying on his stretcher in the darkness of the coach, heard the door open and a heavy load drop upon the floor.

"Mr. Bush," said Hornblower, — the formal "Mr." came naturally again now the action had begun again, — "we are going to escape in the boat."

"Good luck, sir," said Bush.

"You're coming too. Brown, take that end of the stretcher. Lift. Starboard a bit. Steady."

Bush felt himself lifted out of the coach, stretcher and all, and carried down through the snow.

"Get the boat close in," snapped Hornblower. "Cut the moorings. Now, Bush, let's get these blankets round you. Here's my cloak, take it as well. You'll obey orders, Mr. Bush. Take the other side, Brown. Lift him into the stern-sheets. Lower away. Bow thwart, Brown. Take the oars. Right. Shove off. Give way."

It was only six minutes from the time when Hornblower had first conceived the idea. Now they were free, adrift on the black river, and Caillard was gagged and tied into a bundle on the floor of the coach. For a fleeting moment Hornblower wondered whether Caillard would suffocate before being discovered, and he found himself quite indifferent in the matter. Bonaparte's personal aides-de-camp, especially if they were colonels of gendarmerie as well, must expect to run risks while doing the dirty work which their situation would bring them. Meanwhile he had other things to think about.

"Easy!" he hissed at Brown. "Let the current take her."

The night was absolutely black; seated on the stern thwart he could not even see the surface of the water overside. For that matter, he did not know what river it was. But every river runs to the sea. The sea! Hornblower writhed in his seat in wild nostalgia at a vivid recollection of sea breezes in his nostrils and the feel of a heaving deck under his feet. Mediterranean or Atlantic, he did not know which, but if they had fantastic luck they might reach the sea in this boat by following the river far enough, and the sea was England's and would bear them home, to life instead of death, to freedom instead of imprisonment, to Lady Barbara, to Maria and his child.

The wind shrieked down on them, driving snow down his neck — thwarts and bottom boards were thick with snow. He felt the boat swing round under the thrust of the wind, which was in his face now instead of on his cheek.

"Turn her head to wind, Brown," he ordered, "and pull slowly into it."

The surest way of allowing the current a free hand with them was to try to neutralise the effect of the wind — a gale like this would soon blow them on shore, or even possibly blow them upstream; in this blackness it was impossible to guess what was happening to them.

"Comfortable, Mr. Bush?" he asked.

"Aye aye, sir."

Bush was faintly visible now, for the snow had driven up already against the grey blankets that swathed him and could just be seen from where Hornblower sat, a yard away.

"Would you like to lie down?"

"Thank you, sir, but I'd rather sit."

Now that the excitement of the actual escape was over, Hornblower found himself shivering in the keen wind without his cloak. He was about to tell Brown that he would take one of the sculls when Bush spoke again.

"Pardon, sir, but d'you hear anything?"

Brown rested on his oars, and they sat listening.

"No," said Hornblower — "Yes I do, by God!"

Underlying the noise of the wind there was a distant monotonous roaring.

"*H'm,*" said Hornblower, uneasily.

The roar was growing perceptibly louder; now it rose several notes in the scale, suddenly, and they could distinguish the sound of running water. Something appeared in the darkness beside the boat; it was a rock nearly covered, rendered visible in the darkness by the boiling white foam round it. It came and was gone in a flash, the clearest proof of the speed with which the boat was travelling.

"Jesus!" said Brown in the bows.

Now the boat was spinning round, lurching, jolting. All the water was white overside, and the bellowing of the rapid was deafening. They could do no more than sit and cling to their seat as the boat heaved and jerked. Hornblower shook himself free from his dazed helplessness, which seemed to have lasted half an hour and probably had lasted no more than a couple of seconds.

"Give me a scull," he snapped at Brown. "You fend off port side. I'll take starboard."

He groped in the darkness, found a scull, and took it from Brown's hand; the boat spun, hesitated, plunged again. All about them was the roar of the rapid. The starboard side of the boat caught on a rock; Hornblower felt icy water deluge his legs as it poured in over the side behind him. But already he was thrusting madly and blindly with his scull against the rock, he felt the boat slip and swing, he thrust so that the swing was accentuated, and next moment they were clear, wallowing sluggishly with the water up to the thwarts. Another rock slid hissing past, but the roar of the fall was already dwindling.

"Christ!" said Bush, in a mild tone contrasting oddly with the blasphemy. "We're through!"

"D'you know if there's a bailer in the boat, Brown?" demanded Hornblower.

"Yessir, there was one at my feet when I came on board."

"Find it and get this water out. Give me your other scull."

Brown splashed about in the icy water in a manner piteous to hear as he groped for the floating wooden basin.

"Got it, sir," he reported, and they heard the regular sound of the water being scooped overside as he began work.

In the absence of the distraction of the rapids they were conscious of the wind again now, and Hornblower turned the boat's bows into it and pulled slowly at the sculls. Past experience appeared to have demonstrated conclusively that this was the best way to allow the current a free hand to take the boat downstream and away from pursuit. Judging by the speed with which the noise of the rapids was left behind, the current of this river was very fast indeed — that was only to be expected, too, for all the rain of the past few days must have brought up every river brim full. Hornblower wondered vaguely again what river this was, here in the heart of France. The only one with whose name he was acquainted and which it might possibly be was the Rhone, but he felt a suspicion that the Rhone was fifty miles or so farther eastward. This river presumably had taken its origin in the gaunt Cevennes, whose flanks they had turned in the last two days' journey. In that case it would run northward, and must presumably turn westward to find the sea — it must be the Loire or one of its tributaries. And the Loire fell into the Bay of Biscay, below Nantes, which must be at least four hundred miles away.

Hornblower's imagination dallied with the idea of a river four hundred miles long, and with the prospect of descending it from source to mouth in the depth of winter.

A ghostly sound as if from nowhere brought him back to earth again. As he tried to identify it it repeated itself more loudly and definitely, and the boat lurched and hesitated. They were gliding over a bit of rock which providence had submerged to a depth sufficient just to scrape their keel. Another rock, foam-covered, came boiling past them close overside. It passed them from stern to bow, telling him what he had no means of discovering in any other way in the blackness: that in this reach the river must be running westward, for the wind was in the east and he was pulling into it.

"More of those to come yet, sir," said Bush — already they could hear the growing roar of water among rocks.

"Take a scull and watch the port side, Brown," said Hornblower.

"Aye aye, sir. I've got the boat nearly dry," volunteered Brown, feeling for the scull.

The boat was lurching again now, dancing a little in the madness of the river. Hornblower felt bow and stern lift successively as they dropped over what felt like a downward step in the water; he reeled as he stood, and the water remaining in the bottom of the boat surged and splashed against his ankles. The din of the rapid in the darkness round them was tremendous; white water was boiling about them on either side. The boat swung and pitched and rolled. Then something invisible struck the port side amidships with a splintering crash. Brown tried unavailingly to shove off, and Hornblower swung round and with his added strength forced the boat clear. They plunged and rolled again; Hornblower, feeling in the darkness, found the gunwale stove in, but apparently only the two upper strakes were damaged — chance might have driven that rock through below the waterline as easily as it had done above it. Now the keel seemed to have caught; the boat heeled hideously, with Bush and Hornblower falling on their noses, but she freed herself and went on through the roaring water. The noise was dying down again and they were through another rapid.

"Shall I bail again, sir?" asked Brown.

"Yes. Give me your scull."

"Light on the starboard bow, sir!" interjected Bush.

Hornblower craned over his shoulder. Undoubtedly it was a light, with another close beside it, and another farther on, barely visible on the driving snow. That must be a village on the river bank, or a town — the town of Nevers, six kilometres, according to the coachman, from where they had embarked. They had come four miles already.

"Silence now!" hissed Hornblower. "Brown, stop bailing."

With those lights to guide him in the darkness, stable permanent things in this insane world of infinite indefiniteness, it was marvellous how he felt master of his fate once more. He knew again which was upstream and which was down — the wind was still blowing downstream. With a touch of the sculls he turned the boat downstream, wind and current sped her along fast, and the lights were gliding by rapidly. The snow stung his face — it was hardly likely there would be anyone in the town to observe them on a night like this. Certainly the boat must have come down the river faster than the plodding horses of the gendarmes whom Caillard had sent ahead. A new roaring of water caught his ear, different in timbre from the sound of a rapid. He craned round again to see the bridge before them, silhouetted in white against the blackness by reason of the snow driven against the arches. He tugged wildly, first at one scull and then at both, heading for the centre of an arch; he felt the bow dip and the stern heave as they approached — the water was banked up above the bridge and rushed down through the arches in a long sleek black slope. As they whirled under, Hornblower bent to his sculls, to give the boat sufficient way to carry her through the eddies which his seaman's instinct warned him would await them below the piers. The crown of the arch brushed his head as he pulled — the floods had risen as high as that. The sound of rushing water echoed strangely under the stonework for a second;

and then they were through, with Hornblower tugging madly at the sculls.

One more light on the shore, and then they were in utter blackness again, their sense of direction lost.

"Christ!" said Bush again, this time with utter solemnity, as Hornblower rested on his sculls. The wind shrieked down upon them, blinding them with snow. From the bows came a ghostly chuckle.

"God help sailors," said Brown, "on a night like this."

"Carry on with the bailing, Brown, and save your jokes for afterwards," snapped Hornblower. But he giggled, nevertheless, even despite the faint shock he experienced at hearing the lower deck cracking jokes to a captain and a first lieutenant. His ridiculous habit of laughing insanely in the presence of danger or hardship was always ready to master him, and he giggled now, while he dragged at the oars and fought against the wind — he could tell by the way the blades dragged through the water that the boat was making plenty of leeway. He stopped giggling only when he realised with a shock that it was hardly more than two hours back that he had first uttered the prayer about God helping sailors on a night like this. It seemed like a fortnight ago at least that he had last breathed the leathery stuffiness of the inside of the coach.

The boat grated heavily over gravel, caught, freed itself, bumped again, and stuck fast. All Hornblower's shoving with the sculls would not get her afloat again.

"Nothing to do but shove her off," said Hornblower, laying down his sculls.

He stepped over the side into the freezing water, slipping on the stones, with Brown beside him. Between them they ran her out easily, scrambled on board, and Hornblower made haste to seize the sculls and pull into the wind. Yet a few seconds later they were aground again. It was the beginning of a nightmare period. In the darkness Hornblower could not guess whether their difficulties arose from the action of the wind in pushing them against the bank, or from the fact that the river was sweeping round in a great bend here, or whether they had strayed into a side channel with scanty water. However it was, they were continually having to climb out and shove the boat off. They slipped and plunged over the invisible stones; they fell waist-deep into unseen pools, they cut themselves and bruised themselves in this mad game of blind-man's-buff with the treacherous river. It was bitterly cold now; the sides of the boat were glazed with ice. In the midst of his struggles with the boat Hornblower was consumed with anxiety for Bush, bundled up in cloak and blankets in the stern.

"How is it with you, Bush?" he asked.

"I'm doing well, sir," said Bush.

"Warm enough?"

"Aye aye, sir. I've only one foot to get wet now, you know, sir."

He was probably being deceitfully cheerful, thought Hornblower, standing ankle-deep in rushing water and engaged in what seemed to be an endless haul of the boat through invisible shallows. Blankets or no blankets, he must be horribly cold and probably wet as well, and he was a convalescent who ought to have been kept in bed. Bush might die out here this very night. The boat came free with a run, and Hornblower staggered back waist-deep in the chill water. He swung himself in over the swaying gunwale while Brown, who apparently had been completely submerged, came spluttering in over the other side. Each of them grabbed a scull in their anxiety to have something to do while the wind cut them to the bone.

The current whirled them away. Their next contact with the shore was among trees — willows, Hornblower guessed in the darkness. The branches against which they scraped volleyed snow at them, scratched them and whipped them, held the boat fast until by feeling round in the darkness they found the obstruction and lifted it clear. By the time they were free of the willows Hornblower had almost decided that he would rather have rocks if he could choose, and he giggled again, feebly, with his teeth chattering. Naturally, they were among rocks again quickly enough; at this point apparently there was a sort of minor rapid down which the river rolled among rocks and banks of stones.

Already Hornblower was beginning to form a mental picture of the river — long swift reaches alternating with narrow and rock-encumbered stretches, looped back and forth at the whim of the surrounding country. This boat they were in had probably been built close to the spot where they had found her, had been kept there as a ferry boat, probably by farming people, on the clear reach where they had started, and had probably never been more than a half a mile from her moorings before. Hornblower, shoving off from a rock, decided that the odds were heavily against her ever seeing her moorings again.

Below the rapid they had a long clear run — Hornblower had no means of judging how long. Their eyes were quick now to pick out the snow-covered shore when it was a yard or more away, and they kept the boat clear. Every glimpse gave them a chance to guess at the course of the river compared with the direction of the wind, so that they could pull a few lusty strokes without danger of running aground as long as there were no obstructions in mid-channel. In fact, it had almost stopped snowing — Hornblower guessed that what little snow was being flung at them by the wind had been blown from branches or scooped from drifts. That did not make it any warmer; every part of the boat was coated with ice — the floorboards were slippery with it except where his heels rested while rowing.

Ten minutes of this would carry them a mile or more — more for certain. He could not guess at all how long they had been travelling, but he could be sure that with the countryside under thick snow they were well ahead of any possible pursuit, and the longer this wonderful rock-free reach endured the safer they would be. He tugged away fiercely, and Brown in the bows responded, stroke for stroke.

"Rapids ahead, sir," said Bush at length.

Resting on his oar Hornblower could hear, far ahead, the familiar roar of water pouring over rocks; the present rate of progress had been too good to last, and soon they would be whirling down among rocks again, pitching and heaving.

"Stand by to fend off on the port side, Brown," he ordered.

"Aye aye, sir."

Hornblower sat on his thwart with his scull poised; the water was sleek and black overside. He felt the boat swing round. The current seemed to be carrying her over to one side, and he was content to let her go. Where the main mass of water made its way was likely to be the clearest channel down the rapid. The roar of the fall was very loud now.

"By God!" said Hornblower in sudden panic, standing up to peer ahead.

It was too late to save themselves — he had noticed the difference in the sound of the fall only when they were too close to escape. Here there was no rapid like those they had already descended, not even one much worse. Here there was a rough dam across the river — a natural transverse ledge, perhaps, which had caught and retained the rocks rolled down in the bed, or else something of human construction. Hornblower's quick brain turned these hypotheses over even as the boat leaped at the drop. Along its whole length water was brimming over the obstruction; at this particular point it surged over in a wide swirl, sleek at the top, and plunging into foaming chaos below. The boat heaved sickeningly over the summit and went down the slope like a bullet. The steep steady wave at the foot was as unyielding as a brick wall as they crashed into it.

Hornblower found himself strangling under the water, the fall still roaring in his ears, his brain still racing. In nightmare helplessness he was scraped over the rocky bottom. The pressure in his lungs began to hurt him. It was agony — agony. Now he was breathing again — one single gulp of air like fire in his throat as he went under again, and down to the rocks at the bottom until his breast was hurting worse than before. Then another quick breath — it was as painful to breathe as it was to strangle. Over and down, his ears roaring and his head swimming. The grinding of the rocks of the river bed over which he was scraped was louder than any clap of thunder he had ever heard. Another gulp of air — it was as if he had been anticipating it, but he had to force himself to make it, for he felt as if it would be easier not to, easier to allow this agony in his breast to consume him.

Down again, to the roar and torment below the surface. His

brain, still working like lightning, guessed how it was with him. He was caught in the swirl below the dam, was being swept downstream on the surface, pushed into the undertow and carried up again along the bottom, to be spewed up and granted a second in which to breathe before being carried round again. He was ready this time to strike out feebly, no more than three strokes, sideways, at his next breathing space. When he was next sucked down the pain in his breast was inconceivably greater, and blending with that agony was another just as bad of which he now became conscious — the pain of the cold in his limbs. It called for every scrap of his resolution to force himself to take another breath and to continue his puny effort sideways when the time came for it. Down again; he was ready to die, willing, anxious to die, now, so that this pain would stop. A bit of board had come into his hand, with nails protruding from one end. That must be a plank from the boat, shattered to fragments and whirling round and round with him, eternally. Then his resolution flickered up once more. He caught a gulp of air as he rose to the surface, striking out for the shore, waiting in apprehension to be dragged down. Marvellous; he had time for a second breath, and a third. Now he wanted to live, so heavenly were these painless breaths he was taking. But he was so tired, and so sleepy. He got to his feet, fell as the water swept his legs away again from under him, splashed and struggled in mad panic, scrambling through the shallows on his hands and knees. Rising, he took two more steps, before falling with his face in the snow and his feet still trailing in the rushing water.

He was roused by a human voice bellowing, apparently in his ear. Lifting his head he saw a faint dark figure a yard or two away, bellowing with Brown's voice:

"Ahoy! Cap'n, Cap'n! Oh, Cap'n!"

"I'm here," moaned Hornblower, and Brown came and knelt over him.

"Thank God, sir," he said, and then, raising his voice, "The cap'n's here, Mr. Bush."

"Good!" said a feeble voice five yards away.

At that Hornblower fought down his nauseating weakness and

sat up. If Bush was still alive he must be looked after at once. He must be naked and wet, exposed in the snow to this cutting wind. Hornblower reeled to his feet, staggered, clutched Brown's arm, and stood with his brain whirling.

"There's a light up there, sir," said Brown, hoarsely. "I was just goin' to it if you hadn't answered my hail."

"A light?"

Hornblower passed his hands over his eyes and peered up the bank. Undoubtedly it was a light shining faintly, perhaps a hundred yards away. To go there meant surrender — that was the first reaction of Hornblower's mind. But to stay here meant death. Even if by a miracle they could light a fire and survive the night here they would be caught next morning — and Bush would be dead for certain. There had been a faint chance of life when he planned the escape from the coach, and now it was gone.

"We'll carry Mr. Bush up," he said.

"Aye aye, sir."

They plunged through the snow to where Bush lay.

"There's a house just up the bank, Bush. We'll carry you there."

Hornblower was puzzled by his ability to think and to speak while he felt so weak; the ability seemed unreal, fictitious.

"Aye aye, sir."

They stooped and lifted him between them, linking hands under his knees and behind his back. Bush put his arms round their necks; his flannel nightshirt dripped a further stream of water as they lifted him. Then they started trudging, knee-deep in the snow, up the bank towards the distant light.

They stumbled over obstructions hidden in the snow. They slipped and staggered. Then they slid down a bank and fell, altogether, and Bush gave a cry of pain.

"Hurt, sir?" asked Brown.

"Only jarred my stump. Captain, leave me here and send down help from the house."

Hornblower could still think. Without Bush to burden them they might reach the house a little quicker, but he could imagine all the delays that would ensue after they had knocked at the door — the explanations which would have to be made in his halting French, the hesitation and the time-wasting before he could get a carrying party started off to find Bush — who meanwhile would be lying wet and naked in the snow. A quarter of an hour of it would kill Bush, and he might be exposed for twice as long as that. And there was the chance that there would be no one in the house to help carry him.

"No," said Hornblower cheerfully. "It's only a little way. Lift, Brown."

They reeled along through the snow towards the light. Bush was a heavy burden — Hornblower's head was swimming with fatigue and his arms felt as if they were being dragged out of their sockets. Yet somehow within the shell of his fatigue the inner kernel of his brain was still active and restless.

"How did you get out of the river?" he asked, his voice sounding flat and unnatural in his ears.

"Current took us to the bank at once, sir," said Bush, faintly surprised. "I'd only just kicked my blankets off when I touched a rock, and there was Brown beside me hauling me out."

"Oh," said Hornblower.

The whim of a river in flood was fantastic; the three of them had been within a yard of each other when they entered the water, and he had been dragged under while the other two had been carried to safety. They could not guess at his desperate struggle for life, and they would never know of it, for he would never be able to tell them about it. He felt for the moment a bitter sense of grievance against them, resulting from his weariness and his weakness. He was breathing heavily, and he felt as if he would give a fortune to lay down his burden and rest for a couple of minutes; but his pride forbade, and they went on through the snow, stumbling over the inequalities below the surface. The light was coming near at last.

They heard a faint inquiring bark from a dog.

"Give 'em a hail, Brown," said Hornblower.

"Ahoy!" roared Brown. "House ahoy!"

Instantly two dogs burst into a clamorous barking.

"Ahoy!" yelled Brown again, and they staggered on. Another

light flashed into view from another part of the house. They seemed to be in some kind of garden now; Hornblower could feel plants crushing under his feet in the snow, and the thorns of a rose tree tore at his trouser-leg. The dogs were barking furiously. Suddenly a voice came from a dark upper window.

"Who is there?" it asked in French.

Hornblower prodded at his weary brain to find words to reply.

"Three men," he said. "Wounded."

That was the best he could do.

"Come nearer," said the voice, and they staggered forward, slipped down an unseen incline, and halted in the square of light cast by the big lighted window in the ground floor, Bush in his nightshirt resting in the arms of the bedraggled other two.

"Who are you?"

"Prisoners of war," said Hornblower.

"Wait one moment, if you please," said the voice, politely.

They stood shuddering in the snow until a door opened near the lighted window, showing a bright rectangle of light and some human silhouettes.

"Come in, gentlemen," said the polite voice.

Chapter VII

THE door opened into a stone-flagged hall; a tall thin man in a blue coat with a glistening white cravat stood there to welcome them, and at his side was a young woman, her shoulders bare in the lamplight. There were three others, too — maidservants and a butler, Hornblower fancied vaguely, as he advanced into the hall under the burden of Bush's weight. On a side table the lamplight caught the ivory butts of a pair of pistols, evidently laid there by their host on his deciding that his nocturnal visitors were harmless. Hornblower and Brown halted again for a moment, ragged and dishevelled and daubed with snow, and water began to trickle at once to the floor from their soaking garments; and Bush was between them, one foot in a grey worsted sock sticking out under the hem of his flannel nightshirt. Hornblower's constitutional weakness almost overcame him again and he had to struggle hard to keep himself from giggling as he wondered how these people were explaining to themselves the arrival of a nightshirted cripple out of a snowy night.

At least his host had sufficient self-control to show no surprise.

"Come in, come in," he said. He put his hand to a door beside him and then withdrew it. "You will need a better fire than I can offer you in the drawing-room. Felix, show the way to the kitchen — I trust you gentlemen will pardon my receiving you there? This way, sirs. Chairs, Felix, and send the maids away."

It was a vast low-ceilinged room, stone-flagged like the hall. Its grateful warmth was like Paradise; in the hearth glowed the remains of a fire, and all round them kitchen utensils winked and glittered. The woman without a word piled fresh billets of wood upon the fire and set to work with bellows to work up a blaze. Hornblower noticed the glimmer of her silk dress; her piled-up hair was golden, nearly auburn.

"Cannot Felix do that, Marie, my dear? Very well, then. As

you will," said their host. "Please sit down, gentlemen. Wine, Felix."

They lowered Bush into a chair before the fire. He sagged and wavered in his weakness, and they had to support him; their host clucked in sympathy.

"Hurry with those glasses, Felix, and then attend to the beds. A glass of wine, sir? And for you, sir? Permit me."

The woman he had addressed as "Marie" had risen from her knees, and withdrew silently; the fire was crackling bravely amid its battery of roasting spits and cauldrons. Hornblower was shivering uncontrollably, nevertheless, in his dripping clothes. The glass of wine he drank was of no help to him; the hand he rested on Bush's shoulder shook like a leaf.

"You will need dry clothes," said their host. "If you will permit me I will — "

He was interrupted by the reentrance of the butler and Marie, both of them with their arms full of clothes and blankets.

"Admirable!" said their host. "Felix, you will attend these gentlemen. Come, my dear."

The butler held a silken nightshirt to the blaze while Hornblower and Brown stripped Bush of his wet clothes and chafed him with a towel.

"I thought I should never be warm again," said Bush, when his head came out through the collar of the nightshirt. "And you, sir? You shouldn't have troubled about me. Won't you change your clothes now, sir? I'm all right."

"We'll see you comfortable first," said Hornblower. There was a fierce perverse pleasure in neglecting himself to attend to Bush. "Let me look at that stump of yours."

The blunt seamed end still appeared extraordinarily healthy. There was no obvious heat or inflammation when Hornblower took it in his hand, no sign of pus exuding from the scars. Felix found a cloth in which Hornblower bound it up, while Brown wrapped him about in a blanket.

"Lift him up now, Brown. We'll put him into bed."

Outside in the flagged hall they hesitated as to which way to turn, when Marie suddenly appeared from the left-hand door.

"In here," she said; her voice was a harsh contralto. "I have had a bed made up on the ground floor for the wounded man. I thought it would be more convenient."

One maid — a gaunt old woman, rather — had just taken a warming-pan from between the sheets; the other was slipping a couple of hot bottles into the bed. Hornblower was impressed by Marie's practical forethought. He tried with poor success to phrase his thanks in French while they lowered Bush into bed and covered him up.

"God, that's good, thank you, sir," said Bush.

They left him with a candle burning at his bedside — Hornblower was in a perfect panic now to strip off his wet clothes before that roaring kitchen fire. He towelled himself with a warm towel and slipped into a warm woollen shirt; standing with his bare legs toasting before the blaze he drank a second glass of wine. Fatigue and cold fell away from him, and he felt exhilarated and lightheaded as a reaction. Felix crouched before him tendering him a pair of trousers, and he stepped into them and suffered Felix to tuck in his shirttails and button him up — it was the first time since childhood that he had been helped into his trousers, but this evening it seemed perfectly natural. Felix crouched again to put on his socks and shoes, stood to buckle his stock and help him on with waistcoat and coat.

"Monsieur le Comte and Madame la Vicomtesse await monsieur in the drawing-room," said Felix — it was odd how, without a word of explanation, Felix had ascertained that Brown was of a lower social level. The very clothes he had allotted to Brown indicated that.

"Make yourself comfortable here, Brown," said Hornblower.

"Aye aye, sir," said Brown, standing at attention with his black hair in a rampant mass — only Hornblower had had an opportunity so far of using the comb.

Hornblower stepped in to look at Bush, who was already asleep, snoring faintly at the base of his throat. He seemed to have suffered no ill effects from his immersion and exposure — his iron frame must have grown accustomed to wet and cold during twenty five years at sea. Hornblower blew out the candle and softly closed the door, motioning to the butler to precede him. At the drawing-room door Felix asked Hornblower his name, and when he announced him Hornblower was oddly relieved to hear him make a sad hash of the pronunciation — it made Felix human again.

His host and hostess were seated on either side of the fire at the far end of the room, and the Count rose to meet him.

"I regret," he said, "that I did not quite hear the name which my major-domo announced."

"Captain Horatio Hornblower, of His Britannic Majesty's ship *Sutherland*," said Hornblower.

"It is the greatest pleasure to meet you, Captain," said the Count, side-stepping the difficulty of pronunciation with the agility to be expected of a representative of the old régime. "I am Lucien Antoine de Ladon, Comte de Graçay."

The men exchanged bows.

"May I present you to my daughter-in-law? Madame la Vicomtesse de Graçay."

"Your servant, ma'am," said Hornblower, bowing again, and then felt like a graceless lout because the English formula had risen to his lips by the instinct the action prompted. He hurriedly racked his brains for the French equivalent, and ended in a shamefaced mumble of "Enchanté."

The Vicomtesse had dark eyes in the maddest contrast with her nearly auburn hair. She was stoutly — one might almost say stockily — built, and was somewhere near thirty years of age, dressed in black silk which left sturdy white shoulders exposed. As she curtseyed her eyes met his in complete friendliness.

"And what is the name of the wounded gentleman whom we have the honour of entertaining?" she asked; even to Hornblower's unaccustomed ear her French had a different quality from the Count's.

"Bush," said Hornblower, grasping the import of the question with an effort. "First Lieutenant of my ship. I have left my servant, Brown, in the kitchen."

"Felix will see that he is comfortable," interposed the Count. "What of yourself, Captain? Some food? A glass of wine?"

"Nothing, thank you," said Hornblower. He felt in no need of food in this mad world, although he had not eaten since noon.

"Nothing, despite the fatigues of your journey?"

There could hardly be a more delicate allusion than that to Hornblower's recent arrival through the snow, drenched and battered.

"Nothing, thank you," repeated Hornblower.

"Will you not sit down, Captain?" asked the Vicomtesse.

They all three found themselves chairs.

"You will pardon us, I hope," said the Count, "if we continue to speak French. It is ten years since I last had occasion to speak English, and even then I was a poor scholar, while my daughter-in-law speaks none."

"Bush," said the Vicomtesse. "Brown. I can say those names. But your name, Captain, is difficult. Orrenblor — I cannot say it."

"Bush! Orrenblor!" exclaimed the Count, as though reminded of something. "I suppose you are aware, Captain, of what the French newspapers have been saying about you recently?"

"No," said Hornblower. "I should like to know, very much."

"Pardon me, then."

The Count took up a candle and disappeared through a door; he returned quickly enough to save Hornblower from feeling too self-conscious in the silence that ensued.

"Here are recent copies of the *Moniteur,*" said the Count. "I must apologise in advance, Captain, for the statements made in them."

He passed the newspapers over to Hornblower, indicating various columns in them. The first one briefly announced that a dispatch by semaphore just received from Perpignan informed the Ministry of Marine that an English ship of the line had been captured at Rosas. The next was the amplification. It proclaimed in triumphant detail that the hundred-gun ship *Sutherland* which had been committing acts of piracy in the Mediterranean had met a well-deserved fate at the hands of the Toulon fleet directed by Admiral Cosmao. She had been caught unawares and overwhelmed, and had "pusillanimously hauled down the colours of perfidious Albion under which she had committed so many dastardly crimes." The French public was assured that her resistance had been of the poorest, it being advanced in corroboration that only one French ship had lost a topmast during the cannonade. The action took place under the eyes of thousands of the Spanish populace, and would be a salutary lesson to those few among them who, deluded by English lies or seduced by English gold, still cherished notions of resistance to their lawful sovereign King Joseph.

Another article announced that the infamous Captain Hornblower and his equally wicked lieutenant, Bush, had surrendered in the *Sutherland,* the latter being one of the few wounded in the encounter. All those peace-loving French citizens who had suffered as a result of their piratical depredations could rest assured that a military court would inquire immediately into the crimes these two had committed. Too long had the modern Carthage sent forth her minions to execute her vile plans with impunity! Their guilt would soon be demonstrated to a world which would readily discriminate between the truth and the vile lies which the poisoned pens in Canning's pay so persistently poured forth.

Yet another article declared that as a result of Admiral Cosmao's great victory over the *Sutherland* at Rosas English naval action on the coasts of Spain had ceased, and the British army of Wellington, so imprudently exposed to the might of the French arms, was already suffering seriously from a shortage of supplies. Having lost one vile accomplice in the person of the detestable Hornblower, perfidious Albion was about to lose another on Wellington's inevitable surrender.

Hornblower read the smudgy columns in impotent fury. "A hundred-gun ship," forsooth, when the *Sutherland* was only a seventy four and almost the smallest of her rate in the list! "Resistance of the poorest"! "One topmast lost"! The *Sutherland* had beaten three bigger ships into wrecks and had disabled a fourth before surrendering. "One of the few wounded"! Two thirds of the *Sutherland's* crew had given life or limb, and with his own eyes he had seen the blood running from the scuppers of the French flagship. "English naval action had ceased"! There was not a hint that a fortnight after the capture of the *Sutherland* the whole French squadron had been destroyed in the night attack on Rosas Bay.

His professional honour had been impugned; the circumstantial lies had been well told, too — that subtle touch about only one topmast being lost had every appearance of verisimilitude. Europe might well believe that he was a poltroon as well as a pirate, and he had not the slightest chance of contradicting what had been said. Even in England such reports must receive a little credit — most of the *Moniteur's* bulletins, especially the naval ones, were reproduced in the English press. Lady Barbara, Maria, his brother captains, must all be wondering at the present moment just how much credence should be given to the *Moniteur's* statements. Accustomed as the world might be to Bonaparte's exaggerations, people could hardly be expected to realise that in this case everything said — save for the bare statement of his surrender — had been completely untrue. His hands shook a little with the passion that consumed him, and he was conscious of the hot flush in his cheeks as he looked up and met the eyes of the others. It was hard to grope for his few French words while he was so angry.

"He is a liar!" he spluttered at length. "He dishonours me!"

"He dishonours everyone," said the Count, quietly.

"But this — but this — " said Hornblower, and then gave up the struggle to express himself in French. He remembered that while he was in captivity in Rosas he had realised that Bonaparte would publish triumphant bulletins regarding the capture of the *Sutherland*, and it was only weakness to be enraged by them now that he was confronted by them.

"Will you forgive me," asked the Count, "if I change the subject and ask you a few personal questions?"

"Certainly."

"I presume you have escaped from an escort which was taking you to Paris?"

"Yes," said Hornblower.

"Where did you escape?"

Hornblower tried to explain that it was at a point where a by-road ran down to the river's edge, six kilometres on the farther side of Nevers. Haltingly, he went on to describe the conditions of his escape, the silencing of Colonel Caillard, and the wild navigation of the river in the darkness.

"That must have been about six o'clock, I presume?" asked the Count.

"Yes."

"It is only midnight now, and you have come twenty kilometres. There is not the slightest chance of your escort seeking you here for some time. That is what I wanted to know. You will be able to sleep in tranquillity tonight, Captain."

Hornblower realised with a shock that he had long taken it for granted that he would sleep in tranquillity, at least as far as immediate recapture was concerned; the atmosphere of the house had been too friendly for him to feel otherwise. By way of reaction, he began to feel doubts.

"Are you going to — to tell the police we are here?" he asked; it was infernally difficult to phrase that sort of thing in a foreign language and avoid offence.

"On the contrary," said the Count, "I shall tell them, if they ask me, that you are not here. I hope you will consider yourself among friends in this house, Captain, and that you will make your stay here as long as is convenient to you."

"Thank you, sir. Thank you very much," stammered Hornblower.

"I may add," went on the Count, "that circumstances — it is too long a story to tell you — make it quite certain that the authorities will accept my statement that I know nothing of your whereabouts. To say nothing of the fact that I have the honour to be mayor of this commune, and so represent the Government, even though my *adjoint* does all the work of the position."

Hornblower noticed his wry smile as he used the word "honour," and tried to stammer a fitting reply, to which the Count listened politely. It was amazing, now Hornblower came to think about it, that chance should have led him to a house where he was welcomed and protected, where he might consider himself safe from pursuit, and sleep in peace. The thought of sleep made him realise that he was desperately tired, despite his excitement. The impassive face of the Count, and the friendly face of his daughter-in-law, gave no hint as to whether or not they too were tired; for a moment Hornblower wrestled with the problem which always presents itself the first evening of one's stay in a strange house — whether the guest should suggest going to bed or wait for a hint from his host. He made his resolve, and rose to his feet.

"You are tired," said the Vicomtesse — the first words she had spoken for some time.

"Yes," said Hornblower.

"I will show you your room, sir. Shall I ring for your servant? No?" said the Count.

Out in the hall, after Hornblower had bowed good-night, the Count indicated the pistols still lying on the side table.

"Perhaps you would care to have those at your bedside?" he asked politely. "You might feel safer?"

Hornblower was tempted, but finally he refused the offer. Two pistols would not suffice to save him from Bonaparte's police should they come for him.

"As you will," said the Count leading the way with a candle. "I loaded them when I heard your approach, because there was a chance that you were a party of *réfractaires* — young men who evade the conscription by hiding in the woods and mountains. Their number has grown considerably since the latest decree anticipating the conscription. But I quickly realised that no gang meditating mischief would proclaim its proximity with shouts. Here is your room, sir. I hope you will find here everything you require. The clothes you are wearing appear to fit so tolerably that perhaps you will continue to wear them tomorrow? Then I shall say good-night. I hope you will sleep well."

The bed was deliciously warm as Hornblower slid into it and closed the curtains. His thoughts were pleasantly muddled; disturbing memories of the appalling swoop of the little boat down the long black slope of water at the fall, and of his agonised battle for life in the water, were overridden by mental pictures of the Count's long, mobile face and of Caillard bundled in his cloak and dumped down upon the carriage floor. He did not sleep well, but he could hardly be said to have slept badly.

Chapter VIII

FELIX entered the next morning bearing a breakfast tray, and he opened the bed curtains while Hornblower lay dazed in his bed. Brown followed Felix, and while the latter arranged the tray on the bedside table he applied himself to the task of gathering together the clothes which Hornblower had flung down the night before, trying hard to assume the unobtrusive deference of a gentleman's servant. Hornblower sipped gratefully at the steaming coffee, and bit into the bread; Brown recollected another duty and hurried across to open the bedroom curtains.

"Gale's pretty nigh dropped, sir," he said. "I think what wind there's left is backing southerly, and we might have a thaw."

Through the deep windows of the bedroom Hornblower could see from his bed a wide landscape of dazzling white, falling steeply away down to the river which was black by contrast, appearing like a black crayon mark on white paper. Trees stood out starkly through the snow where the gale had blown their branches bare; down beside the river the willows there — some of them stood in the flood, with white foam at their feet — were still domed with white. Hornblower fancied he could hear the rushing of water, and was certain that he could hear the regular droning of the fall, the tumbling water at whose foot was just visible over the shoulder of the bank. Far beyond the river could be seen the snow-covered roofs of a few small houses.

"I've been in to Mr. Bush already, sir," said Brown — Hornblower felt a twinge of remorse at being too interested in the landscape to have a thought to spare for his lieutenant — "and he's all right an' sends you his best respects, sir. I'm goin' to help him shave after I've attended to you, sir."

"Yes," said Hornblower.

He felt deliciously languorous. He wanted to be idle and lazy. The present was a moment of transition between the miseries and dangers of yesterday and the unknown activities of today, and he wanted that moment to be prolonged on and on indefinitely; he wanted time to stand still, the pursuers who were seeking him on the other side of Nevers to be stilled into an enchanted rigidity while he lay here free from danger and responsibility. The very coffee he had drunk contributed to his ease by relieving his thirst without stimulating him to activity. He sank imperceptibly and delightfully into a vague day-dream; it was hateful of Brown to recall him to wakefulness again by a respectful shuffling of his feet.

"Right," said Hornblower, resigning himself to the inevitable.

He kicked off the bedclothes and rose to his feet, the hard world of the matter-of-fact closing round him, and his day-dreams vanishing like the cloud-colours of a tropical sunrise. As he shaved, and washed in the absurdly small basin in the corner, he contemplated grimly the prospect of prolonged conversation in French with his hosts. He grudged the effort it would involve, and he envied Bush his complete inability to speak any other tongue than English. Having to exert himself today loomed as large to his self-willed mind as the fact that he was doomed to death if he were caught again. He listened absent-mindedly to Bush's garrulity when he went in to visit him, and did nothing at all to satisfy his curiosity regarding the house in which they had found shelter, and the intentions of their hosts. Nor was his mood relieved by his pitying contempt for himself at thus working off his ill-temper on his unoffending lieutenant. He deserted Bush as soon as he decently could and went off in search of his hosts in the drawing-room.

The Vicomtesse alone was there, and she made him welcome with a smile.

"M. de Graçay is at work in his study," she explained. "You must be content with my entertaining you this morning."

To say even the obvious in French was an effort for Hornblower, but he managed to make the suitable reply, which the lady received with a smile. But conversation did not proceed smoothly, with Hornblower having laboriously to build up his sentences beforehand and to avoid the easy descent into Spanish which was liable to entrap him whenever he began to think in a foreign tongue. Nevertheless, the opening sentences regarding the storm last night, the snow in the fields, and the flood, elicited for Hornblower one interesting fact — that the river whose roar they could hear was the Loire, four hundred miles or more from its mouth in the Bay of Biscay. A few miles upstream lay the town of Nevers; a little way downstream the large tributary, the Allier, joined the Loire, but there was hardly a house and no village on the river in that direction for twenty miles as far as Pouilly — from whose vineyards had come the wine they had drunk last night.

"The river is only as big as this in winter," said the Vicomtesse. "In summer it dwindles away to almost nothing. There are places where one can walk across it, from one bank to the other. Then it is blue, and its banks are golden, but now it is black and ugly."

"Yes," said Hornblower.

He felt a peculiar tingling sensation down his thighs and calves as the words recalled his experience of the night before, the swoop over the fall and the mad battle in the flood. He and Bush and Brown might easily all be sodden corpses now, rolling among the rocks at the bottom of the river until the process of corruption should bring them to the surface.

"I have not thanked you and M. de Graçay for your hospitality," he said, picking his words with care. "It is very kind of the Count."

"Kind? He is the kindest man in the whole world. I can't tell you how good he is."

There was no doubting the sincerity of the Count's daughter-in-law as she made this speech; her wide humorous mouth parted and her dark eyes glowed.

"Really?" said Hornblower — the word *vraiment* slipped naturally from his lips now that some animation had come into the conversation.

"Yes, really. He is good all the way through. He is sweet and kind, by nature and not — not as a result of experience. He has never said a word to me, not once, not a word, about the disappointment I have caused him."

"You, madame?"

"Yes. Oh, isn't it obvious? I am not a great lady — Marcel should not have married me. My father is a Normandy peasant, on his own land, but a peasant all the same, while the Ladons, Counts of Graçay, go back to — to Saint Louis, or before that. Marcel told me how disappointed was the Count at our marriage, but I should never have known of it otherwise — not by word or by action. Marcel was the eldest son then, because Antoine had been killed at Austerlitz. And Marcel is dead, too, — he was wounded as Aspern, — and I have no son, no child at all, and the Count has never reproached me, never."

Hornblower tried to make some kind of sympathetic noise.

"And Louis-Marie is dead as well now. He died of fever in Spain. He was the third son, and M. de Graçay is the last of the Ladons. I think it broke his heart, but he has never said a bitter word."

"The three sons are all dead?" said Hornblower.

"Yes, as I told you. M. de Graçay was an émigré — he lived in your town of London with his children for years after the Revolution. And then the boys grew up and they heard of the fame of the Emperor — he was First Consul then — and they all wanted to share in the glory of France. It was to please them that the Count took advantage of the amnesty and returned here — this is all that the Revolution has left of his estates. He never went to Paris. What would he have in common with the Emperor? But he allowed his sons to join the army, and now they are all dead, Antoine and Marcel and Louis-Marie. Marcel married me when his regiment was billeted in our village, but the others never married. Louis-Marie was only eighteen when he died."

"*Terrible!*" said Hornblower.

The banal word did not express his sense of the pathos of the story, but it was all he could think of. He understood now the Count's statement of the night before that the authorities would be willing to accept his bare word that he had seen nothing of any escaped prisoners. A great gentleman whose three sons had died in the Imperial service would never be suspected of harbouring fugitives.

"Understand me," went on the Vicomtesse. "It is not because he hates the Emperor that he makes you welcome here. It is because he is kind, because you needed help — I have never known him deny help to anyone. Oh, it is hard to explain, but I think you understand."

"I understand," said Hornblower, gently.

His heart warmed to the Vicomtesse. She might be lonely and unhappy; she was obviously as hard as her peasant upbringing would make her, and yet her first thought was to impress upon this stranger the goodness and virtue of her father-in-law. With her nearly-red hair and dark eyes she was a striking-looking woman, and her skin had a thick creaminess which enhanced her looks; only a slight irregularity of feature and the wideness of her mouth prevented her from being of dazzling beauty. No wonder the young subaltern in the Hussars — Hornblower took it for granted that the dead Vicomte de Graçay had been a subaltern of Hussars — had fallen in love with her during the dreary routine of training, and had insisted on marrying her despite his father's opposition. Hornblower thought he would not find it hard to fall in love with her himself if he were mad enough to allow such a thing to happen while his life was in the hands of the Count.

"And you?" asked the Vicomtesse. "Have you a wife in England? Children?"

"I have a wife," said Hornblower.

Even without the handicap of a foreign language it was difficult to describe Maria to a stranger; he said that she was short and dark, and he said no more. Her red hands and dumpy figure, her loyalty to him which cloyed when it did not irritate — he could not venture on a fuller description lest he should betray the fact that he did not love her, and he had never betrayed it yet.

"So that you have no children either?" asked the Vicomtesse again.

"Not now," said Hornblower.

This was torment. He told of how little Horatio and little Maria had died of smallpox in a Southsea lodging, and then with a gulp he went on to say that there was another child due to be born in January next.

"Let us hope you will be home with your wife then," said the Vicomtesse. "Today you will be able to discuss plans of escape with my father-in-law."

As if this new mention of his name had summoned him, the Count came into the room on the tail of this sentence.

"Forgive my interrupting you," he said, even while he returned Hornblower's bow; "but from my study window I have just seen a gendarme approaching this house from a group which was riding along the river bank. Would it be troubling you too much, Captain, to ask you to go into Monsieur Bush's room for a time? I shall send your servant in to you, too, and perhaps then you would be good enough to lock the door. I shall interview the gendarme myself, and you will only be detained for a few minutes, I hope."

A gendarme! Hornblower was out of the room and was crossing over to Bush's door before this long speech was finished, while M. de Graçay escorted him thither, unruffled, polite, his words unhurried. Bush was sitting up in bed as Hornblower entered, but what he began to say was broken off by Hornblower's abrupt gesture demanding silence. A moment later Brown tapped at the door and was admitted, Hornblower carefully locking the door after him.

"What is it, sir?" whispered Bush, and Hornblower whispered an explanation, still standing with his hand on the handle, stooping to listen.

He heard a knocking on the outer door, and the rattling of chains as Felix went to open it. Feverishly he tried to hear the ensuing conversation, but he could not understand it. But the gendarme was speaking with respect, and Felix in the flat passionless tones of the perfect butler. He heard the tramp of booted feet and the ring of spurs as the gendarme was led into the hall, and then all the sounds died away with the closing of a door upon them. The minutes seemed like hours as he waited. Growing aware of his nervousness he forced himself to turn and smile at the others as they sat with their ears cocked, listening.

The wait was too long for them to preserve their tension; soon they relaxed, and grinned at each other, not with hollow mirth as Hornblower's had been at the start. At last a renewed burst of sound from the hall keyed them up again, and they stayed rigid listening to the penetrating voices. And then they heard the clash of the outside door shutting, and the voices ceased. Still it was a long time before anything more happened — five minutes — ten minutes, and then a tap on the door startled them as though it were a pistol shot.

"May I come in, Captain?" said the Count's voice.

Hurriedly Hornblower unlocked the door to admit him, and even then he had to stand and wait in feverish patience, translating awkwardly while the Count apologised to Bush for intruding upon him, and made polite inquiries about his health and whether he slept well.

"Tell him I slept nicely, if you please, sir," said Bush.

"I am delighted to hear it," said the Count. "Now in the matter of this gendarme — "

Hornblower brought forward a chair for him. He would not allow it to be thought that his impatience overrode his good manners.

"Thank you, Captain, thank you. You are sure I will not be intruding if I stay? That is good of you. The gendarme came to tell me — "

The narrative was prolonged by the need for interpreting to Bush and Brown. The gendarme was one of those posted at Nevers; every available man in that town had been turned out shortly before midnight by a furious Colonel Caillard to search for the fugitives. In the darkness they had been able to do little, but with the coming of the dawn Caillard had begun a systematic search of both banks of the river, seeking for traces of the prisoners and making inquiries at every house and cottage along the banks. The visit of the gendarme had been merely one of routine — he had come to ask if anything had been seen of three escaped Englishmen, and to give warning that they might be in the vicinity.

He had been perfectly satisfied with the Count's assurance upon the point. In fact, the gendarme had no expectation of finding the Englishmen alive. The search had already revealed a blanket, one of those which had been used by the wounded Englishman, lying on the bank down by the Bec d'Allier, which seemed a sure indication that their boat had capsized, in which case, with the river in flood, there could be no doubt that they had been drowned. Their bodies would be discovered somewhere along the course of the river during the next few days. The gendarme appeared to be of the opinion that the boat must have upset somewhere in the first rapid they had encountered, before they had gone a mile, so madly was the river running.

"I hope you will agree with me, Captain, that this information is most satisfactory," added the Count.

"Satisfactory!" said Hornblower. "Could it be better?"

If the French should believe them to be dead there would be an end of the pursuit. He turned and explained the situation to the others in English, and they endeavoured with nods and smiles to indicate to the Count their gratification.

"Perhaps Bonaparte in Paris will not be satisfied with this bald story," said the Count. "In fact I am sure he will not, and will order a further search. But it will not trouble us."

"Thank you, sir," said Hornblower, and the Count made a deprecatory gesture.

"It only remains," he said, "to make up our minds about what you gentlemen would find it best to do in the future. Would it be officious of me to suggest that it might be inadvisable for you to continue your journey while Lieutenant Bush is still unwell?"

"What does he say, sir?" asked Bush — the mention of his name had drawn all eyes on him. Hornblower explained.

"Tell his lordship, sir," said Bush, "that I can make myself a jury leg in two shakes, an' this time next week I'll be walking as well as he does."

"Excellent!" said the Count, when this had been translated and expurgated for him. "And yet I cannot see that the construction of a wooden leg is going to be of much assistance in our problem. You gentlemen might grow beards, or wear disguises. It was in my mind that by posing as German officers in the Imperial service you might, during your future journey, provide an excuse for your ignorance of French. But a missing foot cannot be disguised; for months to come the arrival of a stranger without a foot will recall to the minds of inquisitive police officers the wounded English officer who escaped and was believed to be drowned."

"Yes," said Hornblower. "Unless we could avoid all contact with police officers."

"That is quite impossible," said the Count with decision. "In this French Empire there are police officers everywhere. To travel you will need horses certainly, a carriage very probably. In a journey of a hundred leagues horses and a carriage will bring you for certain to the notice of the police. No man can travel ten miles along a road without having his passport examined."

The Count pulled in perplexity at his chin; the deep parentheses at the corners of his mobile mouth were more marked than ever.

"I wish," said Hornblower, "that our boat had not been destroyed last night. On the river, perhaps . . ."

The idea came up into his mind fully formed, and as it did so his eyes met the Count's. He was conscious afresh of a strange sympathy between him and the Count. The same idea was forming in the Count's mind, simultaneously — it was not the first time that he had noticed a similar phenomenon.

"Of course!" said the Count. "The river! How foolish of me not to think of it. As far as Orleans the river is unnavigable; because of the winter floods the banks are practically deserted save at the towns, and there are few of those, which you could pass at night if necessary, as you did at Nevers."

"Unnavigable, sir?"

"There is no commercial traffic. There are fishermen's boats here and there, and there are a few others engaged in dredging sand from the river bed. That is all. From Orleans to Nantes, Bonaparte has been making efforts to render the river available to barges, but I understand he has had small success. And above Briare the new lateral canal carries all the traffic, and the river is deserted."

"But could we descend it, sir?" persisted Hornblower.

"Oh, yes," said the Count, meditatively. "You could do so in summer, in a small rowing boat. There are many places where it would be difficult, but never dangerous."

"In summer!" exclaimed Hornblower.

"Why, yes. You must wait until the lieutenant here is well, and then you must build your boat — I suppose you sailors can build your own boat? You cannot hope to start for a long time. And then in January the river usually freezes, and in February come the floods, which last until March. Nothing could live on the river then — especially as it would be too cold and wet for you. It seems to be quite necessary that you should give me the pleasure of your company until April, Captain."

This was something entirely unexpected, this prospect of waiting for four months the opportunity to start. Hornblower was taken by surprise; he had supposed that a few days, three or four weeks at most, would see them on their way towards England again. For ten years he had never been as long as four months consecutively in the same place — for that matter during those ten years he had hardly spent four months on shore altogether. His mind sought unavailingly for alternatives. To go by road undoubtedly would involve horses, carriages, contact with all sorts of people. He could not hope to bring Bush and Brown successfully through. And if they went by river they obviously would have to wait; in four months Bush could be expected to make a complete recovery, and with the coming of summer they would be able to dispense with the shelter of inns or houses, sleeping on the river bank, avoiding all intercourse with Frenchmen, drifting downstream until they reached the sea.

"If you have fishing rods with you," supplemented the Count, "anyone observing you as you go past the towns will look on you as a fishing party out for the day. For some reason which I cannot fully analyse a fresh-water fisherman can never be suspected of evil intent — except possibly by the fish."

Hornblower nodded. It was odd that at that very moment he too had been visualising the boat drifting downstream, with rods out, watched by incurious eyes from the bank. It was the safest way of crossing France which he could imagine.

And yet — April? His child would be born. Lady Barbara might have forgotten that he ever existed.

"It seems monstrous," he said, "that you should be burdened with us all through the winter."

"I assure you, Captain, your presence will give the greatest pleasure both to Madame la Vicomtesse and to myself."

He could only yield to circumstances.

Chapter IX

Lieutenant Bush was watching Brown fastening the last strap of his new wooden leg, and Hornblower, from across the room, was watching the pair of them.

" 'Vast heaving," said Bush. "Belay."

Bush sat on the edge of his bed and moved his leg tentatively.

"Good," he said. "Give me your shoulder. Now, heave and wake the dead."

Hornblower saw Bush rise and stand; he watched his lieutenant's expression change to one of hurt wonderment as he clung to Brown's burly shoulders.

"God!" said Bush, feebly, — "how she heaves!"

It was the giddiness only to be expected after weeks of lying and sitting. Evidently to Bush the floor was pitching and tossing, and, judging by the movement of his eyes, the walls were circling round him. Brown stood patiently supporting him as Bush confronted this unexpected phenomenon. Hornblower saw Bush set his jaw, his expression hardening as he battled with his weakness.

"Square away," said Bush to Brown. "Set a course for the captain."

Brown began walking slowly towards Hornblower, Bush clinging to him, the leather-tipped end of the wooden leg falling with a thump on the floor at each effort to take a stride with it — Bush was swinging it too high, while his sound leg sagged at the knee in its weakness.

"God!" said Bush again. "Easy! Easy!"

Hornblower rose in time to catch him and to lower him into the chair, where Bush sat and gasped. His big white face, already unnaturally pale through long confinement, was whiter than ever. Hornblower remembered with a pang the old Bush, burly and self-confident, with a face which might have been roughhewn from a solid block of wood; the Bush who feared nothing and was prepared for anything. This Bush was frightened of his weakness. It had not occurred to him that he would have to learn to walk again — and that walking with a wooden leg was another matter still.

"Take a rest," said Hornblower, "before you start again."

Desperately anxious as Bush had been to be active, weary as he was of helplessness, there were times during the next few days when Hornblower had to give him encouragement while he was learning to walk. All the difficulties that arose had been unforeseen by him, and depressed him out of proportion to their importance. It was a matter of some days before he mastered his giddiness and weakness, and then as soon as he was able to use the wooden leg effectively they found all manner of things wrong with it. It was none too easy to find the most suitable length, and they discovered to their surprise that it was a matter of some importance to set the leather tip at exactly the right angle to the shaft — Brown and Hornblower between them, at a work-table in the stable yard, made and remade that wooden leg half a dozen times. Bush's bent knee, on which his weight rested when he walked, grew sore and inflamed; they had to pad the kneecap and remake the socket to fit, more than once, while Bush had to take his exercise in small amounts until the skin over his kneecap grew calloused and more accustomed to its new task. And when he fell — which was often — he caused himself frightful agony in his stump, which was hardly healed; with his knee bent at right angles the stump necessarily bore the brunt of practically any fall, and the pain was acute.

But teaching Bush to walk was one way of passing the long winter days, while orders from Paris turned out the conscripts from every depôt round, and set them searching once more for the missing English prisoners. They came on a day of lashing rain, a dozen shivering boys and a sergeant, wet through, and made only the poorest pretence at searching the house and its stabling — Hornblower and Bush and Brown were safe enough behind the hay in an unobtrusive loft. The conscripts were given in the kitchen a better meal by the servants than they had enjoyed for some time, and marched off to prosecute their inquiries elsewhere — every house and village for miles round was at least visited.

After that the next occurrence out of the ordinary was the announcement in Bonaparte's newspapers that the English captain and lieutenant, Hornblower and Bush, had met a well-deserved fate by being drowned in the Loire during an attempt to escape from an escort which was conducting them to their trial; undoubtedly (said the bulletin) this had saved the miscreants from the firing party which awaited them for the purpose of exacting the penalty of their flagrant piracy in the Mediterranean.

Hornblower read the announcement with mixed feelings when the Count showed it to him; not every man has the privilege of reading his own obituary. His first reaction was that it would make their escape considerably easier, seeing that the police would no longer be on the watch for them. But that feeling of relief was swamped by a wave of other feelings. Maria in England would think herself a widow, at this very moment when their child was about to be born. What would it mean to her? Hornblower knew, only too acutely, that Maria loved him as dearly as a woman could love a man, although he only admitted it to himself at moments like this. He could not guess what she would do when she believed him dead. It would be the end of everything she had lived for. And yet she would have a pension, security, a child to cherish. She might set herself, unconsciously, to make a new life for herself. In a clairvoyant moment Hornblower visualised Maria in deep mourning, her mouth set in prim resignation, the coarse red skin of her cheeks wet with tears, and her red hands nervously clasping and unclasping. She had looked like that the summer day when little Horatio and little Maria had been buried in their common grave.

Hornblower shuddered away from the recollection. Maria would at least be in no need of money; the British press would see that the Government did its duty there. He could guess at the sort of articles which would be appearing in reply to this announcement of Bonaparte's, the furious indignation that a British officer should be accused of piracy, the openly expressed suspicions that he had been murdered in cold blood and had not died while attempting to escape, the clamour for reprisals. To this day a British newspaper seldom discussed Bonaparte without recalling the death of another British naval captain, Wright, who was said to have committed suicide in prison in Paris. Everyone in England believed that Bonaparte had had him murdered — they would believe the same in this case. It was almost amusing that nearly always the most effective attacks on the tyrant were based on actions on his part which were either trivial or innocent. The British genius for invective and propaganda had long discovered that it paid better to exploit trivialities rather than inveigh broadly against policies and principles; the newspapers would give more space to a condemnation of Bonaparte for causing the death of a single naval officer than to a discussion of the criminal nature of, say, the invasion of Spain, which had resulted in the wanton slaughter of some hundreds of thousands of innocent people.

And Lady Barbara would read that he was dead, too. She would be sorry — Hornblower was prepared to believe that — but how deep her sorrow would be he could not estimate at all. The thought called up all the flood of speculations and doubts which lately he had been trying to forget — whether she cared for him at all or not, whether or not her husband had survived his wound, and what he could do in the matter in any event.

"I am sorry that this announcement seems to cause you so much distress," said the Count, and Hornblower realised that his expression had been anxiously studied during the whole reading. He had for once been caught off his guard, but he was on guard again at once. He made himself smile.

"It will make our journey through France a good deal easier," he said.

"Yes. I thought the same as soon as I read it. I can congratulate you, Captain."

"Thank you," said Hornblower.

But there was a worried look in the Count's face; he had something more to say and was hesitating to say it.

"What are you thinking about, sir?" asked Hornblower.

"Only this — Your position is in one way more dangerous

now. You have been pronounced dead by a government which does not admit mistakes — cannot afford to admit them. I am afraid in this case I have done you a disservice in so selfishly accepting the pleasure of your company. If you are recaptured you *will* be dead; the Government will see that you die without further attention being called to you."

Hornblower shrugged his shoulders with a carelessness quite unassumed for once.

"They were going to shoot me if they caught me. This makes no difference."

He dallied with the notion of a modern government dabbling in secret murder, for a moment was inclined to put it aside as quite impossible, as something one might believe of the Turks or perhaps even of the Sicilians, but not of Bonaparte; and then he realised with a shock that it was not at all impossible, that a man with unlimited power and much at stake, with underlings on whose silence he could rely, could not be expected to risk appearing ridiculous in the eyes of his public when a mere murder would save him. It was a sobering thought, but he made himself smile again, bravely.

"You have all the courage characteristic of your nation, Captain," said the Count. "But this news of your death will reach England. I fear that Madame Orrenblor will be distressed by it?"

"I am afraid she will."

"I could find means of sending a message to England — my bankers can be trusted. But whether it would be advisable is another matter."

If it were known in England that he was alive it would be known in France, and a stricter search would be instituted for him. It would be terribly dangerous. Maria would draw small profit from the knowledge that he was alive if that knowledge were to cause his death.

"I think it would not be advisable," said Hornblower.

There was a strange duality in his mind: the Hornblower for whom he could plan so coolly, and whose chances of life he could estimate so closely, was a puppet of the imagination compared with the living, flesh and blood Hornblower whose face he had shaved that morning. He knew by experience now that only when a crisis came, when he was swimming for his life in a whirlpool, or walking a quarterdeck in the heat of action, that the two blended together — that was the moment when fear came.

"I hope, Captain," said the Count, "that this news has not disturbed you too much?"

"Not at all, sir," said Hornblower.

"I am delighted to hear it. And perhaps you will be good enough to give Madame la Vicomtesse and myself the pleasure of your company again tonight at whist, you and Mr. Bush?"

Whist was the regular way of passing the evening. The Count's delight in the game was another bond of sympathy between him and Hornblower. He was not a player of the mathematical variety, as was Hornblower. Rather did he rely upon a flair, an instinctive system of tactics. It was marvellous how often his blind leads found his partner's short suit and snatched tricks from the jaws of the inevitable, how often he could decide intuitively upon the winning play when confronted by a dilemma. There were rare evenings when this faculty would desert him, and when he would sit with a rueful smile losing rubber after rubber to the remorseless precision of his daughter-in-law and Hornblower. But usually his uncanny telepathic powers would carry him triumphantly through, to the exasperation of Hornblower if they had been opponents, and to his intense satisfaction if they had been partners — exasperation at the failure of his painstaking calculations, or satisfaction of their complete vindication.

The Vicomtesse was a good well-taught player of no brilliance whose interest in the game, Hornblower suspected, was due entirely to her devotion to her father-in-law. It was Bush to whom these evenings of whist were a genuine penance. He disliked card games of any sort — even the humble vingt-et-un — and in the supreme refinement of whist he was hopelessly at a loss. Hornblower had cured him of some of his worst habits, — of asking, for instance, "What are trumps?" halfway through every hand, — had insisted on his counting cards as they fell, on his learning the conventional leads and discards, and by so doing had made of him a player whose presence three good players could just tolerate rather than miss their evening's amusement; but the evenings to him were periods of agonised, hard-breathing concentration, of flustered mistakes and shamefaced apology — misery made no less acute by the fact that conversation was carried on in French in which he could never acquire any facility. Bush mentally classed together French, whist, and spherical trigonometry as subjects in which he was too old ever to make any further progress, and which he would be content, if he were allowed, to leave entirely to his admired captain.

For Hornblower's French was improving rapidly, thanks to the need for continual use of the language. His defective ear would never allow him to catch the trick of the accent — he would always speak with the tonelessness of the foreigner — but his vocabulary was widening and his grammar growing more certain and he was acquiring a fluency in the idiom which more than once earned him a pretty compliment from his host. Hornblower's pride was held in check by the astonishing fact that below stairs Brown was as rapidly acquiring the same fluency. He was living largely with French people, too — with Felix and his wife the housekeeper, and their daughter Louise the maid, and, living over the stables across the yard, the family of Bertrand, who was Felix's brother and incidentally the coachman; Bertrand's wife was cook, with two daughters to help her in the kitchen, while one of her young sons was footman under Felix and the other two worked in the stables under their father.

Hornblower had once ventured to hint to the Count that the presence of himself and the others might well be betrayed to the authorities by one of all these servants, but the Count merely shook his head with a serene confidence that could not be shaken.

"They will not betray me," he said, and so intense was his conviction on the point that it carried conviction to Hornblower — and the better he came to know the Count the more obvious it became that no one who knew him well would ever betray him. And the Count added with a wry smile:

"You must remember, too, Captain, that here I *am* the authorities."

Hornblower could allow his mind to subside into security and sloth again after that — a sense of security with a fantastic quality about it that savoured of a nightmare. It was unreal to be mewed for so long within four walls, deprived of the wide horizons and the endless variety of the sea. He could spend his mornings tramping up and down the stable yard, as though it were a quarterdeck and as though Bertrand and his sons chattering about their duties were a ship's crew engaged on their morning's deck-washing. The smell of the stables and the land winds which came in over the high walls were a poor substitute for the keen freshness of the sea. He spent hours in a turret window of the house, with a spyglass which the Count found for him, gazing round the countryside; the desolate vineyards in their winter solitude, the distant towers of Nevers — the ornate Cathedral tower and the graceful turrets of the Gonzaga palace; the rushing black river, its willows half-submerged, — the ice which came in January and the snow which three times covered the blank slopes, — that winter were welcome variations of the monotonous landscape; there were the distant hills and the nearby slopes; the trace of the valley of the Loire winding off into the unknown, and of the valley of the Allier coming down to meet it — to a landsman's eye the prospect from the turret window would have been delightful, even perhaps in the lashing rain that fell so often, but to a seaman and a prisoner it was revolting. The indefinable charm of the sea was wanting, and so were the mystery and magic and freedom of the sea. Bush and Brown, noting the black bad temper in which Hornblower descended from the turret window after a sitting with his spyglass, wondered why he spent his time in that fashion. He wondered why himself, but weakly he could not stop himself from doing so. Specially marked was his bad temper when the Count and his daughter-in-law went out riding, returning flushed and healthy and happy after some brisk miles of the freedom for which he craved — he was stupidly jealous, he told himself, angrily, but he was jealous all the same.

He was even jealous of the pleasure Bush and Brown took in the building of the new boat. He was not a man of his hands, and once the design of the boat had been agreed upon — its fifteen feet length and four feet of beam and its flat bottom — he could contribute nothing towards the work except unskilled labour. His subordinates were far more expert with tools than he was, with plane and saw and drill, and characteristically found immense pleasure in working with them. Bush's childish delight in finding his hands, softened by a long period of convalescence, forming their distinguishing calluses again, irritated him. He envied them the simple creative pleasure which they found in watching the boat grow under their hands in the empty loft which they had adopted as a workshop — more still he envied Brown the accuracy of eye he displayed, working with a spokeshave shaping the sculls without any of the apparatus of templates and models and stretched strings which Hornblower would have found necessary.

They were black days, all that winter of confinement. January came, and with it the date when his child would be born; he was half mad with the uncertainty of it all, with his worry about Maria and the child, with the thought that Barbara would think him dead and would forget him. Even the Count's sweetness of temper and unvarying courtesy irritated him as soon as it began to cloy. He felt he would give a year of his life to hear him make a tart rejoinder to one of Bush's clumsy speeches; the impulse to be rude to the Count, to flare up into a quarrel with him, even though — or perhaps because — he owed him his life, was sometimes almost irresistible, and the effort of self-control tried his temper still further. He was surfeited with the Count's unwearying goodness, even with the odd way in which their thoughts ran so frequently together; it was queer, even uncanny, to see in the Count so often what seemed like reflections of himself in a mirror. It was madder still to remember that he had felt similar ties of sympathy, sometimes, with the wickedest man he had ever known —with El Supremo in Central America.

El Supremo had died for his crimes on a scaffold at Panama; Hornblower was worried by the thought that the Count was risking the guillotine at Paris for his friend's sake — it was mad to imagine any parallelism between the careers of El Supremo and the Count, but Hornblower was in a mad mood. He was thinking too much and he had too little to do, and his overactive brain was racketing itself to pieces. There was insanity in indulging in ridiculous mystic speculations about spiritual relationships between himself and the Count and El Supremo, and he knew it. Only self-control and patience were necessary, he told himself, to come safely through these last few weeks of waiting, but his patience seemed to be coming to an end, and he was so weary of exerting self-control.

It was the flesh that saved him when his spirit grew weak. One afternoon, descending from a long and maddening sitting with his telescope in the turret, he met the Vicomtesse in the upper gallery. She was at her boudoir door, about to enter, and she turned and smiled at him as he approached. His head was whirling; somehow his exasperation and feverishness drove him into holding out both his hands to her, risking a rebuff, risking everything, in his longing for some kind of comfort, something to ease this unbearable strain. She put her hands in his, smiling still, and at the touch self-possession broke down. It was madness to yield to the torrent of impulses let loose, but madness was somehow sweet. They were inside the room now, and the door was closed. There was sweet, healthy, satisfying flesh in his arms. There were no doubts nor uncertainties; no mystic speculations. Now blind instinct could take charge, all the bodily urges of months of celibacy. Her lips were ripe and rich and ready, the breasts which he crushed against him were hillocks of sweetness. In his nostrils was the faint intoxicating scent of womanhood.

Beyond the boudoir was the bedroom; they were there now and she was yielding to him. Just as another man might have given way to drink, might have stupefied his brain in beastly intoxication, so Hornblower numbed his own brain with lust and passion. He forgot everything, and he cared for nothing, in this mad lapse from self-control.

And she understood his motives, which was strange, and she did not resent them, which was stranger still. As his passion ebbed away, he could see her face again clearly, and her expression was tender and detached and almost maternal. She was aware of his unhappiness as she had been aware of his lust for that splendid body of hers. She had given him her body because of his crying need for it, as she might have given a cup of water to a man dying of thirst. Now she held his head to her breast, and stroked his hair, rocking a little as though he were a child, and murmuring little soothing words to him. A tear fell from her eye on to Hornblower's temple. She had come to love this Englishman, but she knew only too well that it was not love which had brought him into her arms. She knew of the wife and child in England, she guessed at the existence of the other woman whom he loved. It was not the thought of them which brought the tears to her eyes; it was the knowledge that she was not any part of his real life, that this stay of his on the banks of the Loire was as unreal to him as a dream, something to be endured until he could escape again to the sea, into the mad world which to him was sanity, where every day he would encounter peril and discomfort. These kisses he was giving her meant nothing to him compared with the business of life, which was war — the same war which had killed her young husband, the wasteful, prodigal, beastly business which had peopled Europe with widows and disfigured it with wasted fields and burned villages. He was kissing her as a man might pat his dog's head during an exciting business deal.

Then Hornblower lifted his face to hers again, and read the tragedy in her eyes. The sight of her tears moved him inexpressibly. He stroked her cheek.

"Oh, my dear," he said in English, and then began to try to find French words to express what he wanted to say. Tenderness was welling up within him. In a blinding moment of revelation he realised the love she bore him, and the motives which had brought her submissively into his arms. He kissed her mouth, he brushed away the splendid red hair from her pleading eyes. Tenderness re-awoke passion; and under his caresses her last reserve broke down.

"I love you!" she sighed, her arms about him. She had not

meant to admit it, either to him or to herself. She knew that if she gave herself to him with passion he would break her heart in the end, and that he did not love her, not even now, when tenderness had replaced the blind lust in his eyes. He would break her heart if she allowed herself to love him; for one more second she had that clairvoyance before she let herself sink into the self-deception which she knew in the future she would not believe to be self-deception. But the temptation to deceive herself into thinking he loved her was overwhelming. She gave herself to him passionately.

Chapter X

THE affair thus consummated seemed, to Hornblower's mind at least, to clear the air like a thunder-storm. He had something more definite to think about now than mystic speculations; there was Marie's loving kindness to soothe him, and for counter-irritant there was the pricking of his conscience regarding his seduction of his host's daughter-in-law under his host's roof. His uneasiness lest the Count's telepathic powers should enable him to guess at the secret he shared with Marie, the fear lest some-one should intercept a glance or correctly interpret a gesture, kept his mind healthily active.

And the love-affair while it ran its course brought with it a queer unexpected happiness. Marie was everything Hornblower could desire as a mistress. By marriage she was of a family noble enough to satisfy his liking for lords, and yet the knowledge that she was of peasant birth saved him from feeling any awe on that account. She could be tender and passionate, protective and yield-ing, practical and romantic; and she loved him so dearly, while at the same time she remained reconciled to his approaching de-parture and resolute to help it on in every way, that his heart softened towards her more and more with the passage of the days.

That departure suddenly became a much nearer and more likely possibility — by coincidence it seemed to come up over the horizon from the hoped-for into the expected only a day or two after Hornblower's meeting with Marie in the upper gallery. The boat was finished, and lay, painted and equipped, in the loft ready for them to use; Brown kept it filled with water from the well and proudly announced that it did not leak a drop. The plans for their journey to the sea were taking definite shape. Fat Jeanne the cook baked biscuit for them — Hornblower came triumphantly into his own then, as the only person in the house who knew how ship's biscuit should be baked, and Jeanne worked under his supervision.

Anxious debate between him and the Count had ended in his deciding against running the risk of buying food while on their way unless compelled; the fifty pounds of biscuit which Jeanne baked for them (there was a locker in the boat in which to store it) would provide the three of them with a pound of bread each day for seventeen days, and there was a sack of potatoes waiting for them, and another of dried peas; and there were long thin Arles sausages — as dry as sticks, and, to Hornblower's mind, not much more digestible, but with the merit of staying eatable for long periods — and some of the dry cod which Hornblower had come to know during his captivity at Ferrol, and a corner of bacon; taken all in all — as Hornblower pointed out to the Count, who was inclined to demur — they were going to fare better on their voyage down the Loire than they had often fared in the ships of His Majesty King George. Hornblower, accustomed for so long to sea voyages, never ceased to marvel at the simplicity of planning a river trip thanks to the easy solution of the problem of water supply; overside they would have unlimited fresh water for drinking and washing and bathing — much better water, too, as he told the Count again, than the stinking green stuff, alive with animalcula, doled out at the rate of four pints a head a day, with which people in ships had to be content.

He could anticipate no trouble until they neared the sea; it was only with their entry into tidal waters that they would be in any danger. He knew how the French coast swarmed with garrisons and customs officers — as a lieutenant under Pellew he had once landed a spy in the salt marshes of Bourgneuf — and it would be under their noses that they would have to steal a fishing boat and make their way to sea. Thanks to the Continental system, and the fear of English descents, and precautions against espionage, tidal waters would be watched closely indeed. But he felt he could only trust to fortune — it was hard to make plans against contingencies which might take any shape whatever, and, besides, those dangers were weeks away, and Hornblower's newly contented mind was actually too lazy to devote much thought to them. And as he grew fonder of Marie, too, it grew harder to make plans which would take him away from her.

His attachment for her was growing even as strong as that.

It was left to the Count to make the most helpful suggestion of all.

"If you would permit me," he said, one evening, "I would like to tell you of an idea I have for simplifying your passage through Nantes."

"It would give me pleasure to hear it, sir," said Hornblower — the Count's long-winded politeness was infectious.

"Please do not think," said the Count, "that I wish to interfere in any way in the plans you are making, but it occurred to me that your stay on the coast might be made safer if you assumed the role of a high official of the customs service."

"I think it would, sir," said Hornblower, patiently, "but I do not understand how I could do it."

"You would have to announce yourself, if necessary, as a Dutchman," said the Count. "Now that Holland is annexed to France and King Louis Bonaparte has fled, it is to be presumed that his employés will join the Imperial service. I think it is extremely likely that, say, a colonel of Dutch douaniers should visit Nantes to learn how to perform his duties — especially as it was over the enforcement of customs regulations that Bonaparte and his brother fell out. Your very excellent French would be just what might be expected of a Dutch customs officer, even though — please pardon my frankness — you do not speak quite like a native Frenchman."

"But — but — " stammered Hornblower; it really seemed to him that the Count's customary good sense had deserted him. "It would be difficult, sir — "

"Difficult?" smiled the Count. "It might be dangerous, but, if you will forgive my contradicting you so directly, it would hardly be difficult. In your English democracy you perhaps have had no opportunity of seeing how much weight an assured manner and a uniform carry with them in a country like this, which has already made the easy descent from an autocracy to a bureaucracy. A colonel of douaniers on the coast can go anywhere, command anything. He never has to account for himself — his uniform does that for him."

"But I have no uniform, sir," said Hornblower, and before the words were out of his mouth he guessed what the Count was going to say.

"We have half a dozen needlewomen in the house," smiled the Count, "from Marie here to little Christine, the cook's daughter. It would be odd if between them they could not make uniforms for you and your assistants. I might add that Mr. Bush's wound, which we all so much deplore, will be an actual advantage if you adopt the scheme. It is exactly consonant with Bonaparte's methods to provide for an officer wounded in his service by giving him a position in the customs. Mr. Bush's presence with you would add a touch of — shall we say realism? — to the effect produced by your appearance."

The Count gave a little bow to Bush, in apology for thus alluding to Bush's crippled condition, and Bush returned it awkwardly from his chair in bland ignorance of at least two thirds of what had been said.

The value of the suggestion was obvious to Hornblower at once, and for days afterwards the women in the house were at work cutting and stitching and fitting, until the evening came when the three of them paraded before the Count in their neat coats of blue piped with white and red, and their rakish képis — it was the making of these which had taxed Marie's ingenuity most, for the képi was still at that time an unusual headdress in the French Government services. On Hornblower's collar glittered the eight-pointed stars of colonel's rank, and the top of his képi bore the gold-lace rosette; as the three of them rotated solemnly before the Count the latter nodded approvingly.

"Excellent," he said, and then hesitated. "There is only one addition which I can think of to add realism. Excuse me a moment."

He went off to his study leaving the others looking at each other, but he was back directly with a little leather case in his hand which he proceeded to open. Resting on the silk was a glittering cross of white enamel, surmounted by a golden crown and with a gold medallion in the centre.

"We must pin this on you," he said. "No one reaches colonel's rank without the Legion of Honour."

"Father!" said Marie — it was rare that she used the familiar mode of address with him — "That was Louis-Marie's!"

"I know, my dear, I know. But it may make the difference between Captain Hornblower's success or — or failure."

His hands trembled a little, nevertheless, as he pinned the scarlet ribbon to Hornblower's coat.

"Sir — sir, it is too good of you," protested Hornblower.

The Count's long mobile face, as he stood up, was sad, but in a moment he had twisted it into his usual wry smile.

"Bonaparte sent it to me," he said, "after — after my son's death in Spain. It was a posthumous award. To me of course it is nothing — the trinkets of the tyrant can never mean anything to a Knight of the Holy Ghost. But because of its sentimental value I should be grateful if you would endeavour to preserve it unharmed and return it to me when the war is over."

"I cannot accept it, sir," said Hornblower, bending to unpin it again, but the Count checked him.

"Please, Captain," he said, "wear it, as a favour to me. It would please me if you would."

More than ever after his reluctant acceptance did Hornblower's conscience prick him at the thought that he had seduced this man's daughter-in-law while enjoying his hospitality, and later in the evening when he found himself alone with the Count in the drawing-room the conversation deepened his sense of guilt.

"Now that your stay is drawing to an end, Captain," said the Count, "I know how much I shall miss your presence after you have gone. Your company has given me the very greatest pleasure."

"I do not think it can compare with the gratitude I feel towards you, sir," said Hornblower.

The Count waved aside the thanks which Hornblower was endeavouring awkwardly to phrase.

"A little while ago we mentioned the end of the war. Perhaps there will come an end some day, and although I am an old man perhaps I shall live to see it. Will you remember me then, and this little house beside the Loire?"

"Of course, sir," protested Hornblower. "I could never forget."

He looked round the familiar drawing-room, at the silver candelabra, the old-fashioned Louis Seize furniture, the lean figure of the Count in his blue dress-coat.

"I could never forget you, sir," repeated Hornblower.

"My three sons were all young when they died," said the Count. "They were only boys, and perhaps they would not have grown into men I could have been proud of. And already when they went off to serve Bonaparte they looked upon me as an old-fashioned reactionary for whose views they had only the smallest patience — that was only to be expected. If they had lived through the wars we might have become better friends later. But they did not, and I am the last Ladon. I am a lonely man, Captain, lonely under this present régime, and yet I fear that when Bonaparte falls and the reactionaries return to power I shall be as lonely still. But I have not been lonely this winter, Captain."

Hornblower's heart went out to the lean old man with the lined face sitting opposite him in the comfortable armchair.

"But that is enough about myself, Captain," went on the Count. "I wanted to tell you of the news which has come through — it is all of it important. The salute which we heard fired yesterday was, as we thought, in honour of the birth of an heir to Bonaparte. There is now a King of Rome, as Bonaparte calls him, to sustain the Imperial throne. Whether it will be any support I am doubtful — there are many Bonapartists who will not, I fancy, be too pleased at the thought of the retention of power indefinitely in a Bonaparte dynasty. And the fall of Holland is undoubted — there was actual fighting between the troops of Louis Bonaparte and those of Napoleon Bonaparte over the question of customs enforcement. France now extends to the Baltic — Hamburg and Lubeck are French towns like Amsterdam and Leghorn and Trieste."

Hornblower thought of the cartoons in the English newspapers which had so often compared Bonaparte with the frog who tried to blow himself up as big as an ox.

"I fancy it is symptomatic of weakness," said the Count. "Perhaps you do not agree with me? You do? I am glad to have my suspicions confirmed. More than that; there is going to be war with Russia. Already troops are being transferred to the East, and the details of a new conscription were published at the same time as the proclamation of a King of Rome. There will be more refractories than ever hiding about the country now. Perhaps Bonaparte will find he has undertaken a task beyond his strength when he come to grips with Russia."

"Perhaps so," said Hornblower. He had not a high opinion of Russian military virtues.

"But there is more important news still," said the Count. "There has at last been published a bulletin of the Army of Portugal. It was dated from Almeida."

It took a second or two for Hornblower to grasp the significance of this comment, and it only dawned upon him gradually, along with the endless implications.

"It means," said the Count, "that your Wellington has beaten Bonaparte's Masséna. That the attempt to conquer Portugal has failed, and that the whole of the affairs of Spain are thrown into flux again. A running sore has been opened in the side of Bonaparte's empire, which may drain him of his strength — at what cost to poor France one can hardly imagine. But of course, Captain, you can form a more reliable opinion of the military situation than I can, and I have been presumptuous in commenting on it. Yet you have not the facilities which I have of gauging the moral effect of this news. Wellington has beaten Junot, and Victor and Soult. Now he has beaten Masséna, the greatest of them all. There is only one man now against whom European opinion can measure him, and that is Bonaparte. It is not well for a tyrant to have rivals in prestige. Last year how many years of power would one have given Bonaparte if asked? Twenty? I think so. Now in 1811 we change our minds. Ten years, we think. In 1812 we may revise our estimate again, and say five. I myself do not believe the Empire as we know it will endure after 1814 —

empires collapse at a rate increasing in geometrical progression, and it will be your Wellington who will pull this one down."

"I hope sincerely you are right, sir," said Hornblower.

The Count was not to know how disturbing this mention of Wellington was to his audience; he could not guess that Hornblower was daily tormented by speculations as to whether Wellington's sister was widowed or not, whether Lady Barbara Leighton, née Wellesley, ever had a thought to devote to the naval captain who had been reported dead. Her brother's triumphs might well occupy her mind to the exclusion of everything else, and Hornblower feared that when at last he should reach England she would be far too great a lady to pay him any attention at all. The thought irked him.

He went to bed in a peculiarly sober mood, his mind busy with problems of the most varying nature — from speculations about the approaching fall of the French Empire to calculations regarding the voyage down the Loire which he was about to attempt. Lying awake, long after midnight, he heard his bedroom door quietly open and close; he lay rigid, instantly, conscious of a feeling of faint distaste at this reminder of the intrigue which he was conducting under a hospitable roof. Very gently, the curtains of his bed were drawn open, and in the darkness he could see, through half-opened eyes, a shadowy ghost bending over him. A gentle hand found his cheek and stroked it; he could no longer sham sleep, and he pretended to wake with a start.

"It is Marie, 'Oratio," said a voice, softly.

"Yes," said Hornblower.

He did not know what he should say or do — for that matter he did not know what he wanted. Mostly he was conscious of Marie's imprudence in thus coming to his room, risking discovery and imperilling everything. He shut his eyes, as though still sleepy, to gain time for consideration; the hand ceased to stroke his cheek. Hornblower waited for a second or two more, and was astonished to hear the slight click of the latch of the door again. He sat up with a jerk. Marie had gone, as silently as she had come. Hornblower continued to sit up, puzzling over the incident, but he could make nothing of it. Certainly he was not going to run any risks by going to seek Marie in her room and asking for explanations; he lay down again to think about it, and this time, with its usual capriciousness, sleep surprised him in the midst of his speculations, and he slept soundly until Brown brought him his breakfast coffee.

It took him half the morning to nerve himself for what he foresaw to be a very uncomfortable interview; it was only then that he tore himself away from a last inspection of the boat, in Bush's and Brown's company, and climbed the stairs to Marie's boudoir and tapped at the door. He entered when she called, and stood there in the room of so many memories — the golden chairs with their oval backs upholstered in pink and white, the windows looking out on the sunlit Loire, and Marie in the window-seat with her needlework.

"I wanted to say 'good morning,' " he said at length, as Marie did nothing to help him out.

"Good morning," said Marie. She bent her head over her needlework — the sunshine through the windows lit her hair gloriously — and spoke with her face concealed. "We only have to say 'good morning' today, and tomorrow we shall say 'good-bye.' "

"Yes," said Hornblower, stupidly.

"If you loved me," said Marie, "it would be terrible for me to have you go, and to know that for years we should not meet again — perhaps for ever. But as you do not, then I am glad that you are going back to your wife and your child, and your ships, and your fighting. That is what you want, and I am pleased that you should have it all."

"Thank you," said Hornblower.

Still she did not look up.

"You are the sort of man," she went on, "whom women love very easily. I do not expect that I shall be the last. I don't think that you will ever love anybody, or know what it is to do so."

Hornblower could have said nothing in English in reply to these two astonishing statements, and in French he was perfectly helpless. He could only stammer.

"Good-bye," said Marie.

"Good-bye, madame," said Hornblower, lamely.

His cheeks were burning as he came out into the upper hall, in a condition of mental distress in which humiliation played only a minor part. He was thoroughly conscious of having acted despicably, and of having been dismissed without dignity. But he was puzzled by the other remarks Marie had made. It had never occurred to him that women loved him easily. Maria — it was odd, that similarity of names, Maria and Marie — loved him, he knew; he had found it a little tiresome and disturbing. Barbara had offered herself to him, but he had never ventured to believe that she had loved him — and had she not married someone else? And Marie loved him; Hornblower remembered guiltily an incident of a few days ago, when Marie in his arms had whispered hotly "Tell me you love me," and he had answered, with facile kindness, "I love you, dear." "Then I am happy," answered Marie. Perhaps it was a good thing that Marie knew now that he was lying, and had made easy his retreat. Another woman with a word might have sent him and Bush to prison and death — there were women capable of it.

And this question of his never loving anyone; surely Marie was wrong about that. She did not know the miseries of longing he had been through on Barbara's account, how much he had desired her and how much he still desired her. He hesitated guiltily here, wondering whether his desire would survive gratification. That was such an uncomfortable thought that he swerved away from it in a kind of panic. If Marie had merely revengefully desired to disturb him she certainly had achieved her object; and if on the other hand she had wanted to win him back to her she was not far from success either. What with the torments of remorse and his sudden uneasiness about himself Hornblower would have returned to her if she had lifted a finger to him, but she did not.

At dinner that evening she appeared young and lighthearted, her eyes sparkling and her expression animated, and when the Count lifted his glass for the toast of "a prosperous voyage home" she joined in with every appearance of enthusiasm. Hornblower was glum beneath his forced gaiety. Only now, with the prospect of an immediate move ahead of him, had he become aware that there were decided arguments in favour of the limbo of suspended animation in which he had spent the past months. Tomorrow he was going to leave all this certainty and safety and indifferent negativeness. There was physical danger ahead of him; that he could face calmly and with no more than a tightening of the throat, but besides that there was the resolution of all the doubts and uncertainties which had so troubled him.

Hornblower was suddenly aware that he did not so urgently desire his uncertainties to be resolved. At present he could still hope. If Leighton were to declare that Hornblower had fought at Rosas contrary to the spirit of his orders; if the court-martial were to decide that the *Sutherland* had not been fought to the last gasp — and courts-martial were chancy affairs; if — if — if . . . And there was Maria with her cloying sweetness awaiting him, and the misery of longing for Lady Barbara, all in contrast with the smoothness of life here with the Count's unruffled politeness and the stimulus of Marie's healthy animalism. Hornblower had to force a smile as he lifted his glass.

Chapter XI

THE big green Loire was shrinking to its summer level. Hornblower had seen its floods and its ice come and go, had seen the willows at its banks almost submerged, but now it was back safely in its wide bed, with a hint of golden-brown gravel exposed on either bank. The swift green water was clear now, instead of turbid, and under the blue sky the distant reaches were blue as well, in charming colour contrast with the spring-time emerald of the valley and the gold of the banks.

The two sleek dun oxen, patient under the yoke, had dragged the travois-sledge down to the water's edge in the first early light of dawn, Brown and Hornblower walking beside to see that the precious boat balanced on it came to no harm, and Bush stumping breathlessly behind them. The boat slid gently into the water, and under Bush's supervision the stable hands loaded her with the bags of stores which they had carried down. The faint morning mist still lay in the valley, and wreathed over the surface of the water, awaiting the coming of the sun to drink it up. It was the best time for departure; the mist would shield them from inquisitive persons who might be unduly curious at the sight of the expedition starting off. Up at the house the farewells had all been said — the Count as unruffled as ever, as though it were usual for him to rise at five in the morning, and Marie smiling and calm. In the stable yard and the kitchen there had been tears; all the women had lamented Brown's going, weeping unashamed and yet laughing through their tears as he laughed and joked in the voluble French which he had acquired, and as he smacked their broad posteriors. Hornblower wondered how many of them Brown had seduced that winter, and how many Anglo-French children would be born next autumn as a result.

"Remember your promise to return after the war," the Count had said to Hornblower. "Marie will be as delighted to see you as I shall be."

His smile had conveyed no hint of a hidden meaning — but how much did he guess, or know? Hornblower gulped as he remembered.

"Shove off," he rasped. "Brown, take the sculls."

The boat scraped over the gravel, and then floated free as the current took her, dancing away from the little group of stable hands and the stolid oxen, vague already in the mist. The row-locks creaked and the boat swayed to Brown's pulls; Hornblower heard the noises, and felt Bush seated in the stern beside him, but for some seconds he saw nothing. There was a mist about him far denser than the reality.

The one mist cleared with the other, as the sun came breaking through, warm on Hornblower's back. High up the bank on the opposite side was the orchard at which Hornblower had often gazed from his window; it was marvellous now under its load of blossom. Looking back he saw the château shining in the sun. The turrets at the corners had been added, he knew, no more than fifty years ago by Comte de Graçay with a rococo taste for the antique, but they looked genuine enough at this distance. It was like a fairy castle in the pearly light, a dream castle; and already the months he had spent there seemed like a dream too, a dream from which he regretted awakening.

"Mr. Bush," he said sharply, "I'll trouble you to get out your rod and make an appearance of fishing. Take a slower stroke, Brown."

They went drifting on down the noble river, blue in the distance and green overside, clear and transparent, so that they could actually see the bottom passing away below them. It was only a few minutes before they reached the confluence of the Allier, itself a fine river almost the size of the Loire, and the united stream was majestically wide, a hundred and fifty fathoms at least from bank to bank. They were a long musket-shot from land, but their position was safer even than that implied, for from the water's edge on either side stretched an extensive no man's land of sand and willow which the periodic floods kept free from human habitations and which was only likely to be visited by fishermen and laundering housewives.

The mist had entirely vanished now, and the hot sun bore with it all the promise of one of those splendid spring days of central France. Hornblower shifted in his seat to make himself more comfortable. The hierarchy of this, his new command, was top-heavy. A proportion of one seaman to one lieutenant and one captain was ludicrous. He would have to exercise a great deal of tact to keep them all three satisfied — to see that Brown was not made resentful by having all the work to do and yet that discipline was not endangered by a too democratic division of labour. In a fifteen-foot boat it would be difficult to keep up the aloof dignity proper to a captain.

"Brown," he said, "I've been very satisfied with you so far. Keep in my good books and I'll see you're properly rewarded when we get back to England. There'll be a warrant for you as master's mate if you want it."

"Thank 'ee, sir. Thank 'ee very kindly. But I'm happy as I am, beggin' your pardon, sir."

He meant he was happy in his rating as a coxswain, but the tone of his voice implied more than that. Hornblower looked at him as he sat with his face turned up to the sun, pulling slowly at the sculls. There was a blissful smile on his face — the man was marvellously happy. He had been well-fed and well-housed for months, with plenty of women's society, with light work and no hardship. Even now there was a long prospect ahead of him of food better than he had ever known before he entered France, of no harder work than a little gentle rowing, of no need ever to turn out on a blustering night to reef topsails. Twenty years of the lower deck in King George's Navy, Hornblower realised, must make any man form the habit of living only in the present. Tomorrow might bring a flogging, peril, sickness, death; certainly hardship and probably hunger, and all without the opportunity of lifting a finger to ward off any of these, for any lifting of a finger would make them all more certain. Twenty years of being at the mercy of the incalculable, and not merely in the major things of life but in the minor ones, must make a fatalist of any man who survived them. For a moment Hornblower felt a little twinge of envy of Brown, who would never know the misery of helplessness, or the indignity of indecision.

The river channel here was much divided by islands each bordered by a rim of golden gravel; it was Hornblower's business to select what appeared to be the most navigable channel — no easy task. Shallows appeared mysteriously right in the centre of what had seemed to be the main stream; over these the clear green water ran faster and faster and shallower and shallower until the bottom of the boat was grating on the pebbles. Sometimes the bank would end there with astonishing abruptness, so that one moment they were in six inches of rushing water and the next in six feet of transparent green, but more than once now they found themselves stuck fast, and Brown and Hornblower, trousers rolled to the knee, had to get out and haul the boat a hundred yards over a barely covered bank before finding water deep enough. Hornblower thanked his stars that he had decided on having the boat built flat-bottomed — a keel would have been a hampering nuisance.

Then they came to a dam, like the one which had brought them disaster in the darkness during their first attempt to navigate the river. It was half natural, half artificial, roughly formed of lumps of rock piled across the river bed, and over it the river poured in fury at a few points.

"Pull over to the bank there, Brown," snapped Hornblower as his coxswain looked to him for orders.

They ran the boat up onto the gravel just above the dam, and Hornblower stepped out and looked downstream. There was a hundred yards of turbulent water below the dam; they would have to carry everything down. It took three journeys on the part of Hornblower and Brown to carry all their stores to the point he chose for them to re-enter the river — Bush with his wooden leg could only just manage to stumble over the uneven surface unladen — and then they addressed themselves to the business of transporting the boat. It was not easy; there was a colossal difference between dragging the boat through shallows even an inch deep only and carrying her bodily. Hornblower contemplated the task glumly for some seconds before plunging at it. He stooped and got his hands underneath.

"Take the other side, Brown. Now — lift."

Between them they could just raise it; they had hardly staggered a yard with it before all the strength was gone from Hornblower's wrists and fingers and the boat slipped to the ground again. He avoided Brown's eye and stooped again, exasperated.

"Lift!" he said.

It was impossible to carry the heavy boat that way. He had no sooner lifted it than he was compelled to drop it again.

"It's no go, sir," said Brown gently. "We'll have to get her up on our backs, sir. That's the only way."

Hornblower heard the respectful murmur as if from a long distance.

"If you take the bows, beggin' your pardon, sir, I'll look after the stern. Here, sir, lift t'other way round. Hold it, sir, till I can get aft. Right, sir. Ready. Lift!"

They had the boat up on their backs now, stooping double under the heavy load. Hornblower, straining under the lighter bows, thought of Brown carrying the much heavier stern, and he set his teeth and vowed to himself that he would not rest until Brown asked to. Within five seconds he was regretting his vow. His breath was coming with difficulty and there were stabbing pains in his chest. It grew harder and harder to take the trouble to attend to the proper placing of his feet as he stumbled over the uneven surface. Those months in the Château de Graçay had done their work in making him soft and out of condition; for the last few yards of the portage he was conscious of nothing save the overwhelming weight on his neck and shoulders and his difficulty of breathing. Then he heard Bush's bluff voice.

"Right, sir. Let me get hold, sir."

With the small but welcome help that Bush could afford he was able to disengage himself and lower the boat to the ground; Brown was standing over the stern gasping, and sweeping the sweat off his forehead with his forearm. Hornblower saw him open his mouth to make a remark, presumably regarding the weight of the boat, and then shut it again when he remembered that now he was under discipline again and must only speak when spoken to. And discipline, Hornblower realised, required that he himself should display no sign of weakness before his subordinates — it was bad enough that he should have had to receive advice from Brown as to how to lift the boat.

"Take hold again, Brown, and we'll get her into the water," he said, controlling his breathing with a vast effort.

They slid the boat in, and heaved the stores on board again. Hornblower's head was swimming with the strain; he thought longingly of his comfortable seat in the stern, and then put the thought from him.

"I'll take the sculls, Brown," he said.

Brown opened and shut his mouth again, but he could not question explicit orders. The boat danced out over the water, with Hornblower at the sculls happy in the rather baseless conviction that he had demonstrated that a captain in the King's Navy was the equal even in physical strength of any mere coxswain, however Herculean his thews.

Once or twice that day shallows caught them out in midstream which they were unable to pass without lightening the boat to a maximum extent. When Hornblower and Brown, ankle-deep in rushing water, could drag the boat no farther, Bush had to get out too, his wooden leg sinking in the sand despite its broad leather sole, and limp downstream to the edge of the shallows and wait until the others dragged the lightened boat up to him — once he had to stand holding the bag of bread and the roll of bedding before they could tug the boat over the shallows, and on that occasion they had to unstrap his wooden leg, help him in, and then tug the leg free from the sand, so deeply had it sunk. There was another portage to be made that day, fortunately not nearly such a long one as the first; altogether there was quite enough interest in the day's journey to keep them from growing bored.

On that big lonely river it was almost like travelling through an uninhabited country. For the greater part of the day there was hardly a soul in sight. Once they saw a skiff moored to the bank which was obviously used as a ferry boat, and once they passed a big waggon ferry — a flat-bottomed scow which was moored so as to swing itself across the river by the force of the current, pendulum-fashion on long mooring ropes. Once they passed a small boat engaged in the task of dredging sand for building purposes from the river bed; there were two weather-beaten men on board, hard at work with small hand-dredgers on poles, which they scraped over the bottom and emptied into the boat. It was a nervous moment as they approached them, Bush and Brown with their ornamental fishing rods out, Hornblower forcing himself to do no more with the sculls than merely keep the boat in midstream. He had thought, as they drifted down, of giving orders to Bush and Brown regarding the instant silencing of the two men if they appeared suspicious, but he checked himself. He could rely on their acting promptly without warning, and his dignity demanded that he should betray none of the apprehension which he felt.

But the apprehension was quite baseless. There was no curiosity in the glances which the two sand dredgers threw at them, and there was cordiality in their smiles and in their polite "*Bonjour, messieurs.*"

"*Bonjour,*" said Hornblower and Brown — Bush had the sense to keep shut the mouth which would instantly have betrayed them, and devoted his attention instead to his rod. Clearly boats with fishing parties on board were just common enough on the Loire to escape comment; and, besides, the intrinsic innocence of fishing as a pastime shielded them from suspicion, as Hornblower and the Count had agreed long before. And nobody could ever dream that a small boat in the heart of France was manned by escaped prisoners of war.

The commonest sight of all along the river was the women washing clothes, sometimes singly, sometimes in little groups whose gossiping chatter floated out to them distinctly over the water. The Englishmen could hear the "clop clop clop" of the wooden beaters smacking the wet clothes on the boards, and could see the kneeling women sway down and up as they rinsed them in the current; most of the women looked up from their work and gave them a glance as they drifted by, but it was never more than a long glance, and often not as much. In a time of war and upheaval there were so many possible explanations for the women not to know the occupants of the boat that their inability did not trouble them.

Of the roaring rapids such as had nearly destroyed them once before, they saw nothing; the junction of the Allier, and the cessation of the winter floods, accounted for that. The rock-strewn sand bars represented the sites of winter rapids and were far easier to navigate, or rather to circumvent. In fact, there were no difficulties at all. Even the weather was benign, a lovely clear day of sunshine, comfortably warm, lighting up the changing panorama of gold and blue and green. Brown basked in it all unashamedly, and the hard-bitten Bush took his ease whenever the peacefulness of it caught him napping; in Bush's stern philosophy mankind — naval mankind at least — was born to sorrow and difficulty and danger, and any variation from such a state of affairs must be viewed with suspicion and not enjoyed too much lest it should have to be paid for at compound interest. It was too good to be true, this delightful drifting down the river, as morning wore into noon and noon into a prolonged and dreamy afternoon, with a delicious lunch to eat of a cold *pâté* (a parting gift from fat Jeanne) and a bottle of wine.

The little towns, or rather villages, which they passed were all perched up high on the distant banks beyond the flood limits; Hornblower, who already knew by heart the brief itinerary and table of distances which the Count had made out for him, was aware that the first town with a bridge was at Briare, which they could not reach until late evening. He had intended to wait above the town until nightfall and then to run through in the darkness, but as the day wore on his resolve steadily hardened to push on without waiting. He could not analyse his motives. He was aware that it was a very remarkable thing for him to do, to run into danger, even the slightest, when urged neither by the call of duty nor the thirst for distinction. Here the only benefit would be the saving of an hour or two's time. The Nelsonian tradition to "lose not an hour" was grained deeply into him, but it was hardly that which influenced him.

Partly it was his innate cross-grainedness. Everything had gone so supremely well. Their escape from their escort had been almost miraculous, the coincidence which had brought them to the Château de Graçay, where alone in all France they could have found safety, was more nearly miraculous still. Now this voyage down the river bore every promise of easy success. His instinctive reaction to all this unnatural prosperity was to put himself into the way of trouble — there had been so much trouble in his life that he felt uneasy without it.

But partly he was being driven by devils. He was morose and cantankerous. Marie was being left behind, and he was regretting that more with every yard that divided them. He was tormented by the thought of the shameful part he had played, and by memories of the hours they had spent together; sentimentally he was obsessed with longing for her. And ahead of him lay England where they thought him dead, where Maria would by now have reconciled herself to her loss and would be doubly and painfully happy with him in consequence, and where Barbara would have forgotten him, and where a court-martial to inquire into his conduct awaited him. He thought grimly that it might be better for everyone if he *were* dead; he shrank a little from the prospect of returning to England as one might shrink from a cold plunge, or as he shrank from the imminent prospect of danger. That was the ruling motive. He had always forced himself to face danger, to advance bravely to meet it. He had always gulped down any pill which life had presented to him, knowing that any hesitation would give him a contempt for himself more bitter still. So now he would accept no excuse for delay.

Briare was in sight now, down at the end of the long wide reach of the river. Its church tower was silhouetted against the evening sky, and its long straggling bridge stood out black against the distant silver of the water. Hornblower at the sculls looked over his shoulder and saw all this; he was aware of his subordinates' eyes turned inquiringly upon him.

"Take the sculls, Brown," he growled.

They changed places silently, and Bush handed over the tiller to him with a puzzled look — he had been well aware of the design to run past bridges only at night. There were two vast black shapes creeping over the surface of the river down there, barges being warped out of the lateral canal on one side and into the canal of Briare on the other by way of a channel across the river dredged for the purpose. Hornblower stared forward as they approached under the impulse of Brown's steady strokes. A quick examination of the water surface told him which arch of the bridge to select, and he was able to discern the tow-ropes and warps of the barges — there were teams of horses both on the bridge and on the banks, silhouetted clearly against the sky as they tugged at the ropes to drag the bulky barges across the rushing current.

Men were looking at them now from the bridge, and there was just sufficient gap left between the barges to enable the boat to slip between without the necessity for stopping and making explanations.

"Pull!" he said to Brown, and the boat went careening headlong down the river. They slid under the bridge with a rush, and neatly rounded the stern of one of the barges; the burly old man at the tiller, with a little grandchild beside him, looked down at them with a dull curiosity as they shot by. Hornblower waved his hand gaily to the child — excitement was a drug which he craved, which always sent his spirits high — and looked up with a grin at the other men on the bridge and on the banks. Then they were past, and Briare was left behind.

"Easy enough, sir," commented Bush.

"Yes," said Hornblower.

If they had been travelling by road they certainly would have been stopped for examination of their passports; here on the unnavigable river such a proceeding occurred to no one. The sun was low now, shining right into his eyes as he looked forward, and it would be dark in less than an hour. Hornblower began to look out for a place where they could be comfortable for the night. He allowed one long island to slide past them before he saw the ideal spot — a tiny hummock of an island with three willow trees, the green of the central part surrounded by a broad belt of golden-brown where the receding river had left the gravel exposed.

"We'll run the boat aground over there, Brown," he announced. "Easy. Pull starboard. Pull both. Easy."

It was not a very good landing. Hornblower, despite his undoubted ability in handling big ships, had much to learn regarding the behaviour of flat-bottomed boats amid the shoals of a river. There was a back eddy which swung them round; the boat had hardly touched bottom before the current had jerked her free again. Brown, tumbling over the bows, was nearly waist-deep in water and had to grab the painter and brace himself against the current to check her. The tactful silence which ensued could almost be felt while Brown tugged the boat up to the gravel again — Hornblower, in the midst of his annoyance, was aware of Bush's restless movement and thought of how his first lieutenant would have admonished a midshipman guilty of such a careless piece of work. It made him grin to think of Bush bottling up his feelings, and the grin made him forget his annoyance.

He stepped out into the shallow water and helped Brown run the lightened boat farther up the bank, checking Bush when he made to step out too — Bush could never accustom himself to seeing his captain at work while he sat idle. The water was no more than ankle-deep by the time he allowed Bush to disembark; they dragged the boat up as far as she could go and Brown made fast the painter to a peg driven securely into the earth, as a precaution in case any unexpected rise in the water level should float the boat off. The sun had set now in the flaming west, and it was fast growing dark.

"Supper," said Hornblower. "What shall we have?"

A captain with strict ideas of discipline would merely have announced what they should eat, and would certainly not have called his subordinates into consultation, but Hornblower was too conscious of the topheavy organisation of his present ship's company to be able to maintain appearances to that extent. Yet Bush and Brown were still oppressed by a lifelong experience of subordination and could not bring themselves to proffer advice to their captain; they merely fidgeted and stood silent, leaving it to Hornblower to decree that they should finish off the cold *pâté* with some boiled potatoes. Once the decision was made, Bush proceeded to amplify and interpret his captain's original order, just as a good first lieutenant should.

"I'll handle the fire here," he said. "There ought to be all the driftwood we need, Brown. Yes, an' I'll want some sheer-legs to hang the pan over the fire — cut me three off those trees, there."

Bush felt it in his bones that Hornblower was meditating taking part in the preparation of supper, and could not bear the thought. He looked up at his captain half appealingly, half defiantly. A captain should not merely never be doing undignified work, but he should be kept in awful isolation, screened away in the mysterious recesses of his cabin. Hornblower left them to it, and wandered off round the tiny island, looking over at the distant banks and the rare houses, fast disappearing in the growing twilight. It was a shock to discover that the pleasant green which carpeted most of the island was not the grass he had assumed it to be, but a bank of nettles, knee-high already despite the earliness of the season. Judging by his language, Brown on the other side had just made the same discovery while seeking fuel with his feet bare.

Hornblower paced the gravel bank for a space, and on his return it was an idyllic scene which met his eyes. Brown was tending the little fire which flickered under the pot swinging from its tripod, while Bush, his wooden leg sticking stiffly out in front of him, was peeling the last of the potatoes. Apparently Bush had decided that a first lieutenant could share menial work with the sole member of the crew without imperilling discipline. They all ate together, wordless but friendly, beside the dying fire; even the chill air of the evening did not cool the feeling of comradeship of which each was conscious in his own particular way.

"Shall I set a watch, sir?" asked Bush, as supper ended.

"No," said Hornblower.

The minute additional security which would be conferred by one of them staying awake would not compare with the discomfort and inconvenience of everyone's losing four hours' sleep each night.

Bush and Brown slept in cloak and blanket on the bare soil; probably, Hornblower anticipated, most uncomfortably. For himself there was a mattress of cut nettles cunningly packed under the boat cover which Brown had prepared for him on the most level part of the gravel spit, presumably at a grave cost in stings. He slept on it peacefully, the dew wetting his face and a gibbous moon shining down upon it from the starry sky. Vaguely he remembered, in a troubled fashion, the stories of the great leaders of men — Charles XII especially — who shared their men's coarse fare and slept like them on the bare ground. For a second or two he feared he should be doing likewise, and then his common sense overrode his modesty and told him that he did not need to have recourse to theatrical tricks to win the affections of Bush and Brown.

Chapter XII

THOSE days on the Loire were pleasant, and every day was more pleasant than the one preceding. For Hornblower there was not merely the passive pleasure of a fortnight's picnic, but there was the far more active one of the comradeliness of it all. During his ten years as a captain his natural shyness had reinforced the restrictions surrounding his position, and had driven him more and more in upon himself until he had grown unconscious of his aching need for human companionship. In that small boat, living at close quarters with the others, and where one man's misfortune was everyone's, he came to know happiness. His keen insight made him appreciate more than ever the sterling good qualities of Bush, who was secretly fretting over the loss of his foot, and the inactivity to which that loss condemned him, and the doubtfulness of his future as a cripple.

"I'll see you posted as captain," said Hornblower, on the only occasion on which Bush hinted at his troubles, "if it's my last act on earth."

He thought he might possibly contrive that, even if disgrace awaited him personally in England. Lady Barbara must still remember Bush and the old days in the *Lydia,* and must be as aware of his good qualities as Hornblower was himself. An appeal to her, properly worded — even from a man broken by court-martial — might have an effect, and might set turning the hidden wheels of Government patronage. Bush deserved post rank more than half the captains he knew on the list.

Then there was Brown with his unfailing cheerfulness. No one could judge better than Hornblower the awkwardness of Brown's position, living in such close proximity to two officers. But Brown always could find the right mixture of friendliness and deference; he could laugh gaily when he slipped on a rounded stone and sat down in the Loire, and he could smile sympathetically when the same thing happened to Hornblower. He busied himself over the jobs of work which had to be done, and never, not even after ten days' routine had established something like a custom, appeared to take it for granted that his officers would do their share. Hornblower could foresee a great future for Brown, if helped by a little judicious exertion of influence. He might easily end as a captain, too — Darby and Westcott had started on the lower deck in the same fashion. Even if the court-martial broke him, Hornblower could do something to help him. Elliott and Bolton at least would not desert him entirely, and would rate Brown as midshipman in their ships if he asked them to with special earnestness.

In making these plans for the future of his friends, Hornblower could bring himself to contemplate the end of the voyage and the inevitable court-martial with something like equanimity; for the rest, during those golden days, he was able to avoid all thought of their approaching end. It was a placid journey through a placid limbo. He was leaving behind him in the past the shameful memory of his treatment of Marie, and the troubles to come were still in the future; for once in his life he was able to live in the lotus-eating present.

All the manifold little details of the journey helped towards this desirable end — they were so petty and yet temporarily so important. Selecting a course between the golden sandbanks of the river; stepping out overside to haul the boat over when his judgment was incorrect; finding a lonely island on which to camp at night, and cooking supper when one was found; drifting past the gravel dredgers and the rare fishing parties; avoiding conspicuous behaviour while passing towns; there were always trifles to occupy the mind. There were the two nights when it rained, and they all slept huddled together under the shelter of a blanket stretched between willow trees — there had been a ridiculous pleasure about waking up to find Bush snoring beside him with a protective arm across him.

There was the pageantry of the Loire — Gien with its château-fortress high on its terraces, and Sully with its vast rounded bastions, and Château-Neuf-sur-Loire, and Jargeau. Then for miles along the river they were in sight of the gaunt square towers of the cathedral of Orleans — Orleans was one of the few towns with an extensive river front, past which they had to drift unobtrusively and with special care at its difficult bridges. Orleans was hardly out of sight before they reached Beaugency with its interminable bridge of countless arches and its strange square tower. The river was blue and gold and green. The rocks above Nevers were succeeded by the gravel banks of the middle reaches, and now the gravel gave way to sand, golden sand amid the shimmering blue of the river whose water was a clear green overside. All the contrasted greens delighted Hornblower's eyes, the green of the never-ending willows, of the vineyards and the cornfields and the meadows.

They passed Blois, its steeply-humped bridge crowned by the pyramid whose inscription proclaimed the bridge to be the first public work of the infant Louis XV, and Chaumont and Amboise, their lovely châteaux towering above the river, and Tours — an extensive water front to sidle past here, too — and Langeais. The wild desolation of the island-studded river was punctuated everywhere by towers and châteaux and cathedrals on the distant banks. Below Langeais the big placid Vienne entered the river on their left, and appeared to convey some of its own qualities to the united stream, which was now a little slower and more regular in its course, its shallows becoming less and less frequent. After Saumur and the innumerable islands of Les Ponts de Cé, the even bigger Maine came in on their right, and finally deprived the wild river of all the characteristics which had endeared it to them. Here it was far deeper and far slower, and for the first time they found the attempt to make the river available for commercial traffic successful here — they had passed numerous traces of wasted work on Bonaparte's part higher up.

But below the confluence of the Maine the groynes and dykes had withstood the winter floods and the continual erosion, had piled up long beaches of golden sand on either bank, and had left in the centre a deep channel navigable to barges — they passed several working their way up to Angers from Nantes. Mostly they were being towed by teams of mules, but one or two were taking advantage of a westerly wind to make the ascent under vast gaff-mainsails. Hornblower stared hungrily at them, for they were the first sails he had seen for months, but he put aside all thought of stealing one. A glance at their clumsy lines assured him that it would be more dangerous to put to sea, even for a short distance, in one of those than in the cockleshell boat they had already.

That westerly wind that brought the barges up brought something else with it, too. Brown, diligently tugging at the sculls as he forced the boat into it, suddenly wrinkled his nose.

"Begging your pardon, sir," he said, "I can smell the sea."

They sniffed at the breeze, all three of them.

"By God, you're right, Brown," said Bush.

Hornblower said nothing, but he had smelt the salt as well, and it had brought with it such a wave of mixed feelings as to leave him without words. And that night, after they had camped, — there were just as many desolate islands to choose from, despite the changes in the river, — Hornblower noticed that the level of the water had risen perceptibly above where it had stood when they beached the boat. It was not flood water as it was once when after a day of heavy rain their boat had nearly floated during the night; on this evening above Nantes there had been no rain, nor sign of it, for three days. Hornblower watched the water creep up at a rate almost perceptible, watched it reach a maximum, dally there for a space, and then begin to sink. It was the tide. Down at Paimbœuf at the mouth there was a rise and fall of ten or twelve feet, at Nantes one of four or six; up here he was witnessing the last dying effort of the banked-up sea to hold the river back in its course.

There was a strange emotion in the thought. They had reached tidewater at last, the habitat on which he had spent more than half his life; they had travelled from sea to sea, from the Mediterranean to what was at least technically the Atlantic; this same tide he was witnessing here washed also the shores of England, where were Barbara, and Maria, and his unknown child, and the Lords Commissioners of the Admiralty. But more than that. It meant that their pleasant picnic on the Loire was over. In tidal water they could not hope to move about with half the freedom they had known inland; strange faces and new arrivals would be scanned with suspicion, and probably the next forty-eight hours or so would determine whether he was to reach England to face a court-martial or be recaptured to face a firing squad. Hornblower knew that moment the old sensations of excitement, which he called fear to himself — the quickened heart-beat, the dampening palms, the tingling in the calves of his legs. He had to brace himself to master these symptoms before returning to the others to tell them of his observations.

"High water half an hour back, sir?" repeated Bush in reply.

"Yes."

"M'm," said Bush.

Brown said nothing, as accorded with his position in life, but his face bore momentarily the same expression of deep cogitation. They were both assimilating the fact, in the manner of seamen. Hornblower knew that from now on, with perhaps a glance at the sun but not necessarily with a glance at the river, they would be able to tell offhand the state of the tide, producing the information without a thought by the aid of a subconscious calculating ability developed during a lifetime at sea. He could do the same himself — the only difference between them was that he was interested in the phenomenon while they were indifferent to it or unaware of it.

Chapter XIII

For their entrance into Nantes Hornblower decided that they must wear their uniforms as officials of the customs service. It called for long and anxious thought to reach this decision, a desperately keen balancing of chances. If they arrived in civilian clothes they would almost certainly be questioned, and in that case it would be almost impossible to explain their lack of papers and passports, whereas in uniform they might easily not be questioned at all, and if they were a haughty demeanour might still save them. But to pose as a colonel of douaniers would call for histrionic ability on the part of Hornblower, and he mistrusted himself — not his ability, but his nerve. With remorseless self-analysis he told himself that he had played a part for years, posing as a man of rigid imperturbability when he was nothing of the kind, and he asked himself why he could not pose for a few minutes as a man of swaggering and overbearing haughtiness, even under the additional handicap of having to speak French. In the end it was in despite of his doubts that he reached his decision, and put on the neat uniform and pinned the glittering Legion of Honour on his breast.

As always, it was the first moment of departure which tried him most — getting into the stern-sheets of the boat and taking the tiller while Brown got out the sculls. The tension under which he laboured was such that he knew that, if he allowed it, the hand that rested on the tiller would tremble, and the voice which gave the orders to Brown would quaver. So he carried himself with the unbending rigidity which men were accustomed to see in him, and he spoke with the insensitive harshness he always used in action.

Under the impulse of Brown's sculls the river glided away behind them, and the city of Nantes came steadily nearer. Houses grew thicker and thicker on the banks, and then the river began to break up into several arms; to Hornblower the main channel between the islands was made obvious by the indications of traces of commercial activity along the banks — traces of the past, largely, for Nantes was a dying town, dying of the slow strangulation of the British blockade. The lounging idlers along the quays, the deserted warehouses, all indicated the dire effects of war upon French commerce.

They passed under a couple of bridges, with the tide running strongly, and left the huge mass of the ducal château to starboard; Hornblower forced himself to sit with careless ease in the boat, as though neither courting nor avoiding observation; the Legion of Honour chinked as it swung upon his breast. A side glance at Bush suddenly gave him enormous comfort and reassurance, for Bush was sitting with a masklike immobility of countenance which told Hornblower that he was nervous too. Bush could go into action and face an enemy's broadside with an honest indifference to danger, but this present situation was trying his nerves severely, sitting watched by a thousand French eyes, and having to rely upon mere inactivity to save himself from death or imprisonment. The sight was like a tonic to Hornblower. His cares dropped from him, and he knew the joy and thrill of reckless bravery.

Beyond the next bridge the maritime port began. Here first were the fishing boats — Hornblower looked keenly at them, for he had it in mind to steal one of them. His experience under Pellew in the blockading squadron years ago was serving him in good stead now, for he knew the ways of those fishing boats. They were accustomed to ply their trade among the islands of the Breton coast, catching the pilchards which the French persisted in calling "sardines," and bringing their catch up the estuary to sell in the market at Nantes. He and Bush and Brown between them could handle one of those boats with ease, and they were seaworthy enough to take them safely out to the blockading squadron, or to England if necessary. He was practically certain that he would decide upon such a plan, so that as they rowed by he sharply ordered Brown to pull more slowly, and he turned all his attention upon them.

Below the fishing boats two American ships were lying against the quay, the Stars and Stripes fluttering jauntily in the gentle wind. His attention was caught by a dreary clanking of chains — the ships were being emptied of their cargoes by gangs of prisoners, each man staggering bent double under a bag of grain. That was interesting. Hornblower looked again. The chain gangs were under the charge of soldiers — Hornblower could see the shakos and the flash of the musket barrels — which gave him an insight into who the poor devils might be. They were military criminals, deserters, men caught sleeping at their posts, men who had disobeyed an order, all the unfortunates of the armies Bonaparte maintained in every corner of Europe. Their sentences condemned them to "the galleys" and as the French Navy no longer used galleys in which they could be forced to tug at the oars, they were now employed in all the hard labour of the ports; twice as lieutenant in Pellew's *Indefatigable* Hornblower had seen picked up small parties of desperate men who had escaped from Nantes in much the same fashion as he himself proposed now to do.

And then against the quay below the American ships they saw something else, something which caused them to stiffen in their seats. The tricolour here was hoisted above a tattered blue ensign, flaunting a petty triumph.

"*Witch of Endor,* ten-gun cutter," said Bush hoarsely. "A French frigate caught her on a lee shore off Noirmoutier last year. By God, isn't it what you'd expect of the French? It's eleven months ago and they're still wearing French colours over British."

She was a lovely little ship; even from where they were they could see the perfection of her lines — speed and seaworthiness were written all over her.

"The Frogs don't seem to have over-sparred her the way you'd expect 'em to," commented Bush.

She was ready for sea, and their expert eyes could estimate the area of the furled mainsail and jib. The high graceful mast nodded to them, almost imperceptibly, as the cutter rocked minutely beside the quay. It was as if a prisoner were appealing to them for aid, and the flapping colours, tricolour over blue ensign, told a tragic story. In a sudden rush of impulse Hornblower put the helm over.

"Lay us alongside the quay," he said to Brown.

A few strokes took them there; the tide had turned some time ago, and they headed against the flood. Brown caught a ring and made the painter fast, and first Hornblower, nimbly, and then Bush, with difficulty, mounted the stone steps to the top of the quay.

"*Suivez-nous,*" said Hornblower to Brown, remembering at the last moment to speak French.

Hornblower forced himself to hold up his head and walk with a swagger; the pistols in his side-pockets bumped reassuringly against his hips, and his sword tapped against his thigh. Bush walked beside him, his wooden leg thumping with measured stride on the stone quay. A passing group of soldiers saluted the smart uniform, and Hornblower returned the salute nonchalantly, amazed at his new coolness. His heart was beating fast, but ecstatically he knew he was not afraid. It was worth running this risk to experience this feeling of mad bravery.

They stopped and looked at the *Witch of Endor* against the quay. Her decks were not of the dazzling whiteness upon which an English first lieutenant would have insisted, and there was a slovenliness about her standing rigging which was heartbreaking to contemplate. A couple of men were moving lackadaisically about the deck under the supervision of a third.

"Anchor watch," muttered Bush. "Two hands and a master's mate."

He spoke without moving his lips, like a naughty boy in school, lest some onlooker should read his words and realise that he was not speaking French.

"Everyone else on shore, the lubbers," went on Bush.

Hornblower stood on the quay, the tiny breeze blowing round his ears, soldiers and sailors and civilians walking by, the bustle of the unloading of the American ships noisy in the distance. Bush's thoughts were following on the heels of his own. Bush was aware of the temptation Hornblower was feeling, to steal the *Witch of Endor* and to sail her to England — Bush would never have thought of it himself, but years of service under his captain made him receptive of ideas however fantastic.

Fantastic was the right word. Those big cutters carried a crew of sixty men, and the gear and tackle were planned accordingly. Three men — one a cripple — could not even hope to be able to hoist the big mainsail, although it was just possible that the three of them might handle her under sail in the open sea in fair weather. It was that possibility which had given rise to the train of thought, but on the other hand there was all the tricky estuary of the Loire between them and the sea; and the French, Hornblower knew, had removed the buoys and navigation marks for fear of an English raid. Unpiloted, they could never hope to find their way through thirty five miles of shoals without going aground, and besides, there were batteries at Paimbœuf and St. Nazaire to prohibit unauthorised entrance and exit. The thing was impossible — it was sheer sentimentality to think of it, he told himself, suddenly self-critical again for a moment.

He turned away and strolled up towards the American ships, and watched with interest the wretched chain gangs staggering along the gang-planks with their loads of grain. The sight of their misery sickened him; so did the bullying sergeants who strutted about in charge of them. Here, if anywhere, he told himself, was to be found the nucleus of that rising against Bonaparte which everyone was expecting. All that was needed was a desperate leader — that would be something worth reporting to the Government when he reached home. Farther down the river yet another ship was coming up to the port, her topsails black against the setting sun, as, with the flood behind her, she held her course close hauled to the faint southerly breeze. She was flying the Stars and Stripes — American again. Hornblower experienced the same feeling of exasperated impotence which he had known in the old days of his service under Pellew. What was the use of blockading a coast, and enduring all the hardships and perils of that service, if neutral vessels could sail in and out with impunity? Their cargoes of wheat were officially noncontraband, but wheat was of as vital importance to Bonaparte as ever was hemp, or pitch, or any other item on the contraband list

— the more wheat he could import, the more men he could draft into his armies. Hornblower found himself drifting into the eternal debate as to whether America, when eventually she became weary of the indignities of neutrality, would turn her arms against England or France — she had actually been at war with France for a short time already, and it was much to her interest to help pull down the imperial despotism, but it was doubtful whether she would be able to resist the temptation to twist the British lion's tail.

The new arrival, smartly enough handled, was edging in now to the quay. A backed topsail took the way off her, and the warps creaked round the bollards. Hornblower watched idly, Bush and Brown beside him. As the ship was made fast, a gang-plank was thrown to the quay, and a little stout man made ready to walk down it from the ship. He was in civilian clothes, and he had a rosy round face with a ridiculous little black moustache with upturned ends. From his manner of shaking hands with the captain, and from the very broken English which he was speaking, Hornblower guessed him to be the pilot.

The pilot! In that moment a surge of ideas boiled up in Hornblower's mind. It would be dark in less than an hour, with the moon in its first quarter — already he could see it, just visible in the sky high over the setting sun. A clear night, the tide about to ebb, a gentle breeze, southerly with a touch of east. A pilot available on the one hand, a crew on the other. Then he hesitated. The whole scheme was rash to the point of madness — beyond that point. It must be ill-digested, unsound. His mind raced madly through the scheme again, but even as it did so he was carried away by a wave of recklessness. There was an intoxication about throwing caution to the winds which he had forgotten since his boyhood. In the tense seconds which were all he had, while the pilot was descending the gang-plank and approaching them along the quay, he had formed his resolution. He nudged his two companions, and then stepped forward and intercepted the fat little pilot as he walked briskly past them.

"Monsieur," he said. "I have some questions to ask you. Will you kindly accompany me to my ship for a moment?"

The pilot noted the uniform, the star of the Legion of Honour, the assured manner.

"Why, certainly," he said. His conscience was clear; he was guilty of no more than venal infringements of the Continental system. He turned and trotted alongside Hornblower. "You are a newcomer to this port, Colonel, I fancy?"

"I was transferred here yesterday from Amsterdam," answered Hornblower, shortly.

Brown was striding along at the pilot's other elbow; Bush was bringing up the rear, gallantly trying to keep pace with them, his wooden leg thumping the pavement. They came up to the *Witch of Endor,* and made their way up her gang-plank to her deck; the officer there looked at them with a little surprise. But he knew the pilot, and he knew the customs uniform.

"I want to examine one of your charts, if you please," said Hornblower. "Will you show us the way to the cabin?"

The mate had not a suspicion in the world. He signed to his men to go on with their work and led the way down the brief companion to the after cabin. The mate entered, and politely Hornblower thrust the pilot in next, before him. It was a tiny cabin, but there was sufficient room to be safe when they were at the farther end. He stood by the door and brought out his two pistols.

"If you make a sound," he said, and excitement rippled his lips into a snarl, "I will kill you."

They simply stood and stared at him, but at last the pilot opened his mouth to speak — speech was irrepressible with him.

"Silence!" snapped Hornblower.

He moved far enough into the room to allow Brown and Bush to enter after him.

"Tie 'em up," he ordered.

Belts and handkerchiefs and scarves did the work efficiently enough; soon the two men were gagged and helpless, their hands tied behind them.

"Under the table with 'em," said Hornblower. "Now, be ready for the two hands when I bring 'em down."

He ran up on deck.

"Here, you two," he snapped. "I've some questions to ask you. Come down with me."

They put down their work and followed him meekly to the cabin, where Hornblower's pistols frightened them into silence. Brown ran on deck for a generous supply of line with which to bind them, and to make the lashings of the other two more secure yet. Then he and Bush — neither of them had spoken as yet since the adventure began — looked to him for further orders.

"Watch 'em," said Hornblower. "I'll be back in five minutes with a crew. There'll be one more man at least to make fast."

He went up to the quay again, and along to where the gangs of galley slaves were assembling, weary after their day's work of unloading. The ten chained men under the sergeant whom he addressed looked at him with lack-lustre eyes, only wondering faintly what fresh misery this spruce colonel was bringing them.

"Sergeant," he said. "Bring your party down to my ship. There is work for them there."

"Yes, Colonel," said the sergeant.

He rasped an order at the weary men, and they followed Hornblower down the quay. Their bare feet made no sound, but the chain which ran from waist to waist clashed rhythmically with their stride.

"Bring them down onto the deck," said Hornblower. "Now come down into the cabin for your orders."

It was all so easy, thanks to that uniform and star. Hornblower had to try hard not to laugh at the sergeant's bewilderment as they disarmed him and tied him up. It took no more than a significant gesture with Hornblower's pistol to make the sergeant indicate in which pocket was the key of the prisoners' chain.

"I'll have these men laid out under the table, if you please, Mr. Bush," said Hornblower. "All except the pilot. I want him on deck."

The sergeant and the mate and the two hands were laid out, none too gently, and Hornblower went out on deck while the others dragged the pilot after him; it was nearly quite dark now, with only the moon shining. The galley slaves were squatting listlessly on the hatchcoaming. Hornblower addressed them quietly. Despite his difficulty with the language, his boiling excitement conveyed itself to them.

"I can set you men free," he said. "There will be an end of beatings and slavery if you will do what I order. I am an English officer, and I am going to sail this ship to England. Does anyone not want to come?"

There was a little sigh from the group; it was as if they could not believe they were hearing aright — probably they could not.

"In England," went on Hornblower, "you will be rewarded. There will be a new life awaiting you."

Now at last they were beginning to understand that they had not been brought on board the cutter for further toil, that there really was a chance of freedom.

"Yes, sir," said a voice.

"I am going to unfasten your chain," said Hornblower. "Remember this. There is to be no noise. Sit still until you are told what to do."

He fumbled for the padlock in the dim light, unlocked it and snapped it open — it was pathetic, the automatic gesture with which the first man lifted his arms. He was accustomed to being locked and unlocked daily, like an animal. Hornblower set free each man in turn, and the chain clanked on the deck; he stood back with his hands on the butts of his pistols ready in case of trouble, but there was no sign of any. The men stood dazed — the transition from slavery to freedom had taken no more than three minutes.

Hornblower felt the movement of the cutter under his feet as the wind swung her; she was bumping gently against the fend-offs hung between her and the quay. A glance over the side confirmed his conclusions — the tide had not yet begun to ebb. There were still some minutes to wait, and he turned to Brown, standing restless aft of the mainmast with the pilot sitting miserably at his feet.

"Brown," he said quietly, "run down to our boat and bring

me my parcel of clothes. Run along now — what are you waiting for?"

Brown went, unhappily. It seemed dreadful to him that his captain should waste precious minutes over recovering his clothes, and should even trouble to think of them. But Hornblower was not as mad as might appear. They could not start until the tide turned, and Brown might as well be employed fetching clothes as standing fidgeting. For once in his life Hornblower had no intention of posing before his subordinates. His head was clear despite his excitement.

"Thank you," he said, as Brown returned, panting, with the canvas bag. "Get me my uniform coat out."

He stripped off his colonel's tunic and put on the coat which Brown held for him, experiencing a pleasant thrill as his fingers fastened the buttons with their crown and anchor. The coat was sadly crumpled, and the gold lace bent and broken, but still it was a uniform, even though the last time he had worn it was months ago when they had been capsized in the Loire. With this coat on his back he could no longer be accused of being a spy, and should their attempt result in failure and recapture it would shelter both himself and his subordinates. Failure and recapture were likely possibilities, as his logical brain told him, but secret murder now was not. The stealing of the cutter would attract sufficient public attention to make that impossible. Already he had bettered his position — he could not be shot as a spy or be quietly strangled in prison. If he were recaptured now he could be tried only on the old charge of violation of the laws of war, and Hornblower felt that his recent exploits might win him sufficient public sympathy to make it impolitic for Bonaparte to press even that charge.

It was time for action now. He took a belaying pin from the rail, and walked up slowly to the seated pilot, weighing the instrument meditatively in his hand.

"Monsieur," he said, "I want you to pilot this ship out to sea."

The pilot goggled up at him in the faint moonlight.

"I cannot," he gabbled. "My professional honour — my duty — "

Hornblower cut him short with a menacing gesture of the belaying pin.

"We are going to start now," he said. "You can give instructions or not, as you choose. But I tell you this, monsieur. The moment this ship touches ground, I will beat your head into a paste with this."

Hornblower eyed the white face of the pilot — his moustache was lop-sided and ridiculous now after his rough treatment. The man's eyes were on the belaying pin with which Hornblower was tapping the palm of his hand, and Hornblower felt a little thrill of triumph. The threat of a pistol bullet through the head would not have been sufficient for this imaginative southerner. But the man could picture so clearly the crash of the belaying pin upon his skull, and the savage blows which would beat him to death, that the argument Hornblower had selected was the most effective one.

"Yes, monsieur," said the pilot, weakly.

"Right," said Hornblower. "Brown, lash him to the rail, there. Then we can start. Mr. Bush, will you take the tiller if you please?"

The necessary preparations were brief; the convicts were led to the halliards and the ropes put in their hands, ready to haul on the word of command. Hornblower and Brown had so often before had experience in pushing raw crews into their places, thanks to the all-embracing activities of the British press-gangs, and it was good to see that Brown's French, eked out by the force of his example, was sufficient for the occasion.

"Cut the warps, sir?" volunteered Brown.

"No. Cast them off," snapped Hornblower.

Cut warps left hanging to the bollards would be a sure proof of a hurried and probably illegal departure; to cast them off meant possibly delaying inquiry and pursuit by a few more minutes, and every minute of delay might be precious in the uncertain future. The first of the ebb was tightening the ropes now, simplifying the business of getting away from the quay. To handle the tiny fore-and-aft rigged ship was an operation calling for little either of the judgment or of the brute strength which a big square-rigger would demand, and the present circumstances — the wind off the quay and the ebbing tide — made the only precaution necessary that of casting off the stern warp before the bow, as Brown understood as clearly as Hornblower. It happened in the natural course of events, for Hornblower had to fumble in the dim light to disentangle the clove hitches with which some French sailor had made fast, and Brown had completed his share long before him. The push of the tide was swinging the cutter away from the quay. Hornblower, in the uncertain light, had to time his moment for setting sail, making allowance for the unreliability of his crew, the eddy along the quayside, the tide and the wind.

"Hoist away," said Hornblower, and then, to the men, "*Tirez.*"

Mainsail and jib rose, to the accompaniment of the creaking of the blocks. The sails flapped, bellied, flapped again. Then they filled, and Bush at the tiller — the cutter steered with a tiller, not a wheel — felt a steady pressure. The cutter was gathering way; she was changing from a dead thing to a live. She heeled the tiniest fraction to the breeze with a subdued creaking of her cordage, and simultaneously Hornblower heard a little musical chuckle from the bows as her forefoot bubbled through the water. He picked up the belaying pin again, and in three strides was at the pilot's side, balancing the instrument in his hand.

"To the right, monsieur," gabbled that individual. "Keep well to the right."

"Port your helm, Mr. Bush. We're taking the starboard channel," said Hornblower, and then, translating the further hurried instructions of the pilot, "Meet her! Keep her at that!"

The cutter glided on down the river in the faint moonlight. From the bank of the river she must make a pretty picture — no one would guess that she was not setting forth on some quite legitimate expedition.

The pilot was saying something else now; Hornblower bent his ear to listen. It had regard to the advisability of having a man at work with the lead taking soundings, and Hornblower would not consider it for a moment. There were only Brown and himself who could do that, and they both might be wanted at any moment in case it should be necessary for the cutter to go about — moreover, there would be bound to be a muddle about fathoms and metres.

"No," said Hornblower. "You will have to do your work without that. And my promise still holds good."

He tapped his palm with the belaying pin, and laughed. That laugh surprised him, it was so blood-curdling in its implications. Anyone hearing it would be quite sure that Hornblower was determined upon clubbing the pilot to death if they went aground. Hornblower asked himself if he were acting and was puzzled to discover that he could not answer the question. He could not picture himself killing a helpless man — and yet he could not be sure. This fierce, relentless determination that consumed him was something new to him, just as it always was. He was aware of the fact that once he had set his hand to a scheme he never allowed any consideration to stop his carrying it through, but he always looked upon himself as fatalistic or resigned. It was always startling to detect in himself qualities which he admired in other men. But it was sufficient, and satisfactory, for the moment, to know that the pilot was quite sure that he would be killed in an unpleasant fashion if the cutter should touch ground.

Within half a mile it was necessary to cross to the other side — it was amusing to note how this vast estuary repeated on a grand scale the characteristics of the upper river, where the clear channel serpentined from shore to shore between the sandbanks. At the pilot's warning Hornblower got his motley crew together in case it might be necessary to go about, but the precaution was needless. Closehauled, and with the tide running fast behind her, the cutter glided across, Hornblower and Brown at the sheets, and Bush at the tiller demonstrating once more what an accomplished seaman he was. They steadied her with the wind again over her quarter, Hornblower anxiously testing the direction of the wind and looking up at the ghostly sails.

"Monsieur," pleaded the pilot, "monsieur, these cords are tight."

Hornblower laughed again, horribly.

"They will serve to keep you awake, then," he said.

His instinct had dictated the reply; his reason confirmed it. It would be best to show no hint of weakness towards this man who had it in his power to wreck everything — the more firmly the pilot was convinced of his captor's utter pitilessness the less chance there was of his playing them false. Better that he should endure the pain of tight ligatures than that three men should risk imprisonment and death. And suddenly Hornblower remembered the four other men — the sergeant and the mate and the two hands — who lay gagged and bound in the cabin. They must be highly uncomfortable, and probably fairly near to suffocation. It could not be helped. No one could be spared for a moment from the deck to go below and attend to them. There they must lie until there was no hope of rescue for them.

He found himself feeling sorry for them, and put the feeling aside. Naval history teemed with stories of recaptured prizes, in which the prisoners had succeeded in overpowering weak prize crews. He was going to run no risk of that. It was interesting to note how his mouth set itself hard at the thought, without his own volition; and it was equally interesting to observe how his reluctance to go home and face the music reacted contrariwise upon his resolution to see this affair through. He did not want to fail, and the thought that he might be glad of failure because of the postponement of the settlement of his affairs only made him more set in his determination not to fail.

"I will loosen the cords," he said to the pilot, "when we are off Noirmoutier. Not before."

Chapter XIV

THEY were off Noirmoutier at dawn, with the last dying puff of wind. The grey light found them becalmed and enwreathed in a light haze which drifted in patches over the calm surface of the sea, awaiting the rising of the sun to dissipate it. Hornblower looked round him as the details became more clear. The galley slaves were all asleep on the foredeck, huddled together for warmth like pigs in a sty, with Brown squatting on the hatch beside them, his chin on his hand. Bush still stood at the tiller, betraying no fatigue after his sleepless night; he held the tiller against his hip with his wooden leg braced against a ringbolt. Against the rail the pilot drooped in his bonds; his face which yesterday had been plump and pink was this morning drawn and grey with pain and fatigue.

With a little shudder of disgust Hornblower cut him loose.

"I keep my promise, you see," he said, but the pilot only dropped to the deck, his face distorted with pain, and a minute later he was groaning with the agony of returning circulation.

The big mainsail boom came inboard with a clatter as the sail flapped.

"I can't hold the course, sir," said Bush.

"Very well," said Hornblower.

He might have expected this. The gentle night wind which had wafted them down the estuary was of just the sort to die away with the dawn, leaving them becalmed. But had it held for another half-hour, had they made another couple of miles of progress, they would be far safer. There lay Noirmoutier to port, and the mainland astern; through the shredding mist he could make out the gaunt outlines of the semaphore station on the mainland — sixteen years ago he had been second in command of the landing party which Pellew had sent ashore to destroy it. The islands were all heavily garrisoned now, with big guns mounted, as a consequence of the incessant English raids.

He scanned the distance which separated them from Noirmoutier, measuring it with his eye — they were out of big-gun range, he fancied, but the tide might easily drift them in closer. He even suspected, from what he remembered of the set of the tides, that there was danger of their being drifted into the Bay of Bourgneuf.

"Brown," he called, sharply. "Wake those men up. Set them to work with the sweeps."

On either side of every gun was a thole for a sweep, six on each side of the ship; Brown shoved his blear-eyed crew into their positions and showed them how to get out the big oars, with the long rope joining the looms.

"One, two, three, pull!" shouted Brown.

The men put their weight on the oars; the blades bubbled ineffectively through the still water.

"One, two, three, pull! One, two, three, pull!"

Brown was all animation, gesticulating, running from man to man beating time with his whole body. Gradually the cutter gathered way, and as she began to move the oar blades began to bite upon the water with more effect.

"One, two, three, pull!"

It did not matter that Brown was counting time in English, for there was no mistaking his meaning, nor the meaning of the convulsive movements of his big body.

"Pull!"

The galley slaves sought for foothold on the deck as they tugged; Brown's enthusiasm was infectious, so that one or two of them even raised their voices in a cracked cheer as they leaned back. Now the cutter was perceptibly moving; Bush swung the tiller over, felt the rudder bite, and steadied her on her course again. She rose and fell over the tiny swell with a clattering of blocks.

Hornblower looked away from the straining men over the oily sea. If he had been lucky he might have found one of the ships of the blockading squadron close inshore — often they would come right in among the islands to beard Bonaparte. But today there was no sail in sight. He studied the grim outlines of the island for signs of life. Even as he looked the gallows-like arms of the semaphore station on the mainland sprang up to attention. They made no further movement, and Hornblower guessed that they were merely announcing the operators' readiness to receive a message from the station farther inshore, invisible to him — he could guess the purport of the message. Then the arms started signalling, moving jerkily against the blue sky, transmitting a brief reply to the interior. Another period of quiescence, and then Hornblower saw the signal arms swing round towards him — previously they had been nearly in profile. Automatically he turned towards Noirmoutier, and he saw the tiny speck of the flag at the masthead there dip in acknowledgment. Noirmoutier was ready to receive orders from the land. Round and round spun the arms of the semaphore; up and down went the flag in acknowledgment of each sentence.

Near the foot of the mast appeared a long jet of white smoke, rounding off instantly into a ball; and one after the other four fountains of water leaped from the glassy surface of the sea as a shot skipped over it, the dull report following after. The nearest fountain was a full half-mile away, so that they were comfortably out of range.

"Make those men pull!" roared Hornblower to Brown.

He could guess what would be the next move. Under her sweeps the cutter was making less than a mile in the hour, and all day they would be in danger, unless a breeze came, and his straining eyes could see no hint of a breeze on the calm surface of the sea, nor in the vivid blue of the morning sky. At any moment boats crowded with men would be putting off towards them — boats whose oars would move them far faster than the cutter's sweeps. There would be fifty men in each, perhaps a gun mounted in the bows as well. Three men with the doubtful aid of a dozen galley slaves could not hope to oppose them.

"Yes I can, by God!" said Hornblower to himself.

As he sprang into action he could see the boats heading out from the tip of the island, tiny dots upon the surface of the sea. The garrison must have turned out and bundled into the boats immediately on receiving the order from the land.

"Pull!" shouted Brown.

The sweeps groaned on the tholes, and the cutter lurched under the impulse.

Hornblower had cleared away the aftermost six-pounder on the port side. There was shot in the locker under the rail, but no powder.

"Keep the men at work, Brown," he said, "and watch the pilot."

"Aye aye, sir," said Brown.

He stretched out a vast hand and took hold of the pilot's collar, while Hornblower dived into the cabin. One of the four prisoners there had writhed and wriggled his way to the foot of the little companion — Hornblower trod on him in his haste. With a curse he dragged him out of the way; as he expected there was a hatchway down into the lazarette. Hornblower jerked it open and plunged through; it was nearly dark, for the only light was what filtered through the cabin skylight and then down the hatchway, and he stumbled and blundered upon the piled-up stores inside. He steadied himself; whatever the need for haste there was no profit in panic. He waited for his eyes to grow accustomed to the darkness, while overhead he could hear Brown still bellowing and the sweeps still groaning on the tholes. Then in the bulkhead before him he saw what he sought, a low doorway with a glass panel, which must indicate the magazine — the gunner would work in there by the light of a lantern shining through.

He heaved the piled-up stores out of his way, sweating in his haste and the heat, and wrenched open the door. Feeling about him in the tiny space, crouching nearly double, his hands fell upon four big hogsheads of gunpowder. He fancied he could feel the grittiness of gunpowder under his feet; any movement on his part might start a spark and blow the cutter to fragments — it was just like the French to be careless with explosives. He sighed with relief when his fingers encountered the paper containers of ready charges. He had hoped to find them, but there had always been the chance that there were no cartridges available, and he had not been enamoured of the prospect of using a powder-ladle. He loaded himself with cartridges and backed out of the tiny magazine to the cabin, and sprang up on deck again, to the clear sunshine.

The boats were appreciably nearer, for they were no longer black specks but boats, creeping beetle-like over the surface towards them, three of them, already spaced out in their race to effect a recapture. Hornblower put down his cartridges upon the deck. His heart was pounding with his exertions and with excitement, and each successive effort that he made to steady himself seemed to grow less successful. It was one thing to think and plan and direct, to say "Do this" or "Go there," and it was quite another to have success dependent upon the cunning of his own fingers and the straightness of his own eye.

His sensations were rather similar to those he experienced when he had drunk a glass of wine too many — he knew clearly enough what he had to do, but his limbs were not quite as ready as usual to obey the orders of his brain. He fumbled more than once as he rigged the train-tackle of the gun.

That fumbling cured him; he rose from the task shaking his unsteadiness from him, like Christian losing his burden of sin. He was cool now, set completely on the task in hand.

"Here, you," he said to the pilot.

The pilot demurred for a moment, full of fine phrases regarding the impossibility of training a gun upon his fellow countrymen, but a sight of the alteration in Hornblower's expression reduced him to instant humble submission. Hornblower was unaware of the relentless ferocity of his glance, being only conscious of a momentary irritation at anyone crossing his will. But the pilot had thought that any further delay would lead to Hornblower's killing him, pitilessly — and the pilot may have been right. Between them they laid hold of the train-tackle and ran the gun back. Hornblower took out the tompion and went round to the breech; he twirled the elevating screw until his eye told him that the gun was at the maximum elevation at which it could be run out. He cocked the lock, and then, crouching over the gun so that the shadow of his body cut off the sunlight, jerked the lanyard. The spark was satisfactory.

He ripped open a cartridge, poured the powder into the muzzle of the gun, folded the paper into a wad, and rammed the charge home with the flexible rammer. A glance towards the boats showed that they were still probably out of range, so that he was not pressed for time. He devoted a few seconds to turning over the shot in the locker, selecting two or three of the roundest, and then strolled across the deck to the starboard side locker to make a selection from there. For long range work with a six-pounder he did not want shot that bounced about during its passage up the gun and was liable to fly off God-knew-where when it emerged. He rammed his eventual selection well down upon the wad — at this elevation there was no need for a second wad — and, ripping open a second cartridge, he primed the breech.

"*Allons!*" he snapped at the pilot, and they ran the gun up. Two men were the barest minimum crew for a six-pounder, but Hornblower's long slight body was capable of exerting extraordinary strength at the behest of his mind.

With a handspike he trained the gun round aft as far as possible. Even so, the gun did not point towards the leading boat, which lay far abaft the beam; the cutter would have to yaw to fire at her. Hornblower straightened himself up in the sunlight. Brown was chanting hoarsely at the galley slaves almost in his ear, and the aftermost sweep had been working right at his elbow, and he had not noticed either, so intent had he been on his task. For the cutter to yaw meant losing a certain amount of distance; he had to balance that certain loss against the chances of hitting a boat with a six-pounder ball at two thousand yards. It would not pay at present; it would be better to wait a little, for the range to shorten, but it was an interesting problem, even though it could have no exact solution in consequence of the presence of an unknown, which was the possibility of the coming of a wind.

Of that there was still no sign, long and anxiously though Hornblower stared over the glassy sea. As he looked round he caught the eye of Bush at the tiller directed anxiously at him — Bush was awaiting the order to yaw. Hornblower smiled at him and shook his head, resuming his study of the horizon, the distant islands, the unbroken expanse to seaward where lay freedom. A sea gull was wheeling overhead, dazzling white against the blue, and crying plaintively. The cutter was nodding a little in the faint swell.

"Beggin' your pardon, sir," said Brown in his ear. "Beggin' your pardon, sir — Pull! — These men can't go on much longer, sir. Look at that one over there on the starboard side, sir — Pull!"

There could be no doubt of it; the men were swaying with fatigue as they reached forward with the long sweeps. Dangling from Brown's hand was a length of knotted cord; clearly he had already been using the most obvious argument to persuade them to work.

"Give 'em a bit of a rest, sir, and summat to eat an' drink, an' they'll go on all right, sir. Pull, you bastards! They haven't had no breakfast, sir, nor no supper yesterday."

"Very good," said Hornblower. "You can rest 'em and get 'em fed. Mr. Bush! Let her come slowly round."

He bent over the gun, oblivious at once to the clatter of the released sweeps as the galley slaves ceased work, just as he was oblivious that he himself had not eaten or drunk or slept since yesterday. At the touch of the tiller and with her residual way the cutter turned slowly. The black mass of a boat appeared in the V of the dispart sight, and he waved his hand to Bush. The boat had disappeared again, and came back into his field of vision as Bush checked the turn with the tiller, but not quite in alignment with the gun. Hornblower eased the gun round with the handspike until the aim was true, drew himself up, and stepped out of the way of the recoil, lanyard in hand. Of necessity, he was far more doubtful of the range than of the direction, and it was vital to observe the fall of the shot. He took note of the motion of the cutter on the swell, waited for the climax of the roll, and jerked the lanyard. The gun roared out and recoiled past him; he sprang sideways to get clear of the smoke. The four seconds of the flight of the shot seemed to stretch out indefinitely, and then at last he saw the jet of water leap into brief existence, fully two hundred yards short and a hundred yards to the right. That was poor shooting.

He sponged out the gun and reloaded it, called the pilot to him with an abrupt gesture, and ran the gun out again. It was necessary, he realized, to get acquainted with the weapon if he wanted to do any fancy shooting with it, so that he made no alteration in elevation, endeavored to lay the gun exactly as before, and jerked the lanyard at as nearly the same instant of the roll as possible. This time it appeared that the elevation was correct, for the shot pitched well up to the boat, but it was out to the right again, fifty yards off at least. It seemed likely that the gun, therefore, had a tendency to throw to the right. He trained the gun round a trifle to the left, and, still without altering the elevation, fired again. Too far to the left, and two hundred yards short again.

Hornblower told himself that a variation of two hundred yards in the fall of shot from a six-pounder at full elevation was only to be expected, and he knew it to be true, but that was cold comfort to him. The powder varied from charge to charge, the shot were never truly round, quite apart from the variations in atmospheric conditions and in the temperature of the gun. He set his teeth, aimed and fired again. Short, and a trifle to the left. It was maddening.

"Breakfast, sir," said Brown at his elbow.

Hornblower turned abruptly, and there was Brown with a tray, bearing a basin of biscuit, a bottle of wine, a jug of water, a pewter mug; the sight made Hornblower realise that he was intensely hungry and thirsty.

"What about you?" asked Hornblower.

"We're all right, sir," said Brown.

The galley slaves were squatting on the deck wolfing bread and drinking water; so was Bush, over by the tiller. Hornblower discovered that his tongue and the roof of his mouth were dry as leather — his hands shook as he mixed water with wine and gulped it down. Beside the cabin skylight lay the four men who had been left in bonds in the cabin. Their hands were free now, although their feet were still bound. The sergeant and one of the seamen were noticeably pale.

"I took the liberty of bringing 'em up, sir," said Brown. "Those two was pretty nigh dead, 'cause o' their gags, sir. But they'll be all right soon, I fancy, sir."

It had been thoughtless cruelty to leave them bound, thought Hornblower. But going back in his mind through the events of the night he could not think of any time until now when any attention could have been spared for them. In war there was always plenty of cruelty.

"These beggars," said Brown, indicating the galley slaves, "wanted to throw their sojer overboard when they saw 'im, sir."

He grinned widely, as though that were very amusing. The remark opened a long vista of thought, regarding the miseries of the life of a galley slave and the brutalities of their guards.

"Yes," said Hornblower, gulping down a morsel of biscuit and drinking again. "You had better set 'em all to work at the sweeps."

"Aye aye, sir. I had the same idea, beggin' your pardon. We can have two watches with all these men."

"Arrange it as you like," said Hornblower, turning back to the gun.

The nearest boat was appreciably nearer now; Hornblower judged it advisable to make a small reduction in the elevation, and this time the shot pitched close to the boat, almost among the oars on one side, apparently.

"Beautiful, sir!" said Bush beside the tiller.

Hornblower's skin was prickling with sweat and powder smoke. He took off his gold-laced coat, suddenly conscious of the heavy weight of the pistols in the side pockets; he proffered them to Bush, but the latter shook his head and grinned, pointing to the bell-mouthed blunderbuss on the deck beside him. That would be a far more efficacious weapon if there was trouble with their motley crew. For an exasperated moment Hornblower wondered what to do with the pistols, and finally laid them handy in the scuppers before sponging out and reloading the gun. The next shot was a close one, too — apparently the small reduction of range had had a profound effect on the accuracy of the gun. Hornblower saw the shot pitch close to the bows of the boat; it would be a matter of pure chance at that range if he scored an actual hit, for no gun could be expected to be accurate to fifty yards.

"Sweeps are ready, sir," said Brown.

"Very good. Mr. Bush, kindly lay a course so that I can keep that boat under fire."

Brown was a pillar of strength. He had had rigged only the three foremost sweeps on each side, setting six men to work on them. The others were herded together forward, ready to relieve the men at work when they were tired — six sweeps would only just give the big cutter steerage way, but continuous slow progress was preferable to an alternation of movement and passivity. What arguments he had used to persuade the four Frenchmen who were not galley slaves to work at the sweeps Hornblower judged it best not to inquire — it was sufficient that they were there, their feet hobbled, straining away at the sweeps while Brown gave them the time, his knotted rope's end dangling from his fist.

The cutter began to creep through the blue water again, the rigging rattling at each tug on the sweeps. To make the chase as long as possible she should have turned her stern to her pursuers, instead of keeping them on her quarter. But Hornblower had decided that the chance of scoring a hit with the gun was worth the loss in distance — a decision of whose boldness he was painfully aware and which he had to justify. He bent over the gun and aimed carefully, and this time the shot flew wide again. Watching the splash from the rail Hornblower felt a surge of exasperation. For a moment he was tempted to hand the gun over to Bush, for him to try his hand, but he put the temptation aside. In the face of stark reality, without allowing false modesty to enter into the debate, he could rely on himself to lay a gun better than Bush could.

"*Tirez!*" he snapped at the pilot, and between them they ran the gun up again.

The pursuing boats, creeping black over the blue sea, had shown no signs so far of being dismayed by the bombardment to which they were being subjected. Their oars kept steadily at work, and they maintained resolutely a course which would cut the *Witch of Endor's* a mile or so further on. They were big boats, all three of them, carrying at least a hundred and fifty men between them — only one of them need range alongside to do the business. Hornblower fired again and then again, doggedly, fighting down the bitter disappointment at each successive miss. The range was little over a thousand yards now, he judged — what he would call in an official report "long cannon shot." He hated those black boats creeping onward, immune, threatening his life and liberty, just as he hated this cranky gun which would not shoot the same two rounds running. The sweat was making his shirt stick to him, and the powder-grains were irritating his skin.

At the next shot there was no splash; Hornblower could see no sign of its fall anywhere. Then he saw the leading boat swing half round, and her oars stop moving.

"You've hit her, sir," called Bush.

Next moment the boat straightened on her course again, her oars hard at work. That was disappointing — it had hardly been likely that a ship's long boat could survive a direct hit from a six-pounder ball without injury to her fighting ability, but it was possible, all the same. Hornblower felt for the first time a sense of impending failure. If the hit he had scored with such difficulty was of no avail, what was the sense in continuing the struggle? Then, doggedly, he bent over the gun again, staring along the sights to allow for the small amount of right hand bias which the gun exhibited. Even as he looked he saw the leading boat cease rowing again. She wavered and then swung round, signalling wildly to the other boats. Hornblower trained the gun round upon her and fired again and missed, but he could see that she was perceptibly lower in the water. The other boats drew up alongside her, evidently to transfer her crew.

"Port a point, Mr. Bush!" yelled Hornblower — already the

group of boats was out of the field of fire of the gun, and yet was far too tempting a mark to ignore. The French pilot groaned as he helped to run the gun up, but Hornblower had no time for his patriotic protests. He sighted carefully, and fired. Again there was no sign of a splash — the ball had taken effect, but presumably upon the boat which had already been hit, for immediately afterwards the other two drew away from their water-logged fellow to resume the pursuit.

Brown was changing over the men at the sweeps — Hornblower remembered now that he had heard him cheering hoarsely when he had scored his hit — and Hornblower found a second in which to admire his masterful handling of the men, prisoners of war and escaping slaves alike. There was time for admiration, but no time for envy. The pursuers were changing their tactics — one boat was heading straight at them, while the other, diverging a little, was still heading to intercept them. The reason was soon obvious, for from the bows of the former boat came a puff of smoke, and a cannon-ball raised a splash from the surface of the water on the cutter's quarter and skipped past the stern.

Hornblower shrugged his shoulders at that — a three-pounder boat gun, fired from a platform far more unsteady even than the *Witch of Endor*, could hardly do them any harm at that range, and every shot meant delay in the pursuit. He trained his gun round upon the intercepting boat, fired, and missed. He was already taking aim again before the sound of the second shot from the boat gun reached his ears, and he did not trouble to find out where the ball went. His own shot fell close to its target, for the range was shortening and he was growing more experienced with the gun and more imbued with the rhythm of the long Atlantic swell which rocked the *Witch of Endor*. Three times he dropped a shot so close to the boat that the men at the oars must have been wet by the splashes — each shot deserved to be a hit, he knew, but the incalculable residuum of variables in powder and ball and gun made it a matter of chance just where the ball fell in a circle of fifty yards' radius, however well aimed. Ten guns properly controlled, and fired together in a broadside, would do the business, but there was no chance of firing ten guns together.

There was a crash from forward, a fountain of splinters from the base of a stanchion, and a shot scarred the deck diagonally close beside the fore hatchway.

"No you don't!" roared Brown, leaping forward with his rope's end. "Keep pulling, you bastards!"

He jerked the scared galley slave who had dropped his sweep — the shot must have missed him by no more than a yard — back into position.

"Pull!" he shouted, standing, magnificent in his superb physique, right in the midst of them, the weary ones lying on the deck, the others sweating at the sweeps, the knotted rope swinging from his hand. He was like a lion tamer in a cage. Hornblower could see there was no need for him and his pistols, and bent again, this time with a real twinge of envy, over his gun.

The boat which was firing at them had not closed in at all — if anything she had fallen a trifle back — but the other one was far nearer by now. Hornblower could see the individual men in her, the dark heads and the brown shoulders. Her oars were still for the moment, and there was some movement in her, as if they were re-arranging the men at the oars. Now she was in motion again, and moving far faster, and heading straight at them. The officer in charge, having worked up as close as this, had double-banked his oars so as to cover the last, most dangerous zone with a rush, pouring out the carefully conserved energy of his men prodigally in his haste to come alongside.

Hornblower estimated the rapidly diminishing range, twirled the elevating screw, and fired. The shot hit the water ten yards from her bows and must have ricochetted clean over her. He sponged and loaded and rammed — a misfire now, he told himself, would be fatal, and he forced himself to go through the routine with all the exactness he had employed before. The sights of the gun were looking straight at the bows of the boat, it was point-blank range. He jerked the lanyard and sprang instantly to reload without wasting time by seeing where the shot went.

It must have passed close over the heads of the men at the oars, for when he looked along the sights again there she was, still heading straight at him. A tiny reduction in elevation, and he stepped aside and jerked the lanyard. He was dragging at the train tackles before he could look again. The bows of the boat had opened like a fan. In the air above her there was a black dot — a water breaker, presumably, sent flying like a football by the impact of the shot, which had hit clean and square upon her stem at water level. Her bows were lifted a little out of the water, the loose strakes spread wide, and then they came down again and the water surged in, and she was gunwale deep in a flash, her bottom smashed, presumably, as well as her bows, by the passage of the shot.

Brown was cheering again, and Bush was capering as well as he could with a wooden leg, while steering, and the little French pilot at his side was pulling in his breath with a sharp hissing noise. There were black dots on the surface of the blue water where men struggled for their lives — it must be bitter cold and they would die quickly, those who could not find support on the shattered hull, but nothing could be done to help them. Already they had more prisoners than they could conveniently handle, and delay would bring the other boat alongside them.

"Keep the men at work!" said Hornblower, harshly, to Brown, and unnecessarily. Then he bent to reload the gun once more.

"What course, sir?" asked Bush, from the tiller. He wanted to know if he should steer so as to allow fire to be opened on the third boat, which had ceased firing now and was pulling hastily towards the wreck.

"Keep her as she is," snapped Hornblower. He knew perfectly well that the boat would not annoy them further; having seen two of her fellows sunk and being of necessity vastly overcrowded she would turn back sooner than maintain the contest. And so it proved. After the boat had picked up the survivors they saw her swing round and head towards Noirmoutier, followed by a derisive cheer from Brown.

Hornblower could look round him now. He walked aft to the taffrail beside Bush — it was curious how much more natural it felt to be there than at the gun — and scanned the horizon. During the fight the cutter had made very decided progress under her sweeps. The mainland was lost in the faint haze; Noirmoutier was already far behind. But there was still no sign of a breeze. They were still in danger — if darkness should find them where boats could reach them from the islands a night attack would tell a very different story. They needed every yard they could gain, and the men must go on slaving at the sweeps all through the day, all through the night too, if necessary.

He was conscious now that he ached in every joint after the frantic exertions of serving the gun the whole morning, and he had had a whole night without sleep — so had Bush, so had Brown. He felt that he stank of sweat and smoke, and his skin tingled with powder grains. He wanted to rest, yet automatically he walked over to make the gun secure again, to put the unused cartridges out of harm's way, and to repocket the pistols which he noticed reproaching his carelessness from the scuppers.

Chapter XV

At midnight, and not before, a tiny breeze came whispering over the misty surface of the water, at first merely swinging over the big mainsail and setting the rigging chattering, but then breathing more strongly until the sails could catch it and hold it, filling out in the darkness until Hornblower could give the word for the exhausted men at the sweeps to abandon their labour and the cutter could glide on with almost imperceptible motion, so slowly that there was hardly a bubble at her bows, yet even at that faster than the sweeps had moved her. Out of the east came that breath of wind, steady even though feeble; Hornblower could feel hardly any pull as he handled the main-sheet, and yet the cutter's big area of canvas was able to carry her graceful hull forward over the invisible surface as though in a dream.

It was like a dream indeed — weariness and lack of sleep combined to make it so for Hornblower, who moved about his tasks in a misty unreality which matched the misty darkness of the sea. The galley slaves and prisoners could lie and sleep — there was no fear of trouble from them at present, when they had spent ten hours out of the last twenty pulling at the sweeps with hands which by nightfall were running with blood, but there was no sleep for him nor for Bush and Brown. His voice sounded strange and distant in his own ears, like that of a stranger speaking from another room, as he issued his orders; the very hands with which he held the ropes seemed not to belong to him. It was as if there was a cleavage between the brain with which he was trying to think and the body which condescended to obey him.

Somewhere to the northwest lay the fleet which maintained its unsleeping watch over Brest; he had laid the cutter on a northwesterly course with the wind comfortably on her quarter, and if he could not find the Channel fleet he would round

Ushant and sail the cutter to England. He knew all this — it made it more like a dream than ever that he could not believe it although he knew it. The memory of Marie de Graçay's upper boudoir, or of his battle for life in the floodwater of the Loire, was far more real to him than this solid little ship whose deck he trod and whose mainsheet he was handling. Setting a course for Bush to steer was like playing a make-believe game with a child. He told himself desperately that this was not a new phenomenon, — that often enough before he had noticed that although he could dispense with one night's sleep without missing it greatly, on the second in succession his imagination began to play tricks with him, — but it did not help to clear his mind.

He came back to Bush at the tiller when the faint binnacle light made the lieutenant's face just visible in the darkness; Hornblower was even prepared to enter into conversation in exchange for a grasp at reality.

"Tired, Mr. Bush?" he asked.

"No, sir. Of course not. But how is it with you, sir?"

Bush had served with his captain through too many fights to have an exaggerated idea of his strength.

"Well enough, thank you."

"If this breeze holds, sir," said Bush, realising that this was one of the rare occasions when he was expected to make small talk with his captain, "we'll be up to the fleet in the morning."

"I hope so," said Hornblower.

"By God, sir," said Bush, "what will they say of this in England?"

Bush's expression was rapt. He was dreaming of fame, of promotion, for his captain as much as for himself.

"In England?" said Hornblower vaguely.

He had been too busy to dream any dreams himself, to think about what the British public, sentimental as always, would think of an escaping British captain retaking almost single-handed a captured ship of war and returning in her in triumph. And he had seized the *Witch of Endor* in the first place merely because the opportunity had presented itself, and because it was the most damaging blow he could deal the enemy; since the seizure he had been at first too busy, and latterly too tired, to appreciate the dramatic quality of his action. His distrust of himself, and his perennial pessimism regarding his career, would not allow him to think of himself as dramatically successful. The unimaginative Bush could appreciate the potentialities better than he could.

"Yes, sir," said Bush, eagerly — even with tiller and compass and wind claiming so much of his attention he could be loquacious on this point — "It'll look fine in the *Gazette*, this recapture of the *Witch*. Even the *Morning Chronicle*, sir —— "

The *Morning Chronicle* was a thorn in the side of the Government, ever ready to decry a victory or make capital of a defeat. Hornblower remembered how during the bitter early days of his captivity at Rosas he had worried about what the *Morning Chronicle* would say regarding his surrender of the *Sutherland*.

He felt sick now, suddenly. His mind was active enough now. Most of its vagueness must have been due, he told himself, to his refusing in cowardly fashion to contemplate the future. Until this night everything had been uncertain — he might have been recaptured at any moment; but now, as sure as anything could be at sea, he would see England again. He would have to stand his trial for the loss of the *Sutherland*, and face a court-martial, after eighteen years of service. The court might find him guilty of not having done his utmost in the presence of the enemy, and for that there was only one penalty, death — that Article of War did not end, as others did, with the mitigating words "or such less penalty . . ." Byng had been shot fifty years before under that Article of War.

Absolved on that account, the wisdom of his actions in command of the *Sutherland* might still be called into question. He might be found guilty of errors of judgment in hazarding his ship in a battle against quadruple odds, and be punished by anything from dismissal from the service, which would make him an outcast and a beggar, down to a simple reprimand which would merely wreck his career. A court-martial was always a hazardous ordeal from which few emerged unscathed — Cochrane, Sydney Smith, half a dozen brilliant captains had suffered damage at the hands of a court-martial, and the friendless Captain Hornblower might be the next.

And a court-martial was only one of the ordeals that awaited him. The child must be three months old now; until this moment he had never been able to think clearly about the child — boy or girl, healthy or feeble. He was torn with anxiety for Maria — and yet, gulping at the pill of reality, he forced himself to admit that he did not want to go back to Maria. He did not want to. It had been in mad jealousy of the moment, when he heard of Lady Barbara's marriage to Admiral Leighton, that the child had been conceived. Maria in England, Marie in France — his conscience was in a turmoil about both of them, and underlying the turmoil was an unregenerate hunger for Lady Barbara which had remained quiescent during his preoccupation but which he knew would grow into an unrelenting ache, an internal cancer, the moment his other troubles ceased, if ever they did.

Bush was still babbling away happily beside him at the tiller. Hornblower heard the words, and attached no meaning to them.

"Ha — h'm," he said. "Quite so."

He could find no satisfaction in the simple pleasures Bush had been in ecstasy about — the breath of the sea, the feeling of a ship's deck underfoot — not now, not with all these bitter thoughts thronging his mind. The harshness of his tone checked Bush in the full career of his artless and unwonted chatter, and the lieutenant pulled himself up abruptly. Hornblower thought it was absurd that Bush should still cherish any affection for him after the cutting cruelty with which he sometimes used him. Bush was like a dog, thought Hornblower bitterly — too cynical for the moment to credit Bush with any perspicacity at all — like a dog, coming fawning to the hand that beat him. Hornblower despised himself as he walked forward again to the mainsheet, to a long, long period of a solitary black hell of his own.

There was just the faintest beginning of daylight, the barest pearly softening of the sombreness of night, a greyness instead of a blackness in the haze, when Brown came aft to Hornblower.

"Beggin' your pardon, sir, but I fancy I see the loom of something out there just now. On the port bow, sir — there, d'you see it, sir?"

Hornblower strained his eyes through the darkness. Perhaps there was a more solid nucleus to the black mist out there, a tiny something. It came and went as his eyes grew tired.

"What d'you make of it, Brown?"

"I thought it was a ship, sir, when I first saw it, but in this haze, sir — "

There was a faint chance she might be a French ship of war — it was about as likely as to find the king unguarded when leading from a suit of four to the ace. Much the most likely chance was that she was an English ship of war, and the next most likely was that she was a merchantman. The safest course was to creep down upon her from the windward, because the cutter, lying nearer the wind than any square-rigged ship could do, could escape if necessary the way she came, trusting to the mist and darkness and surprise to avoid being disabled before she got out of range.

"Mr. Bush, I fancy there's a sail to leeward. Put the cutter before the wind and run down to her, if you please. Be ready to go about if I give the word. Jib-sheet, Brown."

Hornblower's head was clear again now, in the face of a possible emergency. He regretted the quickening of his pulse — uncertainty always had that effect. The cutter steadied upon her new course, creeping before the wind over the misty water, mainsail boom far out to port. Hornblower experienced a moment's doubt in case Bush was sailing her by the lee, but he would not allow himself to call a warning — he knew he could trust a sailor of Bush's ability not to risk a gibe in an emergency of this sort. He strained his eyes through the darkness; the mist was patchy, coming and going as he looked, but that was a ship without any doubt. She was under topsails alone — that made it almost certain that she was an English ship of war, one of the fleet which maintained unceasing watch over Brest. Another patch of mist obscured her again, and by the time they had run through it she was appreciably nearer and dawn was at hand — her sails were faint grey in the growing light.

Now they were close upon her.

Suddenly the stillness was rent by a hail, high-pitched, penetrating, its purity of quality almost unspoilt by the speaking trumpet — the voice which uttered it was trained in clarity in Atlantic gales.

"Cutter ahoy! What cutter's that?"

At the sound of the English speech Hornblower relaxed. There was no need now to go about, to claw up to windward, to seek shelter in the mist. But on the other hand all the unpleasantnesses of the future which he had been visualising were certain now. He swallowed hard, words failing him for the moment.

"What cutter's that?" repeated the hail, impatiently.

Unpleasant the future might be; he would fly his colours to the last, and if his career were ending, he would end it with a joke.

"His Britannic Majesty's armed cutter *Witch of Endor,* Captain Horatio Hornblower. What ship's that?"

"*Triumph,* Captain Sir Thomas Hardy — *what* did you say that cutter was?"

Hornblower grinned to himself. The officer of the watch in the strange sail had begun his reply automatically; it was only after he had stated the names of his ship and captain that it had suddenly dawned upon him that the cutter's statement was quite incredible. The *Witch of Endor* had been a prize to the French for nearly a year, and Captain Horatio Hornblower had been dead six months.

Hornblower repeated what he had said before; both Bush and Brown were chuckling audibly at a joke which appealed to them forcibly indeed.

"Come under my lee, and no tricks, or I'll sink you," hailed the voice.

From the cutter they could hear guns being run out in the *Triumph;* Hornblower could picture the bustle on board, hands being turned up, the captain being called — Sir Thomas Hardy must be Nelson's late flag captain at Trafalgar, two years Hornblower's senior in the captains' list. Hornblower had known him as a lieutenant, although since then their paths had hardly crossed. Bush eased the cutter under the stern of the two-decker, and brought her to the wind under her lee. Dawn was coming up fast now, and they could see the details of the ship, as she lay hove to, rolling in the swell, and a long, shuddering sigh burst from Hornblower's breast. The sturdy beauty of the ship, the two yellow streaks along her sides, checkered with black gun-ports, the pendant at the main, the hands on the deck, the red coats of the marines, the boatswain's voice roaring at dilatory seamen — all the familiar sights and sounds of the Navy in which he had grown up moved him inexpressibly at this moment, the end of his long captivity and flight.

The *Triumph* had launched a boat, which came dancing rapidly over to them, and a young midshipman swung himself dexterously on board, dirk at his hip, arrogant suspicion on his face, four seamen at his back with pistols and cutlasses.

"What's all this?" demanded the midshipman. His glance swept the cutter's deck, observing the sleepy prisoners rubbing their eyes, the wooden-legged civilian at the tiller, the bare-headed man in a King's coat awaiting him.

"You call me 'sir,'" barked Hornblower, as he had done to midshipmen ever since he became a lieutenant.

The midshipman eyed the gold-laced coat — undoubtedly it was trimmed in the fashion of the coat of a captain of more than three years' seniority, and the man who wore it carried himself as though he expected deference.

"Yes, sir," said the midshipman, a little abashed.

"That is Lieutenant Bush at the tiller. You will remain here with these men under his orders, while I go to interview your captain."

"Aye aye, sir," said the midshipman, stiffening to attention.

The boat bore Hornblower to the *Triumph's* side; the coxswain made the four-finger gesture which indicated the arrival of a captain, but marines and side-boys were not in attendance as Hornblower went up the side — the Navy could not risk wasting her cherished compliments on possible impostors. But Hardy was there on deck, his huge bulk towering over everyone round him; Hornblower saw the expression of his beefy face alter as he saw him.

"Good God, it's Hornblower all right," said Hardy, striding forward, with his hand outstretched. "Welcome back, sir. How do you come here, sir? How did you retake the *Witch*? How — "

What Hardy wanted to say was "How have you risen from the grave?" but such a question seemed to savour of impoliteness. Hornblower shook hands, and trod gratefully the quarterdeck of a ship of the line once more. His heart was too full for speech, or his brain was too numb with fatigue, and he could make no reply to Hardy's questioning.

"Come below to my cabin," said Hardy, kindly — phlegmatic though he was, he still could just appreciate the other's difficulty.

There was more ease in the cabin, sitting on the cushioned locker under the portrait of Nelson that hung on the bulkhead, and with the timbers groaning faintly all round, and the blue sea visible through the great stern window. Hornblower told a little of what happened to him — not much, and not in detail; only half a dozen brief sentences, for Hardy was not a man with much use for words. He listened with attention, pulling at his whiskers, and nodding at each point.

"There was a whole *Gazette*," he remarked, "about the attack in Rosas Bay. They brought Leighton's body back for burial in St. Paul's."

The cabin swam round Hornblower; Hardy's homely face and magnificent whiskers vanished in a mist.

"He was killed, then?" Hornblower asked.

"He died of his wounds at Gibraltar."

So Barbara was a widow — had been one for six months now.

"Have you heard anything of my wife?" asked Hornblower. The question was a natural one to Hardy, little use though he himself had for women; and he could see no connection between it and the preceding conversation.

"I remember reading that she was awarded a Civil List pension by the Government when the news of — of your death arrived."

"No other news? There was a child coming."

"None that I know of. I have been four months in this ship."

Hornblower's head sunk on his breast. The news of Leighton's death added to the confusion of his mind. He did not know whether to be pleased or sorry about it. Barbara would be as unattainable to him as ever, and perhaps there would be all the jealous misery to endure of her re-marriage.

"Now," said Hardy. "Breakfast?"

"There's Bush and my coxswain in the cutter," said Hornblower. "I must see that all is well with them first."

Chapter XVI

A MIDSHIPMAN came into the cabin as they ate breakfast.

"The fleet's in sight from the masthead, sir," he reported to Hardy.

"Very good." As the midshipman went out again Hardy turned back to Hornblower. "I must report your arrival to His Lordship."

"Is he still in command?" asked Hornblower, startled. It was a surprise to him that the Government had left Admiral Lord Gambier in command of the Channel Fleet for three years, despite the disastrous waste of opportunity at the Basque Roads.

"He hauls down his flag next month," said Hardy, gloomily. (Most officers turned gloomy when discussing "Dismal Jimmy.") "They whitewashed him at the court-martial, and had to leave him his full three years."

A shade of embarrassment appeared in Hardy's expression; he had let slip the mention of a court-martial to a man who soon would endure the same ordeal.

"I suppose they had to," said Hornblower, his train of thought following that of his fellow captain as he wondered if there would be any whitewash employed at his trial.

Hardy broke the embarrassed silence which followed.

"Would you care to come on deck with me?" he asked.

Over the horizon to leeward was appearing a long line of ships, close-hauled. They were in rigid, regular line, and as Hornblower watched they went about in succession in perfect order, as if they were chained together. The Channel Fleet was at drill—eighteen years of drill at sea had given them their unquestioned superiority over any other fleet in the world.

"*Victory's* in the van," said Hardy, handing his glass to Hornblower. "Signal midshipman! '*Triumph* to flag. Have on board . . .' "

Hornblower looked through the glass while Hardy dictated

his message. The three-decker with her admiral's flag at the main was leading the long line of ships, the broad stripes on her side glistening in the sunlight. She had been Jervis's flag ship at St. Vincent, Hood's in the Mediterranean, Nelson's at Trafalgar. Now she was Dismal Jimmy's — a tragedy if ever there was one. Signal-hoists were soaring up to her yard-arms; Hardy was busy dictating replies.

"The admiral is signalling for you to go on board, sir," he said at last, turning back to Hornblower. "I trust you will do me the honour of making use of my barge?"

The *Triumph's* barge was painted primrose yellow picked out with black, and so were the oar-blades; her crew wore primrose-coloured jumpers with black neckcloths. As Hornblower took his seat, his hand still tingling from Hardy's handclasp, he reminded himself gloomily that he had never been able to afford to dress his barge's crew in a fancy rig-out; he always felt sore on the point. Hardy must be a wealthy man with his Trafalgar prize money and his pension as Colonel of Marines. He contrasted their situations — Hardy, a baronet, moneyed, famous; and he himself, poor, undistinguished, and awaiting trial.

They piped the side for him in the *Victory*, as Admiralty regulations laid down — the marine guard at the present, the side-boys in white gloves to hand him up, the pipes of the boatswain's mates all a-twittering; and there was a captain on the quarterdeck ready to shake hands with him — odd, that was to Hornblower, seeing that soon he would be on trial for his life.

"I'm Calendar, Captain of the Fleet," he said. "His Lordship is below, waiting for you."

He led the way below, extraordinarily affable.

"I was first of the *Amazon*," he volunteered, "when you were in *Indefatigable*. Do you remember me?"

"Yes," said Hornblower. He had not risked a snub by saying so first.

"I remember you plainly," said Calendar. "I remember hearing what Pellew had to say about you."

Whatever Pellew said about him would be favourable — he had owed his promotion to Pellew's enthusiastic recommendation — and it was pleasant of Calendar to remind him of it at this crisis in his career.

Lord Gambier's cabin was not nearly as ornate as Captain Hardy's had been — the most conspicuous item of furniture therein was the big brass-bound Bible lying on the table. Gambier himself, heavy-jowled, gloomy, was sitting by the stern window dictating to a clerk who withdrew on the arrival of the two captains.

"You can make your report verbally, sir, for the present," said the admiral.

Hornblower drew a deep breath and made the plunge. He sketched out the strategic situation at the moment when he took the *Sutherland* into action against the French squadron off Rosas. Only a sentence or two had to be devoted to the battle itself — these men had fought in battles themselves and could fill in the gaps. He described the whole crippled mass of ships drifting helpless up Rosas Bay to where the guns of the fortress awaited them, and the gunboats creeping out under oars.

"One hundred and seventeen killed," said Hornblower. "One hundred and forty-five wounded, of whom forty-four died before I was removed from Rosas."

"My God!" said Calendar. It was not the deaths in hospital which called forth the exclamation — that was a usual proportion — but the total casualty list. Far more than half the crew of the *Sutherland* had been put out of action before surrendering.

"Thompson in the *Leander* lost ninety-two out of three hundred, my lord," he said. Thompson had surrendered the *Leander* to a French ship of the line off Crete after a defence which had excited the admiration of all England.

"I was aware of it," answered Gambier. "Please go on, Captain."

Hornblower told of how he witnessed the destruction of the French squadron, of how Caillard arrived to take him to Paris, of his escape, first from his escort and then from drowning. He made only a slight mention of Count de Graçay and of his voyage down the Loire — that was not an admiral's business — but he descended to fuller details when he told of his recapture of the *Witch of Endor*. Details here were of importance, because in the course of the manifold activities of the British Navy it might easily happen that a knowledge of harbour arrangement at Nantes and of the navigational difficulties of the lower Loire might be useful.

"Good God Almighty, man," said Calendar, "how can you be so cold-blooded about it? Weren't you — "

"Captain Calendar," interrupted Gambier, "I have requested you before not to allude to the Diety in that blasphemous fashion. Any repetition will incur my serious displeasure. Kindly continue, Captain Hornblower."

There was only the brush with the boats from Noirmoutier to be described now. Hornblower continued, formally, but this time Gambier himself interrupted him.

"You say you opened fire with a six-pounder," he said. "The prisoners were at the sweeps, and the ship had to be steered. Who laid the gun?"

"I did, my lord. The French pilot helped me."

"M'm. And you frightened 'em off?"

Hornblower confessed that he had succeeded in sinking two out of the three boats sent against him. Calendar whistled his surprise and admiration, but the hard lines in Gambier's face only set harder still.

"Yes?" he said. "And then?"

"We went on under sweeps until midnight, my lord, and then we picked up a breeze. We sighted *Triumph* at dawn."

There was silence in the cabin, only broken by the noises on deck, until Gambier stirred in his chair.

"I trust, Captain," he said, "that you have given thanks to the Almighty for these miraculous preservations of yours. In all these adventures I can see the finger of God. I shall direct my chaplain at prayers this evening to make a special mention of your gratitude and thankfulness."

"Yes, my lord."

"Now you will make your report in writing. You can have it ready by dinner-time — I trust you will give me the pleasure of your company at dinner? I will then be able to enclose it in the packet I am about to despatch to Their Lordships."

"Yes, my lord."

Gambier was still thinking deeply.

"*Witch of Endor* can carry the despatches," he said. As with every admiral the world over, his most irritating and continuous problem was how to collect and disseminate information without weakening his main body by detachments; it must have been an immense relief to him to have the cutter drop from the clouds as it were, to carry these despatches. He went on thinking.

"I will promote this lieutenant of yours, Bush, into her as Commander," he announced.

Hornblower gave a little gasp. Promotion to Commander meant almost certain post rank within the year, and it was this power of promotion which constituted the most prized source of patronage an admiral in command possessed. Bush deserved the step, but it was surprising that Gambier should give it to him — admirals generally had some favourite lieutenant, or some nephew or some old friend's son awaiting the first vacancy. Hornblower could imagine Bush's delight at the news that he was at last on his way to becoming an admiral himself if he lived long enough.

But that was not all, by no means all. Promotion of a captain's first lieutenant was a high compliment to the captain himself. It set the seal of official approval on the captain's proceedings. This decision of Gambier's was a public — not merely a private — announcement that Hornblower had acted correctly.

"Thank you, my lord, thank you," said Hornblower.

"She is your prize, of course," went on Gambier. "Government will have to buy her on her arrival."

Hornblower had not thought of that. It meant at least a thousand pounds in his pocket.

"That coxswain of yours will be in clover," chuckled Calendar. "He'll take all the lower deck's share."

That was true, too. Brown would have a quarter of the value of the *Witch of Endor* for himself. He could buy a cottage and land or set up in business on his own account if he wished to.

"*Witch of Endor* will wait until your report is ready," announced Gambier. "I will send my secretary in to you. Captain Calendar will provide you with a cabin and the necessities you lack. I hope you will continue to be my guest until I sail for Portsmouth next week. It would be best, I think."

The last words were a delicate allusion to that aspect of the matter which had occupied most of Hornblower's thoughts on his arrival, and which had not as yet been touched upon — the fact that he must undergo court-martial for the loss of the *Sutherland*, and was of necessity under arrest until that time. By old established custom he must be under the supervision of an officer of equal rank while under arrest; there could be no question of sending him home in the *Witch of Endor*.

"Yes, my lord," said Hornblower.

Despite all Gambier's courtesy and indulgence towards him, despite Calendar's open admiration, he still felt a constriction of the throat and a dryness of the mouth at the thought of that court-martial; they were symptoms which persisted even when he tried to settle down and compose his report with the aid of the competent young clergyman who made his appearance in the cabin to which Calendar conducted him.

"*Arma virumque cano*," quoted the Admiral's secretary after the first halting sentences — Hornblower's report naturally began with the battle of Rosas. "You begin in *medias res*, sir, as every good epic should."

"This is an official report," snapped Hornblower. "It continues the last report I made to Admiral Leighton."

His tiny cabin allowed him to walk only three paces each way, and crouching nearly double at that — some unfortunate lieutenant had been turned out to make room for him. In a flagship, even in a big three-decker like the *Victory*, the demand for cabins always greatly exceeded the supply, what with the admiral, and the Captain of the Fleet, and the flag lieutenant, and the secretary, and the chaplain, and the rest of the staff. He sat down on the breech of the twelve-pounder beside the cot.

"Continue, if you please," he ordered. "'Having regard to these conditions, I therefore proceeded . . .'"

It was finished in the end — it was the third time that morning that Hornblower had recounted his adventures, and they had lost all their savour for him now. He was dreadfully tired — his head drooped forward at his breast as he squatted on the gun, and then he woke with a snort. He was actually falling asleep while he sat.

"You are tired, sir," said the secretary.

"Yes."

He forced himself to wake up again. The secretary was looking at him with eyes shining with admiration, positive hero-worship. It made him feel uncomfortable.

"If you will just sign this, sir, I will attend to the seal and the superscription."

The secretary slipped out of the chair and Hornblower took the pen and dashed off his signature to the document on whose evidence he was soon to be tried for his life.

"Thank you, sir," said the secretary, gathering the papers together.

Hornblower had no more attention to spare for him. He threw himself face downward onto the cot, careless of appearances. He went rushing giddily down a tremendous slope into blackness — he was snoring before the secretary had reached the door, and he never felt the touch of the blanket with which the secretary returned, five minutes later, tiptoeing up to the cot to spread it over him.

Chapter XVII

SOMETHING enormously painful was recalling Hornblower to life. He did not want to return. It was agony to wake up, it was torture to feel unconsciousness slipping away from him. He clung to it, tried to recapture it, unavailingly. Remorselessly it eluded him. Somebody was gently shaking his shoulder, and he came back to complete consciousness with a start, and wriggled over to see the admiral's secretary bending over him.

"The admiral will dine within the hour, sir," he said. "Captain Calendar thought you might prefer to have a little time in which to prepare."

"Yes," grunted Hornblower. He fingered instinctively the long stubble on his unshaven chin. "Yes."

The secretary was standing very stiff and still, and Hornblower looked up at him curiously. There was an odd, set expression on the secretary's face, and he held a newspaper imperfectly concealed behind his back.

"What's the matter?" demanded Hornblower.

"It is bad news for you, sir," said the secretary.

"What news?"

Hornblower's spirits fell down into the depths of despair. Perhaps Gambier had changed his mind. Perhaps he was going to be kept under strict arrest, tried, condemned, and shot. Perhaps . . .

"I remembered having seen this paragraph in the *Morning Chronicle* of three months ago, sir," said the secretary. "I showed it to his Lordship, and to Captain Calendar. They decided it ought to be shown to you as early as possible. His Lordship says — "

"What is the paragraph?" demanded Hornblower, holding out his hand for the paper.

"It is bad news, sir," repeated the secretary, hesitatingly.

"Let me see it, damn you."

The secretary handed over the newspaper, one finger indicating the paragraph.

"The Lord giveth, the Lord taketh away," he said. "Blessed be the name of the Lord."

It was a very short paragraph.

We regret to announce the death in childbed, on the seventh of this month, of Mrs. Maria Hornblower, widow of the late Captain Horatio Hornblower, Bonaparte's martyred victim. The tragedy occurred in Mrs. Hornblower's lodgings at Southsea, and we are given to understand that the child, a fine boy, is healthy.

Hornblower read it twice, and he began on it a third time. Maria was dead, Maria the tender, the loving.

"You can find consolation in prayer, sir — " said the secretary, but Hornblower paid no attention to what the secretary said.

He had lost Maria. She had died in childbed, and having regard to the circumstances in which the child had been engendered, he had as good as killed her. Maria was dead. There would be no one, no one at all, to welcome him now on his return to England. Maria would have stood by him during the court-martial, and whatever the verdict, she would never have believed him to be at fault. Hornblower remembered the tears wetting her coarse red cheeks when she had last put her arms round him to say good-bye. He had been a little bored by the formality of an affectionate good-bye, then. He was free now — the realisation came creeping over him like cold water in a warm bath. But it was not fair to Maria. He would not have bought his freedom at such a price. She had earned by her own devotion his attention, his kindness, and he would have given them to her uncomplainingly for the rest of his life. He was desperately sorry that she was dead.

"His Lordship instructed me, sir," said the secretary, "to inform you of his sympathy in your bereavement. He told me to say that he would not take it amiss if you decided not to join him and his guests at dinner but sought instead the consolation of religion in your cabin."

"Yes," said Hornblower.

"Any help which I can give, sir — "

"None," said Hornblower.

He continued to sit on the edge of the cot, his head bowed, and the secretary shuffled his feet.

"Get out of here," said Hornblower, without looking up.

He sat there for some time, but there was no order in his thoughts; his mind was muddled. There was a continuous undercurrent of sadness, a hurt feeling indistinguishable from physical pain, but fatigue and excitement and lack of sleep deprived him of any ability to think clearly. Finally with a desperate effort he pulled himself together. He felt as if he was stifling in the stuffy cabin; he hated his stubbly beard and the feeling of dried sweat.

"Pass the word for my servant," he ordered the sentry at his door.

It was good to shave off the filthy beard, to wash his body in cold water, to put on clean linen. He went up on deck, the clean sea air rushing into his lungs as he breathed. It was good, too, to have a deck to pace, up and down, up and down, between the slides of the quarterdeck carronades and the line of ringbolts in the deck, with all the familiar sounds of shipboard life as a kind of lullaby to his tired mind. Up and down he walked, up and down, as he had walked so many hours before, in the *Indefatigable*, and the *Lydia*, and the *Sutherland*. They left him alone; the officers of the watch collected on the other side of the ship and only stared at him unobtrusively, politely concealing their curiosity about this man who had just heard of the death of his wife, who had escaped from a French prison, who was awaiting his trial for surrendering his ship — the first captain to strike his colours in a British ship of the line since Captain Ferris in the *Hannibal* at Algeciras. Up and down he walked, the goodly fatigue closing in upon him again until his mind was stupefied with it, until he found that he could hardly drag one foot past the other. Then he went below to the certainty of sleep and oblivion. But even in his sleep tumultuous dreams came to harass him — dreams of Maria, against which he struggled, sweating, knowing that Maria's body was now only a liquid mass of corruption; nightmares of death and imprisonment; and, ever-recurring, dreams of Barbara smiling to him on the farther side of the horrors that encompassed him.

From one point of view the death of his wife was of benefit to Hornblower during those days of waiting. It provided him with a good excuse for being silent and unapproachable. Without being thought impolite he could find a strip of deck and walk by himself in the sunshine. Gambier could walk with the captain of the fleet or the flag captain, little groups of lieutenants and warrant officers could walk together, chatting lightly, but they all kept out of his way; and it was not taken amiss that he should sit silent at the admiral's dinner table and hold himself aloof at the admiral's prayer meetings.

Had it not been so he would have been forced to mingle in the busy social life of the flagship, talking to officers who would studiously avoid all reference to the fact that shortly they would be sitting as judges on him at his court-martial. He did not have to join in the eternal technical discussions which went on round him, stoically pretending that the responsibility of having surrendered a British ship of the line sat lightly on his shoulders. Despite all the kindness with which he was treated, he felt a pariah. Calendar could voice open admiration for him, Gambier could treat him with distinction, the young lieutenants could regard him with wide-eyed hero-worship; but they had never hauled down their colours. More than once during his long wait Hornblower found himself wishing that a cannon-ball had killed him on the quarterdeck of the *Sutherland*. There was no one in the world who cared for him now — the little son in England, in the arms of some unknown foster-mother, might grow up ashamed of the name he bore.

Suspecting, morbidly, that the others would treat him like an outcast if they could, he anticipated them and made an outcast of himself, bitterly proud. He went through all that period of black reaction by himself, without companionship, during those last days of Gambier's tenure of command, until Hood came out in the *Britannia* to take over the command, and, amid the thunder of salutes, the *Victory* sailed for Portsmouth. There were headwinds to delay her passage; she had to beat up the Channel for seven long days before at last she glided into Spithead and the cable roared out through the hawse-hole.

Hornblower sat in his cabin — he felt no interest in the green hills of the Isle of Wight nor in the busy prospect of Portsmouth. The tap which came at his cabin door heralded, he supposed, the arrival of the orders regarding his court-martial.

"Come in!" he said, but it was Bush who entered, stumping along on his wooden leg, his face wreathed in smiles, his arms burdened with packages and parcels.

At the sight of that homely face Hornblower's depression evaporated like mist. He found himself grinning as delightedly as Bush, he wrung his hand over and over again, sat him down in the only chair, offered to send for drinks for him, all trace of self-consciousness and reserve disappearing in the violence of his reaction.

"Oh, I'm well enough, sir, thank you," said Bush, in reply to Hornblower's questions. "And this is the first chance I've had of thanking you for my promotion."

"Don't thank me," said Hornblower, a trace of bitterness creeping back into his voice. "You must thank his Lordship."

"I know who I owe it to, all the same," said Bush, sturdily. "They're going to post me as captain this week. They won't give me a ship — not with this leg of mine — but there's the dockyard job at Sheerness waiting for me. I should never be captain if it weren't for you, sir."

"Rubbish," said Hornblower. The pathetic gratitude in Bush's voice and expression made him feel uncomfortable.

"And how is it with you, sir?" asked Bush, regarding him with anxious blue eyes.

Hornblower shrugged his shoulders.

"Fit and well," he said.

"I was sorry to hear about Mrs. Hornblower, sir," said Bush.

That was all he needed to say on that subject. They knew each other too well to have to enlarge on it.

"I took the liberty, sir," said Bush, hastily, "of bringing you out your letters — there was a good deal waiting for you."

"Yes?" said Hornblower.

"This big package is a sword, I'm sure, sir," said Bush. He was cunning enough to think of ways of capturing Hornblower's interest.

"Let's open it, then," said Hornblower, indulgently.

A sword it was, sure enough, with a gold-mounted scabbard and a gold hilt, and when Hornblower drew it the blue steel blade bore an inscription in gold inlay. It was the sword "of one hundred guineas' value" which had been presented to him by the Patriotic Fund for his defeat of the *Natividad* in the *Lydia*, and which he had left in pawn with Duddingstone the ship's chandler at Plymouth, as a pledge for payment for captain's stores when he was commissioning the *Sutherland*.

"A sight too much writing on this for me," Duddingstone had complained at the time.

"Let's see what Duddingstone has to say," said Hornblower, tearing open the note enclosed in the package.

Sir,

It was with great emotion that I read today of your escape from the Corsican's clutches and I cannot find words to express my relief that the reports of your untimely death were unfounded, nor my admiration of your exploits during your last commission. I cannot reconcile it with my conscience to retain the sword of an officer so distinguished, and have therefore taken the liberty of forwarding the enclosed to you, hoping that in consequence you will wear it when next you enforce Britannia's dominion of the seas.

Your obedient and humble servant to command,

J. DUDDINGSTONE.

"God bless my soul!" said Hornblower.

He let Bush read the note; Bush was a captain and his equal now, as well as his friend, and there was no disciplinary objection to allowing him to know to what shifts he had been put when commissioning the *Sutherland*. Hornblower laughed a little self-consciously when Bush looked up at him after reading the note.

"Our friend Duddingstone," said Hornblower, "must have been very moved to allow a pledge for forty guineas to slip out of his fingers." He spoke cynically to keep the pride out of his voice, but he was genuinely moved. His eyes would have grown moist if he had allowed them.

"I'm not surprised, sir," said Bush, fumbling among the newspapers beside him. "Look at this, sir, and at this. Here's the *Morning Chronicle*, and the *Times*. I saved them to show you, hoping you'd be interested."

Hornblower glanced at the columns indicated; somehow the gist of them seemed to leap out at him without his having to read them. The British press had let itself go thoroughly. As even Bush had foreseen, the fancy of the British public had been caught by the news that a captain whom they had imagined to be foully done to death by the Corsican tyrant had succeeded in escaping, and not merely in escaping, but in carrying off a British ship of war which had been for months a prize to the Corsican. There were columns in praise of Hornblower's daring and ability. A passage in the *Times* caught Hornblower's attention and he read it more carefully. "Captain Hornblower still has to stand his trial for the loss of the *Sutherland*, but, as we pointed out in our examination of the news of the battle of Rosas Bay, his conduct was so well advised and his behaviour so exemplary on that occasion, whether he was acting under the orders of the late Admiral Leighton or not, that although the case is still *sub judice*, we have no hesitation in predicting his speedy re-appointment."

"Here's what the *Anti-Gallican* has to say, sir," said Bush.

What the *Anti-Gallican* had to say was very like what the other newspapers had said; it was beginning to dawn upon Hornblower that he was famous. He laughed uncomfortably again. All this was a most curious experience and he was not at all sure that he liked it. Cold-bloodedly he could see the reason for it. Lately there had been no naval officer prominent in the affections of the public — Cochrane had wrecked himself by his intemperate wrath after the Basque Roads, while six years had passed since Hardy had kissed the dying Nelson; Collingwood was dead and Leighton too, for that matter — and the public always demanded an idol. Like the Israelites in the desert, they were not satisfied with an invisible object for their devotion. Chance had made him the public's idol, and presumably Government were not sorry, seeing how much it would strengthen their position to have one of their own men suddenly popular. But somehow he did not like it; he was not used to fame, he distrusted it, and his ever-present personal modesty made him feel it was all a sham.

"I hope you're pleased, sir," said Bush, looking wonderingly at the struggle on Hornblower's face.

"Yes. I suppose I am," said Hornblower.

"The Navy bought the *Witch of Endor* yesterday at the Prize Court," said Bush, searching wildly for news which might delight this odd captain of his. "Four thousand pounds was the price, sir. And the division of the prize money where the prize has been taken by an incomplete crew is governed by an old regulation — I didn't know about it, sir, until they told me. It was made after that boat's crew from *Squirrel*, after she foundered, captured the Spanish plate ship in '97. Two thirds to you, sir — that's two thousand six hundred pounds. And a thousand to me and four hundred for Brown."

"H'm," said Hornblower.

Two thousand six hundred pounds was a substantial bit of money — a far more concrete reward than the acclamation of a capricious public.

"And there's all these letters and packets, sir," went on Bush, anxious to exploit the propitious moment.

The first dozen letters were all from people unknown to him, writing to congratulate him on his success and escape. Two at least were from madmen, apparently — but on the other hand two were from peers; even Hornblower was a little impressed by the signatures and the coroneted notepaper. Bush was more impressed still when they were passed over to him to read.

"That's very good indeed, sir, isn't it?" he said. "There are some more here."

Hornblower's hand shot out and picked one letter out of the mass offered him the moment he saw the handwriting, and then when he had taken it he stood for a second holding it in his hand, hesitating before opening it. The anxious Bush saw the hardening of his mouth and the waning of the colour in his cheeks; watched him while he read, but Hornblower had regained his self-control and his expression altered no further.

London,
129 Bond Street.
3rd June 1811.

Dear Captain Hornblower,

It is hard for me to write this letter, so overwhelmed am I with pleasure and surprise at hearing at this moment from the Admiralty that you are free and well. I hasten to let you know that I have your son here in my care. When he was left orphaned after the lamented death of your wife I ventured to take charge of him and make myself responsible for his upbringing, while my brothers Lords Wellesley and Wellington consented to act as his godfathers at his baptism, whereat he was consequently given the names Richard Arthur Horatio. Richard is a fine healthy boy with a wonderful resemblance to his father and he has already endeared himself greatly to me, to such an extent that I shall be conscious of a great loss when the time comes for you to take him away from me. Let me assure you that I shall look upon it as a pleasure to continue to have charge of Richard until that time, as I can easily guess that you will be much occupied with affairs on your arrival in England. You will be very welcome should you care to call here to see your son, who grows in intelligence every day. It will give pleasure not only to Richard, but to

Your firm friend,
Barbara Leighton.

Hornblower nervously cleared his throat and reread the letter. There was too much crowded in it for him to have any emotion left. Richard Arthur Horatio Hornblower, with two Wellesleys as godfathers, and growing in intelligence every day. There would be a great future ahead of him, perhaps. Up to that moment Hornblower had hardly thought about the child — his paternal instincts had hardly been touched by any consideration of a child he had never seen; and they further were warped by memories of the little Horatio who had died of smallpox in his arms so many years ago. But now he felt a great wave of affection for the unknown little brat in London who had managed to endear himself to Barbara.

And Barbara had taken him in charge; possibly because, widowed and childless, she had sought for a convenient orphan to adopt — and yet it might be because she still cherished memories of Captain Hornblower, whom at the time she had believed to be dead at Bonaparte's hands.

He could not bear to think about it any more. He thrust the letter into his pocket — all the others he had dropped on the deck — and with immobile face he met Bush's gaze again.

"There are all these other letters, sir," said Bush, with masterly tact.

They were letters from great men and from madmen — one contained an ounce of snuff as a token of some eccentric squire's esteem and regard — but there was only one which caught Hornblower's attention. It was from some Chancery Lane lawyer — the name was unfamiliar — who wrote, it appeared, on hearing from Lady Barbara Leighton that the presumption of Captain Hornblower's death was unfounded. Previously he had been acting under the instructions of the Lords Commissioners of the Admiralty to settle Captain Hornblower's estate, and working in conjunction with the Prize Agent at Port Mahon. With the consent of the Lord Chancellor upon the death intestate of Mrs. Maria Hornblower, he had been acting as trustee to the heir, Richard Arthur Horatio Hornblower, and had invested for the latter in the Funds the proceeds of the sale of Captain Hornblower's prizes after the deduction of expenses. As Captain Hornblower would see from the enclosed account, there was the sum of three thousand two hundred and ninety-one pounds six and fourpence invested in the Consolidated Fund, which would naturally revert to him. The lawyer awaited his esteemed instructions.

The enclosed accounts, which Hornblower was about to thrust aside, had among the innumerable six and eightpences and three and fourpences one set of items which caught his eye — they dealt with the funeral expenses of the late Mrs. Hornblower, and a grave in the cemetery of the Church of St. Thomas à Becket, and a headstone, and fees for grave-watchers; it was a ghoulish list which made Hornblower's blood run a little colder.

It was hateful. More than anything else it accentuated his loss of Maria — he would only have to go on deck to see the tower of the church where she lay.

He fought down the depression which threatened to overmaster him once more. It was at least a distraction to think about the news in that lawyer's letter, to contemplate the fact that he owned three thousand odd pounds in the Funds. He had forgotten all about those prizes he had made in the Mediterranean before he came under Leighton's command. Altogether that made his total fortune nearly six thousand pounds — not nearly as large as some captains had contrived to acquire, but handsome enough. Even on half-pay he would be able to live in comfort now, and educate Richard Arthur Horatio properly, and take his place in a modest way in society.

"The captains' list has changed a lot since we saw it last, sir," said Bush, and he was echoing Hornblower's train of thought rather than breaking into it.

"Have you been studying it?" grinned Hornblower.

"Of course, sir."

Upon the positions of their names in that list depended the date of their promotion to flag rank — year by year they would climb it as death or promotion eliminated their seniors, until one day, if they lived long enough, they would find themselves admirals, with admirals' pay and privileges.

"It's the top half of the list which has changed most, sir," said Bush. "Leighton was killed, and Ball died at Malta, and Troubridge was lost at sea — in Indian waters, sir — and there's seven or eight others who've gone. You're more than half-way up now."

Hornblower had held his present rank eleven years, but with each coming year he would mount more slowly, in proportion to the decrease in number of his seniors, and it would be 1825 or so before he could fly his flag. Hornblower remembered the Count de Graçay's prediction that the war would end in 1814 — promotion would be slower in peace-time. And Bush was ten years older than he, and only just beginning the climb. Probably he would never live to be an admiral, but then Bush was perfectly content with being a captain. Clearly his ambition had never soared higher than that; he was fortunate.

"We're both of us very lucky men, Bush," said Hornblower.

"Yes, sir," agreed Bush, and hesitated before going on. "I'm giving evidence at the court-martial, sir, but of course you know what my evidence'll be. They asked me about it at Whitehall, and they told me that what I was going to say agreed with everything they knew. You've nothing to fear from the court-martial, sir."

Chapter XVIII

HORNBLOWER told himself often during the next twenty-four hours that he had nothing to fear from the court-martial, and yet it was nervous work waiting for it — to hear the repeated twitter of pipes and stamping of marines' boots overhead as the compliments were given to the captains and admirals who came on board to try him, to hear silence close down on the ship as the court assembled, and to hear the sullen boom of the court-martial gun as the court opened, and the click of the cabin-door latch as Calendar came to escort him before his judges.

Hornblower remembered little enough afterwards of the details of the trial — only a few impressions stood out clearly in his memory. He could always recall the flash and glitter of the gold lace on the coats of the semicircle of officers sitting round the table in the great cabin of the *Victory*, and the expression on Bush's anxious, honest face as he declared that no captain could have handled a ship with more skill and determination than Hornblower had handled *Sutherland* at Rosas Bay. It was a neat point which Hornblower's "friend" — the officer the Admiralty had sent to conduct his defence — made when his question brought out the fact that just before the surrender Bush had been completely incapacitated by the loss of his foot, so that he bore no responsibility whatever for the surrender and had no interest in presenting as good a case as possible. There was an officer who read, seemingly for an eternity, long extracts from depositions and official reports, in a spiritless mumble — the greatness of the occasion apparently made him nervous and affected his articulation, much to the annoyance of the President of the Court. At one point the President actually took the paper from him, and himself read, in his nasal tenor, Admiral Martin's pronouncement that the *Sutherland's* engagement had certainly made the eventual destruction of the French squadron more easy, and in his opinion was all that had made it possible. There was an awkward moment when a discrepancy was detected between the signal logs of the *Pluto* and *Caligula,* but it passed away in smiles when someone reminded the Court that signal midshipmen sometimes made mistakes.

During the adjournment there was an elegant civilian in buff and blue, with a neat silk cravat, who came in to Hornblower with a good many questions. Frere, his name was, Hookham Frere — Hornblower had a vague acquaintance with the name. He was one of the wits who wrote in the *Anti-Gallican,* a friend of Canning's, who for a time had acted as ambassador to the patriot Government of Spain. Hornblower was a little intrigued by the presence of someone deep in cabinet secrets, but he was too preoccupied, waiting for the trial to re-open, to pay much attention to him or to answering his questions in detail.

And it was worse when all the evidence had been given, and he was waiting with Calendar while the Court considered its decision. Hornblower knew real fear, then. It was hard to sit apparently unmoved, while the minutes dragged by, waiting for the summons to the great cabin, to hear what his fate would be. His heart was beating hard as he went in, and he knew himself to be pale. He jerked his head erect to meet his judges' eyes, but the judges in their panoply of blue and gold were veiled in a mist which obscured the whole cabin, so that nothing was visible to Hornblower's eyes save for one little space in the centre — the cleared area in the middle of the table before the President's seat, where lay his sword, the hundred-guinea sword presented by the Patriotic Fund. That was all Hornblower could see — the sword seemed to hang there in space, unsupported. And the hilt was towards him; he was not guilty.

"Captain Hornblower," said the President of the Court — that nasal tenor of his had a pleasant tone: "this Court is of the unanimous opinion that your gallant and unprecedented defence of His Majesty's ship *Sutherland,* against a force so superior, is deserving of every praise the country and this court can give. Your conduct, together with that of the officers and men under your command, reflects not only the highest honour on you, but on the country at large. You are therefore most honourably acquitted."

There was a little confirmatory buzz from the other members of the Court, and a general bustle in the cabin. Somebody was buckling the hundred-guinea sword to his waist; someone else was patting his shoulder. Hookham Frere was there, too, speaking insistently.

"Congratulations, sir. And now, are you ready to accompany me to London? I have had a post-chaise horsed and waiting this last six hours."

The mists were only clearing slowly; everything was still vague about him as he allowed himself to be led away, to be escorted on deck, to be handed down into the barge alongside. Somebody was cheering. Hundreds of voices were cheering. The *Victory's* crew had manned the yards and were yelling themselves hoarse. All the other ships at anchor there were cheering him. This was fame. This was success. Precious few other captains had ever been cheered by all the ships in a fleet like this.

"I would suggest that you take off your hat, sir," said Frere's voice in his ear, "and show how much you appreciate the compliment."

He took off his hat and sat there in the afternoon sun, awkwardly in the stern-sheets of the barge. He tried to smile, but he knew his smile to be wooden — he was nearer tears than smiles. The mists were closing round him again, and the deep-chested bellowing was like the shrill piping of children in his ears.

The boat rasped against the wall. There was more cheering here, as they handed him up. People were thumping him on the shoulder, wringing his hand, while a blaspheming party of marines forced a passage for him to the post-chaise with its horses restless amid the din. Then a clatter of hoofs and a grinding of wheels, and they were flying out of the yard, the postilion cracking his whip.

"A highly satisfactory demonstration of sentiment, on the part of the public and of the armed forces of the Crown," said Frere, mopping his face.

Hornblower suddenly remembered something, which made him sit up, tense.

"Stop at the church!" he yelled to the postilion.

"Indeed, sir, and might I ask why you gave that order? I have the express commands of His Royal Highness to escort you to London without losing a moment."

"My wife is buried there," snapped Hornblower.

But the visit to the grave was unsatisfactory — was bound to be with Frere fidgeting and fuming at his elbow, and looking at his watch. Hornblower pulled off his hat and bowed his head by the grave with its carved headstone, but he was too much in a whirl to think clearly. He tried to murmur a prayer — Maria would have liked that, for she was always pained by his free thinking. Frere clucked with impatience.

"Come along then," said Hornblower, turning on his heel and leading the way back to the post-chaise.

The sun shone gloriously over the countryside as they left the town behind them, lighting up the lovely green of the trees and the majestic rolling Downs. Hornblower found himself swallowing hard. This was the England for which he had fought for eighteen long years, and as he breathed its air and gazed round him he felt that England was worth it.

"Damned lucky for the Ministry," said Frere, "this escape of yours. Something like that was needed. Even though Wellington's just captured Almeida the mob was growing restive. We had a ministry of all the talents once — now it's a ministry of no talent. I can't imagine why Castlereagh and Canning fought that duel. It nearly wrecked us. So did Gambier's affair at the Basque Roads. Cochrane's been making a thorough nuisance of himself in the House ever since. Has it ever occurred to you that you might enter Parliament? Well, it will be time enough to discuss that when you've been to Downing Street. It's sufficient at present that you've given the mob something to cheer about."

Mr. Frere seemed to take much for granted — for instance, that Hornblower was wholeheartedly on the Government side, and that Hornblower had fought at Rosas Bay and had escaped from France solely to maintain a dozen politicians in office. It rather damped Hornblower's spirits. He sat silent, listening to the rattle of the wheels.

"H.R.H. is none too helpful," said Frere. "He didn't turn us out when he assumed the Regency, but he bears us no love — the Regency Bill didn't please him. Remember that, when you see him tomorrow. He likes a bit of flattery, too. If you can make him believe that you owe your success to the inspiring example both of H.R.H. *and* of Mr. Spencer Perceval you will be taking the right line. What's this? Horndean?"

The postilion drew the horses to a halt outside the inn, and ostlers came running with a fresh pair.

"Sixty miles from London," commented Mr. Frere. "We've just time."

The inn servants had been eagerly questioning the postilion, and a knot of loungers — smocked agricultural workers and a travelling tinker — joined them, looking eagerly at Hornblower in his blue and gold. Someone else came hastening out of the inn; his red face and silk cravat and leather leggings seemed to indicate him as the local squire.

"Acquitted, sir?" he asked.

"Naturally, sir," replied Frere at once. "Most honourably acquitted."

"Hooray for Hornblower!" yelled the tinker, throwing his hat into the air. The squire waved his arms and stamped with joy, and the farm hands echoed the cheer.

"Down with Boney!" said Frere. "Drive on."

"It is surprising how much interest has been aroused in your case," said Frere a minute later. "Although naturally one would expect it to be greatest along the Portsmouth Road."

"Yes," said Hornblower.

"I can remember," said Frere, "when the mob were howling for Wellington to be hanged, drawn and quartered — that was after the news of Cintra. I thought we were gone then. It was his court of inquiry which saved us as it happened, just as yours is going to do now. Do you remember Cintra?"

"I was commanding a frigate in the Pacific at the time," said Hornblower, curtly.

He was vaguely irritated — and he was surprised at himself at finding that he neither liked being cheered by tinkers nor flattered by politicians.

"All the same," said Frere, "it's just as well that Leighton was hit at Rosas. Not that I wished him harm, but it drew the teeth of that gang. It would have been them or us otherwise, I fancy. His friends counted twenty votes on a division. You know his widow, I've heard?"

"I have that honour."

"A charming woman for those who are partial to that type. And most influential as a link between the Wellesley party and her late husband's."

"Yes," said Hornblower.

All the pleasure was evaporating from his success. The radiant afternoon sunshine seemed to have lost its brightness.

"Petersfield is just over the hill," said Frere. "I expect there'll be a crowd there."

Frere was right. There were twenty or thirty people waiting at the Red Lion, and more came hurrying up, all agog to hear the result of the court-martial. There was wild cheering at the news, and Mr. Frere took the opportunity to slip in a good word for the Government.

"It's the newspapers," grumbled Frere, as they drove on with fresh horses. "I wish we could take a leaf out of Boney's book and only allow 'em to publish what we think they ought to know. Emancipation — Reform — naval policy — the mob wants a finger in every pie nowadays."

Even the marvellous beauty of the Devil's Punch Bowl was lost on Hornblower as they drove past it. All the savour was gone from life. He was wishing he was still an unnoticed naval captain battling with Atlantic storms. Every stride the horses were taking was carrying him nearer to Barbara, and yet he was conscious of a sick, vague desire that he was returning to Maria, dull and uninteresting and undisturbing. The crowd that cheered him at Guildford — market day was just over — stank of sweat and beer. He was glad that with the approach of evening Frere ceased talking and left him to his thoughts, depressing though they were.

It was growing dark when they changed horses again at Esher.

"It is satisfactory to think that no footpad or highwayman will rob us," laughed Frere. "We have only to mention the name of the hero of the hour to escape scot-free."

No footpad or highwayman interfered with them at all, as it happened. Unmolested they crossed the river at Putney and drove on past the more frequent houses and along the dark streets.

"Number Ten Downing Street, postie," said Frere.

What Hornblower remembered most vividly of the interview that followed was Frere's first *sotto voce* whisper to Perceval — "He's safe" — which he overheard. The interview lasted no more than ten minutes, formal on the one side, reserved on the other. The Prime Minister was not in talkative mood apparently — his main wish seem to be to inspect this man who might perhaps do him an ill turn with the Prince Regent or with the public. Hornblower formed no very favourable impression either of his ability or of his personal charm.

"Pall Mall and the War Office next," said Frere. "God, how we have to work!"

London smelt of horses — it always did, Hornblower remembered, to men fresh from the sea. The lights of Whitehall seemed astonishingly bright. At the War Office there was a young Lord to see him, someone whom Hornblower liked at first sight. Palmerston was his name, the Under-secretary of State. He asked a great many intelligent questions regarding the state of opinion in France, the success of the last harvest, the manner of Hornblower's escape. He nodded approvingly when Hornblower hesitated to answer when asked the name of the man who had given him shelter.

"Quite right," he said. "You're afraid some damned fool'll blab it out and get him shot. Some damned fool probably would. I'll ask you for it if ever we need it badly, and you will be able to rely on us then. And what happened to these galley slaves?"

"The first lieutenant in the *Triumph* pressed them for the service, my lord."

"So they've been hands in a King's ship for the last three weeks? I'd rather be a galley slave myself."

Hornblower was of the same opinion. He was glad to find someone in high position with no illusions regarding the hardships of the service.

"I'll have them traced and brought home if I can persuade your superiors at the Admiralty to give 'em up. I can find a better use for 'em."

A footman brought in a note which Palmerston opened.

"His Royal Highness commands your presence," he announced. "Thank you, Captain. I hope I shall again have the pleasure of meeting you shortly. This discussion of ours has been most profitable. And the Luddites have been smashing machinery in the north, and Sam Whitbread has been raising Cain in the House, so that your arrival is most opportune. Good evening, Captain."

It was those last words which spoilt the whole effect. Lord Palmerston planning a new campaign against Bonaparte won Hornblower's respect, but Lord Palmerston echoing Frere's estimate of the political results of Hornblower's return lost it again.

"What does His Royal Highness want of me?" he asked of Frere, as they went down the stairs together.

"That's to be a surprise for you," replied Frere, archly. "You may even have to wait until tomorrow's levee to find out. It isn't often Prinny's sober enough for business at this time in the evening. Probably he's not. You may find tact necessary in your interview with him."

It was only this morning, thought Hornblower, his head whirling, that he had been sitting listening to the evidence at his court-martial. So much had already happened today! He was surfeited with new experiences. He was sick and depressed. And Lady Barbara and his little son were in Bond Street, not a quarter of a mile away.

"What time is it?" he asked.

"Ten o'clock. Young Pam keeps late hours at the War Office. He's a glutton for work."

"Oh," said Hornblower.

God only knew at what hour he would escape from the palace. He would certainly have to wait until tomorrow before he called at Bond Street. At the door a coach was waiting, coachmen and footmen in the royal red liveries.

"Sent by the Lord Chamberlain," explained Frere. "Kind of him."

He handed Hornblower in through the door and climbed after him.

"Ever met His Royal Highness?" he went on.

"No."

"But you've been to Court?"

"I have attended two levees. I was presented to King George in '98."

"Ah! Prinny's not like his father. And you know Clarence, I suppose?"

"Yes."

The carriage had stopped at a doorway brightly lit with lanterns; the door was opened, and a little group of footmen were waiting to hand them out. There was a glittering entrance hall, where somebody in uniform and powder and with a white staff ran his eyes keenly over Hornblower.

"Hat under your arm," he whispered. "This way, please."

"Captain Hornblower, Mr. Hookham Frere," somebody announced.

It was an immense room, dazzling with the light of its candles; a wide expanse of polished floor, and at the far end a group of people bright with gold lace and jewels. Somebody came over to them, dressed in naval uniform — it was the Duke of Clarence, pop-eyed and pineapple-headed.

"Ah, Hornblower," he said, hand held out, "welcome home."

Hornblower bowed over the hand.

"Come and be presented. This is Captain Hornblower, sir."

"Evenin', Captain."

Corpulent, handsome, and dissipated, weak and sly, was the sequence of impressions Hornblower received as he made his bow. The thinning curls were obviously dyed; the moist eyes and the ruddy pendulous cheeks seemed to hint that His Royal Highness had dined well, which was more than Hornblower had.

"Everyone's been talkin' about you, Captain, ever since your cutter — what's its name, now? — came in to Portsmouth."

"Indeed, sir?" Hornblower was standing stiffly at attention.

"Yas. And, damme, so they ought to. So they ought to, damme, Captain. Best piece of work I ever heard of — good as I could have done myself. Here, Conyngham, make the presentations."

Hornblower bowed to Lady This and Lady That, to Lord Somebody and to Sir John Somebody-else. Bold eyes and bare arms, exquisite clothes and blue Garter-ribbons, were all the impressions Hornblower received. He was conscious that the uniform made for him by the *Victory's* tailor was a bad fit.

"Now let's get the business done with," said the Prince. "Call those fellows in."

Someone was spreading a carpet on the floor, someone else was bearing in a cushion on which something winked and sparkled. There was a little procession of three solemn men in red cloaks. Someone dropped on one knee to present the Prince with a sword.

"Kneel, sir," said Lord Conyngham to Hornblower.

He felt the accolade and heard the formal words which dubbed him knight. But when he rose, a little dazed, the ceremony was by no means over. There was a ribbon to be hung over his shoulder, a star to be pinned on his breast, a red cloak to be draped about him, a vow to be repeated and signatures written. He was being invested as a Knight of the Most Honourable Order of the Bath, as somebody loudly proclaimed. He was Sir Horatio Hornblower, with a ribbon and star to wear for the rest of his life. At last they took the cloak from his shoulders again and the officials of the order withdrew.

"Let me be the first to congratulate you, Sir Horatio," said the Duke of Clarence, coming forward, his kindly imbecile face wreathed in smiles.

"Thank you, sir," said Hornblower. The broad star thumped his chest as he bowed again.

"My best wishes, Colonel," said the Prince Regent.

Hornblower was conscious of all the eyes turned on him at

that speech; it was that which warned him that the Prince was not making a slip regarding his rank.

"Sir?" he said, inquiringly, as seemed to be expected of him.

"His Royal Highness," explained the Duke, "has been pleased to appoint you one of his Colonels of Marines."

A Colonel of Marines received pay to the amount of twelve hundred pounds a year, and did no duty for it. It was an appointment given as a reward to successful captains, to be held until they reached flag rank. Six thousand pounds he had already, Hornblower remembered. Now he had twelve hundred a year in addition to his captain's half-pay at least. He had attained financial security at last, for the first time in his life. He had a title, a ribbon and star. He had everything he had ever dreamed of having, in fact.

"The poor man's dazed," laughed the Regent loudly, delighted.

"I am overwhelmed, sir," said Hornblower, trying to concentrate again on the business in hand. "I hardly know how to thank your Royal Highness."

"Thank me by joining us at hazard. Your arrival interrupted a damned interesting game. Ring that bell, Sir John, and let's have some wine. Sit here beside Lady Jane, Captain. Surely you want to play? Yes, I know about you, Hookham. You want to slip away and tell John Walter that I've done my duty. You might suggest at the same time that he writes one of his damned leaders and has my Civil List raised — I work hard enough for it, God knows. But I don't see why you should take the captain away. Oh, very well then, damn it. You can go if you want to."

"I didn't imagine," said Frere, when they were safely in the coach again, "that you'd care to play hazard. *I* wouldn't, not with Prinny, if he were using his own dice. Well, how does it feel to be Sir Horatio?"

"Very well," said Hornblower.

He was digesting the Regent's allusion to John Walter. That was the editor of the *Times*, he knew. It was beginning to dawn upon him that his investiture as Knight of the Bath and appointment as Colonel of Marines were useful pieces of news. Presumably their announcement would have some influence politically, too — that was the reason for haste. They would convince doubting people that the Government's naval officers were achieving great things — it was almost as much a political move to make him a knight as was Bonaparte's scheme to shoot him for violating the laws of war. The thought took a great deal of the pleasure out of it.

"I took the liberty," said Frere, "of engaging a room for you at the Golden Cross. You'll find them expecting you; I had your baggage sent round. Shall I stop the coach there? Or do you want to visit Fladong's first?"

Hornblower wanted to be alone; the idea of visiting the naval coffee house tonight — for the first time in five years — had no appeal for him, especially as he felt suddenly self-conscious in his ribbon and star. Even at the hotel it was bad enough, with host and boots and chambermaid all unctuously deferential with their "Yes, Sir Horatio" and "No, Sir Horatio," making a procession out of lighting him up to his room, and fluttering round him to see that he had all he wanted, when all he wanted now was to be left in peace.

There was little enough peace for him, all the same, when he climbed into bed. Resolutely as he put out of his mind all recollection of the wild doings of the day, he could not stop himself from thinking about the fact that tomorrow he would be seeing his son and Lady Barbara. He spent a restless night.

Chapter XIX

"SIR HORATIO HORNBLOWER," announced the butler, holding open the door for him.

Lady Barbara was there; it was a surprise to see her in black — Hornblower had been visualising her as dressed in the blue gown she had worn when last he had seen her, the grey-blue which matched her eyes. She was in mourning now, of course, for Leighton had been dead less than a year still. But the black dress suited her well — her skin was creamy white against it. Hornblower remembered with a strange pang the golden tan of her cheeks in those old days on board the *Lydia*.

"Welcome," she said, her hands outstretched to him. They were smooth and cool and delicious — he remembered their touch of old. "The nurse will bring Richard directly. Meanwhile, my heartiest congratulations on your success."

"Thank you," said Hornblower. "I was extremely lucky, ma'am."

"The lucky man," said Lady Barbara, "is usually the man who knows how much to leave to chance."

While he digested this statement he stood awkwardly looking at her. Until this moment he had forgotten how Olympian she was, what self-assurance — kindly self-assurance — she had, which raised her to inaccessible heights and made him feel like a loutish schoolboy. His knighthood must appear ridiculously unimportant to her, the daughter of an earl, the sister of a marquis and of a viscount who was well on his way towards a dukedom. He was suddenly acutely conscious of his elbows and hands.

His awkwardness only ended with the opening of the door and the entrance of the nurse, plump and rosy in her ribboned cap, the baby held to her shoulder. She dropped a curtsey.

"Hullo, son," said Hornblower, gently.

He did not seem to have much hair yet, under his little cap, but there were two startling brown eyes looking out at his father; nose and chin and forehead might be as indeterminate as one would expect in a baby, but there was no ignoring those eyes.

"Hullo, baby," said Hornblower, gently, again.

He was unconscious of the caress in his voice. He was speaking to Richard as years before he had spoken to little Horatio and little Maria. He held up his hands to the child.

"Come to your father," he said.

Richard made no objections. It was a little shock to Hornblower to feel how tiny and light he was — Hornblower, years ago, had grown used to older children — but the feeling passed immediately.

"There, baby, there," said Hornblower.

Richard wriggled in his arms, stretching out his hands to the shining gold fringe of his epaulette.

"Pretty?" said Hornblower.

"Da!" said Richard, touching the threads of bullion.

"That's a man!" said Hornblower.

His old skill with babies had not deserted him. Richard gurgled happily in his arms, smiled seraphically as he played with him, kicked his chest with tiny kicks through his dress. That good old trick of bowing the head and pretending to butt Richard in the stomach had its never-failing success. Richard gurgled and waved his arms in ecstasy.

"What a joke!" said Hornblower. "Oh, what a joke!"

Suddenly remembering, he looked round at Lady Barbara. She had eyes only for the baby, her serenity strangely exalted, her smile tender. He thought then that she was moved by her love for the child. Richard noticed her too.

"Goo!" he said, with a jab of an arm in her direction.

She came nearer, and Richard reached over his father's shoulder to touch her face.

"He's a fine baby," said Hornblower.

"O' course he's a fine babby," said the wet nurse, reaching for him. She took it for granted that godlike fathers in glittering uniforms would only condescend to notice their children for ten seconds consecutively, and would need to be instantly relieved of them at the end of that time.

"He's a saucy one," said the wet nurse, the baby back in her arms. He wriggled there, those big brown eyes of his looking from Hornblower to Barbara.

"Say 'bye-bye,' " said the nurse. She held up his wrist and waved his fat fist at them. "Bye-bye."

"Do you think he's like you?" asked Barbara, as the door closed behind the nurse and baby.

"Well — " said Hornblower, with a doubtful grin.

He had been happy during those few seconds with the baby, happier than he had been for a long, long time. The morning up to now had been one of black despondency for him. He had told himself that he had everything heart could desire, and some inner man within him had replied that he wanted none of it. In the morning light his ribbon and star had appeared gaudy gewgaws. He never could contrive to feel proud of himself; there was something vaguely ridiculous about the name "Sir Horatio Hornblower," just as he always felt there was something vaguely ridiculous about himself.

He had tried to comfort himself with the thought of all the money he had. There was a life of ease and security before him; he would never again have to pawn his gold-hilted sword, nor feel self-conscious in good society about the pinchbeck buckles on his shoes. And yet the prospect was frightening now that it was certain. There was something of confinement about it, something reminiscent of those weary weeks in the Château de Graçay — how well he remembered how he had fretted there. Unease and insecurity, which had appeared such vast evils when he suffered under them, had something attractive about them now, hard though that was to believe.

He had envied brother captains who had columns about themselves in the newspapers. Surfeit in that way was attained instantaneously, he had discovered. Bush and Brown would love him neither more nor less on account of what the *Times* had to say about him; he would scorn the love of those who loved him more — and he had good reason to fear that there would be rivals who would love him less. He had received the adulation of crowds yesterday; that did not heighten his good opinion of crowds, and he was filled with a bitter contempt for the upper circle that ruled those crowds. Within him the fighting man and the humanitarian both seethed with discontent.

Happiness was a Dead Sea fruit that turned to ashes in the mouth, decided Hornblower, generalising recklessly from his own particular experience. Prospect, and not possession, was what gave pleasure, and his cross-grainedness would deprive him, now that he had made that discovery, even of the pleasure in prospect. He misdoubted everything so much. Freedom that could only be bought by Maria's death was not a freedom worth having; honours granted by those that had the granting of them were no honours at all; and no security was really worth the loss of insecurity. What life gave with one hand she took back with the other. The political career of which he had once dreamed was open to him now, especially with the alliance of the Wellesley faction, but he could see with morbid clarity how often he would hate it; and he had been happy for thirty seconds with his son, and now, more morbidly still, he asked himself cynically if that happiness could endure for thirty years.

His eyes met Barbara's again, and he knew she was his for the asking. To those who did not know and understand, who thought there was romance in his life when really it was the most prosaic of lives, that would be a romantic climax. She was smiling at him, and then he saw her lips tremble as she smiled. He remembered how Marie had said he was a man whom women loved easily, and he felt uncomfortable at being reminded of her.

THE END